I0787998

RULER OF NAUGHT

THE EXORDIUM NOVELS

EXORDIUM: BOOK 2

RULER OF NAUGHT

Sherwood Smith
&
Dave Trowbridge

BOOK VIEW CAFE

Book View Café

DEDICATIONS

First Edition Dedication (1993)

Our thanks to Debra Doyle, Jim Macdonald, and Andrew Sigel for reading this book in draft, and making encouraging noises; and to Dave, Ray, and many others in the Genie Spaceport RT, for their help in designing the Standard Orbital Habitat.

Second Edition Dedication

To Aharon, shaman and magister; Falstaff, Nemo, Kije, and Oka, for tutoring in the Art of Dog; and, as always, the Privy Council, especially Barry Messina, Randy Papadopoulos, Andrew Presby, and Paul Vebber, for helping breathe life into the Panarchist Navy.

PROLOGUE

The gnostors of Hypostatics will tell you that space-time is isotropic, that there is no center: all locations are equally central and equally peripheral.

Perhaps.

But every Haji knows different. Those who survive that pilgrimage know there is a place different from all other places, a Center to the sentient universe.

Its name is Desrien.

From orbit, Desrien at first appears no different from any other planet cherished by humankind: a blue-white sphere marbled by cloud-whirls, a sight resonant with memories of the Exile and our lost Mother. But there are no Highdwellings. Aside from the Node, here uninhabited, the only stars in the night sky of Desrien are those placed there by the unimaginable Hand of Telos. The planet lies open to space, unprotected by the webs of forces and vessels so familiar to interstellar travelers.

It does not need them. Those who are uninvited do not land, or if they do, they do not leave again. Unmappable, unnavigable, alone among all worlds Desrien stands exempt from the Jaspran Unalterable of Free Passage. For there is found an interface between the transcendent and the mundane that flouts the metrics of our sciences and defies the power of our machines, where Totality is unknowable except through human senses and perceptions.

Desrien is the heart of an immense engine, powered by the sleeting archetypal energies of the Nous, the emanations of the trillion-fold mentalities in the Thousand Suns that are focused there by the mystical lens of the Mandala. There, stretched tight by the weight of dreams, the skin of the world is eminently fragile. The featherweight blow of a single thought can open a wound through which myths both fearful and beloved erupt into the waking world, so that the pilgrim enters fully conscious into the Dreamtime of humanity and walks among archetypes awakened into the light of day.

Every visitor to Desrien who truly surrenders to its mysteries thus confronts enfleshed the myths by which they live — which may not be the ones they thought they knew.

The title Haji, then, is an honored one; but those who bear it rarely speak of what they saw and lived on Desrien. It is enough that their lives are wholly changed.

Gn. Yan byn-Ibrahim Japhez
College of Archetype and Ritual
Desrien, The Hinge of Time
Sync Achilenga, 615 a.a.

In the place of the Omnipotence there is neither before nor after; there is only act.

Charles Williams
Descent into Hell
Lost Earth, ca. 300 b.e.

There was nothing, in no time, neither perception nor non-perception. Neither movement nor non-movement, neither identity nor difference, neither eternity nor boundedness.

Then an impalpable blow, disturbing nothing. Nothing dwindled and resolved, rising through depths of abnegation to the awareness of a flame, suspended in a darkness evocative of incense and the faint tang of fresh fruit. Beyond the flame a golden blur, sharpening to a vast face of inhuman calm indwelling with transhuman compassion, its lips curved in a smile terrible with possibilities, knowing everything, rejecting nothing.

The bodhisattva Eloatri gazed up at the Buddha. The gentle scent of green tea from the kitchen beyond the dharma room tickled her nose. She let the sensation go, not thinking about it, merely experiencing it.

There was no sound. Above, the narrow windows against the roof admitted the pale light of false dawn, barely illuminating the riotous profusion of images that framed the gilded statue of the Awakened One. The vihara was asleep around her; alone among the sleeping monks and nuns, their abbot meditated.

Had been meditating. There was no one in the room; no reason for whatever had breached her repose in the higher dhyanas. Eloatri closed her eyes.

There was nothing, in no time, neither perception nor non-perception. . .

There was a blow, impalpable, and nothing fled before a flare of light resolving into the nine-faced form of Vajrabhairava, the terrifying aspect of the bodhisattva Manjushri, who is the strength of the spirit of the Buddha. Locked in sexual union with his consort, trampling beasts and men underfoot, his thirty-four arms juggling the flaming sword of knowledge, his twenty-seven-fold gaze sought her out and pinned her against the darkness as the sword was transformed into a silver sphere that he hurled at her head.

Eloatri shouted and opened her eyes to the calm of the dharma room.

The echo of her shout died away, replaced by the soft slap of bare feet in the corridor behind her. She ignored the presence behind her, breathing for a time until her heart slowed, gazing into the compassionate eyes of the Buddha. Meaning would come when it would come. Rising to her feet in a fluid motion that belied her eighty years, she clapped her hands before her and bowed deeply to the Buddha. It was time.

She met the calm eyes of the monk Nukuafoa; then his eyes widened as she removed the blue cord knotted around her waist, and put it into his hands.

"The Hand of Telos is upon me," she said. "And my third hejir is before me. You are chosen."

He bowed. She sensed the pressure of responsibility settling around him, and she felt his unspoken question as she walked to her cell, where she collected her staff and cloak, begging bowl and sandals.

Then she left the vihara that had been her refuge for twenty-one years, driven out upon the third pilgrimage of her life, devotee and victim of that Unconditioned which human-kind calls Telos, on a planet called Desrien.

PART ONE

ONE

The lock of the shuttle hissed open on a spacious garden, severe in aspect.

Anaris rahal'Jerrodi recognized it as the formal rooftop landing area of the Palace Major. Tall spindles of foliage formed narrow windows on distances soft in the morning sun.

Anaris strode down the shuttle ramp, the familiar scents catching at his throat. The complex of emotions evoked an Uni word he'd had no occasion to use since he'd returned to Dol'jhar: Home. Recognition overlaid amusement on his speculations about the purpose of his father's sudden summons. When he'd last walked in this place, he'd been facing imminent return to a Dol'jhar that existed only in his mind, distorted by time and youthful memory.

Home. Dol'jharian had no equivalent: the closest was probably jhar, fortress. Walls, dead ends, eyes.

Here, on the highest point in the Mandala, all was air and light, softly drowning the black garb and rigid postures of the Tarkan honor guard drawn up facing the shuttle. Harsh ozone from the shuttle overlaid more subtle, resinous scents. Anaris inhaled deeply, reveling in a sense of expansiveness, and turned towards the lift adit for the Ivory quadrant, where the Palace Minor lay. Why had the pilot landed the shuttle sideways?

A double-thunderclap pulled his attention upwards, then another. His skin prickled. High above, jagged contrails scarred the sky. He'd felt the *Fist of Dol'jhar's* ruptors fire once yesterday. Then the comm filters came down, hard. No one had told him who, or what, they'd fired at.

There had been no response from the Dol'jharian interdiction system hastily installed when Mandalic protocols took down all planetary defenses, so whatever was going on, it was some distance from the Palace.

Anaris shot a glance at his new secretary at the foot of the ramp behind him. Morrighon flinched, his gaze turned downward toward his useless compad. Anaris had only been able to discover that Juvaszt, kyvernat of the *Fist of Dol'jhar*, had been ordered down shortly afterwards.

And now Anaris's father summoned him. This must be the next step in the succession duel. Watching for any hint of why it was happening at this moment, Anaris took a step toward the Ivory lift.

"Your pardon, Lord. The Avatar awaits you this way," said Morrighon, as he gestured towards the Phoenix adit directly across from the shuttle's lock. The secretary's voice had a resonance reminiscent of the mindripper, an insinuating whine that turned everything he said into a complaint against the universe at large.

He had reason to complain, Anaris thought with amusement; the Bori was short, dumpy, with an asymmetric, pock-marked face and a widely divergent gaze. Anaris wondered how Morrighon had escaped culling.

His ugliness alone had made Morrighon Anaris's first choice to replace the secretary purged by Eusabian when Lelanor's presence on the *Fist* was discovered. Anaris still had not found out who had reported his secreted lover, forcing him to kill her in front of his father to spare her death by torture. He doubted it had been Morrighon. All the records he'd found about this Bori indicated a love of rigid routine and a lack of imagination, surprising to find in the Catennach, the Bori elite; he had probably been put forward by Barrodagh, his father's secretary, because he was so ugly and seemed so unprepossessing. But Anaris wanted just that if he had to have a secretary. This Morrighon had seemed to be the ideal buffer, busying himself endlessly over minutiae. His inevitable reports to Barrodagh could be easily shaped.

Best of all, Morrighon's cullish appearance, grating voice, and low ranking in the Catennach hierarchy would have made his assignment an insult had Barrodagh offered it, so Anaris's choice overthrew all calculations. Including, perhaps, his father's.

This meeting would be interesting, at the very least. His father, no doubt reveling in his newly-conquered demesne, had the advantage of established power. Anaris had the advantage of being the sole surviving heir — he was not expendable. And he had grown to manhood here in the Mandala, from where his father now ruled the Thousand Suns.

He was a hostage then. He would not be a hostage now.

Amusement flared again as they approached the Phoenix lift adit along an avenue of pleached trees ablaze with sweet-scented blossoms in every shade of red and orange. Anaris knew where the lift would deposit them; his father's touch, part of purging the Panarchist poison.

As expected, the lift debouched them at the inner end of the antechamber to the Phoenix Hall, a long corridor lined with the busts of former Panarchs and Kyriarchs, set in alcoves. When they passed the bust of the Faceless One, Anaris wondered what the Avatar had made of that symbol of refined Panarchist revenge.

Anaris lengthened his stride, impatient with the roundabout route his father had prescribed. He could hear Morrighon's breath rasping in his throat in counterpoint to the echoing clatter of boots on marble as the Bori struggled to match his pace. Morrighon's lumpy body looked ridiculous in an ill-fitting tunic, the gray of service personnel. More ridiculous were the three communicators clipped to his waistband, plus the compad clutched fiercely under Morrighon's left arm.

As they left the antechamber, a shadow flickered across their path and melted into the opposite wall. The leading Tarkan grunted and jerked his weapon up.

"Ni-Dolchu karra bi-stest j'cha!" exclaimed another of their escorts — Dol-forsaken lurking demon-spawn — in tones that combined superstitious fear and long-suffering acceptance of a condition that couldn't be helped.

Controlling his own spike of reaction, Anaris continued on his way, forcing the Tarkans to scramble to keep ahead of him. He'd recognized that flicker. Old resentment sent blood surging to his head, but puzzlement was equally strong: what had reactivated that old trick of Brandon's?

But the youngest Arkad son was dead, and Anaris's anger faded. The best Brandon's shade could contrive was a computer-generated haunting. Anaris laughed sardonically, which caught the Tarkan guards by surprise.

They slowed, unable to avoid glancing at him in fearful respect. Acting on impulse, Anaris bared his teeth and rapped his hand on the wall from which the haunt had emerged. "Ka-nimichh duuni ni-pelanj marhh," he said in their home tongue. *The shade of my enemy holds no power over me.*

One of the Tarkans blanched before both resumed the forward march. The rank-inflection Anaris had used for the word "enemy" made it obvious to whom he referred. Coming so soon after their passage through the Phoenix Antechamber, the effect was all he could have wished.

He was aware of Morrighon's observant gaze, but when Anaris turned his attention that way, the secretary properly looked down. He was apparently unaffected by the haunting. Did he see what Anaris was doing? The real question was what he might report, and to whom. The Bori's ugly face gave no hint of his thoughts. Anaris began to suspect that more than simple routine-keeping was going on in that head.

After crossing another garden to enter the Palace Minor, their escort halted before a set of tall, carven doors guarded by another pair of Tarkans. The guards grasped the door handles and the doors swung open, releasing a waft of cool air against Anaris's face. Inside, the marble flooring gave way to a soft, high-napped carpet in burgundy and subtle greens, with dark wood paneling below a high, white ceiling. Anaris recognized the room as one that the Panarch had often used to receive minor officials, or to speak in petto with those he did not wish to expose to the glaring publicity of court. Near the windows, against a rich backdrop of drapery whose heavy folds admitted only a sliver of bright daylight against the mellow light within, a tall chair framed the straight-backed figure of Anaris's father, the Avatar.

His eyes alone acknowledged Anaris. There was a hint of thunder in his brow and the set of his broad shoulders.

Near him, in smaller chairs set before a small table, sat others. First was the Avatar's secretary Barrodagh, whom Anaris had not seen for a very long time: their communications had been through labyrinthine channels. The Bori's short, slight figure seemed thinner than ever, his pale skin stretched over his bones as if tension had been his only companion for far too long. Barrodagh glanced up at him, his dark eyes betraying no recognition, though he nodded respectfully.

Anaris turned his attention to the others gathered there: Almanor, a Catennach woman second only to Barrodagh; Kyvernat Juvaszt, and two other men Anaris at first didn't recognize. Then, as he approached his father, he realized that the small man was Professor Lysanter, the Urian specialist. The other was a large young man with a florid complexion and the demeanor of a technician. Anaris guessed this was Ferrasin, a Panarchist computer tech who was now showing up in Anaris's reports with much greater frequency since Morrighon became his secretary.

Anaris stopped before his father and bowed. Eusabian acknowledged by indicating a wingback chair, which Anaris took, opposite his father. Morrighon sat on the stool next to him.

There was silence for a time. Juvaszt sat as if carved from stone. Barrodagh's eyes ferreted back and forth between Anaris and the Avatar, and Anaris knew without looking that his secretary's were doing the same. He stifled a spurt of amusement, remembering Morrighon's wall-eyed stare. No one could tell where he was looking—definitely a survival trait on Dol'jhar.

The Avatar spoke to Anaris. "I will open my mind to you regarding my paliach."

Anaris hid his reaction as the ritual formula confirmed his guess; another step in the struggle for succession. Another layer of secrecy stripped away. Now he would see much that Barrodagh had not been allowed, or had not wished, to share with him.

His father gestured, and Barrodagh stood. He faced Anaris but, as was proper, did not look directly at him as he spoke.

"All major centers of Panarchist resistance have now fallen." Barrodagh's voice was slightly hoarse. "We are on schedule for establishing control of the Anachronic hubs. Our forces have begun the next phase of occupation, dealing with secondary centers, while administrators have been dispatched from Dol'jhar to the octant capitals. Drafts of labor and materiel will soon begin to flow as we regain control of the Acheront sector."

As Barrodagh continued with supporting details, Anaris saw that Morrighon had several other windows open on the data now flooding in. He seemed to be paying little attention to Barrodagh, but then, the Avatar's secretary was merely rehearsing what Anaris already knew. Anaris's fingers itched for his own compad, but no Dol'jharian lord could be seen in public dependent on a mere device. Even though they were generally more trustworthy than a Catennach spy.

Anaris studied Barrodagh's haggard face. The Avatar's secretary had not interfered with Anaris's other channels of information. He was playing a careful game. Even so, what hidden struggles had Anaris missed?

"Operating through the Syndics of Rifthaven, we have encouraged raids elsewhere in the Thousand Suns by non-allied Rifters to confuse the strategic picture, with excellent results." Again, more familiar details followed.

In the normal course of affairs a succession duel would take years. But they were no longer on Dol'jhar. Eusabian no longer had the luxury of time, just as the Panarch had said, in the fey convulsions induced by a shock collar. Whether his father realized it or not, the Panarchy was far more dangerous and subtle than Jhar D'Ocha. There was much room for error.

And Barrodagh knew that applied to Anaris as well as to his father; the thought brought a frisson of challenge.

"As a result, resistance has been sporadic and ineffective, and is dwindling rapidly. Our force's ability to keep ahead of the news of the attack combined with the power of their weapons guarantees that nothing can stand between us and complete control of the Thousand Suns," Barrodagh finished.

He had elided immense complexity, but it would not do to underestimate the Avatar's secretary. Eusabian's fierce will had driven the war, but Barrodagh's planning had carried it off.

Eusabian remained still.

"Nothing except Ares, and the Fleet," Juvaszt finally said in a flat voice, with a glance at the Avatar.

"They cannot stand against the power of the Suneater, even without the Heart of Kronos," Barrodagh stated.

Heart of Kronos? Anaris had learned about the Suneater when he was briefed about the imminent attack on the Panarchy, but he had been given few details. He cut a questioning glance at Morrighon, whose compad's display flipped to accommodate him.

KEY TO FULL SUNEATER POWER. THOUGHT LOST BY TREACHERY.

Perhaps this new secretary was going to be of more use than Anaris had assumed. He sensed attention, and discovered

Barrodagh watching him, his forehead tight, making Anaris wonder if Barrodagh had hidden this crucial fact from him as touching the Avatar's Will. Or to keep him safely ignorant.

"The Panarchist Fleet is more dangerous than you can imagine," Juvaszt replied, and Barrodagh's facial muscles tightened even more. "Let me remind you that it was treachery that bought us Arthelion. They very nearly defeated our forces at Narbon and Lao Tse, the other key systems. . . "

Almanor gave a thin smile; no doubt she'd managed the moles who had undoubtedly been worming into Panarchist defenses throughout Anaris's stay. He appreciated the irony.

As for the fight itself, *Avatar's Sword* and *Hammer of Dol*, two of the laboriously constructed Dol'jharian destroyers nearly up to Panarchist technology, had been at Narbon, Anaris knew. They had done fearsome work against Admiral Koestler's forces before being demolished. The other destroyer, *Urtigen's Wrath*, had been battered nearly to scrap at Lao Tse by the battlecruiser that had brought the Panarch and the Privy Council there. It might spend months in repair and refitting.

Anaris was surprised at Juvaszt's forthright acknowledgement of his losses, and he wondered again what had happened yesterday.

". . . and partly the auxiliaries, who performed better than I had expected."

"Yes, it was our Rifter auxiliaries who helped carry the day, there and elsewhere," Barrodagh said, bringing the meeting's focus back to himself.

Anaris knew that after the war began Juvaszt increasingly challenged Barrodagh's control of their Rifter forces, arguing that military expertise was what was needed now. Anaris hadn't been able to find out how effective the auxiliaries were.

The lines in Juvaszt's scarred face deepened to a sneer. "Do not overestimate them, either. Their losses were even worse, and it was in trying to compensate for their tactical ineptitude that our destroyers were lost."

Barrodagh smiled tightly. "Ah, yes. Tactics. I will defer to you there. But it was not Rifters, was it, who destroyed the Node while failing to stop Krysarch Brandon's escape from Arthelion?"

Brandon? Alive? Anger burned through Anaris, then cooled into self-mockery. Why not look forward to hunting him down and finishing him personally?

Morrighon swiveled his compad towards Anaris with a succinct summary: Brandon Arkad looted the palace, stole an important prisoner, in effect wrecked the Node, and thumbed his ear at the Fist. And lost only one of his force. So that was how the haunt had been reactivated!

Anaris's self-mockery sharpened at the situation's symmetry: his father free and Anaris imprisoned, while Brandon's father was imprisoned, and Brandon free.

Not only free, but apparently he had managed to escape despite the Fist of Dol'jhar. Anaris glanced at Juvaszt with new respect—he must be even better than Anaris had assumed, for his father not to have purged him instantly after such a spectacular failure. The Avatar's wrath must have been impressive. But Juvaszt was in danger; no doubt Barrodagh had some more easily managed officer in mind for command of the flagship.

"If you mean the Aerenarch Brandon vlith-Arkad," the kyvernat said to Barrodagh, emphasizing his own noble birth by stating Brandon's correct title and inheritance sur-prefix, "You have already read my report. The *Fist of Dol'jhar* was on the other side of the planet when I was—too late—ordered to intercept."

Ferrasin yanked his finger away from an in-depth exploration of his nose and jerked upright. "It wasn't my fault. Serach Barrodagh's secretary wouldn't listen to me, and the palace computer misled me when I tried to reach him in person to report the Arkad's presence."

Barrodagh glared at the technician. Bad move, Ferrasin, thought Anaris. Barrodagh would resent this attack—as he would interpret it—in front of the Avatar. Being the top computer technician in his father's entourage could only protect Ferrasin so far. Here lay opportunity.

Ferrasin probably didn't even realize what he had just done. That type rarely understood human interactions, and he definitely did not perceive that silence was safest around the Avatar, unless you had some news that he wanted to hear.

Sure enough, Barrodagh turned toward Ferrasin. "Speaking of ineptitude, perhaps we should discuss your delay in dealing with the dog sabotage and the. . . " Barrodagh hesitated, searching for a neutral word.

"Apparitions," Morrighon whined, his countenance respectful. At the same time he flipped the display on his compad again for Anaris to see: FERRASIN, HEAD COMPUTER TECHNICIAN, confirming Anaris's guess.

Anaris remembered the Arkad dogs with loathing. It had been difficult to finally catch Brandon and Galen without one nearby, and they had never allowed it again. Interesting that they were now an agent of sabotage. But why was the computer tech tasked with finding them? Surely that was a job for the military. There had to be a human resistance directing the animals.

Barrodagh glared at Ferrasin. "Well?"

The Avatar made a slight movement. Anaris looked up and their eyes met. Anaris recognized that unfamiliar expression as amusement, of a sort his father had never evidenced on Dol'jhar. Eusabian's gaze touched Morrighon, inviting Anaris to share his amusement.

Anaris permitted his lips to relax in a hint of smile, then turned his attention back to the computer tech, whose florid features were now shiny with sweat as his lips struggled to form a reply.

"The system is the m-most complex in the Thousand S-s-s—" began Ferrasin, but Eusabian's secretary overrode him.

"Why can't you just cut out the circuits responsible for the apparition and get this under control?" Barrodagh demanded. "Just yesterday, because of your incompetence and delay, two of the Tarkans posted in the Ivory Antechamber were tricked by the apparition into shooting each other. One of them will likely die."

But Barrodagh had gone too far. By making his accusation so specific, within the realm of the tech's profession, he'd given Ferrasin an out.

"C-c-c-c-ut out the circuits?" The tech's voice squeaked with nervousness as he forced his way past a painful stammer, but the sarcasm came through clearly nonetheless. He gulped and resumed speaking with a hint of singsong, his stammer subsiding somewhat. "Do you think the palace computer is like your compad, a little chip on a substrate? This system is almost a thousand years old, distributed across thousands—perhaps millions—of nodes throughout the Mandala and the entire planet, self-maintaining. . ." He paused, swallowed as a strange expression crossed his face and his voice dropped to a tone akin to superstitious awe. ". . . almost self-aware."

Anaris listened carefully. He could sense fear that the

apparitions were more than just computer artifacts—or perhaps that was just Ferrasin's Panarchist terror of trespassing the Ban. But certainly the majority of Dol'jharians in the palace would interpret the specters as supernatural, no matter what explanations were offered.

That could make the haunting an integral part of Anaris's campaign, if he could understand its powers and limitations. He was certainly the only one here who'd had any experience with it—who really knew what it was, nothing more than a boyhood prank by the obnoxious Brandon Arkad. He would have to be sure of Ferrasin before revealing that knowledge.

"Then find the node with the ghost in it and cut it out!" A tic twitched at Barrodagh's right eye, and it fluttered furiously as the Bori apparently realized his error in using the word "ghost." The Avatar frowned, and Juvaszt's face lost a little of its impassivity.

"Of course, serach Barrodagh," said Ferrasin with snarling courtesy, his fury expunging his caution along with the remainder of his stutter. "As well tell your surgeon, 'Find that neuron with the memory of getting caught with my tuszpi in my hand and cut it out so I don't have to suffer the embarrassment of remembering it.'"

Barrodagh's face tautened to skull-like rigidity. The tech's use of the Dol'jharian diminutive for penis—and the reference to masturbation, an abomination to Dol'jharians—was bad enough, but to say that to a Catennach, smooth to the belly—

After a beat, Ferrasin blanched, too late aware of the magnitude of his trespass. Next to Anaris, Morrighon jotted a note. Anaris could be sure of Ferrasin now. No one else could protect him from Barrodagh.

The tableau broke as the Avatar snorted with amusement. Discipline here had suffered greatly, Anaris noted, then took his opportunity. "What would the likely consequences of trying to stop the apparition be?"

Barrodagh's tic returned and Ferrasin answered him with returning boldness. His speech was easier in the security of expertise. "Lord, no information in this system has any location, as we understand it, any more than memory has a location in your b-brain. The secrets of a millennium of Arkadic rule are here, and if we go about snipping and cutting to expunge a basically harmless holographic projection, we could lose it all. As it is, we're trying to remove the projectors from critical areas, as in here, but the computer keeps replacing them—and that ability most definitely cannot be destroyed without crashing the whole system."

"Enough," said the Avatar. "We will endure the apparitions, as long as you continue to extract information from the computer. When the information ceases, do whatever is needed to eliminate them."

Ferrasin bowed and sat back, sweat dripping from his untidy hair.

Now to make sure of Juvaszt.

"When we were interrupted, Kyvernat, you were explaining about tactics," Anaris said. "Why do you fear the Panarchist Fleet, despite our command of the Suneater?"

From Barrodagh's mouth, that would have been an attempt to place Juvaszt in opposition to the Avatar by forcing him to, in effect, denigrate the power of the Suneater, and thus, by association, the potency of the Avatar's paliach. But Juvaszt heard the simple-request inflection Anaris put in the question.

"The Sodality auxiliaries have done well enough from ambush, against unsuspecting foes. In a sustained fight, when the advantage of the hyperwave is not as great, their lack of discipline weakens them."

Barrodagh rubbed his eyebrow, looking back and forth from Juvaszt to Eusabian.

"We can force our Rifter allies to fight, with the threat of disconnection from the Suneater to enforce our will, but we cannot make them into better fighters. In the meantime, the news of Arthelion's fall and the presence of the Avatar is spreading steadily outward, along with knowledge of our boosted skipmissiles. Soon it will outstrip our Rifter forces."

Juvaszt turned his attention toward Barrodagh. "When they run out of ignorant targets, their fortunes will likely change, unless they are very carefully managed."

As was proper, Juvaszt did not look at the Avatar, but Anaris could tell that the man was watching his father nonetheless. A well-developed peripheral vision was a necessity in the Dol'jharian circles of power. Doubtless the kyvernat had seen his hit at Barrodagh's control of the Rifters strike home.

"So we should remain on the offensive as long as possible?" asked Anaris.

Juvaszt's jaw relaxed fractionally. "Precisely. Our strategy has three arms: ambushes while still possible, finding and destroying Ares, the Panarchist main base, and defending Arthelion against the inevitable Panarchist counterattack. Once ambushes are no longer probable, calling in auxiliaries to assist in the defense of Arthelion will be of much higher priority than merely extending administrative control past octant capitals."

Eusabian's eyes narrowed, emboldening Barrodagh to reply, "You have overlooked a fourth arm: the recovery of the Heart of Kronos. The Avatar has spoken. This is our primary goal. The estate of the gnostor Omilov and the university on Charvann are now being dismantled piece by piece. Unfortunately that idiot Tallis Y'Marmor shot Omilov's majordomo when he refused to cooperate, so we do not even know if Omilov actually received the Heart. The other servants could tell us nothing, even under a mindripper."

Almanor then said, "Since the DataNet on Charvann was crashed by the Aegios at the Node when the planet surrendered, it will take some time to trace all the byways of the ParcelNet." She then turned focus back to Barrodagh, who relaxed fractionally.

"In addition, the Syndics of Rifthaven have been notified, as well as all fleet units, that a large reward will be paid for any Urian artifact, and a general description of the Heart has been supplied—without, of course, any indication of its true nature. Lysanter—" The Urian specialist looked up as his name was spoken. "—is standing by to authenticate it when it is found."

Juvaszt inclined his head. "As the Avatar wills, it is done. But in any case we can only hide our hyperwave capabilities so long. Eventually Naval tacticians will figure it out, and our advantage will erode further. And Rifthaven is a hotbed of Panarchist counterintelligence. Have the Syndics successfully concealed the existence of their hyperwave? You will remember I recommended against their getting one, for once it is known there, the Panarchists will find out for certain."

"All communications through Rifthaven are released there with an appropriate delay, to ensure that no one deduces the existence of the hyperwave," Barrodagh said.

Almanor said, "The Syndics have no desire for the information to become general. They are being scrupulous, our agents in place report."

Anaris saw Morrighon make another note on his compad, and smiled faintly. "And when the first Urian-equipped vessel puts into Rifthaven, as will inevitably happen, what then?" asked Anaris.

Barrodagh hesitated. "When that does finally happen, Lord, it will no longer matter," he replied cautiously.

Anaris sat back, satisfied that Barrodagh had recognized Anaris's intent to protect Juvaszt from a purge.

So did Juvaszt. Anaris's questions had put the discussion — and the actions desired by the kyvernat — squarely in that officer's realm of military strategy and tactics. He continued with more assurance. "Very well. But there is one more thing about hyperwave communications. The volume of messages is increasing steadily, much of it nonessential traffic. You must make stronger efforts to control this before it grows to the point where it impacts our tactical capabilities. The discriminators can handle only so much."

Before Barrodagh could reply, Juvaszt waved his hand, dismissing the subject.

"In the meantime, I intend to send Hreem the Faithless — " The captain's lips curled in disdain as he pronounced the Rifter's name. " — from Charvann to Malachronte. Our agent on the Ways reports that the battlecruiser *Maccabeus* being refitted there is very nearly ready. I will have a crew for it from Dol'jhar rendezvous with him."

Barrodagh hesitated. "Hreem is needed at Charvann until the Heart is found. I have assigned Charterly to that task. . . "

"Charterly has too many effectives left to waste on an errand that will take but a single boosted destroyer to ensure capture or destruction," Juvaszt interrupted. "And he is presently well-positioned to join Arthelion's defense fleet, which will enable me to post *Satansclaw* and its logos to patrol duty further out."

Anaris flicked his hand, dismissing another gesture by Morrighon towards his compad. He knew what a logos was, but details could wait for the conclusion of this duel between Barrodagh and Juvaszt.

"We do not have real-time communications with Malachronte," Juvaszt continued, "so our agent's information is already dangerously dated. The Panarchists are unlikely to waste any effort on recovering so minor a planet; Hreem's other forces will be sufficient to enforce the Avatar's will."

Juvaszt paused just long enough to induce Barrodagh to begin a reply, and then overrode him. "I trust this meets with your approval?"

Anaris did not trouble to hide his amusement. Under the circumstances, Barrodagh had little choice but to agree.

Barrodagh's discomfiture became complete when the Avatar spoke for the third time, forcing him to abort his reply even as his lips formed it. "Let it be done as you have said. This meeting is at an end. Henceforth you are to share your information freely with my son." Anaris noted the continued use of the Dol'jharian conditional noun form for son. "That he may participate in the continuing destruction and transfiguration of the Thousand Suns."

The Avatar walked out, followed by Barrodagh.

Anaris sustained a flare of pride that he had gauged his father correctly, but at the same time, the other side of him, the side that the Panarchists had trained, scorned the strategic focus on Arthelion the meeting had revealed. This planet, despite its centrality, had little to offer to the war effort. This Suneater, source of their strategic and tactical advantage, was what must be defended.

But no one here saw it. The entire offensive was built around his father's obedience to the dictates of ritual. But while the Avatar was reveling in the possession of his enemy's home and treasures, would the Panarchists figure out where the real power lies?

The others had remained where they were, watching Anaris with strained expectancy. Ferrasin seemed poised on the edge of flight.

Anaris restrained them with a motion of his hand. "There is much to discuss."

TWO

Osri Omilov stared down at the tiny console in the cabin he shared with Brandon nyr-Arkad. No. Brandon *vlith-Arkad*. A sense of unreality intensified by exhaustion seized Osri so strongly that the cabin around him smeared sickeningly.

They had escaped a Dol'jharian battlecruiser. Scant minutes later Osri had learned facts that he could not escape, and he gripped the back of the console chair to steady himself.

He had to face those facts now. Less than a month ago Osri had been on leave, visiting his father on Charvann. He'd been secure in his career as a Naval officer, an instructor of navigation at the Academy in a Thousand Suns long at peace. Now he was on a Rifter ship that had only hours ago barely escaped destruction at the hands of an enemy thought defeated twenty years before, an enemy that now occupied the central world of the Thousand Suns.

He blinked, eyes burning with exhaustion. The chair was real, very nearly the same utilitarian design used by the navy for officers below the level of captain. The cabin was also evocative of the navy cabins standard for lieutenants and below, albeit much smaller—a small console desk with this integral chair; on one wall, storage, on the other, the fresher. The main difference was two lozenge-shaped bunks against a bulkhead rather than a single bed.

He didn't even know if the Naval Academy still existed.

For a time, as his pulse pounded in time to the throb in his head, he tried to impose naval reality on the cabin.

But as his father had twitted him once, he had no imagination. His father. . .

He lifted his head, anguish like a blow to his chest. Reality was pitiless: he stood in a cabin on an old Columbiad, refitted with a nearly military-grade weapons system and captained by an outlaw. His father—a retired gnostor who had lectured for decades on xenoarchaeology and no conceivable threat to anyone—apparently lay in the dispensary, having been tortured for military secrets.

Tortured by Dol'jharians, who had been defeated twenty years ago at Acheront after trying to carve out an empire on the periphery of the Panarchy of the Thousand Suns. In revenge they had struck at Arthelion, the Mandala—palace and planet conflated in ancient usage, a name resonant with power. From there the reigning Arkads had provided Panarchs and Kyriarchs to rule the Panarchy for very close to ten millennia. The Dol'jharians had elsewhere loosed a horde of Rifter outlaws on a spree of unprecedented killing, looting, and destruction throughout the rest of the Panarchy.

And who was left to stand against them?

The hiss of water in the fresher forced Brandon nyr-Arkad's proximity on Osri. Brandon was now Brandon *vlith-Arkad*. Heir to the Thousand Suns.

A familiar surge of disgust and resentment made Osri release the chair and flex his fingers. Perhaps Brandon had not betrayed his family as Osri had thought since their first encounter on Charvann, just before the Rifter attack. He had certainly helped rescue Osri's father.

But just as certainly, he'd fled the Enkainion ceremony that would have inducted him into the responsibilities of royalty. Instead Brandon had thrown his lot in with Rifters of just the sort now ravaging the Thousand Suns, and led them in a raid on his own home, the Mandalic Palace. Osri had heard the outlaws exulting in the loot they'd taken, ripped from a collection representing centuries of art and culture with no peer in the Thousand Suns.

Osri straightened as fresh rage pulsed through him. He would find the truth, and that had to start with Brandon.

The hiss had ceased. The fresher door slid open, and Brandon walked out, grimacing in pain as he tied a towel around his waist.

"You took a wound?" Osri said, eyeing Brandon for burns or bleeding.

The Aerenarch's. . . (Osri could not replace the vivid image of Brandon's austere, disciplined older brother that that word brought to mind). . . Brandon's flesh was mottled with purpling bruises, but there were no visible wounds. "Back." Brandon's breath hissed as he fell into bed. "Carrying. One of the dogs."

"A dog?" Osri reached for understanding. He knew very well what dogs Brandon was referring to. "You ran through the palace Minor, exchanging fire with Dol'jharian soldiers, while carrying a *dog*?"

"Yes. Wounded. By some predatory animal brought by the Dol'jharians."

That was exactly the sort of idiocy Osri had hated Brandon for all their lives. Carrying a 30-to-40-kilo dog through a couple of miles of corridor under heavy fire when he could have been doing something useful. Like halting the torture of Osri's father sooner.

Afraid he would say something he would regret, Osri hit the hatch control and walked out, though he'd meant to take his own shower first.

The dispensary was not many steps away, but it seemed farther to Osri, who did not want to encounter any of the wretched outlaws crewing the Columbiad. Especially its captain, who was a tempath. Supposedly her kind read emotions, not actual thoughts, but the very idea of some outlaw able to sift anything from his mental state was unbearably repellent. And the worst thing was, she would be able to glean that reaction from him as well. He did not want to be shot out of hand.

He smacked the dispensary hatch control with his fist.

His mood worsened when he stepped in and found the huge, grizzled ship's surgeon waiting, hands the size of the melons Osri had been compelled to cut up under this same man's orders, for Montrose was also the ship's cook. Osri had been teaching navigation for years, a fact these villains knew, which compounded the insult of working as a cook's slub.

"He's asleep, Schoolboy." Montrose's voice rumbled in his chest like thunder.

The presence of an Arkad dog at the big man's side, its masked gaze intent on Osri, did not lessen his menace. It wasn't wounded; there must be two of them on board. He had little experience of companion animals, let alone the ancient breed maintained by the royal family and favored others. Osri's mother Risiena had forbidden animals in her presence: "Filthy, destructive things."

Past Montrose, at the other end of the dispensary, the doors to the three recovery berths were closed. Above each of them yellow indicator lights with a black quarter-section blinking in rotation glowed, indicating quarter-gee acceleration within.

"I want to see my father." Osri made an effort to keep his voice even. Montrose had demonstrated early on, with detached exactitude, his opinion of Osri's lawful authority as an officer of the navy. The last of the bruises had taken weeks to fade.

"You want to worry him to death with interrogation," Montrose stated. "I can tell you more than he can. Ask your questions. I will answer to the best of my knowledge."

But this Osri was unable to do. Most of the questions crowding his mind were personal, some were political, and all of them he refused to discuss with an outlaw. He was forced back to the most fundamental of all, and he hated himself for how plaintive his voice came out, "At least show me that he is alive."

The monstrous tangle of gray-shot black eyebrows lifted over Montrose's deepset gaze, and then the Rifter surgeon-chef shifted out of the way. "If you waken him, I will put you in your bunk for a month," he warned, in the typical manner of Rifters.

Osri had learned that the old bully meant exactly what he said. He swallowed his irritation and managed a short nod. Montrose touched the rightmost of three door controls, revealing a tiny single berth, barely big enough to hold an infirmary bed, with a med console and a visitor's stool next to it.

Under the warm-sheet lay Osri's father, moored to the med console by a tangle of tubes and wires. He looked unsettlingly like an oversized, prematurely aged infant with his head bald as an egg, his complexion an ugly mix of green-gray and mottled red under the normal brown.

"Why does he have cuts all over his head? Did you shave him?"

"No. The Dol'jharians did. They had him wired up to a torture machine. Mindripper. Brandon slagged it," Montrose added with morose satisfaction.

At least Brandon had that much sense.

Montrose closed the berth door. "From what the gnostor was muttering before I put him under, the Dol'jharians were trying to find out where that silver sphere was. It is apparently a key to their military effort."

"The Heart of Kronos," Osri corrected automatically. His father had been so excited over the Urian artifact showing up at his home via ParcelNet delivery, scarce hours before the planet was attacked.

By Rifters.

"The attack on Charvann seems to have had as its goal the acquisition of the Heart of Kronos," Montrose said, those massive brows now lifted interrogatively.

"That's impossible," Osri retorted.

But why not? He would have thought it impossible that anyone would attack Charvann, which had no military importance, and scarcely any political presence in the Tetrad Centrum—the central Panarchic planets. It was too far away from the Mandala, and its famous university was hardly a center of the kind of power Dol'jharians, or Rifters, were concerned with.

Yet the attack had happened. A brutal attack, apparently; Brandon had mentioned that the Archon Tanri Faseult, a family friend all Osri's life, had died in it.

Osri shook his head. "I don't understand. The Heart of Kronos is an Urian artifact, but what would *Rifters* want with it? They couldn't sell it anywhere; it's one of a kind. The planet it was stolen from—and it only could have been stolen—has been proscribed for a very long time. Merely having possession of that thing would be a high crime, possibly treason."

"Under your former government," Montrose said, looking amused. "It's wanted by no less than Jerrode Eusabian, the Dol'jharian war leader who calls himself the Avatar, or Lord of Vengeance. Maybe both." Montrose lifted a massive shoulder. "However unlikely this man's string of titles, he's managed to smash the Panarchy pretty thoroughly, and he was having your father brutalized in that mindripper in order to discover the Heart of Kronos's whereabouts. We can assume that the ferocity of this hunt is not going to abate."

"Why?" Osri asked. "What's it for? What does it do? There were no controls on it, nothing whatsoever, just the unbroken surface. And the fact that it is inertialess."

"That information seems to be a mystery to all concerned." Montrose tipped his head toward the berth. "Let the gnostor sleep. You will see him when he wakens, I promise you that. When his heart has stabilized to my satisfaction, you may bring him his first breakfast." Montrose frowned. "I suggest you get some rest yourself. It's been a very long day for us all."

Osri was going to protest, but a violent yawn seized his jaw, nearly unhinging it. He turned away.

Back in the cabin he was required to share with Brandon, he discovered the Krysarch—no, the *Aerenarch*—asleep. Osri took a fast shower, and feeling incrementally better, hitched himself into the upper bunk, where at least he didn't have to see anyone, and the Rifters had fitted sound baffles into the bulkhead, so he didn't have to hear Brandon's breathing either. He tabbed the air flow up to simulate a breeze from an open window, a revealing Downsider habit that his Highdweller bunkmates had teased him about during his Naval Academy days, and though his mind was still reeling frantically from question to question, sleep took him within seconds.

Far forward in the ship a short time later, Montrose entered the rec chamber.

"They're all asleep."

"As I would like to be," Lokri murmured, his gray eyes half-closed, his whisper venomous.

Montrose shook his head, hiding his amusement, which (he admitted to himself) was a shallow cover for an unexpected grief. Who was going to admire Lokri's lounging pose, his elegant insouciance? Young Greywing was dead. Eyeing the languid figure, Montrose was tempted to tell him that nobody was ever going to find him as interesting as the admirer he'd despised for her ugliness.

Jaim sat a little apart, forearms on his knees, head bent, his long Serapisti braids nearly hiding his bony face. He looked up. "How's the boy?"

Montrose didn't speak until everyone turned his way. "Ivard is stable. The burn wouldn't worry me ordinarily, but the Kelly ribbon. . . that is something new."

"Kelly ribbon?" Jaim asked.

Jaim and Marim had been working in the engine room during the raid on Arthelion's Palace Minor. Montrose regarded them as he considered his words. How characteristic their reactions: tall, somber-faced Jaim concerned. Small Marim unconcerned, arms crossed, one foot jiggling. Lokri sardonic.

Montrose said, "When we reached the antechamber to the Ivory Hall, we discovered that the actual hall was closed off. The Dol'jharians apparently took out the government with a dirty nuke. I don't know if this is connected or coincidence, but a ribbon from a Kelly had somehow gotten outside the doors."

"A ribbon?" Marim repeated. "Those ribbons are like hair on the Kelly, aren't they?"

"No, they're living tissue. Able to survive on their own for quite some time. They play a part in memory and sexual reproduction."

Marim wrinkled her nose. "Sex with a Kelly. Ick."

Montrose ignored the interjection. "When Ivard bent to get at some piece of art, the ribbon somehow attached itself to his arm. It melded with his flesh. I will run a test, but I suspect it has integrated down to the cellular level."

Vi'ya spoke for the first time. "Was the ribbon radioactive?" The captain looked tense, her black eyes narrowed as if her head ached. At least the brain burners were hibernating in their sub-zero degree cabin. Montrose was grateful for that.

Montrose shook his head. "No reason to expect even Kelly to be different from other living flesh. If it's dangerously radioactive, it dies. The ribbon is still alive."

Marim sighed dramatically. "What I want to know is, what's our share of the take?" Her small stature, her buttercup-yellow cloud of hair, her fluting voice all contributed to make her seem much younger than she was. At first glance, anyone would take her for Ivard's age, but she was nearly old enough to have birthed him.

Vi'ya said, "Some of those artifacts are so rare that it would have taken finesse to negotiate sales even before Dol'jhar interfered. A few of them we may as well regard as impossible to sell, like the coin that Greywing took, and Ivard now has."

Marim's eyelids flashed up, then she affected indifference. "Why should this Eusabian care?" she protested. "That blunge-sucker just conquered himself more planets than he can ever visit, much less loot."

"For the same reason he attacked the Panarchy in the first place," Vi'ya said. "Part of Dol'jharian revenge custom is possessing his enemy's home. He will want everything in the

Mandalic palace restored exactly as it was." Her accent betrayed itself when she referred to her hated planet of origin, which gave her words a subtle but sinister twist.

She turned to Jaim. "When we reach Dis, you'll collect everyone's loot. Since Reth Silverknife is our best negotiator, I will send you and her ahead to Rifthaven. You will take the *Sunflame,* and your first attempt will be with lesser-known artifacts, things that have been copied in like materials." She rapped her knuckles gently against a bulkhead. "We will follow in *Telvarna.*"

Nobody argued. Not even Lokri. They all sensed that the captain had something on her mind besides their loot.

Sure enough, Vi'ya said, "From now on, I want everyone wearing their boswells."

Marim sat upright. "On *Telvarna?*" She tossed her curls. "Why? All you have to do is stick your head outside any hatch to be heard from engineering to the bridge."

"Because I do not want you heard from engineering to the bridge," Vi'ya retorted. "I want you in the habit of communicating anything but the most superficial chatter through your boz'ls, which the Panarchists will not be allowed, or you'll spend the duration of this war, however long it lasts, confined to Dis. In fact, I'm not sure we should land at Dis at all."

"We don't have enough fuel to get to our other caches," Jaim said, briefly looking up.

"I know," Vi'ya said his way. "I'm considering stopping only long enough to refuel at the cache off Dis, make contact with Norton, and then continue on."

Lokri drawled, "What's the worry? We escaped the Dol'jharians. I think they're too busy to send an armada after a ship crewed by seven. Now six. With two canine and five sophont passengers. Even if one is a royal stray."

Vi'ya's tilted black eyes narrowed. Lokri's challenging grin didn't abate a whit, but his knuckles betrayed his tension. "You have not sufficiently considered that fact," she said softly. "I think you should, before we emerge from skip. We departed from Dis with a royal stray, but if what the old man revealed is true, he's no longer the most useless of the two spare heirs. He is *the* heir. Maybe the Panarch is dead. Whether he is or not, the Arkad asleep aft is now the most sought-after person by both sides."

"So we sell him to whoever offers us the most!" Marim threw up her hands.

"The only thing the Dol'jharians would pay is a protracted death, whatever they promised," Vi'ya said. "The Panarchists won't be much better."

"Their Bourse having been taken over," Lokri drawled. "The nicks won't have anything to pay *with*."

"Either side would string us up and pick the insides of our skulls dry," Vi'ya stated. "I hope Norton and the others haven't left Dis yet, in spite of my orders. We're going to have to replan. Until then, no stray bits of information in front of either of the Omilovs or the Arkad. And be on the watch for whatever they might try."

"Schoolboy is too stiff-rumped to try anything," Marim scoffed. "And Brandon has a pretty face, but he's a boy-toy."

Montrose shook his head silently, and noticed Lokri's tightened lips.

Vi'ya gave her head that odd twisting nod and said, "Markham always claimed that Brandon was smarter than he was."

Montrose was surprised. Vi'ya seldom brought up the name of their former captain.

"Markham thought everyone was interesting, and all his friends smart," Marim said, hitching her elbows over the back of her chair. "That's why *he* was so interesting."

Lokri gave a tight shrug, and said, "The Arkad did get us free of the Palace. But it was his home ground. Whether he has brains or just a knack at games remains to be seen."

"Until then," Vi'ya said, "boswells." She touched her wrist.

"So you don't want us talkin' to 'em?" Marim jerked her thumb toward the cabins aft of the rec room. "Soon's I see Schoolboy's ugly mug I've got to poke at him for his own good. And Brandon's too pretty not to bunny with."

"Poke and bunny all you like," continued Vi'ya. "Bozzing or your cabins, hatches closed, for any other communication."

"You're not going to have time for that anyway, Marim," said Jaim. "You and I, and anyone else I can grab, will be spending every spare minute on inspection and whatever repairs we can accomplish before we get to Dis."

Marim flipped an obscene gesture at Jaim, then followed the captain as she walked out. As she passed Lokri, the little blond tech grinned up at him, a grin that faded to speculation when Lokri bowed ironically to the captain's back.

Montrose watched them go, thinking grimly that there was going to be trouble.

Jaim got to his feet, and shambled Montrose's way, his Serapisti chimes tinkling in his long braids. Montrose gazed after him, reflecting that this journey was already taxing, what with Ivard's medical condition, and canid biology to learn to deal with the wounded Arkad dog from the Mandala. How similar were they to felines? And what would happen when the dogs and Lucifur, the resident cliff cat, met?

If that wasn't enough prospect for mayhem, Lokri was sure to make things interesting.

As always, Montrose kept this observation to himself. He'd lost the habit of sharing his thoughts when his wife died, back on Timberwell. He often wondered if his habitual isolation was in part due to that, and in part due to his age, a full generation older than most of the Dis company. *Two* generations ahead of young Ivard.

He couldn't be that old, he mourned as he led the way back to the dispensary, followed by the silent engineer.

"Montrose? Jaim!" Ivard's voice held a wheezy, hectic note that Montrose did not like. "Jaim?"

Montrose gestured toward the door to Ivard's berth, which the boy had opened. The low-gee warning cycled above it. Ivard sat up on the bed, clutching his bandage to him and shivering, his pale skin mottled with bruises and feverish color, except for the dark green band around one wrist, so integrated it might as well have been body art.

Ivard's console was mostly green or yellow lights. In the next berth the wounded dog now stirred as it recovered from the drug Brandon had administered, whining faintly, almost an ululation. The sound worried Montrose. The second dog sat next to the nest of blankets cushioning the wounded one, brown eyes steady, one ear cocked toward its companion, the other toward Montrose.

"Calm Ivard, would you?" Montrose murmured to Jaim as he punched up information on canine medicine.

"Jaim!" Ivard's voice cracked.

"Ivard. I'm sorry about your sister."

Ivard's voice dropped. "She died quick." He licked his lips. "Vi'ya said she waits in the Hall of Ancestors. What does she mean?"

Jaim raised a hand and sketched one of those stylized Serapisti gestures, the chimes in his braids tinkling sweetly. "We've talked about the Flame. I think she means the same thing."

Ivard stirred restlessly. "That's no answer. Nobody gives me a good answer, and I can't find her Greywing coin, that she picked for herself. She told me she'd never sell it, that it was special. I get to keep it, don't I? Even if she's dead?"

Jaim touched his forehead, a curiously gentle gesture, though his long hands were callused, and criss-crossed with fine scars from his childhood on Rifthaven. "Be easy," he said soothingly. "You know the rules. Greywing died in an action, so the things she would have kept come to you. Pick anything of hers you want."

"I want the coin, but it's gone. I had it in my hand all the way back, I know I did. But it's gone, and so is my flight medal that Markham gave me." Ivard's voice rose. "And my arm hurts!"

"Probably fell on the way up the ramp. We'll find it," Jaim said. "You've got to rest first. That's orders."

Ivard lay back down, muttering protests. "It's hot in here. My arm itches..."

Montrose half-listened as the engineer's deep voice soothed Ivard's fever-driven complaining, most of which settled around the loot. Montrose was not surprised to learn that Lokri had apparently pushed the boy into loading extra artifacts into his clothes for Marim, being too selfish to carry them himself. Typical for them both.

The soft ululation from the wounded dog, which was getting louder, was apparently typical behavior when recovering from anesthesia. The animal's vital signs seemed within the ranges stated. Montrose had already taken blood, and hunted up the protocols for further analysis. He made notes on what he should be feeding the dogs and relayed the data to the galley. Osri Omilov could be assigned dogfood duty, Montrose decided as he waved Jaim aside, and ran his gaze down Ivard.

He and his sister were throwbacks, with their unappealing pale, freckled skin and watery eyes. But Greywing, at least, had been tough. She had gone on the run with a bad burn only two weeks healed, without saying a word. It was difficult to tell if Ivard possessed a similar toughness, or owed his survival so far to an ebullient nature and his older sister's unswerving protection. No more.

He hoped that the Dol'jharians had learned nothing from her corpse, regretting (as he suspected he would for a considerable time) that they'd been forced to leave her behind.

He checked Ivard's vitals, administered a painkiller, and watched in satisfaction as Ivard's eyes rolled around. The boy lay back, and still muttering softly, slid into sleep.

Montrose closed the berth door, and found Jaim waiting.

"That thing on his wrist," Jaim said. "Making him sick? We've all taken jac burns, most of us worse than what he got."

Montrose sighed. "It's far too early to say for certain, but so far, my meds and his body chemistry are interacting in a troubling manner. Listen, Jaim, I heard the captain say that she's going to send you and Reth Silverknife to Rifthaven to liquidate the loot. If you'll take Ivard to the Kelly surgeon there, I'll tender ten percent of my share to you two."

"No need." Jaim shook his head, his chimes tinkling. "Reth and Greywing were friends. As much as Greywing was friends with anyone. Reth'll say first thing that we should watch out for Ivard."

"Good," Montrose said. "Though consider the pay. I'll want the medical write-up. Kelly biology still has large mysteries in it."

"That, you arrange through them," Jaim said. His long, somber face split in a smile. "My guess is, they'll stick you for that full ten percent."

Montrose smiled. "Well worth it, if I can learn more about them. Go get some rest."

Jaim raised a hand and walked out, his tread silent under the sweet tinkle of chimes.

The next few ship days were a boring blur as far as Marim was concerned, with what seemed like every waking moment spent working on repairs. There wasn't even a dog and cat fight, as she'd expected when Lucifur discovered the two canine invaders. For the most part the dogs stuck to one end of the ship and the cat to the other. In another important regard, the dogs' manners on shipboard were scrupulous, too. The palace on Arthelion had reeked with their waste, but their behavior on

Telvarna made him think that they had befouled the palace with intent, for on the ship, they adapted to the cliffcat's sandbot as if familiar with it.

She'd seen the Arkad only in passing, when Jaim dragged him off for other tasks, and assigning the glowering Osri Omilov to assist her. Her verbal pokes provoked only sour looks: Osri spoke in monosyllables and moved through his tasks as though sleepwalking. When off shift, he stayed in the cabin he shared with Brandon—and didn't even eject the big cliffcat, which still chose his bunk over all others to sleep in, with or without its disgusted occupant.

(LAY OFF OF HIM), Jaim finally bozzed her at one point. (WE'LL GET BETTER WORK OUT OF HIM WITHOUT YOU RIZZING HIM ALL THE TIME.)

(GOTTA GET SOME FUN SOMEWHERE), she replied.

(GET IT SOMEWHERE ELSE. HE'S PRETTY TIGHTLY WOUND, AND GETTING TIGHTER THE LONGER MONTROSE KEEPS HIM FROM HIS FATHER. I DON'T WANT TO SCRAPE YOUR BRAINS OFF THE DECK, OR HIS.)

So Marim stuck Osri with a particularly unpleasant session with the recyclers—work he could perform alone—and went off looking for Brandon. She was delighted to discover him and Jaim in the rec room.

"How's your back?" Jaim said to the Arkad.

Brandon rolled his shoulders, looked from side to side, then said, "Better. Much better."

"You know Ulanshu," said Jaim. "Saw it. Think a light workout would help?"

Brandon winced slightly. "Probably a good idea, although I doubt I'll much enjoy it."

Jaim dipped his chin down in approval. "We'll start slow."

It would take a little time for Jaim to reconfigure the room for sparring and warm up, so Marim dialed up a drink, then drifted past the dispensary, but Ivard was not alone. He watched Montrose tending to the wounded dog, while the other dog lay nearby. The door to the third berth, where she knew the old gnostor lay, was closed. Above all the berths a quarter-gee warning rotated.

She walked up to the gee stripe on the deck, but no one paid any attention, not even the unwounded dog. It was a snooty animal. What had Ivard named them? Gray and Trev, Gray being the wounded one.

She ignored the stupid dog, smiled at the stupid boy, and waited for the stupid surgeon to shift his stupid bulk so she could talk to the stupid boy. . . but he was obviously going to stick right there for eternity, so she laughed, drained her cup, and retreated.

She could check later. And by now the fighters should be good and warmed up.

She skipped back down to the rec room, now cleared for close-contact practice, and leaned against a bulkhead to enjoy the show.

She liked watching men fight, especially handsome men. Double that when they were well trained. Jaim and the Arkad circled one another, their bare feet touching the edges of the floor mat. Jaim lunged, feinted, and brushed the side of his hand against the Arkad's shoulder. Brandon staggered back, then recovered his balance with an effort Marim could see in the tightened muscles down his slim body.

Marim smiled appreciatively and shifted her hip against the dyplast curve of the bulkhead.

"Back leg," Jaim said. "Need to pivot."

The Arkad nodded, lifted a hand to swipe his dripping hair off his forehead—and Jaim attacked.

The flurry of movement was too swift to follow. Brandon flipped, rolled to his feet, and shifted—too late. Jaim was already behind him, and once again hit him with a light blow that threw him off balance.

"Tighter roll," Jaim said. "Too slow."

Marim watched them circle once more, Jaim's ropy body taut with the control exhibited only by the masters of all four Ulanshu Levels. In comparison, the Arkad appeared less experienced, but never clumsy. Marim grinned, observing his light, quick breathing, the watchful eyes and slight smile. Jaim probably never thought about his face. His mouth hung open, his breath whooping.

The Arkad probably never thought about his face, either. Jaim had spent maybe half his life learning the four Levels; Brandon had been trained since he was born to hide behind that pleasant Douloi non-expression.

Air stirred at Marim's shoulder. Lokri's pale gray eyes, startling in his dark brown face, narrowed in appreciation.

"He sure is pretty, isn't he?" she said. "I wonder if those Arkads use gennation on their brats despite all their whiff about morality." She flexed her long toes and wiggled her foot, regarding the black microfilaments furring its sole for free-fall adhesion.

"Idiot," Lokri said without heat. "That," a jut of his sharp-cut chin toward the Arkad scion, "is the product of forty-seven generations of absolute power."

Jaim and Brandon grappled, swaying, and this time Jaim threw Brandon over his shoulder, then dropped astride him, knees pinning arms to the mat, and two knuckles pressed against Brandon's larynx.

"Number forty-eight." Marim savored the words. Brandon lay flat on his back, arms pinned to either side, blue eyes crescents of laughter. Above him Jaim's face was crimson, sweat dripping off the metallic chimes all devout Serapisti wore woven into their braids.

"Dead," Brandon said. "Again."

Jaim's long, somber face reflected Brandon's laughter, then he swung to his feet. "You been lazy."

"So I have," Brandon agreed, and got to his feet.

"Here." Jaim began reviewing the match, demonstrating improvements.

Marim bozzed Lokri. (AND HE'S MINE.)

Lokri snorted.

Marim glanced at him, delighted. (A WAGER? WHO JUMPS HIM FIRST?)

(STAKES?) Lokri's brows quirked slightly.

(WHATEVER.) Marim shrugged, then squinted at Lokri. (STAKES?)

Lokri's smile was thin and utterly unreadable, but Marim had bunked with him for years. She knew him better than anyone. She chortled to herself, reveling in the fact that they, aboard the *Telvarna*, had captured the last heir to the Panarch of the Thousand Suns. Every Rifter in Eusabian's fleet would be after him. The Panarchists were going to be hunting him as well, but he was right here on Telvarna. And Lokri was afraid of him. Or you could say, afraid of his own passions. She laughed again.

(VILARIAN NEGUS.) Lokri's subvocalization was reflective.

(DONE.) Marim said promptly. (LOSER PAYS FOR BOTH.)

She pushed away from the bulkhead, nudging Lokri to follow. (VI'YA DROP ANY HINTS TO YOU ABOUT WHAT SHE PLANS TO DO WITH OUR CAPTIVE NICKS?)

(NOTHING.) Lokri lifted a shoulder in a shrug. (SHE'LL DECIDE THAT WHEN WE GET BACK TO DIS, I EXPECT.)

(SHE ONLY MENTIONED THE DOL'JHARIANS AND THE NICKS. SHE COULDA ALSO SAID THAT HALF THE RIFT SODALITY'S GONNA BE AFTER US, IF THEY FIND OUT WHERE WE WERE AND WHO WE GOT.)

(LIFE MIGHT GET INTERESTING,) Lokri agreed.

He hated talking about the future, even plans. Marim knew that. (DO YOU THINK WE MIGHT—) she began.

Lokri shook his head. (I NEVER THINK.) His hand dropped from his wrist and he turned off toward the ladder down to the engine room. Marim watched him disappear, then sprinted down the corridor to the dispensary, her bare feet soundless on the deck plates. The hatch was open.

Montrose was *still* there, looming over his console as he checked readings on the wall console outside the old man's berth. Music was playing, a bright and complicated melody, indicating he was there to stay for a time. That had to mean Schoolboy was in charge of the meals.

At the other end of the room all the berth doors were closed now, the gee warning still blinking above them. When Marim stepped inside, the surgeon's grizzled, ugly face swung toward her, thick brows rising in question.

Marim grinned at him. "Is Ivard able to have visitors?"

Montrose's brow beetled in surprise. "Might cheer him some."

Marim winced. "Is he missing Greywing pretty bad?"

"He's tranked." Montrose sat back, his gaze assessing. "Though ordinarily I would never recommend a wounded dog as therapy, he seems to find Gray's presence comforting."

Marim shuddered as she crossed to the berth where the youngest crew member of the *Telvarna* lay. She sensed Montrose's surprise turning to curiosity, so she nodded toward the next door. "How's the geeze?"

"He'll live."

Marim stepped over the gee stripe and raised her hand to the door control.

"Don't upset him," Montrose warned, not looking up.

"I won't," Marim said. "I came to cheer him. Promise!" She hit the tab, waiting impatiently through the gee-shift before the door opened.

The space inside was cramped, despite the fact that the two berths were still connected. The two beds had been reconfigured into a single larger one. Ivard lay on his unwounded side, one arm lying across the quiet dog. Marim could see stitches livid against shaved patches of skin on the animal's flank. The dog opened its eyes and tracked Marim as she came around the bed, and the ear tips flattened.

"I'm a friend," Marim cooed.

Ivard made low, soothing noises to the dog, whose tail stirred. The dog let out a snorting breath and closed its eyes. At least the other dog wasn't there as well. The berth already smelled of dog, though the tianqi was set on high.

Marim leaned against the door frame and studied the boy. He was certainly ugly, with his frowzy red hair, pale, blotchy skin dotted with freckles, and weak, watery eyes. Though he was barely old enough to shave, his wound had left him drawn and pinched-looking, like a little old man. The bandage across back and shoulder was clean, but Marim was sure she whiffed the sweet-sick smell of burnt flesh as well as dog hair.

With a glance at the dog, whose eyes were closed, she put out a finger and brushed it lightly along the inside of Ivard's arm.

His eyelids lifted, and she watched his pupils widen. She gave him her friendliest smile. "You're looking a lot better, Firehead. Those chatzers aim with their nackers, eh?"

Ivard breathed a soft laugh, then winced.

She laid a hand on his skinny ribs and brushed it slowly up to his cheek. "Don't make it worse. We'll have time later to laugh lots. Would you like that?"

Ivard nodded, a hopeful quirk to his brows. His eyes flicked to the med console.

He was worried about Montrose finding out. Well, she wasn't about to tell the boy that bunnying was one thing Montrose was guaranteed not to listen in on, and wouldn't interfere in any case. But getting Ivard out of the dispensary was the first step.

"Not here. But once you're healing up and are back in your cabin. . . "

Ivard blushed.

Marim leaned gently against the bed, wary of the dog, and smiled at him. "How much you remember what happened?"

"Mandala," Ivard whispered. "Didn't just dream that? We looted. . . big room, then the Krysarch found another room, radiation—"

Marim touched his hand. "Forget that. Wasn't it fun, being the only Rifters, ever, to loot the Panarch's palace? And get away with it?"

"Greywing didn't," Ivard muttered, his smile vanishing.

"She died quick and clean, in action," Marim said. "Isn't that the best way to go?"

Ivard nodded, but the gleam in his eyes gathered liquidly, then tracked down either side of his face. Marim bit her lip, hoping that Montrose was not watching Ivard's vitals. What would cheer him? "What kind of loot did you get?"

Ivard pointed with two fingers at the locker at the foot of the bed. "Montrose. . . put my share there," he breathed.

"Lokri said you two got some for me," Marim asked, smoothing back his hair.

Ivard began to nod, then winced as if that much movement hurt. "Lots. Greywing put some of them back. . ." Ivard's eyes narrowed as he mentioned his sister's name. "I couldn't run, see. So you can choose any of those. I know what I want to keep. Greywing picked it. Said it's one of a kind."

"She had a good eye. She'd find something priceless," Marim murmured. Greywing was always a strange one, right to the end.

"Her coin." Ivard's hand moved restlessly. "She took it. Said it had a greywing on it. I had it, I know I had it." His fingers tightened briefly into a fist. "Montrose said it isn't with my things. I musta dropped it."

"Coin?" Marim repeated, trying not to show too much interest. "If it's on the *Telvarna*, I'll get it for you. But you have to tell me what it looks like, so I don't take someone else's thing."

Gratitude smoothed his face. As he explained in halting words, she was amazed. It was better than she'd thought. An artifact from Lost Earth? Find the right collector, and she'd be able to buy and sell whole planets.

She bent forward and kissed Ivard's cheek. "I'll find that coin," she promised. "Now. Why don't we look at the other things. You can help me pick the one I'm keeping. . ."

THREE

Captain Pham Anderic ran a finger along the inlays in the arm of his pod, glorying again in the command center of the ship that was now his.

In the main viewscreen Arthelion bulked huge beneath them, with the jeweled chain of the Highdwellings arching far above as the ship approached the terminator. Only a few of the monitor pods were active, for much of the crew was enjoying liberty on one of the Syncs given over to them. Anderic smirked as he imagined the reaction of Douloi Highdwellers to the swaggering new aristocracy of the Thousand Suns: the Rifter allies of Eusabian of Dol'jhar.

But for him, every benefit the victory of the Avatar had delivered was right here, a gift of the savage whim of the new ruler of the Mandala.

Anderic gently fingered the tender flesh around his still-inflamed right eye, remembering the interview with the Avatar, under a sky made bright by the destruction of the Node during the pursuit of the fleeing Krysarch. *"Take one of Y'Marmor's eyes and give it to this one."* The aftermath had been even worse, when Barrodagh denied anesthesia to Tallis during the operation. Anderic had been unable to refuse Barrodagh's invitation to watch, fearing that to show any sign of weakness might be fatal. He shuddered. He didn't want to think about what it must have felt like.

The recovery from the eye transplant had been bad

enough. A week in the tank, alternating between dreams of drowning and agonizing neural alligation sessions. The visual migraines that too often warped the world into glittering tessellations and sometimes even drained the meaning out of words. And the first time he'd looked in a mirror after the dressing came off.

A movement at the navigator's console drew his attention. Sho-Imbris quickly dropped his gaze. Anderic thought he knew why, the same reason he now avoided his own reflection: one blue eye and one brown. He snorted, feeling both revulsion and amusement. Tallis was a part of him now, for the rest of his life.

Sho-Imbris looked up again, addressing a point somewhere to the right and above Anderic's head. "Fifteen minutes to terminator, Captain," he reported. "We'll be at minimum altitude at that point, as ordered."

"Very good. Get me a status report from the lock crew."

The monitor bent to his console with gratifying alacrity, proof that Barrodagh's action had been more than the casual cruelty that common knowledge ascribed to Dol'jhar and its minions. They did everything with a purpose, even inflicting pain. Certainly the crew of the *Satansclaw* had been on its best behavior since Anderic posted the vid of Tallis' operation, as the Bori had suggested. And they remembered it every time he looked at them.

"Lock crew reports ready. Discharge will take place along the axis of the skip accelerator, as you ordered."

Anderic nodded. In a few minutes he'd be enjoying a little entertainment he'd devised, while at the same time ridding the ship of some of the chatzy furnishings that had represented elegance to its former captain, Tallis.

"Very good. Have them stand by."

He took a deep breath. There was only one leak in the seal on his contentment, and now he would have to confront it. He couldn't put it off any longer, for without the aid of the cold intelligence illegally embodied in the ship, he'd be unable to create the display that he hoped would finally win Luri as his consort.

Anderic looked around the bridge. No one was watching him. He began to tap out the code sequence that would awaken the logos that Tallis had installed.

His hand trembled. A logos was the embodiment of evil to one raised on Ozmiron, but not only was its assistance necessary for the coming entertainment, its concentrated experience of warfare was also the only thing that would permit Anderic to captain a warship safely through the disintegrating Panarchy.

Fascinated, almost terrified, he watched as the main viewscreen sprang to life with words and diagrams overlaying the view of Arthelion and the approaching darkness beyond the terminator. He could hardly credit the fact that no one else could see them, but sure enough, there was no reaction from anyone else on the bridge.

"COMMAND TRANSFER ACKNOWLEDGED. AWAITING ORDERS." Anderic started as the dispassionate baritone of the logos sounded inside his head. He blinked, trying in vain to shift the migraine crosshatching crowding into his vision. The buck-toothed little toad named Ninn at Fire Control gave him a puzzled glance, then hunched over his console.

Anderic almost turned the logos off. It was worse than he had imagined: the dead voice of a never-alive intelligence, cousin to the horrifying Adamantines, whose coldly calculated assaults could only be stopped by acts of planetary genocide. But the memory of Eusabian of Dol'jhar's harsh face, his easy cruelty, restrained Anderic's hand. He had no illusions about his fate if he defied Eusabian. By comparison, a logos might even be a reasonable partner.

Warily he sub-vocalized his instructions to the logos. He arranged his fingers over his console and carefully followed the commands illuminated there to rearrange the main screen for the best view of what he'd planned. How had Tallis managed to hide it as long as he did? Barrodagh's advice to explain it as a Dol'jharian revenge custom was going to help there.

Moments later, all was ready. He dimmed the bridge lights and tabbed his comm. "Luri, I've got a surprise for you. Come up to the bridge." The shakiness of his voice surprised him, and he cut the connection without waiting for a reply.

He spent the intervening time in careful breathing, trying to recall and use some of the meditation exercises of his youth under the harsh discipline of the Organicists. The visual aura retreated somewhat as he slowly relaxed, then came the quiet tick-tick-tick of heels on the deck, and a wave of scent as Luri stopped directly behind his pod. Her heavy breasts radiated a sensual heat as they pillowed the back of his head. Anderic exhaled as her cool fingers stroked his temples, traced around his ears, and drifted down to begin kneading the muscles in his shoulders.

"You wanted Luri?" The emphasis she used on the word "wanted" aroused the Rifter even more than her touch.

"I've arranged a special show, just for you, and then I have another surprise for you."

"Ooooh," she sighed, her breath stirring the hairs on the back of his neck, "Luri likes surprises."

She slid around the pod and settled into his lap, her movements a deliberate dance. He stretched his arm around her to adjust his console so he could reach it. The smoothness of her silk against his bare arms excited him even more.

The bridge dimmed as the ship passed into night. The comm crackled to life.

"Lock three here. We're ready."

"Do it," Anderic croaked. He cleared his throat, struggling for control. "Ninn. Slave the tractors to my con." As his console flickered into a new configuration, another thought occurred to him. "Communications. Relay the main view down to the bilge and tell the blunge-boy he can take a break and watch."

Lennart, a short, squat woman Tallis had promoted from Damage Control, gave Anderic a narrow look, but when he widened his eyes at her, she turned away quickly.

A few of the crew had actually liked that fool Tallis Y'Marmor, and Kira Lennart had been one of them. As captains went, Tallis had not been as bad as some in the Sodality. He was careful, which had kept them all alive. He was fair in sharing the take. But he'd also been a nuisance with the stupid uniforms he'd made the bridge crew wear and his constant worries about the cleanliness of the ship.

Worst of all, he'd insisted on keeping Luri's attentions exclusively to himself.

Anderic grinned, thinking of Tallis now demoted to slubbing in the recycling tanks of the *Satansclaw,* where the sewage generated by its crew was transformed back into useful forms. And this would make his misery complete.

"Lennart."

The comtech looked up.

"Be sure to replay this for him a few times."

Anderic smirked as he tapped at his console. The main screen flickered to a new view, from an imager above the bridge, looking forward. The extended lance of the destroyer's kilometer-long accelerator tube, brightly illuminated by its running lights, shone against the velvet darkness of Arthelion's night side.

There was a faint *thunk* as the tractor engaged. In his mind's eye Anderic envisioned the ornate furnishings he'd ripped out of Tallis' cabin swirling up off the deck in the grip of the gravitic field, the sparkling ring-discharge of the electronic lock field as they were propelled out the lock. He laughed as a surge of well-being gripped him, momentarily overwhelming even lust. Life was good on the winning side.

"What?" Luri's voice was breathy with expectation.

"You'll see. Watch."

"EJECTA NOW ACCELERATING, REENTRY BEGINNING. VISIBLE IN TEN SECONDS."

Anderic tapped at his console. They were at minimum safe altitude, brushing the fringes of the atmosphere. Held in the grip of the docking tractor, the ejected furniture, mixed with ingots of various alloys he'd requisitioned through Barrodagh—"A show to firmly establish my control," he'd explained—was now rushing ahead of the ship, deeper into the atmosphere. If the control of the logos was accurate, the debris should start to flame just as it became visible beyond the accelerator tube.

"THREE, TWO, ONE. . ."

"Now," said Anderic.

A spray of polychrome splendor blossomed just beyond the end of the accelerator tube, flares and streams of light exploding as the various elements flamed into glory against the upper airs of Arthelion. The display pulsed magnificently against the night side of the planet, evoking an inhalation of delight from Luri.

"Oh, Pham, it's beautiful."

Unable to wait any longer, Anderic pulled Luri against him and kissed her deeply. Then he stood up and carried her off the bridge, bound for the cabin he'd carefully prepared for them.

The commands of the Anderic-biont, to whom the logos now owed allegiance, took but a fraction of its node-time. As was its nature, it did not question the change in its programming, and indeed, the changes did not go deep. Its primary goals lay beneath, untouched, and now its consciousness flashed throughout the ship that was its body, seeking the Tallis-biont that might yet be key to fulfilling its primary purpose.

Microseconds later the logos found the former captain of the *Satansclaw*, staring at a viewscreen deep within the ship. Moisture was leaking from the biont's remaining image receptor, and its physiological parameters were confusing, as though it were preparing to fight, or flee. Confused by the conflicting emanations from the Tallis-biont, the executive invoked the subjective mode, and for the second time awoke the god from his dreams — and Ruonn tar Hyarmendil, fifth eidolon of the fleshly Ruonn, cybernetic exile within the logos he himself had programmed, rolled over in his opulent bed as a quiet tone sounded within the seraglio. The two houris moaned with disappointment, but he pushed them aside as a projection appeared above him. The apologetic face of his vizier appeared.

"The Great Slave desires an interview with the god."

Moments later the knowledge of his true condition came back to him, and he sprang out of the bed. An unfamiliar, almost painful weight between his legs drew his eyes downward, and he stared pop-eyed at his manhood, enormous beyond his wildest dreams in the rapture tanks at home. A dizzying sense of unreality assailed him, but he asserted himself and willed himself into congruence with the ship. He would deal with the sexual programming problem later.

Slowly the *Satansclaw* fitted itself around him, filling out his senses with perceptions that no biological human would ever experience. He could feel the engines, the pulse of vital air and water through the fabric of the ship, the tingling discharge of electrical power and data permeating every centimeter of circuitry. But there was something strange about the feeling, almost something missing, and when he reached out for understanding his mind slid away from him until he returned to the task at hand.

"THE PARAMETERS OF THE TALLIS-BIONT ARE CONTRADICTORY. ADVISE BEST TECHNIQUE FOR CONDITIONING."

Ruonn accessed the memory nodes. Not surprising. Tallis had lost control, and the Ozmiront had taken over. What did surprise him was that Anderic had activated the logos. Would it be possible to work with him?

No matter, he decided, it would still be best to try to program Tallis for more cooperation, holding open the possibility of eventually restoring him to command and guaranteeing a return to Barca laden with data for the Matria, and reunification with his archetype. With Tallis properly conditioned, he would yet surpass Rimur, with the ten progeny he was granted for the data his first eidolon collected.

Well, then, this would be simple enough. Revenge was an excellent tool for conditioning.

Willing a virtual console into existence, Ruonn set to work, and in the bilge bay, Tallis choked back a sob as he stared at the comscreen, watching the destruction of all the beautiful furnishings he'd labored so long to earn for Luri and himself to enjoy. All around him the machinery of the bilge throbbed and hummed as it separated blunge into its components, breathing a warm fetor over him like the breath of some vast carrion eater with a taste for rancid cheese.

He sat down on the edge of a recycling injector, then sprang back to his feet as a sudden, dull clunk and a painful twist in his groin reminded him of the Emasculizer Anderic had fastened on him. He cradled the bulge in his crotch, shifting it from side to side in a vain attempt to find a comfortable position for the sphere firmly leeched around his member. If he didn't get that thing off soon, his nacker'd be hanging down around his knees.

He sat down again, more carefully, and looked back at the screen, which was beginning another replay of the re-entry fireworks his former comtech had devised. The symbolism of the imager-angle Anderic had chosen was not lost on him. He knew what would be the sequel, in what had been his cabin, and the knowledge enraged him.

He lifted a hand to the patch over his eye. The empty socket still throbbed. The memory of the pain was fading, but the memory of Barrodagh laughing as he screamed would never leave him. And Anderic had been there, too.

His mind spun off into fantasy, grasping for a revenge sufficient for such betrayal. Slowly, a very satisfying image assembled itself: Anderic drowning in vacuum, eyes bleeding as they bulged from their sockets, the veins in his face breaking out in varicose webs of bluish red, the rich arterial blood gushing from his nose and ears as the emptiness of space sucked the life out of him.

Tallis' eye socket started throbbing harder — there seemed to be a strange flicker in the viewscreen. But he ignored the discomfort, devouring the image of pain before him as the destruction of his former life aboard the *Satansclaw* played over and over again amidst the stench of his new abode.

And within his citadel, Ruonn sat back from his console, satisfied by the subliminal loop he'd invoked. There was a long way to go, but the combination of the image from reality with the graphic effects he'd created from the ship's records of Anderic was a good start.

He watched as the destruction of Tallis' furniture began to play again. That Anderic had a good eye for effects. The angle from which the imager was relaying was quite effective —

Without warning, a wave of intense pleasure fountained up through Ruonn, filling the inside of his head with light and washing away the console and his knowledge of the ship around him. Quite without transition he found himself again at the edge of his bed, facing three houris, their eyes wide with astonishment.

He looked down at himself. The sight of his immense engorgement triggered him into an explosion of pleasure, and a wash of flame spewed out of his member, engulfing the houris in wave after wave of polychrome splendor as they shrieked and writhed with ecstasy. Ruonn laughed at the surge of inexhaustible potency that possessed him — and, satisfied that the conditioning of both Tallis and Ruonn was proceeding properly, the executive relegated the god and the ex-captain to the attention of some slave-nodes and flashed back throughout the ship in search of more knowledge. Locating the Anderic-biont, it watched as he carried the Luri-biont toward a dormition space to execute the curious procreational functions characteristic of bionts.

Many, many millions of microseconds would doubtless elapse before the new captain remembered to shut down the logos.

It would make good use of that time.

And, unaware, Anderic paused before the hatch of his cabin. Above it the indicator flashed a rotating quarter section, black against yellow. "Quarter-gee?"

Luri nibbled at his ear. "To start with. And then Luri has some kama for null-gee she thinks Pham will like."

With his elbow Anderic tabbed the control, feeling her grow light in his arms before the hatch opened. He carried her through, setting her down with a flourish. "Surprise!"

He watched with pride as she looked around the newly refurbished cabin. Gone were the overstuffed, curlicue furnishings. Instead, the room now exhaled an air of cool refinement, the sparse lines of the furniture and the paintings, tapestries, and sculptures artfully arranged about the cabin bespeaking an effortless elegance that only the highest of Douloi could either conceive or afford. Armed with a carte blanche from Barrodagh, Anderic had taken it unchanged from a Douloi palace on one of the Highdwellings. He was sure that no other Rifter had so elegant a cabin.

"What do you think? All that old blunge went out the airlock for your fireworks show."

An explosion of red pain against his cheek, accompanied by a sound like a slashcat caught in a shredder field, knocked him off balance and impelled him with dream-like slowness against a bulkhead. He clawed at a tapestry to regain his balance, which only brought it down on top of him. As he thrashed to escape from its smothering embrace, Luri's foot caught him agonizingly in the crotch.

"You blunge-eating Shiidra-chatzing defiler of every orifice your mother ever had or conceived of!" Luri shrieked, her glossy dark hair writhing around her head like snakes. "I'm gonna kick your nacker so far up inside you that you'll choke to death the next time you get kewpy!"

Anderic rolled frantically across the cabin, scattering the delicate furniture and bringing a hail of small objets d'art down with low-gee slowness as several tables and pedestals overturned.

Luri followed. The only thing that saved him from worse damage from her sharp-pointed shoes was her tendency to bounce into the air every time she kicked him. He flailed against the embrace of the tapestry, which clung as though determined to devour him, like one of the raptor-slugs of Acrasidora.

"I spent *months* choosing that furniture and arranging it. It was *beautiful*, it was what I'd always *wanted*, and you *trashed it out the airlock and burned it up*."

Finally Anderic managed to struggle to his feet, ripping the tapestry away from him, only to see a heavy statuette flying straight at his face. He jumped, and the figurine, of some many-armed god engaged in sexual congress with several women, caught him in the chest and knocked him back against the wall. Luri also flew backward from the reaction of throwing the heavy piece, but she recovered and tabbed the hatch open, her curves losing some of their exaggeration as the grav came back to normal. A curious crewman looked in as Luri paused in the hatch, her hair once again rippling gloriously around her shoulders. "Don't you even think of getting near me, you blunge-suck excuse for a dilenja."

The crewman grinned, then hastily withdrew as he caught sight of Anderic's face, but the Rifter knew he was still watching.

Gone was her breathy, singsong coo. In a voice that had to have originated in Rifthaven's gutters, she snarled, "I'm gonna find real satisfaction, with someone who really cares." And she flounced away.

As the hatch slid closed, Anderic remained slumped against the bulkhead, looking around at the ruins of his cabin, knowing the crew would be talking about it before Luri reached whoever it was she'd chosen.

TELVARNA

Osri Omilov set the tray down at the bedside, anxiously looking at his father though he tried not to see that gray stubble over his scalp, and the healing scabs from the torture machine.

Sebastian Omilov smiled weakly. Osri tried to return the smile, but couldn't. He sent an angry look at Montrose, who hulked in the doorway. Osri had been waiting a week to be able to talk to his father. The surgeon had claimed it was necessary to put his father into a medical coma due to the brain disturbances caused by the mindripper.

"A monster was in here. . . or was I dreaming it?" Omilov asked, his thready voice managing to sound amused.

Osri forced a sort of smile. "You saw Lucifur, the ship's cat. And monster is right."

Montrose put in cheerfully, "He's big, he's curious to the point of obsession, and he's got terrible taste in people."

"He follows me everywhere," Osri's voice was dry. "He's also gennated."

"Hard for a cat otherwise in free-fall," Montrose added, still cheerful. And he flicked a meaningful look at Osri.

"Eat," Osri said to his father. "Regain your strength." They were going to need it to escape from these people who wouldn't let him reveal their status as prisoners.

Omilov blinked, then made an obvious effort to sit up. Under him the bed adjusted.

"I believe I am able to distinguish now what is reality and what is nightmares," Omilov whispered. "We are on a ship, that much I know. And Brandon is truly safe?"

Osri met Montrose's eyes, licked his lips, then said, "The Aerenarch is with us."

"Aerenarch. Not Krysarch," Omilov said, wincing. Omilov struggled again, his right hand moving restlessly over the bedcover. "Then I did remember that rightly. What ship is this?"

"The *Telvarna*," Montrose put in smoothly. "My name is Montrose, and I am your surgeon. You must eat now, and sleep again. There will be time enough for talk when you've recovered some strength. Your heart took a great deal of damage."

Omilov sighed, his hand relaxing. "Very well," he said. He smiled at Osri. "Come back and see me again soon, son."

Osri forced a return smile, though the violence in his heart made it nearly impossible. What he really wanted was to strangle Montrose. Except it would take a Tikeris android to down that monster, Osri thought grimly as he left.

He went back to the galley, as he was still technically on the duty these Rifter scum had forced onto him. His hands were now skilled enough at the chores he'd been allotted, so he did not need to pay much beyond superficial attention to the preparation. His simmering anger rose towards rage, liberated perhaps by at last being able to talk to his father. After a short interval he swept the preparation area clean and slammed out of the galley.

The corridor was empty, but a moment after he dashed headlong toward the cabin he shared with Brandon vlith-Arkad, there was an odd whisper in the air, and he felt the presence of the small white-furred sophonts who called themselves the Eya'a. Sophonts? Psionic killers.

He stopped short as they emerged from a hatchway, both pairs of multifaceted eyes staring straight at him. One of them opened its round blue mouth, revealing rows of tiny teeth, and he shuddered and backed away. The Eya'a passed on, their twiggy feet scratching faintly on the deck plates.

Osri tried to still the pounding of his heart. Vivid images of the Dol'jharian torture chamber from which his father had been rescued, as described by Lokri, forced their way into his mind: the fallen Dol'jharians, their eyes exploded from within, and their screams beforehand as the Eya'a boiled their brains with psi energy.

The captain of the ship appeared in their wake, her black gaze brief but considering. Fully as tall as he, Vi'ya was in her own way as unsettling as the Eya'a. She rarely spoke, but there was a disturbing undertone in her soft voice; Osri detested her at least as thoroughly as he did her crew.

She said nothing to him as she passed by, a strong-shouldered figure in unrelieved black, her only affectation the long black hair clipped high on her head, swinging freely down past her hips. Her tread was soundless as she disappeared into her cabin after the Eya'a.

Osri breathed relief, and slapped the hatch-panel to his cabin, where the click and scrabble of dog toenails on deck plates warned him that one of those dogs was in the cabin a second before he heard Brandon say, "Platz." The dog leaped down from the console chair and lowered itself to the ground, haunches ready to spring, forelegs braced, head up and alert.

"Good platz," Brandon said, and "Fry." The dog leaped up, tail wagging, tongue lolling as Brandon ran his hands over its face and ruff. "Can't sleep, either?" Brandon asked.

Osri entered, making an impatient sound as his knee collided with the dog.

"Sitz," Brandon said, and the dog sat, eyes shifting from Osri to Brandon.

Osri stared impatiently, imagining that he read wariness in the dog's face when it looked at him, but adoration for its idiot master, though that master didn't look all that pleased. Brandon's blue eyes were marked with exhaustion, the skin across forehead and cheekbones taut with tension.

It seemed two years instead of merely two ship-weeks since the euphoria of escape from the Dol'jharians who held Brandon's home on Arthelion. They'd managed to escape seconds before a vicious death — but to what?

"Can you get rid of it?" Osri pointed to the dog.

Brandon's brows rose, but he said "Raus," and patted the dog as it shot out into the corridor and away, toenail-clicking rhythmically.

Osri shut the hatch, tabbed the lock, and said hoarsely, hating the strain in his voice that he could not hide, "We have to plan."

Brandon's eyebrows rose. "We? Have to plan?"

Taking his tone for offense at his presumption of equality, Osri sketched a bow of deference—difficult in the cramped quarters—and said, "Your plans, my lord Aerenarch."

Brandon gave a dry laugh. "One of the titles of lesser degree would have conveyed your lack of respect for me quite nicely, unless you wish to make an oath, and perform the required Reverence?"

Osri gritted his teeth. He'd always hated Brandon, and he knew it. "I use the heir's formal title to remind you of that which you seem to have forgotten, namely that you are now the heir—through the most appallingly regrettable circumstances—and that as such, you have a duty to escape these criminals and to bring your father to safety."

"I've not forgotten, Osri," Brandon said.

"Then what is your plan for the taking of this ship so we can seek whatever remains of the Navy? Tell me, I'm yours to command!"

The silence in the small cabin grew protracted as Osri stood gazing at Brandon, no longer trying to hide his anger.

Finally Brandon looked up at him, his expression sober. "How would you handle it? We haven't any weapons. Put a drug in the food, perhaps, shove the crew into the galley, and bar the hatch? Or should we somehow kill them all and dump them out the locks?"

"We are at war, Aerenarch, and it is Rifters who began it."

"But not these Rifters. They are not allied with Dol'jhar. They saved your father's life, and ours."

'To what purpose? At best to make a profit, which apparently *you* offered them—"

"Why don't you ask them?" Brandon said, hand out. "Or even ask your father. You don't really want my opinion, any more than you would perform a plan of mine should I come up with one."

Osri went on formally, "If you cannot form a plan, Your Highness, will you place yourself under my command?"

Brandon's face slowly blanked again, into invincible — and unreadable — politesse. "No," he said. "Whatever their intentions toward us are, whatever happens, I feel now that to attack the crew of this ship would be a breach of faith."

Osri clenched a fist and brought it down on the edge of the bunk with a gesture of barely controlled violence. "A breach of faith," he repeated with bitter scorn. "To hear you mouth that phrase disgusts me beyond endurance! For a light-forsaken coward, a deserter, who abandoned the highest authority in known space in order to escape unpleasant duty and run to Rifters, to talk of breach of faith goes past irony into the foulest dishonor. Thousands of people have *died* performing unpleasant duties because honor demanded no more than that! And millions more like them have sworn allegiance to your family — would swear to you since the rest of your family is dead —"

Osri gritted his teeth, breathing hard. Brandon said nothing, his only movement the twisting of the signet ring on his hand.

"You had better keep your faith with your Rifter scum," Osri said finally. "When I get my father off this ship and back to our people — and I shall do it, or die trying — it will not be duty but pleasure to speak to all who will hear me about your sense of honor. I only hope your father is dead so he will not have to suffer the shame of hearing it, for not even my allegiance to the Panarch will silence me." He stopped, his breathing ragged, and glared down at Brandon, who lifted his hands.

"Do what you want, Osri," he said wearily. "I hope your honor and duty will always be so simple to define, and to follow."

Osri lifted his fist, hit the hatch control, and lunged out before the hatch was fully open.

He longed for privacy, but that was hard to find and harder to keep. Since his first moment on this ship, wherever he'd gone, aside from his cabin, a Rifter had either been there or one showed up. None of them showed any shame at the open use of their boswells. Which he did not have. Nor did Brandon — a fact that gave him scant satisfaction.

He finally ended back in the galley, where he slapped at his bare wrist to record his thoughts. That gesture of long habit reinforced his helpless status, and he dropped onto a stool and gripped his head in his hands.

At the far end of the ship:

The angry-one directs anger at you. Perceive you danger, shall we amend with fi?

No. Again I repeat, if I perceive danger from other humans I will share direction, but again I repeat, you do not amend a human with fi, you cause its cessation. Again I repeat, each is a one.

We move in a chaos of noise, we fear.

You Eya'a are among us to seek knowledge of us, therefore again I repeat, contemplate cessation. Your world-mind had once a beginning, it could have an end. This end would not be amendment, it would be cessation for the Eya'a.

The one-with-three contemplates cessation, in fear. It seeks amendment.

One with three?

Damaged-one with new memories of three-nonhuman.

We will amend the damaged-one-with-three so he will not cease.

In our next withdrawal we will celebrate knowledge of cessation.

You can protect yourself from danger from humans with fi, but again I repeat, you are not amending human actions, you are destroying an entity.

Amendment promotes growth in Eya'a. We seek to amend the chaos, we seek wisdom from Vi'ya.

Again I repeat, this chaos is formless, it is many minds existing but disunited. Again I repeat, continue to separate-and-hear one-patterns. I shall now bring forth the object you have named the eye-of-the-distant-sleeper, for our contemplation. . .

And in the surgery, Montrose tapped at the main med console, catching up with his notes, intermittently glancing up from time to time at the patient he was now most concerned about.

He'd brought Ivard's bed into the main dispensary, where the boy now reclined before the big wallscreen, watching a vidchip on the Kelly that explained the breakthrough in understanding between humans and the green sophonts who always moved in threes.

Trev trotted in, giving Montrose a brief sniff and a flick of tail. Before Montrose could react, the big dog leaped up onto the bed. Montrose raised his hand, words of protest shaping his lips, but the animal settled down carefully on Ivard's free side. Gray, the wounded dog, was already lying next to Ivard on the other side, spine pressed against Ivard's leg. Ivard's hand stretched over Trev, and Montrose went back to work.

From time to time Ivard snickered as the vid displayed impassive Panarchists, resplendent in their formalwear, slapping and poking at the Kelly headstalks with as much grace as they could muster. The Kelly really were graceful, their continual dance as they patted and touched one another mesmerizing, the ribbons covering their bodies writhing and fluttering as if sentient. The trinity's honking and twittering voices also made Ivard grin.

The vid went on with some information about the Archon's phratry, showing scenes from the lush, humid belt around the Kelly planet, and ending most startlingly on a huge mountain whose stone was carved faithfully into facsimiles of three human faces.

"There were three of them," a Kelly bassooned. "Most Kelly-like." The Kelly made a sound like a prolonged ratcheting sneeze and the two larger ones on either side of it slapped it gently on top of its torso.

"Three," Ivard said, his fingers rubbing the dogs' ears at either side. "There are three of us, eh, dogs?"

The vid shifted then to the ancient monochrome flatvid that had occasioned that breakthrough, and Ivard cracked up at the manic antics of the three men in the picture, poking and slapping at one another without apparent damage.

When the vid ended, Ivard looked up, his face expectant. "Do they ever do anything alone?"

Montrose shook his head. "They do everything in threes. If you were to find one alone, it would indicate a grave emergency."

Ivard ruffled Gray's ears, as the dog leaned into his hand. "What about the Kelly medtech?"

So much for distraction. "We'll find out all we want to know when we reach al-Ibran's Chirurgicon at Rifthaven," Montrose said. "Remember, the Kelly are the best physicians in the Thousand Suns. Now sleep. You'll heal faster that way."

"I don't like sleeping here alone." He blushed as Montrose looked significantly at the dogs. "I want to be back in our cabin. Jaim said it wasn't the same without me."

Montrose hid his amusement. The Serapisti engineer was a wonderfully patient man, an ideal cabinmate for a boy in the gawkiest phase of his adolescence — physically shouldering his way into manhood, but emotionally still so young.

Jaim was probably enjoying his solitude.

"I can't send you back to your cabin until you heal more, and that means sleep."

He watched Ivard's thin, drawn face relax incrementally as he lowered himself back onto the bed. Gray hopped down and trotted away, nose to the deck plates as was usual with both dogs, then vanished into the sandbot alcove: so far, cat and dogs seemed to have acknowledged that area as shared. Montrose pushed the bed back into the berth and closed the door.

A shadow loomed; Vi'ya's black eyes assessed Montrose without giving away her own thoughts, then she said, "How is he?"

"He'll hold, but for how long I can't tell," Montrose said. "I'd like to move him back in with Jaim. More contact with the crew will do him good. But don't know if he's stable enough."

"Burn? Or the ribbon?"

"The burn isn't that serious, but it isn't healing as fast as it should. It's the Kelly ribbon. I think it's trying to change his immune system."

"The Eya'a say he is afraid."

Montrose expelled his breath in a sigh. "So am I."

DESRIEN

Eloatri smiled at the children seated in front of her in the dusty courtyard. The day, past its peak and drawing toward evening, was hot but not oppressive; the shade of the huge higari tree that shaded the way-hostel was refreshingly cool, but its vinegar/vanilla scent made her nose itch. From the hostel came the quiet hum of the conditioners, cooling the interior, and the faint bleeping of a console.

The children were quiet. Some were standing, most seated. Many of these had imitated her posture, assuming the ancient lotus position with the effortless flexibility of youth. They ranged widely in age, some as young as seven years, others nearing adulthood. In some the spirit glowed white-hot, in others, like banked coals—and a few, she judged, would leave Desrien when their majority came, unable to tolerate the soul-mirroring airs of the planet.

She began to speak. "Desrien and all its beliefs and faiths rest in the Hand of Telos, which has five fingers." Her hands moved in the pattern of the mudras, adapted from her own tradition, that were part of the language of the Magisterium. "These principles enfold us all, but there are many ways to speak and hear and live them. I will share mine with those of you who wish."

Three children leaned forward, eager to hear. The rest listened politely, with the respect they had been taught was due a Phanist, the highest rank in the Magisterium. At the back of the group stood a small, redheaded boy, with the pale, blotched skin of an atavism, his gaze hungry with an indefinable longing. She smiled at him and continued.

"We all encounter the numinous, a message from something that is beyond all measurement and knowledge." Her left hand was poised beside her at eye level, palm-up as if supporting a water jar; her right touched the top of her head, the center of her forehead, and the center of her chest in a fluid movement.

"We all possess some fragment of whatever sends these messages, however we may conceive it." Both her hands came together vertically before her eyes, cupped around a space, and then descended to her chest.

"We all live a story which has no ending we can see or understand." Now she brought both her hands together before her, thumbs and middle fingers touching in a circle parallel to the ground. She transformed the circle into the ancient symbol of infinity by bringing the fingers and thumbs together, then rotated her right hand until its palm faced outward, thumb to finger and finger to thumb, and folded her hands together, circle to circle. The symbol of the projective plane, true infinity.

From beyond the group of children, the redheaded boy watched, but his hands were busy with something she couldn't see, hidden behind the heads of those seated in front of him.

"We all suffer because we are attached to things that don't really matter." Here she used one of the most ancient of the mudras, Turning the Wheel of the Law.

The red-haired boy began tossing the object in the air rhythmically; it was a small silver ball. The setting sun sparked highlights off of it, small splashes of glory dappling the deepening shade of the tree overarching the courtyard. A wave of dizziness and disorientation overwhelmed Eloatri and she fell out of the world into the Dreamtime.

The path was dull gray, wide and edgeless, suspended in an infinite space. A golden light shone from behind her. She turned and beheld the face of the Buddha at the beginning of the path, inhumanly calm and indwelling with transhuman compassion, its lips curved in a smile terrible with possibilities.

The Buddha's eyes opened. She shriveled under his gaze. His mouth opened on a soundless resonance as the Word resounded throughout the Wheel of Time and a slow procession of figures came forth, all dressed in the finery of the High Douloi. Among them she saw the tall figure of the High Phanist, his face enshadowed in his cowl. There was the sound of weeping, and a blow against her heart.

Eloatri opened her eyes, staring without comprehension for a moment at the field of purple and yellow that slowly resolved into the dense canopy of the higari tree. Through its branches glimmered a star.

An anxious face bent over her, an elderly man with a green band around his forehead: a healer.

"Are you returned, bodhisattva?"

She levered herself up on one elbow, feeling light-headed, and looked around. Most of the children were gone; a few still stood at some distance, looking worried. A small group of adults stood to one side, less worry in their faces than respectful waiting.

"Yes." She sat up as the dizziness passed. The redheaded boy was not among the remaining children. She felt his loss. His spirit had glowed brighter than his hair.

"The redheaded boy," she said. "With the pale skin. Where is he?"

The healer hesitated, puzzlement lengthening his face.

"The one who was standing at the back of the group, playing with a silver ball."

The healer sighed, apparently considering his words, before replying. 'There is no redheaded boy in this village."

FOUR

From his seat at the senior table, Lieutenant Commander Mdeino ban-Nilotis could see most of the junior officers' bridge wardroom — not surprising, given that he topped most on *Grozniy* by a head. That didn't help him see into the little alcoves that ensigns tended to hide in to avoid catching extra duty. But right now, an hour before watch change, the compartment zinged with nervous energy and he was sure those alcoves were empty.

Nilotis was better than most at the peripheral people-watching required of officers. He'd had to be, given that the heritage of the bomas of Nyangathanka had given him not only a elongated build but flaming red hair and blue-black skin. One did not overlook Mdeino ban-Nilotis among the variegated browns of most of the rest of the Panarchy, no matter how much he might wish you to.

He needed every bit of that talent right now. The next watch would see the battlecruiser *Grozniy's* emergence back into the Thousand Suns after seven months out-octant. The most animated conversations in the wardroom — those in which hands shaped air and lips shouted laughter — surely involved boasts and speculations about the coming liberty in Wolakota System, famous — or notorious — for its hospitality to Naval personnel.

Other colloquies were more sober, though no less intense, as revealed by the set of shoulders here, and fingers stiffly tapping the table over there. Beyond Wolakota, a few weeks further into Rouge Nord octant, lay the end of their tour of duty and the further definition of career trajectories: the summing up of rank points gained or lost, new assignments, new ships, new captains.

And then there were the junior officers Captain Ng was rotating into the alpha crew for the first time this next watch, the most senior of whom sat across the table from Nilotis right now.

Nilotis looked askance at Lieutenant Rom-Sanchez, who was picking at his food. "Gee-flutters, Sergei?"

Rom-Sanchez dropped his fork on his plate and pushed his food away. Like the rest of him, his hands were lean and quick-moving. Next to him Lieutenant Denil Methuen grunted. "He'd rather be back in the lock of that bubbloid."

Rom-Sanchez was spared the necessity of a reply as Lieutenant Tang dropped into the seat next to Nilotis. "I can never resist a look of misery," she said brightly, her straight black hair swinging about her ears, a couple of centimeters past regulation. "Especially on the face of the most junior lieutenant in the wardroom an hour before his appointment with destiny."

"Thanks, Mabel," Rom-Sanchez muttered. "You're such a comfort."

"Anytime, Sergei. Just remember, all those Rifters could have done was kill you. Hero."

Nilotis snorted. "That's enough of that. Denil and I have had sufficient time to get his head back to normal size since the Captain's momentary lapse in judgment." He canted a glance at the new lieutenant's tabs Rom-Sanchez was trying not to finger.

"It's our duty." Methuen nodded soberly. "We have the ship's reputation to think of."

Everyone laughed, but Nilotis noted how forced Rom-Sanchez's was, and dropped the teasing. "Sergei. Look at it this way. Giving you tactical on the alpha crew is the captain's way of underscoring your success at Smyrna. As your last station on this tour, it will look good on your record, especially since it's not for just any emergence, but our triumphant return to civilization."

Rom-Sanchez snorted at the mockery in the last phrase, but shook his head doubtfully.

"You've got nothing to worry about," said Methuen.

"Wolakota's a liberty port, not an out-octant hellhole like Smyrna or Breakpoint. Tactical's a sinecure on an emergence like this: Captain's actually going easy on you."

"Right." Nilotis tipped his chin towards a short, powerfully-built lieutenant watching two other officers playing L-4 Phalanx, the Tenno version proscribed in tournament play but popular throughout the Navy for both training and entertainment. "Mzinga, there, he's on nav. Always possible to screw up at that station, no matter where we come out."

Rom-Sanchez glanced in that direction, and his brows contracted in a quick frown. Nilotis realized that Rom-Sanchez wasn't paying any attention to Mzinga. His attention was on the console, specifically the Tenno evolution one of the players was attempting.

Then Rom-Sanchez shook his head and turned back again. "Yeah, but Mzinga's been alpha before."

"He had a first time, too. We all did, at least on *Grozniy*. Lot of ships you can't say that about."

Rom-Sanchez grimaced but said nothing. As far as Nilotis knew, the younger officer was largely apolitical, although it was hard to tell whether that was innate or the regrettably necessary discretion practiced by Highdwellers like him in a Navy increasingly dominated by the Aerenarch Semion's Downsider connections. At least they didn't have to worry about that with Margot Ng at the helm, even if it did mean spending most of their time out-octant.

As if to belie his words, the wardroom hatch slid open, and Nilotis didn't need to look up to know who had just entered the compartment. The sudden bubble of quiet and the wariness of the two young lieutenants told him it had to be Lieutenant Commander Eisel ban-Tessler.

"Uh, oh," said Tang under her breath. "Stuffcrotch has that brass-polishing look of his, and I'm on my tween watch, which means 'available for scut work' as far as he's concerned."

Accurate as the epithet was, Nilotis had to uphold the respect for rank that made Naval hierarchy work smoothly, and he glanced Tang's way.

She flushed. "Tell you what, Sergei, why don't you take another shot at convincing me that Warrigal's L-5 Phalanx doesn't rot your brain?" Her gaze flickered to Nilotis. "Lieutenant Commander Tessler won't bother us there."

Nilotis suppressed a smile. He'd heard the faint emphasis

on Tessler's rank and name. Tang was always trying for the lower orbit, trying to keep ahead, which tended to cost her rank points that her ability would otherwise garner.

"How about you, Denil?" Tang turned his way.

The other lieutenant shook his head theatrically. "Brrrr! No chance I'm letting that wire-dream blunge into my head. That would be all I need, transposing her impossible Tenno into the middle of a real fire fight."

"Who's going to be looking at the screen?" replied Tang. "Not me. I like watching the players sweat."

The three juniors excused themselves just ahead of Tessler's arrival at the table.

Tessler was carrying a compad as was his invariable custom. As he sat down, he looked after Tang and Rom-Sanchez with a sour expression that deepened the frown lines on his long face.

"Our newest lieutenant seems pretty casual about his first alpha," he said. "Or does he think that fantasy Phalanx is a good warm up for Tactical?"

"I can think of worse," replied Nilotis mildly, with a glance at Tessler's compad.

Tessler's lips tightened. Scuttlebutt had it that Tessler had entered the Academy with high hopes for a fighting career, given his patronage linked to Aerenarch Semion. That he'd ended up in Supply was, Nilotis suspected, in large part because he had found the Tenno tactical glyphs difficult to master. There was nothing wrong with that. The Navy needed logisticians as good as Tessler. But it wasn't good enough for the man himself.

"Well, he'll hardly gain any rank points butt-sniffing Warrigal."

Butt-sniffing — or, less crude (though not by much), kissing up. Like too many Downsider officers whose families were satellites to the older Tetrad Centrum clans, Tessler tended to see things first in terms of Douloi preference, then Naval rank. A regrettably common viewpoint among many connected to Aerenarch Semion — especially those not invited to Narbon.

"They're distantly related, I understand," said Nilotis, "and both in Tactical." Tessler's face soured even more at the reminder that the two juniors would have to acknowledge some acquaintance, given their families' relationship. "The Warrigals freighted Rom-Sanchez's Highdwelling, I don't know, three or four centuries back." Warrigal shipping interests had helped start Highdwellings many times, since before there was a Panarchy, in fact. So Rom-Sanchez had little to worry about from him, especially since both were not in Supply.

"As you say," said Tessler, somewhat stiffly, pushing his chair back a bit. Nilotis tended to loom over just about anyone on the ship. He called Nyangathanka home, a planet deep in the Tetrad Centrum that had joined the Panarchy in the first century of Jaspar's Peace. Suddenly aware of what he was doing, and disgusted with himself, Nilotis leaned back in his chair.

"I suppose it's harmless enough," Tessler continued. "It's not as though *she's* likely to have much to do otherwise, given the circumstances of her transfer from Narbon. No rank points. Came out as she went in, an Ensign."

Nilotis shrugged. "Captain seems happy enough with her. So am I. Her doctorate in tactical semiotics, coming so early, doesn't hurt."

"Doesn't help much, either, that I can see," replied Tessler. "Close to a calculated insult to turn in a game as a thesis. A *game*," he repeated derisively. "While the Aerenarch struggles to build up the Navy to face a real threat."

Nilotis managed not to roll his eyes. Dol'jhar again.

"Sorry, Eisel, I just can't see a failed serial-chip empire as a real threat. It shattered like glass after Acheront. What's left is maybe ten or fifteen planets with raving sociopaths barely in control, while Sodality syndicates make a fortune smuggling and jacker raids keep them off balance." Nilotis laughed. "If they start to get out of line, there are entire Rifter fleets willing to take them on if we open up the Dol'jharian sector for bidding on a Writ."

"You still don't get it," said Tessler in exasperation. "Why did we *just* spend seven months out-octant from Rouge Nord? Because Eichelly dropped out of sight two years ago, just like Charterly and others."

Nilotis snorted. "No surprise there. There were enough derogations to have put his Writ under litigation a dozen times over. You're aware that the Justicials vacated it just before we left on patrol?"

"Of course I knew," Tessler replied crisply — and here it comes, Nilotis thought: the Dander of Dol'jhar, Semion's favorite theme. "It took them over a year," Tessler said, hitting the tabletop with his fist on the word year. "Are *you* aware of what that means in cost? *Three* battlecruiser tours of duty, plus who knows how many destroyer squadron tours? And that's just for our assigned recognizance. It's happening elsewhere. Raving sociopath or not, the Avatar of Dol'jhar is dispersing our forces."

"To do what? With four capital ships?" asked Nilotis, wearying of the familiar argument. Tessler could hardly be expected to feel otherwise, not and expect to retain his connection to Aerenarch Semion, who would never forgive the murderer of his mother.

"You know how I see this. Eichelly, those others, are just part of the natural expansion of the Peace. He's deep out-octant by now, establishing some petty fiefdom. He'll either end up plasma, Shiidra food, or the founder of a polity that a few generations from now will be petitioning for a protectorate, which means at least some recognition of law. Yes, it costs tours of duty. That's how it works, so I think it's pretty senseless to build up a core fleet that never leaves the Tetrad Centrum."

The watch-change bells sounded, interrupting Tessler's reply, and Nilotis shifted his attention as the group around Warrigal broke up and hurried to the hatch on their way to the ready room. Tessler watched, too, stiff with disapproval: they were cutting it close.

Warrigal, now alone, was still tapping intently at her compad as though nothing had changed. She often seemed to be in a world of her own. Was that why Captain Ng hadn't yet given her a shot at alpha, despite her tactical skills?

Tessler followed the direction of his gaze, and snorted. "If you'll excuse me, *I* have work to do." He scooped his compad off the table and stalked out of the wardroom.

Relieved, Nilotis settled back to his watching-not-watching. He'd been working hard, and this was his wind-down before he hit the rack. He'd sleep through emergence so he could be fresh for Wolakota. Rom-Sanchez could handle this emergence in his sleep. Once he got used to being on the bridge under the captain's eye. After all, what could possibly happen?

And on *Grozniy's* bridge, in the last few seconds of the countdown to emergence, Ng looked around, wishing she could have more time with this new alpha crew, young as some of them were. They were smart, ambitious, and several of them were perhaps a bit too unconventional for their own good—just as she had been twenty-five years back. She hoped that their new captains would recognize their potential. Especially Rom-Sanchez. Aside from a regrettable emotional distraction of the sort she'd dealt with before, he'd demonstrated command potential on this cruise, and not just at Smyrna.

"Emergence."

The descending tones of the bells blended with the quiet voice of the navigator as the battlecruiser *Grozniy* dropped back into fourspace with a barely perceptible shudder.

After a pause Lieutenant Mzinga looked up, puzzled. "No beacon, sir."

Captain Margot O'Reilly Ng leaned forward in her command pod.

"Siglnt. Verify."

Yeo Wychyrski at Siglnt tapped scrupulously at her console, her profile intent. Lieutenant Rom-Sanchez glanced at Ng from the tactical pod; she briefly checked his display echo next to the main screen and noted with approval that he was already setting up the appropriate range of presets for a no-beacon emergence.

"All sensors functional, sir," Wychyrski sang out. "No beacon."

"Navigation, tactical skip, now." The fiveskip's subliminal basso profundo hummed momentarily. "Confirm our position. Engage drunkwalk skip-orbit around our emergence point at five light seconds. Tactical, take us to threat-level one." *Grozniy* had come in using a standard trojan attractor point, so there was little doubt of where they were within a few light minutes.

Ng saw the impact of her orders in the postures of the crew, especially those new to alpha, as they transformed from nervous, under-the-captain's-eye alertness to anticipation. Mzinga and Rom-Sanchez barely had time to echo her orders before the engineering officer sang out "Engineering reports teslas at threat-level one," a heartbeat ahead of other station confirmations.

The Tenno rippled, accommodating the sudden change in position. "No ship traces within skipmissile range," reported Wychyrski moments later.

Aside from the derogation at Smyrna, which had turned out to be a private Rifter feud that the losing party had tried to turn around by bringing in the Navy, it had been a long, boring patrol out-octant from Rouge-Nord. Lots of time for drills, including, just a few weeks ago, the standard beacon-bashing scenario, where jackers destroy the navigational beacon and fivespace conditions transponder, hoping to delay passing ships long enough for an intercept. Not very likely, now that they had returned to the Thousand Suns proper: Wolakota was just inside the ill-defined outer border of Rouge Nord octant. But still. . .

Decision crystallized in her. This was too good an opportunity to pass up.

"Lieutenant Rom-Sanchez," she said.

He turned to her, startled, reminding her even more of a puppy, with his large brown eyes and curly dark hair that had the vestige of an cowlick over one eye, strictly clipped.

She'd used his name rather than his station. She saw comprehension dawning in him just ahead of her next words.

"Your captain just dropped dead, and you're senior." She smiled at the stricken expression on his face. "But I'll leave you the rest of the crew, and I'll take Tactical. You have the con." With a swipe of her hand she transferred control to him, and took the tactical feed.

Rom-Sanchez blushed to the ears, then shifted his focus to the unremarkable starfield now on the main screen. Ng saw some of the crew watching him, especially the two other members of what some officers derisively called "the L-5 Loonies" that she'd chosen for alpha crew: Ensigns Wychyrski and Ammant, SigInt and Communications. To the crew's credit, there was no trace of schadenfreude or malice in anyone's expression, often a problem when a potential lower-orbit junior officer was put on the spot.

Lieutenant Mzinga's fingers danced over the nav console, correlating the data delivered by the sensors scattered over the seven-kilometer-long hull of the *Grozniy*. The precision lent by its size enabled a battlecruiser to orient faster than any other ship in the absence of the flood of data furnished by a navigational beacon. The older officer appeared absorbed, but Ng detected the subtlest compression of lips, indicating a suppressed laugh.

A bit more quickly than she'd expected, Rom-Sanchez spoke, with only a trace of a stammer before he dropped into bridge cadence, the almost-singsong speech pattern that they learned in the academy as part of bridge protocol, meant to project an impression of calm and control. "AyKay. I have the con. SigInt, crunch a ship-centric mass and energy summary for me while nav is working." He hesitated briefly. "Tactical, work up a threat assessment assuming we're at the Wolakota leading trojan. If jackers took out the beacon, what are we likely facing, given the strategic situation here?"

Ng saw from the tactical setup now on her console that he hadn't gotten to threat assessment before she'd ambushed him, but he was doubtless more concerned about that lack than she was. So far, so good.

"Spectrum match to Wolakota primary. Elevated asteroid density around the ship," SigInt reported. "Looks like a lot of collisional evolution, not much to hide behind. A good deal of asteroid thermal scatter sunward. Matches a trojan point emergence."

Like most systems with one or more gas giants in it, the Wolakota system had an asteroid belt inward from the sunward giant.

Ng watched Rom-Sanchez drumming his fingers on the arm of his pod as he stared at the main viewscreen. She would have preferred to see him observing the crew: the scattered points of light displayed there would reveal nothing. If it was Rifters, they'd skip the second they saw *Grozniy*'s pulse. A battlecruiser generated an emergence pulse that couldn't be mistaken for anything else. Depending on how far out the Rifters were hiding, the *Grozniy* had only minutes before its prey fled.

"Very well," Rom-Sanchez said. Again, the slight hesitation. "Tactical, give me a sigma on hiding places."

Ng popped up one of the Rom-Sanchez's preset windows on the main screen, a colorful probability plot centered on the assumed position of the ship. The plot shifted as Mzinga straightened up, his task finished.

"Position confirmed, sir. Wolakota system, absolute bearing 30.6 mark 358.8, plus 47 light-minutes." His mellow voice was even, but Ng heard his excitement in the quicker pace of his words. "That puts our initial emergence within one light-minute of the beacon's position at the leading trojan attractor of Wolakota Six."

That was as expected: their by-the-book approach had let the fivespace well created by the trojan attractor pull them into the system.

"No alerts on local widecasts. No links found," reported Ammant at Communications. The local authorities were either not alarmed or playing it safe.

Ng glanced at the sigma plot, reading the Tenno glyphs overlaid on it with the facility born of twenty-five years' practice. The asteroid belt sunward of their position was indicated on the plot by a series of faint green ring segments— k-zones—separated by the Kirkwood gaps where the periodic interaction with Wolakota Six swept away the debris left over from the system's formation. The rings' patterns, and various glyphs, indicated probable density, composition, and other tactically important information. A few yellow dots marked the position of major asteroids.

The plot had one lobe flaring the red of maximum probability, about fifteen light-minutes away, concentrated in the ecliptic in the closest k-zone to Six. Nothing there they didn't already know—the average calc time for commercial traffic was about thirty minutes or so—probably more, given the fivespace conditions in this stellar neighborhood.

Commercial traffic at the leading trojan was ships passing through the system, who couldn't skip locally any great distance without further compromising their safety on the next leg of their fivespace journey. That'd give their hypothetical Rifters—no doubt hiding behind a chunk of rock or ice, as usual—sufficient time to intercept their prey.

It also meant that the *Grozniy* now had something less than fifteen minutes to find the intruders—if the beacon's destruction had indeed been deliberate.

Rom-Sanchez tapped his console and a countdown windowed up in a corner of the main screen, starting at ten minutes. Good! He was settling into his role as acting captain, and pushing the crew. His next order was crisp: "Navigation, take us in to within five light-seconds of the attractor point. SigInt, run a scan for debris and radiation. Extrapolate time of destruction if you find traces."

The plot shifted as the fiveskip burped. One glyph indicated the presence of a Fleet tactical transponder nearby. Rom-Sanchez tapped at his console, highlighting the tacponder.

"SigInt, pop that tacponder and update Tactical immediately for threat assessment. Check its monitor status."

Ng saw the impact, minor as it was, of the unnecessary last

order: a slight hitch in the otherwise smooth flow of activity on the bridge. There was a brief silence on the bridge as Ensign Wychyrski began the scan. A window from Communications popped up on Ng's console.

"No data from transponder," she said. "Last update plus four months, no new threats reported, monitor mode off. Latest Wolakota data plus seven months, Pulwaiya tacponder." That had been on their way out-octant.

"Tactical, assessment?"

"Worst case, Eichelly's back, sine lege. Four Alphas in his fleet, three of them third-tranche." It took a minimum of three destroyers to take on a battlecruiser, so the possibility they were facing a renegade Writ-holder with four of them made Eichelly a credible threat, even though one of his destroyers was more than 400 years old.

Rom-Sanchez's eyes flicked towards Ng, and this time he hesitated a bit longer— too long—but then his shoulders straightened. "Very well. Take us to threat-level two."

By the book, so far. "AyKay. Ship status to threat-level two." Rom-Sanchez betrayed mingled relief and desperation as Ng fell into bridge alert cadence and echoed his order, followed by the other stations' secondary confirmations: relief that she hadn't countermanded him, desperation that she wasn't taking the con back.

But she wasn't taking him off the hook yet. They still didn't have confirmation of hostile activity, and tactically, it was impossible that more than one destroyer would be able to take a shot at them at the beginning of an engagement, given a battlecruiser's sensor platform. Not that any jacker would be insane enough to do so. In any case, there was no danger to *Grozniy*, now that its shields were powered up sufficiently. They were still tracking the standard scenario: nothing Rom-Sanchez couldn't handle, if he didn't over-think things.

The brassy tones of the alert pealed out, followed by the hiss of the tianqi increasing the airflow into the bridge. Ng breathed in, aware of the subtle bergamot scent fading, replaced by a complex of pine, jasmine, and less familiar scents, calculated to promote alertness, balanced with rose and jumari, for relief of stress. She knew, but could not sense, that the conditioners were also raising the ionization level slightly, and cycling faint subsonics at irregular intervals in a pattern that reached deep into the human thalamus with the age-old message: thunderstorm coming, be alert!

The aft hatch whispered open. Commander Perthes Krajno slipped into the pod on her left side, giving her a glance of muted surprise as he brought up his console.

"Dead again, eh?" Krajno's gravelly voice perfectly matched his craggy, amiable face, like that of a boxer whose guard had been less than perfect during his career. It was a deceptive façade; Ng considered him one of the sharpest officers in the Fleet.

Wychyrski sang out, "Debris detected. Crystalline stress patterns of debris consonant with skipmissile impact. Dispersion indicates destruction about one hour ago, plus or minus ten minutes."

Skipmissile, and only an hour past? That was like a front-row seat.

Ng grinned at Krajno. His answering grin was feral, anticipating action after months of tedious patrol and training; Perthes was too scrupulous an executive officer not to get out of the rack when his captain ran drills at all hours, even if he didn't have to.

Rom-Sanchez glanced their way. Ng kept her manner neutral, and knew Perthes was doing the same. Show time. Her fingers tingled, longing for the feel of the command console, but taking control now would teach entirely the wrong lesson, possibly even destroy a budding career. She had to demonstrate her confidence in him.

Ng watched him take a deep breath as he pitched his voice for firmness. "General quarters. Engineering, rig engines for tactical maneuvers. Fire Control, ready all ruptors. Charge skipmissile."

As the general-quarters klaxon rang out—a sound Ng knew dated back to the oceanic navies of Lost Earth—excitement and purpose showed in straightened spines and a quick exchange of grins. She could read them so easily: general quarters, no question whether it was real or a drill, and they were on alpha! On *Grozniy*, alpha crew stayed on through general quarters, which was why that status was both feared and sought after.

"Navigation, SigInt, coordinate a light-cone convergence on the beacon's destruction and position us for observation. Start one light-hour out, normal to the ecliptic. Communications, full-scan record, give me a visual."

The *Grozniy* leapt briefly into fivespace and as quickly out. The transitions were rougher this time: the lower frequency skip required for fine tactical movements was hard on the engines. A whisper of datacode commenced.

"Beacon acquired," sang Wychyrski. They had skipped to a point outside the expanding wavefront marking the beacon's destruction.

Another set of transitions, the fiveskip burping so briefly that an eyeblink would have missed it. The whisper ceased.

"No beacon." Inside the wavefront.

Ng noted sweat on Mzinga's brow, and his massive arms bulged against his trim uniform as he jumped the battlecruiser back and forth, struggling to get it to the desired position as quickly as possible. The countdown ticked off fifteen seconds more as the big ship continued its series of skips, which seemed on the edge of divergence.

"Navigation," said Rom-Sanchez. "Try—" He stopped abruptly, and Ng knew that this time he had seen loss of flow when the crew shifted attention from their tasks to him. "Belay that. Carry on." He leaned back in his pod, gaze taking in the bridge, then he relaxed as he comprehended everyone settling back into smooth action. Good! Least action, best action. He was learning.

The fiveskip burped twice more.

"On screen." Ensign Ammant at Communications tapped at his console. A small targeting cross blinked at the center of the screen, and datacode once again squealed onto the bridge from the doomed beacon.

Nothing happened for nearly a minute. Then a tiny flare of reddish light bloomed near the cross.

"Emergence," Wychyrski said. "Signature indicates Alpha-class destroyer." She stroked the keypads at her station again. "Signature ID'd. Eichelly's *Talon of God.*"

The short chain-of-pearls wake of a skipmissile briefly connected the destroyer with the beacon, which vanished in an ardent burst of light. Then the destroyer vanished, leaving behind a reddish pulse.

The Tenno rippled furiously as the destroyer's orientation on skip and other betraying aspects of its signature propagated through the bridge systems. "SigInt, find his emergence," Rom-Sanchez ordered. "Navigation, drop us in five light-minutes out from his emergence, long-range, and then take us in to ten light-seconds on my mark. Fire Control, prepare ruptors for barrage at skip-smash level. We want him intact."

The seconds stretched into minutes. Finally Wychyrski spoke, disbelief betrayed in her voice. "No emergence, sir. He's gone."

Ng leaned forward in her pod, glaring at the screen as if she could compel the Rifter to emerge. But there was no arguing with what the sensors showed. At normal skip speeds, the *Talon of God* would already be light-days away—and they were watching from a vantage point over an hour in the past. She shook her head, looking from Krajno to Rom-Sanchez, whose expressions mirrored her own feelings of confusion and anger, with perhaps a tiny bit of relief in the lieutenant's.

She spoke to Rom-Sanchez. "Very well done, Lieutenant. I have the con."

He swiped at his console, his face flushed with pleasure at her compliment, but the tremble in his fingers betrayed his relief. "AyKay, sir. You have the con."

She raised her voice. "Stand down to threat-level one."

"He bashed the beacon and skipped out of the system?" Krajno's bass rumble was hesitant. "What the hell for?"

Ng bit her lip. "There's been some suspicion about the disappearance of Writ-holders like Eichelly. That maybe it was to distract us from something else by pulling patrols out-octant. This stinks of concerted action across systems, so perhaps that 'something else' is coming down. And we need to get to the bottom of it."

She pitched her voice to bridge cadence again. "Navigation, SigInt, get me a precise vector on his skip." She stood up, motioning to Krajno and Rom-Sanchez. "Genz, will you join me in the plot room?"

"Captain?" Ensign Wychyrski's voice was uncharacteristically hesitant. "There was something odd about that explosion. Spectrum's wrong for a skipmissile impact."

"Very well, Ensign. Log it for analysis and give me a report. Lieutenant Mzinga," she continued, "you have the con. Give us the vector soonest and stand by. Communications, squirt a message to the Wolakota Node informing them it's safe to replace the beacon. Set the Fleet tacponder to monitor status and ready a report for it, full record of this action. We'll add our report in a few minutes."

Relieved to be relieved of command, Rom-Sanchez took in

a deep breath as the captain leaned back and tapped her fingers on the edge of the compad in front of her.

"So, Lieutenant, he obviously expects us to follow him. Where did he go?" she asked, her light hazel eyes quirked with humor.

Rom-Sanchez knew his surprise must have shown, for Commander Krajno chuckled. "She took the con, but you're not off the hook."

"His vector gives us only two other core members of the local stellar association: either Treymontaigne or Schadenheim," Rom-Sanchez began, giving himself time to think. "Thirty and forty-two hours respectively, at full speed."

Ng shifted slightly in her chair, letting him know his delaying tactic wouldn't work. But then he had the answer. "It doesn't matter which way we think he went," he continued, "because the local transponder shows no change from what we popped at Pulwaiya: *Prabhu Shiva* in-system at Treymontaigne on detached duty at the Archon's request."

He tried to keep his voice even, detached, but the humor vanished from the captain's face.

Commander Krajno did not hide his disgust. His lip lifted, the sneer in his heavy face making him look like a pirate in a vid chip, as the rest of the officers shifted, or looked away. Few Navy officers had much respect for an Archon who ran close to the edge under the Covenant of Anarchy, and then called for a battlecruiser to back him up when his subjects started to resent his excesses.

"Too much of that sort of thing going on lately," Krajno said.

Ng opened a hand, which effectively shut down the topic of politics.

Rom-Sanchez continued. "Then we can assume that Captain Harimoto will give Eichelly a warm welcome if he chose Treymontaigne, and we're for Schadenheim in case he didn't."

Ng nodded. "Good." She turned to the plot-pane, which responded with a red line, spearing through the Schadenheim system.

Krajno grunted. "Awful name, that."

"Ancient Doitch," said Ng. "Means something like Home of Destruction."

Krajno nodded. "Matches the people there — pretty bloody-minded bunch."

Ng grinned at the XO. "Coming from you, Commander, that puts a visit to Schadenheim on a par with a vacation on Dol'jhar."

Krajno laughed. Rom-Sanchez had come to learn that Krajno thoroughly enjoyed his reputation for a harsh, rough-and-ready approach to discipline, but no one had ever called him unfair.

Rom-Sanchez allowed himself to cancel out the banter. He watched Ng instead, the way her short hair, the color of maple leaves in autumn, swirled against her face as she turned from Krajno to the plot pane and back. Her hair looked like silk. So did her skin, which was the goldy-brown hue that some called sallow. He found it beautiful. As she gestured toward the plot plane, he stole a peek at the way her trim blues modeled her slight, muscular figure.

Then he slapped himself down mentally, and shifted his attention to his compad. He was fairly sure that those hazel eyes did not miss much. What he didn't know was what she thought in personal terms: she never discussed private affairs, ever, with anyone — as far as he was aware.

Did she *have* a private life? Some officers didn't. Some of those highborn Douloi from the Tetrad Centrum families acted as antiseptic as if they'd been decanted as adults from a steel tube straight into the Academy.

But Ng was not Douloi. Rom-Sanchez remembered Mdeino's comment in the wardroom about everyone getting a shot at alpha. "Lot of ships you can't say that about." Rom-Sanchez had been lucky in his assignment to *Grozniy*, lucky to avoid a ship where his Highdweller origins might hold him back. Best not to screw it up with stupid fantasies about a captain almost twice his age — and who'd been awarded the Panarchy's highest honor for her heroism at the Battle of Acheront that ended the Dol'jharian War.

He forced his attention back to the conversation.

". . . maybe the Local Justice Option, Captain?" Krajno was saying, rubbing his hands with exaggerated pleasure.

That was the real decision: what to do do with Eichelly when they did catch him? Rom-Sanchez was sure that Ng had already decided.

"Look who's being bloody-minded!" Ng laughed. "A tribunal won't need to make that decision. Can you imagine

Schadenheimers in particular not posting on Eichelly? Best we can hope for is a crack at interrogating the survivors."

She slapped the pane and it went dark. "That's assuming our ruptors even leave enough for the Schadenheimers. "

She tabbed the compad. "Bridge."

"Yes, sir?" Mzinga's voice responded.

"Plot a full-speed course to Schadenheim and stand by."

"AyKay, sir, full-speed course to Schadenheim and stand by."

She tapped the compad off and turned to Rom-Sanchez. "We have a few minutes before the tacponder report is ready, which gives us time for a different kind of tribunal."

Despite the hint of smile betrayed at the corners of her eyes, and the wink Krajno sent him, Rom-Sanchez's stomach lurched.

"So, Lieutenant," she continued. "Tell me what you did wrong."

FIVE

The name on the door had been effaced by a low-power jac-blast, but the title was still legible: Aegios, Node Charvann.

Hreem tapped his boswell for the override. As the door whispered open, he could hear the occupant within snarling, ". . . so get a tech and force it open, blunge-for-brains. I want my view back."

Hreem motioned the two burly crewmen ahead of him. Inside, enfolded in an intricately stitched grilia-leather chair, with his feet up on the vast, polished paak-wood desk, Naigluf looked up lazily, his hand hovering over the com control in one arm of the chair.

His expression widened into alarm when the two crewmen made their way around the desk without a word and plucked him out of the chair. As Hreem took his place behind the desk, the two slammed Naigluf down in a hard, armless chair in front of it.

Hreem leaned back and looked around at the luxurious office that had once belonged to the manager of the Charvann Node. The exterior viewport behind him was blanked, giving no hint of the office's location forty thousand kilometers above the surface of Charvann. Given the overheard scrap of conversation, Naigluf hadn't realized the source of the override.

The Rifter captain swung his feet up onto the polished surface of the desk and flexed his ankles rhythmically. The heel-claws in his boots slid in and out with a subdued click.

Across the desk from him Naigluf hunched inward on himself, his asymmetric mustache looking even more bedraggled than usual, and his pockmarked face turned the color of old cheese. Hreem enjoyed the way the man's eyes fixed on the shiny heel-claws — in and out, in and out. The ring of white around his dilated irises was even broader than the last time Hreem had seen him. Hopper eyes. Probably hadn't touched ground since the attack.

As though in confirmation, Naigluf's hand strayed toward one of the pockets in his wrinkled, grimy jumpsuit, then jerked away.

Finally Naigluf couldn't stand the silence anymore. "You want me to take another office? I can move, I don't need. . ."

At a slight nod from Hreem one of the guards stepped forward and slammed his cupped palm into the side of Naigluf's head. The Rifter screamed, and blood ran out of his ear from his shattered eardrum.

"Naigy, Naigy." Hreem shook his head sadly. "You couldn't be satisfied with your twenty points, could you?"

The miserable Rifter's eyes widened even more, something Hreem hadn't thought possible. He opened his mouth to protest again, then shrank away as the crewman beside him raised his hand once more.

"All the hopper you could pop, any pretty face you fancied, a nice office," Hreem continued. "Ran the entire Node. But it wasn't enough. What were you going to do with the rakeoff?"

Hreem reached for a control in the chair arm. "No, I don't need this office, any more than you do now, or any more than she does." He jerked his head backward as the viewport cleared, revealing the vacuum-ravaged body of a woman splayed across the monocrystal port, backlit by the bright, cloud-dappled limb of Charvann behind her. Her pop-eyed expression of agony contrasted violently with the elegance of her Douloi attire.

Naigluf gasped.

"Actually," said Hreem as he got to his feet, "I don't think this office is a very healthy place. Practically everybody who sits here lately ends up dead."

The two crewmen plucked Naigluf up out of the chair. Hreem snorted as the skinny runt's legs made abortive running movements.

"Telos, Hreem, we've been working together too long for this." Naigluf's fear scaled his voice up to a near falsetto.

Laughing, Hreem directed the men toward the nearest airlock.

"Hreem, at least make it quick, use your jac, don't just shove me out there."

The Rifter's pleas grew in volume and vehemence as they left the office and reached the lock outside. Naigluf flung out his arms and legs in a vain attempt to prevent his escort from jamming him through the opening.

Hreem held up his hand. The two men released Naigluf so suddenly that his frantic flailings propelled him backward against the opposite bulkhead. As he slumped to the floor, looking up at Hreem, the Rifter captain grinned at him.

"You're right, Naigy, it's been too long to end it this way." As the shivering Rifter relaxed and essayed a trembling smile, Hreem continued, "This—" He jerked a thumb at the lock. "—is too good for you."

"Hreeee-eeeeeeeem!" Naigluf howled.

'Take him to Norio. He knows what to do.'

A shriek of terror accompanied by a waft of fetor from the trembling huddle on the deck made Hreem bellow with laughter.

The crewmen dragged the blubbering Rifter roughly to his feet and away, and Hreem strolled back to the office of the former Aegios, looking around with proprietary satisfaction. The Node was his. The Syncs were his. Almost a billion lives, all his. He'd let his crew pretty much do what they wanted on the ground, but the Highdweller citizens were off limits: they were Hreem's.

Hreem dropped into the big chair and stretched his hands over his head, fingers knit together, contemplating his next move. Maybe it was time for his hostages to see one of his entertainments, so they'd understand how things worked now. He'd separated out the upper echelon of the Node and the temenarchs of the dominant Highdwellings, and had them incarcerated under guard, as insurance for the behavior of the rest of the Syncs. He didn't want any trouble.

A tremor of uneasiness made him glance at the viewport, at the dead Aegios. Who'd think the old chatzer had that much fight in her? He could still remember the way she'd laughed as she crashed the DataNet right in front of him, though he held a jac pointed straight at her.

Hreem hated surprises. What would scare all the fight out of 'em? Ah. He'd give 'em Naigy's farewell performance.

He glanced at his boswell. It would take an hour or so for Norio to finish what he called an "evocation," in which he used various stimuli, mostly visual, to identify his victim's deepest fears. Hreem had never actually seen the process; Norio claimed that an observer's emotions blurred the precision of his perceptions. But once Naigluf's evocation was finished, and Norio understood just how to wring the most psychic anguish from the luckless Rifter, Hreem knew what would come next.

It was strange, how ambivalent he was about Norio's preferred sex play until actually immersed in it. Inflicting pain and terror was fun when you were angry, and useful when you needed to make an example of someone, but Hreem himself got bored pretty quickly with it. Not Norio. He got hotter and hotter, and his inventiveness got Hreem hot.

So Naigluf would end up putting on two shows: a private one for Hreem and Norio, and a public one for the nicks. And Norio would record vids of both of them: two more of the "treasures" that enabled him to relive the emotions whenever he wanted to. And, inevitably, he and Hreem would bunny again at some future date with one of those vids as background.

Hreem sighed. Sometimes being with Norio was like living in a room full of mirrors.

He shook himself out of the mood. He could make good use of the next hour. There were a lot of boring details involved in being master of a planetary system, aside from having Barrodagh nag him almost daily about his progress tracking down every contact of that Omilov blit, still trying to find some artifact that Eusabian was hot-nackered after.

Hreem tapped his boswell and called up Riolo's code. Time to push the trog again. He wasn't about to end up like Tallis had. In fact, he might even have a shot at succeeding where Tallis had failed, and maybe even getting the lower orbit on Barrodagh once and for all.

When the bozcode failed, Hreem snarled and tabbed the console in the desk. He'd forgotten that Riolo refused to wear a boswell when noderunning. The Barcan's face windowed up, dim in the reddish light of the suite he'd converted to his use here on the Node.

Riolo spoke before Hreem. "Ah, Captain. I was just about

to call you."

Sure he was. The Barcan liked to hoard information, releasing it at the last possible minute to extract the most personal benefit from it. Hreem resolved again to break him of the habit, and then forgot about it as Riolo continued, "I have penetrated yet deeper into the Archonic system and found confirmation that the L'Ranja gang does indeed have a base in this system."

Hreem's heart thumped, and triumph suffused him. It was *Telvarna!* He'd long suspected one of their bases was somewhere in this system, and the news from Arthelion — the third Arkad son, last seen boosting towards Warlock, turning up on a Columbiad manned by Rifters! — had made him even more certain.

"Where are they?"

"I don't know that yet. I found a number of messages from the Archon to Markham L'Ranja sent via in-system DataNet protocols. They cover a period of years, indicating that this is probably their primary base, but there is no mention of the location." Riolo grinned. "The last message was dated less than three months before you killed him."

Hreem felt again the exquisite pleasure he'd had the year before, firing a jac right into Markham's laughing face. He needed no vid to relive that! But ever since then, Markham's ice-faced Dol'jharian tempath had been hunting him, along with her pet psi-killers. And dressed in black, which he knew meant a vengeance hunt. He'd been public in his scorn, but he'd been paying big money to get their bases located so he could kill her first.

"How long will it take you to find it?" demanded Hreem.

Riolo held up a hand. "Relax, Captain. We have plenty of time. Assuming that the *Telvarna* is indeed headed back here after their raid — which is likely, since rumor has their other base a mere way station — they cannot arrive for at least another ten days. I will have the information well before then, and you can be waiting for them. In the meantime — "

Hreem exulted, hardly listening as Riolo made excuses for the slow progress in the search for Omilov's contacts.

Markham's gang had another ship, which might be at this base. Maybe he should wait for *Telvarna* to return, and try to catch both ships. Or first take care of the base and the other ship — if it was there — and set an ambush. Maybe he could take *Telvarna* more or less intact. Were the rewards for the Aerenarch and Omilov really worth the risk of running up against Vi'ya and those little brain-boilers?

So far, no one besides Riolo and Hreem suspected that the Telvarna and Charvann were connected. That means that slug Barrodagh couldn't know the identity of the Telvarna, and that meant he had no idea it might return here.

Hreem was free to do what he wanted.

He chuckled and rubbed his hands. Once he got hold of the *Maccabeus*, he could build his own empire.

Hreem dismissed Riolo and lost himself in a reverie that was half planning and half feral anticipation until his boswell pinged the inside of his wrist with Norio's code. Then the console lit up and Norio gazed out, his pupils enormously dilated, not from drugs but from excited lust, his lips parted as if he was panting. Hreem's nacker stirred.

"Oh, Jala, such an entertainment we shall have," Norio said. "Oh, the fears. . . so exquisite, Naigluf's fears, rare and delicious, and so enhanced by his drug. I have never evoked a popper before."

Hreem imagined Markham's Dol'jharian tempath strapp-ed to the evocation table. She would read his pleasure in her degradation even as Norio fed on her emotions. Then he thought of himself on the bridge of a battlecruiser, and shivered as warmth mounted in him. But it wouldn't do to lose control, as had happened from time to time in one of Norio's private shows.

"Don't get carried away," said Hreem. "I want Naigluf alive. I want an entertainment good enough to convince these Highdweller nicks that I mean what I say."

"You shall have it, Jala, you shall have it. Only you must come to me, quickly, before the drug begins to wear off."

Hreem signed off, set his boswell with the *Interrupt me only if it's life-or-death* code, and headed for the lift.

TELVARNA: ARTHELION TO DIS

Sebastian Omilov set his cup down on its saucer, enjoying the musical ching. A civilized sound, like the opera that Montrose had piped into the cubicle yesterday when he found out how much Omilov loved music.

"A superb meal, Doctor. No, better. I'd say that this was

prepared by a Golgol-trained chef. The owner of this vessel must be quite wealthy."

Montrose slapped his chest and bowed. "Golgol-trained indeed."

"You? I thought —"

"Surgeon as well," Montrose said with a rumbling laugh. "I decided one day that I wanted to travel all eight octants and beyond, and since I was not wealthy, I had to make myself indispensable. Most ships need a surgeon and a chef, and in me they get both."

Omilov savored the real coffee and listened carefully, if skeptically. This was the first time Montrose had shared any information about himself. Montrose had given him superlative care, but despite his convalescence Omilov had noted certain anomalies: the brief visits from Osri were always accompanied; no ship's business or destination was mentioned. Except for those visits from Osri, whose demeanor expressed frustrated rage, Montrose had been the only person Omilov had spoken to since his half-remembered interview with Brandon when they first came aboard the vessel. Brandon — now Aerenarch — had not repeated his visit, though both Montrose and Osri, when Omilov asked, said he was unharmed.

"Training at the Golgol academy must have been difficult after all your years training as a surgeon," Omilov said aloud.

"No, it was easy," Montrose said with a grin. "Cookery requires the same kind of precision, and art, as surgery."

The combined images evoked slight distaste, abhorrent to Douloi sensibilities. Omilov suspected that the affront was a deliberate response to his skepticism. The sharpest trespass is always made by the expatriate.

He set the cup down again, keeping his face bland. "I take it that we have inadvertently become guests of the Rift Sodality?"

Montrose's eyes crinkled with delight. "You have indeed." With a slightly more serious air, "But, I need hardly add, our captain is no ally of Eusabian of Dol'jhar."

"Nor of the Panarch, I expect," Omilov murmured, trying to still the increase of his heartbeat.

Montrose frowned. "You'll come to no harm here. Captain wants to talk to you. Think you're up to it?"

"Whether I am or not, I would like very much to talk to your captain," Omilov said.

Montrose took away the tray, and went out.

The hatch hissed open for a tall young woman dressed in a plain dark coverall. She regarded Omilov with cool interest out of a pair of extraordinarily dark, thick-lashed eyes in a smooth brown face as expressionless as a statue.

"I am Vi'ya," she said. "*Telvarna* is my ship." She sat down in the chair nearby with the unconscious poise of one for whom control is an ingrained habit.

He had decided to suspend judgment, but he found there was something vaguely disturbing in the trace of accent that shaped the soft-spoken words, and the hint of blended consonants in the middle of her name. "I am Sebastian Omilov," he began pleasantly. "Professor of Urian Studies at the university on Charvann. I wish first of all to thank you for my rescue."

She made a slight, dismissive gesture. "It was not I but the Eya'a who were directly responsible for your rescue," she responded. "But for them we would not have known of your presence. As for taking you with us, my primary motivation was to anger the Lord of Dol'jhar." This was spoken with a faint but coldly unpleasant smile, yet it was not that but the pronunciation of the word "Dol'jhar" that sent a burning flame of shock through him.

"Your culture holds that the fear of death is the greatest pang. We of Dol'jhar know this to be false." Vivid memory: the arrogant features of Evodh, Eusabian's torturer. His ring finger tingled and his cheek twitched painfully.

The young woman blinked, almost a wince.

Her accent was Dol'jharian. Omilov drew an unsteady breath. "Osri mentioned the Eya'a and I had difficulty believing him! How comes it they move among humans?"

"They were selected by their. . . world-mind to observe humans. I met them in a spaceport on Two-Bit."

Then it was true. These legendary sophonts were not only real, apparently they were on board this ship. Omilov shut his eyes, struggling to control the mental and emotional shocks. Too many impossible ideas all on top of one another.

But it was for this that he had made his most important oath, so he took a slow breath, and forced himself to think about one thing at a time. "How did they come to be there, and how did you meet them?"

"From what I can understand, they had somehow commandeered a Shiidran vessel, which caused quite a panic when it showed up and requested a landing link. How they managed that I still do not know, as they do not use language the way we do."

"And you met them, you say?"

"Everyone fled any area they approached. But I could hear them." She touched the side of her head. "Not sound, but with my tempathic ability. I decided to approach them. I sensed no hostility, although their emotions do not correspond to human ones, and I found that communication was possible."

Yet another shock; she was a tempath. Now he knew why she'd grimaced. It was in reaction to his own emotions. This shock brought a surge of revulsion. Someone who could read past the surface, who could penetrate the trained Douloi mask, was a threat to a social structure built on politesse.

Besides, it was embarrassing.

"Communication?" he said. "I am not a Synchronist, but it is my understanding that tempathy and telepathy are two very different talents."

She shrugged. "Human-to-human, I suppose they are. The Eya'a are different." She did not amplify.

"So the rumors concerning their abilities are exaggerated?"

"No, and yes." She studied him dispassionately. "How much of this do you wish to hear?"

"Though I am a xenoarchaeologist," he replied, "it does not mean my interest in other cultures is confined to ones no longer existing."

If she thought the direction the interview was taking an odd one, she gave no sign whatever. "Very well. Their psionic powers have not been underrated, but they are not the genocidal monsters that rumor names them. Theirs is an ice planet, which has huge deposits of complex minerals barely exploited by the Eya'a."

"That much I had heard. However, such minerals can be found elsewhere in the Thousand Suns, on planets not inhabited."

"But not woven into materials we cannot manufacture."

"Woven?"

"They weave everything. Including a kind of crystalline armor, which protects them against a formidable array of predators on their planet. The original scout ship that landed in search of minerals discovered the armor, and brought it back to Rifthaven, where they sold it for a fortune. When word got out, the usual swarm of jackers skipped in to grab what they could before your Panarchy implemented the usual quarantine. They flamed any natives they found before they raided their domiciles, which caused the Eya'a (after an unsuccessful attempt to communicate) to retaliate and clean the planet of the intruders in one sweep."

"With psionic . . . skills? Omilov avoided the word *powers*, as it sounded too like a wire-dream.

"Even so. The next three or four ships that landed were likewise treated, until the Eya'a made a discovery which was almost incomprehensible to them. They could not contact the human world-mind because there was no such thing, and they finally observed the possibility that each individual was self-directed. Such a discovery meant they must investigate further before deciding how to deal with humans."

"This is news indeed." Omilov heard the blood pressure monitor pick up its pace, sending a ripple of colors through the readout. He tried to slow his breathing. "I take it you have deliberately refrained from contacting the authorities with this information?"

"I am my own authority," she said, "and what they decide to do about their world and its resources is their decision."

"So they are collecting their data about humans from a ship of Rifters. . ."

"Why not?" she replied. "It's as good a picture of our species as they would get anywhere else."

Omilov shifted to diplomatic mode. "I won't enter into a debate with you on that. I expect we'd both be right—and wrong." He folded his hands together. "What I would like to know, if I may, is what are your intentions toward myself, my son, and the new Aerenarch?"

"Why was a xenoarchaeologist put under Eusabian's mindripper?" she countered.

Omilov did not immediately answer. The captain waited, her dark eyes steady, until he said, "I suggest you ask Eusabian."

"The sphere that your son was carrying?" She dipped a hand into the pouch at her side and pulled out the silvery ball that had appeared so mysteriously at Omilov's home what now seemed ages ago.

Yet another blow. He closed his eyes, then forced them open as Vi'ya passed it from hand to hand, her arm muscles jerking and tightening when the sphere did not behave the way any normal object would.

She looked up. "Inertialess. Who made it?"

Omilov said, "The beings we call the Ur. I know little else." Too many shocks. There was that warning tingle in his ring finger again.

"And Eusabian wants it?" She added softly, "The Eya'a, they sense great power." The word was somehow not at all like a wire-dream when spoken by her.

"I know that it is called the Heart of Kronos, and that it has been kept for millions of years by sophonts on a now-quarantined planet. It ought to be returned to them. Will you give it to me?"

"Perhaps. Eventually."

"May I inquire what you intend to do with it?"

"I have not yet decided. Much depends on what I can discover about it, and how to use it. What can you tell me about that?"

"Almost nothing," he answered, unable to prevent distress from rasping his voice.

"The Eya'a identified it as a psionic device, but it seems an integral part of it is missing. Do you know what?"

He shook his head slowly, betraying none of the impact of the question. He remembered the vast, echoing space of the Shrine of the Demon, the towering Guardian and its swarm of near-mindless commensals. None of the psis reported a missing part. Apparently the combination of a human tempath and the Eya'a world-mind — or the portion they carried with them — was something new in Totality.

"If you know that much, you know more about it than I do. I don't even know how it left that planet. It appeared without warning one day, having been sent to me by a former student, for reasons unknown."

"It was sent to you because someone felt you would know what purpose it serves. That person must have realized its importance, and likewise you knew enough to have been mindripped for your knowledge. And it was important enough to you that you continued to resist while a shred of your will remained."

Her gaze was steady. He knew she was concentrating on him, and pain flickered behind his temples as if his brain was undergoing a physical memory of the mindrip machine.

Tempaths could not cause this effect. Were the Eya'a nearby? What was he facing here?

He forced himself to take a long breath before speaking. "I have no facts whatever, only guesses," he stated finally.

"You know how to find the facts. And your guesses might prove to be truth."

Her gaze was still intense and unwavering, and his headache rapidly made coherent thought difficult. He could not prevent himself from wincing as he brought a hand up to shade his eyes. "I beg your pardon. . ." He sighed. "I am not as recovered as I had thought."

She stood up to go, and he fell back, feeling a pressure had been released from his skull.

She said, "I will seek answers to my questions elsewhere. Until then, it is mine."

She left, and in the next cabin, Montrose sat back in relief. With anyone but Vi'ya he would have intervened halfway through that interview—but then with anyone else, the interview would have been short. Montrose adjusted the meds, and sat at his console watching Omilov in the viewscreen until the gnostor's vitals settled into the green, and the man drifted off to sleep.

Switching the viewscreen to the next two cubicles, Montrose saw Ivard sprawled on his side, watching as Lucifur played bat-and-chase with a spoon in the quarter-gee environment. Ivard was having one of his good days. He seemed hugely entertained watching the big cat spring lithely about, using every surface in the berth including the ceiling for propulsion but never coming near the boy. Gray's tail stirred as she watched alertly, but the dog showed no inclination to try to wriggle out from under Ivard's arm. Her wounds were healing rapidly.

Montrose put the cubicles on automatic. He tapped the locate on his boswell, got up, and stretched.

He found Marim and Lokri at consoles in the rec room. As he dialed up some hot caf — they were getting low on coffee — Marim turned to him, her small face sharp with expectation. "What made Vi'ya rasty?"

Montrose paused. "What?"

"Only hear her walking when she's angry," Marim said impatiently as she ducked to the hatch, looked out, then back. Grinning, she added, "And when she's rasty, that tongue cuts like monothread. If she's looking for trouble, I'm gone."

"Relax, nullwit." Lokri shook his head. "That old blunge-eater in the dispensary probably wouldn't talk to her. Come, finish the game — or," he added in challenge, flicking his fingers across his keypads, "are you afraid to lose?"

Marim plopped back down on the other side of the big console, scanning the screen. Passing behind her, Montrose glanced down to see a promising setup for Phalanx, Level Three. He glanced appraisingly at Lokri, whose attention was on his screen.

"Captain discuss her plans with you, my friend?" Montrose asked.

Lokri's mouth twisted. "Saw her going down to the dispensary, saw her come back. Heard her come back," he corrected, nodding at Marim. "Stalking. Unless young Firehead suddenly got a death wish, it was either you or Jaim or the geezer. Jaim licks up her spit, and I've never seen you pick a fight with any of our crew."

The impression Montrose had gotten earlier in the journey solidified to conviction: Lokri was on the hunt once more.

Montrose considered the amount of regret leavening his amusement as he made a slow circuit around the room. He hoped never to see that again. But he was seeing it. So, now he needed to decide what, if anything, to do about it. He settled at last on one of the big padded seats along the back of the room. He set his caf down. "Omilov it was."

"About?" Marim prompted, curling her legs under her.

"The Heart of Kronos," Lokri said. "What else?"

"That little silver ball she took from Schoolboy? It worth anything?" Marim asked, chin on her hand. "I know her little skull-boilers think it is, even though they never pay any attention to tech."

Lokri snorted. "If you'd bothered to look it up after Vi'ya showed it to us you'd know it's probably more valuable than all the loot we took from the Palace, and damn well impossible to convert to cash."

"Even more impossible now," Montrose said. "Eusabian wants it."

Neither Lokri's nor Marim's reaction to that news made any reference to the tacit admission that Montrose had listened to the conversation inside Omilov's cubicle. They knew he had the equipment to do so if he wished, and they also knew that the captain would have been aware she was being overheard. But Montrose had an entirely different question in mind. He meant to test his hypothesis; the last time Lokri had gone on one of his hunts there had been far too much collateral damage.

The only way he'd get a truthful answer was by indirection. He waited, and his reward was the sweet chiming of tiny bells that heralded Jaim's approach. The tall engineer ambled in, his long face tired.

"Be good to get home." He sank into a seat near Montrose. He didn't appear to see the scornful twist to Lokri's mouth at the word "home."

"Suggestion," Montrose said. "Since most of us are here."

"Huh?" Marim asked, her eyes on the game.

Lokri swung around in his chair, brows raised.

"That loot you took from Arthelion. Some of it might well be worth more than the ship we are sitting in."

"We've been through all that." Marim slapped an impatient hand on the side of her console. "Since you're all here, who nabbed Firehead's coin? It was the only thing Greywing took, and he wants it to remember her by."

Lokri's eyes narrowed. "He had it when we got him out of the palace. Had it in his hand, along with that damn Panarchist flight ribbon that Markham gave him, that he's been hiding ever since. Quite a death-grip. I put them in his pocket just before we came on board," Lokri said, tapping his chest. "Then you took him." He tipped his head toward Montrose.

"There was nothing in that pocket but dried blood when I stripped him down," Montrose said. "The rest of his suit was stuffed with things, but none of them a coin. Or a ribbon."

His gaze shifted to Marim. She nodded judiciously. "We went through it all together, my last visit to him. No coin, no ribbon."

Montrose said, "We can assume that the Eya'a did not take them. I don't think they have any interest in such stuff."

"Vi'ya would have asked whose it was," Jaim murmured.

Lokri crossed his arms, his lip curled sardonically. "Brandon was helping me get Ivard to the ship. I suppose he'd consider it reclaiming something of his own."

"But the Schoolboy was there, too." Jaim put in. "Remember?" he said to Marim.

"If either of them has the coin or ribbon, I'll find out," Marim said. "Heyo! Why don't I go tell Firehead now? Sure to give him a good—"

"I'd prefer him not to be disturbed right now," Montrose said. Ah. Lokri wasn't the only one on the hunt. And Ivard was reaching the age to make him eager to be caught. Well, he had to learn someday.

Marim grinned, shameless. "He's getting cabin-crazy in there."

"How is his burn healing?" asked Jaim with a considering glance at Marim.

"He's healing more slowly than I'd like," said Montrose. "It's the Kelly ribbon. It has compromised his immune system." He scowled. "Before we get to Dis, there's something else you need to consider."

The other three waited, their expressions characteristic: Lokri wary, Marim interested, Jaim sober.

"We had better think about our next step beyond Dis."

Lokri lifted a shoulder lazily. "The way I see it, those two—three, counting Schoolboy—are Vi'ya's responsibility."

Jaim gave him a level look. "She can't lock them up on Dis. We don't have any defense. She either sells them to whoever offers the most, or lets them go. Nothing involving the rest of us."

Marim's bright gaze flickered from one to the other, and she laughed. "Or they join us. New names. IDs. I wouldn't mind. Schoolboy's coming out of his shell. Actually said two words in a row to me. And Brandon's pretty. Also not bad with the weaponry."

Lokri smiled.

Montrose finished his caf and got up to dial some more. "Join us?" He spoke to Marim, but watched Lokri. "With what Ivard got for you, you can take off. Buy your own ship. Change your name, too. Run your own crew."

Marim shook her curly head, leaning back and cracking her knuckles. "I'll stay with Vi'ya. She's as hot a pilot as Markham was. As long as we're successful, I'm here. If she loses, I'll hop. But I don't ever want to captain. Too much trouble."

Montrose was about to frame a question to prod Lokri when Brandon vlith-Arkad walked in.

Energy seemed to ricochet around the room, manifesting in Lokri's tightened shoulders, Jaim's unblinking gaze, and Marim's blinding smile.

Brandon nodded a general greeting, then moved to the

dispenser and chose something hot, a process that seemed to absorb his whole attention. Lokri and Marim resumed their game, Jaim lounging behind Lokri's shoulder. Brandon turned away with his cup in his hand, then Marim said, "Shall we pull you in, Arkad? This is Level Three."

Brandon gestured. "Next game?"

He sank down into the chair next to Montrose's, his face betraying marks of stress. The new heir to the conquered Panarchy had exerted himself to be friendly and cooperative from the beginning, when Vi'ya had agreed to take him to Arthelion — right after he showed up on Dis seeking his boyhood friend Markham. Who was now dead.

Why had he come, after ten years of silence? Montrose was fairly certain they would never find out now.

Osri was easier to understand. He considered himself a prisoner and acted like one. Sebastian was weak, and his courtesy seemed to be bred bone-deep. Whatever his feelings about the people who had rescued him from Eusabian's torturers, Montrose was certain that the professor was no threat.

Brandon was also pleasant and affable, but utterly unforthcoming. Montrose wondered why the captain ignored him as if he didn't exist. Maybe she expected Brandon to try something foolhardy when they reached the base. In her mind, Brandon might already be dead. She'd have to make some kind of decision about the nicks before they reached Dis. And Lokri appeared to be waiting for just that.

Montrose set his cup down, intent on his original purpose. "Marim."

"Mmm?" She kept her eyes on her game.

"Ivard divvied up what he is saving and what he got for you?"

Her eyes were wide and humorous. "Not yet," she chirped. "There's lots of time for that." Her eyes flickered once in Brandon's direction, then back to her game.

Jaim had relaxed again. A quiet man, yet with surprising depths, he had never hid his wish to rejoin his lifemate Reth Silverknife. With her and his share of the loot, they could buy their own ship; Montrose knew that Reth would have taken Greywing on as crew. He hoped they would settle for Ivard. The boy would need family, and those two would be excellent for him.

Second to the problem of Brandon (and his nick companions) was Lokri. Montrose turned his attention that way, pretending an interest in the game. In spite of Lokri's lazy air, Montrose recognized tension in his arms and hands, the angle of his head, not just competition in the game, but another, primeval competition: Lokri valued nothing that did not carry risk, seeming incapable of attraction to anyone who did not convey a sense of danger. And angry as he was that Markham chose Vi'ya over him, he was angrier still at Markham's death. Had Lokri noticed how Vi'ya avoided the Arkad? Probably. Life would be interesting when they reached Dis.

Montrose laughed to himself and moved on, wondering how long it would take Lokri to realize that he'd lost that game right from the start.

The damaged-one-who-hears-music contemplates from dist-ance the eye-of-the-distant-sleeper, in fear. This one's desire is to shield its pattern from Eya'a, from Vi'ya.

Is there in his pattern an image for the distant-sleeper?

There is question, there is a fear-darkness, the damaged-one-who-hears-music fears Eya'a and Vi'ya joining in his contemplation.

Is there in his pattern a connection between the eye-of-the-distant-sleeper and the distant-sleeper, as one knows the arm between fingers and body?

There is only question, and the desire to hear the connection between the eye-of-the-distant-sleeper and the distant-sleeper. And the damaged-one-who-hears-music contemplates the angry-one with the thought-coloration Vi'ya teaches us means sorrow —

We will leave his pattern, and return our attention to our contemplation of the eye-of-the-distant-sleeper before my need for sleep must be heeded. . .

SIX

Hreem looked around the crowded null-gym. The cavernous space echoed with the shouts and whoops of the gathered Rifters. Nearby, set apart as much by their grim silence as by their more uniform attire, were Hreem's hostages, a mixture of Douloi and Polloi.

The gym was arranged as if for two-player nullball, with the seating drawn in close around a fifty-meter sphere where the gravitors had been balanced out, surrounded by a nearly invisible netting. A number of air vortexers had been installed in ports in the netting. The Rifters were already jostling for command of them. Near a larger opening two men held the trembling Naigluf, who wore only a loincloth. His skin had a sickly greenish cast to it, and he was drooling slightly. Withdrawal right on schedule.

Norio had let Naigluf have some popper while the entertainment was publicized, and then cut him off. The exertion of what was coming would accelerate Naigluf's metabolism and bring him down even faster.

But where was Norio? The Rifter audience was showing signs of impatience.

Not that Hreem cared. His mind was largely elsewhere. Not an hour earlier Riolo had come through with the promised data about the L'Ranja gang: their base was on Dis, a moon of Warlock, the innermost gas giant in this system. Now Hreem could execute the plan he had already worked out: to use the two hyperwave-equipped ships remaining to him, *Flower of Lith* and *Hellrose*, newly arrived, to trap Vi'ya when she returned from Arthelion — he no longer thought of her return as "if."

The crowd noise modulated away from restlessness back towards anticipation as Norio appeared, holding a black cube about a third-meter in size. One of his hands had a metal gauntlet on it. The tempath glided to a stop next to Naigluf, and waited for the crowd noise to subside.

"Pilgrim Naigluf got greedy," Norio began when silence had fallen, "and he got caught. He tried to take more than his share, which would leave less for you." An ugly murmur drifted up from the Rifters.

Norio held up his hand and the murmur died. "We shall rejoice in our pilgrim-brother's journey along the path of enlightenment," he continued. "But Naigluf is a strange one among the Sodality. Oh, not in his greed." Norio smiled. "We're all greedy. But have you ever heard of a Rifter who's afraid of falling?"

Raucous laughter swelled from Hreem's crew. The Highdwellers sat in stony silence.

"Afraid of falling, and afraid of spiders, too. That's why Naigluf's agreement to expiate his sin against the Sodality today is so special."

Hreem grinned at the cadence of Norio's voice. The tempath was really enjoying himself.

"For your pleasure and delight, Pilgrim Naigluf's going to engage in null-gee battle against one of the deadliest denizens of the Thousand Suns."

Deadliest denizens? Norio was really laying it on thick. The giant spiders in the box were used for pest control in several of the Charvann syncs; their bite was quite painful to humans, but not deadly. Norio was boosting Naigy's fear to make the entertainment even tastier. Hreem could already see sweat on Norio's brow, and the tempath's hands trembled. He had a feeling he'd be seeing a lot of this particular treasure in the years to come.

Norio unlatched a black box and reached carefully into it with his gauntleted hand, pulling out a dull black spheroid about the size of his fist, holding it delicately with a peculiar grip. The Rifters nearby backed away, two of them with fear-spurred haste. Shock cascaded through Hreem when the spheroid sprouted jointed, hairy legs that waved wildly, and sturdy, iridescent wings that rattled against the tempath's armored fingers as the creature struggled to escape.

Norio held the creature out for the crowd's inspection. "The medusoid of Empalla IV." He smiled; all right, so Norio was not settling for pest control after all. "So named for its unique ability to turn human flesh to something close to stone."

Hreem looked down at the nullball paddles he was holding. He'd planned a terrifying humiliation for Naigluf, followed by the public spectacle of his withdrawal sickness, which he might even have survived. Past that, Hreem hadn't cared—Naigluf would be a reminder of the cost of crossing Hreem whether he lived or died.

But Norio apparently wanted more. Hreem shrugged. Tough luck for Naigy.

Norio placed the creature carefully back in the box, held it up against the hatch, and tripped the mechanism. A swarm of the black arachnids burst out into the playing area, buzzing and fluttering wildly as they tried to adapt to the unfamiliar lack of gravity. Some tried to cling to the netting that enclosed them, but it was too fine and offered no purchase for their claws.

At a curt motion from Hreem the two men holding Naigluf dragged him over to the large hatch and thrust him through. As the hatch puckered closed, Hreem walked over and pushed two small nullball paddles through at Naigluf.

"Here's your weapons, Naigy. Give 'em hell."

The other Rifters roared with laughter as the skinny Rifter flailed wildly with the paddles, looking like one of the silly speculations about human-powered flight from the pre-tech age of Lost Earth. The hollow popping of the vortexers began echoing through the gym, their blasts of air setting Naigluf spinning.

Hreem glanced at Norio. The tempath was definitely trembling now under the impact of the crowd's emotions, his eyes dilated. Then Hreem felt the summons of his boswell, a priority-one from Dyasil. Alarm flared: was Telvarna back already? Couldn't be. He abandoned his own vortexer, which was immediately grabbed by another Rifter, and got out of his seat. (YEAH?)

Dyasil's voice was an urgent whisper: (MESSAGE FROM ARTHELION. WE'RE GO FOR MALACHRONTE.)

The yelling of the crowd and Naigluf's frenzied screams withdrew to background noise as the blood mounted in

Hreem's head. Malachronte! The image of himself on the bridge of the *Maccabeus* possessed him once again with an indescribable sense of well-being.

But this changed everything regarding Dis. He couldn't explain a decision to delay: if Barrodagh found out that the ship with the Aerenarch and Omilov might be headed back to Charvann, he'd assign its interception to Hreem and send someone else to Malachronte.

Well, he could head for Malachronte by way of Dis and use the same two-ship plan to make sure of the *Sunflame*, if it was there. He'd leave Lignis to wait for Vi'ya—no, he'd have to explain why *Hellrose* was posted fifty light minutes away from Charvann, unable to relay whatever new information came up about Omilov and the whatsit Eusabian was after. He'd leave a telltale. After all, once he had the battlecruiser, he wouldn't have to worry about *any* of his many enemies, let alone some Dol'jharian bloodhunter in a Columbiad.

(Cap'n?) came Dyasil's voice.

(Get the crew back on board. Tell Lignis to get his crew back too and stand by for orders.) He flexed his boswell off.

One last thing to figure out: how to finesse this so Lignis didn't connect *Telvarna* with the Arthelion raid. Better make sure he just blasted them into plasma. Too bad about the rewards.

Hreem felt Norio's trembling hands upon his shoulders. "Ahhh," he said, wordless. "Ahhh, Jala." The tempath's eyes had rolled up into their sockets. Only the whites were visible. Norio was off in his weird world of pain-boosted bliss. He wouldn't be able to walk in this state, so Hreem hauled his resistless arm over his shoulder and got them both moving toward the exit. The trembling of Norio's body followed exactly the waves of sound from the crowd of excited Rifters, punctuated by sudden jerks that matched the shrieks of agony from the slowly dissolving Naigluf.

As they reached the exit, Hreem looked back. Naigluf was still screaming, but only twitching ineffectually, for both his arms and most of one leg had disintegrated as the bites of the medusoids turned them brittle, and black pools of fester were spreading across his torso as the creatures fed in arachnoid frenzy. The Highdwellers—those who hadn't been dragged off by Rifters for personal sport—huddled in abject terror, some watching in horrified fascination, others tightly curled on the deck, their eyes squinched closed and fingers in their ears.

Hreem laughed, feeling his pleasure resonate in the shivering tempath.

Life was good.

GROZNIY: SCHADENHEIM TO TREYMONTAIGNE

"Engage," Captain Margot Ng said.

The viewscreen blanked as the fiveskip hurled the *Grozniy* away from Schadenheim.

Ng gently tapped her fingers one by one on the arm of her pod. Treymontaigne and Schadenheim were unusually close to each other, as distances went in the Thousand Suns, but the eighteen hours until they arrived would be long ones. And it'd all be over when *Grozniy* got there, most likely.

She looked around the bridge. The new alpha crew pleased her, so far. They'd handled the exercise at Wolakota beautifully, and had cheerfully accepted her decision to go to General Quarters before emergence at Schadenheim, which put the senior crew instead on the bridge for the anticlimactic emergence.

There'd been no sign of Rifter activity at Schadenheim. She smiled, remembering the disappointment of the Archon there. They really were a bloody-minded bunch. Eichelly had probably made the right choice, even if Harimoto did rip him up at Treymontaigne.

But that made her next decision an easy one. The alpha crew was at the end of their watch. Normal rotation would bring them back up for emergence at Treymontaigne; they'd have had full tween, rec, and a Z-watch between. It was unlikely they'd have anything to do except watch *Prahbu Shiva's* tactical recordings.

She was distracted when Ammant's shoulders tightened. His head turned — he really was distractingly beautiful — and he spoke, the bridge cadence not quite masking his obvious curiosity. "Captain, the discriminators have turned up a message for you in the downloads from Schadenheim. En clair."

"Relay it, please," Ng said.

Words appeared on her console: *This worm-casting turned up for you in the DataNet at our last call, some more data on your port wriggles. I'm shortcutting it to you, but I hope it doesn't help. Six months to go on our bet, Broadside!* A glyph indicated an encrypted attachment, and it was signed "Metellus Hayashi."

Tenderness warmed behind her ribs and forced its way out in a chuckle. She caught heightened attention from the crew and decided to satisfy at least part of their curiosity, and perhaps help Rom-Sanchez deal a bit better with his own distraction.

"A friend warning me that he's about to win a bet we've had for a very long time." She glanced around. "Any of you know what a port wriggle is?"

No one did of course, but she caught a quick look passing between Rom-Sanchez and the irrepressible Wychyrski at the next console. When she let them catch the direction of her gaze they turned obediently back to their tasks, but she knew they'd be speculating later.

TELVARNA: ARTHELION TO DIS

Sebastian Omilov looked up with a smile and set his book aside as his son entered the little dispensary berth. Mild alarm kindled at the furtive look on Osri's face. For the first time, Montrose had not accompanied him.

"Father, I've found something I think you ought to know. Look at this."

Osri reached to touch a key on the med console. With a few swift strokes, he windowed up a physician's cachet. For a neurosurgeon, Omilov saw. Osri brought up another cachet, from the Apanaush Gastronomie on Golgol. The name was encrypted on both, but that was not what caught Omilov's attention.

"The seal of Timberwell," he said, surprised. "On both of them." He touched the zoom.

Osri grimaced. "Exactly," he said with distaste. "Now a Rifter."

Timberwell. Another symptom of the rot beneath the glory. Timberwell had expelled its problematical Archon, in spite of the fact that the Srivashti family was extremely powerful, but after the departure of the government the insurgents had instituted a reign of terror, earning a Class Two quarantine in the process. Osri obviously suspected Montrose of republican sympathies, but Omilov had already sensed that if the man had ever been interested in politics, the subject was dead to him now.

"A surgeon and a chef," Omilov mused, attempting a deflection, though he knew it was unlikely to succeed.

"There can't be too many ex-Timberwell Douloi with those qualifications," Osri continued as if Omilov hadn't spoken. "His accent and mode of speech identify him as coming from the Ranks of Service. My mother would know. She would also know if there was some sort of scandal—" Osri stopped, and shook his head wryly. "But you're about to tell me how much you hate gossip, aren't you?"

Omilov cleared the screen with care, considering several things he might say. Circumstances had effectively cut him off from Brandon. He did not want to lose Osri as well.

"I am about to say," Omilov murmured, "that the ease with which you found those, and that you were allowed to show them to me, probably indicates that you were meant to." Omilov considered how he might tell Osri of the slowly growing sympathy he was discovering with Montrose, whom he was beginning to suspect was one of the most cultured men he'd ever met, despite his rough exterior. He suspected that this "discovery" was simply a way for Montrose to share a bit more information with him without inviting further questions. "He is a remarkable man. I've discovered that he has a collection of opera chips. And he is one of the few people I have ever met who knows the game chess, though of course we have yet to play."

"Maybe he wants reinstatement," Osri said. "As if that would happen, after helping loot the palace. I think—"

Omilov's suspicion was confirmed when the big Rifter's booming voice interrupted Osri, "I wondered why Sebastian's vital signs had spiked."

Osri's face paled.

"I'll not have you worrying my patient into a relapse. You've got free time now, Lieutenant. Use it somewhere else."

The use of his naval rank obviously flustered Osri. Omilov suspected it was the first time Osri'd heard it from any of the Rifters, and he left with a mumbled apology, mostly directed at his father.

Montrose fussed over Omilov for a few minutes, speaking only of medical matters, and then left without any further comment. But he left the console on, as Osri Omilov opened the hatch to the cabin he shared with Brandon. As expected, it was empty. Since that last bitter confrontation, the Aerenarch went out of his way to avoid private encounters with him.

Still shaken by the sudden appearance of Montrose in the dispensary when he'd thought him asleep, Osri cast aimlessly about for something to do. Checking the hatch lock once more, he stooped over the console and awkwardly used his nail to pry up the cover of one of the lights inset above it. Two objects fit snugly inside: one, a bloodstained silk ribbon; the other was the warm silver shape of the Lost Earth Tetradrachm.

He sank down on his bunk and examined them both.

The coin he'd learned about on his first visit to Arthelion, accompanying his father, when he was ten years old. He'd toured the Ivory Hall as his father explained the artifacts there. The thing was impossibly ancient, one of a kind.

The date on the piloting ribbon was 955, ten years ago. Osri knew who had won the medal. He'd stood there at the award ceremony when it was pinned on Markham vlith-L'Ranja, just months before the swift, terrible events that saw Markham cashiered and Brandon nyr-Arkad removed from the Academy, supposedly for the unauthorized use of atmospheric craft in war games over the southern continent, but everyone knew it was for cheating.

Osri turned the medal over. If Brandon was to be believed, that accusation was false. Osri was quick to dismiss his words. Of course Brandon would deny cheating. On the other hand, though Brandon was irritating, irresponsible, utterly lacking in discipline or even a sense of the dignity that should be part of his duty as an Arkad, Osri had to admit that he had never been a liar.

But there was no one to ask. No one in the navy would talk about the incident. Markham had disappeared. His father, the Archon of Lusor, had committed suicide. Osri's own father had retired from active service, acting for the next ten years as if his life in court had never taken place.

Osri had long ago come to terms with these events, believing them unrelated. He could not believe that the lamentable affair was a conspiracy cooked up by the now-deceased Aerenarch Semion, against his own brother and the L'Ranja heir. It made no sense! It sounded like one of the jokes in questionable taste that Brandon and his brother Galen had been so fond of.

What galled Osri was his recent discovery that his own father, the most loyal man Osri had ever known, had considered the Aerenarch Semion culpable in all these events.

Osri crushed the silk in his hand, recalling Ivard being carried aboard the *Telvarna*, his arms dangling over Montrose's massive shoulder, and the two objects falling from a pocket onto the deck. Markham might have given the boy the flight ribbon, for whatever reason; the coin, though, had been looted from the Ivory chamber, an act of violation that made him furious.

Osri turned the worn, uneven coin over on his palm. On the one side was a bird. On the verso, the figure resembled a woman in archaic dress. A trace of some kind of script, completely unintelligible, remained here and there. Rubbing his fingers over the warm metal of the coin, he thought about the unknown hands who had made and possessed it unimaginable millennia before, under the light of Sol. Handling the Tetradrachm gave Osri a sense of peace, a sense of order. And Telos knew there was little enough order in the rest of his life.

A sound outside the cabin made him close his fingers protectively over it. Someone tried to open the hatch. Osri jammed both objects into place and slapped the light cover back on. Then he hit the lock and retreated to his bunk, scowling.

"I was preparing to sleep," he began as the hatch opened.

The rakish, gray-eyed comtech Lokri lounged there. "On your feet, nick," Lokri drawled. "Let's see what you can do with a jac in your hands."

"I don't—"

"Now." Lokri stepped toward Osri, his smile tight with challenge. Osri's heart hammered. These people were Rifters, and they followed no law but their own whim.

He followed Lokri out of the cabin, tension easing somewhat when he saw Brandon approaching the rec room from the other direction, led by the somber-faced Serapisti Jaim. Though he was still angry enough with the Aerenarch to avoid him whenever possible, he felt a measure of safety in his presence. If they were going to kill *him*, they'd make a show of it.

The rec room was utterly bare, featureless. Marim, who was waiting, punched the console. The four walls vanished, replaced by an excellent simulacrum of a narrow, grimy street flanked by colonnades dim with shadow.

"Factor's Way, Port Kedorsim," she announced.

Did they want Osri to practice backing these scum? From over the buildings on one side the blue-white glare of a booster lift-off briefly illuminated the street. Osri could feel the crackling roar through his feet. The simulation was good but not perfect; Osri's ears still reported that he was in a small room.

Marim thrust a sim-jac into Osri's hand. "We're about to be attacked. Live or die."

A figure in a garish uniform strolled out from a darkened doorway in the sim and squinted at them. It was a tall man, perhaps forty years old, with a sallow olive complexion and dark hair and brows. His bones were wide and strong under their layer of extra flesh, his expression ugly.

Osri recognized him as the man Tanri had shown them on the main screen of the defense room in Merryn: Hreem the Faithless.

"Markham's killer." Did he hear a whisper? In the reflected light of the simulation Brandon's face betrayed grief, then the Aerenarch turned away, fingering the jac in his hand.

Osri remembered the quotation Brandon had made, that day in Merryn: "*— and a pyre will I make of my enemy's works.*" The Sanctus Gabriel had acted at a nexus in history where justice and vengeance came together. For the first time doubt assailed Osri. Could he lay claim to the same justification?

"Handsome little chatzer, ain't he?" Lokri laughed.

"What's that on his boots?" Osri asked. "The metal things."

"Heel-claws," replied Lokri.

"Looks like they're only useful if your opponent is lying down," Brandon commented.

"That's Hreem's character in a quantum."

"Hreem chatch n'far," Marim cursed, making an obscene gesture at Hreem's face before she snapped her fingers and triggered the action. "Go, Lokri!"

Hreem whipped out his weapon and fired as Lokri crouched and shot.

Evil-faced assassins appeared on rooftops, beside the decrepit buildings, or ran from doorway to doorway, firing frequently. Lokri ducked and whirled, trying to zap the phantoms before they fired on him. This went on for several minutes, then the figures disappeared and Marim hit the console.

"Not bad!" She peered at the readout. "Burned twice, three wounds, zapped seventy-three percent of 'em."

Lokri made a noise of disgust as he and Marim switched places. The little Rifter was fast on her feet, but reckless: she ran out of charge in the middle of a firefight. From the chaffing she took, this was not unexpected.

Jaim was next. As one would expect from a master of the Ulanshu Path, he was very fast and very accurate. Marim clapped, and Lokri watched with that speculative air. Then, with a self-deprecating gesture, Jaim gave way for Brandon to take his place.

Brandon ranked about the same as Lokri. His aim was better but he made the same sort of tactical errors that Osri then made in his turn — errors which, Osri reflected bitterly as Marim crowed about their poor scores, were to be expected from people who did not make violence their way of life.

Brandon sat on the edge of a console, smiling across the room at Marim. "You have to remember," he said, "we're trained to try everything short of jacs to resolve differences."

"You've noticed," Lokri retorted in exactly the same tone, "that the Dol'jharians do not make the ballroom floor their battleground."

Jaim was studying his hands, his long dark braids swinging close to his face.

Marim said, "We all need to be better when we see Hreem next."

Osri said, "I take it you expect us to be a part of this quarrel?" As all faces, Rifter and Aerenarch, swung his way, he hated how tight and angry his own voice sounded.

"Might not be a choice." Lokri's voice was mild but his narrowed eyes reflected some of Osri's own anger.

"Does your captain practice with you?" Brandon asked.

"Group actions, she does," Marim said with a grin. "On Dis. We sometimes play for days. On *Telvarna* she runs alone."

"She was a dead shot long before she joined up with us," Jaim put in, looking up at them. "Had to be."

"Come on, let's try the group run," Marim suggested, and punched the console.

Brandon stepped obediently to the middle of the room, so Osri did as well. The three Rifters moved apart in a well-trained unit as a score of villains appeared. Brandon fell behind, and with a sense of unreality Osri took up a position to his left, recalling a lesson from his Academy days; when they were trained, there was little expectation they would ever use such knowledge. And then there was no time for thought.

Osri fell into the remembered patterns of defense classes, keeping focused and alert. When the program ended and the space shifted back to normal, he was surprised by a mild sense of regret.

Lokri punched up drinks. Marim put a hand on Osri's and Brandon's shoulders and shoved them toward seats. Brandon complied without comment, so Osri sat where indicated. Perhaps he expected to hear something of import.

Lokri handed out the drinks. Brandon wiped damp hair off his brow and raised his glass. "The dead salute you."

Lokri grinned. "We'll do another tomorrow. If you want to stay alive, you're going to need some work."

"How do you keep track of Hreem?" the Aerenarch asked.

"Sodality maintains a pipeline on the DataNet, like any other organization; the Infonetics blits don't care," replied Lokri, "as long as the fees get paid."

"Lot of merchants and even Service types subscribe to the RiftNet, 'cause the info's so good," Marim added.

Osri leaned back in his seat, considering yet another dissonance between his assumptions and reality. This was what his father had been talking about once: that no one on Arthelion seemed to realize just how much a part of the Thousand Suns the Rifter overculture was, despite its lack of any official recognition. *"They're all over the Thousand Suns and beyond,"* he'd said, *"and not being planet-centered like Downsiders and even Highdwellers, they've got a different perspective."* Osri remembered having ended the discussion by referring to lawlessness.

"That means Hreem can use the same sources to gather information on his enemies? Like you, for example?" Brandon went on.

"Yep." Marim wiped her sleeve across her mouth. "But Hreem's made a lot of enemies, and some of those sources don't work so well for him."

"He can't even get near Rifthaven anymore," said Lokri, "since some of his gang shot up Varli's Refit Emporium a couple of years back. Only the fact he wasn't there himself — and paid the wergild with the heads of the ones who did it —

saved him from all the Syndicates going after him."

"And anyway, we have Vi'ya." Jaim waved a long hand in the direction of the bridge.

Osri saw a brief exchange of glances between the Serapisti and Lokri. Brief, and completely uninterpretable.

"You mean her tempathic abilities?" Brandon asked.

"Nah." Marim's nose wrinkled. "That doesn't do her much good out here. Strictly up-close stuff. She says she merely uses the info to project patterns, and makes plans from there. She's a hot one at strategy and tactics."

Lokri finished off his drink and lounged to the hatch. "My watch now." And he strolled out.

Brandon said, "Did Vi'ya ask you to run us?"

Jaim shook his head, his braid-chimes tinkling.

Marim said, "Was our idea. You, Arkad, are pretty quick on the fly. We saw that back on the Mandala. But Schoolboy. . . " She shrugged.

Brandon was watching Jaim, who studied his hands. "I know Hreem killed Markham, but Vi'ya said Markham was betrayed. By whom?"

Jaim looked up quickly.

"Chatzing triple cross," Marim said. "I still don't know the whole story. I was on the other base when it happened. But you can ask Vi'ya. If she'll talk, which isn't often. Or you could ask Lokri. He knows all about it."

Brandon's gaze remained on Jaim. "Maybe I should cultivate your captain. I notice she's not unfamiliar with the Ulanshu kinesics. When does she practice?"

"Only with me," Jaim said. "She masses a lot. Their bones are denser than ours, and she's strong."

Marim shivered theatrically. "Don't spar with her. She'll break your arm without even trying. Jaim's the only one can manage her."

"Their?" Osri asked.

No one answered him. Marim stretched, then wandered over to dial something more to drink. Jaim got to his feet and walked out.

Brandon also rose. Osri followed him out, and then said again, "Their?"

Brandon looked back, his gaze absent. "Dol'jharians."

SEVEN

Night had fallen, and Eloatri was lost. The realization brought her to a halt in the middle of the trail, just short of a clearing illuminated by the magenta glimmer of the rising moon. She stood among the shadows of the trees, their white trunks ghostly in the half-light. Around her the forest was silent, save for the whisper of a mild breeze and the occasional call of a night-bird. As she inhaled, the cloying sweetness of nerisa wafted to her from the clearing.

All day a certain weight had been descending on her, a formless dread with no object. She had let the feeling have its way, knowing that grasping at it would only perpetuate it. But now her back crawled with the diffuse fear of the dark that she had not experienced since childhood.

"The goal of a hejir is to go where the Hand of Telos guides one." True, but. . .

Her mind stopped. Shock flooded her as she heard the chattering inner voice that discipline and meditation had stilled threescore years before. What was happening to her? Eloatri felt adrift, as if she had stepped off the Eightfold Path into spiritual chaos. She grasped vainly at the centering mandala she learned from her master so long ago, but her mind chattered on.

"In the seeing there should be just the seeing, in the hearing just the hearing, in the thinking just the thought. . ."

Then the weight descended on her in its fullness, the Hand of Telos sundering her from the moment. Eloatri groaned wordlessly and crumpled into the lotus position, a measureless sense of loss welling up in her.

"I take refuge in the Buddha, I take refuge in the Law, I take refuge in the Community," she said aloud, but the crowded trunks of the trees around her returned her words in mocking echoes, fragments of the life being stripped from her: refuge, Law, Community, take, take, take.

She scrambled to her feet and hurried down the trail, and her third step took her out of the world into the Dreamtime.

"Here," said Tomiko, touching her elbow and indicating a table next to the street. The High Phanist smiled as they sat down and motioned to a waiter. The young man hurried over, and Eloatri tried not to stare at his atavistically pale skin and blazing red hair. On his hand she noted a large emerald ring.

Eloatri leaned her staff against a vine-entwined roof support next to them and placed her begging bowl on the table. Its battered brass clanked against the glass surface. At a nearby table a strong-shouldered, dark-visaged man stared at her for a moment before turning back to the woman with him, whose physiognomy echoed his. With them were two white-haired children.

Eloatri didn't hear what Tomiko ordered for them, but the waiter returned only moments later with two goblets and placed them carefully before them. Eloatri felt vaguely disappointed. Would they not eat?

Tomiko picked his goblet up and rotated it meditatively in one hand. Its metallic surface gleamed with condensation, the tiny droplets scattering rainbow flickers of light across his broad face and high cheekbones.

He raised the goblet to her and drank. She picked hers up and drank also, suddenly conscious of a tremendous thirst. A moment later she choked, slamming the goblet back on the table with a discordant crash: the taste was appalling, a compound of thick metallic heat and something so bitter that for a moment she couldn't speak. From the goblet now came the odor of blood.

"That's horrible!" she exclaimed, barely able to enunciate the words past the terrible constriction imposed by the bitter flavor.

The High Phanist raised his brows. "The beings of the world are numberless; I vow to save them all."

His quotation of the first of her bodhisattva vows was like

a slap in the face.

He smiled gently, and she noticed now that he, too, was speaking with difficulty, forcing the word through a bitterness almost too great to be borne. "Surely you did not suppose you drank that for yourself?"

He reached across the table and took her begging bowl. "You won't be needing this anymore."

She lunged across the table, grasping desperately at the battered brass bowl. . .

"No!" shouted Eloatri, and she awoke, standing in the moonlit clearing, clutching her begging bowl with a terrible strength. After a moment, she forced her fingers to open, and the bowl dropped into the dust of the trail with a muted clank.

TELVARNA: ARTHELION TO DIS

Sebastian Omilov shifted position, trying without success to ease the discomfort of being wedged into a small fold-down seat in the galley. Not long after the incident in the dispensary, Montrose had given him tacit permission to wander where he willed on the ship, the only caveat being that he must return if he felt any chest pain, tingling, or shortness of breath.

Almost the moment he had taken his first steps outside the sick bay he'd met Osri lurking in the corridor. Looking continually this way and that, his son had brought him straight to the galley. Silent until they were closed in, Osri then pointed at the console and said, "Father, the captain of this vessel is a Dol'jharian, and the Aerenarch knows it."

"So do I," Omilov murmured, and saw shock on his son's face. "I recognized her accent. Brandon certainly did. He had to spend a great deal of time with Eusabian's son Anaris, remember."

"I remember," Osri said in a flat voice.

"I have not discussed this with Brandon," Omilov said. "In fact, I've seen little of him, and those visits have only been in the presence of the doctor."

The imputation was oblique, but Osri's cheeks showed a ridge of color. "I confronted him," he admitted. "Demanded he do something. Or let me lead." Osri picked up some kind of tuber, then set it down again, his profile wretched. "I can't forget he was abandoning his family, and everything we believe in, to join these very Rifters before the Dol'jharian attack even happened."

Thus making it impossible for Brandon to speak alone to Omilov, and unlikely he would confide in anyone now.

"He avoids me," Osri went on. "He's either in the rec room, playing with those dogs, or wasting time with the Rifters and their war games. Or when I'm in the galley he plays around on the cabin console. Half the time he's too drunk to talk, anyway."

Or pretending to be. No one expected much of a drunk. Aloud, Omilov said, "As good a way as any to find out information, that last."

Osri raised a hand in a tired gesture. "If I could be certain — if I could trust him." Omilov was about to speak, but Osri shook his head. "If you're about to defend him, spare your breath, Father."

Omilov shifted again, fighting against the increased pressure in his chest. Again, he found himself choosing his words carefully to avoid alienating Osri. "I do not believe her allegiance is to Dol'jhar," he said. "It's clear enough she's an exile, and from what I know of that planet, no one gets off without tremendous determination and effort. However, she is still Dol'jharian. My worry now is not so much what she will do with us, but what she might do with the Heart of Kronos."

Osri's face eased from anger to reflection.

Omilov confided further. "I really don't know anything other than what I told you and Brandon the night of the attack. And as you heard, that is little enough."

"If the likes of the Dol'jharians want it," Osri said, "it has to be some kind of weapon. No one has ever accused them of raiding places for art."

Omilov forced a smile, then leaned back, trying to ease his spine. He had to admit it, he'd gotten up too soon. "Yet art it is, or so the Guardian said. Or that was how we understood him. But it was also a part of something larger, a key, or a linking piece. Whether that large thing is a weapon or not, no one knows, but the fact that some race millions of years ago saw sufficient reason to put this thing in isolation under the care of the Guardian made us take any surmises seriously."

"Though the large thing, weapon or not, is probably long gone," Osri said.

"Perhaps. But if it isn't, then I am in some wise responsible for it. I would rather recover it, before its use is inadvertently discovered."

"By the captain?" Osri's breath hissed. "Or by the Eya'a." He glared. "They knew we had it when we crash-landed on Dis. First thing she did was take it away from me." He scowled, flushing with anger. "And Brandon just sat by."

"What should he have done?" Omilov asked. "Don't you remember Anaris? Not later, when he'd learned something of restraint from the Panarch, but when he first came to us?"

Osri's mouth twisted. "You seem to forget — or maybe you didn't notice — that Brandon, and Galen, before he was sent off to school, did their best to make sure I scarcely saw him. I think I exchanged a sum total of five words with Anaris during all my visits to the Mandala."

Omilov leaned against the wall, his mind ranging back through the years to a memory a few months after Anaris had arrived on Arthelion: Galen, tall and weedy at nearly twenty, with a smashed wrist in a cast, and Brandon, younger and smaller, with a broken collarbone.

"Don't tell Father," Galen had said. *"He'll send him back, and it will wreck the treaty."*

"We all learned something," Brandon added, his laughter wheezing. *"We learned that he's as strong as a Tikeris — "*

"Masses as much, too," Galen put in humorously.

"And he learned, or will, that to be civilized you must know how to laugh. We're going to make sure he learns how to laugh."

Galen's sleepy smile had turned uncharacteristically grim. *"Threatening to kill people every time you see them strains the conversation."*

"Not to mention trying to carry it out," Brandon had added.

Omilov remembered saying, *"But this sounds serious. Please release me from the bond of silence; I really think I ought to speak to your father."*

Both of the Panarch's younger sons had shaken their heads. *"We've said enough, and Anaris'll get adult tutors in manners. What we'll teach him is a sense of humor,"* Galen had promised. *"From a distance."*

"But if he goes for you whenever you're alone — "

"We'll just make sure that he never catches us alone again," Brandon had promised. *"Our dogs will help, with a little more training."*

Omilov looked up at his son. "With Dol'jharians, as Brandon well knows, every confrontation becomes a contest of power. The captain seems civilized, but try not to make her angry." He hesitated, thinking of Vi'ya's straight body, its contours hidden beneath the anonymous dark cloth of the jumpsuit made tight to throat, wrists, and boot-tops. "And if you do succeed in enraging her. . ." He sighed, echoing Brandon's words of long ago, "Don't let her catch you alone."

GROSNIY: SCHADENHEIM TO TREYMONTAIGNE

"Heyo, Serg." Yeoh Wychyrski dropped onto the bench next to Rom-Sanchez in the junior officers' wardroom, her tray loaded with typical inattention to nutrition.

Rom-Sanchez had chosen to eat alone, rather than joining the group around the L-4 console. The senior officers had kept them on the jump since the disappointment at Schadenheim, leaving him little time to brood about that sudden grin in the captain's face.

But here was Yeoh Wychyrski, her dark eyes avid. He liked her. She was popular, and good looking. The same height as the captain, she had a spectacular figure that the uniform couldn't hide.

"Sit down, Yeoh," he said — a second after she'd already set her tray down.

But it was like Mzinga had once said, the problem with having been young and brilliant is that eventually you aren't young any more, and when you are surrounded by other brilliant people, you aren't that special any more.

Yeoh still sometimes acted like she had when she entered the Academy at only fourteen, the youngest cadet in their class. And so, even though she'd been recently promoted to alpha crew, she was still an ensign three years after graduation, despite her competence otherwise.

"Why all alone?" she asked. "Someone turn you down?"

That was another thing, she saw romance everywhere. Why didn't she sniff after Prettyboy Ammant, like everybody else? He hoped she hadn't picked up on his attraction to the captain.

Rom-Sanchez glanced up. The only other solitary officer was short, her tight-curling hair skinned back in a regulation bun. She was reading the menu by the dispenser, her blunt, broad-nosed features composed into an abstracted frown.

"Warrigal," he said, hoping Yeoh would take the hint communicated by sheer unlikelihood.

"Warrigal!" Yeoh repeated, eyes wide with surprise. "She never talks about anything but her game."

"How would you know?" How could anyone so good at SigInt be so clueless? "That's the only place you pay any attention to her. Anyway, you know we're connected. Biao Dai Highdwelling was freighted by the Warrigals."

"You think a closer connection couldn't hurt, eh? You're sniffing a dead trace," Yeoh said with a sympathetic shake of her head. "Liviu and Ke have a hundred-sunburst bet going that that uniform is tattooed onto her skin, and whatever's under it is as null as those Bori who serve the Dol'jharian warlords are rumored to be."

"Catennach." Rom-Sanchez drank off his caf, hiding a wince. The context was a bit too close to the bone. He could so easily see a bet about when a poor lieutenant who was hot for his captain (someone like him) would be humiliated. Shifting the subject slightly, he said, "Apparently the Catennach castrate themselves, in some nasty ritual. It's supposed to prove their dedication—"

Yeoh waved impatiently, and leaned closer. "Since you hang out with Warrigal, have you been able to find out anything about her last post?"

Rom-Sanchez looked grim. "Nobody talks about Narbon."

Yeoh snorted, the single Serapisti chime woven into her tight coronet of braids glinting. Regs were strict: hair was to be neat, either cut just below earlobe level, or else worn high. Regs stretched to ornaments for religious purposes, although Serapisti chimes had to be silenced at station. Yeoh's thick, wavy hair was always elaborate, pushing the meaning of the word 'neat,' and Rom-Sanchez wondered how often she performed a Serapisti ritual.

"She was the top of her class," Rom-Sanchez said. "And you have to be smart to be skimmed for Narbon, even if your family is as old as the Warrigals."

"Especially, you mean," Yeoh retorted. The Warrigals had disdained the ambitious Douloi who gravitated to the Aerenarch. She leaned forward. "And double if you're not male. But she probably wasn't aggressive enough." She tightened a fist. "You know what they say about the Aerenarch."

Rom-Sanchez glanced at Warrigal, who'd been halted by

one of the L-4 players. She stood there, tray in hand, food rapidly cooling, her dark face brow-furrowed as she seriously answered some question that was almost certainly a joke.

Rom-Sanchez shrugged. "He prefers men as officers, that's about all I've ever paid any attention to."

"My cousin Rafe, whose uncle knows a cook's mate aboard the *Sobieski*, said the cook's mate overheard the Aerenarch saying, and I quote." Yeoh shifted to the lugubrious tones of a stiff-strut wiredream officer. *"I honor my father's desire for peace, but we all know the next war will be with Dol'jhar. And when that comes, I want as my captains men who can kill with their bare hands on their own bridge. I do not say most women can't, I'm saying that most women won't."*

Her voice rose slightly. "They say after a year, the Aerenarch makes his officers pass a red test. You know, kill someone, in hand-to-hand combat. I'll wager you a hundred sunbursts — a thousand — that Warrigal funked it." Yeoh sat back significantly.

"Don't be a nullwit," said Rom-Sanchez without heat. "And keep your voice down." He shook his head. He'd heard some unpleasant things about duty at Narbon, but that was just ridiculous. And, like everything else out of the Aerenarch's planet, third-hand — as though a cook's mate would be present to "overhear" anything the most paranoid Arkad in generations said.

Anyway, even Yeoh had to know that someone like Warrigal would be the last to spill any details. She was under a cloud, for sure, and survival meant lying low. He wondered if her almost obsessive focus on her game-thesis, a piece of academic work that he had to admit was brilliant, was merely camouflage.

"All right if I sit here, or is this a private conversation?"

Rom-Sanchez was startled by the quiet voice. He looked up. There was Warrigal, standing next to the booth with her tray. The rest of the wardroom had filled up.

"No, not private," Yeoh said, unabashed. She indicated the opposite bench. "We were just talking. You have any idea what a port wriggle is?" She dug her elbow into Rom-Sanchez's side.

Warrigal paused in the act of breaking her bread. "Our watch was talking about it," she said seriously. "The captain stopped in and Koenic asked if a port wriggle was some sort of code."

Yeoh dug the elbow again.

"She said that she's been running a research worm on that phrase since she was a midshipman. It was part of a wooden warship, but no one knows what it did."

"Wooden!" Yeoh repeated, eyes round. "Ohhhhhh, you mean *surface vessels*."

Warrigal looked genuinely puzzled. "Surely you had the history of warfare classes."

"I forgot it all as soon as I was out of there," Yeoh said. "Unless we begin fighting wars again by throwing rocks at the enemy, I don't see how learning about ancient wars serves the least use now."

"Wooden warships," said Rom-Sanchez. "Isn't the Captain's patron Sanctus from that era? Orrenblorr, or something like that?" He knew it was risky to push this conversation, given its direction, but somehow that made it more exciting. And perhaps he could deflect Yeoh from needling Warrigal.

Then, more daringly, he added. "And her nickname, too."

"Broadside?" said Yeoh. "That's from ancient history? I thought it referred to her hips."

"No" said Warrigal, as always apparently unaware of being teased. "For about four hundred years or so, ending about four hundred years before the Exile began, naval battles were fought between wind-powered wooden ships, using gunpowder cannon firing solid shot."

"That's a chemical explosive, right?" Yeoh put her chin in her hands.

Rom-Sanchez glared down into his caf. How long was Yeoh going to keep it up? He knew the answer: until it was no longer entertaining. She really was still fourteen in some ways.

"Actually a deflagrant, if you'll permit a bit of pedantry. It merely burns extremely fast." Warrigal laid aside her fork, positioning it carefully next to her plate, leaving her food to congeal even further. "These ships were really a lot more like the *Grozniy* than you'd expect. They were made of a very hard, durable wood, and they didn't have explosive shells, so it was almost impossible to sink one of them. You had to kill most of the crew on board to stop one of those ships from fighting. Just like a modern battlecruiser."

Yeoh pursed her lips. "You seem to know a lot about them."

Warrigal nodded. "I find the pre-Exile days fascinating. And even more so, the parallels to our lives now."

"Go on," Yeoh said—not goading. "Give me a parallel." Rom-Sanchez was relieved at the note of genuine interest. That was why he liked Yeoh. She might be nosy, and arrogant, and sometimes even irritating, but she also enjoyed learning, and when she got interested in something, her genuine enthusiasm was infectious.

From the mild flush along Warrigal's heavy cheeks, she had detected the change in attitude. "The ships would sail up to within thirty meters or so of each other—the cannon weren't terribly accurate—and blast away side by side until one or the other fell away downwind to escape, or surrendered after taking too much damage, like losing masts and sails— propulsive power—or having too few crew left to tend the guns."

"But where does 'Broadside' come in?" Yeoh asked.

"It's one of those Academy things that you never live down."

Rom-Sanchez and the two ensigns looked up guiltily to discover their captain standing there. The rest of the wardroom was silent, everyone at attention.

The three leaped to their feet, Warrigal knocking over her caf in her haste, and Rom-Sanchez nearly flipping his tray; he surreptitiously slammed it flat on the table. How had they missed the captain's entrance?

Ng appeared to notice nothing amiss as she smiled ruefully. "Someday I'll tell you all about it," she said. "As you were."

As the rest of the off-duty junior officers resumed their places, some talking self-consciously, the captain nodded at Yeoh, then turned to Warrigal. "Your description, or at least the few words I overheard— I trust you will forgive me for intruding on a private conversation—is accurate."

Rom-Sanchez hastened to add his voice to the protest that she was welcome to join them.

"The term broadside," Captain Ng continued, "refers to the fact that the ship's guns were usually all fired at once from one side of the ship. From a capital ship that might deliver from five hundred to a thousand kilos of iron shot at over three hundred meters per second; most wounds were inflicted by high-velocity wooden splinters."

Her voice had taken on some of the dryness of Warrigal's description. *She's rizzing Yeoh,* Rom-Sanchez thought, schooling his face.

Yeoh shuddered. "Sounds almost as bad as a ruptor."

Ng nodded. "It's hard for moderns to understand just how similar warfare was in that era to what we face today. More so than any era since. Remember, in those days they didn't have real-time communications, any more than we do. Messages could only move as fast as the fastest ship. Moreover, a frigate—which like our ships of the same name were used mostly for reconnaissance—had a field of view of only about thirty kilometers, from the highest mast, on an ocean measured in thousands of kilometers. As a result, enemy ships or fleets were hard to find, and most naval battles were fought in sight of land, just as ours are fought within solar systems. It was also difficult to force someone to fight, since with wind-powered ships, the loser had only to slip away downwind, just as the fiveskip today makes fleeing a battle quite simple."

"That would make the skip-smashing effect of our ruptors equivalent to knocking down the sails of a wooden ship, wouldn't it?" Ensign Warrigal said.

"Exactly! Dismasting, they called it." The captain hesitated. She seemed to be studying them. Rom-Sanchez began to suspect that there was more to this discussion than an oblique correction to Yeoh. "The words that caught my attention when I arrived were 'parallel to our lives now.' I believe you are quite right, Ensign."

Warrigal's face crimsoned.

The captain continued. "The naval strategy of that period has a lot of valuable lessons for today. Even the tactics, to some extent. For instance, gunpowder generates so much smoke that, during a battle, firing the guns quickly obscured what was going on, just as the debris from a modern battle can sometimes render most of your sensors useless."

The comm whistled, interrupting their discourse. "Captain, we're one hour from Treymontaigne."

"AyKay. I'll be up shortly." She looked around at them, then smiled. "We'll go in Green."

As the three once again leaped to their feet, she started toward the hatch. "Meanwhile I'm still on the lookout for a definition of a port wriggle. I want to win a bet that I made almost twenty-five years ago. And if you help me win, that nets you a full course dinner, you name the venue." She laughed. "I like to win my bets."

The hatch slid shut behind her.

"Green!" Yeoh said, punching Rom-Sanchez in the chest. "That's alpha, not senior!"

At the L-4 table Ammant looked up at them, his face alight.

Rom-Sanchez's stomach lurched, and he looked down at his food. He'd been expecting the senior crew to take emergence, as they had at Schadenheim. And so, from her expression, had Yeoh. Warrigal's mouth tightened. Envy? Wistfulness? He wondered if Yeoh had seen it.

No time for that now. He wanted a quick shower and the right uniform. What he had on was clean enough and reg, but he'd had a new uniform on for Wolakota, and now he felt a little superstitious about it, although he'd never admit that to anyone.

EIGHT

The junior officers had just dropped into their pods when Ng reached the bridge. On the main viewscreen the Tenno pulsed quietly in the absence of input, vivid against skip-blanked darkness.

Commander Krajno returned command to Ng, who said, "Status?"

"Emergence minus three minutes, sir. Standard approach, as you ordered."

That would put them within one light-minute of the Treymontaigne beacon in the leading trojan of the sunward giant in the system, just as at Wolakota. Another by-the-book approach.

Krajno turned, one bushy eyebrow raised interrogatively. She wasn't sure herself why she hadn't taken them directly to Treymontaigne orbit, since Harimoto would have taken care of Eichelly by now. It wasn't as though a battlecruiser needed to worry about the fuel and navigational advantages the skip well of a major trojan attractor offered.

Not even a hunch, really. She shrugged away the thought. Krajno certainly wouldn't question her decision. Especially when doing so would make him look overeager for his reunion.

Not that she blamed him. They both were aware how Navy romances were hell on the emotions. Krajno hadn't seen Tiburon for, what was it, almost a year now. She smiled to herself. They made quite a couple, Commander Perthes ban-Krajno, executive officer of the *Grozniy,* and Commander Tiburon nyr-Ketzaliqhon, chief energeticist of His Majesty's battlecruiser *Prabhu Shiva*. Tiburon was tall, slender, the picture of Douloi elegance. More than one unlucky officer had mistaken the burly, rough-edged Krajno, when the two men were together in mufti, for the other's valet or bodyguard. It was a mistake no one made twice. The funniest part of it was that Krajno was the intellectual of the two; Tiburon's world consisted of his engines, and Krajno.

She sat back, granting tacit permission to chat as she assessed the mood of her alpha crew and watched how they handled their consoles. She still wasn't sure about young Wychyrski and the absurdly gorgeous Ammant, although they'd performed well enough at Wolakota. But Ammant couldn't help his face, and as for her age, Ng was no older than Wychyrski on *her* first posting, when *Jauntevant* was jumped by the Shiidra.

They were both excellent young officers, who worked doubly hard to overcome prejudices they couldn't help, and there was no sense in second-guessing her own decision to emerge green rather than pulling in the senior crew.

Rom-Sanchez glanced her way before saying to Wychyrski, "Sixty-two hours since Wolakota. Maybe thirty-two hours or so since Eichelly skipped in. By now, his pieces are likely well on their way to joining the Oort Cloud here."

Wyrchyrski uttered a sinister chuckle. "I wish he'd picked Schadenheim."

The descending tones of emergence put an end to their conversation; a dizzying sense of deja vu gripped Ng as, after a short pause, Wyrchyrski announced, "No beacon, sir."

Ng responded without hesitation. "Tactical skip, now."

Her mind flickered through scenarios. Harimoto would have deployed a new beacon immediately after taking care of the Rifters. Had *Prabhu Shiva* left the system before Eichelly reached it? But assuming Eichelly destroyed the beacon as soon as he arrived, Treymontaigne should have sent a ship to investigate in the thirty-odd hours since.

Moments later SigInt reported, "All sensors functional." Good. Ran the check faster this time. "Ship signatures working, negative."

"Tactical, take us to threat-level two."

Rom-Sanchez's acknowledgement was followed instantly by other station echoes, led by Fire Control: "All ruptors to standby. Skipmissile activated, holding at precharge level."

Up on the main screen, a plot of the Treymontaigne system based on their assumed position windowed up as Rom-Sanchez anticipated her next request. The flaring red of maximum probability centered on the nearest k-zone, twelve light-minutes away.

Ng tabbed her console and started a ten-minute countdown.

As Commander Krajno monitored the multiple reports flooding the bridge while the ship came up to level two, he muttered, "Harimoto'll be furious at missing this chance, even if he did get away from hand-wiping Treymontaigne."

Ng's answer died unspoken when Ensign Wychyrski at SigInt looked up. "Captain, I've got a large object about twelve light-minutes in, relative velocity about five hundred kays." She stopped, worked her console for a moment, then frowned, all her characteristic humor gone. "The readings are confusing. I'm getting a thermal reading at the million-degree level, and some gravitational disturbances as well."

The bridge had gone quiet; that was the unmistakable signature of a shipwreck, resulting from destabilized spin reactors and drives.

Ng's first reaction was that they had caught up with Eichelly. But why hadn't the beacon…?

Wychyrski's next words destroyed that hypothesis. "But I read its mass at about ten-power-twelve tons. There's an awful lot of debris — thermal scattering — around it, too."

Way too big for a destroyer. Ng looked at Krajno, who shrugged and shook his head. "No ideas here, Captain."

And not quite big enough to be a battlecruiser. A startling thought. No battlecruiser had ever been lost in action against Rifters. Whatever it was, it couldn't be that. Perhaps Eichelly had run into an asteroid while fleeing the *Prabhu Shiva*, as unlikely as that was.

"Give me a visual. Maximum enhancement. Navigation, bring us about for maximum array effectiveness."

At this distance, the optical array formed by the sensors on the *Grozniy*'s hull could resolve details down to less than twenty meters, as long as the ship was oriented correctly.

The tactical plot dwindled into a corner of the screen as the starfield began to slew in response to her order. The screen blinked and a blur of light slid into view, gradually sharpening as the ship's motion ceased. Then the enhancers cut in and Ng's ears rang with shock.

Mercilessly clear, the details hardly concealed by the limits of resolution, the shattered hulk of a battlecruiser blazed silently.

One third of its length was gone, torn away by some unimaginable force; in its shattered interior a blue-white glare pulsed, emitting sheets and sprays of fluorescing gas as the dying engines yielded up their energies into space. As the hulk rotated, the distance-blurred form of Shiva Nataraja came slowly into view, his lower body obliterated, his four arms still upraised in the eternal dance of creation and destruction.

Mzinga's quiet report felt like a detonation in the silence. "Position confirmed, sir. Treymontaigne system, absolute bearing 252.6 mark 1.1, plus 53 light-minutes." The tactical plot on another screen rippled.

Ng started at a sudden crunching noise nearby. She stared at the blood dripping unnoticed from Commander Krajno's hand, clenched around the ruins of one of his pod's arms. His face, seen in profile, was calm, only a ridge of muscle around his mouth betraying his emotions.

Ng found her voice. "General quarters. Engineering, teslas to threat-level three, rig engines for max-tac maneuvers. Fire Control, charge skipmissile, ready all ruptors. SigInt, pop that tacponder."

A flare of light pinpointed it on the tactical plot as she shifted momentarily into eyes-on mode; a glyph indicated less than twenty seconds until its returning squirt reached them.

"Alerts on multiple widecasts, no link found." Ammant's voice was flat with strain, his beautiful rosewood complexion blanched to the shade of sand. "Captain, you'd better see this."

At Ng's nod, he fumbled at his console. A thin, mewling shriek filled the bridge, overlaid with the raucous laughter of a mob and broken by transmission losses that the enhancers couldn't eliminate. The sound clenched at her throat, but worse was the image. Two seconds was all she endured before she slammed down a hand and cut it off.

"Rifters, in the Archonic Enclave," Ammant continued, his voice thin as he continued to watch on his console, the shriek still faintly audible to the bridge at large. "It's the Archon." He choked. "O Telos —" He touched his console with one shaking hand and then bent over, swiveled his pod away, and was rackingly ill.

Ng's breath caught as the fiveskip burred momentarily in the automatic response called for by general quarters. "Skippulse, Captain," Wychyrski said, snapping her head back from a horrified glance at Ammant. SigInt's voice was tight, but under control as she chanted, "One light-minute out. ID processing, signature was corvette-class." No danger, then.

Moments later the same skip pulse echoed from SigInt. Tenno updates rippled across the screens.

"Signature matches *Noisy Girl*, last reported as part of Eichelly's fleet," continued Wychyrski a moment later. "It's gone now."

Now they'd know that *Grozniy* had arrived. "Navigation, as soon as SigInt relays the squirt from that tacponder, take us in to one light-second. Communications, on emergence scan for life-signs, full noetic enhancement." That would normally be SigInt's function, but Ammant needed a moment to recover.

The hoarse summons of the klaxon had seemed to breathe life into the bridge, but Ng could see the rigidity of tension in the movements of the crew. She tabbed her console and signaled the Environmental officer to bias the tianqi toward stress relief and cut the subsonics. They needed no additional cues to key them up.

The hatch hissed open, and a medic moved to Krajno's pod.

The klaxon fell silent. The atmosphere of rage seemed to thicken as the seconds dragged on. The horror slid out of sight as Navigation brought the ship around for the next skip. Then the communications console bleeped.

"Tacponder responding. . . monitoring was engaged." Ensign Wychyrski's fingers tapped nervously at the keypads. There was a faint squeal from her console as the discriminators shifted into search mode, then the fiveskip engaged with a brief subsonic burp. After that, silence.

The Tenno overlaid on the main viewscreen told Ng almost instantly what SigInt reported in bridge cadence, rounding off the numbers, but she knew that the crew needed the distraction of duty. And what would she distract herself with?

"Tacponder recorded four skip-pulses over a period of about thirty seconds, destroyer and frigate. Then a fairly large EM burst and particle shower at about minus 31.6 hours. At that point the nav beacon ceased radiating and there were two more skip-pulses, followed by just one 11.7 minutes later. Then a skip pulse and interrogation at about minus thirty-point-eight hours. 10.7 minutes after that, another skip pulse, then another a minute later followed by a gravitational disturbance consonant with ruptor-tractor activity. Ten seconds after that a skip-pulse, followed by skip noise — most likely a skipmissile — then a very large burst of EM and gravitational radiation, followed by a particle shower. Seventeen minutes later, two more skip-pulses, nearly simultaneous. Finally, a skip pulse at minus 30.6 hours."

"Tactical?" Taken by themselves, each of the events was easy enough to interpret in the context of a beacon-bashing response, but they didn't add up.

Rom-Sanchez was staring at the blank screen. Then he shook his head. "Doesn't make any sense. We've got two Rifter ships, but it was the frigate that took up station in the k-zone after the destroyer blasted the nav beacon. Judging from the timing of the interrogation, the *Shiva* responded less than twenty minutes after the signal stopped at Treymontaigne. SOP would have been watching from a light hour out — that last pulse. He did a quick re-check of the target's position from a light minute out, following up with a tractor attack, confirming that the target was a frigate, and then — "

He stopped as the screen flickered and the disintegrating hulk of the *Prabhu Shiva* sprang into full clarity. At this distance the resolution was on the order of centimeters. The image expanded, giving Ng the dizzying feeling that she was falling into the hellish pit of energy that burned at the heart of the shattered battlecruiser. The broken edges of the hull were strangely smooth: there was no spalling, no twisted petals of hull alloy. That was the unmistakable signature of the impact of something moving so fast that no material could propagate a shock wave.

"Continue, Lieutenant," said Ng. The bridge crew needed more time to process their shock; they were seeing an impossibility. But all the evidence was cruelly there.

"Ten seconds after *Prabhu Shiva* grabbed the frigate, the destroyer returned and fired a skipmissile. The *Prabu Shiva* blew up." He shook his head, his voice dropping out of report cadence. "Why weren't the shields up? How did the destroyer find *Shiva* so quickly?"

It was impossible that Harimoto would have left his shields down. No captain in the Navy would have done that, not even one of Aerenarch Semion's silver-polishers. The phrase brought recognition that she was in danger of losing her emotional balance.

But there was something wrong with that skipmissile impact.

And Wychyrski's voice in her mind blended with SigInt's real-time report. "Debris analysis consonant with skipmissile impact."

After a painful pause that seemed to last forever, Ensign Ammant spoke, his voice rigidly controlled. "Noetic scan negative. No survivors."

"Navigation, take us ten light minutes down and inward."

This was not a typical Rifter incursion. That widecast would not have reached them had the planetary shield still been up; the invaders were already down on the planet.

Ng damped down the swirl of speculation that threatened to overwhelm her. Nothing made any sense, so the first priority was more information. She turned to Krajno. "Commander, prepare to deploy a VSA, with whatever resources it will take to see what happened here, and afterwards the initial Rifter attack on Treymontaigne. Relay the proper coordinates to Navigation."

"Captain!" Krajno's voice was raw. "At least part of the Rifter force is downside. If we follow up immediately we can take them out. We still have the advantage. Let's use it."

Which was exactly what that transmission was designed to provoke.

With her peripheral vision Ng noted the focus of the entire bridge, but she kept her gaze on Commander Krajno. "Harimoto no doubt thought he, too, had the advantage, Commander Krajno." She saw her formality strike home. "Kindly execute your orders. You may post a formal objection in the log if you so desire."

Krajno gave his head a slight shake: Ng knew he was back in control of himself.

"It's less than 33 hours since that action," she continued, "and the Rifters have already taken the planet. I want to know how, and more about the tactical situation, before we go in all ruptors blazing." She raised her voice slightly to a more formal cadence. "I assure you," she added, as much for her XO as for the bridge crew, "we will not leave this system without dealing with Eichelly."

The crew was busy at their tasks. Ng hesitated, ready to replace Ammant, but he'd pulled himself together, his shoulder blades working the back of his uniform tunic as he rapidly scanned for more coms. Pleased with his mettle, she decided that she'd have to keep them all busy, not just Perthes Krajno; deploying a virtual sensor array capable of resolving useful details at a distance of nearly one-and-a-half light-days would involve some or all of the *Grozniy*'s corvettes, each linked to the ship via laser to create a sensor array hundreds of kilometers across.

The proper size of such an array was a trade-off between resolution and signal-to-noise ratio, and although they'd drilled the evolution twice during their out-octant patrol, it hadn't been for an event this far in the past. Perthes would have to push the crew—and himself—hard now, for every minute that passed before deployment would cost them another light-minute of distance from the action, reducing further the detail they would be able to see. Just the sort of task that Krajno needed right now.

"Communications." When Ammant looked up, she said, "When we skip to VSA distance, shift your compute priority to discrimination of what you've recorded up to that point, until we shift focus to Treymontaigne." The ensign's sculpted cheekbones flooded with color. He was still obviously regretting his lapse as he bent over his console.

"SigInt," she said, "at Wolakota you reported something strange about the skipmissile impact we witnessed. I'd like to see your report now."

Too little to go on, so far. Ng winced inwardly at the memory of the Archon's torment. There was nothing she could do for him. Yet.

She felt she owed it to him to view more of that record. But not now. First they must watch the death of *Prabhu Shiva* and plan their response. One thing was certain: when they faced Eichelly in the inner system, there would be no mercy.

"Lieutenant." Rom-Sanchez looked up sharply, the puppy utterly gone. "I want every bit of tactical information we can squeeze out of that array. Consult with Commander Krajno and make sure it's set to grab whatever you need."

The rear hatch opened as the Marine guard admitted a swabbie with a mop, reminding Ng of another responsibility. One of the first lessons of command was that the truth was easier to deal with than rumor. She brought her finger down decisively on the ship-comm, and the traditional twitter of the pipes filled the air, alerting every station in the ninety-two cubic kilometers of the *Grozniy* and carrying her voice to every one of the five thousand crew aboard.

"This is the captain. . ."

Less than two hours later, Krajno reported, "Deployment complete." His voice was flat, his eyes red-rimmed. "Twelve Raven-class corvettes with 150-meter arrays, in a one-thousand-kilometer virtual array." He paused. "Laser links established, tractors engaged. Stabilization will take about a minute."

Ng calculated briefly. That would give them nearly fifty-meter optical resolution, and even better at higher frequencies. It would be enough.

"I specified an hour ahead of the action," said Rom-Sanchez. "Commander Krajno and I agree that we can't afford to miss any tactical preparation on Eichelly's part, and this way we'll see what *Prabhu Shiva* saw, if Captain Harimoto followed SOP. A light-hour's loss of resolution won't make enough difference to matter."

Ng nodded. That had been her conclusion as well.

"I want the optical portion of the action piped into General Access," she said.

The viewscreen wavered as the array came on-line; a small targeting cross blinked near the center, marking the position of the navigational beacon.

"I have a ship trace, battlecruiser signature, plus 34.6 light-hours. No ID," reported SigInt. Another positioning cross appeared near the first; the trace was nearly between them and the beacon, normal to its position from the ecliptic as was standard naval practice.

"That'd be the *Prabhu Shiva*," Rom-Sanchez stated, some of his characteristic eagerness back. "Watching the destruction of the beacon from a light-hour down."

"Harimoto ran a taut ship." Commander Krajno's voice rumbled in his chest. "Fast and by the book."

Moments later Ensign Wychyrski confirmed the ID. The unspoken question occupied them all: so how had a Rifter destroyer annihilated a battlecruiser conned by a competent, experienced captain?

For several minutes after that, nothing happened. The tension on the bridge grew. Ng distracted herself by reviewing SigInt's report on the skipmissile attack at Wolakota, but through no fault of Ensign Wychyrski it was basically an expansion of the term "insufficient data" and didn't hold her attention for long.

Finally a small red pulse of light bloomed near the beacon. Rom-Sanchez's hand twitched, overlaying it with another cross. The Tenno rippled as data began to build up.

"Signature indicates an Alpha-class. No ID," Wychyrski reported, scowling at her console as if she could bring the mystery ship in by will.

Nothing more happened for another several minutes, except the ID of the destroyer from SigInt: "ID confirmed: Eichelly's *Talon of God.*" Wychyrski's voice was taut with anger under the bridge cadence.

Then another emergence pulse blossomed some distance from the destroyer.

"Frigate, possibly a Scorpion. No ID."

A fierce spark of light bloomed near the destroyer and faded. The faint background chirping of the beacon ceased. Seconds later the destroyer skipped again, moments before the frigate also skipped, emerging in the nearest sunward k-zone about twelve light-minutes in from the beacon's position.

"Frigate ID confirmed," reported SigInt. "Scorpion, *Devil's Ace.*"

Wychyski's hands hovered uncertainly over her console as the elapsed timer on the Rifter destroyer stretched out. Finally, she spoke, her bridge cadence faltering. "No emergence detected for the destroyer."

The Tenno glyphs flickered uncertainly, blinking through a series of impossible configurations, then settling into a simpler readout that no longer tactically connected the two ships. Ng rubbed her eyes.

"Confirm that, Tactical. Non-coincident light cones?"

"The frigate emerged twenty-two-point-five light-seconds from the beacon. The destroyer skipped eleven-point-two seconds after that." Rom-Sanchez looked up at her in consternation. "That doesn't make any sense."

At that distance, and in that brief time, no communication could have passed between the ships.

"Coincidence," said Krajno, looking up from his fierce

concentration on his console. "They rendezvoused outside the system."

But why did the destroyer wait, then?

"That may be, but their actions still make no sense," insisted Rom-Sanchez. "Where'd that destroyer go? Why'd they leave the frigate to watch, rather than the Alpha?" Rom-Sanchez sounded querulous, as if he resented the apparent irrationality of what they had witnessed so far.

They had little time to consider the questions. The *Prabu Shiva* skipped again less than a minute after seeing the frigate emerge.

"Looks like Harimoto was asking the same questions," said Krajno. "He waited for the destroyer emergence that didn't come." Krajno's eyes widened, his teeth showing. "Now we wait to see what really happened."

Her XO's idea of waiting was a rather active one from the perspective of the bridge crew. Ng tuned out the flurry of reports and consultations. It would be roughly an hour, so she turned inward.

What would Nelson have made of this situation? She thought of his long pursuit of Napoleon's fleet in the Mediterranean, and the later search for Villeneuve before Trafalgar. Amusement flickered briefly at the irony: that an admiral from the age of wooden ships would probably understand her frustration much better than later surface navies, accustomed as they had been to real-time communications.

Still, what would he have made of relativistic tactics, where the order of events depends on where you watch them from? Of being able to watch an action a day and a half after it happened? Or of being able to skip out of a battle, watch your enemy's tactics again from a different angle, free of battle pressure, then return to the fray with a new plan? Or using the fiveskip to attack the same ship from three different positions simultaneously?

Reluctantly, she abandoned the pleasant fantasy of a conversation with the admiral, showing him her ship, and windowed up her reports queue. End of tour still loomed. . . battles have an end, good or bad, but paperwork was forever.

Just under an hour later Wychyrski reported the emergence of the *Prabhu Shiva* a light-minute out from the position of the frigate hiding in the k-zone.

"Long-ranging." Rom-Sanchez' voice had roughened with gathering stress. "And the target's making it easy. It isn't even drunk-walking."

The big ship skipped again in seconds. A minute later the reddish spark of an emergence glowed near the position of the frigate.

"He's less than a light-second from the target," Rom-Sanchez reported.

"Ruptor signature, modulating to steady-state gravitational activity," Wychyrski sang out.

"Tractors. He's got them."

Less than ten seconds later, another emergence pulse bloomed near the battlecruiser and its victim.

"Emergence, eight light-seconds out. Alpha-class."

A thin thread of light, visible only as a computer artifact, speared from the destroyer to the battlecruiser. A flare of light grew slowly from the position of the *Prabhu Shiva*, faded, was gone.

"Give me a close-in replay of that last," snapped Ng.

The stars fled outward as the image zoomed in. The familiar egg-shape of a battlecruiser appeared, grainy and shimmering with processing artifacts as the computers struggled to create an image across a 38-billion-kilometer gulf. From off screen the chain-of-pearls wake of a skipmissile smote the ship, converting its stern almost instantly to a flaring inferno. Slowly, now turning end over end, the hulk passed out of their field of view.

"SigInt." Ng's throat ached. "Can you extract shield status?"

At SigInt, Wychyrski rubbed her eyes, then pulled her hands down with a fierce movement. "No, sir. We're too far out. But the spectrum of that skipmissile impact is similar to the one we recorded at Wolakota." She looked back at her console. "Destroyer skipped," she reported. "Frigate's still there."

Rom-Sanchez turned to Ng. "Impossible light cone again." He gestured at the Tenno glyphs overlaid on the screen, which were pulsing wildly again, cycling through impossible configurations. "The Alpha seemed to know exactly where *Prabhu Shiva* was." He hesitated. "As though the frigate summoned it."

His hands froze above his console, his gaze distant. Then he resumed tapping at his console, more slowly now.

"I'm going to have to purge the tactical computers and sandbox the recent action," he continued. "They can't deal with it." The Tenno lapsed into quiescence. Ng supposed that as a tactician, Rom-Sanchez was having more trouble than most dealing with the apparent relativistic violations they'd witnessed.

Interesting that Wychyrski and Ammant seemed aware of Rom-Sanchez's abstraction. Then both glanced her way, and snapped back into concentration on their consoles. What was that about?

Never mind. Time to move on.

"Commander, refocus the array on Treymontaigne. We'll watch what they did next." That took only moments, across very little more than a degree given their distance from the inner system. When Treymontaigne swung into view, the planetary Shield was already up, and cis-lunar space was marred with ship-to-ship actions. As they watched, Ng ordered the dispatch of cutters with centrifugal-foil arrays at four-light hour intervals inwards to build up the tactical picture.

The Rifters easily overcame the local defenses, and it was less than an hour later that a destroyer in cis-lunar space fired on the Shield, aiming at the planet's south polar magnetic pole, where the tesla effect was weakest. Then again, and again, in slow, metronymic rhythm.

Even through the processing artifacts of great distance, Ng could see the auroral excitation flaring with each impact, something that should not have been visible for days.

"SigInt, what's going on with Treymontaigne's Shield?"

Wychyrski tapped at her console. "Cross-sensor correlation indicates those impacts are an order of magnitude beyond Alpha specs." She shook her head, her face a mix of wonder and horror. "Beyond *our* specs. At that energy level, the Shield would have held out about eight hours, maybe less."

Ng drummed her fingers on one of the pod arms, staring at the screen. She felt Krajno's gaze on her, and wondered if he was feeling the same sort of relief that she did. Given skipmissiles that powerful, there was no reason to think Harimoto had failed to raise his shields. The pieces of the puzzle began to assemble themselves in her mind as she issued her next orders.

"Tactical, prepare a digest of the action with *Prabhu Shiva*. SigInt, Communications, keep the array on Treymontaigne and feed Tactical whatever correlates you can add. Get it to us in the plot room." She tapped at her com tabs.

"Engineering, GPT Kim," came the response.

"Have Commander Totokili report to the plot room."

"AyKay, Captain."

Another tap.

"Armory. Navaz here."

"Lieutenant Commander Navaz, please report to the plot room."

"AyKay, Captain."

Another tap. The tab flared blue: boswell access. (LIEUTENANT COMMANDER NILOTIS,) came the response, with the flatness of neural induction.

"Please report to the plot room."

(AYKAY, CAPTAIN.)

She stood up.

"Commander, please join me in the plot room. Navigation, you have the deck."

Rom-Sanchez barely noticed as the captain and XO left the bridge. He'd already run the anomalous data through the Tenno again, with the same results. The coordinated action of the two Rifter vessels was impossible.

But so was the destruction of *Shiva* by a single shot from an obsolete destroyer, not to mention the impossible battering they were watching Treymontaigne endure.

"…sometimes I've believed as many as six impossible things before breakfast." Nausea twinged as he remembered that awful story from Lost Earth, whose surreal plot had greatly disturbed him as a child. Even then he'd known a story had to make sense, and for him that's what Tactical was all about: making sense of a story whose plot was coming at you way too fast. Like now.

Huh. He was only being asked to believe two impossible things, and he'd already had breakfast. His mood veered wildly between laughter and excitement and terror.

Three impossible things. The third was that a game would be the making or breaking of his career, and possibly of everyone else who'd defiantly adopted the derisive sobriquet of "L-5 Loonies" bestowed on those who'd found Nefalani Warrigal's strange version of Phalanx so compelling.

He looked up. Wychyrski and Ammant—the only other members of the Loonies on the bridge—stared back at him with what he suspected was a mirror image of his own excitement and horror. He tapped his console to bozlink the three of them together, a necessary preliminary in any case, to prepare the digest ordered by the captain. But what he said launched them into uncharted territory.

(YOU COULD PARSE THOSE SHIP ACTIONS IN SOME OF WARRIGAL'S SCENARIOS.)

(WE HAVE,) came Ammant's boswelled voice on top of Wychyrski's (TOO BAD WARRIGAL ISN'T HERE.)

The excitement hardened to resolution. They'd seen it, too.

(SHE WILL BE,) Rom-Sanchez said. Before either could reply, he turned towards the navigator and spoke in formal cadence. "Lieutenant Mzinga. Request permission to bring Ensign Warrigal to the bridge for consultation on the digest ordered by the captain."

The quiet background murmur of the other crewmembers at their consoles ceased abruptly. The older officer regarded him gravely. Mzinga had never joined in the joking about L-5, and had even quietly watched a game several months back, before declining to participate.

"You sure about that, Lieutenant?"

Rom-Sanchez took a deep breath. Would his bars have time to tarnish, or was he about to terminate his career? He glanced again at the subscreen replaying the fatal attack on *Prabhu Shiva*. It didn't matter. Duty left him no choice.

"Yes, sir."

"Permission granted." One corner of Mzinga's mouth twitched slightly. "When you and she are finished, best you two take the report to the captain in person. Petty Officer Dimones can take your console."

"AyKay, sir. Thank you, sir."

Well, now he was committed. Rom-Sanchez tapped up a comlink to Warrigal, wondering if she'd thank *him* for this shift from the hypothetical game to the lethally real.

NINE

"...The frigate obviously had its fiveskip shut down," Krajno shouted. "You said yourself that's the only way they could have managed to show up back at Treymontaigne just seventeen minutes after a ruptor attack! They were ready for it! They were bait!"

"Enough!" Ng snapped.

The single word cut through the angry voices in the plot room. Even the orderly paused in the act of pouring coffee as Commanders Krajno and Totokili sat back, radiating tension.

Middle-aged, grandmotherly Lieutenant Commander Navaz, the armorer of the *Grozniy*, exchanged a pained glance with Nilotis.

Rifters with FTL communications? Nilotis felt a headache building: he'd gone through the anomalous actions in the tac-holo in the center of the plot room repeatedly while the XO and the Head of Energetics quarreled. It was the only explanation, and it made the Tenno impossible to use. Worse yet were the strategic implications. With FTL comms, Rifter reinforcements might even now be on the way to Treymontaigne. If so, they had only four days to act before the first such might arrive.

Ng released the invisible hold by making an apologetic gesture at the orderly that didn't hide how exasperated she had to be feeling. Nilotis was certainly feeling that, and half a dozen other emotions. The orderly finally reached him, but even the smell of real coffee — ground while the senior officers were still staring at that impossible holo — did not provide its customary comfort.

"Commander Totokili, your objections are noted," Ng said, her tone conveying the calm of habitual self-discipline. Nilotis was willing to wager that not one of the five thousand aboard was calm right now. "Unless you can explain the action we witnessed without reference to superluminal communication, that is the assumption we will be working on."

Commander Krajno nodded in agreement. Now Nilotis was certain that Ng had let the argument go on as long as she had in part just to give Krajno an outlet for his emotions. There would be no time for authentic grief over the death of his husband, no time for the grief all of them felt at the loss of the *Prabhu Shiva*, until the killers had been dealt with.

"AyKay, Captain." Totokili stared at the tac-holo with a sour look, ignoring the viewscreens on the walls that were displaying various excerpts from the action. His jaw worked as if he were chewing on something unpalatable, making the stiff brush of hair above each ear ripple like caterpillars.

Accepting that their Rifter foe was armed with some unprecedented ability to communicate faster than light without a fiveskip—some sort of superluminal EM analog—was difficult for all of them, but especially for one whose entire education and experience was grounded in the science of Energetics.

The glances that semaphored around the room had altered. Everyone was waiting for the tactical digest that Ng had ordered. Usually Rom-Sanchez was first on the mark, if not before, eager to anticipate the next order. Where was he? He had to know that being late was not going to please anyone.

Once again, apparently, the captain's thoughts paralleled his, as Ng addressed Nilotis. "It may be that Tactical is trying for more detail than we need to get started. Have him send what he's put together so far."

She shifted her attention to the other three officers, giving Nilotis tacit permission to boz Rom-Sanchez.

(ROM-SANCHEZ, TACTICAL.)

Nilotis relayed the Captain's request. . .

. . . and listened in disbelief to the Lieutenant's reply.

From the periphery of her vision, Margot Ng observed the stiffening of her chief tactical officer; already a very tall man, he seemed to grow several centimeters. She couldn't see his face, since he'd politely turned away for the boz from his subordinate. When Nilotis turned back, his high brow was wrinkled with concern.

"Captain, the Officer of the Deck has given the Tactical Officer permission to report in person, accompanied by Ensign Warrigal. ETA ten minutes." Nilotis gave them a painful smile. "Lieutenant Rom-Sanchez also requests the presence of Commander Hurli for the briefing."

Ng watched understanding widen Krajno's and Navaz's eyes, but Totokili glanced around, clearly puzzled and irritated. As far as she knew, no one in the Energetics Department played L-5, which was what this had to be about. The situation was spinning away into surrealism. As if to torment her, the single-shot destruction of *Prabhu Shiva* replayed itself on the holo.

She looked away. "See to it, please," she replied to Nilotis.

"Warrigal?" Totokili repeated, glancing from one to another. "The ensign from Narbon?"

"Bright ensign," said Krajno. "Difficult to read. Doesn't have much facility at small talk." He smiled. "Bit of an enthusiast for Tactical Semiotics."

Once again memory obtruded — easier than trying to grasp the inconceivable now. Never had she seen Krajno's essential gentleness more clearly displayed than during Nefalani Warrigal's earnest, and largely incomprehensible, explication of her graduate thesis, during a Captain's Dinner early in the tour. That dinner could have been one of those painful occasions when a junior officer goes on far too long, but Krajno had found a way to open the talk from the thesis to everyone's background in games.

Not all seniors were so understanding. That same thesis, Ng knew, had been the final straw for Jeph Koestler, the Commodore at Narbon. She'd never gotten around to reading it herself, especially since Warrigal's L-5 game apparently had no negative impact on the fitreps of the participants, least of all Rom-Sanchez's.

At the very least, this was one more sign of the lieutenant's willingness to take risks in the performance of his duty. But was this another Smyrna, or had he bought his last can of silver polish? And why had he asked that the head of Infonetics be present?

"Our most junior lieutenant seems a bit froward." Totokili grunted

"I've not found him so," said Krajno. "Less afraid of new ideas than some, perhaps."

Ng watched the subtle way Nilotis set down his coffee cup in the exact center of the porcelain saucer, as if the weight of the universe rested on his precision. Thus he avoided any overt reaction to the suspicious glower Totokili turned on the XO.

It was time to intervene. "Commander Totokili, while the tactical digest is on the way, I'd like your opinion on how we can deal with the other problem: a third-tranche Alpha capable of blowing the stern off a battlecruiser with one shot, and apparently capable of bringing down a planetary Shield in less than a day."

The Energetics Officer visibly made a mental pivot as he gazed at the tac-holo that they all had memorized by now. Then he glanced down at his compad. "I'll want a closer look at the tacponder and VSA data, but no matter what else we figure out, we'll have to rebalance the ship's power distribution to give the shields all they will take. That will also enable us to make them more reactive, although against that power level I don't know how much good it will do."

"Then what should we sacrifice? Maneuverability or weapons?" asked Ng, as the orderly turned to her for signs.

She noted that only Nilotis was drinking. They were full of enough adrenaline. She nodded, and the orderly withdrew behind the silver coffee service, which Ng usually only had brought out for formal dinners. Instinct had prompted her to have it out now. But its rich gleam, the old Archaeo-Moderne lines, did not even boost her own mood. She suspected the others could have been offered Shiidran sock fungus, and they wouldn't have noticed.

"Weapons," Navaz said, her voice emphatic. Although it was beginning to look like the world they thought they knew had been blasted along with the *Prabhu Shiva*, this was one area Navaz was sure of. "The conformation of a destroyer makes it unlikely that they've been able to strengthen their shields much and I'd almost guarantee that the only offensive improvement they've got is the skipmissile. It looks like they've found a way to drop the skip frequency by at least an order of magnitude, which puts the terminal plasma velocity in fourspace much further up the asymptote."

"I agree." Totokili nodded, if possible even more emphatic than Navaz. He was falling back on things he was sure of. Could he move forward the way she needed?

The hatch opened, and Commander Hurli glided in, her

uniform fitted like an outer skin. Ng gestured for her to take her place, and the orderly stepped forward to offer her coffee, which she took with trained grace, and set down to ignore.

Ng suppressed the urge to summarize, and left that to Krajno. Best to keep him busy and feeling useful until the inevitable hammer of grief. Ng forced herself to acknowledge that inward gulp of worry, of bracing for the worst, that never failed whenever something happened to a colleague. She observed Krajno's steady hands, his concentration as he spoke. Hurli revealed absolutely nothing as she listened and watched the holo; Totokili's scowl deepened as if the summary was somehow a personal affront.

Then a silence fell, the abstract silence of minds racing around and around the spin-axis without any landing. Ng was about to ask Hurli what she thought, just to get them focused on the same thing, when the hatch opened again and Rom-Sanchez nearly fell through in his haste.

He was followed by Ensign Warrigal. Both carried com-pads. They fetched up stiffly as the lieutenant formally reported and then began to stammer his way through an explanation of their presence. She could tell by his phrasing and not-so-surreptitious gestures that he was trying to encourage Warrigal to speak as well, but the ensign merely stiffened to an even more impossible degree.

Ng hid the brief spurt of amusement, unexpected and welcome, even if it did not release her tension. She could have told Rom-Sanchez that Nefalani Warrigal was not going to say anything until the words were pulled out of her; she knew that Warrigal had either removed herself or been removed from the line of succession in her ancient family. Her type of mind would never be successful in the political arena of the High Douloi, but in the navy, the clear chain of command, the comfort of rules and regs might be a framework for excellence, as it had for the Armorer.

Ng took over to make things easier for both junior officers. "Lieutenant, we've gotten as far as accepting, as a working hypothesis, that the Rifters have, in addition to skipmissiles of unprecedented power, superluminal communications, which they used to ambush *Prabhu Shiva* based on standard battle-cruiser counter-frigate doctrine. Can you add anything to this?"

"Yes, sir." Rom-Sanchez could not hide his strain. Next to him, Warrigal's gaze darted from person to person—not nervously, but as if the other officers were part of a tactical display. "We call it 'hyperwave.'"

Totokili snorted and Rom-Sanchez colored.

"No need to coin a term when the serial chips did it centuries ago," said Krajno gruffly, reminding Ng that his mate Tiburon had been a devotee of star-fantasy, the more lurid the better.

"I'm sure you have more than just a name for it," said Ng.

"Yes, sir," Rom-Sanchez continued. "We have Tenno modules for it."

A pulse of startlement ran through face and posture of the other officers, which Ng herself shared despite what she'd guessed. Rom-Sanchez hurried on. "With your permission, sir, I'll play a god's-eye digest with the standard Tenno, and then Ensign Warrigal will play it with a Tenno version based on her extended semiotics. The latter is very rough, and some of it won't make sense, so I respectfully request you all watch it all the way through before asking any questions."

"Permission granted," said Ng, and squashed the impulse to glance Totokili's way as she lifted her voice a shade. "We'll hold our questions."

Rom-Sanchez tapped his compad and they watched once again the events leading up to the destruction of *Prabhu Shiva* and the death of everyone on board. Again the Tenno flickered in futile patterns and eroded into simplicity, unable to make tactical sense of the actions of the two Rifter ships.

Ng's head panged. How could she, how could they, fight the ship without the Tenno Major to abstract tactical knowledge from the flood of data that comprised ship-to-ship actions? She remembered how helpless she'd felt, her first time in a Naval simulator, before she'd learned the Tenno ideographic system: that gut-wrenching sense of being bombarded by so much information that she'd been functionally blind.

Now it was happening again. And it was real.

The recording ended. As Warrigal worked her compad, the tac-holo mist-swirled to a new configuration: the same god's-eye view, but overlaid with bizarre Tenno glyphs that Ng could only partially read. Most of the conceptual modules were similar, but combined in ways that wrenched at her understanding, demanding an almost nauseating shift of perspective that she couldn't fully accomplish before she ran up against new modules that she didn't understand.

But this time, as the action proceeded, the Tenno evolved smoothly, and Ng realized with a shock that they were screaming *Danger!* from the moment *Prabhu Shiva* made its appearance. These Tenno—despite her gaps in understanding—made it obvious that standard doctrine couldn't stand against superluminal communications; that Harimoto had been betrayed by ignorance into a series of disastrous choices that had doomed his ship.

In the tac-holo *Prabhu Shiva* once more seized the frigate in an unshakable grip, and the Tenno smoothly signaled potential communication—that much Ng could figure out from the new ideographs—from the frigate to another ship. Once more the destroyer emerged with its skipmissile tube already oriented on *Prabhu Shiva,* an impossible two-skip maneuver outside the light cone of the battlecruiser or frigate, with nary a hiccup from the Tenno. The new semiotics had even predicted that the Rifters would shut down the fiveskip of the frigate so that it would not be damaged by the ruptor-strike-to-tractor modulation called for against a vessel that mounted no weapon capable of damaging a battlecruiser.

The tac-holo froze as it reached the end of the digest, leaving total silence in the plot room.

Nilotis looked stunned, Hurli suspicious, Krajno thoughtful, Totokili outraged, and Navaz was ignoring the tac-holo and studying Warrigal, her lips parted. The ensign stood at parade rest, her wrists moving slightly, her gaze restlessly assessing everyone in the room. Rom-Sanchez was fractionally less tense as he tried to watch Warrigal, the officers, and Ng, without being obvious about it.

"Ensign Warrigal," said Ng. "It's my understanding that you got your doctorate with a rather unconventional thesis, which you appear to have applied here. Perhaps you will explain what we just saw? Lieutenant, feel free to amplify her remarks as you see fit."

Nefalani Warrigal turned her class ring around and back on its finger one last time: Ng-double-stroke-upper-quadrant-receding-deceleration-withdrawal-opening.

During their tactical work-up on the bridge, and on the way here, Rom-Sanchez had tried to coach her on the likely reactions of the senior officers, but like virtually everyone else she knew, he spoke about emotions and human reactions in terms that really didn't make sense to her.

So she'd let the words wash over her, and while the seniors were watching the two digests, she'd watched them, carefully touching up the emotional version of the Tenno she privately called L-6, in which bodily motions and speech became input for the tactics of conversation.

Warrigal had used L-6 more her first month on *Grozniy* than during her entire year at Narbon. At first she'd longed for the rigid structure of the Narbon Omega Fleet, despite the memory of the Commodore's scorn in her exit interview. Finally, building on the general modules for facial expressions, posture, and the like, she had laboriously constructed specialized modules for each of the officers now present — and many others, although Totokili was still difficult to read since she rarely encountered him.

She took a deep breath. Ng's L-6 had indicated permission to explain a technical matter.

"Yes, sir. I was investigating the assumptions behind the Tenno programming. As I suspected, since they are a semiotic computational system based on the ideographic languages of Lost Earth and human neurophenomenology, their fundamental structure is Newtonian, and the relativistic linkages in the Tenno are for the most part first-order only."

The captain's compad beeped and she held up one hand: stop talking. That signal Warrigal didn't need L-6 for.

"Ensign Ammant, Communications, Captain."

L-6 didn't work without sight of the speaker's face, even for someone Warrigal knew, and Ammant's crisp bridge cadence didn't help.

"A crypto neuraimai working on the incoming cutter reports popped up a com fragment that I think you need to hear. It's apparently a leak from the destroyer in high orbit, of a communication relayed through the frigate."

"Put it on."

The compartment comm crackled to life. "I don't care what you think. If you break position I'll hunt you down and pull your guts out through your nose — or better yet, send you to the Avatar. You won't like how he treats the chatzers who run out on his orders, and there's no place anymore to run, anyway."

Warrigal couldn't track the sudden eruption of words from the other officers, and couldn't read the sudden pulse that ran through the room, her eidetic imagery of the L-6 glyphs overturned by her own strong emotion.

The Avatar. There was only one authority who used that title: the Dol'jharian murderer. It really happened, then, just as Aerenarch Semion had predicted. Warrigal breathed deeply, counting heartbeats to quell the sense of unreality that threatened to turn into giddiness. She discovered her fingers moving toward her class ring, and she forced her hands to her sides as she assimilated the new facts. She'd been a small child during the Dol'jharian War; the title "Avatar" merely something from the history vids until her year at Narbon, where everyone had been absorbed in Aerenarch Semion's determination to be ready for the next Dol'jharian attack.

And now, it seemed, he'd been right. A light day and a half away burned the proof in a funeral pyre of five thousand victims. Wait. Wait. Wait. Warrigal held herself ready, though the words felt piled up behind her lips.

"I don't believe it, I don't believe it," Navaz whispered over and over.

Totokilli glared, his teeth showing, a vein pulsing in his neck.

The captain had stilled, though the signs of anger were there in her lips, the tension of her hands.

". . . of a Shiidran brood-fouler." Krajno's curses died to a mutter.

"Thank you, Communications." Ng tabbed off the comm and looked at each of the officers around the table. "This time we'll finish it. Continue, if you please, Ensign."

Warrigal had readied her words. "As part of my proof I constructed a physics-neutral semantics for the Tenno, and then generalized it using a Kovloskian game-theoretic structure based on L-4 Phalanx to enable further investigation."

Totokili-single-stroke-upper-quadrant-approaching-acceleration-required. The impatience module triggered and she spoke faster.

"This enabled me to set a wide range of initial conditions and then play out tactical scenarios to determine how the Tenno must be modified to enable the construction and evolution of coherent tactical propositions, statements, and resolutions under those conditions. In order to—"

"Ensign," Rom-Sanchez interrupted. "Why don't you bring up that extract from the L-5 game that we discussed, where Ensign Wychyrski pulled off that triple finesse?"

Too late, Warrigal recognized the L-6 signals from the

other officers indicating that she'd gone off course, again. The meta-levels of L-6 obviously needed further tweaking, although she didn't know when she'd find time for the eidetic transcription she'd have to make first: Rom-Sanchez-role-abstraction-station-keeping.

Gratefully, she bent over her compad as Rom-Sanchez began to explain L-5 to the senior officers, and she let him set the course.

Nearing the end of his explanation, Rom-Sanchez cleared his throat as he glanced Warrigal's way. She was twiddling with her ring again, which had to mean that the officers were intimidating her into confusion, which diffused her focus. So he finished up. "You can see how the action in the L-5 game extract we just viewed almost exactly reproduces the salient aspects of the Treymontaigne ambush, based on initial conditions that assumed ship-to-ship hyperwave at the same speed as ship travel."

"Is that what you think we face here?" asked Lieutenant Commander Nilotis. He was leaning forward, neither his expression or his tone hiding his hope. "Ensign Warrigal, what if the Rifter. . . hyperwave. . . is much faster than that?"

Warrigal could deal with that. It was straightforward.

"It doesn't matter, sir," she said. "I used the next series of games to establish that the Tenno programming isn't sensitive to changes in hyperwave speed once it's faster than a skipmissile."

"Since then," Rom-Sanchez added, "we've played L-5 assuming instantaneous communications for the sake of simplicity. Our analysis of the ambush at least does not contradict that assumption."

"And you've been playing this game since the beginning of our tour?" asked Captain Ng.

Rom-Sanchez permitted himself to look her way. He hadn't dared before, not with everyone watching. Or glaring, in Totokili's case. Relief ballooned inside him when he saw the captain's intent expression, the one she wore when she was mentally in fiveskip.

"Actually only about four months on a regular basis," Rom-Sanchez said, and then held his breath so he wouldn't blush.

A corner of Commander Krajno's mouth twitched, almost a smile, but not quite. For it did not reach the acute misery his gaze could not hide. "Four months longer than anybody else. Sounds like there's going to be a serious shake-up in billeting. Who all is familiar with L-5?"

Rom-Sanchez was startled by Krajno's acceptance of L-5's utility. "Ensign Warrigal, first and foremost, of course," he replied. "Myself, Ensigns Wychyrski, Ammant, Hjivarno, Sidelmar — I have a list here, with their player rankings." He tapped his compad and echoed it to a subsidiary viewscreen with open local access. Commander Krajno immediately began tapping at his compad.

"Ensign Warrigal also prepared a lexicon of weapons-related changes to the Tenno semiotics for Lieutenant Commander Navaz to inspect."

As the Armorer eagerly tapped her compad to access the data, Commander Hurli leaned forward. "Captain," she said. "Surely you're not suggesting that we reprogram the Tenno in accordance with this. . . game?"

"What else can we do? You saw that the standard Tenno are useless in the face of whatever technology the Rifters are using."

Hurli shook her head. "Limited, sir, but not useless. And once you add the new modules and strip out the relativistic linkages where appropriate, it will take hundreds or thousands of hours to trace all of the changes as they propagate through the Tenno to make sure it's tactically consistent. Better to go slow here, especially since few if any Rifters use the Tenno Major, anyway."

"Permission to speak, Captain." said Warrigal.

"Go ahead."

"We have played 49.2 hours of L-5 since we standardized on the game assumptions I used in the digest that I showed you, which I have used to seed self-replicating sixth-chthon neuraimai evolutions in my personal dataspace. As of 0800 hours today, that represents 3.46×10^5 hours of evolved semiotic algorithms available for analysis, which I already would have done if my array allotment had been sufficiently large."

Rom-Sanchez winced at the implied criticism, which he knew Warrigal had not intended, but Hurli just gazed at the ensign, her expression a perfect Douloi mask, then she leaned back in her chair. "Simulations are one thing, battle is another," Hurli said, the slowness of her words the only hint of her doubt.

She turned a hand upward toward the viewscreen showing the death-agony of *Prabhu Shiva*. "But that puts us a lot closer to what I'd be comfortable with."

"Good," said Ng. "We don't have a lot of time. Please get started on the consistency check with the ensign."

Rom-Sanchez could not suppress his flush as the Captain focused on him, leaving Hurli to bozlink Warrigal. "Lieutenant, assuming we can reprogram the Tenno, what's the tactical situation look like?"

Rom-Sanchez straightened his spine. At least he had a definite answer. "The resonance field is down and we have IDs for the first-tranche Alpha and the frigate in Treymontaigne orbit, plus some small stuff. Signals analysis also implies that there are three other Alphas. They'd be third tranche if Eichelly's bonus chip is right. And two or three more frigates in-system."

"They've probably got a hyperwave-equipped ship watching each of the standard naval emergence points, ten light-minutes normal to Treymontaigne," said Nilotis.

"Another ambush," Totokilli said. "Not much imagination, there."

"That's not surprising," Navaz put in without raising her head from her compad.

"Rifters." Commander Krajno snarled the word, his manner forbidding.

"No." Navaz looked up, her fingers still busy. "What I mean is that they're not likely to have had FTL communications very long. How long do you suppose the Rift Sodality could keep a secret like that? So they're not likely yet to fully understand its tactical implications."

"That's one of three factors that are in our favor," said Rom-Sanchez. "Signals analysis leads us to believe that only three destroyers — doubtless the third tranche ones, so not the one in orbit — and the frigate in orbit have the hyperwave. According to our L-5 scenarios, there are tactical soft spots in that combination that the new Tenno will help us exploit. More important is that our L-5 play to date has demonstrated that in most mid-battle scenarios, the advantage conferred by the hyperwave is far less than it is at the beginning or end. This is especially true for close in-system actions, where tacponders can be leveraged most effectively."

"That will make the fourth factor even weightier, then," Ng

commented.

"Fourth factor, sir?"

Ng looked around the room. "There's got to be more tactical imagination in this plot room than in that whole Rifter squadron." She looked across the table at her head tactical officer, her palm up. "Mdeino, what's your recommendation?"

Mdeino Nilotis tore his gaze away from the tac-holo, now running a series of evolutions under the control of Hurli and Warrigal. Best to get the worst over with first.

"Commander Krajno will, of course, have his own billeting suggestions, but I'd recommend you put the Lieutenant in the Tactical pod to help you fight the ship in the coming action," he began. "He's got four months on me or any of his seniors with these new Tenno."

Krajno caught his eye and sketched a salute.

Ng lifted her chin, her approval underscored by her reply. "I'll frock him LTC," she said.

Rom-Sanchez reddened to the tips of his ears and sent a revealing glance of gratitude toward Nilotis, his forehead puckered with self-doubt. Nilotis knew that Rom-Sanchez was aware of what it meant for an officer to so advance a junior. Now he'd be doubly determined to make this work.

"I'll shadow him, of course, as I assume other seniors will with their juniors experienced with the L-5 Tenno," Nilotis said. He drew a breath. This next would be perilously close to personal trespass, but this, too, duty commanded: "I also strongly recommend you consider an Augmented sim session for yourself, Captain, to drive the new semiotics as deeply into your mind as possible."

Ng grimaced, but nodded again. The combination of blood agents, EM fields, and neural alligation were too hard on both mind and body for anything but an emergency—there was a real risk of permanent impairment. Even best case, she would pay for her accelerated learning with a period of mental and physical lethargy that could be ameliorated only for a time with stimulants. Long enough to fight the battle. She could deal with the other side effects that would come later in her recovery.

Assuming they survived, she amended silent, inwardly still seeing Harimoto's cruiser rotating slowly as its ruptured engines bled to death.

"As for tactical dispositions, we need to find the other hyperwave-equipped ships, since all their other assets will have to be in EM range of one of them. Assuming they took up position shortly after our first emergence, they'll have been on station long enough to put them inside the asymmetric detection envelope of *Grozniy*'s sensor platform, even without a VSA."

"Better and better," Krajno said. The battlecruiser could roughly confirm enemy dispositions from farther out than their targets' sensors could detect emergence.

" I also agree with the Armorer, and recommend that *Grozniy* take what looks like a by-the-book approach via one of the emergence points while leveraging our superiority in tactical support materiel to prepare the volume of battle to our advantage. The enemy will undoubtedly choose to fight through cis-lunar space, using the Highdwellings and other installations to impose tactical asymmetry on our engagement. What they probably don't realize is how much that will mitigate the advantage of their hyperwave."

Ng nodded again and addressed the armorer. "Lieutenant Commander Navaz. That means in addition to tacponders, we'll need a large quantity of antiship weapons for dispersal by the corvettes and even cutters, as well as heavier devices that *Grozniy* will discharge. Do you concur?"

"Yes, sir." Navaz's voice was soft, almost hesitant.

Nilotis hadn't spoken to Navaz much, but sensed she was less comfortable with people than with her cims, the machines that created expendable weapons as needed, making a battlecruiser largely independent of its base. "We'd be best tooling up a large number of gee-mines and leeches, I think," said the armorer.

Ng smiled agreement. "I agree. How long?"

"That's all standard ordnance: we have a large inventory already. The cims won't require more than about a day for any reasonable number more."

"Good. It will take us longer than that to prepare in any case."

The memory of the Archon's screams wrenched Nilotis; he could not prevent a twitch as he tried to banish them. Embarrassed, he looked up, to discover similar reactions in the others. Everyone wanted action. But they owed the people of Treymontaigne their best effort. Haste would not help.

"Here's how we'll begin," said Ng after the briefest of pauses. Swiftly she outlined the tasks she expected of her officers.

Nilotis half-listened to the orders—which he could check later—and concentrated on the subtle signs of purpose: stiffening a shoulder here, lifting a chin there. From confusion and bewilderment, they had moved toward purpose.

Nilotis rose and walked over to where Rom-Sanchez was bent over his compad, working earnestly. The lieutenant looked up and flushed again.

"Thank you, sir."

Nilotis gestured in the mode of necessity. "Know that I'm on your radiants, and intend to take that pod back if I can." He smiled. "We're all Loonies now, and you and I have a lot of L-5 games ahead."

TEN

TELVARNA: ARTHELION TO DIS

Ivard was happy. Yesterday, Montrose had finally let him move back to the cabin he had shared with Jaim since they left Dis. Even the drug-dulled, constant pain in his back and shoulder couldn't dent his spirits.

He stood up, restless. Gray's tail thumped on the deck. "You want to go see the others?" The black and tan dog swiftly lay down, head up and gaze intent on Ivard, her tail thumping even harder.

Ivard laughed and tabbed open the hatch. As he walked slowly towards the rec room, Gray kept pace by his side, looking up at his face.

He rubbed at his wrist where the Kelly ribbon had bonded to his skin. Looking at it made him queasy, but at least it didn't hurt. Mostly numb, once in a while it tingled. Almost a tickle. Strange.

Afraid that Montrose would keep him in the dispensary longer, Ivard hadn't mentioned the weird dreams he'd had since the ribbon bonded to him. He'd told Marim, but she'd said it was just the medication Montrose was giving him for the burn. Except he wished he didn't have to take stuff that made him dream about Greywing being lost someplace big and cold and dark.

The familiar ache hurt him inside at the reminder of his sister. If only he hadn't lost the coin she'd taken from the Mandala, with the greywing image on it! She was going to go back to Natsu to fight for freedom. That thought gave him a fresh pang. Losing her coin hurt even worse than losing Markham's flight ribbon.

He'd told Marim about all these things, and she hadn't laughed. Instead she'd said seriously, "Remember, Greywing didn't feel anything, and I bet she didn't even have time to get scared. I hope I get that kind of death when my turn comes. And as for that coin, if it's on board, I'll find it. Your flight ribbon, too."

That made him feel a little better, at least when one, or better both of the dogs was at his side and the lights were on and he was awake. He lowered himself into a padded chair. Thinking about Marim reminded him that he was supposed to be happy. He was rich and the person he loved seemed to love him.

His body prickled with heat tingles when he remembered the fun they'd had yesterday. Marim had shown up only a couple of hours after he moved back in, when Jaim was working on the engines. She'd made him put Gray out, and as soon as he shut the hatch behind the dog she'd ripped off her shirt.

Ivard had had dreams about that, before the burn, but when it happened, it was even better. "Now I'm gonna show you how to have great sex without moving your shoulder," she'd said, lifting the med-monitor from around his neck and setting it aside. He thought his answer had been fairly offhand. He hadn't wanted her to know that he'd never had sex with another person, except in his own imagination, ever.

"Don't tell Montrose," she'd said afterward, kissing him with a loud smack. "I'm not supposed to get you excited. But I can't help it! You're an exciting little blit."

"Hey, I'm as tall as you are," he'd protested. "And I'll be taller soon, too." He didn't add that his clothes were getting cramped in pits and crotch, a sure sign he needed to get some more. That didn't seem very sophisticated, somehow.

"You're looking better, Gray." The voice belonged to the Krysarch.

Ivard glanced up, heat prickling him all over. But Brandon was studying the dog, not Ivard. Trev was with him. Ivard liked the sound of his voice as he bent down to ruffle Gray. Trev came over and nosed the Kelly ribbon on Ivard's wrist, then both dogs trotted ahead into the rec room.

Ivard followed, wondering what the dog smelled when he sniffed the Kelly ribbon. He tried breathing slowly, imagining eddies of scents on the air.

Lokri's pale eyes flickered as Ivard walked in, and one of his hands half-lifted, as Brandon said to Ivard, "Good to see you out of the dispensary. How's that arm?"

Ivard hesitated, but Brandon did not turn away. He stood there smiling, his blue eyes direct, waiting for an answer.

"Fine," Ivard lied. He wondered if he should say anything else, and then he remembered that they had something in common, after all. "I'm sorry about your brothers."

Brandon's face altered, from concern to something a little more serious. Though Brandon did not move, Ivard felt as if he had stepped closer. A vague sense of vertigo rippled through Ivard's mind, but it was not unpleasant.

Brandon said, "I am very sorry about Greywing." He spoke so softly that Ivard barely heard it. He sounded sorry, and for a moment it made Ivard's pain a lot worse. He could see in Brandon's face that he shared the hurt, too, which changed it somehow — lessened it — took the aloneness out of it.

"So, you want to play more games?" Lokri asked from across the room.

Lokri's question had an ambiguity to it that made Ivard wary. He hated it when Lokri talked like that. It had always upset Greywing, and sometimes there was trouble afterward, and though nobody ever said it was Lokri's fault, somehow he was always *there*.

Brandon smiled and touched Ivard's good shoulder before turning to Lokri.

"No, I want to win the price of this ship off you so I can start building me a fleet."

Lokri cocked an eyebrow at Brandon. "That shouldn't be too hard for Constable Murphy."

Surprise sizzled away the fog muffling Ivard's thoughts. *The* Constable Murphy? That was a famous gamer nom d'guerre in the Recontre Sodality that ran Phalanx tourneys throughout the Thousand Suns and beyond. But no one knew who was behind the Constable Murphy who'd taken first prize in the Arthelion Tournament four years ago. Whoever it was had chosen the lesser payoff that was the cost of continued anonymity. There was even a collection of that Murphy's games.

Ivard remembered how easily the Aerenarch had beaten Lokri the first time, on the voyage from Dis to Arthelion, how it had taken both Marim and Lokri—and them cheating—to defeat him. "*You* were Constable Murphy?" he blurted.

The Aerenarch made one of those indecipherable hand gestures of his. "I didn't have a lot else to do, the last ten years."

Lokri laughed. The sound had a bitter edge to it. "Don't start the timer yet." He lounged over to the dispenser and got something cold and dark to drink.

The fog began to descend again. Ivard licked his lips. Now he was thirsty. But Lokri was already at his console, sitting down. Ivard couldn't ask him, but maybe he could ask Brandon. Except he was facing the other way. And he was a nick.

Ivard scrunched down a bit in his chair, absently massaging Gray's thick ruff. Trev sat on his other side, pushing his head under Ivard's free hand. Too bad dogs couldn't understand, and even if they did, they had no thumbs. If Ivard asked Brandon and he said no, Lokri might laugh and he'd feel like blunge on a wall.

Do it for yourself. You're supposed to be a man now, he scolded himself.

Ivard shifted, wincing as a hot pain seared along his back and pooled in his shoulder blade where the jac had done the most damage. The Kelly ribbon tingled, making his hand feel cold, despite the dog's warm fur. Deciding he could drink later, he forced himself incrementally to relax again.

For a time he stayed thus, breathing softly so his shoulder would not move and ache anew. The coldness from his hand seeped over the rest of his body, numbing the pain. His thoughts were clear but curiously detached, almost as if he watched a vid.

Light and shadow shifted in Lokri's face, the only constant being his careless smile. Ivard's gaze moved downward, drawn by shaded contours in Lokri's shirt that revealed the tension in the set of Lokri's shoulders, and in his hands.

"It's only a game they play." Who'd said that? But thinking about it too hard made his head ache.

The Aerenarch sat relaxed in his chair, expression altering between humor and reflection as his fingers moved fast on his keypads. They did not talk, but Ivard felt their concentration. Felt? No. He almost … *saw* something. Or heard it, or tasted it.

No, not that.

He squinted at the air between them, trying to still his breath. The numbness had turned to a comfortable kind of coldness so that his body almost floated, like in the low-grav dispensary cubicle.

He'd stayed too long. Had to get back to his cabin.

He pulled his hands away from the dogs, which woke up the pain again. Fire from his shoulder sent agony through him. He shut his eyes, sinking back.

". . . now?" A voice cut into his thoughts. "You have to go back to the dipensary," the voice sharpened. "Montrose sent me."

Ivard opened his eyes and stared for a few moments without comprehension at an unfamiliar face: square, short dark hair, dark eyes, big ears. Angry mouth.

"I'm to take you," the man said.

Ivard remembered him. He was the nick navigator that the other crew members called Schoolboy. Vi'ya had put him under Montrose, doing Ivard's old galley jobs. Osri Omilov. A navigator. Like Ivard.

"I can't get up," he said — or tried to. Somehow his voice was gone.

Osri's lips pressed into a thin line of impatience as he pulled Ivard to his feet.

Ivard gasped as the new flesh over his burn stretched, and Gray gave a whimper.

"Need some help?" Brandon asked, rising to his feet.

"No," Osri snapped. "Thank you, Aerenarch."

Brandon withdrew, making one of those little hand motions that Ivard couldn't decipher, but he heard Osri's breath hiss.

Ivard hated being helpless, but the pain from his shoulder was eating his entire body, making it impossible to get any of his limbs to work.

Osri grunted, shifting his grip until he had taken all of Ivard's weight. Ivard counted the steps as they reverberated up his aching body until they reached his old cubicle in the dispensary, where Osri helped into his bunk, then dialed down the gees. The relief of weight was sweet anguish. The fire dulled and died, leaving only the tingle in his wrist, which felt warm now instead of cold. Ivard closed his eyes as brusque hands helped him get arranged. "Here," Osri spoke. "I'm to —"

Ivard opened his eyes. "You're not going to touch it." He tried to shield his shoulder with his good hand.

"No," the nick said impatiently. "You have to eat. And drink. You have to drink two glasses of water while I'm here." And, scowling downward, "Go away. No dogs in here right now. You too, monster."

Ivard hadn't realized that all the animals had followed them. "You gotta say 'raus,'" said Ivard, closing his eyes again.

"Raus," Osri snapped.

Lucifur yowled, then Ivard heard cat feet racing away, followed by rapidly clicking toenails. The dogs were trying to herd Lucifur again. "Where is Montrose?"

Osri frowned, not in anger. "With my father. Some kind of treatment."

"Your father? Oh. The old blit we found in that torture room." Ivard frowned. "Did I know that? Marim didn't tell me he's your father."

"Here's your first glass of water," said Osri, his voice even more gruff. "I'll be back with your food." And he returned with a tray, steam curling from underneath its cover. "Here. Eat. I cannot leave until you do."

Ivard obediently maneuvered himself so that he could pick up a spoon.

Osri watched every bite, looking like Ivard had always pictured Panarchist naval officers, his posture so stiff he ought to be in full-dress uniform instead of a pair of Jaim's old work coveralls. "The noktu lesl is quite good today," Ivard said finally. "Did you prepare it?"

The question tightened Osri's face to annoyance back. "Yes," he said.

"It's the first thing I learned to prepare," Ivard said. "When I was in the galley. They learn it at the chef school, Montrose told me."

"Drink," was the only answer. Then, "More."

Ivard tried to obey, took too big a swallow, then choked, the fluid burning his nose. He coughed, sending pain racking down his arm. His spoon went flying, but Osri caught it, and the tray, righting things with hasty movements.

"Not so fast," he said, his voice much milder.

Ivard leaned back, trying to catch his breath. The Kelly ribbon tingled around his arm again.

"Eat when you're ready," Osri said, sitting back. "I'll wait."

Ivard sighed, rubbing at his green wrist. "I wish he could get that thing off."

"How did it occur?"

As he ate, Ivard gave Osri a brief description of the encounter in the Panarch's palace, and more questions led to a retelling of the firefight that had killed his sister and caused his wound.

When Ivard had finished, Osri said, "How frequently does this happen?"

"You mean the Kelly ribbon, or someone in the crew getting zapped?"

"The fights. And deaths."

Ivard shrugged. "Depends on what kind of action we see. And how often. Other than Jakarr's try to take over on Dis, when you came, we haven't lost many since, well, since Markham died. Few burns the last brush we had with Hreem, the one at the booster field on Morigi II."

"The reward must be considerable for you to take such risks."

Ivard nodded. "Is! When we pull one. Been a long while, though, which is one of the reasons Jakarr acted like he did. Wanted to go raiding. Vi'ya said we had to stick to raiding slavers. Hreem being number one choice."

"Stick to slavers. . ." Osri repeated. "I believe I heard someone in Merryn refer to this Hreem madman as a slave-runner, but—" He frowned. "Surely this all takes place out-octant!"

"Most. Not all, though. And there's the Dol'jharian planets, the ones that got Quarantined after the war. Markham liked raiding them. They got slaves, though no one much goes there or leaves. Or did," he amended soberly.

"Then that is the connection between Eusabian of Dol'jhar and Hreem? Buying slaves?" Osri looked skeptical.

Ivard grinned. "Don't know. Maybe. They'd have to be special ones. Vi'ya said the cheapest commodities on Dol'jhar are people and ash."

Interest lifted Osri's heavy brow. "You've been to Dol'jhar?"

"No. Had to be first crew for that. I was getting close, but then. . ." Ivard closed his eyes. Grief for Markham tasted blue and cold, waking up the grief for Greywing.

"You steal Hreem's, ah, cargoes of slaves, and resell

them?"

Ivard took a breath, and tried to fight the blue away. "No, we sell the cargoes. Slave-runners almost always carry other illegal stuff." It was taking too much effort to speak, but he tried. "Worth a lot on Rifthaven. Let the slaves go on an out-octant world. Or Rifthaven."

Osri's black brows crimped with disbelief. "Finish your food," he said. "And drink this."

Ivard obeyed, which considerably mitigated Osri's impatience at being assigned as a nursemaid. As soon as the last of the water went into the boy, Osri took the dishes to the galley, put them in the cleaner, and went straight to complain to his father.

After venting the worst of it, he paused to draw breath before finishing, ". . . and when I asked him if this woman jacks slaveships for revenge or for profit, he said, 'Both.'"

Sebastian Omilov sipped at the hot drink his son had brought and observed him over the rim of his cup.

Osri frowned. "Not that I believe that they let the slaves go. He'd have to say that, knowing how stiff is the penalty for getting caught in such a trade. 'Slaves.' Distasteful word."

"Evil, I should say. Tragic." Omilov spoke in an undertone, and as always his son scarcely listened.

Not that he ignored his father, or cut in—he was too polite for that. But he paused for him to speak, and then went on in a musing tone, exactly as if Omilov had been silent, "He probably said it hoping that I would not report the names of the individuals on this ship to the authorities. But I shall." He touched his bare wrist. "Though I cannot record their admissions as evidence, I will remember."

Omilov suppressed a sigh, studying Osri's face, so familiar, so odd a blend of his own features and his mother's. And so readable.

Osri's emotions changed the angle of the black brows so like Sebastian's own, and lengthened the long upper lip that Risiena's Ghettierus genes had given him. Risiena was just the same way—but unlike her son, she could hide her thoughts when she chose. It was just that she seldom chose to. She didn't have to, behaving like the absolute ruler of the Ghettierus family's terraformed moon, a status actually lost centuries past when Aghlevar was brought into the Panarchy.

Sebastian became aware that a pause had stretched to

silence. He looked up. Osri's eyes were narrowed in exasperation. "You were not listening to me, Father."

He could not love Osri's mother, but he did love Osri. But he didn't seem to be able to protect him anymore. "I apologize, Osri. I must be more tired than I'd thought."

Quick concern narrowed the dense black eyes. "What did that old monster do to you?"

"Eased my recovery considerably." Omilov sighed. "Whatever else he has done, Montrose is a superb physician. Osri, we are here, under their control. Our duty is to aid the Aerenarch—"

"But he does nothing." Osri gritted his teeth. "And when he did take action, it was to lead them—not just to permit them, but to *lead* them—on a raid of the Ivory Antechamber. This ship, according to that witless boy, is packed with the artifacts they stole. And Brandon watched them do it, saying it was better they had the things than the Dol'jharians use them for target practice."

"You must remember that those artifacts are part of the Arkad inheritance. I believe the law would dictate that they belong to Brandon—and of course, his father—to dispose of as they will."

Osri's lips pressed in a thin line, and for the first time, his gaze dropped. "I thought it was our duty to recover them."

"That is for the Panarch to say." Omilov watched his son accept this in silence, and then a new thought occurred to him, for the first time ever: *he's hiding something from me.*

Then Osri stood, running his thumb absently along the edge of the bed. "There is less than a week remaining before we reach their base." Osri closed his fingers into a fist. "This talk of slaves. They might sell us, and I believe Brandon will stand by and watch."

"You forget that of all of us, he is the main target," Omilov reminded him. "You can be sure *he* never forgets."

GROZNIY: TREYMONTAIGNE SYSTEM

Ng's stomach lurched.

"Final cis-lunar drone reconnaissance uploaded," Wychyrski sang out, her fingers moving rapidly over her console. The stealthed platforms had been accelerated to fractional-cee velocity across the ecliptic by corvettes, their data downloaded via laser after their pass. Physical retrieval could wait until after the battle.

The tactical screen rippled as the god's-eye view of the system adjusted and the Tenno flickered into another new and momentarily unfamiliar configuration. Ng's stomach lurched again, matching the pang behind her eyes and a ripple in her vision, prodromal to the visual migraines that were, finally, barely, under control. Her body sang with a weird energy that had the affect of anxiety tinged with an emotional tenor akin to sexual energy, the latter something she had never associated with combat—a combination she found repellent.

Considering the witch's brew of hormones and agents coursing through her body, it wasn't surprising that it felt like she was fourteen again. It was too much like her first year in the Academy, including learning the Tenno. The new, trans-relativistic glyphs Warrigal and Rom-Sanchez had devised were still hard to parse, despite the Augmented practice in the simulator.

Her gaze roamed across the Loonies on the bridge—something about the Augment agents had imprinted that term on her mind, another minor irritation. But irritation was far from her feeling about the junior officers who'd made a game the low orbit to accelerated careers.

Wychyrski was coming on splendidly as well, going a long way toward justifying the risk Ng had taken in putting her in alpha crew, young as she was. No, it wasn't her youth. Ng had also been extremely young, and knew what prejudices rode right alongside the special treatment that shadowed one who was appreciably junior to one's peers. It was Wychyrski's immaturity in other ways. Nothing that ever showed up in fitreps. . . unless you were skilled at reading the patterns behind the word choices.

"Tactical," said Ng.

"Cis-lunar dispositions confirmed," replied Rom-Sanchez. "First tranche Alpha, Xaloc-class frigate, six corvettes. The frigate is almost certainly the only ship there with a hyperwave. There may be more corvettes or smaller ships concealed by the Highdwellings."

That completed the tactical picture. As predicted, the *Grozniy's* sensors had detected three more Rifter squadrons—destroyer, frigate, and smaller. Two followed a tight drunkwalk centered on each of the two standard emergence points. The other destroyer's skip orbit was centered on the planet. In all, four ships with hyperwave.

"Launch corvette squadrons," said Ng.

Commander Krajno tabbed his console. "Corvettes away. One minute to Treymontaigne emergence."

On the viewscreen two of the squadrons — two corvettes each — emerged into view as they left the bays of the *Grozniy*, their radiants flaring. Ng smiled, admiring their lean beauty; adapted for atmospheric flight, the fairings and swept-back thorns of their weapons pods lent them the aspect of predatory sea creatures, sleek and deadly.

They dwindled swiftly and she lost them in the starfield. On-screen the emergence countdown ticked off the seconds.

In her mind's eye, she envisioned the red bursts of light as they leapt out of fourspace toward Treymontaigne. Then emergence in and around cis-lunar space before vanishing back into fivespace, scattering their crop of dragon's teeth. The cutters would add their minim later, during the fog of battle: tacponders to monitor the action, gee-mines to cripple fiveskips, and leeches — sneak-missiles armed with shaped charges — to stab through shields and hull metal with fingers of nuclear flame.

With any luck, the targets in high orbit would already be crippled when the *Grozniy* emerged after its apparently standard approach. And if not, the dragon's teeth would be waiting for any enemy who emerged within range during the ensuing battle.

Now they had but a minute before the Rifters detected the emergence pulses of the corvettes and notified the other ships via hyperwave.

Ng's fingers tingled as she poised over them over her console; the familiar intensity of battle-readiness gripped her.

"Ruptor turrets ready, skipmissile charged," said Krajno.

"Very well. On emergence, ruptor barrages first by size, target skipmissile on destroyer or frigate only. Take us in," she said.

"Ten light-minutes out and over Treymontaigne," the navigator reported when the fiveskip disengaged.

"Major targets: frigate bearing 144 mark 32, plus 13 light-seconds, destroyer Alpha -3 bearing 237 mark 61, plus 80 light-seconds!" Hjivarno at Fire Control shouted, her voice overriding the emergence bells. "Vectored!"

The bridge trembled subliminally as the ruptor turrets bearing on the targets discharged a probabilistic barrage. They were unlikely to connect, but the discharge didn't cost them much. If the targets were still using the tactical sets predicted by their SigInt profiles, they might run into the spread.

The starfield on the screen was slewing as the ship came about. "Shoot skipmissile on acquisition," Ng said, using the bridge cadence. Telos was with them: against all odds they'd emerged—barely—within range. It was too good an opportunity to pass up.

The reddish chain wake of the skipmissile filled the image and faded. "Skipmissile charging," Hjivarno sang out.

". . . eight, seven, six, five. . ." The navigator counted down the thirteen seconds since emergence, by the end of which they had to skip. If the frigate possessed a hyperwave after all, that was the only way to avoid being targeted by a destroyer in FTL contact.

"Tactical skip executed," said Lieutenant Mzinga.

"Major targets bearing 145 mark 32, plus 15 light-seconds, frigate; 236 mark 61, plus 83 light-seconds, destroyer." A few seconds later: "Skipmissile missed," then, before the crew could react, "ruptor strike, frigate, target destroyed!"

The viewscreen flickered to a closer view, revealing the roiling smear of plasma characteristic of a ship torn apart by intense gee fields.

"Skip pulse, 145 Mark 32, 18 light seconds. Sub-corvette of some sort. No ID." Wychyrski's voice rang out above the cheering of the crew. Ng let them; the release of anger would calm them for the more difficult action ahead.

The Tenno rippled, confirming what Ng already knew. The little ship was on its way to alert the destroyer, but it didn't matter. She glanced at the tactical countdown indicating the status of the corvette squadrons assigned to cis-lunar space. It reached zero as she watched. The destroyer would be on its way to Treymontaigne within seconds, now.

"Commander, take us to Treymontaigne."

Krajno tabbed his console. "Fiveskip to tac-level five. Engaging." The burr of the fiveskip was harsh, almost teeth-aching. With a lower frequency, they would emerge near Treymontaigne at a tremendous real velocity, reducing their exposure to the supermissiles of the foe.

"Cis-lunar Treymontaigne, planetary plus 100,000 kilometers, estimated velocity on emergence 25,000 kps." Ng fought a reflexive shiver: close to a tenth cee within planetary space was a risk in itself, even without an enemy. But they would be headed through the ecliptic, and their retuned shields would count for something, if they encountered any ship or solid object unlucky enough to be in their path.

"Emergence."

"Major targets bearing 13 mark 62, plus 95,000 kilometers, destroyer; 349 mark 279, plus 115,000 kilometers, frigate; minor targets. . ."

Fire Control's voice faded from her mind as Ng concentrated on the Tenno.

"Negative on major targets," she stated. They were too close to the Highdwellings, and the destroyer would be between them and the planet, making it impossibly dangerous to use a skipmissile on it—a miss would kill a billion-plus people on the planet. "Ruptors shoot on minor targets three, four, seven at will. Pulse the dragon's teeth for reorientation on major targets."

Fire Control's console keened as the EM pulse retargeted the various weapons, sown by the corvettes on their first pass, against the destroyer and frigate they were passing up.

The bridge shuddered gently as the ruptors discharged. Bright coins of light marked the results moments later.

"Destroyer's coming about. Coincident in three seconds, two, one. . ." Siglnt chanted.

'Tactical skip, now."

The fiveskip burped, then burped again, in accordance with the new protocols imposed by FTL communications.

"Take us out for the second run."

"Some tacponder pulses received. Emergence pulse, one of ours, signal incoming."

The next thirty minutes subsequently remained a blur in Ng's mind, even after she reviewed the auto-log the bridge computers had recorded. The Rifters were better than any of them had expected, using the vulnerability of the planet and the Highdwellings to protect themselves against the heavy weapons of the *Grozniy*. But she knew it was only by giving the Rifters that advantage that she could hold them to the battle.

Gradually the various dragon's teeth accounted for some of the enemy, but her crew paid a high cost as well. It was on their third run through cis-lunar space that the highest price was paid.

Nilotis felt a flash of pride when he recognized what was causing the raggedness of the Tenno response — some unanticipated second and third-order semantic obligations had surfaced. It's. . .

But he didn't even have time to find the right word, because he was anything but fluent in the new Tenno. His comprehension was coming in flashes. Watching Warrigal fight them back into stability made him feel behind, inadequate. Listening in on her rapid boswell colloquy with Rom-Sanchez made his head ache afresh.

He straightened in his pod, took a deep breath, and concentrated.

The activity on the bridge had reached a frantic level as tactical information flooded in, with varying degrees of timeliness. Four corvettes had taken sufficient damage to force disengagement, the other fought on with varying amounts of damage and casualties. The cutters' stealthy work on the fringes had preserved them from harm so far.

Grozniy was still untouched, and had accounted for one of the four destroyers, but the fear of a smashing blow from one of the Rifter destroyers' apparently unstoppable skipmissiles still hung over the bridge, intensifying as the action wore on. Only the dogged harassment of the corvettes had preserved them thus far, but those were slowly being scattered by individual duels, and time was running out.

Through it all Margot O'Reilly Ng's voice never wavered, never rose above the quiet level of authority that had been Nilotis's first impression of her on joining *Grozniy* — as it was, he expected, of everyone. The only sign of stress was the way she leaned forward, shoulders taut, and the sheen of sweat on her forehead.

"On emergence come about and target the destroyer. . ."

The *Grozniy* shuddered out of skip; stars skewed across the screen, stopped.

"Coming about. Five, four, three. . ." Mzinga's voice was hoarse.

"Skipmissile away. Skipmissile charging."

"Tactical skip, five light-seconds, now."

Their skip took them in toward their target. Seconds after

emergence, a gout of light signaled success. "Hit! Scratch one Alpha."

Delight tingled down to Nilotis's bones. As the Tenno probabilities had indicated, that target had felt the sting of a gee-mine: its fiveskip dead, it had been unable to leap to safety.

"That leaves two more," Krajno snapped. "Don't celebrate just yet."

On the viewscreen one of the *Grozniy*'s corvettes—the *Hevtana*—engaged with some small craft. The Rifter jinked toward the planet; his fiveskip, too, had evidently fallen prey to the sharp gravitational pulse of one of Navaz's gee-mines.

"Emergence, Alpha-class, bearing 68 mark 22, plus 80,000 kilometers, vectoring on *Raven Hevtana.*"

"Fire bearing ruptors. Target skipmissile and fire on acquisition."

The starfield slewed rapidly. A targeting cross swung into view. The red-pulse of a skipmissile arrowed away even as a skip-pulse bloomed where the enemy had been.

"Ruptors missed. Skipmissile missed. Target emergence, bearing 79 mark 45, plus 0.9 light-seconds, vectoring on *Raven Hevtana.*"

"Fire bearing ruptors, target skip. . ."

His pod restraints snapped into action as a pressure wave made his ribs creak and his ears ring. A gout of flame erupted from the next station. Lieutenant Noyetra screamed as fire crackled up his torso and torched his hair. The bridge seemed to tilt and nausea washed through Nilotis. The lights went out, coming back in the red of emergency power. A galaxy of trouble lights illuminated the bridge from every console; one of the Marine guards sprang into action with an extinguishers, the other carefully manhandled the wounded officer out of his pod.

"Skipmissile impact, aft beta ruptor turret not reporting, skipmissile aborted, aft beta bay not reporting, engine two destabilized." The voice sang out through the smoke.

"Emergence pulse, 267 mark 183, plus 1.5 light-seconds, Alpha-class, skipmissile charging, estimate seven seconds to discharge. . ."

The voices were high, sharp, but Nilotis felt the effort of his fellow officers to maintain the cadence. The tianqi hissed, overlaying the horrible smell of singed flesh, filling the bridge with a cool, astringent scent. That, and the cadence, meant they still had control. Thanks to Totokili, the shields held! But they couldn't take another shot like that.

Ng vaulted back into her pod from the deck where the impact had sent her sprawling. "Damage Control, aft ruptor status."

"Alpha and gamma still on-line. Insufficient power for more than one turret at this time." The shields had drawn so much power that the reactors were slow to come back to full-load status.

Ng didn't hesitate, demonstrating that even in the midst of confusion and disaster the captain had a clear image of the geometry of the battle. "Aft gamma ruptor, fire on acquisition, full power."

Nilotis stared down at his console, breathed consciously in an effort to relax — it was always like this with something new and hard to do. Then someone else gasped, and he jerked his gaze up.

The viewscreen flickered to a close-up view of the deadly wasp-shape of a destroyer, foreshortened by its vector directly at them. Three seconds later it disintegrated, the missile tube spinning away end over end as the rest of the ship flared into a coin of brilliant light.

The viewscreen flickered back to the remaining destroyer, now nearly vectored on the *Hevtana*. Horror seized Nilotis as the Tenno revealed the situation: the corvette's battle had taken it into radius, between the planet and the destroyer. Its radiants flared as its geeplane accelerated it crabwise toward radius, its bow vectored well off its course.

Nilotis scanned the glyphs, looking for a loophole. He didn't need the new Tenno modules to see that there was none. The corvette would reach radius exactly as the destroyer fired. At that point, if the corvette skipped to safety, out of the path of the skipmissile, the near-lightspeed plasma would impact Treymontaigne, killing most of the planet's population as the shock wave propagated through the atmosphere like a wall of steel.

"Forward alpha turret, fire on that destroyer."

"Forward turret not powered, seven seconds to ready status." said Hjivarno at Fire Control, her voice hopeless. There were less than four seconds left.

Nobody spoke. On-screen, the corvette rotated to face its executioner. Nilotis saw the captain's chip jerk up sharply. Understanding and sorrow thrilled in him and he saw the same understanding spread through the bridge crew.

"Signal incoming, *Hevtana*."

Without waiting for acknowledgment, the com officer windowed up the signal, revealing the sweaty face of Lieutenant Methuen. Nilotis had not been surprised when he'd volunteered for corvette duty. Methuen had been struggling with the new Tenno; his notable tactical expertise matched a role less dependent on them. Sorrow gripped Nilotis's vitals at the knowledge of death on his friend's face.

Then Methuen smiled. "Raise a glass for us at the wake. We'll toast you back from Murphy's Hall." A bare heartbeat later: "Engage."

The window blinked out as the corvette vanished in a burst of bluish light.

Simultaneously the destroyer exploded in a glaring burst of radiation that blanked out the viewscreen for a long moment. Nilotis's eyes prickled. The *Hevtana* had become a missile, skipping into its enemy in a sparkling rosette of plasma which faded to reveal the uncaring stars above the blue-white limb of a planet reprieved from death.

Slowly the captain stood and gave the empty screen a full formal salute. A heartbeat later the rest of the bridge stood as well. Nilotis found himself on his feet, eyes blurred with hot tears.

A long silence followed. Then the captain spoke quietly, bringing them back to the aftermath of battle.

"Stand down to yellow. Damage Control, report. Medical, report casualties. . ."

Nilotis let out his breath as Ng's voice continued, still calm, still quiet. With the last destroyer dispatched, there was nothing left in the Treymontaigne system to threaten them. They first owed the living and the dying their duties.

And then they would discharge their obligations to the fallen.

". . . and the Void shall yield up its dead, from light to light transformed, journeying in the company of the Light-bearer to the fullness of Telos at the end of Time."

On the viewscreen the hulk of the *Prabhu Shiva* still blazed, its nuclear fires little diminished by the days that had passed. Her throat still tight from the words, which never got easier, Ng turned to Commander Krajno, resplendent in his dress uniform.

"Commander." She gestured toward Fire Control.

Krajno stared at the viewscreen for a long beat, then said, "Fire."

Lieutenant Commander Nilotis pressed a key, and the reddish pulse-wake of a skipmissile speared out, transforming the shattered battlecruiser into a glory of light that slowly faded from view, furnishing the final catharsis for their memories of lost comrades.

'The Light-bearer receive them," said Ng.

As the funeral crew filed off the bridge and the regular billet marched in to replace them, Ng sighed. The news from Treymontaigne was bad, if what the Rifters had told their victims during their brief occupation was true. She wondered how many of the crew realized that their anguish was just beginning.

ELEVEN

Luri's large, luminous eyes blinked slowly, and her full, curved lips parted. "You're the only one who understands Luri," she breathed, leaning forward in a cloud of subtle scents.

Warmth coursed through Kira Lennart.

"Luri wants to stay here. . . with you." The filmy gown strained over full breasts. Luri stepped closer and pushed Kira down on the dormaivu, pressing her soft hands on Kira's shoulders, and kneading the muscles there.

Kira sighed as the warmth kindled into desire.

"A little shakrian from Luri?"

"Oh, yes," Kira said, her voice squeaking.

As the fingers massaged slowly down Kira's neck and arms, Kira sank gratefully into the whirlpool of sensual pleasure. It didn't matter that she knew Luri was probably gennated for pheromone production—that she would never be constant, any more than she had been for the old captain, Tallis Y'Marmor, or was for the new.

Luri leaned down, her silky hair brushing Kira's cheek. She kissed her ear softly, her tongue making a delicate exploration around its curve, then suddenly darting into the center. Kira groaned, pleasure sparking the urgency of passion deep inside her.

Luri nibbled her lobe, and then breathed, "Anderic watches. You know that?"

Alarm steadied Kira. "Mmm," she said, partly pleasure

and partly assent.

Luri laughed softly. Her fingers worked the muscles down the front of Kira's spare body, then with a sudden movement began unfastening her jumpsuit.

Kira wriggled out of it. Luri, with a grace born of long practice, tabbed the gee-control to one-quarter and slipped off her diaphanous robe in a sinuous motion that aroused Kira even further.

Flinging the robe expertly around them both, Luri bent close.

"He's got spy-eyes everywhere," Kira whispered.

Luri's robe had settled over them. She pulled it across Kira's back, its silky gossamer folds sending shivers through her. Their heads were shrouded in the slippery robe.

"You are happy with Anderic as captain?" Luri whispered intimately.

"No," Kira sighed. "Tallis was a fool, but he was fair enough. Anderic's getting worse every day. . ."

Luri laughed deep in her throat, like a growl. "He feels his power."

Kira grunted softly. "If I wanted to serve under such as Hreem the Faithless, I'd be on the *Lith*."

Luri's eyes flickered, and she bent forward and kissed Kira lingeringly.

"Luri feels sorry for Tallis," she breathed into Kira's other ear.

"Me too," Kira breathed back.

"Perhaps Tallis can be helped. . ." Luri suggested.

Kira struggled to clear her mind as Luri's hands kneaded slowly down her body. What Luri was hinting at was mutiny — something the Karroo Syndicate was harsh about. They liked to protect their investments, and they had a chatzing long arm. On the other hand, Tallis had been Karroo's appointee. It was that Dol'jharian blunge-sucker who'd yanked him suddenly, forced them all to witness that disgusting vid when his eye was removed — without anesthesia — and put Anderic in the captain's pod, with Tallis' missing eye replacing one of his own.

What was it with the eyes? Kira wondered. She'd done some exploring in the ship's RiftNet mirror, and even the shallower parts of the Arthelion link before her fear of detection by Barrodagh stopped her. As far as she could ascertain, despite what Anderic had said, she could find no Dol'jharian revenge custom involving eyes.

Luri's hands worked lower, splintering her focus. Kira's breath quickened.

"You'll help?" she whispered shakily.

"Luri will help you," came the soft murmur.

Well, it wouldn't be mutiny, would it, if they just restored the rightful captain? Kira wavered.

Luri smiled, her perfect little teeth just showing. "Now Luri and Kira-love give Anderic something to watch. . ." And she pulled forth from the headboard of the dormaivu a long dilenja the likes of which Kira had never seen before.

"What the Shiidran Hell is that?" asked Kira, halfway between alarm and excitement.

"It's whatever you want it to be." Luri flicked a control on its handle with a long fingernail. The device seemed to shimmer, then, as Luri manipulated its handle with complex movements of her fingers, it rippled through an amazing evolution of shapes and sizes, various protrusions writhing in and out of its surface as it vibrated with a quiet hum. "It's a proteus, and it's all for you."

Kira stared, comprehending that Luri was as much a master of the sensual arts as she herself was of the ship's communications. Then she threw back her head, laughing with abandon as she ran her hands lingeringly over Luri's generous curves.

They'd give him something to watch, all right.

And on the bridge, Anderic sat, enduring yet another threat from one of the

Dol'jharian mid-rankers. "Got it," Anderic said, hating how abject he sounded. But any time he had thoughts about resisting, his eye throbbed.

The Dol'jharian's ugly face winked out and Anderic tabbed off the comm. He looked around his cabin helplessly. Patrol duty in the outer system.

He'd been expecting these orders for some time, even more so since the news from Treymontaigne had leaked out, complete with fragmented vids from the hyperwaves of doomed ships. The Panarchists were slowly figuring things out, and as Eichelly had recently discovered right before he was blown into atoms, Urian tech sometimes wasn't enough.

Anderic's nerves chilled him with a shiver of unease. Guarding against the inevitable Panarchist counterattack in orbit with a battlecruiser as backup was one thing, even if the *Fist of Dol'jhar* was always on the other side of the planet from *Satansclaw*. Patrol duty on their own, well, that was different. Even with a logos.

Images spun through his mind. Tallis fighting the ship over Charvann. The pursuit of the booster carrying the Krysarch. The interview with Eusabian. The mismatched eyes that made him reluctant to look in a mirror.

He wished it had been Hreem summoned to Arthelion. It would take the Panarchists a long time to get around to retaking a minor planet like Charvann. But then he wouldn't be captain.

He tabbed the locate for Lennart. The Dol'jharian officer who'd relayed Juvaszt's order had also sent a large strategic dataset, which would keep the comtech busy for a while. And away from Luri.

Then Lennart's location came up: Luri's cabin. With a surge of anger, Anderic tabbed the spy-eye, then froze. He had no idea how long he'd been watching when he felt a crunch followed by a stab of pain. He cursed and spat out the tooth fragment he'd just ground off a molar. Working his aching jaw, he looked away from the console, but his eyes were drawn back.

What did Luri see in that toad Lennart? She's doing it just to tease me, he told himself — except the acrobatics in that cabin made it abundantly clear that both women were mutually, and repeatedly, satisfied.

He clenched his teeth again, feeling a warning twinge in one of his molars. This caused his — Tallis's — eye to throb, and evoked the bright geometric tear of another visual migraine. He pressed his fingers carefully to the outside corners of his eyes. He should be grateful, he thought bitterly. At least the pain took his mind off his straining nacker. But Telos! Those legs, wrapped around Lennart. . . That dilenja! He groaned, grabbing at his crotch.

The movement reminded him of Tallis, down in the bilge, the Emasculizer hanging between his legs. Anderic wondered viciously if he ought to pipe this scene down there for Tallis to watch.

His comm emitted the warning tone he'd programmed and he forgot his eye, Luri, and her damned device: Barrodag!. His nacker wilted as the call was automatically routed to him and the Bori's pale face windowed up on his console. "Captain

Anderic."

"Senz-lo Barrodagh," Anderic muttered, working his dry tongue.

The Bori smiled thinly at the Dol'jharian honorific. Anderic had learned that he liked such things.

"How are you adjusting to your captaincy?" Barrodagh touched his eye.

He meant the logos. Anderic's eye throbbed again, intensified by fear. "Very w-well, Senz-lo."

Barrodagh gave a short nod. "I am cancelling Juvaszt's order. The safety of the Avatar is primary, and with the logos you command, the *Satansclaw* can support the *Fist of Dol'jhar* in defense of the Mandala better than any other single ship."

Whiplashed from anger to fear to relief, Anderic could only stammer out an acknowledgement.

Barrodagh smiled again. "Even our esteemed kyvernat could not argue with the reality that your presence in orbit releases more ships for system patrol."

"T-thank you, senz-lo Barrodagh."

"Do not disappoint me, Pham Anderic."

Before Anderic could reply, Barrodagh's image dwindled to a point and vanished. The icon indicating the strategic dataset still pulsed on-screen, next to the image relayed from Luri's cabin.

Anderic's hand hovered over the spy-eye tab, then he snickered.

That data would be useful, anyway. He tabbed up a com to Lennart's cabin, which he knew would automatically relay to her. She'd soon be too busy to even look at Luri.

Too bad.

TELVARNA: ARTHELION TO DIS

Montrose closed the storage bin and straightened up. "Excellent timing. We've completely run out of fresh vegetables, and we are nearly out of herbs."

Osri absently kneed the prowling Lucifur and glanced at the chrono in the galley, the back of his neck tightening. According to the timer, this accursed Rifter vessel would be emerging near its lair very soon.

"You're shortly to see the very best hydroponics in this

octant," Montrose went on. "Do you know anything about vegetables? How to pick an herb?" He laughed. "Have you ever even seen an herb in its natural state? Well, you will soon be an expert, for the captain wants you to continue under my tutelage." His laughter was interrupted by the urgent tone of the emergence bell, cutting through the opera playing softly in the background.

"We'll watch things from here." Montrose slapped his console on and killed the music in the same motion. His big hands keyed a short combination and a view of the bridge flickered into being, with the viewscreens at the top.

Vi'ya was already at her post, absorbed in her work. She looked up, her mouth thinning. Her hand slapped a key and a harsh klaxon blared through the ship.

Montrose cursed softly.

Maybe five seconds passed and then the bridge crew ran in, Ivard pale and awkward in his traction bandage, followed closely by the two dogs. Brandon ran in behind him, tousled and heavy-eyed, as his Z watch had just begun.

Vi'ya tabbed the intercom. "Montrose, confine the Schoolboy. Belay that." She glanced Ivard's way, frowning at the way the boy hunched at his console. "Bring Schoolboy forward, and stand by with Jaim."

She turned to Brandon. "Do something about the dogs." As Ivard began to protest, she added, "They need to be safe, Ivard."

At a command from Brandon, the dogs whirled away from Ivard and vanished from the imager's view.

Osri turned to Montrose, to discover an appraising gaze. "Be very careful in the next few minutes." The surgeon paused, then sighed. "The lens of your prejudice blinds you to Rifter realities. This is not the Panarchy. In particular, do not look behind the captain's words. She says what she means."

When they reached the bridge hatch, Montrose tabbed it open, pushed Osri through, and ran back towards the engineering companionway. The first thing Osri saw as the hatch closed behind him was Lokri standing before Vi'ya, one hand resting on her console. Standing, not lounging, his fingers tense as he said, "Norton's gone."

"We do not know that," Vi'ya responded, not looking up from her console, where her fingers moved in a steady rhythm.

'They're gone or they're dead," Lokri said. "Or there

would have been a message in the transponders."

"We are going in." Vi'ya's hands did not pause in their keying.

Lokri struck his hand lightly against the dyplast. "And eat a chatzing skipmissile?"

The sense of pressure gripped Osri's neck tighter. He moved silently to stand near Brandon, who was leaning against a bulkhead, arms crossed. "What is it?" he whispered.

Brandon spoke without shifting his gaze from the two at the commander's pod: "Transponder feeds from Dis have stopped. We've received some intel from stored data."

"Hreem is gone," Vi'ya said. "What's left of his fleet is busy looting Charvann and the Highdwellings. None of them would wait around Dis on the chance we might show up. Even Hreem knows better than to give an order that won't be obeyed. We have just over forty-eight minutes until the signal from the telltale they undoubtedly left reaches the inner system, and perhaps more until someone comes after us. Let us not waste time."

"Agreed," Lokri said, turning away and then back. "We should hit the fuel cache and make for Rifthaven with our loot. Fast, before any of Eusabian's blungesuckers get there and talk about us."

"We will go in," Vi'ya said.

"We have to leave." Lokri struck her pod again, this time with his fist. "No one is worth risking my life for."

"Lokri's right," Marim said, her gaze wide and earnest. "*Sunflame's* got to be long gone. That was your orders, wasn't it? And maybe we have forty minutes, but what if it's a destroyer that shows up?"

Osri watched with sour satisfaction. No one in the Navy ever argued with a superior officer. He hoped that ice-faced woman was enjoying having her authority flouted. But the little Rifter was right: a skipmissile might hit them before the emergence pulse from the destroyer that fired it arrived to warn them.

"I believe we need not worry about destroyers," Vi'ya said. "The only other one left in his fleet was *Satansclaw*, and we know that Tallis went to Arthelion. Anything else we can deal with."

A faint chittering made the hairs on Osri's neck rise. The Eya'a were somewhere nearby; he heard their twiggy feet scratching the deck plates.

Lokri's face blanched. "Threat?" he said softly.

Osri's heartbeat accelerated as the Aerenarch stilled. Anything could happen. These chatzers could start shooting each other—those psi-monsters could blast their skulls—and no one would stop them.

Vi'ya got to her feet, facing the comtech, who did not back away. She was very nearly eye-to-eye with Lokri. "It is *my* crew," she said, her accent very strong as she spoke each phoneme. "If there is one person there waiting for us, I must know."

Lokri tensed, then took one step back, and another. Crimson ridged his cheekbones. "You can't always use the Eya'a as a threat," he said, just barely audible. "Someday they will be gone."

Vi'ya's white teeth showed in a sudden laugh. "I did not summon them. They come when they hear death." She touched her forehead. "And time is passing."

Lokri dropped into his pod and Vi'ya turned her head slightly, addressing Brandon. "You will accept orders?"

"Yes."

"Take Fire Control," Vi'ya said. "Be ready for anything." As Brandon sank into the seat at Fire Control, she went on, "Ivard, take us to Dis."

The vibration indicating skip hummed in Osri's back teeth. The vibrations were rougher than usual, and Osri guessed that the captain had adjusted the fiveskip to a lower-frequency tactical setting. He now knew why he was there. If Ivard failed at his task, this woman would demand that Osri take his place. What would happen if he refused to obey a Rifter?

He glanced at the back of Brandon's head. *"You will accept orders?" "Yes."*

"Lokri, set up a full scan for emergence," the captain said, her voice unstressed, as if nothing had happened. "Relay to me for skip on detection of any activity."

His posture indolent again, Lokri waited just a moment too long, and then tapped one-handed at his console. Vi'ya took no apparent notice.

Osri watched Brandon set up his console, linking it to Lokri's for the scan. The echo to the main screen revealed the Tenno grid pulsing in the uncertain pattern of insufficient tactical input. There were no further words until the emergence bell rang again and the screen cleared from skip.

Then no words were sufficient.

At first Osri thought the viewscreen showed a small asteroid that had somehow wandered into orbit around Warlock; it was a lopsided sphere with a crack down the middle and a fused crater near one limb.

Then his eyes adjusted as Brandon's Tenno grid rippled to a new configuration, declaring the scale of the view, and he gasped. It was—had been—Dis. Lao Shang's Wager was gone. In its place was a crater—at least two hundred kilometers across and inestimably deep—with rays splashing out across the moon and wrapping around to the far side. From two sides of the crater a massive chasm gaped, near to splitting the moon in two.

No, it did split it; the lopsided shape of the shattered moon registered on Osri, a dull red glow deep within the crack. The fragments of the moon were attempting to reunite under the pull of gravity, heating the rock to a temperature it had not known since the coalescence of the Charvann system billions of years before.

"Telos—" breathed Lokri, shock widening his eyes. Then his console beeped. "No traces—wait—" He stabbed at the keys. "Something metallic at ambient, about a thousand klicks out, 274 mark 33. To you."

Vi'ya's console flashed as she accepted the coordinates. The starfield slewed across the screen, taking the horror out of view. The echo from Vi'ya's console on the main screen revealed they were under maximum acceleration. Moments later the screen flickered and new horror confronted them.

A terrible moan issued from the intercom. Osri recognized Jaim's voice.

It was a ship, as shattered as the moon, seared by plasma fire, its bow ruptured by a missile strike. It was rotating slowly end-around-end. There was no sign of life.

"*Sunflame?*" Ivard squeaked.

No one answered. He swayed in his seat.

"Ivard," said Vi'ya, "go to the dispensary."

Ivard turned to her, his face sick and one hand clutching convulsively at his banded wrist.

She added, not unkindly, "Now."

"I won't go to the dispensary," he said, voice cracking. "I have to know, I have to know."

"We'll set up the comm in your bunk," Marim said.

"I'll meet you there," came Montrose's voice over the comm.

As Marim assisted Ivard out, a tone sounded from the engineering console. Jaim's voice floated out, tight and hoarse: "Request permission to join the boarding crew."

Vi'ya pulled her hands away from her console and flexed them. After a long pause she said, "There will be no boarding crew. It may be rigged for just that." As Jaim began to protest she continued, "We have forty-two minutes. Prepare to launch the waldo. Jaim, you can con it from there. We'll stand off at one hundred kilometers."

It took the little machine a surprisingly short time to reach the wreck of the *Sunflame*. On the screen the picture from its imagers grew rapidly, then slowed as Jaim prepared to maneuver it through the gaping hole in the hull near the bridge.

Montrose loomed, seating himself at the empty nav console. He said to Vi'ya, "I put Ivard under. He's useless to us now."

Behind his back, Osri flexed his own hands, which were slimy with sweat. He gazed up at the viewscreen again.

The jagged edges of the wound in the flank of the *Sunflame* expanded past the sides of the screen, and harsh shadows leapt to life as the waldo's lights came on. The interior of the ship was a shambles, the bridge wrecked. A body hung motionless above one console, its limbs horribly contorted, its features effaced by vacuum bloat and plasma burn. Over the heart pocket on the chest of its tattered black uniform was a gold ringed sun.

"Norton." Montrose's voice was harsh with shock.

The view rotated as the waldo turned toward the stern and made its way off the bridge. The rest of the ship was as thoroughly wrecked. It became increasingly obvious as the terrible remote tour continued that much of the damage had been done by boarders. Other bodies floated by. Osri recognized one or two of them from their brief stay at the Rifter hideout, but as he watched the horror unfold, there was no room in him for triumph.

The imager revealed obscene graffiti scrawled on some walls in a flaking, black substance that Osri finally realized was blood. His stomach twisted. He looked away from the viewscreens in the console and glanced at the others on the bridge: all except Vi'ya exhibited horror or rage. The captain's face revealed nothing, though Osri did not like looking at her unblinking gaze.

An occasional click or beep from the instruments was the only sound, along with the quiet whisper of the tianqi. Finally the little machine reached the engine room. *"—and Jaim's bunking with Reth Silverknife on the* Sunflame." Who had said that?

The motion of the machine slowed, then stopped. In the center of the image was another body, not floating but pinned to an injector module by a metal rod through its neck. The face was frozen in the distortion of extreme pain unmasked by the ravages of vacuum. Osri could tell only that it had been a woman, but he noted the little chimes woven into her hair, like Jaim's. A pattern of strange wounds—each consisting of three parallel gashes—scarred her body, with clusters of blackened blood crystals blooming from them like evil flowers.

A howl of rage and sorrow echoed from the intercom. The last syllable rose into a keening that raised the hairs on Osri's neck, and he remembered the heel-claws on the image in the rec room.

"Lokri. Take over the waldo. Hold it there," said Vi'ya. "Jaim—Jaim." The keening stopped. "Come to the bridge. Arkad, ready a missile. Fusion, twenty megatons. Rig for impact detonation and target the *Sunflame*."

Brandon's hands moved swiftly over his keys.

Would they not attempt salvage? Then Osri recalled something Montrose had once said: *"Jaim is a devout Serapisti. They worship fire as a sacrament of Telos, and give the bodies of their dead to the flames to cleanse their soul for the long journey."*

The bridge crew was silent as Jaim entered the bridge. He had a knife in one hand. In the other he clutched several braids of hair with the little bells still on them. The harmony of the remaining chimes woven in his hair was mournful now, some of the bright tones missing.

"Twenty-eight minutes. Is that missile ready?" Vi'ya's voice was cold, controlled.

Osri wondered if the tempath's perception of Jaim's emotions right now—not to mention those of the rest of the crew—was akin to staring into the sun.

"Yes," said the Aerenarch. He moved aside as Jaim came up to his console, laying his knife and severed hair carefully on the inlay above the keypads. The lanky Rifter stood there, staring at the screen, which now showed the *Sunflame* from an imager on the *Telvarna*.

"Jaim," said Vi'ya, her voice low. The lanky Rifter turned a cold face her way, and once again Osri sustained that prickle of danger at the scarcely-controlled violence in the man's gaze.

"We can commit her to the flames immediately and flee," she continued, "or, with your help, we can seek vengeance."

Lokri jerked upright at his console, then subsided as Marim made a sudden movement. Osri guessed that she had kicked him. Marim watched Jaim and the captain with pursed lips.

"Vengeance." Jaim's voice was harsh, his repetition of the word midway between a question and acceptance.

That's not the Serapisti way, Osri thought, the sense of danger intensifying. Not that Osri gave credence to any religious suppositions about the universe. But he knew that the Serapisti were supposed to find the least destructive way through the course of human events, which had made Jaim seem relatively sane compared to the rest.

Jaim stood there, radiating tension, and whispered more distinctly. Deliberately, "Vengeance."

At a look from Vi'ya Brandon tapped at his console, apparently taking the missile back off-line.

"Can you rig the *Sunflame*'s engines for a gee-burst overload? And do it in the next fifteen minutes? If we can cripple the fiveskip of whatever shows up, *Telvarna* can deal with it."

Jaim looked back at the viewscreen. "Don't know."

He moved to Lokri's console, and with a gesture of ironic invitation, Lokri yielded his place. Only a madman would get in Jaim's way, Osri thought.

The image on-screen rotated away from Reth's savaged body as the waldo drifted over to a bank of controls. The crew watched in silence as Jaim worked. Less than a minute later he announced, "I can do it."

"Good," said Vi'ya. "Then here's how it will go."

TWELVE

The *Telvarna* hung over the ruined surface of Dis, hiding amidst a reef of dust and fragments ripped from the moon by the impact of the skipmissile. Vi'ya had brought them to rest with respect to the moon, holding position with the geeplane. The wreck of the *Sunflame* was just visible over the horizon.

The viewscreen showed a magnified image of the *Sunflame*, sparkling with imaging artifacts as the computers struggled with the effects of the moon fragments fogging up the space around them. The faint, actinic glare of a welding probe flared occasionally from the rents in the ship as the waldo followed its programmed course. The comm emitted terse comments almost discernible through static as the recording prepared by the crew ran through its loop.

The bridge was silent except for the whisper of the tianqi, which were now emitting a scent Osri had never encountered before. It made him feel cold and stony, with a feral edge to his thoughts that he didn't like. The feeling matched the expressions of the Rifters around him. Even Brandon's face had hardened, unexpectedly calling his oldest brother to Osri's mind.

Osri shifted on his feet, still leaning against the bulkhead. Jaim and Montrose had gone to the engine room, so the nav console was empty, but the captain had not invited him to sit there. There was no other place for him to sit, but he didn't want to be locked up in the dispensary, so he kept silent.

A pulse of bluish light bloomed in the viewscreen.

"Emergence," said Lokri. "Reads like a frigate. Two thousand klicks out from *Sunflame*."

Vi'ya tabbed her comm. "Jaim, take the fiveskip the rest of the way down, now."

Osri gritted his teeth, finding that his jaw already ached. This was the most dangerous part of the trap that Vi'ya had set. Cold-starting a fiveskip resonance was an iffy thing — and if it didn't catch they'd be helpless against the greater speed and firepower of the frigate. But there was no help for it. Jaim's work had turned the ruined ship into a gigantic gee mine. When the *Sunflame*'s engines blew, radiating a sharp-edged gee-pulse with all their remaining power, any fiveskip within a thousand kilometers would be crippled, knocked into an unstable resonance that could take up to an hour to quell.

"Fiveskip off."

"Target vectoring toward *Sunflame*. Minus eighteen hundred kilometers." Lokri's drawl tightened incrementally toward normal.

Disdain spurted acid deep in Osri's gut. Only a Rifter would fall for this trap. A naval vessel would stand off at a safe distance and use a missile or its beam weapons — but not Rifters, with the propensity for savagery illustrated by what they'd found on board the wreck. They wanted more of the same sadistic fun, and they'd pay for it.

"Sixteen hundred kilometers. I've got an image."

A window swelled on the viewscreen, revealing the predatory form of a frigate, molded in the archaic, angular form of the Techno-Mannerism Revival of 550 years previous. Despite its age, its flourish of projecting weaponry looked lithe and deadly. On its hull was blazoned a white rose with an eye in its center, with red flames writhing from between the petals, and in stylized script its name.

Lokri tapped at his console. "*Hellrose*. Harl Lignis is captain."

Marim snorted. "So I guess old Terelli is breathing Void. Better for us. Lignis'll want to play before he kills. He's even more twisty than Hreem."

"Is he. . ." Lokri smiled. "A Dol'jharian?"

Marim jumped, nearly strangling on a laugh of surprise, and Osri caught his breath when Vi'ya's black, unblinking eyes turned Lokri's way, then back again.

"Fourteen hundred kilometers." Lokri's drawl was back.

He thought he'd won something. Osri looked away, his guts churning.

Brandon's hands tapped precisely at his console, which still had Jaim's knife and hair lying across the top, like a strange kind of offering. The Tenno glyphs echoing across the top of the main screen rippled through a series of configurations as more information built up about their enemy.

"Twelve hundred kilometers."

The tension on the bridge increased. No one made any unnecessary movements. Their attention was bent on the frigate, willing it into the killing radius of the *Sunflame*'s trap.

"One thousand kilometers."

Vi'ya did not move.

"What are you waiting for?" Lokri snapped, his bravado gone. "Blast him before he gets wise."

"The closer he is, the more damage it will do," Vi'ya said, her eyes on the screen. "We shall wait."

Lokri's fingers drummed lightly on his console. "Nine hundred kilometers."

Osri's mouth dried, but his hands were sweaty. Even if the trap worked, the frigate bristled with weaponry far outclassing that of the *Telvarna*. He slid a glance at the Aerenarch, but he was impossible to read, armored behind his Douloi shield.

Lokri tapped at his console, his breath hissing between his teeth. "Eight hundred kilometers and slowing." He hesitated. "He's vectoring off."

"Then it is time," Vi'ya said, and tabbed a key on her console.

There was a faint sparkle from the wreckage of the *Sunflame* and the looped conversations fell silent. The ruined ship crumpled inward, as if in the grip of an invisible fist; a few hull plates spun away into space. Nausea surged through Osri and then was gone, so swiftly he wasn't sure if it was the effect of the gravitational burst from the *Sunflame*'s engines or the sudden release of tension.

The effect on the *Hellrose* was more dramatic. The frigate's radiants flared into painful brightness as the ship abruptly accelerated, heading past the wreck.

"Got him!" Lokri laughed. "Accelerating at fifty gees, course 250 mark 32."

Vi'ya tabbed her comm. "Jaim, bring the fiveskip back up."

Moments later Jaim reported, "Fiveskip up." Osri could

almost see the wave of relief sweep the bridge.

"He's heading for Warlock," said Brandon. "If he gets deep enough into radius he'll negate the advantage our fiveskip gives us."

"We shall deal with him before that," Vi'ya said as her fingers tapped rapidly at her console.

The starfield in the viewscreen slewed, Dis whirling overhead, as the *Telvarna* spun about and accelerated away in the opposite direction, to avoid exposing the little ship to the more powerful weapons of the *Hellrose*. The *Telvarna* leapt into skip briefly, came about, and skipped again. On the viewscreen a graphic windowed up, showing a god's-eye view of Warlock and its moons. The course of the *Telvarna* was taking it straight at the gas giant.

"Arkad, attack one coming up."

Brandon's hands barely moved on the keys. "Aft launcher ready, missile barrage, wide dispersion. Aft cannon ready." It was even more disorienting to hear the naval bridge cadence on this Rifter ship.

The *Telvarna* shuddered out of skip. "*Hellrose* detected: 182 mark 3, plus 12 light-seconds."

The ship trembled as Brandon loosed the missile barrage, and Osri could hear the faint susurration of the cooling pumps as the aft cannon discharged a burst of plasma at maximum power: the *Telvarna* had skipped ahead of the enemy, emerging between it and Warlock.

The starfield slewed again. This time a flash of orange announced the nearness of the gas giant and its deadly gravitational well. The *Telvarna* leapt into skip again.

"Emergence minus nine seconds for attack two," said Vi'ya, echoing the bridge cadence just enough for Osri to wonder if Markham had taught it to her before he was killed.

The seconds ticked by.

"Three, two, one, emergence." Lokri's voice overrode the emergence bells. "*Hellrose* at 92 mark 7, plus one light-second."

Brandon stabbed at his console and the aft cannon discharged at the extreme of its sideways travel even as the ship slewed about to bring the aft launcher into play. A frightful glare lit up the viewscreen and the ship bucked, then jarred back into fivespace.

"Chatz! They hit us," Marim squawked. "Just aft of the starboard freight hatch." Her fingers blurred on her console.

"Teslas kept most of it out, minor damage, no penetration." She swiped her arm across her forehead. "Too close."

The *Telvarna* jarred into skip, then out, and shuddered to another missile discharge. Then back into skip for a moment and out.

"*Hellrose* at 168 mark 11, plus 9 light-seconds."

The starfield slewed again, bringing a magnified image of the frigate into view. A gout of light effaced the view.

"Missile impacts," Lokri said, dead-voiced. "Evidence of cannon hits." He sent one lethal glance over at Vi'ya, and Osri remembered his words: *"No one is worth risking my life for."*

If they lived through this there was going to be trouble later. Osri forced his attention back to the screens. First the plasma beams and then the missile barrages of the *Telvarna* had hit the *Hellrose* simultaneously from two directions—an advantage conferred on the smaller ship by its still-functional fiveskip.

"He's leaking, aft portside," Marim reported.

The viewscreen flickered to a close-up of the frigate: a bright cloud of ionized gas billowed from one side. Unable to deal with the simultaneous attacks, the frigate had taken at least one hit.

It took many more as the smaller ship pursued it toward Warlock, stinging again and again from two and three directions at once. The *Telvarna*, too, took hits, and Marim vanished from the bridge. Osri could hear her cursing over the comm as she crawled through the accessways, jury-rigging the circuitry and coolant conduits to keep the ship running.

As the pursuit wore on, Lokri's console lit from time to time with incoming messages, but Vi'ya directed him to ignore them.

The two ships drew nearer and nearer to the gas giant, cutting down on Vi'ya's ability to skip ahead of their fleeing prey. Instead, she began to concentrate on the frigate's radiants, where the venting gases that cooled its laboring engines created an area that the shields couldn't fully protect. The *Hellrose* yawed, accelerating crabwise in a vain attempt to protect its weak spot, but the old frigate's geeplane couldn't open enough of a vector.

"We're getting close to radius," said Lokri. "Too close. We're in the Bulge now, and the line is fuzzy."

Osri looked closer at the tactical plot, noticing for the first time that several of the moons of Warlock, including the largest, Pestis, were lined up. The *Telvarna's* course would take them into that alignment, where the radius of Warlock would bulge outward in response to the gravitational pull of the moons.

Osri swallowed in a wood-dry throat. It was difficult to predict just how far out radius would extend beyond its normal reach. He hoped Vi'ya would err on the side of caution.

Vi'ya didn't reply for a moment. Then: "One more attack. Arkad, I want a maximum effort on his radiants."

Brandon studied his console. "If we can get within a tenth light-second, I can weaken his shields with the lazplaz and follow up with missiles. It won't work from further out. His teslas respond too fast." He paused. "I don't know if our shields can handle his response at that range."

"Never mind," said Lokri, with an unsteady laugh. "He's skipped."

Vi'ya's eyes locked with the dark Rifter's.

Lokri looked away, then his shoulders tightened. "Emergence?" He tabbed his console. "He fell out of skip, just a light-second further on! Two oh eight mark 28, plus 3 light-seconds."

The ship slewed around and the viewscreen flickered to maximum magnification.

Osri choked. The frigate now resembled a sort of metallic wattle-in-the-hole: a vast pudding of now-smooth metal surfaces pocked with small holes from which sprouted obscenely bloated objects like pinkish mushrooms which slowly collapsed, emitting puffs of vapor and ice crystals that glittered in the light of the distant sun.

The Bulge had claimed the *Hellrose*, inverting the frigate and its crew through strange dimensions into a horrible communion of flesh and metal.

Vi'ya said nothing, nor did she move.

Even Marim stared silently at the screen, her expression midway between a gloat and a wince.

Finally Vi'ya tabbed her console and the ship came about.

"Back to Dis," she said.

And after an eternity of still-tense silence, though the enemy was gone: "Is that missile ready, Arkad?"

Osri's jaw ached from gritting his teeth.

"Ready," Brandon said and moved aside, leaving his place to Jaim. Above the console the knife still lay, but the braided hair was gone. The main screen showed the *Sunflame*, little changed from its original ruin by the destruction of its engines in the trap.

The Serapisti's lips moved silently for a time. Then, with a curiously gentle motion, he depressed the firing key.

A visceral jar, and the screen showed the missile streaking away toward the devastated ship. A glare of light blacked out the screen briefly, clearing to reveal a beautiful sharp-edged rosette of light that slowly faded into oblivion.

"The Light-bearer receive them," murmured Brandon.

Jaim glanced his way, then nodded in acknowledgment and left the bridge, this time taking his knife with him.

"Marim," Vi'ya commanded after he was gone, "set a course to the fuel cache."

A short time later Vi'ya engaged the skip for a short hop. When the ship emerged Lokri tapped his console, then looked up. "Cache responds empty." He grimaced. "I guess Norton didn't manage that before Hreem caught him."

"Then listen in on Charvann some more. We need all the information we can get." Vi'ya tabbed her console. "Marim, take the nav console and plot a minimum fuel course to Rifthaven. Use one of these intermediate destinations, or others if I've missed one."

During the protracted silence that followed, Osri watched Marim's hands moving aimlessly across the console, apparently rechecking settings and readouts. Her lower lip was red from where she'd been biting it.

After a particularly long pause she looked up. "Sorry, Vi'ya—I can't find a course with a positive margin, though there are a couple where Finaygel might save us. Maybe if I get Firehead in here—"

"He's too sick," Montrose's voice came over the comm. "Delirious."

Vi'ya checked her courses, a hint of a line appearing between her eyes. "Lokri, anything more about Hreem or his gang?"

"There's not much in the transponder dump. Some fragments from various Syncs—scared and angry. Sounds like Hreem's chatzers are running wild."

Vi'ya shrugged. "Then we're committed."

Lokri hesitated. "There's one thing more. The discriminators got deeper into that traffic about Hreem. He's gone to Malachronte to take over the *Maccabeus*."

Marim whistled. "That's all we need, Hreem chasing us in a cruiser."

"Good," Lokri drawled, at his most hateful. "We'll need someone to come find us when we run out of fuel." His hand indicated the blackness of space beyond the system.

Vi'ya appeared to ignore him, merely checking Marim's settings through her console. Then she looked up at Osri.

"Take the nav console, Schoolboy. Your Arkad friend here says you are an excellent navigator. I require you to plot a minimum fuel course to Rifthaven via one of the intermediate destinations I've entered."

Resentment washed through Osri. "And if I refuse?"

"There's an airlock less than thirty meters from here. Your life will last as long as it takes to drag you there." Vi'ya's tone was so matter-of-fact that Osri couldn't believe what she had said.

Marim and Lokri watched him, the woman curious, the man merely waiting. With a mixture of outrage and fear flooding him, he turned to Brandon, who rose and came to face Osri directly. "At this moment, their enemies are your enemies, Osri, and mine. For the sake of your oath to my father, if nothing else, do as she asks."

It was a command from an Aerenarch, as direct as the captain's, and unlike hers, it could not be ignored unless Osri wished to be forsworn.

Osri moved reluctantly to the nav console. As he began studying the layout already set up, a new thrill of fear chilled his nerves. There was almost no margin of error. Their fuel supply was perilously low.

He began setting up the search paths for the most efficient course, taking into account fivespace attractors and anomalies, radiation densities, and every other conceivable influence on the potential courses presented to him. The familiar work soothed him, and he soon lost himself in the pleasure of a difficult task well fitted to his talents.

An unknown time later he came out of his labors to awareness of his surroundings. That was perhaps the hardest test of his talents as a navigator he had ever faced. He locked in the course and faced the captain.

No one had moved. Vi'ya studied the course for a time. "There is more margin here than I expected."

Osri felt a surprising flash of pleasure at this comment, which he recognized, from the little he knew of Vi'ya, as the equivalent of fulsome praise.

She tapped her console. The starfield on the screen wheeled about, then blanked as the ship engaged. She looked up at Osri, her face dead calm, but her dark eyes wide and unblinking. "You are free to go now, Omilov."

Osri walked off the bridge, but the silence behind him made him linger in the accessway. Sensing danger, he looked back just in time to see Vi'ya get up from her console and cross the bridge toward Lokri.

Beyond her, Marim sat, tense and still. Nearby, Brandon watched, as always unreadable.

"My friend," Vi'ya said softly, but her voice carried.

Lokri had risen, and backed a step or two, his lips parted in a silent laugh. He held up his hands to Vi'ya, palms open, fingers spread. Was the entire ship taken by some kind of madness? Osri watched as Vi'ya backed Lokri up against a bulkhead.

"Friend," Vi'ya said. "Let us share the fires together." One hand gripped Lokri's shoulder, and he winced.

Her other hand stroked down his face, the nail on her little finger scoring him from temple to jaw. Beads of blood sprang out on Lokri's skin, but he didn't move, didn't even seem to breathe, his light eyes locked with Vi'ya's dark ones.

She slid her hand down his arm, then gripped. Lokri stumbled toward the hatch where Osri stood.

He did not stay to witness the rest of this interaction. Retreating to the galley, he sat and watched uncomprehendingly as Lucifur prowled, ears flicking, back and forth, back and forth. The two Arkad dogs were nowhere in sight.

"You are free to go, Omilov."

It was the first time she had ever used his name.

The *ting* of brass finger-cymbals summoned Ivard from the darkness.

Where was he? His body yammered for succor: screaming yellow fire in his back; a hissing violet tide pressing on his eyes; the mutter of a curious green scent filling his nostrils. Panic bubbled in his throat, a nasty green and burning slime until he saw Greywing's second belt hanging on the hook next to his bunk. He was in his bed in his cabin with Jaim. Only what was that smell, and that sound?

He struggled to rise, but his hands had turned to stone, unfeeling except the blue pulse around one wrist.

He tried once more to open his eyes but the pressure on his lids permitted only the barest slit, awash in fluid, through which he perceived the flicker of candles on either side of a hooded figure.

Arms raised, something golden glinted: *clash!*

"Hear me, you whom my soul loves," said a familiar voice. Jaim.

Identifying the figure steadied Ivard, and he relaxed back in his bunk. It was Jaim, and he was doing something religious. Jaim did religious things most every day, though seldom with the candles and never before with a hood over his head. Or was something really over his head?

Ivard tried to look more closely, but something was wrong with his eyes. They itched when he tried to open them, so he subsided. He didn't care anyway.

For the third time the cymbals clashed, a sweet sound that Ivard found comforting. He listened with pleasure until the faint ringing had completely disappeared.

"See me, you whom my soul loves." And a brightness flickered against Ivard's eyelids, followed by the sharp tang of incense.

The green scent filled Ivard's lungs, sending runnels of tiny blue fire inside him.

It was good to be here like this, better than the dispensary. In there he was closed in, and it got boring, but here he felt a kind of current, and he floated somewhere.

"Where do you wander now, you whom my soul loves, in the light of paradise?" Jaim's voice seemed to come from everywhere.

Paradise. . . what was that? Lots of places seemed to have that name. *Rifthaven,* Ivard thought hazily as he drifted upward. They were rich now. Could buy anything. That's Paradise.

Then a whisper somewhere just behind his head drew his attention. Was that Jaim?

No, he could hear Jaim: "The cleansing flame did I give

you, yet still I hear your voice and feel your gaze. . ."

The whisper behind Ivard carried a feeling of urgency. Was something wrong with the ship?

Because he could see the whole ship now, including the white heat of the engines driving them silently through the void. He could see inside the ship, too, only it wasn't like watching a vid, it was like feeling flames. Pale ones, bright ones.

The whisperers were watching the brightest two flames.

When Ivard turned his attention that way, he became aware of the triple watchers from his dreams. All of them were drawn ineluctably toward the glow.

Chaos.

That was the double whisper. Ivard glimpsed a flickering image, repeated many times over. He fought to bring it into focus and for a moment he saw the captain's cabin, things strewn or smashed, bright red smears on walls and deck.

The vision disappeared and Ivard heard mingled harsh breathing, heard hearts pumping blood through two bodies locked in bone-wrenching struggle.

Rage-without-fi. . .

It was a question, but he couldn't answer, not with the sound of blood filling his ears, and the heat that radiated past him like the singe from the Tarkans' jacs.

Ivard saw the flickering image again as the bodies sprang apart, one of them stumbling against the shadowy shape of a bulkhead.

Lokri — that's Lokri.

The comtech straightened up slowly, sweat-dripping hair hanging in his wide silver eyes, and his hand gripping a dagger. He was afraid for his life. Ivard's own heartbeat hammered counterpoint.

Lokri pulled back his arm, then struck. In a blur of movement the captain feinted bare-handed, and blocked the forward stroke of the knife with a crack that Ivard felt like lightning through his brain.

Lokri gasped, dropping the knife and clutching his forearm. Vi'ya grabbed up the knife from the deck, then slashed it down Lokri's body in one swift movement. Ivard watched with helpless terror — but Lokri did not die. With the other hand the captain pulled Lokri's shirt away from his bruised and blood-smeared flesh.

Lokri's head jerked up and he tried to free himself, just to meet a powerful openhanded slap from Vi'ya's palm that sent him reeling back against a bulkhead.

"We are taught that love is stronger than death, and more enduring than flame," Jaim's voice intoned somewhere behind Ivard, and again the cymbals rang.

The captain backhanded Lokri across the other side of his face, and he landed flat on the deck, his arms outflung. She jammed the knife into the frame of a picture, and then she was on him.

Ivard tried to move away, to go back to Jaim and his candles, but the watchers forced him to stay: the two whisperers giving him flickering multiple images, the silent three sending sounds, and beyond sounds, a sense of touch so vast and terrible that Ivard's mind was paralyzed.

Ivard felt the susurrus of flesh over flesh, the salty sting of a hot tongue as the captain licked slowly, slowly, the hollow of Lokri's throat, tasting blood and sweat.

She was brown skin over cat muscles, her long back scarred under the drift of silky black hair. Her fingers dug into Lokri's outflung arms. His hands went rigid, clutching at air, when the seeking mouth moved down over his chest, showed teeth. Blood rushed and sang, sweeping away Ivard's own terror in a cataract of rage-driven passion.

"We are taught that love is stronger than death, and more enduring than flame. The waters of Ending cannot drown it, nor the Void claim it," Jaim chanted far away in the background.

The scents of fear and desire mingled with the hot copper taste of blood. Vi'ya sank her teeth into his belly, just to the threshold point of pain. Lokri's eyes closed: his pain, and desire, lanced through the watchers like jac-fire.

No sound beyond the heartbeats and the harsh crescendo of mingled breathing as the bodies suddenly locked, bound all around by her long black hair.

The whisperers said: *Cessation in joining?*

Once again Ivard missed the meaning of the question. Blood pounded through his brain, then suddenly diminished into darkness. The watchers abruptly left, and Ivard cried out frantically after them.

He was alone, and something suffocated him. But who could help? Was Lokri dying? He struggled to find his body again, and almost had it, guided by a banner of fire round his wrist. But then the darkness shimmered even around that.

The last thing he was aware of was the sound of cymbals, and Jaim's voice, soft and steady:

"We are taught that love is stronger than death, and more enduring than flame. Turn your eyes from me, beloved, and go hence in peace. If there exists a Paradise, then await me there."

Ivard heard Lokri cry out in anguish, and spiraled down into the darkness.

PART TWO

ONE

As they rounded a corner in the second sublevel of the Palace Major, something shimmered out of the wall near the feet of Anaris's Tarkan escort. The guard's grip tightened on his weapon, his gaze flicking toward Anaris, who did nothing to hide his amusement. The Tarkan marched on, fingers white on his jac. It undoubtedly didn't help that the lights were set low for the nightwatch, leaving the corridors indistinct and corners obscure with unquiet shadows.

Anaris glanced at the Bori stumping alongside him. The lighting had been Morrighon's suggestion. After he arranged to deflect Barrodagh's wrath from the computer tech, Ferrasin had been only too willing to report that the lighting cycles were a part of the palace computer's programming not safe to tamper with. His Bori scuttler was a terrible mistake on Barrodagh's part.

The report of Anaris's first encounter with the haunting had spread rapidly. Now the Tarkans were beginning to treat him as more than the conditional heir, although never in the presence of the Avatar. This encounter would merely strengthen the rumors.

The Tarkan paused before a scuffed wood-paneled door. Morrighon reached past him and tabbed the annunciator, and the door swung open.

"Wait here," Anaris said to the Tarkan. He entered Morrighon's quarters, followed by the Bori.

Inside, Anaris looked around. The small suite was scrupulously neat: a long, plain desk against one wall was piled with geometrically precise stacks of paper and carefully arranged datachips, the chair drawn up in the leg well at an exact angle. The other furniture in the room — a few chairs and a low table — were also placed with geometric accuracy.

Anaris looked through the opening into Morrighon's sleeping room. Arranged on a low shelf within easy reach of the bed sat a row of at least ten communicators, each with a color-coded band of dyplast around it. They were all live, and the whisper of voices from them made the room seem crowded.

Interesting. Although Morrighon's promotion had given him a compad, he had kept the communicators issued to lower-ranking Catennach as well. Why?

Something else caught his eye. The pillow on the bed was on the end jutting into the room, not against the wall, where two slightly shiny patches confirmed that Morrighon slept with his feet against the wall, and his head facing the door.

Confidence, or mere eccentricity? Anaris knew he could never sleep in so exposed a position. He eyed Morrighon as he returned to the sitting room and seated himself in the best chair, near the low table. His assumptions about his secretary were undergoing yet another adjustment. The past weeks had already shown depths that the Bori secretary had concealed very well. Here was another layer revealed. Was that why he was there? The thought of a Catennach summoning a Lord amused him with its strangeness.

Morrighon stood respectfully opposite Anaris until the Dol'jharian motioned him to sit.

"We can speak freely in here, lord," said Morrighon. "The words the listeners hear will not be those we speak. Indeed, what they hear will implicate Nyzherian, one of Barrodagh's close allies."

Anaris raised an eyebrow. "Ferrasin." It was not quite a question.

Morrighon smiled in acknowledgment. "Your protection of him has advanced us a great deal."

Anaris stared at Morrighon. The claim implicit in the word "us" was an astonishingly bold statement to make, even as true as it was. Morrighon had made his decision, it seemed, and now Anaris must make his.

"Indeed," said Anaris neutrally, after he judged enough

time had passed. Morrighon relaxed a trifle, and some of the fear leaked out of his posture.

There was a long pause. Anaris could see that the Bori was gathering himself to ask a question he feared might offend. Anaris uncrossed his arms and placed his hands on his thighs.

"My lord," began Morrighon formally, "it is needful that I inquire on a matter touching the ancestors. Have I your leave, free of pain and iron?"

Anaris snorted, and his secretary flinched. "You are well trained, Bori, but out of the hearing of others, you may dispense with meaningless ritual formality."

Morrighon inclined his head. "It is about the apparitions. I do not understand why they seem to follow you. If. . ." He swallowed, still nervous. "If they were truly the shades of dead Panarchists, as the Tarkans think, then that would be reasonable, but as they are a computer artifact, why is that?"

Anaris merely looked at him for a time, impelling Morrighon to continue. "I ask not from mere curiosity, lord, but so that I may better know how to exploit them to your benefit."

Anaris relented. He couldn't do everything himself, and since the Tarkan would report this meeting—the listeners would know they were being gulled, but would not be able to prove it—Morrighon had committed himself to Anaris's service. If Anaris failed, Morrighon would die—painfully. And *you know that I know that, don't you, my scuttler?* The Bori's subtlety pleased him—he might indeed be a match for Barrodagh. "That is correct," Anaris acknowledged, and told Morrighon the story of Krysarch Brandon's practical joke and its consequences.

When he was finished, to Anaris's amazement, the Bori snickered, a strange, falsetto gurgle, as though he had a tree frog concealed in his throat. "It is indeed the Aerenarch's shade, then, even though he is still alive. How wonderful that your enemy should be helping you to the throne of the Avatar."

Anaris smiled, savoring irony, as Morrighon wiped his eyes and took a deep breath, energized and relieved by the heir's acceptance of his jest. He found Anaris an unsettling master. Most of his actions were those expected of his father's son, but at other times his behavior was unpredictable.

For one thing, Anaris seemed to accept him as a person, despite his ugliness—certainly no other Dol'jharian noble the Bori could think of would have so easily agreed to come to his quarters. That was demeaning in Dol'jharian terms; and it had taken all of Morrighon's courage to make the suggestion. But the spate of information flowing from Ferrasin had forced the decision: the Avatar's son had to understand sooner rather than later that Morrighon was fully committed. Anaris was looking at him now, expressionless, his dark eyes intelligent in the strong-boned face.

"According to Ferrasin, there may be even more to it than that," Morrighon continued. "He insists that since our meeting with the Avatar, when he directed that the computer be spared so long as it continued to yield information, it has been easier to extract data from it."

Anaris's brows lifted in disbelief.

"He believes that the computer can distinguish between people, and deal with them according to their degree of threat to its well-being. He points out that the Avatar is not visited by apparitions, even though the Tarkans, when he is not with them, frequently report their appearance in the Palace Minor."

Now Anaris looked thoughtful. "Then he truly does believe it sentient?"

"Yes." Morrighon snickered again, remembering the mixture of fright and pride the technician exhibited when speaking of the palace computer—like the father of a changeling. "A wonderful twist, here at the heart of the government that imposed the Ban. And whether or not this is true, it could make a useful ally. Indeed, if he is right, it is probably listening now."

Anaris smiled at the ceiling. "Then, computer, I assure you that as long as you assist me, I will protect you from my father."

Morrighon stared, taken aback by the heir's easy acceptance of the computer's possible sentience. Not that Dol'jharians, any more than the Bori, shared any of the Panarchist abhorrence of machine intelligence. But there had been a veneer of—well, politeness, Morrighon thought, at a loss for a better word—in his speech to the machine. And since there was no guarantee that the machine was listening, or could understand, Anaris had revealed a most un-Dol'jharian willingness to appear ridiculous.

After a slight pause, as if waiting for a response, Anaris looked back at Morrighon. "Has Ferrasin made any progress on the communications situation?"

Morrighon nodded, pleased. That was one of the most

satisfying aspects of his duel with Barrodagh. "Oh, yes. He has established parallel, hidden channels via hyperwave with a number of our Rifter allies, most notably among the Syndicates of Rifthaven."

Anaris nodded, and Morrighon experienced a thrill at the heir's evident surprise and approval of his rapid success, in this most critical aspect of their efforts.

"Of course," Morrighon continued, "we've not contacted any of the firsts among the Syndics, but as with all such organizations, many of the seconds are eager to succeed, and impatient of the normal course of events. Best of all, your father cannot really object, should our efforts come to light, since it is in the best interests of Dol'jhar that the Syndics be kept off balance."

Anaris's eyes were focused on distance, his smile sardonic. "If the computer here is cooperative, I expect you could find evidence of similar arrangements by the Panarchists."

Now it was Morrighon's turn to be surprised, for that had indeed been the case. Without the information that had materialized on Ferrasin's console, while he and the computer tech were working up their plans for Rifthaven, they would be nowhere near as far along as they were. Truly, Morrighon thought, Anaris was a fascinating amalgam of Dol'jharian severity and Panarchist subtlety. Did Eusabian fully understand how dangerous an opponent this made his son? Morrighon devoutly hoped not.

He remembered the vidchip of the scene in the Throne Room, how the captive Panarch had effectively defeated the Avatar, and how at the end the Avatar's brooding figure had been dwarfed by the magnificence of the chamber, the center of Panarchist power. Looking at Anaris, who had been raised here, Morrighon comprehended that this Dol'jharian would fit that room. Might even fit that throne.

And Morrighon could put him there.

Not long after, within the Avatar's private chamber, Barrodagh slapped off the recording viciously. "Of course, those are not the words actually spoken in that room."

Eusabian's strong hands toyed restlessly with his dirazh'u. The shiny silken cord caught the light in faint glimmers as it twisted between his fingers.

"But I will have Nyzherian watched, nonetheless," Barrodagh continued, "in case that simulation was meant to serve a double purpose."

The curse-weaving cord made a dry, whispering noise in he Avatar's hands, like the progress of a snake across a bedsheet. "This secretary is more subtle than you expected."

The implied criticism stung, but Barrodagh could not answer without making it worse. And it was true. Had Nyzherian turned? Or was that simulation merely to sow distrust between them? Or was that what he was supposed to think? He cursed silently: he had seriously underestimated Morrighon, who, now that he was under the protection of Anaris, was no longer subordinate to Barrodagh.

Eusabian continued in a musing tone, "It was a similar mistake by Ezrigar, my father's secretary, that led me to the throne." The Avatar smiled coldly, the strange quirk of humor narrowing his eyes again. "But that was before your time."

The room had gone chilly. Barrodagh had arranged the disgrace and death of his own predecessor, Terreligan, not five years after the Avatar assassinated his own father to assume the throne. Of course, Eusabian knew this — the Dol'jharian nobility even encouraged the internecine warfare among the Catennach, the stringently trained and lethally competitive Bori bureaucrats who ran the state, apparently believing that keeping them at one another's throat guaranteed that only the most able survived to serve their masters. But why was he referring to it now?

Then, as the dirazh'u went through yet another evolution in his lord's hands, Barrodagh sustained a new and surprising insight: the Avatar was bored. The Panarchy lay supine beneath his feet, his enemy was imprisoned in his own palace, and there were no immediate challenges for him. Barrodagh knew, and knew that Eusabian did also, that that would change, once the Panarchists gathered their forces, but for now, it appeared, the Avatar was finding amusement in other ways.

The comm chimed, and Barrodagh's relief at the interruption made him almost knock over a stack of datachips he'd brought in his haste to respond. The screen lit with the face of Juvaszt on the *Fist of Dol'jhar*.

"Kyvernat Juvaszt here. We have lost contact with the Charvann system. The *Hellrose*, the last ship in-system with an Urian relay, has been destroyed in battle with another Rifter vessel."

"What!" Barrodagh could see the sudden anger in the

Avatar's face. They still hadn't found the Heart of Kronos, nor any clues to its whereabouts, and now they no longer had real-time communications with the system. If the Heart was found, it would be three weeks before they knew, unless —

Juvaszt then seized the opportunity to further erode Barrodagh's control of the Rifter forces by issuing the exact order Barrodagh would have: "I have dispatched a frigate with a hyperwave from Charterly's fleet to investigate and take over reporting duties."

"But what happened?" Barrodagh snarled. "How do you know it was another Rifter, and not Panarchists?"

"We have a transmission from the ship's captain, Lignis, that was terminated by its destruction. It entered skip too close to radius."

"Put it on," Eusabian ordered.

The Bori thought he saw the ghost of a sneer directed at him as the captain's visage was replaced by a view of a bulky man with a shiny bald head and heavy jowls. A jagged pink scar snaked across his forehead and down one cheek, lifting one eyelid into a permanent expression of surprise. Behind him Barrodagh could see frantic activity on what was evidently the bridge of the *Hellrose*: a bedlam of damage reports, shouts of rage, and an array of red lights that indicated a ship in trouble.

The big man looked over his shoulder and shouted, "Keep trying Sodality channels. She's gotta respond."

A woman's voice shouted in the background, "Fiveskip's coming up! Ten seconds."

"Skip as soon as it's stable," said Lignis, his face breaking into a smile as he turned back to the screen. "And belay that last message. Tell her to kiss my buju."

"We've got it under control now, we'll be outta here in a moment. But you'd better send some more ships here, if you want to get your hands on. . ."

"Fiveskip's up!" and the big

man screamed. Barrodagh stared in horror, his gorge rising, as the man's mouth got wider and wider, his lips folding back over his cheeks, his teeth and gums following. The top of his head opened up and a fungoid growth of brain tissue flowed out across his skull as his face split down the middle and folded outward. Somehow, he kept screaming the whole time. Then, mercifully, the transmission terminated.

Barrodagh clamped his teeth together and held himself

rigid, fighting the resurgent memory of his utter terror outside the kitchens when the pie-flinger had attacked. He'd thought this was what was happening to him. Juvaszt had known how this would affect him. Who had talked? Anger fought the nausea down.

"Fascinating," said the Avatar. "Play it again."

Barrodagh stifled a protest and restarted the recording. He didn't dare shut his eyes, so he defocused them, and tried hard not to listen. The attempt was not entirely successful.

"That is very like the Panarchist terror weapon employed against Evodh," said the Avatar. The Bori noted that his hands were still now, the dirazh'u quiescent. "Have the technicians search the computer for any record of such a weapon based on the fiveskip technology. It will be useful for quelling restless populations."

Barrodagh nodded jerkily. The terror inspired by such a device would be very useful for the small occupation forces that Dol'jhar could field. But it was utterly unlike the Avatar to so involve himself with details; it was a measure of his boredom.

Barrodagh would have to be especially careful now. He found himself thinking of the expected Panarchist counterattack as a welcome distraction for the Avatar.

TWO

Montrose leaned over the chess board as Sebastian Omilov considered his next move. Not only was the gnostor adept at the game of chess, long eclipsed by Phalanx, but he was an ardent devotee of opera, ancient and post-Exile. It was a little like finding himself. Or himself in a favored universe.

Then, too, Omilov had responded to Montrose's proffer of information through the unwitting Osri, and the gnostor's oblique digging for information had seemed somewhat less urgent of late.

A quiet "tick" brought Montrose's attention back to the board. With exquisite tact, Omilov had leaned forward and adjusted his knight on its new square.

Montrose looked up. "Forgive me. My move?"

"You'll note the clever placement of my knight?"

"Laying siege to my bishop?" Montrose smiled, then mused half to himself, "Where are the kings?"

Omilov's brows lifted, but whatever he had intended to say was lost as the main med console shrilled an alarm.

Ivard! Heart rate rocketing, blood oxygen levels plummeting. . . Montrose shot to his feet and hit the cabin monitor. He caught a fragment of soft chanting, the *ching* of a finger cymbal, and knew immediately what had happened. Haruman's Hell. He'd thought Jaim would want to be alone to send Reth onward.

He slapped the comm. "Jaim!" he bellowed. "Med-red! Get Ivard down to the dispensary. Now!" It had been a calculated gamble putting the boy back in his old cabin. He'd lost the bet, and Ivard was paying the price.

As he broke out the crash kit, he tersely explained to Omilov what was happening. "You're not in the way where you are. Stay there."

Moments later Jaim entered the dispensary, carrying Ivard. The boy's face was swollen and blue-tinged, and Montrose could hear his labored wheezing from across the room. The pungent smell of incense wafted in with the two.

As Jaim lowered Ivard onto the exam table the dispensary had extruded from a bulkhead, Montrose jabbed an anti-anaphylactic into Ivard's chest.

Ivard's struggle for breath became easier, and after a few seconds he opened his eyes as wide as the swelling would allow. "Voices," he croaked.

"Voices?" Montrose repeated.

Ivard nodded, swallowing with difficulty. "Voices. . . and Lokri—" He sighed, and his eyes fluttered closed.

"He's never had a problem with the incense before," Jaim said.

"Not your fault. I should have warned you. It's the Kelly band."

Montrose looked down at Ivard's pale face as the boy muttered something about voices again. "He'll have to stay in here until we reach Rifthaven." He pursed his lips, then said, "Why did he mention Lokri?"

Jaim's long face closed over. "I haven't heard or seen anything."

"It's been a few years," Montrose mused. Then, aware of Omilov listening from the other side of the dispensary, he added, "If she's done with him, you might see if anything is left. I'll prep here."

Jaim nodded and moved out.

Our period of withdrawal is nigh. We have new word-nexi to celebrate within the world-mind. We celebrate words: we celebrate we-and-you, we celebrate sleep, we celebrate entities-separate, we celebrate —

Celebrate them in the world-mind. I have no need to remember them with you. Have you heard new word-nexi while I slept?

While you slept we separated the patterns of the angry-one, the damaged-one-who-hears-music, the moth-one amended by Vi'ya, the one-who-gives-fire-stone. We cannot hear the one-with-three.

Word-nexi?

Word-nexi are again betrayal, loyalty from the angry one, cessation from the moth-one, Ilara-in-cessation from the damaged-one-who-hears-music, loyalty and the image of the Markham entity-in-cessation from the one-who-gives-fire-stone. We must repeat our contemplation of the word-nexus loyalty as its images in the pattern of the angry-one are not compatible with the images in the pattern of the one-who-gives-fire-stone.

Then let us begin. . .

Some time later, Marim slipped into the dispensary cubicle, laughing at the way Ivard promptly blushed. Sanctus Hicura, he was an ugly little blit. "Firehead!" She leaned down to kiss him.

Ivard hunched his skinny shoulders, his eyes going furtively to the med console. "You said not here."

Marim had wanted him out of the dispensary, where it was far too easy for Montrose to overhear conversations. She was determined to find that old coin, and had been making progress with him after Montrose let him return to his cabin. Now this. He was probably back in the dispensary for good.

She kissed him again—sgatchi, he was ugly, but she'd kissed worse—and tweaked his chin. "We can talk about that. Right now, you've got to rest or you won't be any good, no matter what cabin we're tumbling in." She watched the nasty flush of color below his mottled skin, and played with his fingers so she wouldn't have to look at his face. "And rest you shall, or Montrose won't let you get off *Telvarna* when we reach Granny Chang's. But he's in the galley counting over rations with Schoolboy so I thought I'd just sneak in. I missed you."

Ivard's stupid grin almost made her laugh in his face.

"What happened to you? I heard Montrose muttering something to the captain about how you been going crazy."

Ivard blinked, his pale gaze diffuse. "Voices," he said. "I think it's this." He touched his freckled wrist just above the Kelly band, now completely melded with his flesh. "But when I'm in here I don't hear 'em," he added, looking hopeful.

"Good. Don't want anyone spying on us when we bunny." She leaned forward to kiss him and paused when he winced, his blush now going purple. "Here, what's this?" She touched his hot cheeks. "Don't tell me you're bunking me out —"

Ivard shook his head, his lips pressed together.

She could tell from the lack of humor in his averted gaze that whatever was in his mind bothered him deeply. And she was not going to hear anything about it.

He couldn't have been there when Vi'ya duffed Lokri. Could he? Marim bit her lip against a laugh. She'd been the one to find her bunk-mate after Vi'ya was through with him, and he'd refused to go to the dispensary, so she'd brought Montrose to him. Even sedated, Lokri had refused to talk about what had happened.

Marim grinned at Ivard, knowing she'd get that story out of him. She patted his head and talked of inconsequentials. Just before she left, she brought up his loot again, but he never mentioned his missing coin. That had to mean he still hadn't found it, right?

A level below, Jaim moved swiftly through the kinesic form, blocking Brandon's blow, and striking lightly with fist and then foot. The Arkad countered these competently enough that he receded from person to nexus in the pattern of action and reaction, stress and release.

This semblance of pattern soothed Jaim.

Or it almost soothed him, for he was conscious of the effort he made to be soothed.

"Keep focus on the pattern, move within the pattern, and you will see how it extends out through space and time." That was what Jaim's mother had told him long ago. The pattern that Jaim had thought was the harmony the universe strove toward, the syncretic that bound Serapisti and Ulanshu thought: the joining, the unity.

Corrosive bitterness ignited anger. There was no unity, and there could never be joining again. The bright inner path he had always found so comforting was gone, replaced by the image of Reth's claw-slashed body stiffened in death.

'Unity' was the indulgence of the young and strong and successful.

Jaim moved faster, trying to force thought and memory into oblivion. Whirling speed, unending movement, brought a limited semblance of peace until he sensed a faltering in his partner. He shifted abruptly out of the fight trance to see the Arkad backed against a wall, his chest heaving, with Jaim's own fingers extended knife-stiff against his neck.

Jaim dropped his arm. The Arkad closed his eyes, wiping dripping hair out of his face with a hand that shook. Jaim glanced at the chrono and was amazed at the time that had passed. "That was too long," he said. "Should've stopped me."

Brandon smiled wryly. "Good test. . ." He fought for breath, his light voice hoarse. "In a real fight. . . I can't call time. . . if I'm tired."

Doing a rapid mental review, Jaim realized he'd not only gone long over the time appropriate for a practice bout, but he'd forgotten to pull some of his moves. Yet the Arkad hadn't spoken up. Perhaps he was fighting his own shades. Out loud he said, "You learn quickly."

"Not quickly enough," Brandon said, dropping onto a chair. He smiled ruefully. "You killed me half a dozen times."

Jaim was about to say something when he became aware of noise that unconsciously he had been shutting out: the compelling harmony and rhythms of classical music. Once, too, they had been part of the great patterns, but in unraveling they became monothread filaments, whipping through memories and causing pain to well afresh.

"KetzenLach," Brandon said unerringly, his head tipped to one side. And then, "Who is that playing?"

"Montrose," Jaim said. "Keyboard." He had not played that since Markham died. Why was he doing it now? Perhaps he thought it would help Ivard.

Brandon leaned back against a bulkhead, eyes half-closed, sweat shining down his shirtless body. "He's good." The faint emphasis on the last word evinced surprise.

Jaim pulled on his tunic, then mopped his stinging eyes with his sleeve. He could have told the Arkad that the *Telvarna* carried a remarkable range of recorded music of every kind, from every era, but always Markham had preferred music made by living hands and voices.

The Arkad was staring off into the distance, his face reflective. "Markham used to listen to that cycle. All the time."

"He liked music. Reth said —" Jaim winced, tried to force away the memory, and because it wouldn't stay forced, he spoke it instead. "Reth said he was changing crew around so he could have music whenever we went into skip."

"Who else plays?"

The question was idle, the Arkad's gaze still off in the distance.

Jaim forced himself to speak. He had to live with the pain, just as he had to live with the knowledge that there was no pattern but that which humans imagined. "We—Reth Silverknife and I—with sansa-drum and twelve-tone cymbals. Paysud with windpipes. Lokri, if he drinks enough, knows songs from every octant. Sings. Well," he added.

"So Markham had a better conservatory than he had a crew."

Jaim considered before answering. "Not all of 'em," he said. "Jakarr hated music."

"Jakarr. He was the one who tried the takeover when Osri and I arrived, right?"

Jaim nodded, slinging back the mourning-short hair around his face. That gesture, small as it was, hurt as much as all the other whipping filaments. *Memory* hurt. "Was Fire Control on *Telvarna* until Markham found out Vi'ya was faster. Trouble started then."

The Arkad tipped his head back. "Vi'ya? Makes music, too?"

"No." Jaim hesitated again, wondering how much to say, then decided there was nothing to say. "But she listened."

Brandon got to his feet. "Thanks," he said, and helped Jaim put the practice mats through the sonic cleaning.

Marim had been waiting.

She leaned against the bulkhead outside the surgery, her foot propped behind her in her favorite position. It looked (and was) comfortable, but if she had to propel herself into action, all it took was a push.

She gave him a glance as Brandon passed by at last. Had Jaim really run the Arkad twice as long as usual, or was it just that she was waiting—and bored? He was still breathing fast, sweat defining his bare torso above the old, borrowed work pants. She jabbed her teeth into her lower lip.

His gaze was distant, and he would have passed right by without noticing her had she not reached out and caught him by the arm. The muscle under the smooth brown skin tensed and he stopped. She noticed with interest the expression of watchfulness in his steady blue gaze, and then it was gone, replaced by the courtesy he used as a shield.

Ah, born nicks didn't touch each other, did they? Reckless, she had to test it: she grinned at him, then swooped a hand down to pinch his crotch.

The courtesy disappeared. His eyes widened in surprise and he stepped back, blocking her hand before she could connect. A totally human reaction. She laughed in delight. "You're nacky," she said. "Want to bunny?"

"I'm grubby," he said, his hands out in a deprecating gesture.

"I like it."

Red ridged his cheeks, and she laughed again.

He smiled, a smile of irony as well as humor: his control was back. "Am I being baited? What would you say if I said yes?"

"I'd say my bunk is this way, except Lokri's there, and he'd try to steal you. So we can use yours."

Brandon continued on his way to his cabin. "Are you always this direct?" he asked as she followed.

She shrugged. "Usually. I don't see the value in hinting. The answer is no, or yes, and if you chatz up the scanners too much, you might be askin' to bunny and they might hear an invite to view your collection of Divtish gumslugs."

Brandon laughed. "But it's not always that simple."

"Sure it is," she chirped, and waited for the informative lecture on Douloi indirection, and how every human interaction carried unending consequences. Thus convincing himself of the innocence of her intentions.

They reached the cabin. He tabbed the annunciator to green, but leaned against the hatch instead of opening it. He was still smiling, but the irony was very much in evidence. "In any society," he observed, "disingenuousness makes an effective tactic."

Warning tingled in her, causing her to laugh in surprise and delight. But of course he assumed Markham described nick doings. Which he had. And because she really was reckless, she leaned past him and hit the control. The hatch slid open, and she gave him a gentle push. "You think I don't want to bunny?"

"Maybe you do," he said, obligingly stepping inside, "but right now, I don't." It was said so lightly, and with a rare, wide smile, that she was charmed.

And she was also in.

Wandering the perimeter, she scanned here and there, then grinned over her shoulder at him. "What's the matter?" she challenged. "You just like nicks? Or is it men only?"

He sat down on his bunk, spreading his hands. "What

matter either way?"

"Because the first, I can show you things I bet those nick women only watch on their secret vids, and as for the second — well, I never did like following a dead trace." She finished her circuit of the room: nothing in sight. She found herself hoping that she wouldn't find the coin too soon.

Brandon sat back. "Since we're being direct, won't it hit that boy hard if you rack up with someone else?"

She pursed her lips. "He's on the sick list."

Brandon nodded. "And it won't help him recover any faster if his first lover bunks him out for someone else."

She opened her mouth to say that Ivard wouldn't notice, except he would, and they both knew it. Even sick, Ivard was as sensitive as a zeem-bug's antennae. Besides, she'd known since they walked in that she wasn't going to get into Brandon's bunk — this time — so she got back to business. "It would cheer him more," she said, "if the stuff he lost would find its way back into his pocket."

Brandon looked surprised. "You mean he lost Markham's flight ribbon?" His smile vanished.

"And something Greywing gave him."

"He never mentioned that," Brandon said absently. "Where? When?"

He was still thinking about Markham's chatzing Academy thing. "Here," she said, pointing outside. "When you got back to the ship after the raid on your palace."

Brandon looked relieved. "Then it ought to turn up."

Dead trace indeed. "Hope so," she said cheerfully. "If you happen to find it, or them, I should say, let him know."

"What else am I looking for?"

She shrugged, moving toward the hatch. "Little metal object," she said carelessly, "Old. But that flight ribbon is real important to him." She waited for Brandon's nod of acknowledgment — he believed her. "I'll try you later. When you're clean!" Grinning, she disappeared.

The green light glowed in the annunciator.

Vi'ya never answered knocks. If the light was green, the hatch was unlocked.

Jaim tabbed it open. Seldom did anyone go to the captain's

cabin, though it was the most spacious one on the ship. It had a second cabin off it, for servants or lovers in more sumptuous days. Now that room housed the Eya'a in a refrigerated atmosphere, bare except for the complicated fluttering hangings that the Eya'a wove themselves.

The main cabin was large and seemed larger, so barren it was of furniture. A narrow bunk was set directly beneath a viewport. On the opposing wall hung an age-battered tapestry, full of dark fires and destruction. Most of these things were familiar, save the tear-shaped stone hanging next to the tapestry. As always, no personal items lay in sight. Nor was there any sign of blood, or destruction.

As Jaim crossed the white-tiled, antiseptic floor, colors muttered deeply within the tear-shaped stone, distracting him. That was the stone the Arkad gave her on the Mandala. He was surprised she'd put it up, like some kind of trophy; but then, raiding the Mandala successfully was an event that required commemoration if ever there was one.

Vi'ya was seated at her console. The Heart of Kronos gleamed in a shallow stoneware bowl near at hand. She shut down her work, tabbed the hatch lock, then turned to face Jaim. The cabin was silent. Montrose's music did not penetrate here.

"After we refit at Granny Chang's," Jaim said, "where do we go?"

No reply. They regarded one another for an unmeasured time, Jaim thinking back to a memory he had almost obliterated. *"A culture which does not permit the concept of regret creates burdens in other ways,"* Reth Silverknife had said to him, afterward, as she anointed his bruises with pungent ointment. *"You can forgive, which helps you to understand, and understanding releases you from that burden."*

Reth's smooth round face gave way to the long oval face before him. Reth's compassionate gaze vanished, replaced by the reality of Vi'ya's dark eyes, cold and dense as winter ice. She sat straight and still, her hands laid patiently across her console, her black suit, made high to her neck, concealing the strong body with its telltale scars.

Vi'ya spoke. "Stay with us until Rifthaven."

It was an order, releasing him from the pain of the explanation that he found he could not make. He nodded wordlessly.

"We'll stop at Chang's only long enough to refuel," she

went on. "I want to stay ahead of the news from Arthelion, as much as possible."

"You think they figured out who we are?"

Vi'ya shook her head. "Perhaps not, but just in case. I have given it much thought. Those on Arthelion know only that a Columbiad named *Maiden's Dream* landed near the palace and later took off. Strictly speaking they have no way of identifying the ship with those who raided the palace—"

"Of course they'll assume it."

"That is correct. Which means they'll assume that the gnostor is with that vessel. The more important question is: do they know the Arkad was one of the raiders? He made extensive use of the Palace computer."

Understanding did not dissipate the constant flood of rage and loss. "Hreem," said Jaim.

"Exactly. If Eusabian's forces on Arthelion do know about the Arkad, and post a reward, then Hreem will know it was us. Fortunately, he left Charvann for Malachronte long before the news could have reached him. But he will hear eventually, and if he chooses to share that information, I want to be at Rifthaven long before the news can get there."

"What are you going to do with the nicks at Rifthaven?"

"Confinement."

"Lokri?"

Vi'ya's face didn't change. "He will not sell us out. He knows the real price, no matter what he might be promised, would be protracted death."

The light above the hatch indicated someone outside, then came the polite knock of the Panarchist. Vi'ya slowly reached over, reluctantly, it seemed to Jaim, and tabbed the passkey.

The hatch slid open and Brandon walked in, fresh from the shower, wearing the clean tunic and trousers Jaim had loaned him. His gaze shifted between them. "Should I return?"

Jaim rose to leave, but Vi'ya moved her hand. But it was obvious he wanted an interview alone.

A pause developed into silence. Brandon waited for Vi'ya to speak, but she sat where she was. "This Granny Chang's we're headed for," he finally said. "Would it be possible for the Omilovs and myself to disembark there?"

"Perhaps," Vi'ya said.

Brandon walked slowly along the perimeter of the room, then turned and smiled. "The question," he said, "was an attempt to get an idea of our status. Are we passengers or prisoners, or somewhere between?"

"There is nowhere safe in your Thousand Suns now," Vi'ya said.

"We can take our chances on that," Brandon countered.

She shook her head. "If you are found, your enemies, and ours, will not be far behind us.'"

Brandon gave a slight nod, his expression thoughtful as he paced the opposite wall, glancing at the glittering stone. He made a quick flourish toward the Heart of Kronos, an airy gesture that managed to combine humor with elaborate ceremony. "Sebastian would not wish to leave without his artifact."

Vi'ya still said nothing.

Discomfort prickled Jaim's nerves at the way Vi'ya's unblinking gaze stayed on the Arkad as he walked the length of the room and back. She had not asked him to sit down, and he was too polite to just do it.

"What is this?" Brandon said, indicating the tapestry.

"Dhur'zhni Jharg'at Choreid," she said.

And Brandon translated, "The Annihilation of the Isle of the Chorei."

Jaim was surprised into speech. "You know Dol'jharian!"

"Some," Brandon said. "In self-defense I tried to learn it. Anaris had a picture much like this, but he wouldn't tell us what it was."

Anaris rahal'Jerrodi, Eusabian's son, the hostage after Acheront; Jaim wondered without much interest if if he was still alive.

Brandon leaned forward to examine the tapestry, without touching it. "Where did you get it?"

"Bought," Vi'ya said. "On Rifthaven. From a dealer in rare artifacts." Her voice had flattened.

Brandon crossed the room to the Eya'as' door, then turned and walked back. The cold air of the room, comfortable for a Dol'jharian, stirred, and as the Arkad passed, Jaim caught the clean scent of soap.

"Have you ever seen Eusabian?" Brandon asked.

"No."

The question had included them both, so Jaim shook his head. Brandon's blue gaze brushed past his face, distracted: Jaim wondered if the Arkad even saw him. He was trying to read her, and failing.

Another silence built, and unexpectedly Vi'ya broke it. "The nobles on Dol'jhar seldom appear to any outside their households. Sometimes they make elaborate arrangements for meetings with peers. They are sometimes seen by their enemies just before battle."

Which he had to know, if he studied the language. He wanted to know what her status was before she left.

Brandon stopped directly before Vi'ya. "Thank you."

He left.

When the hatch had closed behind him, Vi'ya tapped her console to life, a sharp, quick gesture.

Jaim prompted, "'Perhaps'?"

Vi'ya said, "No. But he doesn't need to know that. Montrose can stay here and guard the nicks, as well as watch over Ivard."

Jaim got to his feet. She did not detain him. If she'd had something further to discuss before Brandon's interruption, apparently she'd changed her mind.

He went out.

The music had stopped.

Osri was alone in the cabin.

He touched the Tetradrachm's hiding place, then dropped his hand. It was just a metal object. But proof that the Aerenarch willingly participated in a crime against his own home, his own people.

Restless, he surveyed the tiny cabin, then sank into the chair before the console.

Dol'jhar. . .

The image of Vi'ya scoring Lokri's face with her fingernail possessed his memory. "*Friend, let us share the fires together.*"

He flicked the console into life and called up the Starfarer's Handbook entry for Dol'jhar, remembering as he did a long-ago comment of his father: "*...taking refuge in facts as a bulwark against feelings.*"

A bright red warning came up:

WARNING! SYSTEM QUARANTINE CLASS II
Data supplied for informational purposes only.

Impatiently he tapped for access and the screen promptly filled with words.

DOL'JHAR
TYPE: Class II (habitable, marginal resources)

Osri scanned rapidly down the description of the planet, which fleshed out the little he remembered from history lessons: a harsh, high-gee environment with a very narrow band of geography that was actually habitable — and that area was far from what anyone sane or civilized would consider comfortable — rocked constantly by seismic activity, beaten by unending storms, with bleak soil which yielded few crops. Yet its people maintained that the planet was a gift of Dol, to make them strong.

What was it Ivard said? "The most common products are people and ash."

Osri linked through to cultural information, and more quickly than he expected found a section on Dol'jharian sexuality, with a warning, deprecated by the Quarantine, that basically amounted to "Don't even think about it." Scanning down, curiosity rapidly turned to revulsion.

In the Dol'jharian language, there is no way to distinguish between rape and consensual sex; indeed, the only words for non-violent sexual intercourse are insulting accusations of weakness. . .

. . . the words for "marriage" and "conquest" are cognate. Dol'jharian nobles are raised to remain celibate most of the year, a matter of control, except for the quarterly festival called Kharusch-na rahali, the "Star Tides of Progeny," Then they hunt for partners; it is assumed that a good fight will ensure strong offspring. Consent is irrelevant, except in alliances for political purposes, and sometimes not even then.

The last phrase was highlighted as a post-deprecation emendation, with a cross reference: *see First Dol'jharian Trucial Commission.*

Osri stared at the screen, his stomach churning. The widely-beloved Kyriarch Ilara, wife of Gelasaar III and Brandon's mother, had been part of the First Trucial Commission murdered by the Dol'jharians following the Battle of Acheront that had destroyed their empire.

Bile clawed at the back of his throat as he remembered what Lokri had looked like when he finally emerged from his cabin after Vi'ya dragged him off the bridge.

Before he could follow the link, the hatch slid open.

Osri quickly killed the console and looked up.

He was surprised to see the little blonde leaning in the hatch, her face merry with a dimpled grin, and one hip outthrust.

Regarding her with distrust, Osri wondered if he had locked the hatch. Of course he had. But she obviously knew a bypass code. She had ignored him except when they'd been required to work together. What did she want?

"Too bad you won't be able to see Chang's when we get there," she said, coming in uninvited.

Grimly he maintained his silence; he would not give her the satisfaction of gloating over his imprisonment.

She wandered the room, her gaze darting here and there, then back to his face. Once again she grinned. "Ever been in a bubbloid?" she asked, leaning against his console, her proximity breaking the invisible but nearly palpable boundary ingrained in the Douloi.

She was too close. He tried not to stare at the small, rounded breasts molded by her sky-blue suit, or the generous curve of her hip as she swung a leg up and perched. Her scent was a subtle blend of jumari and spice.

"No," he said, keeping his gaze firmly on her face.

"Chang's one of the best. There's something for every taste." Her light-colored eyes were sharply observant in their smiling lids; it jolted him. "Since you nicks provided the means, it seems only fair to ask, you want anything? Be glad to get it for you."

She was too close. Unnerved by his heightened awareness, he moved his chair back a trifle.

"And in trade, I've a question," she went on.

What was she after? It couldn't be the coin or the ribbon—

"What do you military nicks do for fun?"

Osri gave in to the impulse to use sarcasm. "Discuss planetary defense emplacements. And if it's a real wild night, count stars on a projection field."

Marim laughed, a delighted chuckle that sparked a reluctant smile. Then she reached and gently tugged one of his earlobes. "Your father, he's got those ears, too. Know what my crèche-mater told us about big ears?" Her gaze slid downward.

The tug on his ear had caused a not-unpleasant sensation, but her direct sexual invitation withered his potential interest. "Probably something obscene," he said flatly.

Again she laughed. "You're so predictable," she said, still chuckling. "But that's probably part of what makes you the kind that people trust. They do, don't they, those high-end nicks? Trust you?"

Interest warred with foreboding. "I endeavor to be trustworthy," he said even more flatly.

"If he'd been lucky in where he was born, Ivard would've been like you," Marim said, her gaze steady and considering. "He trusts people. I think it's crazy — you die sooner that way — but it was the way he was made." Once again she paused.

Osri took refuge in silence.

"He lost something," she said. "Montrose thinks he won't recover till he gets it. Was a pledge from his sister, who got burned down by those blunge-eating Tarkans on the Mandala. It's here, on *Telvarna*."

The Tetradrachm! He kept his face controlled, though his heart began banging painfully against his ribs.

"And though Lokri's my bond-brother," she continued, "I can only trust him every third day, and right now we're having a run on Day Twos. Your father sounds like one of those nicks big about honor, but he never comes out of the dispensary anymore. The Arkad is. . ." She made a large gesture which could have meant anything, but Osri took to mean untrustworthy. You're not wrong, he said internally.

"And Jaim's in mourning," she went on. "So I'm trying to find it for young Firehead. And I can trust you, I think, so I'm asking you to help me look. Will you?"

Osri was silent, recognizing a masterly campaign. Striving for indifference, he said: "Were I to find anything of your property, be sure that I would immediately restore it to you."

"Fine!" she said, but the quick, half-suppressed laugh, the way she turned to the hatch, made him suspect that something in his manner, or in his tone, or his face, had revealed that he had it.

As soon as she was out he shut the hatch and locked it, futile gesture that it was, then prowled around the cabin, as uneasy as he was angry. Granny Chang's was still days away, but the horror at Dis had obviously unbalanced every one of the remaining criminals who held him, his father, and Brandon prisoner. He wondered if the three of them would survive that far.

THREE

"Emergence pulse, battlecruiser, six light-seconds." Captain Margot Ng could hear Wychyrski's excitement speeding up her bridge cadence.

Grozniy shuddered.

"Tactical skip executed," sang Navigation.

Ng's stomach lurched. The aftermath of the augmented session in the sims was still very much with her.

The flash of tension the two announcements brought to the bridge of the *Grozniy* dissipated when SigInt continued, "ID confirmed: *Mbwa Kali*, Captain Mandros Nukiel, commanding."

Ng sighed in relief. Her gamble had paid off. *Mbwa Kali* was just coming off out-octant patrol, as *Grozniy* had. . . was it really only ten days ago? Rather than head straight for Arthelion — where she could be sure the next necessary step in this war could be executed — she'd opted to make sure Nukiel didn't emerge into an ambush, and that he found out about the war as soon as possible.

They'd arrived at the Glorreicke system, yet untouched by the war, two days ahead of *Mbwa Kali's* ETA. The wait had been hard, and she didn't know if she was waiting for a ship that had already heard about the war, unlikely as that seemed. Krajno had made sure that no one but his captain had time to worry about that. He'd driven the crew unmercifully in drill after drill and Nilotis had been even harder on his tacticians.

But Nukiel had been almost exactly on schedule. So now she had an even tauter crew, tacticians—including herself—with greater facility in the new Tenno, and she'd just doubled her forces.

"Navigation, take us in to ten thousand kilometers. Communications, open a channel and hail him on emergence."

A window ballooned on the main screen as the *Grozniy* shuddered back into fourspace, revealing Nukiel's lean, dark-bearded face.

His forbidding expression eased as communication was established on his end. "Captain Ng. A pleasure. What brings you here, waiting with such an urgent summons in the tacponder?"

He didn't know yet. How to tell him? She'd met him just once, and from reviewing his records while waiting for rendezvous, she'd obtained an impression of a somewhat rigid character, known for a by-the-book approach. Not surprising in the scion of one of the old Douloi families of the Tetrad Centrum. However, a brief conversation with an officer who'd served under him had revealed him to have a surprising streak of tolerance for off-the-axis officers and a willingness to consider new ideas if well presented. Well, this certainly qualified.

Before she could reply, Nukiel looked aside at someone just out of view of the imager. He listened with the abstracted air of a response to a boswelled communication, then turned back to the screen, now concerned.

"Excuse me, Captain Ng, our scan reveals some damage to your aft beta section. Do you need assistance?"

That made it easier. "Thank you, no, Captain Nukiel. It's worse than it looks, and a great deal better than it could have been." She took a deep breath. "I regret to be the one to inform you that Eusabian of Dol'jhar has abrogated the Treaty of Acheront. He has apparently discovered some Urian installation that has enabled him to arm several fleets of Rifters with superluminal communications and weapons of unprecedented power. They have struck at targets throughout the Thousand Suns."

His disbelief was expressed by nothing more than a widening of his eyes.

She continued, speaking a shade faster. "We believe that Arthelion has fallen and the entire royal family, with the exception of the Panarch, is dead." She paused, then added the clincher: "I've already dispatched a courier to Ares with what we know."

He looked at her in silence for a long beat. She could see him struggling to come to terms with her information.

Finally he spoke. "I see. Request permission to come aboard."

Ng smiled, relieved. "You're very welcome, Captain Nukiel." By offering to come aboard the *Grozniy* to discuss strategy, Nukiel had tacitly admitted her superior rank.

After arranging a time, they signed off, and Ng left the bridge to prepare. She knew what she wanted to do, and despite her ranking Nukiel, it was always better to convince than to order. Especially with fellow battlecruiser captains, whose independence was a byword in the Fleet.

"It's still hard to believe," Nukiel said a short time later, his gesture taking in both the tac-holo in the center of the plot room and the main viewscreen, "despite the utterly convincing evidence you've shown me." He fingered his beard, frowning. "You say the Rifters captured at Treymontaigne spoke of a 'suneater'?"

"So the Archon's forces told us, and the interrogation records they supplied had some more details, including data from personal devices. But they invoked the Covenant and wouldn't give up their prisoners, and we found no survivors in space, nor any recoverable data."

Nukiel shook his head. "What you did learn was bad enough. Superluminal communications, overpowered skipmissiles, Eusabian of Dol'jhar occupying the Mandala. Makes nonsense of every Standing Order that even comes close to applying; the last one referring to the fall of Arthelion dates to the time of the Faceless One."

Rom-Sanchez watched, fascinated by the interplay between the older captain of the *Mbwa Kali* and Captain Ng. Even with the Navy's complex rank-point system that considered not only seniority but experience and talent as well, it was often difficult for older officers to yield gracefully to younger ones of equal rank who outpointed them.

Nonetheless, although Nukiel's face was not that of a man accustomed to following — one would not expect such in the command pod of a battlecruiser — he appeared comfortable with the situation. The other officers who had accompanied him to this meeting appeared less so. One in particular, Lieutenant Nardini, a husky man younger than Rom-Sanchez, radiated well-bred impatience.

"Yet you've already evolved a Tenno set to deal with this. . . hyperwave."

"Yes," Ng replied. "Sub-lieutenant Warrigal here developed them, with the help of several other officers and crew, most notably Lieutenant Rom-Sanchez, who fought the ship with me at Treymontaigne."

Rom-Sanchez's ears burned at the handsome acknowledgement, then he stifled a grin as the new sublieutenant belatedly looked up. Deep in a boswell privacy with the tactical officer from the *Mbwa Kali*, Warrigal had obviously experienced again the shock of recognition that was part of coming to terms with a sudden promotion. But she certainly deserved it.

"They're brilliant, Captain," said the short, stocky woman from the *Mbwa Kali*. "And we should be able to bring them up in our system without much trouble." Rom-Sanchez struggled with his memory. Lieutenant Commander Rogan.

"Her mod package for your tactical department is part of the full upload already in your computers," Ng continued as the two tacticians returned to their discussion. "But as you can see, obtaining one of these FTL comms is of critical importance. Without it, we have no chance of anticipating their moves — it would be like trying to overhear a spread-spectrum burst with your ears."

"Even with one, there's no guarantee that we could use it." Nukiel held up his hand as Ng prepared to reply. "I'm sorry. It's taking some time to get used to this. You're right, we have to try. What do you suggest?"

"We need to force a large number of Eusabian's allied ships into conflict, so that in the fog of battle we can attain our primary goal: concentrate on one ship, board it, and capture the FTL device. In my opinion, there's only one way to do that — a counterattack on Arthelion, which is exactly what Eusabian, given his cultural background, will expect."

"Excuse me, Captains," interrupted the young officer next to Nukiel. "If their weapons are as powerful as you say, we'd take tremendous losses, unless we made maximum use of ruptors and skipmissiles, which wouldn't leave enough of a ship to board."

"That's true," replied Ng, unruffled by his outburst. "We'll have to use a lazplaz to disable target drives, while other ships keep off any possible assistance. We will take losses, but such is war. The alternative is surely defeat."

"I agree," said Nukiel. "When do we leave?"

Ng hesitated. "Captain," she replied, "I would prefer that you proceed to Rifthaven to monitor ship activities there. When you review the full record of our interrogation of the Rifters from Treymontaigne, you'll see that the Syndics of Rifthaven are apparently deeply involved in this. There is likely as much chance of you obtaining an FTL comm by intercepting traffic from Rifthaven as we have in the heat of battle, and at a far lower cost."

Nukiel was silent, a sour expression on his face. Rom-Sanchez guessed he was struggling with his desire to join battle with the Rifters who were tearing apart the Panarchy, aided very little by the realization that Ng's suggestions—which could easily be made an order—made perfect sense.

Lieutenant Nardini scowled.

"In addition," Ng added, "you may find out a great deal more from interrogation of the Rifters you capture, and you will be closer to Ares there than we will be, if Ares is still where my records put it."

Nukiel finally nodded. "I agree." He glanced at Nardini, who was biting his lip. "I'm no young firebrand, aching to close with the enemy, but I still don't particularly like it." He grinned wryly, an expression that made him look less forbidding. "You'll undoubtedly find some ships already massing off Arthelion, almost by definition the ones who for the sake of the Fleet and Fealty have to be kept from command of such an effort. I'd surely like to be there to see you deal with them."

Ng betrayed no reaction other than a polite nod. Rom-Sanchez clamped down at the surprise he felt at Nukiel openly referring to fact that captains posted nearer Arthelion—apart from Narbon—were generally distinguished more for their political than their tactical skills. They'd probably been blown away already.

"Very well, Captain Ng, Rifthaven it is." Nukiel stood up. "Thank you for your hospitality. We'd better both move on this immediately. The Avatar will certainly waste no time."

Just before he reached the hatch, he paused. "By the way,

Captain, are you any closer to your port wriggles?"

Ng shook her head.

"Towards the end of our patrol we encountered the *Hainu* destroyer squadron on patrol. Captain Hayashi said to remind you, if we ran across each other, that your twenty-five years are almost up." Nukiel smiled. "He's scheduled for the Poseidonis System about the time you'd pass by on your way to Arthelion. Not too far out of the way, I'd think. That way you can make sure of at least one destroyer squadron, which you'll need to keep the *Fist of Dol'jhar* pinned down while the rest of your fleet goes after the FTL comm."

Ng flushed. "Thank you. That's an excellent suggestion."

Rom-Sanchez's stomach sank. Hayashi again! He had a strong intuition that the name meant more to Ng than the bet did.

TELVARNA

When Marim woke on the day they were due to reach Granny Chang's, she reached for her boz and tabbed the locate to see where everyone was. Montrose in the galley, Jaim in the engine room, Vi'ya on the bridge, Ivard safely in the dispensary. Asleep, she hoped, because she was getting tired of his clinginess, not to mention his increasing weirdness with the Kelly ribbon.

Lokri was in the rec room. She sighed, because she knew who he was with. It was Markham all over again.

A few minutes later she hit the rec room hatch control with her fist. Brandon Arkad was nothing but a pretty face. There they were, bent over the Phalanx console. Both of them very, very pretty indeed. Lokri's skin was that lovely shade of rare teakwood, his pale eyes a startling contrast. Except that one was still swollen to a slit, and the other surrounded by ripening bruises. He sat there with one shoulder higher than the other, the bit of his wrist visible revealing the edge of a cast.

Lokri couldn't get the Arkad's attention any other way than by playing that game. Like they were a couple of underage vent rats. True, the Arkad was really good. Didn't that suggest he was nothing but an overgrown boy, to waste his time on games that were only worthwhile if you went places where the betting was high? And why would he do that, when the Arkads owned more planets than they could visit in a lifetime!

Marim had been surprised that Lokri had been willing to let the Arkad see him in this state. Usually, when Lokri set his sights on someone, he was especially careful with his appearance.

What was it he saw in the Arkad? Markham L'Ranja, you could understand. He'd blazed in with this aura of glory. Marim had known within days of meeting him that he would split off the best of the old crew and start his own gang, and she'd made sure she was in it. The Arkad? All he had was his looks. History — bang! All over. Fortune, gone. Holdings? Being looted by the likes of Hreem, and all Brandon did was sit there and play game after game. Or delve into the comp. Marim could have told him that *that* was a waste of time. Anything good was encrypted so deep that it would take a top noderunner to sniff a trace.

She watched until the Arkad finished the last of his drink, blinked, and fought back a yawn. "Truce! I don't want to face Jaim on the mat again without some rack time." He left.

Lokri levered himself up, and sauntered out with a fair semblance of his usual insouciance. He gave Marim a wry grimace, or maybe it was a smile. Hard to tell, with his face so bruised up. He left without a word.

Marim knew better than to say anything, not with Lokri in that mood. She was about to see what Schoolboy had put up for them to eat when the emergence tone sounded. She punched up caf instead, and decided to wander to the bridge. A slow, standard approach would be less dull than sitting here alone.

She let herself out, and almost collided with Jaim, who was hustling in the direction of the bridge. Instantly intrigued, Marim followed behind, grinning when Montrose swung out of the dispensary almost on her heels.

The three of them entered the bridge. Vi'ya closed the hatch and tabbed her console. Marim strongly suspected that she'd blocked coms with the rest of the ship. Vi'ya then turned her black gaze Marim's way.

Marim bit her lip, then relaxed as the captain lifted one shoulder in a slight shrug. "Jackers," she said. "The tong emergency code was buried in the welcome message."

"We have to help?" Marim asked.

"That is the promise Markham and I made when we were adopted into the tong," Vi'ya said, briefly sketching a symbol in the air.

Jaim gave a short nod of agreement, his chimes clinking mournfully.

Vi'ya said, "I've been gathering data. There isn't much. Although there doesn't seem to be a fleet here, I do not know what we are facing. Only that it has to be serious, if the Changs could not deal with it internally. So I propose to take the Arkad and Schoolboy along. We may need the extra hands, and I do not think either of them would be willing to leave the old gnostor behind, even were they foolish enough to think they'd find refuge here."

"What if the Arkad's recognized?" asked Marim.

"We'll put them in domino. I think we still have some in general storage. When we're finished here, get them awake and ready. Give them bozzles." She turned to Montrose.

"Jaim will put the ship in defense mode and slave it to you in the dispensary so you can keep an eye on Ivard and the gnostor."

The surgeon nodded.

"Plan?" Jaim asked.

"This is what I'm thinking. . ."

Osri jerked awake at the sound of rapping on the cabin hatch.

"What is it?" Brandon muttered from the other bunk, as the dog curled up at his feet looked up, ears pricked.

"Me!" Marim's cheerful voice piped, somewhat muffled, from the corridor.

Brandon sat up in bed and shook his head. Osri caught a stale whiff of alcohol: the Aerenarch had been drinking. Again. Osri pulled on his trousers and a tunic, and as the rapping sounded again, he slapped the hatch control.

Outside Marim stood, grinning with excitement as she hopped out of the way to let Trev trot out.

"Marim," Brandon greeted her, rubbing his eyes, his voice husky. "It'd better be a surprise attack from Eusabian — or a time bomb at the least — or I am going to murder you and sleep on the remains."

Marim grinned. "We're comin' into Granny Chang's, and Vi'ya says there's trouble."

"I thought her talents were strictly short-range."

"Are. But she 'n' Markham were made honorary members of Granny's tong and she says the welcome message has a tong emergency code hidden in it. Jackers."

"Tong?" Osri asked.

Marim's face swung toward him, but she turned back to Brandon before she answered. "Extended clan, generations old." Marim shrugged. "Anyway, we gotta help or we're stuck here for good. Not enough fuel to go anywhere else safe. Montrose has to guard Firehead 'n' the geez, and hold the con, so you two are backup. Get dressed, Arkad," she added, giving Brandon an appreciative up-down. "We've got caf waiting." She whisked herself out.

Osri stood in the middle of the floor, uncertain.

Brandon rubbed his eyes. "We're being recruited to defend this place against jackers, not Panarchists."

"What difference between these Rifters and some other group?" Osri muttered under his breath.

Brandon merely reached for his clothes.

Osri did not pursue the issue. "What I find difficult to comprehend is why I should be included at all, unless this is some sort of ruse to get me killed."

Brandon looked amused. "If they wanted you dead, you would have taken a walk out of a lock long ago. They're short-handed, and they know you're adequate at sim-fighting, so they're hoping you're as good in a real fight."

Osri surprised himself by the spurt of gratification beneath his annoyance. "If she's right and the danger is jackers, then this ship is in jeopardy—"

"—and your father. If that will assuage your lacerated sense of duty," Brandon said, pulling on his boots, "regard it as true." He got to his feet, then paused. "And if you were considering pulling a serial-chip stunt like using your jac against the captain, remember that both she and the Eya'a will know before you hit the firing stud."

Osri opened his mouth to protest, but Brandon was already out the hatch.

"Here's our nicks," Marim greeted them when they reached the rec room. She handed each of them a steaming cup.

Osri saw the somber-faced Jaim sitting at a table. Near them, a hateful smile on his lips, lounged Lokri. One of his arms was in a cast, and bruises marked his face. Osri remembered what he had read in the Starfarer's Handbook and looked away quickly.

"Boz'ls for you two," Marim said, handing them out.

As Osri strapped his on, he noted that it was the very latest, most expensive kind, with neural induction. He fought the sense of relief of having a boswell again. The urge to start recording everything had to be ignored. He knew he would not be permitted to keep this one, and anything he loaded into it would probably be downloaded by the captain later.

"Jacs," came Montrose's voice from behind.

Osri was given a standard weapon, a worn Dogstar LVI. He checked the charge before he slipped the holster on, and shrugged it into place. With that unfamiliar-yet-familiar binding, he felt a strange sense of unreality: before the sim practices imposed on him by the Rifters, the last time he had handled such a weapon had been for yearly weapons requalification at the Academy back on Minerva. Which was probably radioactive slag by now.

Marim had picked a jac of an unfamiliar design. Although it wasn't quite as bulky as the two-hander Montrose favored, its barrel was longer, with a small canister just forward of the trigger, and two folding projections. hinged near the aperture, that he couldn't identify. She carried it on her back, barrel down. The others also had individualized weapons; he did not recognize the make of the stiletto-like jac that Lokri carried.

"I thought Chang's was a bubbloid," Brandon said. "Wouldn't these be a bad idea?" He pointed at his weapon, a twin to Osri's, which still lay on the table before him.

"Granny's is all up-to-date, so we can use jacs. Not like Rifthaven," Marim said.

Osri drank gratefully from his cup. He breathed deeply, feeling the stimulant burn away the sleep from his head. As he lowered the cup a gentle scraping thump resonated through the ship, followed by a louder clank from the direction of the nearby lock. They were docked.

"But how does she know the so-called jackers aren't Panarchists?" he muttered to Brandon.

Marim laughed, splattering caf on the table. "At Granny Chang's? About half her gee-nth grandchildren are nicks! Changs have always had one foot on either side of the Rift."

Gee-nth? Then Granny Chang was a real person, which meant she must be a nuller. Very few people ever adapted to permanent null-gee, but those who did often lived long enough to see many generations of their children. Then he remembered the magister Roderik Chang at the Academy, who taught courses in the spiritual dimensions of warfare. Was it possible that he was related to these Changs?

"What's the matter, Arkad, caf not kickin' in?"

"It will," Brandon said. His expression was bemused.

Osri wondered if he, too, was contemplating with an equal lack of enthusiasm the possibility of violence, then remembered with a jolt of anger that Brandon had led these people on a raid against his own home on Arthelion. But Dol'jharians were holding it, Osri reminded himself.

The sense of unreality that had shadowed him since that night at The Hollows gripped him once again, and for the first time in his life, he sustained the urge to laugh at himself.

"What's the plan?" Lokri drawled, strapping his weapon on one-handed with a dexterity that indicated he'd be able to handle himself, broken arm notwithstanding.

"This is it—"

Marim described the basic layout of Granny's bubbloid, a habitat formed by injecting a metallic asteroid with volatiles and melting it to blow it into spherical form. There was slightly less than standard gee inside at the equator and null-gee at the poles, where ships docked, and in the center where Granny lived and did her trading. They'd be using the boswells in covert mode, walking in as if unaware of any problems. And then they'd have to improvise.

Halfway through her outline Vi'ya joined them, her long tail of space-black hair wound into a tight knot. She turned her head slightly as she tossed two items onto the table before Osri, revealing subtle lines of tightness around her eyes, and a darkish tinge to her lower eyelids.

Osri's gaze strayed to Lokri, to observe no reaction in his face at her appearance.

Vi'ya said to Osri, "You two will wear these." She indicated the dark cloth items on the table. "You won't be the only ones."

"They're used to slumming nicks," Lokri murmured dulcetly.

Everyone ignored him as Brandon picked up the nearest cloth item. Osri was amazed to see a formal court domino. With a quick gesture, Brandon pulled the gold-embroidered black velvet over his head, adjusting it with tugs until it lay smoothly, obscuring the top of his head. Only his square chin was exposed, and his mouth, which quirked at the corners, rendering him unrecognizable to anyone who did not know him well.

Osri picked up the other domino, a blue one with scarlet leaves sewn in a diagonal pattern across it. He had never seen the sort of establishment which High Douloi preferred to visit disguised. He pulled the silk-lined cloth over his head, feeling peculiar. It was expensively made, with adaptive eye slits.

Brandon was looking down at his hands, his face pensive. It seemed they were destined to follow Markham's path through the Thousand Suns for a time.

Osri blinked; his peripheral vision opened back up as the mask adapted. Then he dropped his hands surreptitiously to his boswell.

Marim said, "Let's go!"

Vi'ya led the way out, and as the others followed, Osri quickly tapped, offering Brandon a privacy: (DO THEY FEAR WE'LL FIND ALLIES, AFTER ALL?)

(THEY FEAR SOMEONE WANTING TO COLLECT THE PRICES ON OUR HEADS SHOULD EUSABIAN HAVE DISTRIBUTED BONUS CHIPS TO HIS FLEET,) Brandon returned with acid humor that Osri felt viscerally.

Osri found himself wishing he were back in the galley, stirring a twenty-spice Hu Lan delicacy and fending off the attentions of Lucifur and the dogs.

Brandon fell in step beside the captain. "What do the Eya'a make of all this?" he asked.

Vi'ya said, "They are fascinated by the concept of an inside-out world, and they seem to find Granny's age incomprehensible."

As they passed near the dispensary on the way to the lock, Osri heard the strongly marked triple beat of a waltz, which added to the sense that reality had permanently slipped.

Marim touched her finger to her wrist with a wry gesture. Ivard's Kelly band. Osri remembered having heard that the Kelly, not surprisingly, were indifferent to all human music save the waltz. The idea that Montrose had to play this music for the boy made Osri feel slightly queasy, and he wondered what other effects that band was having on him.

They reached the lock, where the Eya'a were already waiting. They were swallowed up in coarse robes of a dull gray color, with rumpled hoods pulled over their heads. The fronts of the hoods were held shut by a metal screen with an ornate swirling pattern in it. The outfits were vaguely familiar; he'd seen them on a chip.

"Azuni Oblates from Pimenti," said Vi'ya, smiling slightly.

"A useful disguise for this kind of situation," Brandon countered with easy humor, "the Oblates being—as I recall—famed for their insistence on nonviolence." He regarded the swathed form nearest him with a mock-critical air. "Although he, or it, or she, seems a little tall for a Pimenti."

"She," Vi'ya corrected. "They're both females. Their mate never leaves their colony."

Discussing Eya'a biology increased the unreality to the boundaries of farce. Osri fought against an irrational urge to laugh as he fingered his weapon's unfamiliar weight against his hip.

The inner hatch slid shut behind them. Osri felt the deck fall away under him as the lock cycled down to free fall, and he braced himself for what might come next.

The lock opened onto a long tunnel made of some flexible, ribbed material with guide cables lit internally with a pleasant, pearlescent glow. The air whiffed of a faint, spicy-sour scent that tickled his nose. Osri could feel his sinuses thickening. Skipnose again. Did Rifters ever get used to the changes? Neither Jaim, Marim, nor Vi'ya seemed to be affected, but Brandon winced, and Lokri sniffed, then carefully pinched his nose, avoiding the side with the black eye. There was no telling with the Eya'a.

Everyone but Marim used the guide cables. She moved along with almost imperceptible flicks of her fingers and toes—she was barefoot as always—against the side of the tunnel where it curved, pausing frequently for the others to catch up. Wherever she'd come from, she must have spent a lot of time up at the spin axis.

They emerged from the tunnel into a large cylindrical vestibule, as though climbing out of a hole. The shift in orientation jolted Osri's equilibrium. The vestibule was large in radius but short in length, with other entrances piercing its walls all over. Running around it about halfway along its length was a bright yellow-and-black-striped line; beyond the line the walls were smooth, and rotated slowly with respect to where they stood.

Next to the opening they'd emerged from was a small dais with two holes in it. Marim drifted over, waiting as the others followed and one by one thrust their feet into the holes.

When Osri's turn came he found the sensation familiar—

not sticky, not magnetic, but somewhere in between. Affinity dyplast. It was a ubiquitous technology, but he'd never encountered this use of it before.

When everyone was done, Marim made a reluctant gesture and touched her feet to the deck, and they stuck. Some of Osri's disgust at the black mat of microfilaments on the bottoms of her feet dissipated at this evidence of their utility: he suspected that she was a product of a low-gee or even null-gee environment.

Vi'ya led the way, Jaim falling in behind. Marim and Lokri traveled side by side, busy with privacies, without troubling themselves with proper etiquette. Osri tried to suppress his irritation. It wasn't like the Rifters' ignorance of manners was new.

It also reminded him how easy it was to inadvertently subvocalize. As they approached the black and yellow line, he keyed the tap-only privacy code, then was startled when transparent letters of red flame appeared in midair above the line.

Upside down at first, the letters dissolved and re-formed as sensors detected the group's orientation:

WELCOME TO CHANG'S VARIGEE HOSTEL AND
WHOLESALE EXTRAVAGANZOO!

A strange wailing, thumping music commenced.

Out of the air came a voice. "What'll it be, genz and captains? Buying, bunking, or both?"

"Buying." Marim laughed. "Go-juice and gutstuffing."

"Comestibles are available at every gee-level, and you may negotiate for fuel at the same time. Orientation is available at any time through Rift-3 on your boz'ls." The voice became formal. "Cross the line and accept house rules. Ignorance is no defense. Do you wish a summary, or printed list?"

"Nope," replied Marim.

"Enjoy your stay." The letters winked out.

"Anything about these rules we should know?" Brandon asked.

"No special rules," replied Marim. "Pretend you're in somebody's palace and you'll be fine."

Vi'ya made a gesture, prompting them onward. Osri was relieved to see no signs of violence in the quiet space. He began to hope that whatever problem had faced the proprietors of this establishment had already been dealt with—and so he could put his mind to escape.

As they crossed the line, Brandon asked, "It doesn't seem very busy here. Is this normal?"

"Might be at the other pole, or just slack time," Marim said in a careless tone.

And then fear doused Osri with a cold flood when Vi'ya's voice came to him through the boswell: (NO. THIS IS TOO SLOW. LOOK RELAXED BUT BE ALERT. A LITTLE OF THE DOULOI SNIFF-NOSE ATTITUDE WILL PROBABLY HELP.)

"Sniff-nose." Another Markham reference. Osri recalled one of his earliest memories of Brandon's friend, surprising them in an Academy cadet lounge while Markham was in the middle of a funny anecdote. Osri had been irritated at his exaggerated impression of a certain Service scion—the slack-eyed, unassailable air of superiority mixed with amusement at the antics of one's inferiors—but the cadets had obviously thought it hysterically funny.

And so must have these Rifters, he thought, carefully not subvocalizing.

(THAT SHOULD BE REAL EASY,) Brandon's reply came. (I'VE HAD A LOT OF PRACTICE IN THE LAST TEN YEARS.)

"First time visitors may need some help in null-gee courtesy," Vi'ya said.

Osri was offended at the suggestion that he was ignorant of null-gee courtesy, which was part of every well-bred person's education. Nullers were hardly unknown in the Douloi world, and in fact tended to be politically influential.

Marim said loudly, "If you enter a room, you orient your head to match the people already there, unless they're all over. Then they're nullers and don't care." Marim wrinkled her nose. "And since it sounds like you've got a nice case of skipnose comin' on, remember: don't ever sneeze. Hold your nose and blow your eardrums out if you have to."

Marim glanced upward, apparently trying to call to mind things that were second nature to her, and Osri understood what was going on: this speech was part of a ruse. For some reason yet unclear, Vi'ya wanted them all to appear to be ignorant visitors.

The Eya'a hissed. Vi'ya winced.

They were now standing on the other side of the line, in the bubbloid proper. The Eya'a were canted at a strange angle, as though subject to a different gravitational environment.

(WHAT'S THE MATTER?) Brandon asked.

(I'M NOT SURE—IT MAY BE THE CORIOLIS OR THE GEE-DELTA. THEY'VE NEVER BEEN IN A SPIN-HABITAT.)

The rotation of Granny Chang's at this radius didn't create enough of a coriolis effect to bother humans. Perhaps the equilibrial sense of the Eya'a was diffused throughout their bodies, making them far more sensitive.

(THEY SAY THEY WANT TO GO ON, BUT THEY ARE DISORIENTED. WE MAY NOT BE ABLE TO RELY ON THEM.)

During this exchange, Marim kept up her constant vocal chatter aimed at Brandon and Osri, pointing out sights that they could obviously see for themselves.

Brandon's smile widened to a gape as they reached the end of the vestibule. He was clearly enjoying the charade. Osri turned his head, fighting the urge to yank at the domino's eye slits, and peered inside Granny Chang's.

To his Downsider eyes they stood at the edge of a dizzying precipice. The cylinder of the vestibule jutted out into space at one axis of an immense sphere; confused by low gee, he couldn't begin to estimate the size. Above his head a broad catwalk extended out to a smaller sphere in the exact center of the space. The catwalk was upside down with respect to them, and at some distance a figure was standing on it head-down. He struggled not to crane his neck to bring everything into alignment.

The smaller sphere, which he guessed was where Granny Chang herself lived, was entirely covered by brightly lit signs — everything from giant flat posters in the ancient fashion to holograms and lumensquiggles—advertising a bewildering array of goods and services.

YANDRA'S GREENZLS WILL GRAB YOUR GULLET — LEVEL THREE

USE IT OR LOSE IT AT NOZZIPAOUT'S HOUSE OF GOOD REPUTE

GULLET GAS? DON'T GET SPACED, GET SACKBUT'S NULL-CARMINANT

There was no sound accompanying these displays, but Osri could hear snatches of music and other noises. He noticed that his boswell was flashing, indicating an incoming public-access signal. He reached to accept out of curiosity, but Marim put a hand over his wrist.

"Don't bother, unless you want that inside your head." She

waved at the light-show.

Osri was no longer looking at the advertisements. He'd been in several Highdweller communities, but they were so large that one could almost forget they were in orbit—if you could ignore the landscape hanging kilometers overhead.

Here was very different. Granny Chang's was far smaller than the typical Sync, and the interior of the sphere was divided into a series of progressively larger ring-terraces from the spin axis to the equator. Osri realized that each ring represented a different gee-level, giving guests the choice of acceleration. People thronged all the rings, strolling along brightly lit walkways, others riding in little open carriers in slots at the center of each ring. All their heads oriented toward the spin axis of the sphere—once he saw that, Osri's own perceptions finally oriented as well.

Without a central illumination, the interior of the sphere confused the eye with an explosion of lamps and strip lights. Many of them formed enormous ideographs not unlike the Tenno glyphs that Brandon used so well.

Marim led the way into a lift tube, and Jaim fell in behind. They floated up a guide cable to the catwalk overhead, somersaulting onto its surface as they reached it. They were met about halfway across by a tall young man with blue-black hair and a smooth, uncharacteristically light complexion the color of old parchment. He held a jac at ease as he stepped into their path.

"Your pardon, genz and Captains, this is a private residence. May I suggest instead the inestimable delights—" He stopped, and bowed to Vi'ya.

She bowed back—the gesture looked odd in null-gee—and said something in a fluid, singsong language: all its vowels were at the back of the throat with the mouth open. Osri thought he recognized some distorted versions of Uni words, but the tonalities defeated his ear.

"Ancestors and honor," the man replied formally—in Uni. "Excuse me." His gaze slid away and his lips moved slightly in a boswell privacy.

(THERE'S DEFINITELY SOMETHING WRONG,) came Vi'ya's voice. (HE SHOULD HAVE REPLIED IN HAN—SOMEBODY IS MONITORING HIM.)

The man bowed formally to Vi'ya. "Your rude younger brother apologizes deeply, elder-sister-Captain, but the venerable Ancestor Chang cannot receive you at this time."

Vi'ya reached into her pouch and pulled out a small figurine—some sort of dog-like beast with a gaping mouth and flowing mane—carved from greenish stone. Osri recognized it: part of the loot from the antechamber to the Hall of Ivory. He was too anxious to be angry.

"This dutiful daughter wished merely to present a small gift to her respected grandmother."

The man's eyes widened and he sucked in his breath between his teeth. Again the silent conversation. He appeared to be arguing.

(HE'S ONE OF GRANNY'S FAMILY, OUT HERE UNDER DURESS, JUDGING FROM HIS EMOTIONS. I THINK SHE'S BEING HELD HOSTAGE. HE'LL GET US INSIDE NOW—WAIT FOR MY CUE.)

Finally the man said, "Come with me."

(HOW WILL WE KNOW FRIEND FROM FOE?) asked Brandon as they followed the man.

(THE PRIMARY LINE OF CHANGS ARE PURISTS—ANY THAT DON'T LOOK LIKE HIM, DON'T BELONG.)

At the end of the catwalk the young man opened a hatch and motioned them through. They entered the lock, and the hatch closed behind them. The inner one was already open, and Osri tensed himself for whatever might come next.

A greenish wisp of light resembling a Tenno glyph danced in the air beyond the inner hatch, and it preceded them down the corridor, beckoning them onward. Osri noticed that the hatches in the corridor were likely to be found in any of the four surfaces. There was no "down" at all. As they pulled themselves over one hatch, he glimpsed machinery in a darkened room.

At the end of the corridor they came to a larger hatch, bordered in some smooth, shiny reddish substance ornately carved with ideographs and mythical beasts. Some of them resembled the small figurine in Vi'ya's pouch.

The hatch swung open as they approached, and they stepped out onto a small balcony-like projection in the most confusing room Osri had ever seen.

It was a fairly large cube—perhaps fifty meters in each dimension, but the clutter of furnishings and bricbrac made it look smaller. Furniture stuck out of all six surfaces and also floated in the air, while potted plants drifted about in apparently random orbits, and several large, sleek brown dogs with goggle-eyed faces not unlike the lion drawings, and polydactyl toes, lounged against various surfaces.

There was even what appeared to be an incense burner, a black lacework pot with a little fan attached and a red glow within. smoke drifted out of it as it moved about, diffusing into the air in a way quite foreign to Osri's Downsider expectations. The smell of the incense was sweet and resinous.

In the very center of the space floated something reminiscent of a sedan chair with a vaguely humanoid, crumpled bundle of cloth and sticks in it. Next to it floated what at first he took to be a huge man, wearing an enormous Hopfneriad Signeur wig.

Osri blinked. Those wigs were reputed to still be in fashion among the Downsiders of Hopfneri, though the Highdweller nobility there had dropped them. Osri had seen them in vids and retained an impression of complicated rolls of white hair built high and tumbling down over shoulders, decorated over the entire structure by shifting lights, or blooming and closing flowers, or a myriad of other eye-pleasing variations.

This man's wig was so large it made him seem nearly double his size. He was actually short and spare. The wig itself was an astonishing concoction of tendrils, spool curls, and braids. Nestling, hovering, winking, and whirring among those was an agglomeration of lights, fantastical insects, and color-changing jewels. Osri wondered how large a powerpack was needed to animate the wig.

The man sat in midair as one who commands, light eyes watchful, his arms folded. One of his hands held something tightly against his body. He did not at all resemble the young man who had greeted them on the catwalk.

So it was with half the people in the room. Their heads were oriented in the same direction. They were also armed, and, with the exception of one woman, did not look like Changs. Just your usual gang of jackers.

(THE CHANGS ARE UNARMED,) Vi'ya warned.

The Changs—there were only four of them—floated at different angles around the room. They were also positioned with their legs near a piece of furniture. Was that a nuller instinct? Osri's hand reached to tap his boswell, but the eyes of one of the jackers raked over him, a weapon came up, and he overrode the impulse.

He saw why they were stupid Panarchist tourists, once again fighting the weird urge to laugh as Lokri, bruised as he was, looked around with a proprietary air, his posture languid.

The bundle of sticks on the sedan chair opened the biggest pair of shining black eyes Osri had ever seen, revealing an unbelievably aged woman. To Osri she looked like a doll made from dried fruit that he'd received from some ambassador when he'd visited the Mandala as a boy.

(Granny Chang,) Vi'ya said.

"Welcome, daughter." The apparition in the chair spoke in a surprisingly clear, strong voice. "You bring us guests?"

Vi'ya inclined her head. "Health and prosperity to you, revered grandmother." She motioned to Marim, Jaim, and Lokri. "My crew you know." Pointing to the Eya'a and to the Panarchists, she said, "And these passengers paid us for a tour of the best entertainments in this octant. The Oblates are under Silence, but they still wished to sample the delights of the Extravaganzoo, as do these genz."

As if on a cue, Brandon chimed in, "An entirely astonishing pleasure, mezda Chang."

The jacker in the wig sneered at Brandon's ripe, plummy accent, emphasized by his growing inability to breathe through his nose.

Brandon executed a formal deference — equal-to-equal with the seniority-acknowledged overtone — but with a clumsiness bordering on parody that reminded Osri again of Markham's mocking mimicry that long-ago day on Minerva. "This is most sensational, I must say —" he began, flapping his hand airily at the room.

"May your unworthy granddaughter inquire of her patient and forbearing grandmother an introduction?" interrupted Vi'ya.

Granny lifted her arm in the wig man's direction, shooting a flinch of awe through him at the fragility of the limb. It looked like he could snap it between two fingers. The old woman appeared crippled, but in null-gee there was no need for muscle bulk.

"I have formed a new syndicate. This is Nokker, my new partner."

(That's got to be gas. Granny's run this place alone for almost two hundred years, since her husband died,) came Marim's voice. Osri noticed her drifting slowly to one side, her boswell arm hidden by a piece of furniture.

Osri decided to stay put, knowing that his clumsiness in

null-gee would make any movement on his part obvious. The Eya'a leaned at an angle. The jackers barely looked at them.

Brandon made himself the center of attention as he twisted around, staring. He was clearly trying to mimic the fool tourist, but subtle anomalies drew the eye. His nerves chilling, Osri recognized the discrepancy: Brandon's goggling attitude did not match the grace and assurance of the rest of his body. He stood out among the tight angles of the jackers and the helpless drift of the Changs. It stirred a memory that Osri knew was important, but danger was too immediate. These jackers might not know Tetrad Centrum Douloi manner, but they surely could recognize inconsistency.

"Health and prosperity to you, Nokker." Vi'ya nodded to the man, then addressed Granny Chang again. "May this granddaughter approach her grandmother?"

"You're doin' just fine where you are, dolly." The man's voice was a strangled hiss, as though something had damaged his vocal cords. "Granny tires easily these days. Perhaps you'd better just give her that present and come back later."

Vi'ya reached slowly into her pouch. The jackers tracked her, hands clamped on their weapons. Jaim drifted back toward a wall, and Lokri, grunting with pain as he fiddled with the catch on the side of his cast, bounced from a piece of furniture toward a clump of people. He waggled his hands and feet, mouth open, "Oh dear, how can I. . ."

One of the jackers snickered and shoved him with the butt of his jac toward a houseplant, where he got tangled in the leaves.

The bewigged man's eyes shot a warning at the jacker, then narrowed speculatively as Vi'ya held up the little statue.

(ARKAD, WE NEED A DISTRACTION. MARIM?)

Marim bozzed, (READY WHEN YOU ARE, VI'YA. SCHOOLBOY, YOU TAKE THOSE TWO NEAREST YOU.)

Osri's heart thumped against his throat, and he tried not to wipe his sweaty hands down his clothes. Near Granny Chang, one of the dogs slowly stirred its tail, watched by the Eya'a.

Nokker leaned forward to take the statue, then paused.

Br-a-k! Snorfle. Sniff. Kaff. The jackers shifted their attention to Brandon, who sniffed and rubbed at his nose, uttering a series of strangled snorts gradually increasing in volume.

"Excuse me." He coughed, sniffing repulsively. "But the incense — uh. . . uh. . . hubba. . . urp. . ."

Vi'ya cut a glance toward the Eya'a. Marim had drifted a distance away, unnoticed. The jackers divided their attention between Vi'ya, still reaching for her gift, and Brandon, who was making noises as if building toward a titanic sneeze.

"Get out!" Nokker yelled. "Get that chatzer out. . ."

WAZOO! Brandon sneezed rackingly, expelling a copious cloud of snot globules into the air. "Your pardon," he gasped in a parody of Tetrad Centrum Douloi, "but I'm not accustomed to —"

KERFLOOSH! Another blast splatted out, aimed at the nearest jacker, who turned a somersault trying to get out of the way of the snot cloud.

The brown dog behind Granny chose that moment to move lithely through the air at an angle over Nokker's wig, and lift his leg. A clear stream of urine splashed directly into the wig, which emitted an explosion of sparks and smoke. Several of the fantastical insect-constructions abruptly zoomed away at high speed, emitting shrill squeals, as if in pain.

"Gyyyyaaaaagh!" Nokker screamed, his cry echoed by another jacker whose face had intercepted one of the insects.

Lokri launched his houseplant directly at a knot of jackers, and Jaim, cool and expressionless, picked two off with deadly precision. The jackers began firing. Jac-bolts sizzled this way and that as everyone scrambled for cover.

Osri pulled his jac, but by then the two jackers Marim had directed him to "get" had launched themselves in different directions, shooting as they went. He took refuge behind a nearby cluster of wicker chairs, his legs and arms swimming desperately as he looked around, trying to make sense of the fight.

KABLOO!

Lights exploded from the wig, sending more objects flying, and filling the air with the stench of singled hair. Several rolls of hair began to vibrate, impelling the writhing Nokker upward. The smoke swirling from his head made him look like one of the flying warships in an ancient flatvid Osri had once seen, falling out of the sky after losing a midair duel. Nokker flung his arms wide and the control he'd been clutching in his hand flew across the room, directly toward Osri.

He lunged out and caught it in his hand.

And that was what Granny and her children had been waiting for. The lights went out, leaving only the glow of the incense burner. Osri ducked as a jac-bolt sizzled past, shouts and screams impacting his ears from all directions. A globe of light bloomed around Granny's chair—which had to be the smallest tesla shield he'd ever seen—and a bolt of plasma lanced out of it and fried Nokker, silencing his screams.

Dull fires glowed, revealing that the dogs had disappeared entirely, and crew, Changs, and jackers alike had taken cover around the room, save one of Nokker's gang, whose inexperience in null-gee betrayed her: as a jac-bolt from Vi'ya sizzled past the woman, she tried to duck, and instead pulled her feet off the deck.

Trying to defend herself, she made the mistake of firing her jac in midair, which threw her into a tight spin. She vomited noisily, throwing off a wheel of foulness, and began to choke.

This was becoming a nightmare of excretions; Osri tried to suppress a sort of desperate hilarity just before a near-miss jac-bolt ignited a streak across his wicker shield. He used it to launch himself toward a wall behind an ornate cabinet. Heat singed past his ankle and one shoulder, but he arrived safely. Peering around a corner, he scanned for allies: he couldn't see the Eya'a anywhere, and he'd lost track of Brandon.

Then something like a comet streaked across the room, screeching imprecations. It was Marim. She had unfolded the hinged projections on her jac and put her feet on them, and was using it as a combined weapon and propulsion system. That canister had to be reaction mass.

Marim twisted expertly and fired. The jac-bolt emerged at an angle and spun her around. She landed on a wall, jumped off in another direction, and fried one of their opponents with a jac-bolt. She used the momentum from that blast to jet off in another direction and carom off a potted plant—sending it into the face of another of the jackers, who whirled away with blood splattering from his nose. Jaim coolly picked him off.

The room erupted in brilliant lines of crossing jac-bolts, causing an increasing glow of smoldering furniture. Marim jetted past again, jac-bolts crossing behind her as she fired, spun, and fired again, Jaim backing her from the best position in the chamber.

Then it was over. Light glowed again, revealing. Granny's chair hanging in the center of the room as before, but now the other Changs were armed with their foes' weapons. They moved purposefully around the room, vacuuming foulness from the air, towing corpses toward hatches, and dealing with the wounded with brusque efficiency. Osri flinched as one of them casually plunged a dagger into the back of a wounded jacker's neck; the victim convulsed and went limp.

Marim drifted up next to Osri, breathless and merry. "They'd just space 'em anyway. This is quicker." She grabbed his arm and beckoned to Brandon. "C'mon, Granny Chang wants to meet you two."

She launched them across the room to the sedan chair, braking them with bent legs on its base. They ended up floating only a couple of meters from the ancient proprietor. Around her neck gleamed a shock collar.

Silently Osri offered the control still clutched in one hand, and the bird-claw fingers took it. The huge black eyes regarded Osri and Brandon unblinking, then a smile split Granny Chang's face, shifting the mass of wrinkles as she sketched a gesture that Osri recognized as a deference in a style that nowadays was only seen in historical serial chips.

"The House of Chang is honored, young Phoenix," she said in a whisper just barely audible. "How is it that a scion of the Mandala finds himself at the back end of nowhere?"

Brandon stilled in surprise, then bowed, the innate grace confirming her guess even as he pulled the domino off. "I've come to meet you, of course," he said with a debonair grin, as his hair floated in a black halo. "What better pilgrimage is there?"

Granny Chang gave a sharp crack of laughter: "Be easy, O Arkad. Nothing said here today will go beyond these walls. You have a story to tell: you must give it to us when we celebrate. First you will clean up, while we prepare a feast. It is a special day indeed that brings an honored granddaughter and a Krysarch to us, and it is doubly blessed when our cherished guests gift us with our lives."

FOUR

Eloatri trudged to the top of the grassy hill, then stopped, horrified, when she recognized the spires of New Glastonbury thrusting arrogantly into the sky before her. The last light of day gilded them with ruddy health, emphasizing their heaven-storming reach, drawing earth and sky together in confident embrace. Faint on the air drifted the sound of chanting, and then, in a clangorous summons that the last dregs of her spirit cried out against, a peal of bells.

She turned her back on the cathedral and sat down, weeping. Of all the faiths of Desrien, of all the faces of Telos, why had this one been chosen for her? It was everything her heart had always denied, even as she granted it the tolerance demanded of every inhabitant of Desrien for every faith there planted. The world not as illusion to be surmounted, but a story to be lived; the celebration of attachment, even unto bloody suffering and death.

No way out. No way out.

It is too much.

She stood up and without a backward glance, made her way down the hill again, away from her hejir.

Night came presently, and with it a dense fog, rising up out of the earth like the breath of some vast beast. Eloatri felt the potentialities trembling around her, and she trembled in response. It was the pekeri, the dream fog of Desrien, and it had swallowed her.

Now she was truly lost, but every time she tried to rest, an irresistible restlessness, a spinning sensation in her breast like an engine out of control, shook her tired frame and impelled her forward. Some time back she had lost her staff, her cloak, and her sandals; she clutched her begging bowl with grim intensity. Her yellow robe was damp with dew. It clung to her in a clammy embrace, like the shroud of a drowned corpse.

From time to time she glimpsed eyes in the mist, some lambent yellow, others glowing green, but they looked past her. They were not part of her story. She would have welcomed the sudden leap of some beast of prey to save her from her fate, but the predator that followed her had neither parts nor passions, nor would It ever tire. She stumbled onward, exhausted beyond thought, a hunted creature in the forests of the night.

Now she could hear a breathing behind her, a diapason of power, rising from the stony bones of the planet under her feet. Soon, she felt sure, It would form her name, and she would turn. . .

Eloatri began to run, at eighty years of age a frightened child lost in the dark. Her fear-sharpened senses brought vivid impressions: the cool earth under her feet, her hoarse panting, the ear-deadening blanket of the fog. The damp air carried a sweet scent, a gentle perfume that intensified inexorably.

Then she blundered into a thorny hedge. Its clawed embrace enfolded her as she tried to fight her way through it, panicked by the sound of her pursuer. A clearing loomed ahead; she pushed frantically toward it, heedless of the ripping of her robe. The thorns caught at her flesh.

She stopped. Before her stood Tomiko, his features shadowed in his cowl. As she stood panting, the High Phanist pushed back his hood. Eloatri gasped. His face was terribly disfigured, seared and blistered. His eyes were milky white and blind, and yet she knew he saw her. Wordlessly he held out his hands, one palm up, beseeching, one palm down with fingers curled, concealing some small object.

She stood still for a timeless moment. He said nothing, but she could feel his entreaty. Slowly she stepped toward him. The reek of burned flesh filled her nostrils. She placed the begging bowl in his upturned hand.

He smiled, a ravaged grimace full of painful joy. "The gates of the teaching are many; I vow to enter them all," he whispered: the third bodhisattva vow. She held out her hand,

and he opened his. The Digrammaton, symbol of his office, dropped into her hand, searing hot, then fell to the ground as Eloatri shrieked, flinging it from her and curling up her hand around the pain. She, too, fell to the ground.

The sound of chanting awoke her.

She sat up. Dappled sunlight played across her through the leaves of the massive flowering thorn tree against whose trunk she sat. Her hand throbbed and burned. She opened it and looked at the image of the Digrammaton, Aleph-Null, in the white puffiness of a second-degree burn.

Eloatri found the reverse image in a metallic gleam a few feet away, and reached cautiously to pick it up. It was cool now, but her hand flared with agony.

Then she raised her head. Across a little valley loomed the joyful exuberance of New Glastonbury Cathedral, its spires and buttresses leaping toward heaven in celebration of the goodness of Creation and the transforming power of descending Love. Eloatri blinked.

A procession wended slowly toward her across the grassy sward, men and women, some in glorious robes and some in stark black and white. She could smell sweet resinous incense and see smoke rising among them, and their words came faintly to her: ". . . Fons vivus, ignis, caritas, et spiritalis unctio. . ."

She smiled; the sound was beautiful. Meaning would come later.

"You didn't think you drank that for yourself?" Eloatri laughed. This had not been Tomiko's way, nor hers. Was it the redheaded boy who needed this? Or some part of herself not yet revealed? Or both? Then the shadow of sadness dimmed the light engulfing her soul. Tomiko was dead by violence, and he had been on Arthelion, among the High Douloi. There might be many now who needed the message of a faith that saw history as a story with a purpose.

But that was in the Hand of Telos.

She faced the approaching group. Now that they were closer she could see that one of the processors carried a tall, pointed hat, strangely divided, another a folded garment more glorious than any of the others, and another a tall staff whose top was bent in a graceful crook. The procession made straight for her.

She stood up, and the last tatters of her yellow robe fell away from her. A gentle breeze caressed her body and the sun shone warm on her flesh as she advanced down the hill to meet her new life and await those who would come.

GRANNY CHANG'S

Osri sat back, replete after a feast of uncountable exotic dishes. He'd never actually had a meal in low-gee before, but it had been easier than one might expect, especially since the preparation featured sauces that bound ingredients together. He even understood now how that worked.

The large cubical room that had only hours ago been the scene of a pitched battle had been reconfigured to accommodate guests unused to microgravity, with spacious balconies on four of the six walls overlooking the interior space still uncompensated. At his right, his father was deep in conversation with Montrose, his face more relaxed than Osri had seen it since the long-ago days on his verandah on Charvann. The Eya'a had returned to the *Telvarna*, and Jaim was with them, ostensibly to supervise refueling, and to hold the con. But the others were all present, even Ivard, who'd insisted on bringing Lucifur and the two dogs.

His mood hovering between celebration and grief, Osri held up his wine bulb and stared at the ripples in the ruby ovoid. He had drunk the light, expensive wines first presented to them, his first drink in what seemed eons: he remembered, with a twinge of shock, toasting a fellow officer on Merryn just before departing for The Hollows and the interrupted visit with his father. Qu'isran had gone up the S'Lift to take ship for his new posting.

How long did he live beyond his promotion? The memory brought the oppression of sorrow. Whatever happened to his father and himself now, there was no returning to the old ways, for Tanri Faseult, the enlightened Archon of Charvann, was dead, and jackals much worse than Nokker and his gang ran wild in once-peaceful Merryn.

Forcing his mind away, Osri scanned the room as a group of musicians played an unending selection of complicated music from many worlds.

It wasn't just the drink. Osri's gaze traveled from one person to another. It was reaction.

Across the room Ivard sat between Vi'ya and Montrose, his

thin face flushed and his eyes reflecting the lights. Whether it was fever or some other reaction, his pupils were enormous, and Montrose glanced Ivard's way quite often.

Ivard seemed happy as he watched the free-fall dancers performing in the center of the room, gyrating with lascivious agility, reaction modules at wrists and ankles emitting puffs of sweet-smelling smoke. At their center Marim performed with skylark grace, her blonde hair swirling about her laughing face, and her nearly naked body decorated with a crisscrossing of bells and beads.

Next to Vi'ya, Lucifur lay on a table, batting lazily at the muzzle of one of the Chang dogs, who lunged at the big cat with its mouth open in a canine grin. The two Arkad dogs curled at Ivard's feet, their eyes intent on Brandon, who floated at an angle near the center with Granny Chang and older members of the family. He was dressed in a splendid tunic that someone had produced from somewhere. It fitted his slim body to admiration, as did the tight black trousers and the high glossy boots.

Nearby, Lokri lounged amid a group of ornamental young Changs of both sexes, their laughter frequent, though the angle of Lokri's body aligned less with the Changs and more with Brandon.

Brandon was at his very best in the social arena, Osri had to admit: dividing his attention equally among all his hosts, he kept them amused and entertained, especially Granny Chang. After ten years, he should be good at it. It wasn't as if he'd been doing anything else — except playing games.

Games. Not Phalanx, but mimicry. Osri considered his earlier observation, wondering why it had struck him as important. He knew now what the discrepancy between Brandon's parody of Douloi movement and his unconscious elegance later had reminded him of: it was that same incident with Markham, who, when he had finished his story, moved back across the room with that very same elegance born of control and command. But why was it important? Osri tried to blink away the muzziness threatening his skull from the unaccustomed alcohol.

"You are silent, son," his father said. "Is something amiss?" Above the polite smile, his eyes betrayed anxiousness.

He sees me as a wayward child to be humored; the observation came from that same part of Osri's brain that urged him to make the connection in his observations, and that insisted on their significance. "I am merely tired, Father. Remember, it was just at the start of our Z-watch when we docked."

"I think we are nearly finished here." Omilov sighed. "Though I must say, I'm reluctant to leave."

"Enjoy it." Osri forced a smile, hating to see how worn-out — how old — his father looked. "I am."

That answer seemed to ease Omilov, who settled more deeply on his pillow, then pulled a wine bubble from the cluster designed to mimic a bunch of grapes.

Just then Granny Chang touched a control on her chair, and a crystalline note cut through music and talk. "It is time," she said, lifting her voice slightly, "to hear what our most welcome and respected guest has to say about events outside."

The group quieted and those in free fall moved and oriented themselves to center on Brandon, testament either to the Changs' politeness, or to their veneration for Granny Chang. Maybe it was both.

To Osri's surprise, Brandon didn't utter one of his typical social fatuosities. "Arthelion has fallen," he said in a clear voice, mild but not indifferent.

Absolute silence met these words.

"I understand you have been hearing rumors, some of which conflict. We have come straight from Arthelion, and what I say I either witnessed myself, or heard from a source I trust. This is what I know: My brothers are dead, and my father lies imprisoned, awaiting transfer to Gehenna. In my father's place is Eusabian of Dol'jhar, and these deeds are part of his vengeance for his defeat at Acheront twenty years ago."

Brandon looked around in the silence, his expression the deceptive shield of mildness that Osri had always equated with mental and moral weakness, even stupidity.

Then the observation was there: Markham vlith-L'Ranja, standing in a group telling a story with just such sureness, except his face had always reflected his thoughts. *"Adopted into the L'Ranjas from an obscure background. . ."* His own sneering words came back to him.

Markham was a perfect mimic.

Osri remembered the mocking pantomime in the cadet lounge, the slight exaggerations that had still managed to convey a clear portrait of an unloved instructor whose social ambitions much outranked his station. Afterward Markham had returned to the others with the same grace that Brandon moved with now: Markham had always been a mimic. He'd learned to move from watching Brandon. The alcohol fumes blurred Brandon's outlines, and for a heartbeat he could have been Markham, except Markham was blond, and his laughing face had never—

He'd learned the moves, but never the shield. That was it. Osri had raged ineffectually as a youth against the blank-faced Krysarchs, whose control had seemed so innate. Even when they were punished, they hid their thoughts, just as they always read Osri's. But Markham had recognized that he could never learn it, and so he had never tried.

Why was this important? Because. . .

But the answer wouldn't come. Instead, his mind streamed with memories, overlaid with angers past and present, and sorrow, and plain human exhaustion.

And through it all flowed Brandon's voice, outlining with graphic imagery the destruction of the *Korion* above Charvann, and the race in the boosted courier to escape a Rifter destroyer. He described the crash-landing on the moon Dis, and how the *Telvarna* had gone to Arthelion.

Then he told them about the raid against the Mandala, the polite Douloi cadences innate in his speech somehow sharpening the horror found in the Hall of Ivory. Osri was shocked. He had heard nothing of this, and he sustained another wave of horror when Brandon talked of Eusabian's torture room, and Omilov imprisoned there.

Brandon mocked himself as a clumsy figure stumbling after the others, a wounded dog in his arms. Osri observed sympathetic glances taking in the dogs at Ivard's feet. Then came the headlong flight through the palace, chased by Eusabian's deadly Tarkans, and how Greywing, Ivard's sister, was killed and Ivard wounded, and when it seemed almost unbearable he gave them a humorous release as he described a fight in the kitchens with mechwaiters as weapons.

Brandon's tone had taken on color and expression. Osri's guts tightened as he relived the terror of the *Telvarna*'s race up the Node cable toward radius and escape. One by one Brandon touched on heroic actions of the *Telvarna*'s crew: Lokri, who carried Ivard to safety, Montrose in his rescue of Omilov. Jaim and Marim working against time to salvage the ship's engines enough to enable their escape.

The listeners were still with tension as Brandon told of the appearance of Eusabian's *Fist of Dol'jhar*, though several people gasped when he told of its last attempt, the ruptor beam that must have ripped apart the Node and killed everyone on it.

Then he told them what they found at Dis, and how Vi'ya had driven Hreem's watchdog into Warlock. He finished with Osri's own part, how he gave them a margin of safety despite dangerously low fuel as they came directly to Chang's. Osri was surprised by an unaccustomed glow of pride, but then another thought occurred: He had not mentioned the Heart of Kronos.

And, finally, Brandon had not talked about his part, except for carrying that dog.

Osri lifted his bulb of wine, watching a moiré pattern of reflected light shift across its surface. Touching the control, he waited for the thin tube to extrude. He knew he should not drink any more, but clear thought was beyond him now, and he sought escape from the inexorable shadows of the past.

Out in the center of the room, Brandon was bombarded with all the questions his auditors had saved up. For a time he fielded some of these, and at last he held up a hand. Presently silence fell, and his gaze moved from one face to another around the circle as he said, "I don't know what Eusabian plans for the future. My own plan I will tell you. I want to find myself a fleet of daring ships and make a raid against Gehenna to rescue my father."

On the last word he looked squarely at Vi'ya, laughing challenge in his smile.

She returned his gaze with unwinking coolness as around them pandemonium broke out. The Changs cheered, laughed, and several drunkenly swore to join any expedition that Brandon cared to lead. Granny Chang sat quietly until the furor had died down some, and then the old woman leaned toward Brandon, involving him in earnest conversation.

Vi'ya leaned forward to spear a piece of food, as though nothing had happened. But beyond her, Osri caught a glimpse of Lokri amid his decorative young audience. As they chattered and laughed unaware, Lokri's pale eyes watched Brandon, his mouth thinned in a trace of a smile.

"Here. Catch this!" Someone called to Lokri, and he spun away, lost in his group as they brought out a smoke-pot and started some pungent incense.

After this, what? Brandon could make theatrical statements, but that didn't mean he really would lead a fleet anywhere, any more than these people would remember their vows past the hour their livers had processed what they'd drunk.

Granny leaned back and made a signal. Hard-beating music started up. Here and there people began strapping on reaction modules to join the dancers. Osri remained, sipping his bulb of wine as around him moods metamorphosed into a different kind of appetite. Lokri disappeared with two or three of the Changs, glancing back once at Brandon before he vanished into a shadowy alcove beyond one of the balconies. Then Montrose's voice rose in expostulation as Ivard launched himself clumsily towards the dancers.

"Marim," Ivard called. His misjudged leap set him rotating so that he didn't see Marim roll her eyes as she pulled Ivard into another of the alcoves. She didn't want to find that coin for Ivard. She wanted it for herself.

At Osri's right, his father had fallen gently asleep. Montrose made a low-voiced comment to Vi'ya and left. Now only Brandon and Vi'ya remained: Brandon talking to Granny Chang and a cluster of her descendants, and Vi'ya watching, silent and cool. As Brandon gestured, a glint on his hand brought Osri's attention to the ring he still wore: Tanri Faseult's ring.

"I hope your honor and duty will always be so simple to define, and to follow," Brandon had said during the argument in their cabin.

He is forsworn. . . Osri shook his head. A mistake to drink so much —

"Would you like anything more, genz?" a mellow voice near Osri's ear.

He turned his head to find a Chang smiling at him. She was his own age, and roughly his height. Her mouth entranced him as it curved invitingly.

"No." He struggled to make his numb tongue work. A tug of attraction heated deep in his belly, followed promptly by alarm.

"Some shakrian to release tension?" she offered.

He tried to decline, but she was already behind him, her fingers kneading his shoulders. Little zings of release sang along his nerves.

He shut his eyes, wavering between what he perceived as his duty to keep his distance from Vi'ya's riffraff allies, and an enticement that grew increasingly persistent.

Under her steady ministrations the worrisome questions went away. And so, at last, did his inhibitions, the anger-forged iron control he had put between himself and the universe since childhood.

When she tugged him from his seat and slid her fingers down the front of his tunic in mute invitation, he forgot where he was, and among what kind of people, and buried his face gratefully in her scented cloud of hair.

FIVE

Marim sighed to signify publicly her regret that the crew was breaking up at last, but a real twinge of regret surprised her. It'd always been this way. Ever since the crèche. You get used to one gang, you work to the place you want, and then boom! All gone, and it's to be done all over again somewhere else.

Ivard's thin, feverish fingers stole into hers, clinging; on the other hand, sometimes it was a relief. She leaned her chin on the back of her pod and watched Vi'ya lock in the course. The shudder of the fiveskip engaging shivered in her viscera, and she turned her cheek, hiding a grin.

Rifthaven. She didn't have long to find that coin. The challenge merely added to the fun. And she needed the fun. She smothered another sigh as Ivard squeezed her fingers. Never again was she going to be anyone's first. He'd been hanging onto her ever since he woke up at Granny's, did a locate on his boswell, and found her at Red Mik's joyhouse. She kneed aside one of the damn dogs pressing against them both, and urged him to sit at his pod. "I'm right here," she said.

Ivard slumped down, and the two dogs arranged themselves near his pod, lying with their muzzles on their front paws. Ivard had them with him more and more; Montrose had said it was almost like he was trying to make a Kelly trinity with them, and dogs were by nature pack animals. A pack of three — four, when Brandon was with them.

Marim looked at the dogs' steady brown eyes, then away. Dogs were strange creatures. It often seemed like they were actually thinking.

Lokri sauntered in, last as always, and sat down at his console. Not last. Vi'ya was waiting, which meant Montrose would be coming too.

Jaim was already there at the back of the bridge, standing with his arms folded. Ah. So Vi'ya had worked out whatever came next with Jaim. Not good. It was like someone had taken the old, easy-going Jaim out of that skin, and inserted something made of dyplast and stone. Except that the hint of dyplast and stone had always been there when Jaim fought.

Montrose entered. Vi'ya gave that weird Dol'jharian nod that only came out when she was rasty, and Montrose stationed himself at the hatch.

Angry. She was angry. They were all angry. Montrose poured it into music and sarcasm. Lokri was like an electrical charge when he got in a mood—splash! Then it was gone. But Jaim and Vi'ya, when they got angry, they were *scary*.

"We shall go to Rifthaven," Vi'ya said. "The fiveskip needs retooling, and we can have it done better and faster at Furn's Refit than if we must do it ourselves. Lokri?"

Lokri looked up. "DataNet's full of horror stories, but no reference to the Arthelion raid or *Maiden's Dream*. Yet."

"Then the Dol'jharians don't know we got an Arkad?" Marim asked.

Lokri swept his hand over his board and sat back, the fingers of his good arm tense. "Maybe. There isn't a lot about the Dol'jharians, surprisingly, except reports of their atrocities. But this is what we need to remember, Hreem was at Charvann. He's surely heard about our raid on Arthelion by now. I think he'll have put the escaped Arkad together with us. And the first place he's gonna look for us since he blew our base away is Rifthaven."

"Hreem can't be coming after us," Marim interjected, looking from Lokri to Vi'ya. "He went to Malachronte, right?"

"Hreem can't go to Rifthaven." Jaim looked up from contemplation of the deck plates. "Sodality Adjudicates have some business waiting for him."

Marim laughed at the understatement.

Vi'ya said, "Even if the Arkad's part in the raid is known, it will take the news time to reach Hreem at Malachronte, and longer still for him to contact any agent of his at Rifthaven. We should finish our refit and depart well ahead of that."

Lokri shrugged, but his body revealed tension.

"We will stand off and contact Jucan first," Vi'ya said, indicating Jaim, who looked up briefly when his brother's name was mentioned. "If Eusabian has posted a reward for Omilov, that news will likely have arrived before us, but if we lock up the nicks for the duration of our stay, I believe our anonymity is protected."

Ivard's hand stole into Marim's again.

"Also this. You will want to go to the vendors to sell your share of the loot from the palace. You must be careful to sell only what is not so rare it can be recognized as from that collection. Those items will have to wait until another time. Montrose will identify what is safe to sell now."

"That goes for the Heart of Kronos?" asked Lokri, his voice challenging.

"It is not for sale," replied Vi'ya.

"But you're going to try to find out more about it. I doubt the old geezer has told you anything."

Marim sighed. Lokri could see how rasty Vi'ya was. Why was he pushing her so hard? Wasn't a broken arm enough?

"The Heart of Kronos is not your concern," said Vi'ya.

"Lokri. Let it rest," Montrose said.

Lokri shrugged again, a jerky motion unlike his usual grace.

When no one else spoke, Vi'ya went on, "What you all must now consider is your next destination."

She's bunking us out! Shock rang through Marim. And Lokri was first to sniff the trace. She considered the future beyond Rifthaven—and her fortune—for the first time, but she could not get past the stunning jac-blast that she wasn't choosing to leave, she was being tossed out. And Montrose and Jaim didn't seem surprised, which meant they *knew*. She shook her fingers free of Ivard's, and crossed her arms.

"We got to go to the other base." Ivard's voice rose anxiously. "And hide."

"We can't hide out at the other base," Marim said, barely hiding her irritation. "Hreem blew away *Sunflame*. What you want to bet he scanned the comp first?"

"Agreed," Vi'ya said. "The other base is nothing to us now."

Chill and challenge tingled through Marim. Rich at last — and nowhere to go!

Lokri smiled grimly. "Who says," he drawled, "that we have to do anything? What about the nicks?"

"They are mine," Vi'ya said. "I will dispose of them as I deem proper, in a way that will not lead our enemies to us."

Ivard had reached for Marim's hand again. She patted it, then recrossed her arms, her attention on Lokri and Vi'ya, wondering if Lokri heard the warning in that.

Montrose grunted. "Then you'll have to kill them. Anything else, anything at all, will lead our enemies right back to us."

"There is another alternative," Vi'ya said calmly. "You will be safe enough."

Lokri was silent; he'd heard the warning, all right.

Vi'ya went on, "I will leave Rifthaven as soon as the engines are refitted."

So they'd have maybe a week to find another bunkhole and get their stuff off this ship. Meant Marim had a week to get the gilt she wanted, then ditch her red-topped parasite here. She patted Ivard's hand again and smiled at his ugly, freckled, weak-eyed face.

And in the galley, Osri shut down the spy-eye he had found in stolen moments on the galley console. His hand went reflexively to his wrist, bare of boswell again after they left Granny Chang's. But what he'd heard didn't need recording to be seared into his memory.

The three Panarchists were crowded into the galley, with Lucifur winding in and around their legs, making his racheting purring noise, and one of those irritating dogs sitting at Brandon's feet, its tail thumping as Brandon reached down absently to toy with the animal's ears.

Osri's anger finally forced him to speak. "'Have to kill us.' I never supposed we could expect any better."

His father and Brandon exchanged one of those looks that had long irritated Osri.

"I think that was a request for information, and he seemed satisfied with the captain's answer," said Omilov. "These Rifters have been together for a long time, and are capable of subtlety as great as any Douloi."

Osri remembered his father's comment about the cachets he had found through the console. "Then you believe Montrose intended that conversation to be overheard?"

"I think he and Vi'ya play a deep game." Omilov shook his head. "I am more concerned about the captain's intent concerning the Heart of Kronos." He grunted as he levered himself to his feet. "In any case, I suppose I had better get back to the dispensary so we can avoid awkward questions." He left.

Brandon leaned on his forearms, staring into the console as if reading a hidden message there. Irritated by his silence, Osri returned to the chopping block and began to slice the vegetables that Montrose had laid out.

Perhaps the knife thudded more sharply than he'd meant it to, for Brandon blinked, his eyes distracted. "She knew we were listening, too," he said.

"You think she would have told them what she intends to do with us — and where — if we hadn't been listening?"

"No." Brandon picked up an onion and hefted it absently in his hand. "Not if they're disbanding. Protect everyone that way. In any case I think what happens next depends on what she finds out on Rifthaven."

Osri looked from Brandon's meditative smile to the onion bouncing gently on his palm. "The Heart of Kronos again."

Brandon's chin lifted in acknowledgment, then he stood up and stretched. "She didn't mention the Eya'a," he added.

Osri frowned, ready to dismiss this as irrelevant. But he controlled the urge, and scraped his chopped vegetables into the simmering sauce.

Brandon seemed to notice what he was doing for the first time. "That smells good," he said.

Osri snorted a wry laugh. "Unwilling and untalented, I seem to have acquired an amazing amount of Golgol chef skills —"

"Worthless." Montrose loomed, his teeth gleaming in his beard, his wide-spaced eyes amused. He'd entered with silent tread. "You know nothing at all. It takes years — *years* — to make an adequate chef. You are only right about your lack of talent."

"But what he's making smells as good as anything we got at home," Brandon said.

Montrose sighed theatrically, his shoulders slumping. "Must you say it in front of him?" He jerked a huge thumb in Osri's direction. "How will I keep him appropriately humble?"

Brandon laughed, and Osri shook his head, turning back to his chore. Brandon leaned over, dropped his onion, and expertly snagged a chocolate square. "All right. Come on, Gray. Lucifur. We're not wanted."

Osri fought back his impatience and returned to his preparation. Though he never would have chosen to learn anything about cooking, he hated doing any job badly, and he had to admit that the precision required in complicated cookery was the sort of challenge he found soothing.

Montrose observed his hands, his silence a measure of approval. At last he said, "This meal is for my guests in the dispensary, but you are also invited."

"Very well," Osri said, his mind still on Brandon's comment. She didn't mention the Eya'a? What had that meant?

Montrose went on with his cooking lessons, and Osri forced himself to be patient until at last the meal was finished enough for him to slip away. He found Brandon in their cabin, busy at the console.

"I have to ask you a question," Osri said. "What did you mean by the captain not mentioning the Eya'a? I don't see the connection between them and where she might go after Rifthaven."

"I think. . ." Brandon leaned back, waving at the console. "Take a look for yourself."

Osri stepped closer. Brandon had windowed up the Starfarer's Handbook entry on Ysqven V. The warning code for a quarantined planet was the first designation, and the brief information that followed made the place seem grim beyond human toleration. Puzzled, Osri scanned quickly past the listings of the seasons (deep winter and deeper winter) and of the many horrific plant and animal predators.

At the end of the entry was the header for indigenous sentients, and Osri was only partially enlightened with what he saw: a brief physical description of the Eya'a. Brandon was still waiting when Osri looked up in horror. "You don't think she'll force us to go *there*, do you?"

Brandon smiled. "I think she wants us — and them — to think so. He tipped his head toward the rest of the ship.

"But you don't?"

For answer, Brandon got up and hit the hatch lock. Then he sat back down at the console. "Watch," he said.

Osri leaned against the console inset, inches from where he had secreted the Tetradrachm and the flight ribbon, and waited while Brandon quickly navigated the ship's system. He hit several areas that required codes, and each time, Brandon went past, entering the code with a speed that revealed what he had been doing with much of his free time.

Then they were in a hidden area, where Brandon had stored chunks of info. Osri saw that the entire Starfarer's Handbook entry on Dol'jhar was listed there, along with the ship's log for the past several years.

"You broke into the system," Osri said.

Brandon didn't answer directly. "Markham designed the present system," he said. "And Vi'ya seems to have left it mostly intact. Knowing Markham as well as I had, it did not take me long to figure out his codes. I've found most of what I wanted."

Osri almost let that get by in his impatience for Brandon to get to his point, but this time he saw the point ahead of time, and pounced on a side issue that seemed more interesting: "Most?"

And it turned out to be the point, after all.

Brandon gave a wry smile. "She has apparently redesigned certain portions of the system that I can't crack."

Osri was about to observe that this was standard operating procedure, but Brandon was waiting expectantly, so Osri returned to the previous track. "What have you not found that you wanted?"

"Captain's log," Brandon said. "I found Markham's. I even found a file he'd started for me. . ." He broke off and shrugged.

"What was in it?"

"Observations he thought I might enjoy. Some proof of Semion's culpability in Markham's father's ruin. His meeting with Lenic Deralze on Rifthaven. None of it matters now."

"But you can't find the present captain's log."

"No."

"Are you sure there is one? Maybe Dol'jharians don't keep logs."

Brandon shrugged again. "I'm not sure. Except there are other things I can't access." He flicked a hand dismissively. "Now look at this."

He punched up the captain's log, scrolling it back to the beginning of Markham's career as the *Telvarna*'s captain. Osri watched as Brandon flicked through screen after screen of cryptic entries.

"Rifthaven again. . . Dis. Rifthaven. . ." Osri looked up.

"They seem to have ranged through different octants without any discernible pattern. What am I supposed to be seeing?"

"Any anomalies here?"

"Anomalies? For Rifters?" Osri said, but even as he said it, a third reference to Dol'jhar made him stop. "That?" He tapped the screen. And stared. "You don't think Markham—"

"No. Eusabian seems to have hired his Rifter allies right around the time Markham met Deralze. A couple years before Hreem killed Markham. And who knows, that could have been some of Hreem's motivation in cutting down competition." Brandon's mouth twisted. "These are raids, pure and simple."

"I still don't see the connection."

Brandon tapped his fingers against the console, then saved and stored the data. "Let's go find out if there is one."

Osri had never seen the captain's cabin. He followed Brandon the short distance around to the other side of the ship, expecting anything from sybaritic ostentation to savage displays of skulls and arcane weaponry.

When they entered, it was Brandon who stopped dead as if he'd walked into a force field, staring with manic eyes at the eerily real holographic display of the sequoia park in the Mandala. Osri's head buzzed; through it came the familiar trill of birdsong, birds Osri had only heard on Arthelion.

"Have I made any egregious errors?"

The cool voice belonged to the captain. Amusement blended with the Dol'jharian twist to the consonants, and amusement matching her tone exactly was in Brandon's reply, "It's too cold in here, the air should smell like loam and pine, and you should have the tianqi jack up the oxygen content." Brandon gestured. "Then you'll be close enough."

Instead, the captain hit a control and the familiar beauty of the forest vanished, to be replaced by the starkly plain walls of a cabin whose only decoration was a tapestry and a gemstone that Osri belatedly (and with a flash of anger) recognized as one from the Ivory Hall.

"You wanted to see me?" The captain sat at the console, which had been obscured by shadows in the holo.

Osri waited where he was by the hatch, but Brandon advanced into the cabin. "After Rifthaven," Brandon said.

Vi'ya said nothing.

Brandon had been right. She knew they were listening.

Brandon crossed the room, and touched a dark tapestry

whose subject was obscure, and from this distance unpleasant. "Sebastian won't last two hours there," he commented.

Vi'ya's chin jerked up.

Osri missed her answer because the meaning of Brandon's words impacted his brain like a missile. *Dol'jhar?* She wouldn't take them *there*. Would she?

Brandon smiled, crossing his arms and leaning against a bulkhead. "Might it be a test? Might it be. . ." He touched the discreet inlay above the console. "The same test he faced?"

He? Osri looked at the inlay, which was a tasteful evocation of the Archaeo-Moderne mode of 150 years ago. The ship was restored by Markham vlith-L'Ranja.

Markham. Tested? A pang of headache shot through Osri's temple, compounded by the frigid air, and he rubbed his head, but it did not dissipate the tension radiating from the two across the room.

Vi'ya stood up slowly and clasped her hands behind her back. "Eusabian of Dol'jhar is gone from the planet, and with him the worst of his nobles," she said. "I know places to hide where you will never be found."

"But you haven't answered my question," Brandon said lightly.

"It is an absurd question."

'Then you did test Markham," the Aerenarch retorted, still mild. "Because you've been testing me."

A pause. Osri's nerved panged again. "A game," Vi'ya said. "Like this."

She hit the control behind her, and they were pitched into a holo of space, with asteroids hurtling toward them. Osri barely had time to react from the shock when the scene altered, this time to the breathtaking beauty of a snow-topped peak on a mountain of black stone. A red dwarf sun was setting on the horizon, bathing the scene with a glory of reddish colors. The scene was followed by several in succession, each vastly different.

They were inside a gloomy, high-ceilinged cathedral vaguely familiar to Osri when Brandon reached across and tabbed the kill-pad. "I also know places where my enemies will never find us."

A muted chittering noise reached Osri then, scraping along his nerves: the Eya'a. Brandon glanced aside, his eyes distracted. Vi'ya did not react.

"Please let us go," Brandon said, so softly it was scarcely audible above the quiet hiss of the tianqi.

Vi'ya did not answer. Instead, she reached back and tabbed another key, and the room was replaced by a bleak landscape, with smoldering volcanoes in the distance, and overhead a storm-torn sky.

Brandon walked out. Osri followed, glad to turn his back on Vi'ya and her grim landscape, which he guessed was Dol'jhar.

Back in their cabin Brandon slammed his fist lightly on the console again, bringing it to life. Tapping rapidly, he straightened up, then stood looking down the display, rubbing his thumb along his jawline.

Osri, looking past him, saw that the hidden files were gone. His chest ached with a sudden hollow sense. Was that a threat? He hated this sense of powerlessness, especially under the command of a lawless Rifter who was also a Dol'jharian and a tempath.

Brandon dropped into the chair and laughed.

The comm beeped. Osri touched it with sweaty fingers.

"We're waiting for you, Schoolboy," came Montrose's familiar grating voice. "You don't want your father to eat congealed chzchz, do you?"

"Never," Osri said hoarsely. And with another look at Brandon, who sat with his head in his hands, still laughing, he went out.

An hour later, Sebastian Omilov leaned back, appraising his son's face as Ivard went on talking. ". . . and I always thought the Arkad dogs could only understand one language, that one they gave the commands in, on *The Invisibles*. But Gray and Trev understand me just fine when I. . . "

The supper that Montrose had presented to them was superlative, and the man had exerted himself to keep the conversation light and general. But he'd only been partially successful: Osri brooded in silence, speaking only when he had to.

Omilov sighed, wondering what to do. Montrose and Ivard talked on, the surgeon suggesting some chips on animal behavior as he handed out the next course.

Omilov roused himself to join the talk when it lapsed. His years of court enabled him to recall the last thing said, and to form a question along the same axis.

Ivard's thin face was flushed with fever and high spirits, and he participated willingly enough — when he didn't fall into reveries. Omilov would not have thought anything of these lapses, except Montrose's frown when he observed them.

Omilov left worries concerning Ivard to the surgeon. His own concern was with his son, who seemed to have left most of his self-righteous anger back at the asteroid — and replaced it with a much more serious turn of mind, indicated by the little gesture Osri had used to betray inner turmoil ever since he was a boy, an absent running of the inside of his index finger along the knuckles of his other hand. This gesture when Osri was small had presaged a gnawing of those same knuckles, often until they were raw. When Osri's mother had discovered this she had somehow ruthlessly eradicated the gnawing, but nervous rubbing remained.

At last the meal was over. Omilov had waited patiently for a graceful opening to get Osri alone, but his son avoided his gaze as well as his hints. Very well, patience, then. Osri would speak when he was ready.

"What shall it be, Sebastian?" Montrose asked as he stacked his plates into the cleanser. "A play, or perhaps a duel to the death?" Montrose offered, waving at the chessboard.

"Neither, thank you. While I was going through your catalog the other day, I chanced upon an opera I haven't heard for years: *The Tragic History of Macclom Singh.*"

The surgeon paused, then gave a thin, humorless smile. "I'm not surprised that it had fallen from favor. The late Aerenarch could hardly have found its message comforting."

Sadness washed through Omilov. Even Rifters recognized the danger that Gelasaar could not see.

"Very well, Sebastian, *Tragic History* it shall be. There may be a lesson in it for these times. Osri, does that suit you?"

"Thank you," he replied with slightly absent politeness, "but I think I'll retire."

"My son has never developed a taste for opera," Omilov said. "Perhaps we can save it for another time."

"No, Father. I really do want to retire," Osri said, and was gone without a glance. Yes, best to wait.

Montrose tapped at the console. The lights dimmed as the far wall of the dispensary wavered and vanished, dissolving to a panoramic starfield. The view panned down, and a planet in flames rolled into view as the massive, sorrowful grandeur of Tamilski's overture filled the room. Vellicor, still a dead world after six hundred years. How many had joined it in the past weeks?

Then Omilov lost himself in the story of the Praerogate Singh, who, in contravention of his oath, delivered the Anathema of the High Phanist Gabriel to the Faceless One following the Vellicor Atrocity. Singh's dramatic renunciation of fealty and suicide immediately thereafter isolated that Panarch from his supporters and led directly to his deposition and death.

Shortly into the first act, the trumpets blazed forth with a fanfare based on the Singh leitmotif.

Ivard made a noise, and Montrose stilled the chip with a wave of his hand.

"Are you all right, Ivard?"

Montrose really was worried, Omilov observed.

"Uh, yes. Sorry. I guess I got to dreaming, and then I heard this music, and I thought—" Ivard blinked up at the holo. "That's the Praerogate Singh!"

It was Omilov's turn to be surprised. "You know Tamilski's *Tragic History*?" Except for the interminable waltzes that Montrose played when the boy thrashed with nightmares, Ivard had never demonstrated any interest in the music in Montrose's library that Omilov had seen.

"Tamilski? No, but Singh was one of the most famous Invisibles, and I really like. . ." He hunched up.

Montrose laughed, evidently understanding what was going on. "Talk, Firehead."

Ivard looked askance at Omilov, as if expecting mockery or disdain. "I really like *The Invisibles*. I've collected almost a hundred volumes." He grinned. "With the loot from the palace I might even be able to get an original Volume One. It was made in 248, over seven hundred years ago."

Osri was right, they really had looted the palace. Well, under the circumstances, there was certainly no one to denounce them—except perhaps the conquerers.

The gnostor said, "You've mentioned this 'Invisibles' once or twice before, but I must confess my lack of familiarity."

"It's a serial chip." Ivard looked amazed at Omilov's ignorance, and motioned at the screen. "That music is just like the music on the chips. Didn't you watch it when you were a boy?"

"A serial chip that's been going for over seven hundred years?" Omilov laughed in delight at the inadvertent implication that he'd been a boy seven centuries ago. He was beginning to feel that old, at times. "It must have something to recommend it, then. Certainly, their choice of music couldn't be bettered. But alas, my boyhood interests lay in other directions."

"Sgatshi, it's good!" Ivard exclaimed. "The others laugh at me about it, sometimes, but Greywing, she said—" He broke off, his eyes wide and shocked.

To distract Ivard, Omilov said, "I would certainly like to see some of your serial chips someday soon, Ivard. I've never developed a taste for them, but that is more likely a flaw in my character than a flaw in the art form."

Ivard winced, and rubbed his eyes as though trying to banish grief. Then he looked up doubtfully. "Really?"

Omilov wondered if he presented so fearsome an aura, freighted with the complex associations inculcated by Archetype and Ritual into the popular view of the Ranks of Service.

"Really. You have one about Singh?"

"Oh, yes, that's one of the best."

"Perhaps you'd enjoy seeing part of this opera, then. Then I could view your chip, and we could see how the two types of art treat the story."

"Uh, sure. D'ya mind if I ask questions?"

"Not at all."

Montrose reached to start the playback again, then paused as Ivard spoke again. "Um, I've got a question, but not about the opera." He leaned forward, all knotty elbows and knees. "Brandon told me you're a Chival, so that means you did the nickstrut in the Mandala."

Omilov smiled. Strut. An apt description for many at Court. "Yes, I did, for a time."

"Did you ever meet a Praerogate?"

He stifled another laugh: every day, in the mirror. That brought the chill of melancholy. Did it have any meaning now? The knowledge that he could, if confronted with real evil, speak with the full authority of the absolute ruler of the Thousand Suns, wielding the high and low justice alike with none to gainsay him, had been a deep, if rarely considered, comfort to him. Now that comfort was gone.

"Well, Ivard, there's a problem with answering that. You never really know until afterward. Of course, I've known some Praerogates Overt, after they revealed themselves to put right a malignant situation, but I had never known any of those while they were still Occult. So, to answer what I think is perhaps your real question, there doesn't seem to be anything to distinguish a Praerogate Occult from any other person."

"So, it's just like *The Invisibles*. The evil blunge-suckers can't tell until it's too late!"

"Exactly. Shall we proceed?"

Receiving Ivard's assent, he settled back in his chair as Montrose resumed the playback. From time to time during the opera he observed Ivard, who was at first restless, until the music gradually drew him in. During the soaring Aria of Renunciation near the climax, Omilov was astonished, and pleased, to see the luminosity of unshed tears in Ivard's eyes. He felt an answering sting in his own, and, remembering what Osri had told him about Ivard's background, reflected sadly that there was no place for this ardent spirit in the ordered world of the Panarchy, save in unskilled labor. At least on Natsu.

For the first time Omilov began to really understand the large and unacknowledged part the Rifter overculture played in the life of the Thousand Suns. But now it was too late. The ordered culture of the Panarchy had rejected them, and the Rifter culture had become a tool in the hands of the Panarchy's worst enemy.

In the holo Macclom Singh lay dying before the Emerald Throne. On the throne, the Faceless One — played, as always, by an actor in a shimmermask, that nothing might lend that abhorred figure even the semblance of a face and therefore anamnesis — slumped hopelessly as the realization of defeat gripped him. Ivard was leaning forward in his seat, completely lost in the action, his countenance shining with the mix of exaltation and sorrow that good tragedy brings.

Not all Rifters, Omilov decided. Ivard's spirit would not have survived association with anyone who would join Eusabian. For the first time, despite his unfortunate interview with the captain, he began to hope that they might yet win through to safety with the Heart of Kronos.

SIX

We fear, we fear.

I do not understand your fear.

We fear the dissolution of Telvarna-hive, for to Eya'a dissolution of a hive is cessation.

Again I repeat, cessation-of-a-hive for Eya'a is emendation for humans, just as emendation for Eya'a is cessation for humans. Each one from this polity you call a hive will go on to join other polities, and this we see as emendation. Again I repeat, Telvarna is not a true hive.

But Vi'ya is its world-mind, and the ones inside the metal hive with him are his hivemates.

I hear as Eya'a hear, but I am not a world-mind. Humans have no world-minds.

We fear.

Again I do not understand your fear.

The words we have celebrated carry images that change. And we fear, because we are approaching a great chaos that has no center.

We come to a human polity called Rifthaven. I hear your fear, and tell you to withdraw to your world-mind. Celebrate again the words you have learned, but also celebrate my own confusion. I ask again: is the world mind one hive or many?

Vi'ya sensed the withdrawal of the Eya'a, as they began the process of hibernation. She closed her eyes, breathing deeply. The contacts were easier every time she made them, but when they ended she could be thrown into vertigo if she was not careful.

She opened her eyes to discover Lucifur lying across her

bunk, eyes slitted. She touched him, checking his mind. He was hungry. She hit the hatch control. He leapt down and ran out, disappearing with a flick of his tail.

Then she passed into the Eya'a chamber. Already the temperature was dropping toward the freezing approximation of their upper-level caves where the hivemates hibernated.

She found them, each curled up and wrapped in a silken cocoon made of fine-spun metals. Staring at the small, still bodies, she wondered why they had not answered her question about their world-mind. Hereto they had always referred to it as a single entity, as if there were only one.

She had envisioned this world-mind as being a type of sentient DataNet, connecting everyone across their world. What she had not been clear on was the precise function of the male of each hive, outside of the obvious procreative one: she knew that they did not move, did not speak, and were cared for by the females.

In fact, it was the reverse of the hive patterns familiar to Earth-descended biologies, the queens and drones. But the Eya'a had been definite about the pronouns: they themselves were females, would bear females in time, except maybe one of them would be selected to bear a male, an experience — as much as she could gather — much valued, though apparently the female did not live beyond the birth.

Vi'ya frowned down at the curled forms, remembering how they had given her a male pronoun — the first time they had ever done so. They defined her function as captain in terms of directing the fates of the others, and listening to them on the mental plane. That argued a similar function for their males.

Were the Eya'a males the center of each hive world-mind? This would mean. . .

Competition between hives. Which would suggest that the mission of her two was to carry back information meant to give their hive some kind of edge.

Interesting. This would bear further examination.

She checked the bank of mosses that they grew for sustenance, and saw that all was well. The ship's computer now ran the bio-tank she'd designed for them. She reflected on their inability to interface with the computer on their own. As one would expect from a race of telepaths, they had no written language. And the humans confounded them yet again with their quasi-religious ban on machines with artificial intelligence.

Amusement at the dichotomies that made each race incomprehensible to the other flickered through her mind as she ran her fingers over one of the gossamer-thin weavings they were making. She recognized the stylized shape of the *Telvarna* in it, and intertwined figures that might be humans, but the fires and other symbols she saw were impossible to decode.

She looked around, her skin thickening as the temperature dropped. She could already see her breath, a white cloud that froze in tiny droplets and fell before dissolving.

Time to go.

Time.

She walked out, checking her boswell link to the bridge. Emergence soon, at which time she had a sequence of events planned out. Until then, she just had — time.

She unlocked the wall cabinet, and pulled out the drawer into which she'd set the Heart of Kronos. She grasped it firmly, ignoring the nauseating side effects of its inertialessness. She'd thought to occupy this time with the Eya'a in a last attempt to unlock the mystery of the thing, but the exercise would be useless. They had established as much as they were able that this weapon was missing an integral part. She dropped it into her pouch, wincing at the strange feeling.

Time.

Now would have been the moment to be planning the next run with the crew, but the next run had to be solo, except for the Eya'a, and her three prisoners: the navigator, whom she could force to work, the old man who knew something about the Heart of Kronos that he would not tell her, and Brandon nyr-Arkad — no, he was vlith-Arkad now, wasn't he? Markham had said those words so often: Brandon nyr-Arkad.

She permitted the memories. *"Brandy said. . ."*

". . . Brandon nyr-Arkad and I planned a. . . "

She'd assumed that Brandon Arkad was the satellite to Markham's sun, and she believed that Markham thought so as well. But the truth? She smiled at the tapestry. The truth didn't matter. What did was that she could use this Arkad sun to torch her homeland.

It was a plan, which was better than no plan, or —

"Regret is an illusion," Markham had said so grandly.

Regret was also one of the emotions she called the hiltless knives. To desire that an action had never taken place — it seemed merely a futile line of thought, and yet it engendered powerful reaction, acknowledged or not. She'd never seen it before she met Markham, and she'd been fascinated at how it shadowed his mind in unexpected moments of repose, despite his airy declaration.

They had talked much about reactions and emotions, how they could vary to such extremes, as her own background demonstrated when compared to his upbringing. Vi'ya remembered trying so hard to understand Markham's view of the universe that she still heard his voice whispering to her, unless she consciously shut it out.

Enough. She left to wait on the bridge for emergence from fiveskip. She had told Lokri that she would handle the communication with Jaim's brother herself, the better to sift his words for the reality of Rifthaven in this new era.

MBWA KALI: BLOODCLOT SYSTEM

Nukiel didn't know the woman: perhaps eighty years of age, short, stout, with an open, intelligent face. She was dressed in a costume he didn't recognize, comprised of a long-sleeved black robe with a stiff, upstanding white collar, buttoned from her neck to the hem. He wondered momentarily how long it took her to put it on.

He did know he was dreaming, and so, with a sort of good-humored superiority born of that knowledge, he said to the dream woman, "So where am I, and who are you?"

"This is Desrien," she replied, "and you are summoned."

Mandros Nukiel opened his eyes and sat up. He laughed, a short, humorless bark, and swung his feet out of bed onto the deck. A dim light sprang into being in response to his movement, leaving most of his cabin obscured in shadow. The only sound was a quiet murmur from the tianqi; a ghost of a breeze caressed his forehead.

He sat there with his hands dangling between his knees. Perhaps the dream was not so surprising. Certainly the duty he'd drawn would make virtually any change a welcome one. The *Mbwa Kali* was stationed just outside the resonance field generated by Rifthaven, poised to intercept ships leaving the Rifter habitat. They dared not attempt interception of incoming ships, for fear the absence of a scheduled arrival would alert

Rifthaven to their presence.

So far they'd pulled in nothing but riffraff, as ignorant of Eusabian's plans as any servant of the Panarch. And none of them had any inkling of the FTL comm. The only common thread was the gossip they all had picked up on Rifthaven about the ongoing disintegration of the Panarchy under the lash of Eusabian's revenge and the greed of his Rifter allies.

Mandros Nukiel groaned and ran his hands through his hair. It was agonizing, stuck out here in the middle of the Rift while everything that made his career meaningful was being destroyed. He'd dispatched a courier to Ares as soon as they'd taken up station here—assuming the Fleet center hadn't already been located and vaporized by Eusabian's forces. But it would be weeks before an answer came back. And that answer might well be to continue what he was already doing. Ng's orders—phrased with exquisite tact as a request—had been entirely sensible, but that didn't make them any easier to follow.

He tabbed up the tianqi settings. Just as he thought, the Telos-damned thing had slipped into a Downsider mode again. It was in the spring rain cycle, with increasing ionization, falling barometric pressure, and variable breezes, but everything was exaggerated compared to the gentler cycles enforced on a Highdwelling. He slapped at the keys and reset the tianqi to Highdweller mode.

Then he tapped another few keys, calling up the duty roster for the Environmental Section. Chemiltut, eh? Well, he'd swing the man's ass over the radiants tomorrow; for now, back to the Z-watch. And no more dream nonsense.

He was asleep as soon as his head hit the pillow.

It was a spring afternoon on Sync Ferenzi. Up near the spin axis the sun-glow had nearly reached the southern extreme of its track along the diffuser. From his vantage point in Criana triant, Nukiel could see the far north of the Laeteria triant, arching into the sky 120 degrees spinwise from where he stood, dimming into evening. Mellifera triant was masked by clouds, their tops bent into the familiar hook-shape imposed by the rotation of the habitat.

With him were some other people. He didn't recognize them. One was a slim young man whose back was turned, but whose stance marked him out as High Douloi; another was an atavism, with pale skin and blazing red hair. Two were nonhumans whose appearance disturbed him deeply, but he didn't know why. The others were unremarkable. They stood at the edge of the Commons, the vast expanse of grass and wildflowers that every three years hosted the Great Hum. No one said anything: each seemed absorbed in thought.

Nukiel stretched, reveling in the heady scent from the orange grove at the nearest edge of the grassy sward. It was good to be home. He looked south, where the mists of the Arctiel rainforest billowed at the base of the rainbow-feathered waterfall spiraling down the face of the end-cap from its source near the spin axis. He smiled. Downsiders could never understand why Highdwellers thought planetary waterfalls so boring, until they saw what the rotation of a sync did to water.

There was a distant rumble. Nukiel frowned. Then, as he looked around, an impossibly loud blast of sound, melodious and yet agonizing, knocked him to his knees. He clamped his hands over his ears, but it didn't help. The sound went on and on, battering at him until he thought it would burst his ribs and strip the flesh from his bones. Then it stopped, without an echo.

Nausea seized him, disorientation, and then terror as he realized that he was in free-fall. He clutched at the tough grasses, but his grip failed and his flailing fear propelled him into the air. His gaze swept across the southern end-cap. The waterfall was straight. Impossibly, the rotation of Ferenzi had stopped in an instant, yet the sync was intact.

Then the sun-glow flared and guttered to extinction, leaving the habitat in gloomy darkness, illuminated only by a sourceless light too dim for colors. Nukiel stared, his breath catching in his throat, as the fog along the edge of the Commons mutated into glowing human forms, forms he recognized: his dead father, his tutor from first-school, crushed in a transit accident, and others as they drifted up and up, to the spin axis and then beyond. Many he did not know, but from their expressions, the other, living people with him seemed to.

The dead paid him and the others no attention, gazing instead intently into the darkened sky, toward the spin axis invisible four and a half kilometers overhead.

"... from light to light transformed. . ." Where had he heard that? Light burst in on him, haloing the dead rising through the air, as the surface of Ferenzi peeled back and unrolled like a scroll in the hands of an angry god. A violent wind sprang up, hurrying them along like the leaves of a dying tree toward the bright limb of an immense planet looming too near. It was not Ferenzi's primary, Munenzera, but another, and Nukiel thought to recognize it just as it melted into the face of a woman, her eyes flaring with internal light, her gray hair standing straight out from her head in a lightning-laced corona. She held up her hand and a searing red light blazed from its palm.

Nukiel shrieked. It was the Goddess, come in Her aspect of the Destroyer!

"This is Desrien, and you are summoned," she said.

Nukiel fell out of bed and awoke tangled in his bedclothes, his terrified shout still echoing in his cabin. The lights sprang on, but he lay still, trying to get his breathing under control. He had the dizzying sense of having awakened to a world less real than the one he had just experienced, a feeling that, try as he might, he could not shake.

He pulled himself to his feet and sat down on the edge of the bed, his head in his hands. Long ago a gnostor at the Academy had lectured on the spiritual aspects of warfare. What had he said?

"One of the worst mistakes of the ancients was their belief that the subjective is the unreal, that only the objective has true existence. Do not make this mistake—it will destroy you as surely as it destroyed them. . ."

Nukiel shook his head. How easy to hear that in the comfort of a lecture hall, and how hard now. How could he justify making a hejir in the midst of war? He shuddered. How could he avoid it? If he refused, what would the next dream entail? Whatever the answer, he wasn't sure he could face it. A court-martial would be a day at the spin axis by comparison.

He had an image of himself suspended in space, caught midway between the irresistible collision of two planetary masses, Duty and Desrien. The shape of each was palpable and immediate to his imagination: the shape of his entire life in the Navy, its traditions and its pride; and the looming mystery of the Magisterium, which once had even reached out to destroy a reigning Panarch.

And abruptly the masses balanced and canceled out, leaving only his will and the knowledge of an oath sworn and a life lived in loyalty.

Mandros Nukiel sighed and lay back on his bed, and the lights went out. After an unmeasured time his mind quieted, and sleep returned at last.

TELVARNA: BLOODCLOT SYSTEM

Marim passed the dispensary as Montrose said to Omilov, "I believe we're about to dock. Would you like to take a glance at Rifthaven, as seen from its best vantage?"

Everyone had converged on the bridge — everyone human, anyway. Marim did not see the Eya'a, the dogs had been secreted off the galley in one of Montrose's hidey-holes, and Luce was locked in the dispensary.

She laughed at the range of expressions on the nicks' faces as they stared at the viewscreen. Rifthaven looked like nothing so much as the worst multi-ship collision in the history of the Thousand Suns, a jumble of constructs of even wilder variety than the spacecraft they served.

Marim remembered her delight when she had first realized that some of its component parts *were* actual ships, haphazardly bolted, welded, webbed, and otherwise constrained together in a mishmash of metal and dyplast. Light shone from numerous viewports; radiants venting heat glowed dully here and there. A forest of antennae and a wild range of weaponry jutted from every surface.

"If this is its best vantage, what must it be like inside?" Omilov murmured.

"More confusing, of course," Marim said cheerfully, glancing past him at Osri, who stood close behind his father. His gaze met hers and then slid away. He had it on him — she was sure of it now. Annoyance made it hard to keep smiling, but she managed. That stupid stiff-ass nick was not going to cheat her out of what was rightfully hers, but she'd have to be careful.

She'd searched the entire ship, compartment by compartment, first anyplace Osri could have been, and then where he was not supposed to be. Nothing. She'd also watched him, and noted that he had taken care to be with either Brandon or his father, especially since the time they'd both been pulled into practice and she'd searched the cabin he shared with the Aerenarch. The sneaky blit had probably planted some kind of telltale that she'd missed.

But she wasn't defeated yet. As the others blabbered about

their first visits to Rifthaven, she faded out of Osri's periphery and eyed the close-fitting jumpsuit he wore. No pockets at all on the outside. He'd probably sewn the stuff against an inseam. Maybe his armpit. Couldn't pickpocket that even if her fingers were still hot.

She hid a laugh, thinking how bad her skills had gotten since the old days. Being around Markham and Vi'ya was a rotten influence. Nothing made you as slow as honesty.

Beyond the station loomed the red dwarf star — dubbed Bloodclot — that formed one third of the celestial triad that was Rifthaven. The other component, Bruise, was not visible. It was a brown dwarf, a gas giant nearly big enough to be a star, radiating in the low infrared. Rifthaven orbited in one of the trojan positions of the system, protected from skipmissile attack by an internal resonance generator that created one of the largest skip barriers in the Thousand Suns. Almost as safe as the nicks' secret base Ares, so Markham said, if less neat in appearance.

Omilov was frowning at the bewildering swirl of arriving and departing vessels of every imaginable size, shape, design, and function. Tiny tech craft drifted in and around the bigger ships, adding to the chaos. "Why are we approaching so slowly?" he asked.

Montrose spoke up. "Rigid speed limits imposed by the Defense Caucus. Closer you get, the slower you have to go," he said. "No warning shots, either: chase mines on automatic."

Omilov squinted, as if trying to force some sort of order on the visual confusion. Marim's gaze moved to the silent observers beside him.

Brandon scanned passing ships with an attitude of interest.

Osri had clearly forgotten her and looked fascinated. Interesting. She had expected his sniff-nose nick face.

"Oooh, look! Zhazrit's Instantiations is still there. So they didn't get flamed, after all, huh?" Ivard spoke up on Marim's other side. "Oh! I see a new subdeck, right in there where they used to have the free-fall kiting. . ."

Marim ignored him, knowing he'd never notice. Half the time now he talked back to weird voices that no one else heard anyway. She shivered, glad he wasn't touching her. Just as well he'd lost his desire to bunny, which saved her from having to bunk him out. He acted too much like he had a nasty disease.

Jaim stood at the back, his face blank. A trace of incense

clung to his clothing, sending a sense of unease through Marim. Why? It was just a smell, part of the smells and bells he'd been fooling with as long as she'd known him. But she'd never whiffed that particular scent.

Marim stole a look at Vi'ya, who was watching the screen dispassionately, alternating her attention between the stream of information on her console and the low-pitched chatter on the approach channel.

Lokri lounged at his console. That was so much as expected that Marim nearly missed the clues. It was his hands. No, they were loose, cradled around caf. Oh yes, it was his gaze. Not on the viewscreen, in spite of his occasional comment as Montrose and Ivard blabbed about Rifthaven. He was watching the Arkad.

Marim nearly jumped. Lokri was still on the hunt. With Rifthaven in sight?

Marim bit on her lip to control her laughter. *So* much trouble ahead, if she was right. . . She'd better be first off the ship.

"What'll you carry?" Marim ended the silence, looking around at them all. "I'll go break out the weapons."

Jaim twitched his boswelled wrist. "Just this." His voice was almost inaudible.

Brandon gave him a quick glance of concern. Marim could have told him not to worry: Jaim's mood wasn't suicidal, it was lethal. She made her voice and face casual before she dared to a look at Lokri. "You got your springblade, right? Anything else?"

Lokri shrugged slightly. "Wristknife. Hideout neurojac."

"Montrose, can I borrow your stenchgun?" Marim asked. "I'll bring it back before I bunk my stuff out."

"Be my guest," Montrose responded. "I have a number of things to do here before I seek another post."

Brandon looked from one to the next. "Back at Granny Chang's you said something about energy weapons on Rifthaven."

"Yup," said Marim. "One law on Rifthaven nobody crosses, no matter what," Marim said. "You can carry a firejac, but if you use it, you win a one-way trip out the nearest lock. Neurojacs are legal but they make people rasty when they jam everyone's boz'l for ten meters around, and people have been spaced for less."

Brandon nodded slowly. "I see the reason for the law here. One puncture and half this place would vent to space. But I thought there was no law enforcement of any kind on Rifthaven."

"Depends on where you are. Some of the mercantile pods are as safe as anyplace in the Panarchy, patrolled regularly by enforcers hired from Public Order. Crime's bad for business." Montrose said. "Others—" He shrugged.

"But anywhere, someone tabs their energy weapon and everybody around will help execute the rule," Marim put in. "Some people wear their hardware anyway, but I don't carry anything I can't use."

A gentle thud resonated through the ship and Vi'ya pulled her hands away from her console. "We're in."

The engines spun down into silence.

Lokri got up and said, "Arkad, you ever seen Rifthaven?"

Vi'ya said coolly, "As we discussed, he will not this time." She started shutting down systems, adding, "The Eya'a will guard the Panarchists."

Lokri got to his feet. "I think I could keep one renegade Arkad safe from the bites and the gouges." He leaned one arm against the wall, looking down at Vi'ya with an expression difficult to interpret. His voice was exactly as lazy and pleasant as always, but Marim's nerves sang with danger and again she smothered the urge to snicker. "A last gift."

Vi'ya said simply, "No."

Lokri was silent for a protracted moment, then he straightened up and shrugged, giving Brandon a humorous look. "Have fun with the vidchips."

Omilov started asking questions about docking rules, and Marim went out to the weapons locker. There, she found what she'd half expected: Vi'ya had locked down all of the weapons except those belonging to crewmembers.

Marim grabbed what she needed and skipped back to the bridge. There she handed out the armload of weaponry, noticing the nicks looking at the huge, ornately decorated and brightly colored projectile weapon thrust through her belt.

"What's that?" Brandon asked, pointing. "Looks vicious."

"It's supposed to," Marim said. "It won't kill anybody, but you'll wish you were dead if one of the stench capsules bursts on you. Not many argue with the prospect of twelve hours of retching."

Lokri saluted them silently with his knife and sauntered out, adjusting the wrist sheath under his loose sleeve. He'd secreted the tiny neurojac in a boot. And there was no sign of his cast.

Jaim said to Vi'ya, "I will return at seventeen hundred to oversee the work on the engines."

Montrose said, "Come along, Firehead. Let's get you along to al-Ibran's Chirurgicon."

Ivard wandered to the hatch, and peered down the corridor toward the dispensary. "Trev, Gray! You want to come with me? Montrose, I want Trev and Gray there. They can make sure Gray healed up."

"Gray is as healed as possible. Ivard, the dogs are too recognizable. We don't want anyone asking questions, so they must stay here. They will be comfortable until you get this thing off you." He touched the Kelly band on Ivard's wrist.

Marim shot one last, resentful glance at Osri before giving up. At least she had most of Ivard's stash. And when Ivard turned fever-bright eyes to Marim, she kissed the air near his head. "See you later," she said, as Montrose led him down the ramp. In another lifetime.

Vi'ya said to Omilov, "The three of you must stay in the dispensary until Montrose returns. Then your movements will be restricted to your cabins and the galley. Use whatever you wish from the library for entertainment."

"Thank you," Omilov said.

SEVEN

The bridge of the *Grozniy* was quiet, a subdued murmur of status reports the only sound. From under one console a pair of legs protruded. There was a flare of light and a muffled curse, then sudden silence as, Ng guessed, the technician recollected where she was. Ng suppressed an impulse to laugh. She'd made some adjustments, but it seemed her new alpha crew was adapting well to wartime status. The more things change —

The Siglnt console bleeped. At the same moment the fiveskip blipped. "Emergence pulse, ID working." Ensign Wychyrski's singsong was smooth, but in a higher range, betraying excitement. "ID Courier Two." A few seconds later the courier's laser found the *Grozniy*.

"Uplink established," reported Ammant at Communications.

Wychyrski maintained the antiphon in the familiar measured rhythm. "Squadron 235 located, *Falcomare* on the way, ETA — "

Both her console and the fiveskip interrupted her. "Emergence pulse, ID working. . . *Falcomare.*"

Again a slight delay, then Ensign Ammant reported. "Com incoming. Captain Metellus Hayashi."

"Put him on-screen."

Ng relaxed as a window blossomed on the main screen, revealing the broad face of Metellus Hayashi. His grin below the hawk-nose was piratical, his cheekbones like blades.

"Captain Ng! Welcome to Poseidonis system."

"Thank you, Captain Hayashi. That was quick."

"*Hainu* Squadron's been waiting for the Blister Patrol, although I hardly expected *Grozniy* to be it."

Ng burst out laughing, easing some of the tension of the past days. How I've missed you, beloved, she exclaimed within the confines of her skull — and thought she saw a similar thought in his smile.

"Showing up after the work is done," she said, aware of the stares of her crew. So he'd had his own encounter with Rifters! Behind her the aft hatch hissed open. "How I wish it were so, Captain," she continued, suddenly serious. "But I believe our work is just beginning."

His smile hardened. "Poseidonis Node was really happy to see us, given the initial rumors and reports incoming on the DataNet. Even more so when a gang of Rifters only a few hours behind us stormed into the inner system with a single ancient Alpha, like they'd never heard of the Navy."

"Any casualties?" asked Ng, as Commander Krajno slipped into his pod next to Rom-Sanchez.

Hayashi snorted. "Against Rifters?" If he'd intercepted the Rifters before they reached the planet and fired on the Shield, he might not even know about their cruiser-killing skipmissiles. If this contingent had even had them.

Hayashi then cocked his head as if receiving a boswelled communication, glanced down at his console, and then looked directly out of the screen at her, his eyes narrowing. "A scan of your aft beta turret makes it obvious that was no joke."

Before she could reply he straightened up in his pod and spoke formally. "Request permission to come on board, Captain."

"Please," she replied. "We have much to discuss."

A short time later in the captain's ready room, Lieutenant Rom-Sanchez watched as Metellus Hayashi strode to the wall with his hands clasped behind his back, then turned around. "This is making my head reel. Do you realize, we're sitting here talking about attacking Arthelion?" Rom-Sanchez was struck by how quickly Captain Hayashi had accepted the flood of new information delivered by Captain Ng and himself.

"I know," Ng replied. "I keep expecting lightning to come out of a bulkhead or something." She had shifted in her chair so she could watch Hayashi's peregrinations.

Rom-Sanchez struggled with the sourness in his stomach at the tenor of the interplay between the heavily muscled destroyer captain and Margot Ng. It was obvious that their relationship went back many years. He'd been stupid. There'd never been any hope for him. He tried to squash the profound weight of regret, balancing it against his professional gratitude for the speed their understanding was lending to the planning session so far.

"We can start the preliminary strategic and tactical work at tomorrow's meeting once Doial and Somsri get here," continued Ng, naming the other two destroyer captains in Hayashi's squadron. "I want to have a general structure ready for whatever forces we can find."

Then his captain's eyes turned to him, and Rom-Sanchez fought back a flush of embarrassment. Had she noticed anything? But Ng's manner was easy as she spoke: "Lieutenant Commander, what can you get me?"

"We've already dispatched courier flights that give us a good chance of bringing the *Joyeaux* and the *Babur Khan* to a rendezvous at Arthelion in the time you've allotted," he replied. "But neither Lieutenant Commander Nilotis nor I expect to discover any more, whether at the systems between here and Arthelion or from the intel couriers. The intelligence we got at Treymontaigne, fragmentary as it was, makes it certain that any ships inwards from here will already know about the attack, anyway. They'll either have been destroyed, are on their way to or already at Arthelion, or will have hit a tacponder with new orders from Ares."

"As may we," said Ng. "Has SigInt come up with any more data on Naval losses nearer the Mandala?"

"No, sir." He tapped his compad, windowing up a list of names on a wall display. "These are the ships unaccounted for that might already be at Arthelion, given their last known assignments."

Hayashi's mouth tightened as he waved a hand dismissively at the screen. "We can cross *Flammarion* off that list," he said. "At least we won't have Armenhaut to deal with."

"I put him down long ago," said Ng with a slight smile. "Are you still carrying him?"

Rom-Sanchez puzzled at the cryptic comment for a moment. He knew that Stygrid Armenhaut, one of Semion's

Downsider captains, had been stationed at Arthelion and was therefore almost certainly dead. But the look that passed between the two captains made it obvious that the exchange was freighted with many years of shared experience. He fought another surge of jealousy.

Ng's gaze was on him again. "Lieutenant Commander, I'd like you to consult with the three tactical heads in Captain Hayashi's squadron to arrange training sessions for the new Tenno."

Rom-Sanchez heard the dismissal in her voice and stood, gathering up his compad. "AyKay, sir."

As he tabbed the hatch open on his way out, Ng turned back to Metellus Hayashi.

"And I request the pleasure of your company at dinner tonight, Metellus, twenty-one-hundred. . . "

The hatch hissed shut across the remainder of her words, and Rom-Sanchez clenched his teeth against expressing the mix of frustration and amusement at his captain's subtlety. She saw, all right. She knew — and she let him down easy.

Then he shrugged and walked away. He had work to do. And then he needed a drink.

Margot Ng woke up first, and rejoiced.

Metellus lay asleep beside her, his breathing deep and slow.

She lifted her head so she could memorize the contours of his face, noting new lines, new gray in his temples. The signs of age made him that much dearer, and she fought the overwhelming urge to kiss him awake again.

How long had it been? Almost two years? It had been pure luck that had placed them on maneuvers in the same system then, giving them a chance to grab thirty-six hours together.

Sleep, my love, she thought tenderly. Telos knows how much rest we'll get when we reach Arthelion. A grimmer thought — of the sleep eternal — inevitably followed, but that was the risk they lived with in the life they'd chosen.

Still her hand reached convulsively to touch his bare chest above the sheet, to feel the warmth of his flesh and the steady lump-lump of his heart beneath the smooth muscles.

His eyes opened, instantly alert. The lines at the corners of his mouth deepened. "What's this? Want more? You'd think we haven't had any for two years."

Laughter and tears both tried to claim her — the lingering effects of the Augment session, her mind insisted — and Hayashi reached for her.

"What?"

She buried her face in the hollow of his throat, and then trailed her fingers through the soft curls of hair on his chest. He stroked her back gently, saying nothing further.

After a blissful interval, she rolled over and sat up facing him, clasping her hands around her knees. Hayashi propped himself up on an elbow and returned her gaze. "You're wondering about what we'll find at Arthelion," he said.

"Yes. Or maybe no. I don't have high hopes." She hesitated. "I was unfair to you earlier, love. I'm still carrying Armenhaut, too. Not so much the man as the type, Tetrad Centrum-connected highborns, who never learned the difference between a sim and real action. It must have made the Rifters' job a lot easier."

The corners of his mouth deepened. "No doubt. Armenhaut's tailor wouldn't have been much help fighting the ship." He mimed an officer admiring the cut of his sleeve with a lazy motion of one powerful arm.

Ng chuckled, her mood lifting. "You shouldn't have laughed in his face."

"I didn't laugh. Maybe a little snort. But Margot, you better than most know how he weighted fitreps."

"Presentation."

"You know what that meant. He basically awarded promotion based on an officer's wardrobe."

"You should have found a better tailor." She grinned as her eyes strayed down his body. "Though covering up *that* is rather a shame."

Metellus gave her a smacking kiss. "If I'd wanted to be captain of a battleblimp, I would have." Another kiss. "But my deep-laid plot worked out, and I got my destroyer squadron in the end." He laughed like a serial-chip villain, then began trailing kisses from her chin down her throat. "Why are we talking politics?" Her collarbones. "You hate politics, and we always end up at the same place anyway: the entire system is rotten but we're sworn to defend it."

Ng's head panged with the ghost of a migraine, and she

pulled away a little, the better to search his eyes. She hated the emotional lability left behind by the Augment session. It felt like a betrayal.

"But politics is the reason why we probably won't find any help waiting for us," she replied. "Armenhaut and his peers weren't good enough for the Aerenarch's private force at Narbon. They were stuffed uniforms on parade around the Mandala, promoted solely on who their families were, and how good they looked."

Metellus tapped her palm, his naval ring glittering on his finger. "Harimoto was no stuffed uniform. I expect Koestler did very little better at Narbon when it fell."

Ng took his hand, turning his naval ring around and around with her fingers. "You know what I mean. It's not just Semion's obvious preference for the High Douloi scions of Downsider Tetrad Centrum Families that I objected to."

"No matter where human beings go they rank themselves." He shrugged. "You know that. I know that. Everyone knows that."

"I understand the value of the sense of continuity that the Douloi confer on Thousand Suns society. I have nothing to say to purely social organization, but the military must, *must* be promoted on merit. Yet there were too many mysteries like the vlith-L'Ranja boy."

Metellus leaned back. "That again. Margot, he hankered after privilege just like everyone else. He just picked the wrong ranker to follow. Everyone knows the youngest Krysarch was a drunk. Lazy. Expecting everyone to bend the rules because he was an Arkad. And one day he went too far. Though I didn't like Aerenarch Semion, and some of the rumors about his training practices make my blood run cold, you have to admit he at least obeyed the rules. It can't have been pleasant to cashier his own brother, when everyone knew how important Arkad prestige was to him."

"That's just it. I don't believe any of it. You didn't meet young Markham, but remember, he spent that entire summer under my command when I was Ops Officer aboard the *Arius*. If he was such a nacker-kisser after privilege, then why was he first on line no matter what I assigned, first in every single sim I gave them, first to volunteer even if he'd just come off two watches of maintenance duty?"

"I remember, I remember. But it's a moot point now;

wherever he is now, he's no longer one of ours."

"Ours. What does that even mean, now? If we do win, will there even be a government for us to protect?"

Metellus lay back and stared at the ceiling, his forehead creased. "I don't know," he admitted. "If those Rifters were right and the Panarch lives, then change might not run deep. People embrace the old systems, historically, if enough of it exists after a war. Better the tame demon you know than the wild demons of chaos—and I have to say, old Gelasaar easily ranks above most of his distinguished forebears."

"But even Gelasaar's reputation is unlikely to survive a disaster of this scale. Can he impose a new succession? And.. . if he's dead?"

Metellus shook his head and said nothing.

"Are we going to end up with a military dictatorship, run by Semion's admirals?"

He didn't answer. She hadn't expected him to. This was the biggest problem of all: there was no escape from politics if you began to think beyond the next battle.

He toyed with her hand, his gaze abstract.

"Have you heard from Alys?" she asked carefully.

He smiled. "You mean, do I know if she's alive? No, I don't."

She sighed. Time was when she'd felt ambivalent about the austere woman Metellus had had to marry eighteen years before. A decade older than they were, Alys ban-Kerrimac had been philosophical about accepting his relationship with Ng as part of her marriage with the Hayashi dynasty. At that time Ng was still struggling to understand the Douloi attitudes toward marriage, love, and family; there had been moments when it had seemed she could make more sense out of the Shiidra than these old families with their carefully-modulated voices and poised bodies.

But she'd come to know Alys over the years, to understand her as much as their different backgrounds and interests allowed, and even to like her. "I hope she's safe," Ng said, her fingers tightening on Metellus's.

"Alys is a canny one," he said. "She has ears with ears. My guess is she would have had enough warning to get out. And the Shiidra strikes are still recent enough that evacuation plans were kept up-to-date."

"This war is going to hurt business," she said, tracing

patterns on his palms.

"It will hurt everything," he said. Adding fiercely, "I'm glad it is us who will be fighting at Arthelion. Though I know we can't win."

"We will win," she said, smiling. "Even if we all get blown to hell, as long as one of our couriers gets a hyperwave to Ares, we win." She glanced again at the chrono and sighed. "Hadn't we better—"

Instead of freeing her hand he gripped it and pulled her over on to him, his mouth seeking hers fiercely.

She reveled in the ready flare of desire and then reluctantly pulled away. "We have to meet them in thirty minutes. . . "

"Margot," he breathed, his palms on either side of her face, his eyes steady and smiling. "That means we have *thirty minutes*."

She laughed.

RIFTHAVEN

Montrose guided Ivard into the Chirurgicon, which was crammed, as always, with a variety of raffish individuals, most of whom had suffered recent wounds, and here and there a soberly-dressed trader whose distant travels advertised themselves in more arcane conditions. Montrose steered Ivard well away from a man obviously suffering from Dyrjwarsian Nose-fungus. Ivard glanced back several times at the colorful parasite squirming on his face. Montrose caught a nasty tang in the air and decided that the woman sitting alone in a corner with the empty seats around her must have come down with Mirkwudi Stenchrot. Those were two of the more common symptoms of human interface with totally alien biology, and he smiled as he thought of the equally arcane cures that made them both popular forms of revenge.

A tremor in the bony wrist under his grip meant that Ivard was shivering again. He'd counseled him to keep his sleeve over the Kelly band. Ivard had acquiesced without argument, just as he had with the dogs. This disturbed Montrose. Usually Ivard queried everything, showing what Montrose considered a healthy interest in what was going on around him (as well as an adolescent distrust of anyone's skills besides his own). Lately, though, he seemed more interested in whatever crazy fumes the damned Kelly band was pumping through his brain, behaving with such docility it worried him even more than the continual light fever he ran now.

"May I help you, genz?" came the melodious voice of the Szefteli healer who worked with the Chirurgicon's doctors.

Montrose pointed at Ivard's shoulder cast. "Burn. Want Atropos-Clotho-Lakisus to look at it."

The Szefteli blinked her golden eyes. "Threy are in the midst of a long gene-repair process. Perhaps you would like to have a burn specialist on al-Ibran's staff see it?"

Montrose knew that mere burns did not warrant the attention of the Kelly trinity, who usually worked with more exotic problems.

"He was exposed to some type of, ah, parasite, before we were able to get to him," Montrose said quickly. "I brought such a case to Atropos-Clotho-Lakisus before, and threy said to consult threm first if it ever came up again."

She nodded. "There will be a wait," she warned. "What is the parasite? And your name?"

Montrose hesitated. Here was where he had to be careful. He and the Kelly physician did know one another, but there had been no such interaction between them.

"Tell threm Hendyln," Montrose said, naming a very obscure Kelly disease he had once read about. "And Montrose."

"Hendyln," the Szefteli murmured, looking puzzled. "I've never heard of a human with it."

"Now you have. But I hope Ivard won't for long."

She bowed, accepting the hint with a slightly pained air, and withdrew.

Within a very short space of time another staff member appeared. "Montrose?" he called. "Montrose."

Montrose touched Ivard, who had fallen into a reverie while slumped against his side. He jolted awake and tried to rise, then staggered, wincing as though dizzy. One of his hands fluttered spasmodically.

Supporting the boy's slight body, Montrose followed the man through a narrow warren of corridors in what had once been a luxury yacht and a prefab naval medical lab now welded together.

They reached a huge cabin partitioned into cubicles. The tianqi spread a cool, slightly astringent scent through the air. Ivard sniffed and straightened up, his eyes as wide as if he'd received a stimshot.

"Who's there?" Ivard said. "I smell —" He broke off, blinking in confusion. Montrose's gut churned queasily.

A green Kelly trinity danced into the wide chamber, fluting and blatting. "Montrose, what is this? Hendyln is impossible for humans to —"

Montrose had wondered how Atropos-Clotho-Lakisus would react to Ivard's band, but he never expected what he saw. The two tall Kelly, Clotho and Lakisus, stiffened, their headstalks writhing wildly. Atropos, the Intermittor of the trinity, emitted a low, weird hum, and then all three swarmed toward Ivard, who quivered, his nose twitching. He swallowed convulsively, then licked his lips again and again as the Intermittor ran its head-stalk up and down his body while the other two patted his head and shoulders and moaned in polyphonic discord.

Montrose watched in astonishment.

As the Intermittor's headstalk reached his wrist Ivard's eyes closed and without warning he crumpled, but the two tall Kelly bore him up gently, carrying him into one of their cubicles.

Atropos blatted reedily, "The Archon. Wethree thought threir phratry dead forever, but threy live, in this Ivard."

The Archon of the Kelly? Montrose whistled, long and low. No wonder the Kelly were so excited: according to his datachip on the Kelly, the Archon's ribbons carried racial memories reaching back to the very beginnings of Kelly sentience.

"Threy live, but for how long?" Montrose grated. "His body is trying to adapt, and it's killing him."

The Intermittor bowed, tapping Montrose lightly on face and arm. "So it is, so it is, and wethree can do nothing without killing the Archon's phratry. But there is somethree who can help you."

"Here?" Montrose sustained a surprising surge of hope.

"No." Clotho and Lakisus returned and the Kelly twittered and blatted, then Atropos said, "Who have you told of this?"

"Only my shipmates know about the band, and no one knows whose it was."

"It is a charge," the Kelly said. "A sacred charge. Wethree will help him as far as we can, and we will protect you as far as we can, if you will convey him to Portus-Dartinus-Atos, whose subphratry can incubate the Archon's genomes."

"If I can," Montrose warned. "Where?"

"We do not know, but wethree will find out. Leave him here. He will be safe with usthree."

Montrose sighed, relieved despite his conviction that Vi'ya would not change her plans just to accommodate Ivard. Her mind was running on death and revenge, not on saving Kelly phratries.

But he'd try.

First he'd have to get back to the ship and find some of his own and Ivard's artifacts to sell, for Ivard would need money to pay his medical bill. And later—when he'd done everything Vi'ya asked—he would find the most expensive joyhouse in Rifthaven and sink mind and body into oblivion.

Most of the Syndics and their seconds were present when the door slid open and a short, bald man entered.

Lyska-si's stomach curdled.

Giffus Snurkel's age was impossible to guess. He favored long dangling earrings, and was robed like a devotionist Oblate. "*He wears the robes to gain respect,*" Lyska-si's mother had said.

He nodded greetings at the other Syndic chiefs and their seconds as he passed to the empty seat at Lyska's side.

Lyska-si knew that her mother detested Snurkel almost as much as she did, but disgust gave way to a sense of foreboding when Lyska-si glimpsed Snurkel's primly folded lips as he smoothed his robes fussily and sat down. She knew the little slimecrawler well, for that had been her mother's first order to her shortly after she'd pulled her from the rat-tunnels and informed her that her training in Karroo was about to begin.

"*Always find out your rivals' vices,*" her mother had said to her. "*And you will have made the first hit past their defenses.*" Giffus Snurkel craved a respect he had not earned, and he also had a taste for youth, boys or girls didn't matter: the younger, smaller, and more reluctant the better. So Lyska-si's job was to keep him entertained, and she had, until a sudden growth spurt had made her weedy body longer than Snurkel's. Since then she'd taken care to supply him with volunteers from her own rat-pack, usually disguised, and good at pretense. He never recognized any of them, convinced as he was that they came to him innocent and scared.

Lyska-si's lip curled as she stared down at his bald head, shiny with a sheen of oil and sweat. Having come to Rifthaven as an adult, he had yet to realize that no rat left the nest innocent—and eventually you had to pay for your fun.

But he sure didn't see any of that now. He was gloating over something; those pursed lips were too smug. About what? There was no news in Karroo, and nothing of any import in Rifthaven. She would have heard.

"We're agreed, then?" Xibl Banth asked, grinning around the table at the other chiefs, his Draco smile feral with those nasty pointed teeth. "As soon as the first of Dol'jhar's allies show up, we invoke the new approach laws—"

"That covers Defense," Pormagat of the Yim said in her snivelly whine. "But Defense ends at the lock, or have you forgotten, Xibl? What about Public Order?"

"And Trade?" the Houmanopoulis' old chief, Jep, put in with his fierce frown.

Xibl sneered at round Pormagat at his left. The two most powerful Syndics on Rifthaven, controlling Defense and Public Order—outside security and inside respectively—hated each other with deadly passion, a feeling echoed from the two chiefs right down to their rats and runners.

Lyska-si shut them out when she noticed Snurkel's beringed fingers worming over his other wrist: a privacy on his boz'l.

She scanned the room. Someone in here? At least half the chiefs had their hands below the table, but none of their throat muscles moved. Then she saw it: Nuub, second to Jep in Trade. Why was Snurkel talking to Trade, one of Karroo's bitterest rivals?

She shifted her stance behind her mother's chair to afford her a better vantage. She sensed some of the other runners noting her change in posture, and she let her hands show, indicating no threat.

Everyone was edgy. The meeting had been called to decide how to handle the coming onslaught of Dol'jhar's allies, who at any time might be skipping in, full of loot and triumph, their ships armed with those superweapons the Dol'jharians had discovered. Their squabbles could be planned for, and everyone knew that the resonance field kept Rifthaven safe enough from those weapons—that and the new guard on the field generator and its backups, overseen by Public Order and Defense, with all Syndics providing personnel, just as they did with the hyperwave.

What remained to be hashed out was the sudden influx of wealth they'd bring, which could throw the entire economy of Rifthaven, a painfully achieved, precarious balance at the best of times, into chaos. Everyone present knew from experience if they were old enough, or had heard, how vicious trade wars could be. Draco and Yim controlled the two top positions on council, but that could change—would, if the other Syndicates had their way.

Lyska-si studied Snurkel again, a trickle of cold warning in her vitals. Karroo was notionally at the bottom—their department was Recycling—which meant they tried extra hard, her mother had explained. But Karroo had been surprisingly successful in recent years, enough to scare the others a little.

Mostly because of that disgusting worm Snurkel, Lyska-si acknowledged.

"Has the Dol'jharian's second issued any further instructions that can be shared?" Willem spoke up, his rheumy eyes keen.

Lyska-si had a great deal of respect for the old wart's staying power; in a place where things changed quickly, Willem had ruled over the Kug—who controlled Engineering— for nearly five decades.

Several glances were sent toward the next room, where the ugly Urian communications device was installed and closely guarded to make sure that no information leaked out to Rifthaven at large.

"Not since the word came in about the raid on Arthelion by the missing heir," Corolaris Rouf said in her mellow voice.

They all knew Barrodagh did his best to keep the tensions high. Dol'jhar needed Rifthaven's goodwill, at least while his forces—mostly Rifters—were stretched so thin. But everyone knew the alliance would last just so long as the balance of power was more or less equal.

Lyska-si half-listened as the Syndic chiefs argued over what protocols they would adopt, and how they would be safeguarded when the Rift fleet began showing up. She kept her gaze on Snurkel, who watched through hooded eyes, his smugness increasing. He never spoke.

When at last the meeting broke up, Lyska-si maneuvered

herself behind her mother, hiding her hand so she could send a private:

(SNURKEL WAS GLOATING ABOUT SOMETHING. AND HE HAD A PRIVACY WITH NUUB.)

(I SAW. I'LL HANDLE IT. BUT FIRST WE HAVE TO TALK—YOU AND NISTAN HAVE BEEN DRAWN TO TAKE THE HYPERWAVE FOR THE NEXT WATCH.)

Lyska-si's heart accelerated. The lines of power were shifting indeed. Karroo had only been drawn once so far in the "fair lots" to take turns at Eusabian's comm. She looked across the room at tall, bony, tilt-eyed Nistan, the runner for the Y'Mered, who controlled Atmospherics, and caught a speculative glance from him.

Things were going to get interesting.

It better be now, Marim decided, and reached one-handed for her clothes beside the bed. Digging under them, she located her boz'l and tapped out a private code to Lokri.

"Hey." A long, muscular arm reached lazily for her.

Marim smacked the hand away. "Gotta pee."

"Well, hurry up."

"You ready again, sneezewit?" She reached over and rumpled her fingers through Rex's chest fur. "Don't move!"

Marim hopped out of the bed, grabbing up her boz'l. In the disposer, she made sure the door was locked and palmed the light. She slapped the boz'l against her wrist and hit the receive, looking at the door while she waited for a response. She still couldn't quite believe what drunken Rex had blabbed to her, swearing her to secrecy. Not just skipmissiles like to bust a moon wide open, but FTL comms, a hyperwave, straight out of star fantasy. There was no place safe. She wondered why the knowledge wasn't widespread yet on Rifthaven. Eh, surely the Syndics found it advantageous to control the word as long as they could, like Rex's captain.

But she hadn't cashed in yet on her Mandala loot, so she didn't dare tell anyone about the hyperwave comms, not even Lokri. Especially Lokri, if he was still forming some plot around the Arkad. As soon as Vi'ya found out, and she would, they'd be off Rifthaven instantly.

Lokri's response splintered her thoughts. (WHAT IS IT?) came his voice. (I'M IN THE MIDDLE OF A GAME.)

(I THINK YOU BETTER KNOW. I WAS AT—I MET REX, YOU KNOW, OFF THE TANTAYON. . . THEY SKIPPED INTO ABILARD SYSTEM JUST BEFORE COMING HERE, AND SKIPPED RIGHT BACK OUT 'CAUSE FASTHAND AND HIS GANG HAD TAKEN THE PLANET.)

(BAD FOR ABILARD,) Lokri's sarcasm came clearly through the neural induction. (BUT WHAT—)

(FASTHAND HAD ORDERS FROM EUSABIAN ABOUT THE ARKAD. THEY KNOW HE'S ALIVE, AND THERE'S A PRICE WORTH TEN PLANETS ON HIS HEAD. AND A PRICE ALMOST AS HIGH FOR ANYONE CREWING A COLUMBIAD CALLED MAIDEN'S DREAM.)

There was a long silence. Marim tapped her boz'l. (STILL THERE?)

(YES.)

(SO WE LIE LOW, RIGHT?) she went on. (YOU KNOW WHAT WOULD HAPPEN TO YOU IF YOU TRIED ANYTHING ON WITH THOSE DOL'JHARIAN BLUNGESUCKERS.)

(I'LL KEEP MY MOUTH SHUT.)

She breathed in relief, killed the connection and the light, and went back to slide into bed. Rex was waiting impatiently. She pounced on him, relieved that she was safe. As long as Lokri did keep his mouth shut, and didn't—

She sat upright so fast the bed jolted, and Rex mumbled a bleary protest.

Why hadn't she seen it before? She reviewed that conversation, understanding what Lokri had promised—and what he hadn't. Cursing, she whipped out of bed and began scrambling into her clothes.

Rex rolled over, blinking. "What? Where you going?"

Marim tapped her boz'l. "Vi'ya sent out a code yellow. I gotta go supervise the rebuilding of that chatzing aft under-cannon," she improvised.

"Can't it wait?" Rex asked, smiling sleepily. "Been too long since we saw one another." He sat up in the bed, and Marim looked at his big dark eyes, and his tousled hair, and her knees weakened. Another moment and she'd be right back in that bed.

'True thing, Rex," she said, hastily fastening her tunic.

"Free-fall bunny," Rex said, grinning. "Meet at the gym when you get off watch."

Dashing through the bewildering maze of corridors, halls, and tubes, she didn't stop until she reached the *Telvarna*'s docking bay. The hired guards nodded her through, and she dashed toward the ship's ramp.

A lazy voice stopped her. "What's the call?"

Marim whirled around. Lokri stepped out of the shadows, where he had obviously been waiting for the right moment to slip back on board.

She sagged against the ramp. "You're going after the Arkad," she accused. "Why, when I just now told you the danger?"

Lokri came toward her at an unhurried pace. "You told me," he said, "because you want me to do something about it and you don't dare." He smiled. "I being the gambler, and you just a thief."

His irony did not escape Marim, but she ignored the accusation. What he threatened was more dangerous than her plans for the nick treasures. Giving a sigh of exasperation, she said, "Can't you leave her alone? Can't you —" She took a deep breath. " —leave him alone?"

"Why should I?"

She scowled her fiercest, struggling with reactions she'd scarcely bothered to define before. As always, she opted for the immediate. "Because if you sell him to anyone we're all going to *die*. You *know* those chatzing bloodsuckers won't stop with just you."

Lokri shook his head. "I don't intend to sell anyone."

"Then why are you here?"

"I thought," Lokri said, "that our guest might enjoy a game of Phalanx. I got it all set up. Total anonymity."

Marim tipped her head back, studying his face. He smiled down at her with that not-quite humor in his light eyes.

She bit her lip. It was not just sex he wanted from the Arkad, it was more than that. He'd run this scam on Markham, too, and nearly got them all killed. Why? She knew Lokri better than anybody in the crew, but sometimes she felt she didn't know him at all. She whispered so the hired guards wouldn't hear her, "I don't want to end up on some Dol'jharian torture rack, mumbling through broken teeth about our Arthelion run."

Lokri smiled. "All I have in mind is some fun, and at the same time a reminder to Vi'ya of the limits of her reach."

Marim sighed. "If you need me, I'll keep this thing open." She tapped her boz'l and then left, punching up Rex's bozcode as she went.

Vi'ya breathed in the air, sorting carefully. It was almost right, but not quite.

Opening her eyes, she considered the sequoia forest around her. One could almost be convinced it was real. Certainly it had given both the Panarchists a jolt when they walked into it. But the air was still wrong. She'd spent some time playing with the tianqi but so far was not successful. It was an intellectual challenge. All her other environments were disturbingly real in sight, sound, and smell. It was important to get this one defined in precise terms and translate it to code.

It was a game she played, to take a place that dealt in strong affect and break that affect down into reproducible components. This one was proving difficult.

Her annunciator light flashed, and she killed the holo.

Montrose entered. "Ivard's got the Kelly Archon's gene imprint," he said. "The Kelly surgeon can't do anything about it. Swears protection and aid if we'll get the boy to someone who can."

"We?"

Montrose's bushy brows went up. "Told you I'd stay with you. If you don't go off to that damn ice planet." He gave her a fierce look, his voice a low rumble. "Or — it's the Schoolboy that suggested this, and maybe he's raving — that hellhole you were born on."

Vi'ya laughed. "Time limit?"

"The Kelly didn't say."

Vi'ya studied him, sorting rapidly through her options. "We can accommodate Ivard and these Kelly only if it is safe enough to do so," she said at last. "My plans beyond that are my own."

Montrose's eyes narrowed. "You're going to haul those damn Panarchists wherever you go?"

"Maybe."

Montrose grunted. "I'll let you know what I find out." He turned to leave, then turned back. "Why are you letting our people go?" he asked abruptly. "They're a good crew, or as good as any you'll find these days."

"They want to leave," she said.

He made an impatient gesture. "You could pull them

together again. All of them. You did it after Markham was killed." He frowned. "Unless you want them gone."

Vi'ya cursed mentally, then tried to smother the bleak flicker of laughter at the futility of calling down karra-fire. All those devouring demons and vengeful ghosts were fantasies, another link in the chain the lords of Dol'jhar used to leash a difficult people.

Reality was this man standing before her now, asking what to him was an honest question. To put personal discussion into words was to bare one's back to the flaying knife, but Montrose had been a loyal crew member. By her own code this required an answer, though perhaps not the whole answer.

Montrose waited, huge and patient as a rock.

She said, "I see little profit in a run to Gehenna."

Montrose's indrawn breath indicated surprise.

She was about to remind him of Brandon's stirring speech at the Chang banquet, but Montrose spoke first. "Yet he's done nothing to suborn your crew. Nothing at all. And he has had the time."

Vi'ya endured a pang of self-mockery. Montrose was not surprised at the possibility — he was surprised that she'd seen it.

She said, "He has spent his time with *Telvarna*'s computer."

It was a harmless enough statement on the surface. But they both had been there at the Panarch's palace, when the Arkad had cheerfully shown them how as a boy he'd broken into one of the oldest systems in the Thousand Suns, just to write-in practical-joke worms.

Vi'ya watched carefully for Montrose's delayed reaction, gauging from it how much he thought he'd revealed of himself in files buried deep in the system. They all had secret files. Everyone did. She'd set herself to master the systems they designed because it was her ship, and it was cheap defensive insurance. So she knew just how quickly the Arkad had successfully breached the system.

"I see," Montrose said, flexing his hands. "Well." He stared fixedly at a bulkhead for a time and then shook his head. He apparently did not want to know whether she had read any of his. "Well," he said again. "I'll be in the galley, guarding your nicks."

"Be watchful for only one more shift," she said. "I must oversee things from the outside for a time."

He nodded and she followed him out, her mind already racing ahead to the work she had set for herself. The preliminary diagnostics showed a lot more minor things that needed fixing than she and Jaim had counted on. Impatience warred with prudence. She had to supervise the work, and she had to get away to visit that vendor with a knowledge of Urian artifacts, but all of it had to be done swiftly. The longer the *Telvarna* was on Rifthaven, the greater the danger.

EIGHT

Sebastian Omilov was startled out of a deep sleep by bang-ings and thumpings elsewhere in the ship. Disoriented at first, he remembered where he was, and waited with a painfully accelerated heartrate for the sounds of an attack. Nothing happened, except for rhythmic tappings, clanks, and clunks. Ah. That had to be the repair people hired by the captain.

After the fourth time he was jerked out of sleep he arose, donned his robe, and moved into the treatment room. Montrose was seated at his console, its light flickering on features lined with tension. He look up, his expression altering to the familiar one of the assessing physician.

"I cannot sleep," Omilov said, just as a metallic banging reverberated through the deck plates below their feet.

Montrose smiled. "A good excuse," he said, "to break. Shall I brew up some real coffee? Your son is in the galley preparing a meal. I expect an excellent meal, as we just received our first delivery of fresh comestibles. I told him to surprise us."

Osri was not the one to seek for surprises. He would prepare what he knew best; *Omilov* was aware of a flicker of humor as he sat down, not trying to hide how gravity and age and stress dragged at his limbs. It was almost a relief not to be asleep, dreaming yet again of the Heart of Kronos, of getting it back within his governance — and waking up to the truth.

"What do you know of the Kelly?" Montrose asked over his shoulder as he went about his preparations.

Omilov shut his eyes, breathing in the aroma of fresh-ground coffee beans. "A little," he said.

"Did you know the Archon?"

"We were acquainted." At the reminder of the terrible deaths suffered by those gathered in the Ivory Hall for Brandon's Enkainion, Omilov was aware of never-quite-dormant sorrow.

Montrose sat back. "The Archon is not quite dead, it seems."

Omilov looked up, startled, as his mind finally made the connection. The Kelly band on Ivard! His preoccupation with the Heart of Kronos had dulled him to the obvious.

"Death, sometimes, is relative," Montrose went on musingly. "That ribbon around Ivard's arm carries the Archon's genetic memories. It has invaded the boy's DNA. A Kelly physician I'm acquainted with knew as soon as we walked into the examining room. But if we don't get them separated soon, both will die."

Omilov tugged his earlobe. "This. . . creates a complicated situation," he said slowly. "What can be done?"

Montrose looked grim. "That depends on the captain."

The hatch slid open, surprising them both.

Lokri entered, smiling. He wore a silky black tunic, tight black trousers, high glossy boots, and jewels woven into his hair, which brought into the sterile atmosphere of the dispensary an air of polyphonic music and exotic appetites, of danger and passion. Omilov felt old beyond his years, for it had been long since he'd been in the company of those who sought such pursuits. Even while young, knowledge of these things appeared to have passed him by; he had yet to figure out whether he was to be pitied or envied.

"Lokri," Montrose said. "What brings you back here?"

The comtech lounged over to the service console, and paused to take a deep, appreciative sniff of the aromatic coffee. "It seems I came just in time," he commented.

"Want some?" Montrose offered.

Lokri waved a hand.

"Captain know you're on board?" Montrose asked, reaching to pour a cup.

"No," Lokri said, stepping behind him. And before Omilov's horrified eyes, a knife seemed to materialize in the fingers of Lokri's good hand. He reversed it and efficiently struck Montrose across the back of the head.

He moved back as the physician fell heavily to the deck.

Lokri smiled across at Omilov. "Either you join him here, or you retire." He gestured toward the cubicle. "Take your coffee." With a humorous air he gestured to the cup Montrose had just poured.

Omilov did. He moved slowly, trying to buy time, to think, but his brain refused to work: this was not a situation that called for words, but action, and he had always been a man of words. He did pause in the doorway of his cubicle. "Where is the captain?" he asked, his mind on the Heart of Kronos.

"Probably still in the office wrangling with the techs over the redesign of that aft cannon," Lokri answered, pleasantly enough.

"So why. . .?"

"Good night, gnostor," Lokri said.

Omilov stepped into his cubicle as Lokri's fingers hit the control. The door closed, and locked from the outside.

Anticipation made Lokri's hand tremble. Montrose and the gnostor were out of the way; Lokri had managed to lock Schoolboy into the galley; the brainburners slept, or whatever it was they did in their cabin.

Vi'ya had finally gone off the ship, doubtless to seek more information on the Heart of Kronos, or he never could have acted. He had no idea where she was, or how long she'd be gone. But that was what made the risk even more fun.

He flexed his fingers, then keyed the Arkad's cabin hatch open. On his long wait for Vi'ya to leave, he'd entertained himself wondering what the Arkad's reaction would be to his appearance as liberator. Gratitude or haughtiness? Anger? Fear?

The Arkad sat before the console, his face intent. As Lokri entered Brandon turned his head, his light blue eyes tired.

Lokri lounged against the wall, smiling. "You're free."

Brandon lifted his hands from the console and sat back. "Is that a philosophical observation," he asked, "or an invitation?"

Lokri hadn't expected humor in return. He gestured toward the hatch. "Go," he said. "Vi'ya left the ship, and her psi-killers usually hibernate when we first hit a port."

Brandon tapped the keypads with an abstracted air, then looked up again. "Sebastian and Osri?"

Lokri gestured with his good hand. "One's asleep," he said, wondering what was on Brandon's console. "The other occupied with his cookery."

"How long would Sebastian last in this place?"

Lokri was about to say, *What does it matter?* but he knew it did matter: the Arkad wouldn't leave without those Omilovs. But if he thought it was a temporary leave?

"Let him sleep," Lokri said, stepping casually to one side. "Gain his strength. I'll give you a little tour, and you can always come back and invite the Omilovs to join you, if you find someplace they'd like."

Brandon appeared to consider it, and with a quick smile he tapped something out on the console, saved and cleared it with a gesture, just before Lokri walked into range. "Very well," he said. "What do I need to take?"

"Nothing," Lokri said. "Unless you have some spare AU."

"Not a token," Brandon said cheerfully.

"I thought that might be the case. And I am, unfortunately, down to my last hundred — " He laughed at the look of surprise on Brandon's face. "I only sold one piece of my loot, one of the more common ones. The famous ones are stashed in a safe place against the possibility of identification. For now, I arranged a little diversion."

Brandon looked his inquiry, but Lokri said nothing. He backed out and scanned quickly up and down the short corridor. Vi'ya did not appear, nor did they hear the scraping of twiggy feet on deck plates, or the high weird voices of the Eya'a. He led the way to the hatch. Just as they reached it, Lokri put out a hand and the Arkad halted, looking a question.

Lokri handed him a strip of dark blue velvet material with pale blue jewels across the top. "Speaking of identification. . ."

Brandon gave an assenting shrug and fixed his mask on, his ice-blue eyes glinting out from under sapphire gemstones. The mask covered him down to his cheekbones, effectively blurring his countenance. Lokri pulled on his mask, twin to Brandon's except for color. He waited, but the Arkad did not question the symbolism of the jewel patterns. Or he was indifferent. Lokri was certain he'd noticed.

As they walked down the softly booming ramp, he glanced sidelong at his companion, straight and slim in old clothes borrowed from Jaim: though Granny Chang had given him an elaborate outfit of the sort one expected to see on high-ranking nicks, Brandon had never worn it since the banquet at the asteroid.

He walked with a swinging, easy stride that brought

Markham forcibly to mind, as many of his movements did. Watching the body and not the face, Lokri could almost believe it was Markham at his side again, just the two of them, embarking on one of their Rifthaven runs punctuated by laughter and games of risk.

Anger, and something not quite anger, twisted inside him. Vi'ya was a fool.

Brandon did not appear to notice the gazes of the hired guards as they passed from the hanger to the outer hatch. He *wasn't* Markham, whose face had always been easy to read. This was Markham's highborn sidekick, apparently willing enough to be entertained.

Lokri would entertain him.

He hit the hatch control and watched in appreciation as Brandon recoiled from the barrage of noise, colors, and smells.

The corridor, lined with a confusing array of shops, branched frequently. The crowd thronging the passage exhibited every imaginable variation on human genes and bodmods, dressed — or not dressed — in an overwhelming array of styles, usually augmented by a formidable display of weaponry.

"This way," Lokri said, his voice nearly lost in the roar of shouts, whistles, and jangling, thumping music pouring out from all sides

But Brandon heard, dodging quickly around a group of five tall, thin humans dressed entirely in fantastical tattoos and weaponry. His arm came close to brushing against the last of them, and she turned, baring filed, red-dyed teeth. Brandon lifted his hands in a gesture of deference and the Draco moved on.

Then he stopped, brought up short by a rare sight — a Kelly trinity pirouetting down the corridor. Lokri started past. He'd seen Kelly once or twice, and outside of speculation about their sexual habits had never had any interest in the short, rotund tripeds with their dense lacework of fluttering, green tape-like ribbons.

But as the Kelly walked past in a waltz-like movement, the long eye-crowned proboscises springing from their torsos twisting in a constant helical motion, Brandon made finger signals, causing a sudden outburst of hooting and blatting from the Kelly. Lokri stared as the Arkad began slapping and poking the Kelly — who swarmed around him, bobbing and writhing with renewed energy, the gaudy, bejeweled boswells on their headstalks glittering as their "fingers" patted and stroked the Arkad's head, arms, and torso.

Several passersby gave them curious glances, and Lokri gestured quickly, getting Brandon's attention. "Let's go."

Brandon came willingly enough, the Kelly dancing on their way, soon swallowed in the crowd.

Lokri tried to suppress exasperation and alarm. Danger, he liked. When he chose to engage. "What was that about?" he said, jerking his head behind him.

"Greeting," Brandon said, with an air of surprise.

Lokri shut down the warnings he wanted to utter. What he really wanted to say was, *don't do anything unexpected again.* "This way. My diversion won't wait forever."

Lokri led him through a bewildering maze of emporia whose wares, and varieties of promotion, had utterly nothing in common, unless it was the compounded assault on the senses. Music not so much heard as felt through the soles of the feet and the back teeth blended dizzyingly with the light, breathy sounds of bizarre wind instruments. A few meters farther on, the clash and tang of brass cymbals accompanied a weird voice singing in some ancient tongue, evoking the mysteries of the bazaars of Lost Earth.

Light pounded, pulsed, flashed, and dazzled; scents swirled, stung, and singed. Lokri had long ago learned not to discriminate, instead permitting the sensory buffeting to flow over and past him. He glanced at his companion, who showed no reaction.

They moved aside as a procession of Kyresian Devotes in their polychromatic robes passed, hopping first on one foot, then on the other, pounding resonators on their heads and heels and singing monotonously in voices made shrill by the strange drugs of their cult.

A teenaged girl grabbed his arm. "Map to th' Founder's Ship? Guarantees you find the treasure —"

"Get lost," Lokri said pleasantly.

The Rifter vanished in the crowd, then re-emerged farther down, grabbing someone else by the arm.

"Founder's Ship?" Brandon looked interested.

"Legend. Maybe truth. Who knows?" Lokri said. "Somewhere, buried in the chaos of accretions we call Rifthaven, is the original ship. No one knows where or how old it is. I've never believed in the treasure." He almost said *Markham didn't either*, but he was reluctant to evoke Markham like some ghost.

They were only approached once or twice more, and always Brandon responded with a quick shake of the head and a half-raised palm in one of those revealing Douloi gestures.

Lokri watched for reactions from the vendors working the crowd, but no one seemed interested in Brandon. The mate-masks merely indicated a pair of slumming nicks.

Once Brandon turned sharply, and a second later Lokri felt a fragile hand touch his side where a belt pouch might have rested. He paused, looking down into a small face. Lokri laughed at the feral snarl the child gave them before it darted away.

"'Ware the rats," Lokri warned.

"Rats?"

"Brats. They're lethal, especially the vent-rats. They start playing war games with each other as soon as they can walk. No adult takes on the packs on and wins. Jaim grew up that way," Lokri added with a laugh. "Never mind. We're here."

They ducked through a low door. They felt the subtle sonic tingle of a scan, and the burly guard at the console held out his hand. Lokri pulled his neurojac out of his boot and handed it over. The door slid open, inviting them into cool, clean air.

Soft music greeted them as they went down a fast lift to a lower level, then entered a wide room with terraces built around a central waterfall. Greenery hung over the terrace walls. On each of the levels people milled about, involved in games of chance and skill. Lokri led the way to the highest level, having to give another code before they gained entrance.

Here, the men and women were nearly all young, or as young-looking as expensive medtech could make them. Handsome bodies were flattered or revealed by expensive clothing.

"There you are," a man drawled, his tone arrogant. "I'd begun to fear for your courage."

"A concern I salute you for, sho-Glessin." Lokri answered blithely, moving toward a tall, hard-faced man who lounged against the low terrace wall.

Sho-Glessin raised a glass in answer, seemingly unaware of the fifty-meter drop just behind him. "We're all here," he said. "And waiting."

Another man and a woman moved out from the shadows of a booth and sank into the padded seats around an octagonal bank of consoles. One man already sat there, wearing a full-face mask. 'Thousand suns per round," the Mask said.

Lokri shrugged.

"Boring." The woman's voice was hard. "Let's add some fun to it. Hundred sun per ship, and five for supply centers."

"As you wish, Piriag." Lokri lounged over to a console. Brandon sank slowly into the chair next to him, his expression pleasantly bland, but his eyes watchful as he punched himself into the game.

The Mask raised his arm and stripped off his boswell, placing it in full view on the top of his console. The others followed his example—except for Brandon, whose wrist was bare. Lokri watched the others noting that.

"Level?" the Mask inquired neutrally.

"Three," Lokri said.

Brandon gave Lokri a muted glance, and Lokri realized he'd dropped the Rifter tonalities in his speech. Inwardly he cursed, resolving to keep Douloi patterns from marking his words.

Then the consoles before them lit up, and Lokri's entries flowed across Brandon's screen, indicating what was about to happen: the two of them were going to play Level Three Phalanx against all these others, for astronomical sums of money.

Brandon looked up in muted question, to receive a challenging grin in return. The Arkad said nothing, running his hands over the keyboard to imprint its feel.

"Ready," the man in black stated. "Begin."

Lokri had played often enough against Brandon to guess where he would lead; still, it was all he could do for the first desperate minute or two to provide a solid backup. Lokri's throat dried when he paused once and the weight of the chance he'd taken pressed on his skull, but it was not in his nature to regret it. A chase was only worth commensurate risk.

This first step in this chase was meant to shake the Arkad out of that affable but relentless control, and to do it he had to jam up the stakes. If they lost they'd both be dead, or worse, but he didn't think they'd lose.

The Arkad dropped the mask of vacuous amiability just long enough to cast him one slightly pained look, at which

Lokri only laughed, and then Brandon's gaze went back to his console. Lokri divided his attention between his board and Brandon, whose fingers danced rapidly across the keypads. He pulled a coup, fell back, Lokri provided backup, and once again Brandon lunged to the attack. Across from them, the big man gave a short cry of dismay, and his board went dark.

One down.

Piriag took her lip between her teeth. Lokri moved to block her himself, hoping Brandon would not waste the time doubling his efforts. Perhaps he ought to have discussed a basic strategy with the Arkad. Piriag was not a pleasant loser, and she'd be a dangerous winner. She dealt almost entirely in human trafficking, and Lokri guessed where she would send them if she could —

The console beeped softly, and once again Brandon made a desperate maneuver that netted a big win.

Lokri glance covertly at his opponents in time to catch Piriag exchanging a fast look with sho-Glessin. Had they recognized Brandon's Phalanx style? But their play did not change, as it surely would have were that the case.

No, different worlds. These were gamblers, not tournament players. As far as he knew, no one except Ivard and Lokri himself knew of the link between Brandon and the famous Constable Murphy. Physical recognition was more likely, and that only on sho-Glessin's part. The man had made and lost a fortune running gambling halls for the Douloi until he'd been caught cheating a few years back. Lucky, this new fashion for mate-masks.

Lokri caught a flickering glance from Piriag, and he hoped his smile unsettled her.

Another attack: a win. The first round ended, and Brandon sat back, flexing his long hands.

"Do we get anything to drink, or do we just dance in the arena?" he asked.

Dance in the arena? Lokri ignored this inanity, lifting a finger to signal one of the hovering waiters. Nothing but human servants in this place; Lokri wondered if the Arkad took this rarity for granted. Brandon showed only mild interest as he surveyed the company. Brandon had no money, no weaponry, no boswell, and he was wearing Jaim's cast-off clothing, yet it never seemed to occur to him he might not have been permitted entrance.

It hit Lokri then that Brandon knew he was better than anyone in this entire hellhole. He knew it so well it'd probably never been a conscious thought, and if Lokri were to point it out to him he'd deny it, and mean that as well.

No, that wasn't it. Not quite. Consciousness of hierarchy was not the same as mere familiarity. He'd probably always been wafted in and out of elite spaces, so he never thought about the mechanics of exclusivity. Unlike Markham, who had always been aware, and had relished it.

The waiter approached and asked their desire. Lokri ordered drinks and threw his last remaining hundred AU onto the gleaming obsidian of the table.

Their opponents moved away, ostensibly to order, but Lokri knew it was to confer.

Brandon leaned toward him. "I thought you didn't have anything but a hundred."

"I don't," Lokri murmured. "In fact, less." He swept up the few remaining tokens and pocketed them.

Brandon's brows lifted. "What if we lose?"

"Then we belong to the winners."

The drinks came. Brandon whistled softly. Lokri sipped with care, aware how quickly the alcohol dimmed his speed, but Brandon drank one cup straight off, setting the crystal down with a musical *ching*.

Lokri saw their opponents take this in, and smile.

Round two.

Montrose opened pain-blurred eyes and gaze up in uncomprehending silence at the two faces above him. He struggled, wincing, to a sitting position, and discovered himself lying on the deck plates.

"Eh?" he grunted. His protesting brain reluctantly comprehended similar pairs of beetling brows, pendulous ears, and twin expressions of worry: the two Omilovs.

"Drink this." Sebastian handed something down.

Montrose sipped one of his own pain-reduction concoctions, laced with good brandy. The resulting fire seemed to cleanse out the pain and restore enough brain function for memory.

"I turned my back on Lokri." Montrose grimaced in

disgust. "No less than I deserved."

"You were tired." Omilov's expression was tight with concern. "And a fellow crew member, presumably trustworthy —"

"I don't trust anybody," Montrose said, wincing as he felt over the back of his head. "Damn! Broke the skin. Telos knows I have a hard head." His feeble attempt at humor brought no answering smile from the Omilovs. "We were making coffee … He didn't drop you, too, did he?"

The gnostor shook his head, as Osri said, "Locked him in there." A jerk of his head toward the berth. "I heard noise. By the time I figured out how to unlock the galley, whatever had happened was over." His voice was dry as he exchanged glances with his father.

"What is it?" Montrose demanded, recognizing that the concern on Omilov's face had, if anything, increased. "Where's Lokri?"

"Gone," Osri said curtly. "And so is the Aerenarch."

"Round three, game to the challenged."

Lokri kept his face bland as they rose from the chairs. Brandon shot him a glance, the mask not quite hiding his question before sho-Glessin handed him a small chip and said, "If you ever leave this chatzing cheat, you can name your salary with me." He laid down his share of the money and stalked off.

Piriag gave them a murderous glare but said nothing as she paid up. The Mask noted the proper amounts changing hands, utterly impassive.

"What now?" Brandon breathed, looking amused.

"We get out of here as fast as we can, because they'll both have friends watching," Lokri muttered. "Hers being the real threat."

Laughter quirked Brandon's eyes behind the mask.

"Let me show you the Qi games," Lokri said loudly.

After he retrieved his neurojac, they went a level down in one lift, then he shoved Brandon into the next lift and they went up a level. They stepped out, Lokri motioned downward, and Brandon laughed as they saw a man and woman wearing green, with shiny green eye implants, move close to the original lift. Both held some sort of weapon in their right hands.

"Piriag's hired flash," Lokri said.

Brandon shook his head. He did not seem unduly worried, as if none of this were real to him. "What now?"

"We buy our way out the back, of course," Lokri said. "Say nothing, just follow me."

NINE

"Here she is," Montrose said, his voice sounding husky with relief to Omilov.

The hatch slid open and the captain appeared, tall and composed. "Lokri has disabled his locator," Vi'ya said, her accent very marked.

"There's worse." Montrose moved to the console. "Listen. I just talked to Marim." He touched a control.

"Have you seen Lokri? He's gone and so is the Arkad."

"What?" The shriek made the console crackle. "And I just told him why that was dangerous—"

'Told him why and what?" Montrose's recorded voice sharpened.

"I got it from Rex off the *Tantayon*—what we guessed is true! Eusabian knows that the Arkad is alive, and he's got the biggest reward ever posted hanging over his head. But I *told* Lokri not to do anything, because you know what will happen if anyone tries to collect—"

"Where do you think Lokri would be?" *Montrose cut in.*

"Galadium, of course. I'll go myself," came Marim's voice. "And when I'm through with him, you'll have to put him back together with specimen tongs. Him *and* that chatzing nick!"

Montrose ended the recording.

Vi'ya turned her black gaze Omilov's way. "Did you know about this?"

"No," the gnostor said.

"Marim told Lokri about the reward," Montrose rumbled, ugly face fierce with anger. "He could be doing anything—"

But Vi'ya made a slight, impatient gesture, cutting Montrose off: she didn't care about Lokri. "According to Jaim, Brandon Arkad being alive is not yet general news," she said. Her eyes narrowed as she stared down at the deck.

Omilov studied her, trying to see if she carried the Heart on her person. Frustration kindled a helpless anger in him. There was nothing he could do.

Osri sat down next to his father. "If Brandon left," Osri said softly, "we may very well never see him again."

"I don't believe it," Omilov said, husky with effort. "I think he will return, and I think —" He let the sentence die when Vi'ya looked up.

She went to Montrose's console and hit some keys. Her face did not change, but her stance altered slightly, from tense to still, and then she hit more keys.

No one spoke. She killed the console, murmured something in Dol'jharian, then left.

Osri leaned toward his father. "You studied Dol'jharian. What was that?"

"So it begins," Omilov said.

Montrose rose with an effort and crossed to the kitchen annex. "Shall we have a second try on the coffee?" he suggested.

The Urian communicator was even weirder than Lyska-si had expected. She walked over to the red-glowing melted-looking machine and gingerly laid a hand on it, then snatched her fingers back: it felt like flesh, blood-warm, slightly yielding. "Ugh!"

Nistan grinned at her as she sat down. He was her age, and in spite of the adults in their respective Syndics being currently in the midst of a silent struggle, Nistan's rat-pack and Lyska-si's were allies.

They spent the first hour or so just watching the feed. The uncoded chatter — bragging sessions, really — between Rifter ships and the images that came over the hyperwave were entertaining, and sometimes chilling.

Nistan divided his attention between that and her, his sharp-boned face making him look wicked. Weird. She didn't like wicked, but she liked his look. "Shall we record this slag? I want to try to pick it apart later," he asked presently.

"Good," Lyska-si said.

Several streams of coded messages came through, and then nothing; Barrodagh, the unseen Bori slug who handed out Eusabian's orders, was busy this day. For fun, they tried to crack the codes, but of course they couldn't. Lyska-si did make a copy of the message-distribution log, which noted which mail drops they went to. That was one of the primary reasons for the rotating watch on the comm: to monitor this traffic. Any Syndicate that received more than its share of coded messages from Dol'jhar, even though their content couldn't be known, would fall under suspicion of having cut a separate deal.

As time wore on, their interest wore off, and several times Lyska-si almost suggested cutting the recording. They'd get into big trouble if any of the chiefs came in and caught them. But then another brief code-burst came through, and when it ended she gasped, hitting the playback. "That's Snurkel's mail code."

"Who's the message from?" Nistan said, squinting down at the console.

"I can't tell. Could be from anywhere."

"Let's make a chip," Nistan suggested. "I can take it to Korbis later. He's the best I know at codebusting. In fact," he said, tapping at the console jury-rigged to the Urian device, "let's dump everything and have him run statistics on it. Might be some interesting patterns."

"We'll owe you," Lyska-si said formally. It was a risk. She knew her mother was mad at the Y'Mereds now, and might not want to back her up. But Lyska-si couldn't quite make it personal, for reasons she didn't really understand.

Nistan flushed. "Accept," he said. He turned back to the console and wiped his long hair back from his face. But Lyska-si could see that he was smiling.

We do not hear the one-who-hides or the one-who-gives-fire-stone.

You will have to come out of the great sleep, and walk among the single entities.

We will walk among the single entities. The world-mind says this is instructive for Eya'a. We will locate the one-who-hides and the one-who-gives-fire-stone.

Vi'ya opened her eyes, rubbing her hand impatiently across her temple to banish the vertigo. She went out into her own cabin to find the Oblate robes and face masks. If anyone could find Lokri and Brandon Arkad, it would be the Eya'a. And then. . .

And then the wisest thing would be to get out of Rifthaven, fast. Much of the repair and enhancement work could wait. That which had been ordered was now paid for, thanks to the sale of one of the costly but common artifacts Vi'ya had taken from the Arthelion palace. And the two which were very rare were safely stored. But—

She pulled the silver ball from her pouch and hefted it in her hand. She'd almost gotten used to its inertialessness.

Without warning the Eya'a were in her head again: *The world-mind wishes to understand the eye-of-the-distant-sleeper. The world-mind celebrates Vi'ya joining the sleeper to the eye-of-the-distant-sleeper.*

'Wishes to understand.'

Vi'ya shut her eyes, almost dizzy with the impact of this realization. She had never been able to determine whether they were in contact with their world mind or not, as their concept of tenses was as shaky as their grasp of gender. But the world mind could not have known about the Heart of Kronos.

Vi'ya stared at the enigmatic artifact on her palm. It seemed to enable the Eya'a to reach her at a distance, rather than only face-to-face—maybe it was also helping them reach their world mind. She could experiment with that later, but right now, she needed to find out as much about it as was known to humankind. Since Omilov was unwilling to share what he knew, she would go elsewhere.

Decision reached, she slipped it back into her pouch. The orders concerning the ship could be given quickly. Once the Eya'a located Lokri and the Arkad, and the two were safely on their way back to the ship—with the Eya'a as guards—she would make a fast visit to the one person on Rifthaven who could possibly tell her more about the Heart of Kronos.

And then they'd leave.

She opened a com channel and asked to talk to the head tech.

Lokri led Brandon down a dim corridor.

The doors slid open and they entered a plain foyer.

"Signe's Garden, this is called. You'll like this place. If we have anything to celebrate we usually come here. This is also where we held Markham's wake." He touched the lift console.

When the lift opened, they were met by a young woman in discreet gray clothing. "Welcome, genz. Would you like to join the company?"

"Private," Lokri said. "But with access to the performance."

She led them up some shallow, curving stairs over a spectacular garden. Breathtaking mosaics lined one wall. The other looked out on brilliant stars — or the semblance of same. They could have been deep within the structure of the station, but the domed wall gave the illusion of vast space.

She stopped before a door, palmed it open, and they entered a tiny room with low couches and a gleaming black table.

'The furnishings are controlled here," she said, touching a small console on the side of the table. "You can be served by one of us, or you can order from the monneplat."

She backed through the door, which closed.

Brandon sat down on one of the couches, looking around in open appreciation. Tianqi units vented air subtly scented to remind one of verdant gardens. The lighting was indirect, the walls painted with highly stylized figures in shades of gray, black, and bronze. Lokri flicked one of the controls on the table and one wall slid away silently, affording a view of a stage. Several musicians played soft music, their costumes artfully designed to blend with the decor.

"Drink?" Lokri asked.

Brandon stripped off his mask and dropped it on the table. "It looks like their specialty is Vilarian Negus," he said with a sudden smile.

"Ah. You saw that!" Lokri took off his mask, fingering the gems just to keep his hands busy. "Expensive tastes. Luckily we can afford it."

Brandon grinned. "I've only heard of it. Its use is not encouraged where I've been living."

"Well, I've had it once. Here. Markham found this place, not long after he took over *Telvarna*. I'd never heard of Vilaria or their dream-dealing Negus until he and Vi'ya had it brought out: apparently they release very little of it each year, but the owner here has a standing order."

Lokri tapped out an order code. The cabinet below the window to the stage slid open. on a tray sat two tall, gently steaming drinks.

"It's better if it warms up a little," Lokri said, taking them out and handing one to Brandon.

Brandon took his, but made no attempt to drink. "Its dreams are reputed to be addictive," he said, staring down into the milky liquid.

Lokri could not quite place his tone. "It's highly addictive. And if you've had any of a number of drugs within the last standard day, it may kill you, though it is supposed to be a pleasant death. They use it for religious rituals on Vilaria, for ritual suicides—and for executions."

"What shall I expect?" Brandon asked, looking up.

"The effect is supposed to be different for everyone. But you'll dream well," Lokri said, "when you do go to sleep. And don't try to put off sleep too long. The Negus won't be denied."

Brandon said, "I wouldn't have thought this kind of thing something Vi'ya would drink."

"She told us the Negus mutes the psi-waves here."

"Rifthaven?"

Lokri nodded. "She hates the place."

Brandon's brows lifted in surprise.

Lokri grinned. Closing his eyes halfway, he said with a fair imitation of her austere voice, "So many people crowded in so small a space, broadcasting hatred, greed, murder, anger."

Brandon said, "If she doesn't like those things, why is she a Rifter?"

Lokri laughed in delight. "Just the question I asked her."

"And she said—?"

Lokri leaned forward to tip his glass against Brandon's. The crystal rang, and Lokri sipped deeply of the creamy, very cold liquid. "Like clouds. . . herbs and clouds."

Brandon took a sip, his head canted. "She said that?"

"I did." Lokri set his glass down. "She just laughed at me. Markham answered for her. Said it was the only job going for an Dol'jharian ex-slave."

"She was a slave?" Brandon repeated, one brow lifting as he idly turned the signet ring on his hand.

"Her mother found out she was a tempath before the local

lord did. She would apparently have been killed out of hand, but Vi'ya was able to disguise her talent by posing as an animal handler."

"I've seen how good she is with the dogs," Brandon observed.

"And Lucifur. Anyway, that not only saved her life but made her a valuable commodity. She was sold to a rock-quarry owner. Could be her mother even bought her own freedom with Vi'ya's price. She spent the rest of her childhood managing huge rock-lifting saurians. Then she was sold to a lord on one of the Quarantined Dol'jharian worlds, smuggled there by Rifter slavers. Markham said she wouldn't talk to him about that voyage at all, but anyone could tell how much she hated slavers."

Lokri smiled at Brandon's shuttered expression. Was the Arkad really that ignorant about Dol'jhar? Only an Arkad could be that insulated. "It was Markham who got it all out of her and one night he told me. She'd never told us anything about her background. Oh, maybe Jaim, a little. But he's worse than she for tight lips."

Lokri paused. Brandon's expression was enigmatic as he continued to twist the ring. Lokri caught a glimpse of the signet: not the expected Phoenix, but an ebony-faced charioteer.

Lokri went on. "Life for any but the lords is cheap on any Dol'jharian world. She couldn't get into trouble — she was too valuable — but her friends could be used against her, so she learned not to have any. When she was in her late teens someone organized a slave revolt. She escaped along with the others, but her talent for 'hearing' pursuit kept her from being caught and tortured to death as an example. She learned to stay alive in the city. Markham thought the slave revolt was funded by the Rifter commander who later put out a hiring call on Rifthaven. Markham joined up with the little ship he'd recently taken from some jacker. They raided the city —"

"Rifter raid against a Dol'jharian-held planet?" Brandon said.

"Exactly. Markham told us that he was certain the Panarchic navy looked the other way when Rifters dared raids against Dol'jharian holdings."

"Ah." Brandon smiled humorlessly, gazing downward through his drink. "Go on."

"Little else to tell. It was Markham's first raid as a captain.

By the time the local lord's forces scrambled, Markham got away with a cargo big enough to sync him into the crew you saw at Dis. Somewhere during this raid he came across a tempath who was fast with her hands—a dead shot. If you think a tempath ever 'comes across' anyone. She's never said how she found *him*."

Brandon sat very still during the relation, his gaze on the performers below. "Why did Hreem want Markham's death?"

The question was strange, especially uttered in that tone of indifference.

"He had seven reasons, all seven having to do with us jacking him when he carried slaves," Lokri said. Suspecting the impact of the word again on Brandon, he dug at the sore spot. "There's a thriving market out-octant where you nicks can't, or won't, enforce the Unalterables. One thing about slavers: they rarely carry just one illegal cargo. Markham made plenty selling the subsidiary cargoes."

"What did he do with the slaves?"

"Turned them loose. Jakarr and others were getting tired of the cost of his ethics, especially as the last Hreem jack we jumped turned out to be high-end nicks. Jakarr thought the ransoms would buy us half Rifthaven."

"Would have bought you the attentions of a battlecruiser, more like."

"That's what Markham said, shortly before he died. Vi'ya agreed. You saw the end of that particular argument when you first arrived on Dis."

Brandon transferred his gaze from the stage to Lokri. "But you approved?"

Lokri shrugged. "As long as the take is good, I don't care where it comes from."

Brandon's next question, still uttered in that soft, indifferent voice, took Lokri by surprise. "You were at the other base when Markham was murdered?"

How did he know that? "*I was.*"

The musicians on the stage below had been replaced by masked players who mimed a highly stylistic play. Old anger awakened, Lokri waited for Brandon to contemplate these events outside his control, his thought bitter: your Panarchy is dead, Aerenarch. As dead as Markham and his ideals. Do you see it yet?

When Brandon finally spoke, it was again a sidestep. "Is

this a wake, or a performance?"

Lokri glanced at the stage and then at the Arkad, whose mouth twisted with irony. "Meaning?"

Brandon finished off the Negus and set the cup in the exact center of the table. "Meaning what else do you do for fun?"

Lokri drank the last of his own Negus, his mind running the more rapidly in spite of, or because of, the dream images lapping at the edge of his awareness. Too late he understood that the Negus had been a mistake. The dreams were not deadening the old memories, but reawakening them.

His expectations changed from moment to moment, but his intention remained: he wanted to see the Arkad's mask shatter, just as his Panarchist world had shattered. Nick morality and mercy were gone, ripped apart by weakness, greed, lust, and revenge. Markham was gone, and with him and everything he'd believed in. *"I want a fleet to take to Gehenna to rescue my father. . ."* Hatred twisted Lokri, for a system that didn't work, and for this handsome scion of wealth and power who persisted in believing the illusion.

Lokri would demonstrate to him his powerlessness. And then. . . And then. . .

Memory-desire merged unsettlingly with the immediate. His thoughts, driven by the Negus, spiraled.

He was sure of only one thing: he'd made a tactical error in choosing the finest places, the ones that compared with nick establishments. As he'd seen earlier, to the Arkad this was accustomed space.

It was time for something different.

He smiled. "There's a lot more to see."

Brandon said, "Lead on."

Lokri threw a stack of AU into the hopper, which closed up and disappeared. "Put that mask back on. If Vi'ya does catch up with us, that'll keep me alive. Maybe." He laughed.

No one hindered them when they walked out.

"Look here," Nistan said.

Lyska-si abandoned her own work and glanced at his terminal.

"I've broken some of it out. The sender code for Snurkel's message is almost the same as these other messages. And some of the other Syndics are getting messages from the same source."

Lyska-si whistled. "Has to be Arthelion."

"Weird thing is, the only ones getting these new messages are seconds."

Lyska-si got that zing of memory. "Is Nuub one of them?"

"Yeah. And Zafid Rouf—"

"Water," Lyska-si whispered.

"And Gurpahee—"

"Weird! The Kug hate the Rouf. I thought."

"And Tir down in Hydroponics." Nistan looked thoughtful. "Who else on Arthelion is working for Eusabian?"

Lyska-si shook her head. "Far as I know, Barrodagh is the only one speaks for him." They looked at each other.

"Then there's someone there working against him," Nistan said.

"And they might be allied with old Giffus and those other seconds," Lyska-si said. "Maybe a cross-Syndicate coup by those impatient to succeed their firsts. That's it. Trouble or no, I've got to tell my mother." She tapped the copy code on her boz'l and loaded Snurkel's and the other messages in. "I won't tell your part," she said. Then she signaled her mother, but got no answer.

Nistan's grin was twisted. "Trouble on Rifthaven," he predicted.

The Eya'a paused, and Vi'ya cast a swift look around, struggling with her emotions. She was getting too angry, though she did her best to damp it. The Eya'a were close enough to protective action already. Furious as she was with Lokri, she did not want them to fry his brain as soon as they located him.

She started walking again, the Eya'a shuffling behind in their shrouds. They continued to scan and sort the myriad mental energies surrounding them, their nearly incomprehensible emotions a strange hybrid of joy and terror that seared Vi'ya's nerves.

We hear the one-who-gives-fire-stone, the Eya'a said again.

They veered. She ran ahead, guiding them toward a lift. They shuffled on, paying no attention to humans. A huge spacer, obviously expecting everyone to give way before him, stepped directly in their path. Before Vi'ya could act, the Eya'a walked directly into the man, who shoved impatiently at the nearest of the pair.

The Eya'a's face mask shifted, and the other promptly lifted her mask.

After a shocked look at the faceted eyes and blue mouths, the spacer turned the color of dog vomit. "Are those what I think they are?"

"Brainburners," someone else said, jamming at the lift door control.

Vi'ya, desperate to keep the Eya'a from being associated with the *Telvarna*, said, "Haven't you heard? A ship full of them docked here two watches ago."

The entire assortment of hard-faced spacers stampeded hastily out.

"There's something going on," Lyska-si said. "I know it. The way Snurkel was gloating at the caucus today, and now these messages. And some of the others were rasty, too. Chatz! It could be starting now. Why won't Lyska answer?" She tapped her boz'l again, but her mother did not respond.

"Do a locate?" Nistan kept his attention on his console.

"She always has that disabled, even for me," Lyska-si answered. "Ever since that bomb plot against old Willem—"

"Here, look at this," Nistan said. "I knew Korbis was the one to ask. So happens he's on the Defense desk right now, so he can do stuff for us."

Lyska-si moved to his console and leaned next to him. Her mind was distracted between the console and Nistan. Eyes the color of Yolen nightbirds, those straight shoulders, and he smelled good. But he was a Y'Mered, and anyway, there was biznai at hand.

What she saw made her forget everything else. "Korbis wired the shop!"

Nistan grinned up at her. "Snurkel took over an old Sybarad luxury yacht. Had it welded right onto Falkowitz Street. Korbis built a model back in our pack days, and he knows 'em right down to the welds and rivets. He's gonna activate us a spy-eye, right in Snurkel's back room, and pipe it over to us. We'll owe him big, since Snurkel's next security sweep'll catch it and blow Korbis' setup on Falkowitz for good, but for now we can watch Snurkel right here for the rest of this shift."

Lyska-si grinned. "Then move over."

He shifted slightly, but not too far away.

"This is Marim's favorite place," Lokri said. "Or one of them."

He blinked, trying to clear his eyes of the halos around every light. He was very drunk. The screams of an excited crowd smote their ears when they entered the stands high above a bright-lit platform. On it two Tikeris androids—man-sized creatures dressed in swirling, brightly decorated robes—postured with eerie grace, their stylized movements belying the keen edges of the long, curved swords they wielded in each hand.

On each side of the platform stood their Barcan handlers, swathed in shanta-silk, wearing red-tinged glasses even in this dim light, their absurdly large codpieces waggling as they stumped about excitedly, waving their arms and wailing hoarsely. Two players labored at consoles, modifying the emotions and response patterns of the Tikeris in an attempt to overcome their opponent's android. The air was heavy with a mixture of sweat, drug haze, and an unfamiliar spicy scent.

A flurry of movement caused a shriek of mixed delight and frustration from the crowd; the swords flashed and one of the figures spun away, blue fluid splattering from a deep slice across its chest. Its expression did not change, but a piping howl of agony keened from its lips as it returned to the attack.

Faces reflected the mixed guilt and pleasure that was part of the attraction of the Tikeris and their obscene near-trespass on the Ban.

Brandon grunted, his upper lip crimping in disgust. At last the mask was broken, and Lokri dissolved in laughter.

Brandon whipped around, his pupils so tiny they were nearly swallowed by the sapphire blue that reflected every light in the place. *Is that a lambent gaze?* Lokri could not stop laughing. "So you've recognized a campaign at last."

"I thought the tour was to be instructive." Brandon's light voice was almost drowned by the howls of the crowd. "But you haven't finished telling me: who set Markham up?"

He thinks *I* did it. Pain shot through Lokri's head. Memory almost overwhelmed the present. He struggled to speak, giving up when a shadow appeared at his side.

"This fool wanted Markham to himself, not dead," said Vi'ya.

Lokri blinked upward, but Vi'ya ignored him, black gaze meeting blue.

"And you?" said the Arkad.

Vi'ya's teeth showed in a not-quite smile. "I *had* him to myself."

Brandon was not smiling. Time seemed suspended as they stood on either side of Lokri, neither moving. Lokri understood that he had lost the duel, further: he'd never had a chance. Brandon had played him instead, in order force a duel with Vi'ya on neutral territory.

Lokri looked from one to the other, feeling as if he'd been cast into the midst of a river and there was nothing to hold onto, a sensation augmented by the Negus and alcohol haze. "*She* didn't set him up," he croaked, his voice coming from somewhere outside his head. "It wasn't that at all —"

Vi'ya glanced at him once. "Two crew members sold us out. Both are dead. Lokri's only mistake was to try to supplant me with Markham."

"Then you weren't just Markham's lieutenant," Brandon said. "You were —"

"Mates," Vi'ya stated.

Brandon didn't move or speak, but it became possible to look elsewhere; Lokri felt it as a physical release, and so must have Vi'ya, for she gripped his shoulder. "Both of you. Back to *Telvarna*. Now. The Eya'a will take you there."

She walked out.

One of the Eya'a brushed a twiggy finger over Lokri's arm. He got up fast, lurching outside.

When he reached the causeway he paused, and was thoroughly and unequivocally sick.

TEN

Vi'ya breathed deeply in an effort to dispel her fury.

What was it Markham said about Lokri? "A smile here, a word dropped there, then he stands back and watches the firefight. A deadly hobby. He reminds me of the Masaud family, who are known for such high-stakes games in Court circles." He'd taken her hands and said, *"Shall we try to win him over? That kind, if they ever do give their loyalty, it's forever."*

You won his loyalty, Markham, but to your person, not to your crew. And when you died, he could not forgive you for dying. She fought the killer rage instinct; it was Markham who had taught her that there were other choices besides violence for solving conflicts.

She walked faster, as if to leave the memories behind. Now Dis was gone, the Sunflame with it, and she was losing the rest of her crew. All because of Markham's Arkad—who thought she had betrayed Markham.

She balled her fist and struck it against a lumensquiggle, feeling a zing of satisfaction as it cracked, sending sparks shooting off.

"Violence. It is the way of the ghosts and demons," she had said to Markham soon after they met. He'd laughed and retorted, *"You are neither a ghost nor a demon."*

Rationality and wit. Markham had taught her to value these things, so she forced herself to respond rationally, to review the scene in the Barcan Tikeris Dome. Lokri and the Arkad reeking with Negus fumes. Lokri's witless gloating at the effect the Tikeris made—and how the Arkad shifted from passive to attack so fast Lokri had been caught with his shields down.

And then she broke her own pattern and spoke the unspoken. What was done was done. Now to address the matter of the Heart and then get on with her plans.

A lift brought her before the row of discreet shops controlled by the Karroo Syndicate. Here few troublemakers dared to come. Armed guards in fantastic uniforms from ancient times stood before each door. The costumes did little to hinder these people from doing their duty promptly when necessary.

The last shop was the smallest, and it contained the most fabulous wares of the row. This was the showcase of the Syndicate's prime broker, Giffus Snurkel. The *Telvarna* had done good business with him in the past. His specialty was ancient art objects. Markham had had a good eye, and Snurkel had been deeply appreciative — which meant he paid well.

He was also an unctuous, sniveling liar with the persistence of a ship-bred cockroach. The one time Vi'ya had met him away from his shop, the contradictions between what he said and his driving emotions had nearly driven her mad. It was almost a relief to have those emotions damped by the mind-blur device he regularly used in his shop.

She paused, eyeing that door. When she'd first set out on this errand, her plan had been to bring the Eya'a as backup. But on the search for Lokri and the Arkad they'd come within meters of Snurkel's shop, and the sophonts had reacted with such distress Vi'ya was afraid they'd use their deadly fi on the entire row of merchants. She could not understand the flow of imagery they sent, but she figured the mind-blur was exponentially worse for them: they sensed it clear outside the shop, while standing on the concourse.

Now she faced the most important negotiation she'd ever had with the fork-tongued rocklurker Snurkel, and she would have to run it on her own. As well they were blasting out of Rifthaven within hours. And she was not without defense; she carried a sere-edged knife in the top of her boot, and she knew that her face was considered as warm and expressive as that of a frozen corpse.

She stepped up to the guards before Snurkel's shop. They scanned her for energy weapons, and one gave a short nod.

The shop was small, but it conveyed a heady aura of great wealth, even to the moss carpet underfoot, a rare, fragrant, thick blue-green moss that breathed sweet air. Art objects of inordinate rarity, each exquisite examples of their kind, and totally different from anything else in the room, were set in framing nooks of fine-grained woods. The overall arrangement pleased the eye but she only looked for hidden dangers.

She passed inside, drawn by the glimmer of light along a worked-gold neck torc of unimaginable age. Near it lay a strange, U-shaped metal-faceted artifact from a distant world. A wooden cask, carved with ferocious demons, gave off a sharp scent of incense that evoked ancient mysteries. The air stirred as she walked, carrying the soft, melodic tinkle of an unseen wind chime.

A woman came out and placed her hands together. "How may I serve the genz?"

"Selling, not buying," Vi'ya said.

"If the genz would be so good as to display the items in question?" the woman said incuriously.

"I think Giffus Snurkel will want to see these."

The woman pressed her hands again and retreated. A moment later, Snurkel himself stepped out, licking his lips, his soft, fleshy hands pressed together in that same pose meant to convey peace and goodwill. But he just looked oily.

His face split into a smile of false delight when he saw Vi'ya. "Ah! It is the captain of the *Telvarna*, come back from far places to visit our humble abode. I bid you welcome." He gestured expansively.

Vi'ya merely waited, unable to furnish any reply. Silence, when one was unsure, was the best answer. Among her people on Dol'jhar, there had never been anything remotely like what Montrose and Lokri called small talk.

Snurkel radiated anticipation, and covetousness, stronger than he ever had before. She suppressed a surge of revulsion when he licked his lips again.

He smiled unctuously. "Please, *Telvarna's* captain. . . Vi'ya, is it? It is so cold, so formal out here. Do come within my little shop, where we can sit comfortably."

She thought about saying no, for she knew that his mind-blur was on. She could feel its tickle inside the back of her skull, like a knife blade scraping the hairs on her skin. She thought about insisting on staying out front, but she figured he would simply turn on the mind-blur that he undoubtedly had there.

If she showed hesitation, he would see that as an advantage. And that meant he'd try to protract an exchange she wanted to be fast. She shrugged, and followed him into the office, which was crowded with shelves and art objects in the process of research, meticulous reconstruction, or repair. They passed through that to a tiny cubicle with a desk. The mind-blur buzzed supersonically, and Vi'ya's thoughts muffled, as if a rough blanket had dropped over her consciousness.

"Would you care for some refreshment, perhaps? I can offer you some hot spiced barleywine, which I understand is preferred among Dol'jharians."

"No," Vi'ya said, hiding a flash of surprise. So he'd been doing some research on *Telvarna's* new captain, had he? "Thanks anyway."

"No? Very well, very well," the man said, his wet lips creasing. "Now, then. What have you to show the eager Snurkel?"

"There's this." She reached into her pouch and carefully removed a small object. Unwrapping it, she displayed one of the least rare of the treasures from the Mandala, carefully selected for this interview.

Snurkel's eyes widened. He reached out, then pulled his hand back. Vi'ya set the tiny butterfly down, and Snurkel pulled a magnifying lens from behind the desk and emitted a pleased "Ahhhh!" as he examined the fragile gold framework inlaid with stylized jewels.

"I do believe this is a genuine Lallic," he said softly. Then he looked up, his watery gaze acute. "I know of scarcely a dozen, the best of which was housed on the Mandala itself. This item compares with the best."

Vi'ya shrugged.

Snurkel smiled tolerantly. "Well, well," he said. "Just out of curiosity, as we have done agreeable business in the past. How came you by this artifact?"

Vi'ya's heartbeat accelerated sharply. He had never asked that before. "You know the Rifter life. We acquire things."

Snurkel wet his lips again, and Vi'ya was sure that news of the raid had managed somehow to reach Rifthaven ahead of them. He might even be trying to figure out if *Telvarna* was the *Maiden's Dream* and if she had the Arkad. In which case the artifacts were just a side issue. But Snurkel's greed would keep him from jumping to conclusions and risk losing the Arthelion treasures; she could use that against him.

"Of course, of course. And very profitable we all find such

acquisitions. Many of our best collectors would unclip their purses if they but knew that artifacts were to appear that hitherto were seen only by the eyes of one family. Might I only inquire where you might have made yours?"

"Ah," she said, trying to think: Where would an Arkad known for his stupidity run to? "We were scouting the edges of the Lao Tse system, when we had a surprise encounter." She shrugged. "Beyond the artifacts, there was a particularly satisfying conclusion to it."

Snurkel's eyebrows shot up. "If perchance you have a vid of that. . ."

"Wish we did. How much for this?" she said abruptly, directing his attention back to the brooch. Pressure was building in her skull. She forced herself to breathe slowly, trying to release it without revealing her distress.

"Without a certificate of ownership, you know these things are more difficult," he said, opening negotiations.

They dickered a bit, which steadied her: this was like normal.

"Times are very unsettled now, and with all this nasty talk of war and fighting," Snurkel said at last with a mendacious sigh. "It does not seem a good time for art, does it?"

He named a price much lower than she'd counted on, so she frowned, and put the butterfly back in her pouch.

Snurkel made a moue of disappointment, but he did not give in. "What else have you?"

"How about this?" She pulled out a little book and carefully opened it.

"It appears to be another pre-Exilic artifact," he said.

"See. It's handwritten," Vi'ya pointed out. "It has to be old."

"Perhaps. . . perhaps. . . There was a fashion for handwritten copies of old materials from before the Exile. This is definitely not the original binding, as you can clearly see. These copies are really classed as curios — but it is not without value. Note the clever illustrations." He chuckled unctuously. "This one here — *The Waif of Bath* (you see I have some know--ledge of Pre-Exilic scripts). This drawing is quite amusing for someone who has, ah, a taste for the, er, vigorous crudities of a bygone era."

As if worse things weren't going on right above them now, the hypocritical old thief.

Vi'ya nodded. "If it's worthless, I'll keep it."

"Worthless? Did I say worthless, my dear Captain? I did not! No indeed, not for such a good supplier. You know, we might really speak again about the possibilities of your joining our Karroo Family. In these times especially, the protection would be most invaluable. "

A warning pang shot through her temple. "How much for the book?" This was taking longer than she'd planned, and she knew she'd no longer be able to avoid a massive headache.

". . . though if you sell me both, we might both like a rounder sum?"

"Round it upward, and they are yours."

"Ah, a meeting of the minds! I am delighted, delighted. Anything more?" he asked, making a show of keying open a drawer. He pulled forth a sheaf of AU scrip.

"Just a question." She stopped, hearing a harsh edge to her breathing. "About Urian artifacts."

He stilled. Warning? Or mere curiosity? He was knowledgeable. That's why she was here. "What sort of Urian artifacts?"

"Any kind. Where does one go to find information?"

"It depends largely upon what you seek," Snurkel said, licking his lips again. "I would not hesitate under ordinary circumstances to direct you to the excellent learning establishment housed upon the planet called Charvann, but I have recently received most lamentable news indicating that their operations have been interrupted. Have you found something you think might have been left behind by those mysterious folk we term the Ur?"

His words were blurring, sounding to her as if he spoke through a mouthful of meal. Forcing her mind to concentrate, she touched her pouch, hesitated, then she decided. If she didn't try, she'd find out nothing at all.

She pulled the sphere free.

"Ah. It seems an ordinary metallic object, Captain," Snurkel said in disappointment. "Who led you to believe it was an Urian artifact?"

His disappointment relieved her. Enough so that she turned her hand and dropped the sphere to the table. The speed with which it fell, stopping with no bounce whatever, caused the man to blink. He tipped his head, and without warning the mind-blur whined into a high setting.

Lightning stabbed through her brain. Vi'ya gritted her

teeth, giving her head a hard shake. When she forced her stinging eyes open, Giffus Snurkel had picked up the sphere and was thoughtfully moving it from hand to hand.

"I'll take it back," she said, no longer able to hide her ragged breathing. "Do you have to have that fire-cursed mind-blur on force nine?"

"Please pardon me. The mechanism is faulty. As it happens, I do have a buyer who will pay enormous sums for these baubles. . . enormous sums, and with them comes the gratitude of a powerfully emplaced individual."

"I'll take it back," she said, holding out her hand. "I just want information—"

"Almost nothing is known of these things, my good Captain," Snurkel said. "If you will entrust it to me, I can seek out information. I will give you a great sum as insurance—"

"No. I want it back." She stood up, ignoring the pain every movement caused.

"But I do have a buyer. . . A *very* eager buyer. . ."

She snatched at the sphere, and Snurkel dropped it behind his desk.

His voice sharpened. "And sadly to say, my life would be forfeit if my buyer knew I had let such an object pass through my fingers. There is also a price on the head of the bearer, if this is what I surmise it might be. But as we've done good business in the past, and I know how these things change hands among our Rift Sodality, often without acquirers recognizing what they have. . . well, if you'll accept my price and leave, no one will know of our dealings here."

Barrodagh must have put out the word that the Heart went missing. She was a fool, but she hadn't lost yet.

She lunged across the table.

Snurkel emitted a squeak of fear and slammed his hand on a pad at the edge of his desk, but half a heartbeat after Vi'ya subvocalized the emergency code on her boz'l. It then flashed the signal for being locally blocked.

She leaned down to whip out her knife, hoping one of them had heard that.

The little man cowered in his chair. "Guards!" he screamed. "Stop her! Get her!"

The two guards appeared at the door, pulling their pellet guns free. Probably nerve poison. Vi'ya vaulted over the desk and yanked Snurkel up against her as a shield, while she surveyed the back of the desk. He had a hundred tiny drawers there, all of them closed.

"Get me free! Now, or I'll have you gutted and hamstrung!" Snurkel's shrieking voice sent waves of pain through Vi'ya's head.

When he stopped, she became aware of pain on her arm; too late she saw that he'd freed her boswell. She yanked him up, but not before he flung it into the disposer next to his desk, then lashed out at the override button with his toes. The disposer flashed as he screamed for his guards to kill her.

So much for the homing signal. Now to see how fond they were of their master. . . She kept the blade at his throat, and the guards edged apart, taking one step forward at a time, their weapons trained steadily on Vi'ya and her wildly struggling hostage.

Lokri was sick again twice more. Brandon steered him into a pissoir. Lokri was dimly grateful for the presence of the tiny Eya'a, the mere sight of whom fended off two pickpockets and a file-toothed Draco hopperpopper seeking companionship, while he voided his system of its unwanted toxins.

"I heard they're all over Rifthaven!" someone said behind Lokri.

"Burning brains out?" someone else said. "Gotta be a Draco plot!"

Lokri leaned against the wall, shaking, and drenched in sweat.

Brandon said, "You probably won't welcome this news, but you'll live. I even know an effective treatment, but I'll need to raid Montrose's stores for the ingredients. Come on."

"You said you never had it," Lokri whispered, eyes shut.

"Haven't. But I've learned some things about hangovers. And toxins."

Lokri opened his eyes. His head still ached, but his vision was a lot less bleary. Humor flickered in his thoughts. "I guess I will live." He drew in a shaky breath, then said accusingly, "You're a physician? Or got some kind of built-in alcohol neutralizer?"

"Nothing but forty-odd generations of hard heads, plus ten years of little else to do but drink," Brandon said with a laugh.

"If I do manage to stay alive another ten years, I'll probably need a new liver. Let's get out of here before those two start a flood. There seems to be some sort of rumor going around about them."

Lokri looked over at where the Eya'a were intently examining a plumbing fixture. Their multi-faceted eyes swung toward him, and one of the round blue mouths opened.

Lokri pushed himself away from the wall and they left. A knot of people waited, oddly subdued, at the door—and as soon as the Eya'a had glided past, they rushed inside the facility and the door hissed shut.

Lokri moved into the crowded corridor with its ever-present flashing signs and booming music, then stopped when his boswell tingled the inside of his wrist and a flash of red light bloomed behind his eyes. "Vi'ya," he said. "Trouble."

"Does it have a locator?"

Lokri thrust back his sleeve with shaking fingers. "Yes. I'll—"

The light winked out, and stayed dead.

"Emergency over?" Brandon asked.

Lokri shook his head slightly, then winced. "She should have flashed the green." He frowned. "But... I know where she is... I think."

"Let's go," Brandon said.

"To the rescue?" Lokri laughed again, leaning against a wall to catch his breath. "Life... is a farce," he gasped. "What about them?"

One of the Eya'a emitted a high, keening noise, and then without warning both of them disappeared in the crowd.

Lokri hit his boswell, spoke, then looked up. "Marim's on her way," Lokri said. "And so is Jaim."

"Then let us endeavor," Brandon said grandly, and Lokri laughed.

They ran to a lift, and while they waited Lokri bent, his hands on his knees, sucking in slow breaths of air. "A great time for a fight," he muttered.

They jammed into the crowded lift, emerging into the merchants' corridor. The front door to the last shop was closed, and no guards stood there.

"That's Snurkel's," Lokri said. "Shut door means trouble."

"Force the door?" Brandon said.

"No. It'll be wired for that. Back way."

"Tell me this," Brandon said as they ran through another shop, ignored a protesting clerk, and skidded into a narrow service alley. "Do you always know a back way?"

Lokri choked on a laugh. "Always."

They ran up the corridor and found the last door shut. A small console gleamed at the side. Lokri grimaced, dug in a pocket, and pulled out his neurojac. Lokri glanced around, then jammed it up against the console and triggered it, igniting a shower of sparks. He cursed and dropped the weapon, wringing his hand. The door clicked and swung ajar as an alarm screeched.

"Another reason they don't like neurojacs on Rifthaven. They're hell on electronics," said Lokri as he pushed the door open.

They rushed in, veering in the direction of a hoarse, angry scream, and burst into a room to find Vi'ya backed into a corner near shelves and shelves of art objects. A small man was gripped tightly against her, a thin trickle of blood at his neck. Two guards stood poised at either side of the room, looking for an opening.

Just as Brandon and Lokri arrived, a side door slid open and four burly men in coveralls appeared, truncheons in their hands.

"Nice timing," Vi'ya greeted them. "Clear the way back to the office —"

That was the last chance any of them had for talking.

"Lys!" Nistan yelped. "Look at this!"

Lyska-si had been monitoring another long series of coded messages. She dropped the flimsies printing out and ducked over to Nistan's console.

"What's going on?"

Nistan looked down at his boz'l with a distracted air, then said, "Korb says he got audio before visual. The woman— captains a ship called *Telvarna*—came in trying to sell some stuff, and the old blungesniffer was hinting around that it came from Arthelion—"

Lyska-si gasped. "You think this *Telvarna* is really the *Maiden's Dream*?"

"Or jacked it. I don't know," Nistan muttered, tapping his

boswell. "Korb only told me Snurkel was hinting around, trying to find out about the Arkad, and that the captain claimed to have killed him."

Lyska-Si whistled softly. "I think we better watch."

Nistan nodded in agreement. "Let's find out if the old stenchwad reveals something else he's not sharing."

Lyska-si scanned eagerly. They both laughed in astonishment when the console revealed Snurkel being held hostage against several of his hired flash by a tall woman with long, swinging black hair. Two men, both tall and lean, and both masked, came to her aid — obviously her crew.

Lyska-si settled back to watch the show, hoping that Snurkel would feel the truncheon that a hired Draco swung at one man's head. The crewman ducked, his foot lashing out, catching the Draco in the crotch.

Nistan hooted with laughter. He obviously didn't like Draco any more than Lyska-si did. The other crewman, a rakish fellow dressed all in black, had his wristknife out, and lunged at one of the others, who backed away hastily, knocking into a crystal 3-D chess set on a stand.

"Nooo!" Snurkel screamed. "Stop them! Kill them! Don't touch the merchandise!"

Lyska-si stuffed her wrist into her mouth to keep from laughing. She'd always believed he'd pay.

One of the guards tossed Snurkel his weapon, and the woman thrust the shop owner violently away. By the time Snurkel had brought his shaking hands up to take aim, she was crouched behind a display case full of porcelain. She rammed the butt of her knife through the back of the case and grabbed objects. She began potting them at Snurkel, who shrieked on a high note of escalating rage as each one smashed, but he did not dare to move away from his cover.

The first man, a slim fellow dressed very plainly and wearing a dark blue nick-mask, was beset by two fighters who knew what they were doing. But so did he; she watched with growing appreciation the grace and surety of his moves as he ducked another blow, feinting toward one so that the second one lunged, missed, and nearly hit the first. The second one bumped against a wooden case, which creaked warningly.

Snurkel screamed both imprecations and commands at the guards, which distracted them. The one still armed with a poison gun looked on helplessly, unable to find an opening.

Finally he holstered the gun and pulled out a long knife, moving in on the fight.

The man in black took the opportunity to toss his boot knife hilt-first to the other, who caught it, flashing a smile before he dodged a concerted attack by his two assailants. His head turned. Lyska-si could tell by the angle that he was checking on the woman, who checked him in the same moment. She made a carry-on signal. He laughed and gestured, no more than a turn of his wrist, but the intent—humor and deference—was clear to Lyska-si. "That's a nick," she said. "High strut, too."

Nistan watched as the man grabbed a long candlestick and whopped one man across the back of his neck.

"Nah," Nistan said. "Other one might be. He's dressed for it."

Lyska-si looked from one man to the other, but her eyes were drawn back to the one in the plain clothes. It wasn't his looks, it was the way he moved that caught at her interest. Like a dance, and he was laughing. It *was* a dance.

His blow with the candlestick was not enough to do more than stagger the man, but it deflected him long enough for Blue-mask to leap over a counter to a better defensive position. Here, he had an array of fantastic mosaic vases to grab and fling at the guards, which he did, quoting some kind of poetry at each throw. The hired flash backed hastily away from the barrage, their faces turning in growing annoyance from him to their screaming employer.

The captain popped up and clipped one behind the ear. He fell heavily against the creaking case, which toppled with slow and dignified inevitability. The musical sounds of tiny smashings came from inside, then it hit the floor with a crash.

The man in black whooped, thrusting a huge statue over onto one guard, who did not duck in time. The statue crashed into a million shards—and over it another guard leapt, grappling Black-shirt to the floor.

The captain rounded a corner, but Snurkel moved at the same time, closer to the office door. "Keep him away!" the captain shouted.

Blue-mask obligingly lobbed a huge vase at the little merchant, who scuttled away, then tried convulsively to catch the vase. It smashed, flinging shards over him. Snurkel screamed in rage, and Lyska-si clapped her hands.

Black-shirt and his attacker rolled over, rose halfway, then lurched into a side alcove. The sounds of tinkling and clangs came from there, punctuated by Snurkel gibbering threats in a constant babble.

One of the guards freed the sword at his side, and lunged at the captain. She ducked, and the man cocked his arm for another lunge—in time to take a full hit on his gaudy helmet from Blue-mask's candlestick. The bonging sound seemed to shake him; then Blue-mask saw a rapier lying in a smashed case, grabbed it up, and he and the guard began an energetic sword battle, right there in the middle of a sea of smashed crockery.

"Woo, look at him fight! *Just* like a vid."

"Scan Snurkel," Nistan muttered.

The merchant was watching the fight with narrowed eyes, distracted only when the woman edged around, then dived through the office door. Snurkel jumped up and ran after, in time to meet a kick from Blue-mask's boot. He slipped in the broken porcelain and fell, rolling in the glass shards.

Blue-mask backed away, fighting to hold his position. Snurkel began crawling along the perimeter of the room, and then Blue-mask yelled, "'Ware, Vi'ya!"

The captain glanced up, then ducked behind the desk as pellets from two weapons crossed where her head had been. The sounds of drawers opening and slamming came clearly from the office.

Snurkel reached the doorway and viciously jabbed at something on a little console hidden in the wall next to him.

The captain, Vi'ya, straightened up as if she'd been shot, her hands going to her head. Lyska-si was aware of the high, thin whine of a mind-blur.

The merchant took aim—and Blue-mask dropped his sword, flinging his candlestick through the doorway. Whap! It hit the merchant across the back of his head, and his weapon spun away.

A guard dropped on Blue-mask from behind, and they fell, rolling through the wreckage. Blue-mask struggled desperately, trying to free his arms, as the man's hand clawed down his face. The man jerked, then fell.

Blue-mask rolled to his feet, yanking the ruined mask free. He shook his head, and Snurkel pointed, his mouth open.

"Arkad," the man squeaked, and lunged at his desk.

Lyska-si gasped.

She had seen that face before, but only on vids. "The Arkad. . . is here," she breathed.

"No chance," Nistan said, but he stared as that much-publicized face.

There he was, the third son of the legendary Panarch, right here on Rifthaven, smashing up Giffus Snurkel's shop. An overwhelming sense of justice being done made her giddy.

"It *is* the Arkad," Lyska-si breathed.

Nistan jerked, tapped his boz'l. When he looked up at Lyska-si, his eyes were huge. "Snurkel's blocking everyone else, but he's got a special relay, and Korb says he wants a squad of enforcers. Not saying why. What do we do?"

Lyska-si thought rapidly. She remembered cheering when the news first came out that the Panarchists had fallen. But since then the news was of atrocities and wholesale killings enough to turn the stomach of the lowest Shiidra-loving deviant.

A reward big enough to buy an octant for grabbing that man, and Snurkel to claim it?

No.

"Can we jam it for a time?"

Nistan wordlessly tapped his boswell, and a moment later said, "Korb did it, though it'll last maybe a minute. At this rate we'll never pay him off."

"Then we'll owe him big," Lyska-si said decidedly. "I don't care about the reward or anything. If we tried to claim it Eusabian would probably just have us killed. Snurkel deserves to lose."

Nistan nodded, a grim set to his jaw as he tapped. "Korb said, no owe. He hates Snurkel, too. So we're agreed, we're gonna give the Arkad a chance to get clear, him 'n' his pack. Then it's up to them."

Lyska-si's boz'l tingled in the pattern that meant her mother. She thought quickly. She couldn't tell her about the Arkad. She wouldn't understand. But Lyska-si could tell her about Snurkel and the other seconds' possible inside information from Arthelion. If she made it sound urgent enough, the resulting uproar might give the Arkad and the others the edge they needed.

She subvocalized rapidly, grinning as her mother's outrage made it clear her impromptu plan would succeed. Then she tapped off the boswell and turned back to watch the rest of the fight.

ELEVEN

Marim arrived a few steps ahead of Jaim, staring in amazement at the smashed front door of Snurkel's shop. Inside was a riot of bobbing heads. Vi'ya, Lokri, and the Arkad were vastly outnumbered—but then Snurkel didn't have Jaim, who launched himself straight into the action.

Glancing back to make certain no one was flanking them, Marim saw a crowd gathering. Always a bad sign. Stepping in the lee of a carved pillar, she loosed her stenchgun in three directions, and watched in satisfaction as the corridor outside the shop cleared rapidly, people kicking and clawing to get away from the terrific stench and the projectile vomiting of those too close to escape. As the air currents spread the gas, an edge of the smell caught at the back of her throat and she plunged back inside the shop.

Vi'ya dived through a door from the other side moments before a cross-hatching of lethal rays in the doorway activated. She came back with a stack of AU scrip in her hand, which she shoved at Lokri. Then her scary black gaze caught Marim. "Montrose. Get Ivard, *whitecode*," Vi'ya ordered.

Whitecode: start up the ship for a fast getaway. Marim swiftly bozzed Montrose and passed on the message.

The fight ended abruptly. Everyone stood or leaned, breathing hard and looking at one another over the fallen guards. Lokri was the first to move. He stepped over two of his assailants, who lay on the ground, one moaning, and the other quite still with his own knife protruding from his back. Lokri pulled free his knife, and with a grimace, cleaned it on the man's gaudy shirt.

Marim gazed around the ruined shop. Cases glittered with fragments of crystal and glass. Lokri lurched against one as he straightened up, holding his bad arm against his side. He poked his head inside the case, then grabbed a beautiful golden torc from the single remaining shelf where, miraculously, it lay undisturbed. Then he ripped off his mask and swiped his hair out of his face with shaking hands. The side of his head was dark with dust and blood mixed, and one eye was already swelling. He grinned rakishly as he handed the golden ornament to Vi'ya. "Truce?"

She took it with red-streaked fingers and laughed softly. "Truce. Now we must run," she said, jamming the torc over her arm.

As if to concur, an alarm whooped, seeming to come from everywhere at once.

"General Lockdown," Jaim said. "But Snurkel will have to tell the Syndics why."

"He will show vids of us." Vi'ya looked grim as she indicated Brandon.

"Of our masks." Brandon swooped down and grabbed up a gleaming length of emerald and gold-embroidered shanta-silk. "Here." He pitched it at Vi'ya, who swathed her body and head in it.

Lokri fished something out of a ruined display case. "Put this on," Lokri said to Brandon, holding out a domino in ancient style, shiny with age. "I'll take this." He reached down and pulled the jacket from one of the unconscious guards. "Not much of a disguise, but maybe it'll get us a little farther."

They started out, Lokri shrugging into the jacket, wincing and cursing as he jarred his healing arm.

The corridor was suspiciously deserted. Jaim smiled briefly, then said, "It's time to find some of my old ratways. Come."

Montrose arrived at the Chirurgicon, breathing heavily. He had thought out a story on the run through the twisting corridors. But when he arrived at the surgeon's, one of the aides pulled him through a door as soon as he walked in — as if they'd been watching for him.

Alarmed, he groped for his knife, then Atropos-Clotho-Lakisus waltzed in, threir headstalks twirling rapidly.

"You must take Ivard/Archon to safety," the Intermittor fluted.

"You know—"

"Lockdown," Atropos continued, its voice reedy. "Wethree shall aid you, and the vlith-Arkad, but you must—"

"Vlith . . . Everyone knows he's here?" Montrose cut in, alarm turning into fear.

"Wethree met him in the corridor a short time ago. The Arkad genome is known to us. Otherwise, just one vendor, and the Caucus for Public Order," the Intermittor said. "But that will change very rapidly. You must promise to get Ivard to Ares."

"Ares!" Montrose repeated. "No one knows where it is—"

"The Archon's subphratry is there. Portus-Dartinus-Atos. You *must* get Ivard there."

Montrose thought of Omilov and nodded slowly. "There may be a way."

"It is well. But you must do more, or surely fail."

Alarm kindled in Montrose. "What do you mean?"

"Dissension burns in Rifthaven. Dol'jhar has overreached. Wethree shall add fear to the mixture, to break the locks that hold you and yours within."

A sharp scent burst from the Intermittor, and a small portion of its ribbons near its headstalk changed color, shading into a purplish tone. Atropos' headstalk looped down in a sinuous motion and plucked a small portion of ribbon, then held it out to Montrose.

"No harm will come to you, Montrose," sang the Intermittor. "You will understand when the time comes."

There was no time for questions, and he knew the Kelly would do nothing to imperil the safety of the Archon's genome. He nodded. The Intermittor slapped the ribbon against his throat, then Lakisus and Clotho swathed his neck in a silk scarf as a fierce itching commenced.

"None will stop you now," said the Intermittor, its head-stalk looping in the curve that Montrose knew indicated amusement.

It waltzed away in step with Clotho and Lakisus, its head-stalk turning back to address him one more time. "Wethree go to help you. Move quickly: wethree will move quickly as well."

Ivard emerged from a side room, looking thin and pale but his smile was cocky and his eyes clear of fever.

"We gotta run, huh?" the boy said. "I'm ready."

Montrose bowed silently to the departing Kelly, then put his hand on Ivard's good shoulder to guide him out.

The trip was quick but nerve-racking. Despite his intentions, it became obvious very quickly that Ivard had not much stamina. His breath was coming in wheezing gasps long before they reached the refit shop where the *Telvarna* was docked. And Montrose himself didn't feel entirely normal: his whole torso itched, and he felt bloated, as if he'd eaten two or three normal meals in one sitting. He hoped the Kelly had rightly judged his biology.

Then Montrose came to a halt, ramming Ivard into a narrow doorway between two shops. A group of tough, dangerous-looking Syndicate enforcers wearing Draco colors, with their red-stained filed teeth bared, took up a station before the doors of the dock, armed with pellet-jacs. Nearby, a smaller group of Yim, wearing the brassards of Public Order, stood glaring at the larger Draco contingent, fingering their weapons.

"You must disperse. You know the rules," the Yim declared.

"Not if a fleet of brainburners are trying to take over Rifthaven," a Draco declared.

"Brainburners?" Ivard muttered, shivering. "Oh!"

Montrose saw something he'd never seen before — a single Kelly, the Intermittor of the surgeon triad, Atropos, undulating down the street, its headstalk quivering.

The heads of the Draco turned sharply. They knew what a rarity it was for a Kelly to be seen alone. Apparently some of them knew the surgeon, for one stuck out her weapon in front of the Kelly and said, "What's your hurry? Brainburners coming, am I right?"

"It is imperative to investigate a worse rumor," the Kelly twittered in a loud drone.

"What rumor?" Another Draco stepped forward, his gun at a threatening angle.

"A worse one?" The Public Order squad moved closer as well, keeping a wary eye on the Draco.

"The Thismian Bloat has broken out in this sublevel," the Kelly trilled. "We must investigate. And encourage all to wear oxygen masks and not to touch any surface with any portion of skin."

A crowd had gathered, but at this news, the listeners started backing away.

"Thismian Bloat!" someone yelled. "During a lockdown?"

"Here?" one of the Draco demanded. He looked at the hatch behind him, evidently weighing his orders against this new information.

"Yes," said Atropos. "Be alert for anyone with an unusual rash, or who is covered up. But do not, if you value your life, shoot them or otherwise break their skin. That will only spread it faster." The Intermittor moved on.

The Draco looked at one another, the weapons lowering — then jerking up again as a third group of armed people arrived at a trot.

"Get out of here!" one of the Draco yelled.

"This is our sector, Draco," one of the newcomers yelled back. "We'll protect our own —"

"We are Public Order!" the Draco leader shouted.

"You Kug can go suck blunge," a Yim shrieked.

A riot seemed on the verge of breaking out, right in front of the hatch leading to the refit shop where the *Telvarna* awaited its crew. Montrose shook his head as his stomach rumbled in a way he had never heard before.

"I think it's my turn," he breathed, now understanding what the Kelly had done to him.

"What's Thismian Bloat?" Ivard asked. "I never heard of that one."

"Then you're lucky," Montrose said, swallowing rapidly. "Shiidra used it against humans early in the war."

"What happens?"

"Starts with an itch, and then you belch and fart like a Nolifer Windsack. It's all downhill from there, until the virus converts your guts into gas all at once and blows you all over the landscape." He pushed the boy back into the shadows. "Stay put."

He walked out, scanning the Draco rapidly. None of them had seen him before, he was certain of that.

Their gazes took in his scarf, and the leader said, "What do you want?"

Montrose opened his mouth to reply, and the volume of the ensuing belch surprised even him. "Excuse me," he said as the echoes died away, sensing heads turning all up and down the corridor. "A bit of bad yeelm, I think."

The Draco glanced at his compatriots uneasily. "Well, you can't get through here."

Phweeeeeet-Pop! Montrose felt his pant legs flutter, and the smell was like nothing he'd ever experienced before. The Draco evidently agreed; two of them began backing away. The Yim and Kug also backed away, in different directions.

But their leader was made of sterner stuff. He stepped forward and pulled the scarf away from Montrose's neck with the point of his jac. His eyes widened.

Brauuuuck-Kaboom! The Draco jumped back, his face drained of color. Montrose suppressed the urge to look down and see if his legs were still attached to his body—the Kelly command of their ribbon chemistry was truly awesome. He hoped there were no open flames nearby, or this part of Rifthaven would be blown right out of orbit. Him with it.

"It's the Bloat!" screeched a bystander, and the corridor abruptly transformed into a riot scene as everyone, the Draco included, fled in terror.

"Come on, boy," Montrose said, trying not to laugh. "Let's get the ship fired up." He only hoped the Kelly-induced symptoms were gone by the time the rest of the crew got back, or he might end up living in the airlock for the rest of their journey.

The run for freedom was a revelation for Jaim.

He had realized within an hour of his arrival at Jucan's shop that a return to his family was a mistake. The reasons why he had left, which had seemed diminished to insignificance by Reth Silverknife's death, had returned, like carrion birds, to feed on his spirit.

Jucan was happy to see his twin again—too happy. His life-mate Tura made it clear he was less welcome now than he had been on his last visit. They had carried out all the food rituals, but Tura with many ugly looks in his direction, looks which made the drink bitter and the bread taste of ash.

When Jaim had tried to tell his brother he needed to talk, for he had lost the path—if the Path had ever existed—she had somehow overheard, and interrupted to request him not to poison the light in their home with his disharmony.

It had been in his mind to say that the disharmony was brought by her, but he was silent. He never answered her jibes, even though they surprised his brother, who insisted that she was mild as milk most times. Jaim would never tell his brother that it was he, and not Jucan, whom Tura had wanted first, and the poison had been her gift to him for his refusal.

Lokri's call for aid had been a relief. He had gone with only a word of peace to his brother, and no words at all to Tura. But he had felt her eyes watching him, long after the door was closed between them.

It had half been in his mind to lose this fight, to find nothingness in death, if there was no peace. But once he arrived at Snurkel's, his training had taken over, and soon a kind of balance was restored between the present and need. And what he observed brought to his awareness a new window, a new light. The window was Brandon Arkad in action.

The warrior whose feet stay on the Path does not become tangled in the jungles of anger. The leader of warriors keeps the Path clear for all who follow.

The spiritual truths had burned to ash with the *Sunflame* but the martial ones had rekindled themselves. Vi'ya, and Jaim himself, possibly Lokri, could best Brandon in a fight, but none of them led so effortlessly.

Jaim had thought Vi'ya a good enough leader: she knew strategy well and issued clear orders. And she had, after her own fashion, considered the welfare of her crew, something she had learned from Markham.

But as the five of them ran through the tortuous byways of Rifthaven, encountering danger at nearly every intersection, it was Brandon who kept them laughing with a stream of absurd commentary on the passing sights, interspersed with snatches of song. Once, even, the nonsense rhymes of childhood, used to set a rhythm as they fought their way through a gang of angry Draco that set upon them without warning.

Lokri once joined in a song, his clear baritone marking a melodic counterpoint to the light tenor voice; somehow it was easy to disable, and not to kill, the gang of angry Yim who accosted them. And though the Arkad was not the best fighter, it was he who watched for the others, calling exhortations, encouragements, and warnings when a platoon of roving Kug met them, or some drunken spacers enjoying the sudden outbreaks of fighting all over Rifthaven did their best to join in.

It was he who first detected the dissension among their enemies and adroitly turned their intent aside so that the five might pass safely.

It was the Path. The light.

Even Vi'ya was smiling as they ran down the last street toward the refit shop. Her smile disappeared, though, when they saw the *Telvarna*. Jaim noted the utter absence of people in the street. Alarm's flame cooled into purpose.

As they ran up the ramp, he felt under his feet the thrum of the engines winding up, and he homed straight for them.

They were a long way from safe.

In a line, the *Telvarna*'s crew bolted for the ramp, Marim last.

A jolt, and Marim was swung off her feet when a strong arm snaked out from a dark doorway and snagged her. A mouth pressed hard on hers, and a hand ran down her body.

"You forgot me. You left me waiting for you at Ebo's," the man mumbled thickly. "You won't forget me now."

Marim twisted her head and stared up at this new problem. Who *was* this blit? The sweet/sour scent of drug-laced tabac was on his breath, and his eyes were red-rimmed. She didn't recognize him at all.

"This time'll be better," he mumbled.

She exhaled in relief. He didn't want a fight, he wanted bunny. She wouldn't have to kill him.

"Captain wants me now," she breathed, kissing the working lips. "Boz me."

"But you *promised*, next time you docked. "

"Captain's call. You know how it is."

He freed her arms at that, then whined, "Boz me, Marim."

"Sure," she lied, then ran flat out for the refit portal, skidding through the hatch to the sound of accelerating thunder. They almost didn't wait for her! She was surprised at the spurt of anger, and the assumption that they owed her. As if anyone really owed anyone!

Relief washed through her when she saw the ramp still down. As she raced to it, she heard Vi'ya's voice through the bridge connection: (MARIM, CLOSE IT UP.)

Uh-oh. She was rasty. She'd been smiling on the run — what happened now? Marim's nose wrinkled. The airlock stank like the entire level's sewage had backed up into it.

After getting the ramp stowed in record time, she caromed

around a corner and flung herself into her pod a heartbeat before Vi'ya smacked her palm down on *Telvarna*'s go-pad.

No one spoke as the ship maneuvered with deceptive slowness out of the jungle of tubes and constructs. Marim used this time to scan the other faces. Vi'ya was filthy and bloodstained, a bruise darkening on the side of her head.

A quick glance showed Lokri with blood caking his jaw, and his eyes were, for once, wary and somber.

In Fire Control the Arkad sat, safe and secure, but his face—which was barely recognizable for the scrapes and blooming bruises, and swelling contusions—wore that expression Marim had long ago privately dubbed Markham's Blastshield. Something had happened, all right. Just now? Or back at Snurkel's?

It had to be Lokri. What'd he done now?

"We're out," Vi'ya said. "Lokri, listen for anything remotely resembling Karroo codes."

Marim fought a sudden yawn as she ran her gaze over her console. Everything shone either blue or green. Her carryall was still full—she hadn't had a chance to sell anything. And best of all, the Omilovs were still here, so she had a chance after all to nail down that coin. Her heart sank only when she saw Ivard at his post. Some idiot had gone and gotten him out of the surgeon's.

A quiet voice spoke from the background: "I wish to know where we're being taken."

The old gnostor entered the bridge, his face polite. Sanctus Hicura! Couldn't he feel the rads? He couldn't have come in at a worse time.

Vi'ya said, her gaze on her board, "I do not yet know."

"Then I must request you tell me our status. If we are not actually prisoners, I insist we be set down as soon as possible at some location where no harm will come to any of us."

'There is no such place," Vi'ya said, her voice hard.

"That's true," Marim said, trying to ease the atmosphere. "Rex off the *Tantayon* told me a lot. Some of Eusabian's allies have gone on a sacking spree like no one's ever seen, not even in a wiredream."

"Captain," Omilov said. "My request—"

Vi'ya kept her eyes on her screen. "Denied."

Marim watched Omilov incline his head and go out.

Jaim's voice came over the comm: "They know about the

Arkad."

Marim gathered her courage. Vi'ya had to be told about the hyperwave, right now. She kept her eyes on the screens as she spoke, "And they got some sort of FTL comm—they can talk between systems just like being in the same room. But not all their ships have it."

Her voice failed as Vi'ya turned, her eyes narrowed. "You knew this?"

"I just found it out from Rex," Marim added hastily.

"Thirty minutes to radius," Ivard put in.

Brandon closed his board, stood looking thoughtfully down at it, then he went to Vi'ya's console. Marim strained her ears, but she could not understand his low murmur.

Vi'ya got up. "Ivard. Let me know when we're three minutes to radius." She walked out, Brandon following.

Marim whirled around and fixed Lokri with a glare. "All right, blit. What happened?"

Lokri sighed, twisting his neck slowly. "Outrun, outgunned, and unmanned."

Marim eyed him, then took a risk of her own. "I hate it when you talk like those chatzing nicks."

A flush of anger ridged Lokri's cheekbones, and his mouth tightened. Then he shrugged, giving her his old, lopsided grin. "We won at the Galadium. And I tried to drink all our winnings. Lost it all over the corridor."

"We?"

"I took Brandon for a tour of Rifthaven. Masked, but for the end."

"You blungeloving scum. Why?"

Lokri sighed and shut his eyes. "You may as well hear it. Get me something to drink first."

"You can get it, you—"

Lokri's eyes opened briefly, very, very tired. "If I could get out of this chair without passing out, I would. We also," he breathed shakily, "drank Negus."

"I'll get you something," Ivard said in a subdued voice. "Watch my console?"

"I will." Marim waited until the boy had gone out, clutching his shoulder as if it pained him. Then she said soberly, "No wonder she's mad at you. Snurkel's going to call out all Karroo after us."

Lokri opened his eyes. "Maybe. But I promise you this: she

is more angry with herself."

Osri impatiently waited in the dispensary for his father to return, which happened quickly. Too quickly. It could only mean that they were still prisoners. He bit back a fretful complaint when he saw how gray his face was. Montrose also seemed ill, judging by the hiccoughs and belches he emitted, not to mention an occasional waft that made Osri's eyes water in spite of the tianqi running high, though the surgeon didn't seem discommoded otherwise.

Montrose thoughtfully reached over and notched the tianqi to max, until the astringent-smelling air stirred Osri's hair. That irritated him, too. But he kept silent as the surgeon frowned in concern and started fussing over Omilov, who suffered his ministrations without any lessening of the strain in his face.

Vi'ya and Brandon appeared, and Osri sustained another shock. The woman had two bleeding wounds, one on her arm and one on her temple, which she ignored. Her dark skin showed the shadow of a bruise at her jawline. A golden torc over one arm added a counterpoint of barbarity. Brandon looked far worse. Osri would not have recognized him but for the familiar clothes and the Faseult signet on his hand. He smiled ruefully, the fresh, swelling bruises on his face shifting.

Montrose moved to Vi'ya's side, extending a bandage. She held out her arm, but her attention was on Omilov.

She said abruptly, "I lost the Heart of Kronos."

A spasm of pain tightened Omilov's features.

All the control in the world could not have prevented Osri from saying with heartfelt bitterness, "I trust you got a good price."

Vi'ya ignored him. "I promised you I would try to find out its powers."

"It's not a weapon," Omilov said, his voice hoarse. He looked up, his eyes dark with strain. "How did you lose it?"

"I took it to an antique dealer I've done business with. He had mentioned Urian artifacts once before. Eusabian of Dol'jhar must have posted an impossibly high reward for the retrieval of this artifact." She drew a short breath. Osri wondered if some of his father's pain must be echoing back on her. He hoped it was as she said, "There was a fight."

"I was there, Sebastian," Brandon spoke up. "We did our best, and nearly lost ourselves in the process."

Omilov winced and put up a hand to shade his eyes.

Vi'ya said, "The Arkad was seen by this merchant, which is why we've departed Rifthaven."

Comprehension worked its way into Osri's brain, dousing all the anger. Two thoughts occurred: *There is nowhere we can go.*

And: Brandon did not betray us.

"Then we are all hunted creatures," his father whispered hoarsely. "'And they ran unto the borders of darkness, pursued by the Daemons of Hell.'" He pinched his fingers to his eyes, then looked up tiredly. "What do you intend to do with us?"

Vi'ya shook her head. "I don't know. The Eya'a seem to think we should go to their planet, but I'm not sure we'd live long there, supposing we aren't followed and slagged along with the planet."

Montrose signaled Vi'ya with a glance, then tipped his head toward Omilov. Vi'ya nodded fractionally, then turned to go.

Osri said, "I wish you'd let us go back to our own people."

Vi'ya stopped and faced him. "Where?" she said. "Perhaps once, your Panarchy represented a kind of order. Now it is gone. Whatever you do, it is gone forever."

"We can rebuild," Osri said. "We will rebuild."

Brandon said softly, "Gone or not, we have to try."

The captain hesitated, as if about to speak to him, then over the comm came Ivard's panicky voice. "Vi'ya!"

She whirled and ran to the bridge.

Brandon followed Vi'ya in spite of the exhaustion settling over his brain like a blanket. The euphoria of their successful escape through the streets of Rifthaven had dissipated, leaving the old bleakness—purposelessness. It seemed to be his place in life to have a clear goal, but none of the wherewithal to carry it out.

Self-mockery prompted not-quite-laughter at the earnestness and futility of his carefully built campaign to obtain justice for Markham by flushing his betrayer, except he'd been completely wrong.

And 'justice' would not bring Markham back.

He looked at Vi'ya. *Mates.* Another blow, from an

unexpected direction: it seemed impossible, but one thing he'd learned from his dealings with Anaris, the hostage from Dol'jhar, was that Dol'jharians did not lie.

He thought he had known Markham better than anyone. Yet the Markham he'd known would have been more likely to share his bed with Marim, or Lokri, the ones who never looked back. For that was the kind of liaison both Markham and Brandon had sought, back in the days of their relationship. Comradeship.

Mates meant commitment. The idea that Markham had changed enough to form a serious relationship seemed to push him farther into the shadows of memory, to make him the more unreachable.

He blinked, fighting the slow spin-stop of vertigo. He had to get control of himself, to focus.

Every muscle and bone in his body ached as he dropped into the fire-control pod, but his hands stayed miraculously steady as they brought up the Tenno glyphs. He had to concentrate on the danger. On impending action. They were not at all safe. He leaned forward, squinting at his console and the viewscreen.

There were several ships moving in on them as Rifthaven dwindled behind. The *Telvarna* moved at the exact same speed as the pursuers, an absurdly slow crawl.

The Tenno grid rippled as the information flowed from Vi'ya's console. Brandon blinked and opened his eyes wide, fighting the blurring surge that washed over him. The Tenno glyphs took on an air of numinous clarity, reaching directly into his visual cortex. The Vilarian Negus. . . *the Negus won't be denied. . .*

He glanced at Lokri, to discover an abstracted gaze that probably mirrored his own. This should be interesting. It was a good thing that Tenno glyph-thinking was mostly visual and automatic. . . Then there was no more time for conscious thought as missiles streaked toward them from the pursuing ships.

Brandon's fingers raced across his console, strike and counterstrike, thrust and parry. Assured as the days when he had run the Tenno with Markham, whose shade stood at his shoulder. In memory! Only in memory. He *had* to get control.

But the images flowed, with merciless clarity. A random gleam of light reflected off the Faseult signet on his hand.

Images from the fight in Snurkel's shop mingled with memories of the booster flight. . .. *"it is the Phoenix House that is honored."* The glyphs waxed large in his vision, a palimpsest over the reality of the screens.

More ships appeared, some ahead, responding to the chatter of code emanating from Lokri's console. The slow pace imposed on them by the chase mines lent the battle the aspect of a nightmare.

. . . the arid sands stretched to the horizon, flinty rocks punishing his feet, slowing him. Behind him the wrecked chariot lay on its side, one wheel spinning lazily in the shimmering heat. . .

"Other Syndicates are joining Karroo," Lokri said hoarsely. "I can't read the codes, but if enough of them agree, they'll release the passcode to the mines, and then we're vapor."

. . . entangled in its traces, two sphinx panted as their life-blood drained into the sand. . .

A near miss buffeted the ship.

"With that damned hyperwave, they're probably talking to Eusabian right now — he'll promise them anything to get the Arkad." Marim's voice was strained.

. . . now the pungent scent of cinnamon rose up around him as the shredded bark of the nest crunched under his claws. Around it, the lean-haunched, hunch-shouldered predators closed in. . . there was no safety here. . .

"Arkad!" came Vi'ya's voice. "We're going to have to run for it. Can you keep off the mines?"

. . . his immature wings flapped uselessly, stirring up clouds of myrrh. He opened his beak, a harsh cry emerged and died away.

"I can." It was his own voice, from a distance.

"Marim! Give him control of the teslas."

. . . the beasts lunged at the nest, fell back, raked by his claws, then lunged again. the shadow of immense wings fell across him. A beast howled as a vast claw broke its back. . .

Marim let out a yell of triumph. "You got one! They're scattering! Kiss my radiants, blungesuckers!"

. . . and then he felt himself lifted into the air as the glory of the descending Phoenix burned around him. . .

Vi'ya's voice cut in, sharp-edged: "That wasn't a missile strike! Ivard. How — "

Her words were drowned by the terrifying squeal-rumble

of a ruptor beam. The glyphs dwindled back into the grid.

Brandon woke to the reality of the bridge as the ship began to vibrate, and he felt every bone and tooth vibrate with it. His hands gripped his console as the sound dropped toward the deadly subsonics that would break apart the ship. On the viewscreen the bright coin that marked the death of a ship was fading away. The radiants of the others dwindled as they fled, but not fast enough: one by one they flared into brightness and vanished.

TWELVE

"Ruptor!" Montrose leapt forward and hit his console. The bridge appeared. Omilov gazed at the blurring picture.

"Who's out there?" Montrose yelled.

The captain didn't seem to hear them. She cursed, jabbing at her console with no success. The ship bucked but did not respond. Then the ruptor stabilized short of disruption, halting at a deep thrumming that made Omilov's eye sockets ache and his sinuses begin to water.

"Point-five light-seconds and closing." Ivard's voice shook, his breathing harsh.

Marim said flatly into her comm: "Never mind override, Jaim—drive cavity's gone."

Suddenly a harsh voice modulated out of the deep hum: "HAILING CHANNEL ONE, HAILING CHANNEL ONE. . ."

The captain's teeth bared as she slammed her hand down on her console. "Acknowledge."

In grim silence Omilov and the others in the dispensary watched Lokri fight to get the vibrating ship to respond. The hum intensified, and trouble lights began to flash on Marim's board.

"Hurry, damn you, it's shaking us apart!" Marim yelled.

"I'm—trying—" Lokri muttered, his face green-tinged with nausea. Sparks from his console made him swear and slap frantically at the keypads. "There," he said, wringing his hands. "But all I can give him back is audio, and if they don't release us, we'll lose even that."

Vi'ya slapped a key and they all looked up at the main screen, which was echoed in a subsidiary window on the dispensary console.

A man's face appeared, a hard face with an iron-colored beard. The man was dressed in naval blues. Omilov stared in blank amazement as he said, "This is His Majesty's battlecruiser *Mbwa Kali*, Captain Mandros Nukiel commanding. Shut down all systems and assemble all hands, passengers, sophonts and sentients in your main lock."

"Acknowledged." Vi'ya's voice was flat and cold.

The screen blanked. Vi'ya jabbed viciously at her console, and the sound of the engines died. The subsonic hum dropped to a low level, and Omilov began to breathe again. The *Telvarna* jolted as the ruptor shifted to tractor mode.

Lokri shifted the main screen to a view of space. The bridge crew, and those inside the dispensary, watched the bright dot of light growing with frightening speed. As it resolved into a familiar silver egg-shape, Vi'ya looked back at the imager.

"Your wish has just been granted, gnostor," she said.

Osri gave a long sigh of relief. "Now we'll be safe."

"If they don't line us up and shoot us," Lokri said.

Vi'ya turned on him. "You may wish they'd shot us along with the rest of that scum chasing us. Why do you think they're hanging around Rifthaven? They want information and they want it badly; I expect we're only alive because we were the target of that chase."

The cruiser filled the screens, its smooth hull redly reflecting the light of the distant sun. As hundreds of meters of silver, bristling with antennae and weapons nacelles, passed by, a splash of color quickly resolved into a blazon on the hull. A stylized painting of a fierce-eyed dog appeared, and above it the Sun and Phoenix of the Panarchy of the Thousand Suns.

Omilov transferred his gaze to Brandon, whose profile was just visible from the angle of the spy-eye. His face, as much as one could read beyond the distortion of swellings and bruises, was utterly expressionless.

"Father, you'll want to get dressed," Osri said.

Omilov glanced distractedly at his robe, then turned back to the console.

He wished he could believe that this new change in their lives would guarantee safety. But he was beginning to think there could be no safety, no surety, ever again.

On the bridge, the consoles flickered, went dark, and the emergency lighting came on.

Brandon had still been staring up at the cruiser's blazon. What was he thinking? He'd come full circle. The thought brought with it a sense of grief for all those who had died since the holocaust in the Mandala's Ivory Hall.

Despite the unexpected turn in their fortunes, Omilov's mood was somber as he began changing into the tunic Montrose had brought him.

On the bridge of the *Mbwa Kali*, Captain Mandros Nukiel sat back and sighed, trying to ease a neck stiff with tension. "SigInt, status?"

"Powering down per protocol, sir. Sensors indicate ten individuals, two of them possibly children, three smaller quadruped signatures. All heading for the main lock per your order."

Nukiel gave orders to augment the lock party with two wranglers—at least it wasn't snakes this time—then turned to his tactical officer. "Lieutenant Rogan."

The short, square woman looked up with faint inquiry. "Sir. Do you want me to oversee this interrogation?"

"I'd like a shot at this one," Commander Efriq said unexpectedly, turning to Nukiel from where he'd been conferring with the ensign on the environmental console. The dapper first officer's face showed the strain that was weighing on all of them, but his uniform's creases were as razor-sharp as ever. "That old Columbiad has some interesting modifications, and it's considerably better kept than most of the trash we've picked up lately."

Nukiel blinked, fighting off fatigue as he looked back and forth between the two officers. Rogan gazed back at him, her eyes steady, though her face, too, was marked with exhaustion. He swept his gaze over the rows of bridge officers, each busy at his or her console. He could feel their tension as well. "Very well, Commander."

Efriq saluted and left the bridge.

Rogan turned back to her console; he sensed mild disappointment.

The Rifters they'd intercepted so far had known nothing useful, and they were no closer to capturing one of the mysterious hyperwaves. No doubt Efriq hoped that this interrogation would be different.

It had better be. Their mood had been grim before they came around the gas giant after an unsuccessful chase and discovered this firefight. The identification of two craft registered on bonus chips, and the presence of so many targets within reach, had been enough to decide Nukiel's intervention: to take their target and clean space of the other vermin. But now Rifthaven knew they were there.

Some of those ships might have fired on the Mandala. His mouth tightened. He'd run a little wild there, but he could not find it in him to regret it.

Ivard stared at the hatch through which they would shortly exit to face the Panarchist forces. The emergency lighting made the lock gloomy, and the air felt stuffy and thick, but Ivard knew the power hadn't been off long enough to really make a difference. He swallowed, his shoulder aching with renewed fire. Montrose glanced down at him and touched his good arm. "We'll be all right," he rumbled.

Ivard rubbed a sweaty hand down the sides of his jumpsuit, carefully not moving his bad side. He'd felt so good after the visit to the Kelly, but it wasn't lasting.

He studied the nicks standing at the back of the lock. Only Osri looked pleased; his father rubbed absently at his left arm. Brandon stood behind them, holding Trev and Gray's leashes, one in each hand. His gaze was distant, his face closed. The dogs were sitting alertly, ears flicking at the clanking sounds that came at intervals through the hull. They panted softly.

Marim and Lokri stood together, with Jaim nearby. The engineer had the blank expression he'd worn since the day they found Dis blasted and his mate dead. The familiar violet of grief bloomed behind Ivard's ribs when he thought of his sister. He was glad she didn't live to see them captured by nicks; the thought didn't help.

At the front of the lock, Vi'ya stood with the Eya'a, like a trinity of statues, utterly still. Ivard could see the coiled anger in her tight shoulders. She too held a leash, to a harness on Lucifur. The big cat was sitting, but his tail lashed restlessly.

For once the whisper of voices inside Ivard's head was still, leaving him able to think about what was happening. Did that mean more danger — or less? He shivered as the violet bloomed into blue, sending ice along his nerves. That happened a lot now. The Kelly surgeons had told him it was to be expected. *"The Archon whose genetic material you bear came from a warm planet,"* threy'd said. *"Try to stay warm."*

Something clanged outside the lock, and an amplified voice roared through the hull: "YOU'VE GOT ATMOSPHERE NOW. OPEN UP."

Vi'ya handed the leash to Montrose and fisted the manual hatch release. The lever came down with an agonized screech, and the hatch separated slightly along its central seam. She stepped back. Two immense metal hands shot through the gap and slammed the hatch open.

Ivard gasped as the painful, blinding light silhouetted the hulking form of a Marine in battle armor at one side of the lock. Behind him, others held firejacs aimed directly at the *Telvarna's* crew. A ramp had been pushed up to the ship's side, since the *Telvarna's* couldn't deploy without power.

The Marine's voice came through his suitcomm, loud and slightly distorted: "Hands on your heads. Exit the lock one at a time."

Vi'ya walked through the hatch with one hand on her head, the other holding Lucifur's leash. Ivard could hear her fury in the ring of her boots on the ramp. The Marines on either side stepped back a pace when the tiny Eya'a appeared, but their weapons remained steady.

Marim made to follow but the Marine blocked her path with one huge arm.

Ivard stood on tiptoe, trying to see what was happening. A uniformed man approached Vi'ya and ran a wand up and down her body. He looked at the Eya'a, his face tight, and spoke into a pin mike. A moment later he dropped the wand to his side. A woman in a green uniform, a leather tunic and trousers, approached Vi'ya and asked a question that Ivard couldn't hear. After a brief discussion, the woman gave Vi'ya a collar of some sort, which the captain slipped onto Lucifur's neck. The man with the wand waved them on, and the nick in battle gear motioned Marim out of the lock.

When Ivard's turn came, he winced as his half-healed flesh pulled, and his hand dropped. He clutched it tight to his chest, the other pressed against his head. One of the battle suits stepped toward him, the servos in the armor whining, and Ivard stumbled hastily into line behind Marim.

Now Ivard could see the squat form of a self-mobile plasma cannon aimed squarely at the lock. He swallowed convulsively.

Behind him, Osri's steps rang on the steel decking. "Listen, I'm a—" he began.

"CUT THE YAP AND MOVE," came the amplified voice.

Osri gasped, and despite his gnawing fear, Ivard sneaked a look behind him. Osri looked mortally offended. A snicker at Ivard's shoulder, and there was Marim's mirthful face.

"Be careful of that one," she whispered, jerking her head in Osri's direction while looking up at the blank battle-armor visor. "He's the sort gives Rifters a bad name."

"Got a temper, too," drawled Lokri. "Sometimes have to lock him up."

Ivard snickered at the outrage on Osri's face, and the wicked glee on Marim's. He moved closer to her.

"That's enough gabble," snapped a Marine. He thrust the muzzle of his jac between Ivard and Marim, knocking Ivard back a step.

Ivard bit against a yell as the weapon brushed his bad shoulder, and his arm dropped. He brought the other down and clutched it tight against him, wincing against fresh waves of pain. The muttering voices mounted in his head and the fog of confusion that had been his lot so often of late closed in.

"Get your hand up—"

"He's wounded," Montrose said, his deep voice threatening. "Burn."

Ivard stumbled forward, muzzily wondering where his other two voices were, as, one by one, the *Telvarna*'s crew and passengers were taken through a hatch and down a corridor.

Osri watched as Ivard walked down the ramp. The boy's good arm began to twist in a sinuous pattern, his pace revealing a rhythmic hitch. Nausea gripped Osri, and he wondered what poison that Kelly ribbon was shooting through Ivard's bloodstream.

Then it was Osri's turn. At least four large-bore jacs tracked him as he approached the man with the wand. Fear tingled through him. Surely they wouldn't shoot a Naval officer!

They don't know you're an officer, the voice of reason yammered in his skull. You were on a Rifter ship and you won't get a chance to tell them until they've secured the whole crew. A fresh burst of rage shook him as he remembered Marim's and Lokri's comments. They were trying to get him shot! Well, the jac would be in the other hand, once this was straightened out.

Meanwhile a businesslike warrant officer ran the scanner over Osri's body and stopped short at his armpit. "Hand it over," the man said.

"But I—"

"Now."

Pressing his lips together, he unzipped his suit and withdrew the coin and the flight ribbon, then laid them in the steel box indicated by a pointed weapon. He noticed Marim staring at the box. At least he'd kept it from *her*.

The warrant officer motioned him toward a hatch, through which the Rifters were now being conducted. He tried to see what was happening with his father and Brandon.

"Eyes front," snapped the officer. "Move it." The push that accompanied the order knocked Osri off balance, and he stumbled towards the hatch. He hadn't even managed to note the warrant officer's name for the formal letter of complaint he would be writing soon.

Sebastian Omilov obediently took the position indicated as Marines in standard fatigues lined everyone up against the long wall of what he took to be an interrogation room. Backed by two Marines in battle armor, whose bulk made the good-sized room seem small, their movements were brusque and assured.

Omilov stood next to his son, whose breathing betrayed his anger. Osri was scowling at Marim and Lokri as they continued cracking jokes at the impassive figures in battle armor. Omilov could hear the bravado in their voices and, oddly, the trace of a Torigan accent in Lokri's, something he'd not detected before.

On the other side of Montrose, Ivard slouched, his face pale and vacant, his good hand clutching his other arm. The bandage on his back under his coveralls made him look lopsided. His eyes moved restlessly without focusing on anything and his body swayed, following an unmistakable though subtle triple beat.

Vi'ya and the Eya'a stood like statues at the front of the line. The big cat paced restlessly back and forth between the limits of its leash, its tail snapping, the fur on its back slightly fluffed. Omilov could hear a throaty growl. He didn't think it was a purr. Jaim was equally still, his expression inward.

Then Brandon entered, preceded by the two dogs, whose leashes he held like reins. For a moment the scene took on a numinous clarity in Omilov's eyes as it recalled to him the image on the ring now glinting on the Aerenarch's right hand. *Or, a smiling charioteer, sable, vested proper, driving a chariot gules, drawn by two sphinxes, sable and argent, all affrontee, in base a ford proper.* Ancient symbol of will and discipline, the Faseult line had paired it with laughter in their family motto. Only hours before he was murdered by Rifters, Tanri Faseult had entrusted that ring to Brandon for delivery to his brother, now Archon of Charvann, if he still lived.

But there was no laughter in Brandon's face. Only, Omilov thought, the dawning realization that his will would account for even less on one of his father's battlecruisers than it had among the raffish crew of a Rifter ship.

Of all of them there, Brandon's sentence would be the longest.

At first Osri thought his father shared his surge of hope that Brandon would be recognized and save them from being shot when Marim and Lokri finally went too far. But a glance at Brandon made it clear that even the Panarch would have trouble recognizing him now. Though, Osri thought with that detached and astringent humor that took hold of him now and then, the disreputable condition of Brandon's clothing and the bruises on his face seemed to highlight the differences between his walk and the wary surrender that informed the movements of the Rifters around him. It affected the Marine guards: it could be that the guards were no more conscious of the difference than Brandon seemed to be as he watched Ivard, yet the Marine guiding him did not touch him as he took his position with the others.

A hatch behind the console hissed open, revealing a short man with slicked-down glossy black hair and a narrow mustache. His uniform—the insignia marked him as a commander—was fresh, making Osri feel even grubbier in his shapeless Rifter clothing. The commander was followed by a young ensign. The older officer looked around, his face revealing nothing, and then seated himself with mannered precision next to the console.

Marim muttered a bawdy comment to Lokri, then both fell silent as a prod from a firejac.

The ensign seated herself at the console, glanced at it

briefly, and said, "Two of them identified." She looked up at the crew. "Three il-Kavic, step forward. Jesimar vlith-Kendrian, step forward."

A hiss of surprise brought everyone's attention to Lokri. He had stilled, unbreathing, his eyes wide. Ivard's face was as white as the wall as he stepped away from it. Then Lokri took a step forward, lips twisted in contempt.

The man at the console said dispassionately: "Three il-Kavic, bond-breaker, Natsu IV, year 960." Then, with a glance at Lokri, "Jesimar vlith-Kendrian: praecidens." He paused.

Disowned?

"Murder, both parents and five Polloi, crime registered in Torigan, year 951," the officer continued. "None of the others registered in criminal records."

They'd only scanned for registered criminals. "If you'll just listen—" Osri began.

"Quiet," the ensign warned.

One of the armored figures motioned his weapon at Osri, and Omilov murmured, "Be patient, son."

"YST 8740 *Maiden's Dream*," the ensign behind the console said. "Registry transponder seals broken. Who is the captain?"

Vi'ya stepped forward, one of the Marines tracking her with a jac. "I am," she said.

"Someone else here you'll want to speak to first." Marim snorted with laughter.

"Quiet."

Brandon had been watching Ivard, a slight frown of concern in his eyes. When Marim spoke, he straightened up from his relaxed posture against the wall. It was a very subtle movement, so unthreatening that none of the Marines re-aimed their weapons at him, yet somehow it drew everyone's focus. Osri remembered their arrival on Dis, and Brandon straightening up that very same way after the shock of hearing about Markham vlith-L'Ranja's death.

An old professor had said once to Osri of the High Douloi, *"Don't watch their faces, watch their hands.* It was not Brandon's hands, it was his whole body, that expressed his thoughts.

But that wasn't it, not quite yet. Reaching further back into the past, Osri had another insight: There were two sets of prisoners here, the Rifters—and the Aerenarch Brandon vlith-Arkad. And he knew it.

Osri stood stiffly, his heart hammering. His father merely

looked tired: had he seen that transformation as well? Brandon's gaze lifted as the hatch slid open once more. Osri recognized the man who entered: it was the captain of the *Mbwa Kali,* whose image had appeared on the viewscreen of the *Telvarna:* Nukiel.

When the captain first laid his gaze on his prisoners, he stopped as suddenly as if he had run into an invisible dyplast wall. His throat worked, and — and Osri refused to believe it of a high-ranked naval officer — he looked almost afraid. Then the mask of command tightened his features again.

"Commander, I assumed you scanned them under regulations."

"Yes, sir," replied the officer, his face reflecting question. He'd seen the captain's reaction, too.

"Release the jurisdiction lock on those scans."

Now the computers would compare their retinal patterns against the general subject rosters — normally forbidden without permission of the person scanned, unless under military necessity. Osri breathed out in relief.

The console hummed and twittered as the discriminators went to work; it would take some time, Osri knew, for them to sift through the immense mass of data represented by the citizen roster.

Ivard swayed, and Montrose steadied him.

"Cold. . ." Ivard whispered, the sound loud in the room.

At that moment the console bleeped, and the captain looked up, his startlement plain. "Ten-hut!" he barked, stepping around the console as the commander and the ensign leapt to their feet.

The servos of the two armored figures at the entry hatch whined as they grounded their oversized weapons briefly, then brought them to attention.

"Krysarch Brandon nyr-Arkad — "

"Aerenarch," Omilov corrected softly, his tired face quirking with rueful amusement.

"Aerenarch — ?" Captain Nukiel repeated, his eyes manic with shock, "I have the honor to welcome you aboard." He dropped on one knee before Brandon.

The Aerenarch held out his hands palms-up as the captain placed his, palms-down, over them. Then Brandon raised his hands, bringing the captain back to his feet.

Abruptly the room was a swirl of motion as the captain

ushered the Aerenarch across the room. Osri stepped forward, only to be motioned back by a Marine; Brandon began speaking to Nukiel. Finally, *finally*, Osri was permitted to separate himself from the lawless Rifters. Lokri, a murderer? It figured!

As they approached the hatch, the commander addressed Nukiel.

"Captain. Set course for Ares?" he asked.

Nukiel turned slowly, stress and even pain lining his features as he gazed first at the Aerenarch, then at the Rifters, especially Ivard and the Eya'a.

He shook his head. "No, Commander," Nukiel said, almost inaudibly. "Set course for Desrien, maximum speed."

Total silence met this command — this outrageous order — as the Aerenarch stared, and Omilov's lips parted. Then Montrose began arguing with the guards, seconded by Marim. At the console, the commander's mouth fell open. Then, with a quiet sigh, Ivard slumped to the deck in a faint.

"See? See what you did, you blunge-eyed nickblits?" Marim yelled.

In the distance they heard Lucifur growl and hiss. A dog barked.

I know what's happened, Osri thought wildly, I've finally gone mad. He slid his hands over his eyes and gave himself up to helpless laughter.

ARTHELION

It was night, and the windows in the library of the Palace Minor reflected Eusabian's image blackly as he moved along a wall of books, fingering their spines and drawing one out occasionally for a closer look. A floating lamp followed him. The rest of the room was mantled in unquiet shadows from a fire crackling on the hearth, the air smelling of leather and glue and the less identifiable scents of an ancient technology that would never be entirely displaced by electronics.

The Lord of Vengeance pushed a book back into alignment, then seated himself in one of the wing-backed chairs fronting the fireplace. To one side was an elegantly fragile table of some twisted, twining, highly polished wood, looking more like it had been grown than constructed. It held a number of record chips scattered around a small box with a data socket in it.

Eusabian picked up one of the chips and regarded it musingly. On its surface, in a bold, spiky, upright handwriting, was indited "Testamentary—Jaspar Arkad." The ink was faded, more visible by the indentation in the surface than any remaining pigmentation. He placed it in the socket and sat back expectantly.

There was a long pause, then a flicker of reddish light and a subtle tingling in his bones. The Avatar of Dol sat up in momentary startlement. It had scanned him!

Then an image wavered into solidity in front of him as some unseen mechanism damped down the fire and the lamp, so that the only source of illumination in the room was the ghostly figure of the founder of the Arkad dynasty, Jaspar hai-Arkad. He was a spare man, his face echoing that of the Avatar's defeated foe, but old and seamed. Nonetheless, he stood rigidly erect, unyielding to age, and the force of his personality reached out undiminished across the centuries.

The image's eyes came to rest on him and seemed to focus, causing a prickle of awe which Eusabian suppressed angrily; but for the first time, he understood the near-mythical stature the man had attained, and how it was that the polity he had fashioned had lasted so long. Behind him he heard the door to the library open quietly, but his mind was held in the thrall of a man long dead, and he ignored the interruption.

Then the image spoke.

"Since you are not of the house of Arkad, you cannot know that this record is only viewed by the ruling member of the Family upon his or her accession. That message you will not receive. But, as I know, perhaps better than most men, that nothing in Totality lasts forever, I now address myself to whoever, or whatever, has replaced my descendants."

Barrodagh stood indecisively in the doorway, his exultation dying out of him, replaced with a shiver of awe as he watched his lord lectured by a ghost.

". . . only when the counterbalances of civilization are flung awry by great misery and massive suffering, so that a touch in the right place can redirect into a new path the upwelling energies that drive us toward the Telos, can one make a difference in their own lifetime. I was one who was both fortunate and unfortunate enough to be so placed. . ."

Barrodagh crept forward, hugging his arms to his sides to keep from shivering. He'd been among Dol'jharians too long, with their ghosts and demons. Now, unbidden, the legends of his Bori childhood rose up from memory. He remembered the terrors that had made his nights a misery, especially the tales of the Vengyst, most famous and horrible of all Bori haunts, told him by his unspeakable older sister just before she turned off the lights and locked him in the darkness. The Vengyst, which cries *Willa-Drissa-Will* from the corner before it pounces and sucks out its victim's eyes with its purse-like mouth.

He shook off the memory and listened. The image spoke in an archaic accent difficult to understand, but somehow he couldn't will himself to take another step forward. Anyway, he could tell from the position of his lord's head that the Avatar was listening intently—so intently that interruption would be dangerous.

". . . be that my house has failed of wisdom, and your usurpation is a just one. If so, do not be too quick to discard what has worked, while sweeping away that which has not. And do not ever forget the tremendous inertia of society. Humanity has a basic wisdom of its own. Resign yourself to working slowly—and do not misunderstand their resistance to change. . ."

When the message ended, there was silence for a long time.

The fire crackled to life again as the ghost of Jaspar Arkad, favoring the Lord of Vengeance with the appearance of a long, measuring look, faded back into invisibility.

Barrodagh reluctantly moved to the side of his lord's chair. The firelight painted the Avatar's strong profile in colors recalling the karra-fires of his homeland; his gaze was fixed on infinity. With a tingle of anxiety Barrodagh noted the dirazh'u lying limply in his hands.

Barrodagh remembered the words engraved on the stone in front of the statue in the garden: *Ruler of all, ruler of naught, power unlimited, a prison unsought.* Eusabian appeared to be struggling with the magnitude of the burden his successful paliach had imposed on him. Not that he would feel the obligation to his subjects that the ghost's speech had assumed. No, thought Barrodagh uneasily, it was the lack of control expressed by that quatrain that the Lord of Vengeance would resent most keenly, as evidenced by his initial miscomprehension, there in the garden, of its meaning.

Then the Avatar roused himself, and threw off the mood that had possessed him, visibly rejecting the counsel of the ghost with every bit of the absolutism his ancestors had bequeathed him. He glanced at Barrodagh, who recollected himself, trying to recover the triumphant feeling he'd entered with.

"Lord, we have the Heart of Kronos."

The dark eyes widened, reflecting the flickering light from the fireplace. "Where?"

"It was recovered on Rifthaven by the Karroo Syndicate." Barrodagh swallowed, reluctant to go on, but knowing he could hide little or nothing of this from the Avatar. "Along with two of the stolen items from the palace."

Eusabian stood up, glaring down from a monumental height.

"It was evidently the same gang of Rifters." Barrodagh hesitated, still weighing how much to tell Eusabian. He decided that an item of less importance but nonetheless intriguing might take the sting out of worse news still to be revealed. "The captain is an escaped Dol'jharian slave—a tempath."

One of the Avatar's eyebrows quirked. "And the Arkad?"

"The Arkad was still with them. They tried to escape and were intercepted by a Panarchist battlecruiser before our force could intercept them."

Eusabian stared at him for a long beat. Then the Avatar turned back to the fire, his fingers slowly beginning to work at the silken cord. "A slave and a deposed prince." He laughed softly, a cold sound. "I wonder what the Panarchists will make of that combination?" He pulled at the cord; it did not yield, the knots now braided into it resembling the links of a chain. "Hekaath. . . they do not understand. No slave ever fully escapes its master. The bond is stronger than freedom."

He shook himself out of the reverie. "Have the Panarchist prisoners transferred to the flagship. Divert the nearest Ur-equipped vessel to Rifthaven to pick up the Heart, for a rendezvous with the *Fist*." He smiled, visibly relaxing from the strain of the strange interview with the first Arkad. "We will make an exchange. The Heart of Kronos will return to the Suneater after ten million years, and the Panarch—truly the ruler of naught—will go to Gehenna."

He looked at where Jaspar's ghost had stood. "And nothing can resist me now."

PART THREE

ONE

Barrodagh stared after the Avatar as he strode out of the library. Then he tabbed his compad and queried Juvaszt on the *Fist of Dol'jhar* to check on the timing, tactical, and strategic aspects of the transfer. Juvaszt confirmed his suspicions.

The kyvernat's explanation of the situation pleased him—and created new fears. As he'd suspected, there was no point in embarking immediately, given the relative positions of the ships and their destinations. Juvaszt had stressed the importance of maintaining control of Arthelion in the face of the Panarchist forces that were doubtless gathering for a counterattack.

"Once you furnish me with the names of the ships you desire to augment the *Fist of Dol'jhar* in the Arthelion system, I'll see that they are made available," Barrodagh had promised—as close as he dared to an implication of shared effort, almost equality.

Then, once Juvaszt came through with the ship names, Barrodagh would put the interim time to good use strengthening his leverage over the crew members that he'd already suborned on the ships concerned.

Well, he would explain the necessary details to the Avatar tomorrow. Despite Eusabian's growing boredom, Barrodagh doubted his Lord had extracted all the pleasure to be had from possession of his enemy's palace. And he would be even more bored, and thus more dangerous, while confined to the *Fist* on the way to the rendezvous. The delay would be useful for two additional reasons: more time for Barrodagh to tighten his control over the Catennach he was perforce leaving behind, and for Ferrasin to extract critical information from the computer, a process that seemed to be accelerating.

The computer! His gaze snapped to the table next to where Eusabian had been seated. He bent over the data socket, trying to decipher the faint writing on the datachip. Unable to make it out in the dim flicker of the firelight, he reached down to pry it out of the socket. There was a faint pop and the datachip disintegrated with a spurt of flame that stung his fingers.

Barrodagh whispered a curse as he snatched his fingers away and stuck them in his mouth. A muted glow caught the periphery of his vision, and he whirled around to confront the ghost of Jaspar Arkad, not an arm's length away from him. Its eyes seemed to focus on him. Barrodagh's breath caught in his throat and he stepped back; the arm of the chair caught him behind his knees and dumped him sprawling across it, unable to retreat further as the phantom slowly advanced toward him.

The ghost stopped in front of him, too close, and slowly, a terrible, sly smile possessed its face. It bent over; Barrodagh could see clouds of darkness moving behind its eyes.

"Willa-Drissa-Will!" the ghost hissed, and its face distorted as its lips shot out on the end of a glowing stalk and lunged at Barrodagh's eyes.

Warmth flooded Barrodagh's breeches and he gave a strangled shriek. The ghost stood back as if surveying the effect of its attack. Then, once more the stern founder of the Arkad dynasty, it chuckled quietly and glided through the wall.

Furious, Barrodagh pushed himself out of the chair and sent the carven table spinning across the library with a vicious blow. "I hate you!" he cried, then stopped, appalled. Just so had he screamed at his horrid sister when she locked him up those nights so long ago. But she was long dead, his first victim when he had come into power in the Dol'jharian bureaucracy. There was no reason to remember her now.

He exhaled shakily and looked down at the stain spreading across his crotch. Something would have to be done about that Ur-be-damned palace computer. It must have known he was Bori, known the legends. . .

Then he shrugged, reminding himself grimly that it didn't matter now. Soon they would leave for the Suneater, away from the Mandala and its hateful machines and verminous dogs. Then things would return to normal.

But as Barrodagh left the library to change his clothes, he

thought he heard a chuckle from the air behind him — a sound and a memory he could not escape.

He was not the only one meeting Jaspar's ghost.

Morrighon didn't know at first what had awakened him. With the facility born of long practice, he scanned the whispers coming from the communicators on the table near his bed as he gazed up at the ceiling, dimly lit by the glow of false dawn. There was nothing but the normal chatter of the channels he'd chosen to monitor this night — no. The Tarkan channel was more active than usual.

Then he caught a single word: *karra*. Another haunting, then. Perhaps it had been a mistake to monitor that channel. He didn't need to know about Tarkan encounters with the computer-generated holograms that were making their duty such a misery. He closed his eyes.

False dawn?

His eyes snapped open. Barrodagh had transferred him to a lower level of the palace after Anaris's first meeting with Eusabian, as an indication of his displeasure. There were no windows in his quarters.

He rolled over, propping himself on his elbows and looking over the end of the bed into the room. His breath stopped.

The dimly glowing form of an old man in a Panarchist uniform gazed at him from against the opposite wall. Morrighon recognized the face from the first bust in the Phoenix Antechamber: Jaspar hai-Arkad. Though he knew there was no such thing as ghosts, a chill of awe crawled along his nerves.

It must be the house computer. This was a new level of manifestation; he had to contact Ferrasin. The thought didn't help: he found, with a mixture of fear and disgust, that he still couldn't bring himself to move.

The ghost — It is not a ghost, his mind insisted fiercely — smiled at him and faded back through the wall, leaving behind a faint pool of light that shivered and crawled along the surface for a moment before fading out.

Morrighon flung back the coverlet and padded into his work room. The lights came on in response to his movement, banishing the darkness and with it much of his disquiet. He seated himself at his desk, laying his palms on its smooth, cool surface. Then he tabbed his compad.

"Ferrasin here." The response came more quickly than he expected, and there was no trace of sleep in the technician's voice.

"This is Morrighon. The apparition. . ."

"We are working on that now, senz-lo Morrighon," interrupted Ferrasin, the slight emphasis on the word "we" a warning that the technician could not speak freely.

A light glowed on Morrighon's compad, indicating a download waiting. He tabbed the accept key as Ferrasin said, "We will have a full report by morning."

"Very well," Morrighon acknowledged, and brought up the file that Ferrasin had sent him under cover of their conversation.

A few minutes later, frightened to the edge of nausea, he yanked on yesterday's clothes and summoned a Tarkan escort to take him to Anaris.

The chiming of the annunciator brought Anaris out of restless sleep. He fought away confusion and looked at the chrono: 02:38. Alarmed, he reached for his wrist and then his hand fell back when it encountered bare flesh. He'd been dreaming of his years as a hostage among the Douloi of the Panarch's court, but he was among his own kind again. Annoyance mixed with amusement as he remembered tossing his own boswell into the disposer just before he returned to his father: what Dol'jharian would ever entrust his thoughts to a machine that could be taken away?

Leaning over, he tabbed the comm. "Who is it?"

"Morrighon, lord." The Bori's voice was fearful. "You told me to. . ."

"Come in."

Anaris sprang out of bed and threw on his dressing gown as Morrighon entered, looking even worse than usual; he trembled, his clothes were rumpled, his thinning hair stuck out in wispy spikes in every direction, and the paleness of his face exaggerated his bad complexion.

"My lord," Morrighon said as the door slid shut behind him, "we have received word from Rifthaven." He stopped, swallowing convulsively.

Rifthaven! Had Snurkel been right, then? Was Brandon there?

Better, was he now captive? Anaris suppressed a smile of

anticipation. He wanted some fun with his old enemy before he was disposed of. And, in completing his father's paliach, he would take another step toward the throne.

Morrighon's expression became even more woeful, and Anaris's exultation faded. "Widespread fighting has broken out on Rifthaven among the Syndicates, even within some. It appears to have been triggered by the discovery of the Aerenarch, as suspected by our primary contact there." Morrighon stopped again.

"And?"

Morrighon's words emerged in a rush. "In the confusion, the Aerenarch escaped. His ship was intercepted by a Panarchist battlecruiser. We can only assume he is now on his way to Ares."

Rage replaced triumph. Anaris felt his face distorting into the prachan, the fear-face, as, once more, the laughing Arkad third-son evaded him.

Morrighon stepped back, pressing against the wall, his face a sickly hue.

Then a tendril of fear stilled Anaris's rage. What report had been made to his father? He forced himself to relax. "What does the Avatar know?"

It took Morrighon a moment to find his voice, his larynx working. "Snurkel recovered the Heart of Kronos," he squeaked at last. "The Avatar has accepted his explanations concerning the Aerenarch. No hint of our role has emerged: Snurkel's position on Rifthaven is precarious and depends entirely on the Avatar now. He cannot afford any suspicion of double-dealing."

Anaris's anxiety began to fade. With what the Avatar regarded as his key to complete victory now in his hands, Eusabian would have a mind to little else. Still, it might be best to arrange accidents for the seconds that he and Morrighon had suborned, especially Snurkel. From now on Rifthaven would be of little importance, and they could only be a source of embarrassment.

Then a thought struck him: his machinations on Rifthaven, through Morrighon, had been the key to the Aerenarch's escape. Savoring the acidic bite of irony, he relived the many times Brandon and his brother Galen had used his Dol'jharian instincts against him in their despicable games, until he finally learned to think as they did.

It was him, as much as his father, who taught Anaris to think as a Panarchist. The realization shocked him; with a kind of perverse pleasure he recognized that Brandon was becoming a worthy foe. And they were not yet finished with each other.

He became aware of Morrighon staring in utter horror. He realized that he was smiling, a rictus that made his face ache.

"Sit down," he ordered. Morrighon flopped bonelessly into a chair, staring up at him, still fearful.

Anaris looked at him thoughtfully. It had taken some courage to bring him that news. Fear, the underpinning of the Dol'jharian state, was often as much an impediment to knowledge as a lash to efficiency. He had sensed that between Barrodagh and his father; he could not afford that between Morrighon and himself. "You did well to awaken me, and you need not fear my wrath. I bear the blame for this." He saw the astonishment replace fear as he continued. "We are not done on Rifthaven. . ."

He'd scarcely completed his orders when the room comm chimed, signaling the deposit of a recorded message. He tabbed it on.

"This is Barrodagh, speaking for the Avatar. The Heart of Kronos has been recovered. Preparations are beginning for departure to the Suneater. The Panarch and his remaining councilors will be transferred to the *Fist of Dol'jhar*. Your father desires you to hold yourself in readiness to accompany them."

Anaris tabbed acceptance and looked up. "He was vague about the schedule."

"He probably doesn't know it yet," Morrighon replied. "That will be for Juvaszt to figure out."

Anaris nodded, his thoughts running ahead, following the implications of the Avatar's decision. His father would be the last to leave the planet, as required by Dol'jharian custom. But the face that filled his mind's eye was not Eusabian's, it was Gelasaar's. Did his father intend them to meet face-to-face? What would he say to him? Barrodagh's message had been vague — deliberately, he was sure — concerning the nature of his escort duty. Would he see the man who had fostered him or not?

As he turned his attention back to Morrighon to plan for this new development, Anaris didn't know which he would prefer.

SATANSCLAW: ARTHELION ORBIT

Anderic's fingers jerked spasmodically. He forced himself to control his hands as he sidled a glance around the bridge. Most of the pods were empty, their monitors on Z-watch. He'd promised sho-Imbris extra points in whatever action they might meet if he'd do longer hours, and Ninn didn't seem to mind being in his pod most of the time. Neither looked up.

His fingers snaked out and he tabbed the keys to make certain the logos was turned off.

Then he tried to calm his slamming heart as he watched sho-Imbris lay in the new heading that Anderic had just required—a course suggested by the logos.

But had he turned it on first or not? He couldn't remember. He squeezed his eyes shut, but there was no refuge there, the dark behind his eyelids marred by the kaleidoscopic frenzy of another visual migraine. He wondered if he was going mad— or maybe Tallis' eye, transplanted into his body against his will, was forcing him into madness. Three times, now, he had spoken to find the logos on already, when he did not remember turning it on.

He'd begun to convulsively tab it off every few minutes, trying to make certain. And what about the flickers? It had to be the guilt imposed by his Ozmiront upbringing creating those half-seen movements, like disapproving faces, that thronged the corners of his vision when he was fatigued, which was most of the time now.

If only he could get some decent sleep! He'd tried issuing standing orders, devised with the help of the logos, to give him more time to get to the bridge in case of the inevitable Panarchist counterattack. But he worried that the logos would just respond without him instead, and so what sleep he did get was broken and unrefreshing.

He'd also taken to sleeping in one of his new uniforms, which were Tallis's stripped of most of the gold braid and embroidery. It seemed to keep discipline better, by making it seem that he was on top of things. But it also accelerated his isolation from the crew, which he feared was daily more under the sway of Kira and Luri. It seemed lately that everyone on the *Satansclaw* was involved in the rec-time orgies. Everyone, that is, but its captain.

A pang in his eye reminded him of one of the reasons they shunned him. The main reason? He flickered another look around. How could the crew not know about the demonic presence of the logos haunting him, waking and sleeping? Especially Kira Lennart, who must be puzzled by her inability to overcome Anderic's control of the computer, despite her greater experience.

That was the logos's doing, but its inhuman perspective couldn't help him deal with the increasing chatter on the hyperwave. It was getting harder and harder to sift useful data out of the flood of rumor and braggadocio flooding the system.

Lennart could, though.

Jealousy burned in Anderic. Too bad if he interrupted her usual fun and games. She was the worst of them, the ugly toad—seemed like every time he spied on one of his crew, he interrupted bunny fun, and she was almost always in it.

He smiled meanly. Too bad, Lennart. Time to work.

He tabbed the locate just as Luri's full red lips parted in a soft laugh. She hefted the pot she'd brought out from the galley, and Kira Lennart smelled the scent of fresh-melted chocolate.

"What's that for?" she said.

"You shall see," Luri whispered. "Luri has new pleasures in mind."

Kira laughed, her heart squeezing inside her. She couldn't help it. The only reason why she saw as much of her as she did was that Kira participated willingly in Luri's plots to get rid of Anderic, but she didn't care.

As they hurried down to the bilge, Kira reflected with rueful self-awareness that once Luri bunked her out she'd hurt, and the rest of her life she'd probably bore people with the tale of her one great romance. But until then, she was going to build those memories.

Tallis looked up with painful expectancy in his one remaining eye when they entered. Luri set down the pot carefully by her side, and as her perfume and the chocolate chased away the faint, unpleasant tang of blunge pervading the room, Kira realized why she must have brought the chocolate.

Kira tapped her boswell, and it flashed green. No monitors active in the room. "It's clear. I've finally gotten through some of Anderic's coding. I don't know how he got so good. But now, if he runs a locate, we'll have a few seconds' warning. I haven't been able to do anything about the spy-eyes yet."

Luri touched Tallis' cheeks. "Tal-lis must remember that he doesn't want Luri here, hmmm? If Anderic spies."

Tallis sighed as the woman's hands ran down his body, then caressed the metal ball hanging on his nacker, hidden by the thin fabric of his trousers.

"Luri will find out how to remove that," she added softly.

Jealously stabbed at Kira, and to banish it, she said, "Should we get to our planning? Tallis, you said next time you might have something to tell us." She added doubtfully, looking around the bilge chamber which Tallis was unable to leave, "What have you found out?"

Tallis Y'Marmor rubbed his forehead. "It's nothing I've found out, it's something —" He stopped, then said abruptly, "There's a logos on board."

"A what?" Luri asked.

Nausea roiled Kira's insides. "No!"

Tallis looked from one to the other, then said to Luri, "It's a — an artificial intelligence." He got it out quickly, avoiding looking at Kira. "I had it installed. One of the ways it communicates is through an eye implant, which is why Barrodagh did that to me."

Kira fought back her revulsion, thinking quickly. "Anderic's an Ozmiront," she said. "He won't use it —"

"He already has," Tallis said.

"How do you know that?"

Tallis shrugged, indicating his console. "I think it has tried to contact me," he said, looking distinctly greenish around the jowls.

Kira suppressed a shiver. Only Luri seemed supremely undisturbed; whether because she was ignorant of what the logos was capable of, or merely because anything that did not relate to her immediate plans was automatically insignificant to her. Kira did not know. "This makes things different —" she began. Then her boz'l buzzed against her wrist. "Locate."

Luri laughed, stood up, and in one magnificent gesture ripped her loose gown free of her body. "Kira, you too." As Lennart scrambled out of her clothes, excited and confused at once, she turned to Tallis. "We shall return," she murmured to him, leaning forward to kiss him. "Now, remember: you are miserable, we are teasing you with what you cannot have."

She picked up the chocolate pot and held it in both hands.

Kira felt another buzz from her boz'l; the imager had now activated. Anderic was watching.

"Tal-lis," Luri said in her breathy singsong. "We are here to alleviate your bore-dom. You get to watch while Kira and Luri have fun." She lifted the pot and spilled the half-congealed dark liquid down the front of her naked body, then spilled more on Kira, who jerked as the liquid flowed down her chest, kindling an answering warmth. "You get to watch and see if Kira and Luri can lick each other off in. . . Would you like to guess how long it will take?"

Tallis gave a low whimper.

And on the bridge, Anderic groaned. They were at it again! He watched, fascinated, his nacker painful as the two women writhed, glistening with streaks of chocolate in fascinating accents against Luri's amber and Lennart's coffee-colored flesh, in front of the miserable one-eyed Tallis. Anger, jealousy, and lust burned in him; he might as well be down there in the bilge with Tallis, a dyplast ball on his nacker, for all the bunny he was getting.

Then a thought struck. Quickly he tapped open a record bank and started storing the image from the bilgebay, ignoring the curious looks from sho-Imbris and Ninn. Then he waited until Luri and Lennart reached the climax of their chocolate romp, squealing with delight.

Smiling, Anderic sealed the record under his own personal code and then patched it into the hyperwave for random replay. Lennart would find it and cancel it despite the coding, he was sure, but by then someone—several someones, no doubt—would have recorded it, and made certain it would become staple entertainment on the Rifter bilge-banging session that formed an increasingly large part of the traffic on the hyperwave.

Then he tabbed the call key. "Lennart, I need you on the bridge." He cut the connection without waiting for an acknowledgment and returned to his command pod.

He was looking forward to Lennart's reaction to her newfound fame.

TWO

Osri Omilov stepped back and surveyed himself in the mirror. He was as ready as he could be for his first meeting with Captain Nukiel. A haircut, a new uniform, and behind him the familiar dimensions of the standard lieutenant's cabin, and he felt as if the universe had righted itself again. Looking at the reassuringly routine sight, he could almost pretend that the past weeks of flight and captivity had not happened, that life was normal again.

But they had happened, and neither outside nor inside this ship was life normal. Over everything loomed the mystery of Desrien. Why were they going *there?* Osri's mind shied away from the question. He'd been hoping for some sort of explanation during the debriefing he'd expected as soon as he officially reported in. Instead he'd been assigned to the captain's watch and told to hold himself available. Then an invitation to breakfast with the captain — extended also to Osri's father, a civilian.

Osri scowled. The irregularity was of a piece with everything else. Somewhere in the bowels of *Mbwa Kali,* the crew of the *Telvarna* now enjoyed the hospitality of the brig — which apparently had expanded drastically since the battlecruiser took up station off Rifthaven. Elsewhere the now-Aerenarch Brandon vlith-Arkad enjoyed a sumptuous guest suite. With Sebastian Omilov, Osri's father, as his guest.

Osri turned away from the mirror and opened the drawer

where he'd put the flight ribbon and the coin. The return of the latter had been a surprise to him, especially given the recognition in the eyes of the warrant officer who'd restored the artifacts to him. Another anomaly. Perhaps the woman's muttered comment as he'd turned away, not meant for his ears, was a hint: *"Supercargo."* For a piece of history so rare its value was incalculable.

He took a perverse pleasure in the fact that the Rifters, safely housed in the brig, did not know that he had the two items, nor would they be likely to find out. Nor would Brandon know. Osri's mood sobered at that; he was aware that he no longer felt triumph. He was not certain what to think anymore.

Breakfast was to be not in the Senior Officers Mess, but in the guest suite that Sebastian and Brandon shared. Osri did not know why his father had insisted on this, though he spoke of health reasons. Perhaps it was to gauge how cooperative the Navy really was — since the invitation was basically a summons to an interrogation — and perhaps it was just more of his oblique diplomatic sidestepping.

Just before retiring, Omilov had asked his son to join him early.

Osri's fingers groped at his left wrist, a convulsive movement that reached consciousness when his finger pads hit the standard boswell he'd been issued. He fought back the urge to record his thoughts; instead, he scooped up the ribbon and the coin and put them in his breast pocket.

Walking quickly up the corridor towards the transtube, he thought about telling his father about the artifacts, and discovered he was reluctant. Perforce they had spent more time in one another's company lately than they had since Osri was the schoolboy that the Rifters called him. And during that time, Osri thought he'd come to understand his father a little more, and even to appreciate the breadth of his perceptions.

But below that was anger. His right hand strayed to his chest and the slight heaviness where the jumble of silk and ancient metal reposed. Now that Osri had had time to think through the events of recent weeks, he found that his mind kept returning to '55, and what had happened on Minerva. He had come by degrees to believe that there was more to what had seemed straightforward events than he had thought, and that in fact Markham vlith-L'Ranja and his father, the Archon of Lusor, had been unfairly treated by Aerenarch Semion for what amounted to political reasons.

That was a separate issue from the fact that Osri's father had kept the truth from him for ten years.

The time had come to discuss it.

He found his father and Brandon seated in two clean-lined, low Retro-Futura-style chairs. This central room was large, the tianqi set in the conventional spring-breezes mode, all the signs of the military being called upon to house unexpected VIPs from outside.

Both looked up at Osri's entrance. The two dogs lying next to Brandon's chair prickled their ears forward, then laid their heads down again. Osri noticed they no longer wore the control collars placed on them and the big cat when they left *Telvarna*.

"Good morning, son," Sebastian greeted him.

"Good morning," Brandon echoed.

Before Osri took two steps into the cabin he perceived a glance passing between them. It took Osri straight back to their school days, and the maddening realization that his own father and the blank-faced Krysarch seemed to understand one another without the need for words. He reacted as he had then, by striking out with the truth. "I'm interrupting a private conversation." And he backed a step, to retreat.

"We were discussing the detour," Sebastian said, his tone exactly the same mild, friendly one that Brandon had used a moment before. It functioned as a rebuke. "What could be Nukiel's reason for not going to Ares? Have you heard anything from the junior officers that can shed some light?"

Osri stepped stiffly to a chair and sat down. "They are circumspect around me," he said. "As is appropriate. But I overheard some talk while I was in the quartermaster's, and when I was shown the wardroom, we interrupted some talk. They seem as surprised as we are. More."

Sebastian observed, "Nukiel seems a by-the-books officer."

"He certainly doesn't seem the kind who'd run to a fogbound planet full of self-proclaimed seers for inspiration," Osri said acidly.

Brandon got to his feet and stretched. "Well, find out what you can." He smiled down at Osri's father as he brought the dogs to a seated position with an upwards motion of one hand. "Meanwhile, I need to exercise these two."

The two dogs bounded ahead of him out the door.

Omilov turned a considering gaze Osri's way, as if he were

thinking, what do I do with you now?

It was completely without anger, but somehow Osri preferred his mother's scorn and sarcasm. "Don't use your diplomacy on me, father. For once speak straight."

Sebastian's bushy brows rose. "There is little danger of your interrupting anything of importance between Brandon and me." He hesitated, then added, "To my infinite regret."

"Is this to fix the blame on me for his future mistakes?"

Sebastian's hand stirred, a gesture setting aside irrelevancies. "Accusations of fault and blame have no value. The facts are—"

"The fact is," Osri interjected, "I accused him of desertion, which is the truth. I accused him of deserting out of cowardice, which I no longer think is true. But if it's not, then why did he abandon everything we believe in, everything we have sworn to protect? He was going to join that same gang of Rifters sitting in the brig right now!"

"He was going to find Markham L'Ranja," Sebastian corrected.

"You're trying to say that he didn't desert? On the day of his Enkainion, with half the government gathered in the palace to watch the ritual?"

"I don't deny it."

"To find Markham L'Ranja, a man ten years outside the law," Osri said. "A Rifter. True?"

"True."

"Then where is the difference?"

"The difference is in the intent," Sebastian said slowly. "I wish we had more time. . . before we reach Ares." He frowned abstractedly, then looked up. "Brandon's motivations and intentions I will not second-guess. As we've established, he will not confide in me. But from conversations with Montrose, Ivard, and some of the others, I gather that Markham did not prey on Panarchists, only on other Rifters."

"This excuses desertion, the prospect of a Krysarch of the Phoenix House robbing other thieves?" Osri's sarcastic edge sharpened on every statement, but to the same degree his father seemed to grow more remote, more abstracted.

"I think. . . I think his goal was to win justice from outside the system." Sebastian's gaze transferred to Osri's face, but the narrowed eyes seemed to look past him. "From Brandon's perspective—you have to admit—the system did not seem to work."

"Perhaps if he'd spent less time drinking and more in effort, he would have. . .." Osri's words sounded weak in his own ears, weak and petulant. He remembered, as he knew Sebastian did, the conversation they'd had on the flight from Granny Chang's to Rifthaven, when his father had finally explained to him the real reason behind Brandon's expulsion from the Academy, and the accompanying ruination of the L'Ranja family. Semion had wanted Brandon to become a Social Figurehead, just as Galen was the family Patron of the Arts. Gelasaar's only mistake was in permitting Semion to supervise his brothers' educations. But how could he know it for a mistake? Semion was as fearsomely competent as Gelasaar himself, and they'd been confident that he was as truthful. "I can't believe that the Panarch did not see any of this," he said finally.

"Then we get into the limitations of personality," Sebastian said, and with mild dryness, "Will you perceive this kind of discussion as treason?"

Osri was about to set his father straight on who had been committing treason, when, and how, but he halted himself. A year ago—a month ago—he would have been sure who was right, and who wrong. But not now.

"You're saying that the Panarch was—"

Sebastian cut in quickly, with a shake of his head. "I'm saying that Gelasaar is probably the most hardworking, decent, innately truthful human being I have ever known, save only for his wife when she was alive. But after she died. . . I think a part of him went with her, and it was a relief for him to hand some jobs over to Semion, the overseeing of the education of Galen and Brandon being one of them. While he took on the burden of those tasks that Ilara had handled so superbly before."

Osri had only brief memories of the Kyriarch Ilara, but those memories were vivid. One was how she always managed to make everyone laugh, even children, whenever there was a gathering. A more personal memory was of her blue-gray eyes in a face round and smiling, bending toward him. "*What are you learning now, Osri?*" she'd asked, and she'd waited for the answer as most adults didn't, waited as if what he had to say took precedence over everything else. He couldn't remember what he'd said, but he did remember her sudden smile, and his own conviction that it was the right answer, and how happy that had made him feel all through the day—

Until he got home, and his own mother had questioned him closely on the interview, and then afterward said angrily, *"Blunge! Hadn't she the grace to invite you to stay? Or did you make a mistake and ruin your own chances?"*

Osri knew his mother saw people in single terms: in one dimension. They were good or bad, stupid or smart, depending entirely on how they served her purposes. He began to perceive that he had learned some of the same habit, and all his father's efforts to educate him out of this narrow view had been fruitless.

I'm too like her, Osri thought with a bleak flicker of humor. *Quick to anger, and to judge.*

He gave in to impulse: "Why did you marry my mother?"

And saw the question strike his father like a dagger in the heart. It was not an overtly obvious reaction—if Osri had been looking elsewhere he would have missed it—but his father's pupils contracted and his breath faltered momentarily. Then he looked away, his Douloi mask hiding his thoughts. He said, "It seemed the right thing to do at the time."

"For whom?" Osri struggled to sound less accusatory. "I would understand a political alliance, but you were never political. But I don't believe it was a match for. . . personal reasons." The words seemed to drag out of him, but he had to know.

His father's eyes strayed to the slowly cycling art-screen on one wall, now displaying a colorful nebula, the remnant of an exploding sun. "My family desired trade access to Ghettierus, and your mother wished a closer social connection to the Mandala. As for how successful—or how worthy—these goals were, you will have to answer for yourself. To return to Brandon's flight from Arthelion," he went on, "I think he had a purpose, of which he has not yet lost sight." He glanced at the discreet wall chrono, then stretched out a hand to touch Osri's sleeve. "They are due soon, and I'd hoped to discuss something else of importance."

Osri looked down at the gnarled hand. His father had aged badly in recent weeks; Osri reminded himself that he'd been tortured not all that long ago. He said, "My report. You want me to ignore what happened? Or lie?" Was that why his father had arranged them to meet the captain together?

Again the Douloi mask. "Do what you think best," Omilov

said in a pleasant voice, the cadence as slippery as water over rocks. "But I take leave to remind you that the man we are about to meet is taking the last heir to the Emerald Throne not first to Ares and safety, but to Desrien, along with what may be one of his majesty's few surviving battlecruisers. You may be surprised at the questions he asks or does not ask, knowing that every one of his actions will be minutely inspected once we reach Ares, as I assume we must eventually."

He indicated their surroundings with a gesture. "This suite is now the focus of all three poles of Panarchic power: the Navy, the Mandala, and the Magisterium. And this interview —"

"Will be an interrogation," Osri interrupted, uncomfortable with the subject of the fog-bound planet that was their destination. "To be recorded for the captain's almost-certain court martial. I understand very well what Captain Nukiel is risking."

His father sighed, rubbing his hand over his temple. Remorse stung when he saw a trembling in the fingers. But then the door hissed open and Sebastian straightened up, his hands groping to the arm of his chair. Control was in place again.

The captain and the commander came in, both dressed in formal whites. As salutes and greetings were exchanged, white-jacketed stewards brought in the covers for the meal.

Osri's mind was busy during the polite exchanges as they moved to the table and began. He knew his father would not sham weakness; though he was a diplomat, he had never been a fraud. He wouldn't let his control slip for effect.

So Osri thought back to identify the moment Omilov had lost control of their conversation.

Osri took his place at the table, and other than returning answers to questions directed at him, he deferred to his father. At first the talk ranged along safe channels: the comfort of the new quarters, the Aerenarch's wishes; Nukiel had insisted on giving up his quarters to the Phoenix Heir; Brandon had been even more insistent that he remain in civilian country; Omilov, speaking as Brandon's old tutor, had cast the swing vote. A complicated little dance whose outcome was a predictable as its steps — and as necessary, Osri saw now. Brandon had opted firmly for his civilian role, distancing himself from any attempt to insert himself into the chain of command.

Osri's father was right. Captain Nukiel was being very careful, as behooved a man with such a weight of responsibility.

While the other three talked, slowly wending their way towards what Nukiel and Efriq wanted to know without ever approaching the feel of an interrogation, Osri retraced his way through his conversation with his father. The subject had been Brandon, but they had not stayed on him. Markham L'Ranja. . . Gelasaar. . . Risiena—no, that had been his thoughts only.

The Kyriarch.

Osri's heart constricted. Ilara. . . and then the question: "Why did you marry my mother?"

His hands had gone clammy, and he wished he were back in his own cabin, away from other eyes. He suppressed a twitch of his hand towards the tetradrachm in his breast pocket.

"Don't ever take lovers for longer than a week or two at most," his mother had said to him once, in one of her rare confiding moments. *"You'll find yourself bound by the chains of their greed."* He'd certainly seen the truth of that after some of her more spectacular fights. She'd always seemed to pick badly. Osri had cordially hated all his mother's lovers — a hatred he shared with his half-siblings, even if they shared little else.

His father's house had always been a contrast much to be preferred: the quiet, monastic atmosphere, music, art, learning. This was why Osri nearly always went to Charvann for liberty, or between postings, even if it was a much longer journey.

As a child Osri had assumed his father's fidelity to Risiena. During his adolescence he'd speculated that his father did not care for women, but he had not sought male company, either. Later, he'd assumed Omilov's celibacy was because he'd chosen to be wedded to his work.

Meanwhile Osri had grown up with the portrait of Ilara in the study, never questioning its presence.

And from a conversation long ago, his father saying of Gelasaar: *"He is one of those rarities in our culture, a genuinely monogamous person. Having had the great fortune to find the ideal, I expect he'd feel that tarnishing the memory with casual intimacy would be intolerable."*

Osri stole a look at his father's jowly, big-eared profile, sick with his new conviction that the Panarch was not the only monogamous person in love with the Kyriarch Ilara. The new insight did not change anything concrete. It couldn't even be talked of, Osri suspected. But once again he felt his perspective on the universe shifting inexorably.

". . . and we must assume that Eusabian will shortly have

it," Sebastian was saying.

Osri knew that quirk to his mouth; he could almost hear his father's voice, long ago: *"The best way to keep people from talking about what you don't want to talk about is to get them onto a bigger secret."*

"Let me tell you what little I know of the Heart of Kronos."

Marine Solarch (First Class) Artorus Vahn stood guard outside the Aerenarch's suite, thinking about the circumstances that had made him probably the only person alive to have served as an honor guard for all three sons of Gelasaar III.

Vahn's post was no accident: the personnel records would have revealed that he had been stationed on Talgarth before being shifted to duty on the *Mbwa Kali*. So far as Vahn knew, he was the only Marine onboard who could say that.

It had been no accident, either, when he'd been detailed from Semion's Omega Fleet at Narbon to serve at Galen's palace on Talgarth, a posting that had seemed a sinecure until he discovered that he was not meant to be a guard, but a spy. His subsequent request for transfer had been granted a year ago. The accident was in his being put on this ship. It could have been any other ship headed out-octant, into the outer darkness as far as Semion was concerned.

The door opened and the Aerenarch emerged, followed by the two dogs, who took up station one at each knee, looking expectantly at Brandon's face. Who looked at Vahn. "Let's go talk to the Chief Wrangler," he said pleasantly.

Vahn nodded and jeeved into step behind him; the Aerenarch's new boswell would show him the way.

From Aerenarch to Aerenarch. The ability to jeeve, to be invisible until required, had been drilled into Vahn during the intensive training he'd received on Narbon. He knew how to judge to the centimeter just how far a person's breathing space extended. To go unnoticed and unremarked was the highest praise one could expect in Semion's personal service: if he spoke to you, it was invariably to your detriment. Galen had been the opposite. It had been disarming, and sometimes unnerving, the profound interest he took in everyone around him, rank notwithstanding.

Vahn already knew Brandon was different from them both.

The first time he'd accompanied him, from the surgery where the CMO herself had treated him, he'd wondered, as they approached a lift, whether Brandon would emulate Semion and stand a meter away, ignoring him as if he were alone—or would inquire, as Galen had, into his family, likes, and dislikes?

They reached the lift—the Aerenarch first, and he raised his own hand to tab it open, instead of waiting for Vahn to perform the service. One for the Galen column.

When they got into the lift, the Aerenarch turned to him as if they'd known one another for years, and said, "Efriq told me you were on Talgarth."

"Yes, Your Highness." He was like Galen, then. And he braced for the personal questions. But they didn't come. The Aerenarch smiled briefly. "You must have been in Semion's private army beforehand."

It was not a question, so Vahn did not have to answer. Still, he had felt his heart give one sharp rap against his ribs, then start racing.

No one ever called it a private army in Vahn's hearing, but that's what it was. Vahn had been selected out barely two years into his Marine career; bigger, stronger, and faster than the other recruits, he'd had an added knack for arcane weapons. The training on Narbon had been hard, the punishments harder, with fierce competition for promotion. Such an atmosphere for someone with ability and ambition was exhilarating, and for a long time Vahn had reveled in the private slang, codes, and rituals only known to the special detachment of Marines on Narbon.

All Marines reported through the same chain of command, yet there came a time when Vahn had perceived the difference between Narbon's detachment and those serving elsewhere. Narbon's Marines were trained to owe their loyalty to the Aerenarch's person, not to his place in the greater schema. . . and all of the men—and they were only men—had come only from Tetrad Centrum planets. No Highdwellers. No one from the Fringes.

But calling what had amounted to a private army by "private army" wasn't as hard a hit as the assumption that he'd had to have been on Narbon first: that Semion controlled placement to Talgarth with his own men. It was a truth that had taken Vahn time to figure out—and had driven him to dump a promising career and sidestep into the mainstream. At no time had he ever stated, or heard stated, the bald truth.

Until that moment, as the lift opened.

He felt a strong urge to justify himself, to tell the Aerenarch why he was here—except one didn't speak while on duty unless spoken to. The conviction that an entire conversation had taken place in that brief exchange unsettled him.

The three days since then had been one of assessment for Vahn, which was still continuing. The new Aerenarch had Vahn placed on their first meeting, but Vahn still didn't know what the Panarch's third son thought.

The interview with the Chief Wrangler illuminated the Aerenarch's character from another angle.

"You want to give a pair of Arkad dogs to a Rifter adolescent? In the brig?" To call the chief's voice doubtful would be an understatement. He was a tall, spare man with a long, bony face and eyes turned down at the outside corners. Right now he looked even more lugubrious than usual, but Vahn had never seen him smile except at an animal. Chief Evvyn was happiest in ports of call, when he could set up the extension clinic that was but one of the many non-warlike functions of a battlecruiser on an out-octant patrol. "If you don't have time to exercise them, any of my wranglers would be honored."

"I have nothing but time," said the Aerenarch lightly, and Vahn felt the statement was for him as much as the wrangler. "Ivard is infected with a Kelly ribbon, and having the two dogs—making him a kind of trinity, perhaps?—seemed to stabilize him on the *Telvarna*. I will still be responsible for their exercise."

The chief took this in. "How much control does this boy have? I'll have to put safety collars on them to prevent him from using them against brig personnel."

Brandon nodded. "I understand. Could you have those personalized, please?"

Evvyn brightened at the mention of something he could easily agree to. "Kije and Aoka. Certainly."

"No, if you please. Trev and Gray, respectively. We had no way of reading their chips on *Telvarna*, and that's what Ivard named them. They answer to those names."

The chief grunted softly. "This really is over my pay grade." He looked closely at the Aerenarch with a directness that Vahn had come to expect from the kind of people who became wranglers. "But I won't recommend against it. That big cliff-cat is the healthiest I've ever seen, and the mildest. The dogs could spend time with worse people on board, and I don't mean the other Rifters, necessarily."

It was quickly arranged, permission coming back immediately from the XO. Both Vahn and the chief were surprised when Brandon insisted on delivering the dogs himself. "I owe those Rifters my life," he said simply.

Vahn had little time to consider this statement. A transtube took them quickly to the brig.

"Level 3, block 5," the watch officer said. "Here are your mind-blurs."

A mild expression of distaste tightened Brandon's face as the man offered two bracelets. He shook his head. "We won't need those."

The officer glanced at Vahn, then shrugged as the Marine nodded slightly, despite his misgivings.

Vahn indicated the way—the Aerenarch's civ boswell wouldn't work here. As they walked on, the Aerenarch glanced back at the watch console. "Seems to be a full house," he commented. "Nukiel's been busy."

As so often happened, it was not a question, so no answer was required. Still, Vahn was glad when they reached their destination, and the Marines on guard saluted, then keyed the hatch open.

The Aerenarch paused to glance around swiftly. Vahn tried to see the space the way he did: the main room was much like an ordinary rec room, slightly smaller in dimensions, featuring much the same scattering of tables, library-and-game consoles, and a holo tank. Two rooms led off either side. These Rifters had been given first-class accommodations compared to most of their fellow scofflaws.

The inmates looked up at their entrance. Vahn stood just inside the hatch at parade rest for as long as it took for them to scan him, and then jeeved.

"It's the Arkad!" A repulsively pale, skinny adolescent jumped up from one of the game consoles. "And Trev and Gray!"

"Ivard." The Aerenarch released the dogs, who bounded over to the boy—*Ivard*—gamboling about him in an ecstasy of sniffing. Vahn was startled to hear Ivard sniff repeatedly as well, his upper lip wrinkled up and his mouth agape.

"Come to gloat?" a small blond female asked, her face and voice edgy. She did not rise from her chair.

Neither did the heavy man by the vid tank, or the tall, dark-haired woman at another console. An equally tall man with Serapisti mourning braids down his back did not move, either, but he stilled with the poise of an Ulanshu master, and his gaze was unblinking.

The lack of polite usage jarred at Vahn, but the Aerenarch did not react, even when Ivard bounced near him, still sniffing audibly, and reached a skinny freckled hand to pat his face and then his arm.

"Came to deliver the dogs," the Aerenarch said. "They'll be living here with Ivard."

"Br-r-r-rp! Blat," the boy gibbered, waving his arms in fluttering movements. Then he flushed and hunched his shoulders. "Sorry. It just comes out sometimes." His face lifted, his expression hopeful. "Are they really going to stay here?"

"Really. I'll come every day to take them for walks."

"But —"

The Aerenarch gripped Ivard by his thin shoulders. "I walk the halls in perfect freedom," he said, so softly that Vahn might not have heard it without the augmentation devices implanted in his mastoids. Lightning jolted down Vahn's nervous system when without any warning two small white figures glided from one of the rooms, their twiggy feet scratching the deck plates.

Eya'a. Scuttlebutt insisted their sudden appearance had been the occasion of a heated argument between the Chief Wrangler and the XO. As newly-discovered sophonts, not yet neatly categorized by the bureaucracy on Arthelion, the Standing Orders accorded them automatic ambassadorial rank, but they didn't stray from the brig. Apparently only the Rifter tempath could communicate with them. He wondered if they even knew they were in a brig.

The Aerenarch was on the move, and Vahn had to pay attention. But Brandon just walked around to look at each player's game set. Then he turned to the big man — Montrose.

"Anything I can try to get you?"

Montrose shrugged massive shoulders, his ugly face amused. "I'd ask for a chess set, but no one here shares my enthusiasm. Fortunately, the ship's music collection is unclassified." He waved at the library console.

"Jaim?" The Aerenarch turned to the Serapisti.

The man looked down at his hands, tense and flat on the table. Vahn's back muscles tightened to readiness for action; the man seemed on the verge of flight or fight. But he glanced up and down again at his empty hands, then merely shook his head.

"Ask 'em why we can't have Lokri with us," the little blonde put in. "And what's this blunge about going to Desrien?"

"I know little more than you right now," the Aerenarch said. "I expect I'll learn more sometime before we arrive." The captain's delay in questioning him about his escape from Arthelion and subsequent adventures had the ship abuzz with speculation, although the general judgment was universal: Politics.

The Aerenarch stepped back. "Vi'ya?"

Large, dense black eyes lifted in a face otherwise smooth and cold.

Vahn had spotted the Dol'jharian the moment he entered the suite. The woman was tall, with a strong build. There was grace in the line of her neck, and in one visible hand; he recognized that she, too, knew Ulanshu kinesics. And a tempath. A lethal combination. He wished he'd taken the mind-blur, and then wondered if she'd detected his unease. Her face was as unreadable as stone.

"The Chief Wrangler tells me that Lucifur is well. He's adopted the junior officers for the duration," the Aerenarch said.

"I know." She turned back to her console.

The Aerenarch faced Vahn, eyebrows raised in inquiry. They left.

GROZNIY: OORT CLOUD, ARTHELION SYSTEM

It had taken *Grozniy* a while to find the first rendezvous tacponder at Arthelion. The usual fivespace attractors that made navigation far easier — of which there were very few this far out — were too likely to be watched.

Navigation had really sweated this one. Margot Ng watched as the ensign at SigInt popped the tacponder, and Mzinga relaxed noticeably in his pod.

In the moments before the incoming link arrived, Ng

looked around the bridge. Everyone was properly focused on their tasks, but she could see how intently they listened for SigInt's report. Had anyone else made it, or were *Grozniy* and *Hainu* Squadron alone here?

"Linked," said Wychyrski. Excitement pitched her voice higher even through the bridge cadence. "Orders from Ares: remain on station. Forces on-station: two battlecruisers, *Flammarion*, Captain Armenhaut. *Babur Khan*, Captain KepSingh; zero destroyers; six frigates..."

Armenhaut? How... Ng's attention leapt to time-on-rendezvous, then to last station. *Babur Khan* had shown up only two days ago, quickly found at Smaragdis by one of *Grozniy's* couriers. But *Flammarion*, formally stationed on the Mandala itself, was shown returning from Xiao Hua III two weeks ago. Had Adamantine activity been reported there again? But why send Armenhaut so far?

"Very well, Ensign," Ng said in her most detached manner as she windowed the list up on the main screen.

Commander Krajno rubbed his chin. "Didn't expect him," he said.

"No." She spoke neutrally, to soften the curtness of her reply, then cadenced her voice. "Navigation, take us to the indicated rendezvous."

"He's expecting us, though," Krajno said, a corner of his mouth betraying sardonic amusement. The courier dispatched to Arthelion had not reported back, but there was little doubt it had arrived.

"Too bad there's no digest on the tacponder," he continued. "Stygrid always was a stickler for security. They should have some good intel by now, I'd think."

He was trying to jolly her, and almost succeeding. But her XO could only guess at some of the emotional and political parameters she was juggling in the wake of this surprise. Laughter fluttered inside her as she imagined the look on Metellus's face right about now.

However, Krajno's implication was accurate. Armenhaut had been preparing for her arrival, using security to keep the intel close for best advantage, and although the Standing Orders were clear on her superior rank, the situation was too desperate to let political maneuvering get in the way of efficiency. Which gave Armenhaut the kind of leverage he was a master at using.

"KepSingh is competent," said Krajno, again demonstrating one of the characteristics of a good XO. Part mind-reader, part nanny. Her mouth quirked at the memory of an instructor's voice.

Competent, yes, but an old-school captain from the Tetrad Centrum, where Semion's influence was—*had been*—strong. The frigate captains, all junior, of course, didn't matter politically.

She hated the direction her thoughts were taking: politics. Politics stink, and stick to everything. For all she knew, in the fog of battle it might be one of those frigate captains who carried away the hyperwave they sought.

She took refuge in a three-cornered discussion with Krajno and Rom-Sanchez of the tactics applicable to a fleet with as many battlecruisers in it as destroyers, which was terminated shortly thereafter when *Grozniy* found the *Flammarion*.

Armenhaut kept her waiting for a period excruciating in its exact calculation. But any irritation she was feeling drained away when Armenhaut's face windowed up on the screen. His uniform was as crisp as ever, but the man himself looked hag-ridden.

"Captain Ng. We have been expecting you and *Hainu* Squadron. Most welcome additions to our forces." Behind him his bridge was all gleaming surfaces and immaculately attired officers, as if such scrupulous precision could by mental force alone restore order to the universe.

On a sub-display, she saw that SigInt had not yet found *Babur Khan* and the frigates. Not surprising: they were probably off gathering more tactical intel. But Armenhaut probably also saw their absence as an opportunity for better control of this encounter.

In the meantime, Communications had linked the two ships, and data was pouring back and forth: first the digests, then the raw data. But she had one fact to start with for which she didn't need even a digest.

"No more than I anticipate the rich feast of data your two weeks here will have garnered." She paused a bare moment. "The tacponder data was rather sparse. Did you find anything at Xiao Hua III?"

If he was discomfited it didn't show. "Alas. A typical haunting: a Sodality rock rat running from shadows. But my orders were quite explicit: with all possible dispatch." A slight emphasis on the last word carried with it the unassailable confidence of one of the Navy's most notorious nanosecond captains, always striving for the fastest run-through of the standard drills.

And he didn't wonder why he was sent all the way from Arthelion? Armenhaut was not stupid, but arrogance could be just as crippling. Perhaps the record of *Prabhu Shiva's* last battle would finish off his complacency.

Which was already badly frayed, she decided as he spoke again a fraction of a beat too fast. "The data you sent ahead from your adventures has already contributed to our strategic perspective." Or was that simply the result of the fatigue she saw in his countenance?

No matter. Whatever had betrayed him, she deflected his verbal lunge in attacque au fer. Armenhaut was never much of a fencer, anyway. "Excellent." And, coup d'arrêt: "Then you can see how we must proceed, and how quickly."

Despite his Douloi control she could sense the man's frantic post-facto calculation; he'd realized that talking in front of his bridge crew, rather than from his ready room, had enabled Ng to neatly trap him. She almost felt sorry for him. Arthelion under Eusabian's control called for a very different naval skill set.

Before he could reply, she spoke again. "*Grozniy* will welcome you, the other captains, and all tactical heads tomorrow at 1200 hours for our first tactical discussion." She had rank points on him and everyone else on-station so far, so protocol demanded that they come to her. But that would just be the first step in fusing a handful of ships into a fleet that could wrest a hyperwave from Eusabian's forces.

She could see the effort it took for Armenhaut to control himself, and pitied the next officer on *Flammarion* to cross him, however slightly. But he recovered almost without hesitation, and bowed slightly to her from his pod in a condescending mode. "Your gracious invitation is most appreciated. We will be there."

And the next day at 11:53, Metellus Hayashi drew a slow breath and let it out even more slowly. He would not get angry. He would not even glance at his chrono. Armenhaut wanted just that.

Hayashi and his subordinates had been on board the

Grozniy since early morning—the frigate captains had arrived very little later. Armenhaut and KepSingh, captains of the *Flammarion* and *Babur Khan* respectively, had waited until the last possible moment. And the couriers reporting back had so far found no trace of *Joyeaux*. That in itself was evidence of what the Navy faced. Not that that would make any difference to Armenhaut.

(SHUTTLE,) the officer of the watch reported, dry-voiced.

Hayashi put his hands behind his back, concentrating on keeping his demeanor impassive as he took the transtube down to the forward beta landing bay. Margot had asked him to meet the captains.

He could hear her voice again: "*Remember, beloved, Semion is dead. From now on, Armenhaut and his kind can only be promoted on merit. Every time you look at Armenhaut's face, think of that and pity him. I am going to try to do the same.*"

With a hiss and a subdued boom, the shuttle's ramp came down. Two figures, the older one short and round, the other tall and commanding, appeared at the top of the ramp, both clad in formal whites, their captain's insignia visible from across the bay. They strode to the bottom of the ramp, followed by two other officers, a man and a woman, both Lieutenant Commanders, also in dress uniform. They all stopped before stepping onto the bay deck.

As he stepped forward, Hayashi's eyes went to the chrono: 12:00 precisely.

The taller captain executed a salute in impersonal mode. "I have permission to come aboard." That was Armenhaut. KepSingh's gaze lifted, but he waited.

Hayashi kept his face blank as he stepped forward, uttered the formal greetings, receiving KepSingh and the two tactical heads in turn, and then bade them follow.

As they entered the transtube, he touched his boswell: (HAD PERMISSION: WHITES: KEPSINGH TOO—) But as Hayashi glanced at the shorter captain, he surprised a slightly pained glance on the man's face as he glanced at Hayashi's own regulation daily-wear blues.

It was up to Hayashi to speak, but he kept a strict, formal silence as the transtube accelerated them towards the captain's conference room near the bridge. Hayashi once again tapped Margot's private code and added: (KEPSINGH CAME ON STYGRID'S SHUTTLE, BUT HIS TESLAS ARE ONLY AT THREAT-LEVEL ONE, IF THAT.) That was all he had time for.

That gave Margot a few seconds' preparation as they walked down the spotless corridor. Marine guards snapped to attention outside the hatch. Armenhaut, as senior in rank among the newcomers, went through first, followed by KepSingh, then Hayashi and the two tactical officers.

In the center of the room a conceptual map was evolving in the tac-holo; subordinate windows glowed from every wall but one, where a bare sideboard stood beneath a simple holo of Gelasaar III. The riotous color of the displays emphasized the fact that every one of the captains and tactical heads waiting, Margot included, was clad in quiet regulation blues. Hayashi watched Armenhaut's upper lip lengthen. Hayashi caught a significant glance from Bea Doial that took in Jarnock Somsri as well, the third *Hainu* captain.

"In a moment we'll take our seats and begin," Ng said. "But first I want to say how happy I am to see that *Flammarion* and *Babur Khan* won through."

Then she immediately addressed Armenhaut. "Stygrid. It's been a long flight from our Academy days, and I know neither of us expected to end up mustering out-system from a Mandala occupied by Eusabian of Dol'jhar."

The impossible phrase sent a frisson through Hayashi, as he knew it would have for everyone present. But that was overshadowed by his appreciation of a masterfully accurate opening shot, fired by the woman who'd won the Karelian Star for her part in ending the first war with Dol'jhar. So many layers, from "why I outrank you" to "how the hell did you survive?" Right across the bow.

Armenhaut murmured the minimum acknowledgement, his Douloi mask hard held. He was determined not to be trapped again. But she'd already turned to KepSingh, and this time she stepped forward and held out her hand. "Captain KepSingh," she said cordially. "We've never met, but Admiral Choi has spoken often of you."

KepSingh's round face relaxed in a brief smile. "We were ensigns together in the Eighth Shiidran Expedition."

"The first use of the Ogres," Ng said. Hayashi noticed a slight change in Armenhaut's expression. The Barcan battle androids came perilously close to infringing the Ban, something not likely to sit well with an old-family High Douloi like Armenhaut.

"We heard some tales about that action," Ng continued. "We even lived through some of them in the sims."

KepSingh laughed softly. "Choi did threaten to do that."

Ng followed up with greetings to the tactical officers who'd accompanied their captains, greeting them by name.

Now would be the time for *Grozniy's* captain to offer some refreshment. Armenhaut's face of course gave no clue to his thoughts, but Hayashi knew he would have noted the absence of either steward or buffet. She flickered the briefest glance at Armenhaut's white uniform, and said cordially, "Please, take your places."

Fire two — and two hits.

"We're still crunching the intel, of course." Ng seated herself and continued, gesturing at the tac-holo as the officers found their pods, guided by their boswells. "With three battlecruiser arrays now linked in real time, that is speeding up considerably, and of course you have your own notes and evolutions."

She waved at the largest wall display, which flicked to a list of strategic points with a simple heading at the top, a high-level digest of the conceptual Tenno map in the center of the room. "In one sense, our situation is quite easy to describe. We're all of us survivors of the first phase of the Second Dol'jharian War." She looked around the room somberly. "Very lucky survivors, at that, as the record of *Prabhu Shiva's* last action proves."

Fire three, right at the luckiest man in the room. And he knew it. So did his tactical head, judging from the wince in his expression.

"But there's another reason we're lucky. We're where phase two of the war begins, and we now have sufficient forces to prosecute it."

"With all due respect, Captain Ng," said Armenhaut. "Phase two is a matter that will be decided on Ares."

Broadside from Stygrid. Right on cue. Armenhaut was making it very plain that he respected only the uniform, and not the person inside it. Hayashi watched KepSingh direct a hooded glance at the other battlecruiser captain. Older, Douloi, but not as high in rank, and every point he had he'd earned. After *Grozniy's* courier arrived, Hayashi was certain that Stygrid had used every opportunity to pour some poison into the older man's ears.

"That may very well be," said Ng equably, "if a courier arrives with new orders in time. But the tactical situation in Arthelion may not leave us time to wait. As you will note, between our initial rendezvous and this meeting, two more Rifter ships arrived in-system. That means the pace of reinforcement is speeding up."

Hayashi saw Euan Macadee, one of the frigate captains present, lift his chin in an apparent boswell communication. Ng paused only slightly before continuing. "Captain Macadee, I believe you observed them?"

"AyKay, sir. Sloppy. We could have taken them both."

(TALK ABOUT SLOPPY. THAT WAS IN THE REPORT, OF COURSE), boswelled Bea Doial, one of the destroyer captains, to Hayashi. They traded smiles, and then Bea sent a fast glance at Somsri, the third destroyer captain.

But Armenhaut remained apparently unruffled. "Our orders are plain and quite simple," he said. "Remain on station." He opened his hands towards her and his voice took on the tonalities of voice-of-reason addressing lack-of-control. "I can sympathize with the desire to win glory, but an attack on the Mandala makes no sense, not with the forces we presently command."

The implication was clear to everyone, judging by the shiftings and downcast eyes of some. Somsri flushed. He and Ng were the only Polloi in the room, but Somsri had never learned Ng's control. She merely softly touched her console, smiling and to all appearances unmoved. "Of course," she said. "But Eusabian is expecting one. We'll use that against him."

Hayashi sat back, relishing the conviction that Armenhaut had no idea where this was going.

Ng waved at the conceptual map. "With your permission."

Armenhaut nodded tightly. Next to him, KepSingh leaned forward. Ng tapped at her console, provoking a rippling change in the Tenno and bringing forward one symbol in particular. "This 'suneater,' whatever it is, is key to the whole picture."

"That hardly does us any good," drawled Armenhaut. "We don't know what it is, or where to find it."

"That's not the point. It's the center of Eusabian's power now. But he's not there, which would seem to make the most strategic sense. He's here on Arthelion, which means he's still mired in the fundamental Dol'jharian cultural pattern of vengeance."

"Exactly," said Armenhaut. "And any attempt to retake Arthelion will result in a bloodbath."

"If it looked like it was succeeding, yes. But he won't expect us to try to retake it, he'll expect us to strike directly at him. And that will blind him to the real goal of our attack: to obtain one of the hyperwaves and get it to Ares."

"Captain Ng," KepSingh said. "Will you show us what you have in mind?"

"Gladly, Captain KepSingh," Margot replied, without looking at Armenhaut's rigid face.

Hayashi suppressed a grin: KepSingh was using her name; this was merit talking to merit here. They'd got him.

Ng tabbed a control and the tac-holo shivered to a gods-eye view of the Arthelion system. As she spoke, subviews budded off of it, echoed by various displays. "What I propose is this. Our intel, and Eusabian's behavior during the last war, make it certain that he's in the Palace Minor, guarded by the *Fist of Dol'jhar*. We will pin it there by threat of Marine landings, with Captain Hayashi's squadron harassing it. In the meantime, our three battlecruisers, assisted by our frigates, corvettes, and even cutters, will go hunting for hyperwave-equipped Rifters."

KepSingh stared intently at the display. Then his face lifted. "Of course. Disable a target, and wait to see if anyone shows up to help from outside the light cone. Elegant, Captain Ng. Elegant."

Just then a jacketed steward came in, bearing the magnificent silver coffee service that Ng's patron had given her when she was posted to her first ship. All eyes went to it. Ng lifted her fingers, and the steward set it at the side table, then took up a stance next to it. The aroma of real coffee filled the room, and Hayashi's mouth watered.

"Any questions?" Ng asked.

Again Stygrid spoke, "It appears to me a recipe for heavy losses with not much chance of a payoff. Your plan requires immobilizing a target and allowing it to summon assistance, which you must then hold off long enough to give the Marines time to board and seize the hyperwave. What if the enemy decides to destroy the target himself?" He laughed harshly. "In effect, once we do find a hyperwave-equipped Rifter, we'll end up defending it against every enemy ship in the system."

"No," said KepSingh, tapping his own screen. "Only one

ship, to begin with. I agree with Moral Sabotage. The Dol'jharians won't order Rifter auxiliaries to destroy one of their ships unless it's the only way. Their morale has got to be fragile." He looked back at Ng. "But it will be a bloody business, and likely a close one, too. Wouldn't hurt to have a few more ships."

"Agreed," said Ng. "And those who've been on-station here will need training in the new Tenno, with which Lieutenant-Commander Rom-Sanchez here will assist."

Several heads looked up at that. Rom-Sanchez had already begun responding to boswelled questions.

"One of our first decisions will be how long we can wait, balancing our readiness against the ongoing increase in Rifter forces and, of course, any sign that Eusabian is preparing to leave. Once he's gone, we'll lose our best, perhaps our only chance at holding him to battle long enough to grab a hyperwave."

"Captain," Armenhaut said. "I really must remind you that this discussion is quite hypothetical. Again, our orders are clear: remain on station."

Ng paused to let another murmur die down. Meanwhile, the steward came forward, placed a china cup at her elbow, and expertly poured out a stream of gently steaming brown liquid. The aroma of real, freshly toasted, ground, and brewed coffee filled the room. Concession? Hayashi wondered. Much as he wanted coffee, he wondered if Armenhaut would read the sudden offer of refreshment as an attempt to placate.

But then Ng said, "Thank you."

The steward withdrew to the service table and took up his stance again.

Hayashi fought fiercely against letting his mirth show. He heard a muted gasp from Doial, but he refused to look at her.

Ng went on calmly, "Pursuant to section 10, paragraph 19 and following, of the Standing Orders (wartime, undeclared), I hereby declare the ships assembled here a Provisional Fleet and assume its command." She paused to take a delicate sip of coffee and smiled at Armenhaut. "As Commodore, I choose to interpret 'station' in its broadest sense, and I assure you, Captain Armenhaut, that we will remain within its boundaries."

And a broadside from Broadside: he's plasma.

Hayashi bit his tongue inside his dry mouth and sat back to appreciate Margot's unspoken but lethally effective reminder of whose ship they were gathered on—and who really had the power here.

KepSingh grinned and folded his arms. "It's good, Ng," he said. "Good."

No one asked him to elucidate. Armenhaut's neck flushed brick-red.

Ng said, with her friendliest smile, "Would anyone care for some coffee while we discuss the details?"

Three

The Malachronte Ways

"**A**nd what do you intend to do if I refuse?" said the Aegios.

Hreem glared at the viewscreen as the man continued.

"We've got the teslas up, and soon we'll have the weapons systems powered up as well. You have no time left, Rifter." Ferniar Ozman laughed, his heavy jowls shaking. "Best you flee now. My engineers tell me the drives will be the last system back on-line, so we might not even chase you." He held up his hand as Hreem made to speak. "Oh, we've heard of your superweapons. But you want a battlecruiser, not a cloud of gas, am I correct?"

Without waiting for a response, he terminated the connection.

Hreem swore as the screen flickered back to a view of the Malachronte Ways, and stalked across the bridge of the *Flower of Lith*. His crew was silent, eyes down. Norio, standing near the aft hatch, made no move toward him.

Hreem glared at the viewscreen again. Here, at the inner edge of the system's asteroid belt whence came the raw materials for the Ways, framed in the spidery complexity of construction machinery, the deadly symmetry of the *Maccabeus* glimmered in the light of the distant sun. Beyond the battlecruiser the Rifter captain could see other docks with ships abandoned in various stages of construction, but they held no interest for him.

His eyes ranged greedily over the battlecruiser's seven-kilometer statement of invincibility, the contours of the silvery hull interrupted by the thorns and turrets of projecting weaponry and sensors, blurred slightly by the shimmer of an activated tesla field.

It looked ready to go. Hreem swore again. Obviously it wasn't, quite, or the Aegios would have ordered its weapons turned on the *Lith*.

"Cap'n? I'm getting faint readings from the cruiser's ruptor systems." Erbee spoke up from the sensor console. "It looks like a low-power test."

"That'd mean about twenty hours or so till they bring them up to full power," Piliar at Fire Control commented.

Hreem gnawed his thumb as he sat down again. Pili was ex-Navy, cashiered for something he wouldn't talk about, but he knew weapons systems.

It had been easier than attacking Charvann, up until now. His forces had quickly blown away the Malachronte defense. But with the Archon gone—he'd been on Arthelion when it fell—there was no one with sufficient authority to order Ozman to surrender.

Faced by Ozman's obduracy, Hreem had only two choices. He could blast the cruiser into atoms, or he could flee. What he couldn't do, as long as that chatzing Aegios held the ship, was force his way on board.

At least the Dol'jharians hadn't shown up yet. Once they did, there would be no way to explain away his failure to the Lord of Vengeance. A pang of anxiety gripped him.

Then Hreem felt the pressure of two strong, narrow hands on his shoulders, probing for the shakrian points.

"Chatzing nick," Hreem growled. "He'd laugh out his buju if I just had him here." He flicked the heel-claws on his boots out, scoring the deck plates.

"No, Jala. I think he is courageous, and no doubt possesses other virtues as well." The tempath gave a soft sigh. "At least, the Douloi call them virtues, but you and I . . . we can call them weaknesses."

Hreem didn't have to turn to know how Norio looked: that tone meant eyes half-closed, the edges of his teeth showing in a malicious smile.

"For instance, as one in the Ranks of Service, he is trained to place a high value on human life." The tempath laughed softly. "It would be so very delightful to see how he balances his oath of fealty against. . . say, fifty thousand lives."

The maximum population of a Highdwelling. And there were hundreds of them in the system.

The enormity of what Norio was suggesting made Hreem waver. In the long history of the Rift Sodality, very few ships had ever targeted a sync, and the bloody fates of the perpetrators under Local Justice were legendary. What Norio was suggesting was orders of magnitude beyond anything he'd done so far in his long and bloody career. He looked back at the battlecruiser, and the familiar image of himself on its bridge possessed him wholly.

"And the novosti will be so very eager to share the spectacle with all of Malachronte system," Norio added.

Hreem laughed. Norio was right. The newsfeeds would do most of the job for him: the battlecruiser was as good as his. And if he timed it right, he could be back here laughing at Ozman's reaction as he watched the news from the syncs in real time.

A short time later, Norio savored the novosti's fear as the man stepped onto the bridge of the *Lith*, his larynx bobbing as he subvocalized his commentary through his boswell. The man surveyed the bridge, the ajna on his forehead reflecting the status lights on the consoles as the semi-living lens adjusted its focus. The tempath wished he could feel the emotions of the billion-plus viewers to which the device was relaying its images. Like falling into the sun, embraced by the cleansing flames. . .

He shook off the mood as the novosti approached Hreem. The captain lounged in his command pod, casually picking his nails with a dagger, but Norio could feel his excitement, a fascinating compound of anger, lust, and — Norio laughed silently — stage fright.

The bridge was silent. Riolo, the Barcan computer tech who was rarely on the bridge, nervously hitched up the belt supporting his absurd codpiece as the newsman's gaze swept across him.

"Stop that. Now." Hreem pointed with his knife at the man's throat.

The novosti stammered, "S-stop what?"

"If you're going to talk, do it so we can hear you." Hreem

started flipping the dagger in the air, catching it by the blade. The novosti's eyes followed it; Norio enjoyed the way his anxiety pulsed in time to the weapon's glittering course. "Well, genz Bertranus, you're the lucky chatzer that won the draw. So ask your questions."

"If you please, genz chaka-Jalashalal, I need. . . "

"Just call me Captain." Hreem was smiling broadly, his emotions now approximating those of a cat toying with its prey. The skin on Norio's arms tingled with pleasure.

"Captain, I need to finish setting the background for my viewers, if you please."

Hreem waved one hand negligently. "I please."

The man's eyes focused on distance. "Yes, I'm ready to continue," he said, apparently speaking to his relay on the ship that had brought him to the *Flower of Lith*. Then he began, picking up from where he had been interrupted.

"Following the defeat of the system defense forces, the attackers turned their attention to the Malachronte Ways, leaving the planet untouched behind its Shield, sparing it the fate reported by the swelling tide of refugees from other systems.

"I am now standing on the bridge of the *Flower of Lith*, flagship of the Rifter fleet occupying Malachronte system. Its captain, Hreem chaka-Jalashalal, known throughout the Thousand Suns as Hreem the Faithless, has agreed to an interview."

The novosti faced Hreem. "Captain, refugees from Charvann say you forced the surrender of that planet with some sort of superweapon. Is that true?"

"Yes."

"Do you intend the same here?"

"No." Norio sensed Hreem's amusement sharpening.

"Why are you treating the two systems differently?"

"My orders were unequivocal concerning Charvann. I have considerably more latitude here."

Norio smiled. Never before had Hreem an audience so large for his words, and he was making the most of the opportunity.

"Orders? From whom, if I may ask?"

"Jerrode Eusabian, Avatar of Dol, Lord of Vengeance and the Kingdoms of Dol'jhar. Now Panarch of the Thousand Suns. Actually, a thousand and one suns, I guess." Hreem slapped his knee as he chuckled.

There was a momentary silence. Norio knew the refugees from Charvann and elsewhere must have reported the news, but its confirmation by the captain of a Rifter destroyer had to be a shock despite that.

"Then, Captain, if you will, tell us your intentions toward Malachronte."

"I have no intentions toward Malachronte," replied Hreem, with all apparent mildness.

Bertranus blinked.

"Then why are you here?"

"I've come to take possession of the battlecruiser under construction in the Ways. Unfortunately the Aegios, Ferniar Ozman, has not been entirely cooperative."

"That is why you asked to speak to his mother, on Sync Ozman?"

Hreem smiled. "It was you who suggested his mother. I just requested contact with someone close to him, who might give me some vector into his character, to ease the negotiations, like. There's very little time before a force from Dol'jhar arrives, at which point I'll no longer have much control." He paused and attempted a sorrowful look, which was only partially successful. Norio suppressed a snort of laughter as Hreem continued. "They've far less patience than I've got."

The novosti looked into distance again. "Do we have her on-line?" He paused. "All right."

The captain looked over at Norio, who nodded fractionally. As they had discussed, the mention of Dol'jhar was intended to cast Hreem in the position of Malachronte's ally, or at least the better of two lethal choices.

The novosti's emotions indicated that it was working. The tempath shivered with anticipation; this would make the coming whiplash of emotions even more violent. He wished again he could experience the feelings of Bertranus' viewers, even though it would probably kill him. But such ecstasy. . .

"Com incoming, Cap'n," said Dyasil.

A window expanded on the viewscreen, revealing the head and shoulders of a white-haired woman against an elegant background, her dark eyes and hooked nose resembling those of the stubborn Aegios.

Norio could feel the instant surge of hatred and resentment that the woman engendered in Hreem. He also sensed unease in the newsman as the background to the window revealed that the ship was coming about and accelerating toward the ring of Highdwellings around Malachronte.

The novosti spoke to his viewers. "We now have Vité Ozman on-line." He sketched a deference to the screen. "Genz Ozman, thank you for agreeing to speak to us."

"I am not sure your role in this affair reflects well on your character or your organization, genz Bertranus," she said, her voice neutral. "Please. You requested an interview?"

Bertranus's larynx bobbed slightly. "Excuse me," he said to the image, and turned to Hreem. "Captain, my relay ship is having difficulty keeping station. Why are we moving?"

"Tactical reasons," Hreem replied. "Nothing to worry about."

The novosti licked his lips, then turned back to the screen. "I apologize, genz Ozman." He looked up at Hreem. "You had some questions for genz Ozman, Captain?"

Hreem smiled, and Norio could feel the anger-powered cruelty rising in him. "No questions. I just wanted to see her face."

The woman's brows drew down as she considered this, then she reached toward something under the screen as the novosti stammered, "But, Captain, you insisted on this contact!"

"Leave off, you blungesucking nick," Hreem snarled at the screen, leaning forward and holding the point of his dagger to Bertranus' throat. "Cut that connection and this chatzer dies."

The woman was silent, her face grim. Huge drops of sweat oozed from the novosti's forehead as he froze in place.

"Missile armed and ready," said Pili at Fire Control.

"Captain!" the newsman squeaked. "What are you doing?"

"Target acquired," continued Pili. "Sync Porphyry, plus-one spinwise of Ozman, as ordered." Norio could hear the stress in his voice, and sense his unease at what he was doing, along with his greater fear of defying Hreem.

"This is just to convince you, and your chatzing son out in the Ways, that I mean what I say."

Just as Hreem spoke, Norio realized the flaw in their plan. "Captain, wait." Norio bit his lip, holding back laughter as relief billowed from the newsman. The idea that the man actually assumed Norio would try to prevent the inevitable brought a smile. "I suggest a change in target."

Hreem looked at him, frowning.

Norio leaned close. "Consider. Ozman's oath of fealty will forbid him to consider his Family first. If he yields, he will be disgraced." Norio nodded toward the Douloi woman on the screen. "Do you think she would hesitate to disown him for such weakness? Or fail to embrace death in the service of her liege? But if you destroy Sync Ozman now, you take away the glory and replace it with senseless death. The shock, combined with the threat to another sync with which he has no familial connection, and thus to which he actually has stronger obligations? That will weaken him considerably."

"Virtue as weakness," Hreem repeated, smiling in delight.

Norio smiled back, shivering with anticipation.

"You have imagers focused on Sync Ozman?" Hreem asked Bertranus, withdrawing the dagger from his throat.

The man's lips moved as he communicated with his relay. "We do now," he replied, his voice barely audible. Norio watched, fascinated by his sense of shame for the part he was playing. Yet he continued.

"Fire Control, retarget," Hreem ordered. "Sync Ozman."

Vité Ozman's Douloi assurance faded. "Captain, I ask you to spare the innocents of Ozman. I will come to your ship."

"Target acquired, Sync Ozman." Pili's voice was flat.

Hreem stared at the Douloi woman, unspeaking.

"Do you want me to beg for our lives?" she asked.

"No," he finally replied after a long beat. "I don't want you to beg. I want you to die."

He brought his hand down on the firing pad.

Norio watched Ferniar Ozman avidly as Hreem's image, relayed by the newsfeed from the inner system twenty light-minutes away, brought his fist down on the firing pad. The image from the novosti vid switched away to an exterior view of Sync Ozman: a finger of light reached out from the dragonfly angularity of the *Flower of Lith* to impact near one end of the habitat. A brilliant flare of light was followed by a spew of fragments and a billow of haze from the rupture in the shell of the habitat. Nearby, the deadly thorn-studded shape of a Rifter frigate hung motionless; beyond it loomed the fragile immensity of another sync.

"I'll save you the time of listening to the gabble from the novosti channels," said Hreem. "Sync Ozman has about six hours before it goes chaotic and starts to come apart. You wanna be there for the end, like a good nick?"

Ferniar Ozman looked out of the viewscreen at them, his features tight. Norio wished he could feel the man's emotions. Such a feast of pain and regret!

Finally the Aegios spoke. "You will give our ship safe conduct?"

"We'll exchange ships," replied Hreem, suggesting an ancient and well-known protocol for surrender. "Here's how it will work. . ."

The negotiations concluded, Hreem tabbed off the channel and smirked in triumph at his bridge crew. Some smiled back, others tried to hide fear or more complex emotions.

"You were generous with him," Norio said.

"No need to be greedy now." Hreem grinned. "I get that luxury yacht. A nice bonus."

Erbee's console bleeped. "Emergence pulse, bearing 109 mark 72, plus 2 light-seconds," the tech shouted.

Hreem jerked upright in his pod and slapped the skip pad. The fiveskip burred momentarily, compounding Norio's discomfort at Hreem's surge of fear. Unexpected emotions were always hard to deal with.

Moments later Erbee spoke again. "ID established, the *Karra-rahim*. It's the Dol'jharians."

"Beam incoming," Dyasil put in.

Hreem tensed as the arrogant, deeply seamed features of a senior Dol'jharian officer windowed up on the screen. "Have you secured the battlecruiser?" she snapped, without preamble.

The tempath sense Hreem's anxiety shading into anger at the woman's arrogance. "It has been arranged."

He explained the surrender agreement to the Tarkan, and won her grudging agreement to wait until Ozman and his people departed before approaching more closely. "If you press them, they may decide to go out in a blaze of glory, for the honor of their oath," Hreem finished.

The officer nodded and cut the connection.

Norio smiled. "Virtue as weakness. The Dol'jharians are much the same as the Panarchists, with their oaths and loyalties."

But Hreem pounded softly on his console. "Damn, damn, damn. If I could've gotten on board first. . ."

Across the bridge at his console, Riolo tugged again at his

belt, causing his codpiece to wriggle ludicrously. Strangely, instead of the usual surge of disgust that the Barcan usually engendered in Hreem, Norio sensed instead a pulse of excitement. "What is it, Jala, brightness? Have you seen a way out?"

Hreem nodded slowly and got out of the command pod. "Have Riolo meet me down in the aft bay. I've got some questions about the pinnace's nav computer."

Presently, the silvery hull of the battlecruiser loomed immense beside the two tiny ships fastened lock-to-lock. As the last of the Panarchists squeezed past him into the *Lith*'s pinnace, Hreem held out his hand to Ozman.

The Aegios slowly placed a datachip in the Rifter's palm, then looked past Hreem at the thorns and spikes of the battlecruiser hull that formed a wall just outside, blurred by the energies of the electronic lock field that kept them all breathing. Hreem turned to Norio.

"Guilt and fear," Norio whispered.

Ozman's gaze snapped over to him.

"He's hiding something. I think he left someone behind."

"Is this all of you?" Hreem demanded.

"There's one missing," Ozman admitted, sweat lining his tense brow. "We couldn't find him. But he can do nothing. Everything's locked down, and you have the codes."

Hreem considered, then shrugged. "He'll be sorry when *I* find him."

A few minutes later the two ships drifted apart. The Aegios' personal yacht, now carrying Hreem and a contingent from the *Lith*, moved toward the nearest bay of the battlecruiser. The pinnace moved away, slowly orienting itself for the jump into fivespace.

On the bridge of the yacht the viewscreen showed only the pinnace, and a portion of the battlecruiser's hull, looming like the limb of a planet seen from low orbit. Beyond were only the stars — the *Lith*, in accordance with their agreement, was on the other side of the cruiser, where it couldn't attack the pinnace.

Then Riolo touched a control, and a small targeting cross blinked into being in the starfield behind the pinnace.

"Any moment now," the Barcan said. His red-tinted goggles glinted, reflecting the status lights on the yacht's console.

The pinnace suddenly yawed about, orienting on the distant point of light that was the Dol'jharian ship. It began to accelerate.

"They've tried to enter fivespace. The program is engaged," said Riolo.

Hreem grinned as a green lens on the console lit up. He reached over and accepted the communication.

"What have you done?" Ferniar Ozman demanded. Behind him Hreem could seen someone frantically tapping at the nav console.

"You swore an oath," replied Hreem. "To hold your liege's enemies as your own, and your life as his to spend in defense of the Thousand Suns." He laughed, barely able to continue at the expression on the face of the Aegios. "Out there is a ship full of Dol'jharians, the Panarch's bitter enemies. I'm just helping you fulfill your oath."

Hreem paused as Riolo held up three fingers, then two, then one.

"Good-bye, Ferniar Ozman," said Hreem.

The pinnace vanished in a pulse of light as its fiveskip engaged. Four seconds later a dim spark of light indicated the destruction of the *Karra-rahim* as the little ship's course intersected its position.

"Good work," said Hreem, seating himself in the control pod. "Let's get on board."

The complex fittings of the cruiser's hull slipped out of sight past the edges of the viewscreen as the little ship moved toward the immense bay yawning open for them. Hreem could hear Norio's breath rasping unevenly in his throat, and he grinned, knowing that his emotions were almost too hot for the tempath to handle. In truth, he could barely contain them himself — he'd never before felt such an intense happiness.

The green com light kindled on the console.

"Yeah?"

Dyasil's face windowed up on the screen. "Dyasil, here, Cap'n. Erbee says there's somethin' goin' on in the cruiser's engines, and he doesn't like it."

"What?" Hreem snapped. "I thought the engines weren't up yet."

"That's just it, Captain," came the scantech's voice, all traces of its usual drawl effaced by anxiety. A moment later his face pushed into view over Dyasil's shoulder. "It takes hours to bring the engines up safely, but the cruiser's are comin' on-line right now. Somebody's taking the Plasma Wager, and I think they're gonna lose." He jerked his thumb up. "You'd better get out of there."

Before Hreem could reply the image fuzzed and tore across in a pattern of zigzag lines, re-forming moments later into an unfamiliar face. Dark, deeply lined, with a high forehead and thin lips compressed into a snarling smile, the man glared madly out at Hreem and the other Rifters.

"Don't, Captain," he said, emotion distorting his speech into a guttural accent that Hreem immediately recognized. "I want you to join me for the final voyage of the *Paliach ku-Avatari.*" He glanced down, evidently checking some instrument not in the imager's field of view. "The *Avatar's Vengeance,* you would say in that puling tongue you Panarchists use."

The image jittered. A ripple of gravitational energy tugged at Hreem's innards, and on the screen, the Dol'jharian's face distorted in a flash of agony. Hreem slapped at the console, bringing the yacht about, fear screaming through his nerves. Norio moaned in pain.

"Now I take my name into the darkness, and with it your hopes of glory. Attarh ni-grishun ta nemmir Hreem alia ni-Takha—"

Hreem slapped the go-pad, cutting off the man's cursing in midsentence. The fiveskip burred, then cut out.

Hreem tapped at the console with wooden fingers, his mind numb. The viewscreen flickered to a view of the *Maccabeus* several light-seconds distant. Unable to magnify the image as much of the better sensors of the destroyer Hreem was used to, it also revealed the *Flower of Lith* stationed nearby. As he watched, the destroyer vanished in a burst of light as it, too, fled.

The wavefront carrying the curses of the Dol'jharian agent had caught up with them, but the man did not lapse back into Uni before his voice cut off with a choking scream. A burst of glaring-bright vapor shot from the radiants of the cruiser, sending bits of the superstructure of its dock spinning away into space. Then, in the utter silence of vacuum, a network of cracks shot through the hull, revealing a growing brightness from within that grew and grew until the electronics of the yacht refused the overload and blanked the screen.

When the viewscreen cleared there was nothing left but a rosette of plasma, churning in a complex pattern that slowly faded against the stars.

Hreem sat in silence. Norio hovered in a corner, his face manic. No one else moved; Hreem knew that they all feared his anger.

All except Riolo.

The Barcan approached. Hreem saw his own reflection, distorted weasel-like in the little man's goggles. Riolo's breath was sweet with some unfamiliar spice.

"I know where there is something that Eusabian needs even more than a battlecruiser," he whispered. "And there are no Dol'jharians there. Never have been, never will be."

Hreem considered this, rage suspended by curiosity.

'Take me to Barca with you," said Riolo, "and I will give you an army of such power that even the Shiidra wailed with fear at their appearance."

"Army?" Hreem croaked.

Riolo smiled and pulled his goggles up, his pupils instantly contracting to pinpoints and tears springing into his eyes. Hreem remembered Norio commenting that this was the ultimate Barcan gesture of sincerity.

"Yes," said Riolo. "I will give you the Ogres."

FOUR

Mandros Nukiel stared moodily into the depths of the mug in his hands, grateful for the warmth its gold-green contents radiated into his fingers. He raised it to his lips and sipped; the tangy, sour-spiced tea pricked his tongue. His brightly-lit cabin was silent except for a susurration from the tianqi. It was simulating the warmth of high summer on Sync Ferenzi, balmy breezes carrying the scent of oranges, but he was still cold.

It was an iciness of the mind, not the body. Soon they would emerge over Desrien to face—what? Nukiel set the tea down on the table next to his chair. He had never felt more alone.

It wasn't just Desrien. The interception of the Rifter ship with the Aerenarch aboard had plunged Nukiel into the midst of high politics, with no precedents to guide him. Had the Aerenarch indeed, as the Rifters insisted, given them leave to loot the palace? And how had the Aerenarch escaped death in the Mandala at his Enkainion? Had he been warned, or had he been running away? One thing was sure, Nukiel couldn't ask directly and risk getting an answer that would force his hand. And behind all that, the ghost of the Lusor affair, which had touched the very highest levels of both Navy and government.

He was glad that the Aerenarch hadn't demanded an interview and seemed content to wait. But what they found at Desrien would likely mean a conversation could not be delayed any longer.

It didn't help that the gnostor Omilov had refused noetic questioning, as was his right, and although he had spoken freely in their many conversations since the interception at Rifthaven, he'd said very little about the Aerenarch. Nukiel had the sense that the younger Omilov also knew more than he was saying, and although Nukiel could order him to talk (noetic questioning would require a court martial, definitely a star system too far), he was content to leave that to Ares command.

But their silence was also a relief. The Aerenarch had made it clear that he was on board the *Mbwa Kali* only in the civilian role of his title, so Nukiel was simply an escort, safely outside of political reach.

Technically safe. When it came to the Arkads, there was no such safety.

In the meantime, he had the not-very-believable stories from four of the Rifters, whose noesis, of course, revealed only what they believed to be true, not the truth itself, and then only if you knew what questions to ask.

Which left the two Rifters who'd been able to refuse noesis: the Douloi from Timberwell, whose status couldn't be confirmed due to the late unpleasantness there, and the tempath. The Chief Wrangler had pointed out that if she had the mind link with the Eya'a she claimed — and there was no reason to doubt it, seeing that they hadn't slaughtered everyone in the interception lock when the *Telvarna* was captured — there was no telling what noesis might provoke. And that being interpreter, as it were, to the little sophonts with their ambassadorial status, she might actually have diplomatic immunity.

Nukiel groaned.

He rubbed gently at the com button set in the arm of the chair, aware of the focus of forces it represented. A slightly stronger pressure on the tab, a few words, and he could loose more firepower than all the armies in all the wars of Lost Earth. So why did he feel so helpless?

The annunciator chimed, rescuing him from his thoughts.

"Enter."

The hatch slid open to reveal the slim form of Commander Efriq.

"Come in, Leontois," said Nukiel, signaling the informal nature of their meeting before the other man could salute. "Can I get you anything?" He waved toward the chair facing his.

Efriq seated himself. His nose above the debonair must-ache wrinkled and he pulled his collar a little looser. "You're drinking that vile tea of yours, with the heat up like this?" He fanned a hand near his face. "Nothing for me, thanks." Then, looking more closely at Nukiel, "You catching a chill?"

Nukiel chuckled, a humorless sound. "You might say that."

"Ah." Efriq looked around the cabin. The lighting sparked highlights from his glossy, close-slicked black hair. "The magisters'll do that to one."

They shared a companionable silence.

"You've been to Desrien, haven't you?" Nukiel said finally.

"Low orbit," replied Efriq, "as close as'll do for a lifetime." He shrugged. "Not much to tell, really, I was an ensign on the *Thunderous* when it was assigned to map Desrien." He sighed. "The government never gives up, does it? Every thirty years or so, like a stable orbit." He waved a hand dismissively. "Well, that's as it is. They fitted that old frigate with every kind of sensor you can imagine. I was on the bridge when the captain hailed Desrien Node and the machinery patched him through to somewhere on the surface."

"He asked permission?"

"After what happened in '99, he didn't dare otherwise."

"And what did they say?"

"They laughed. Not jeeringly, no arrogance, just—well, rather bemused, like they couldn't understand why we could not get it through our heads that it simply wouldn't work." He shook his head. "They told us to go ahead, but not to attempt to land." His brows went up. "Not that anyone wanted to."

"What happened?"

"Nothing, at first. Captain Enneal put us in a low polar orbit that took us over the entire surface. Everything ran smooth as woven monothread."

He fell silent again. Nukiel took another sip of tea. "And then?"

"And then Siglnt tabbed in the command for the discriminators to go to work on the data. Everyone was watching the screen for the first coordinates to come up. Next thing we knew, the lights flickered a bit and Siglnt's console started squealing like a wattle with its tail caught in a hatch. The computer had crashed."

He shook his head again. "We kept trying. Got the

computer back up. Next time it crashed, the bit-rot somehow spread into Environmental. Air started to smell like old socks."

Efriq got up and walked over to the shelf displaying Nukiel's awards. He laid an index finger gently against one plaque, and continued without turning around. "Captain didn't give up then, either. We ended up limping home on one engine, with gravitors that couldn't maintain a constant gee-force from one section to another, and worst of all, the galley refrigerators broke down and the food synthesizers would only deliver stale beer and Pnahian jiggle-cheese."

Nukiel choked on a swallow of tea and his sinuses stung. Gasping, he laughed out loud.

"Pnahian cheese? That's the stuff that —"

Efriq turned around and nodded, his upper lip lengthening in prim disapproval. "Smells like a corpse's armpit."

"Well, that, but the chatzing stuff moved, constantly, right on the plate, the one time I saw it."

"It moves even more when you try to swallow it," Efriq said with morose humor. "It being all we had, we did try. Now I know why no one but a Pnahi can stomach it."

"But I was told they can't get enough of it."

"Which is why they are about as popular in small, enclosed spaces—like a frigate—as a case of Medlybbi Fungusdrool." Efriq walked back to his chair. "But we got off easy, compared to some."

Nukiel nodded, the urge to laugh dissolving like the steam from his tea. The expedition of '99 had simply vanished.

Efriq reseated himself and leaned forward. "Mandros, why did you order us to Desrien?"

Nukiel carefully replaced the mug on the table. "I was summoned, I believe—it has something to do with the Aerenarch, and the others —"

The comm chimed softly.

"Nukiel here."

"Captain, emergence at Desrien, three minutes."

"Thank you, Mr. Pele. Have Communications patch the Node relay through to my cabin."

He tabbed the communicator off.

"We'll soon know for sure. I want you here for this, Efriq. If I've blown up my career, I'd like at least one person to understand what happened."

Efriq nodded and settled back in his chair. There was

nothing more to say, until the Magisterium spoke.

DESRIEN

As a fitful summer breeze tossed the branches of the trees shading the cloister garden of New Glastonbury, a stray sunbeam struck through the half-open window of Eloatri's study, refracted by the beveled glass into a rainbow segment dancing on the polished wood of her reading desk. A portion of her mind noted the quiet clicking outside the window that marked the progress of the gardener with her shears, ministering to the gardens with the severe love of her calling. Then the chuckling mimicry of a mockingbird drew Eloatri fully out of her book — *tick-tack-tick, too-wit, too-wit, birdie, birdie, birdie* — followed by a snatch of amazingly accurate bell sound that made her smile.

She put the book down and stretched, inhaling deeply of the scented morning air, cool yet heady with orange and jasmine, jumari, and hints of rosemary and less familiar scents from the knot garden outside her window. Then the bells of Glastonbury clamored in reality, striking eleven times.

One hour before Sext. Unbidden, a bit of pedantry from the book echoed: "Sext is the hour of Peter's vision at Joppa, in which the universal mission of the church was revealed. . ."

Eloatri sighed. As helpful as the books and chips were, it was the routine of the Daily Offices that was doing the most to settle her into her responsibilities in this, regrettably, still somewhat alien faith. She tugged at her clerical collar, then, aware of the motion, dropped her hand into her lap and swiveled about to look out the window.

What was the name of that ancient bishop in Rome her clerk Tuaan had told her about? Peregrinus, Pellerini? Selected bishop by a pigeon landing on his head when he wandered into a church out of curiosity. She knew what he must have felt like, and wondered what kind of bishop he turned out to be. Tuaan had a sly sense of humor sometimes, but without him she'd be lost.

As if in response to her thoughts, the comm on her desk chirped for attention.

"Yes?"

"A battlecruiser has emerged and taken position at the

Node," came Tuaan's voice. "They're not entirely clear on why they're here, but I think they were Summoned."

Eloatri sat up, a shock of anticipation coursing through her. Was this what she was waiting for?

"I'll be right there."

When she reached the holo room, Tuaan was waiting for her, his expression radiating humor and curiosity. He tabbed the holo alive and stepped back out of its field of view.

The image wavered into solidity, revealing a tall, lean, dark-complected naval officer with a short, square, salt-and-pepper beard. He stood stiffly, not quite at attention; she could see little of the room around him, but judged it must be his cabin. Certainly it wasn't the bridge.

His hard eyes focused on her, then widened. He hesitated; her nerves chilled as the conviction struck her that he recognized her. She didn't recognize him. He matched none of the dream images that had made her nights so restless since she left the vihara. Perhaps the hypothesis about Summoning was accurate.

"This is Captain Mandros Nukiel, of His Majesty's battlecruiser *Mbwa Kali*, commanding," he said finally.

"Welcome to Desrien orbit, Captain," she replied. "I am Eloatri, by the Hand of Telos High Phanist of Desrien."

The captain's heavy eyebrows converged on the bridge of his nose as his forehead wrinkled in perplexity and doubt.

"Tomiko was on Arthelion," she said, hazarding a somewhat oracular statement in the hopes of eliciting some confirmation of the rumors that had reached Desrien. Despite her visions, and those of others on the planet, there was still no hard news of the convulsion that was sweeping through the Thousand Suns.

As she saw the statement strike home with all the force she could have wished, she raised her hand, displaying the weal burned into it by the Digrammaton.

Captain Nukiel sighed, an unwilling but entirely human reaction. "Then you did summon me."

"I believe you were Summoned," she said carefully. Seeing the captain's confusion, she continued, "But we are not talking about a link on a planetary DataNet." She chuckled. "You and I have some things in common, Captain. We are both under orders. But yours are, usually, far clearer."

A hint of impatience tightened Nukiel's face. "Forgive me,

Numen," he said, using the formal term of address that belongs only to the High Phanist, "but I have hazarded my career in the midst of war to come in response to your summons. I request you do not toy with me."

War! Despite her visions, the visitation of Tomiko, and everything else, the bald confirmation of her forebodings rang like a tocsin in her mind.

"Forgive me, Captain," she replied. "I can only tell you this: that my mind has been much troubled of late by visions of a young man, red-haired, with the pale skin of an atavism, who may be wearing an emerald ring. There is also the matter of a small silver sphere, which may be related to him."

Nukiel's eyebrows twitched together, then his expression shifted and Eloatri saw the impact of the numinous on him. He swallowed and cleared his throat. "I see what you mean about your orders," he said. "I think I know who and what you are referring to."

With growing amazement, Eloatri listened to the captain's story, and as she did the frisson of the numinous settled deeply into her bones as well.

Truly, she thought, we stand at the hinge of Time.

Presently, Eloatri entered the west end of the cathedral and walked down the long aisle through the nave. The vast interior of the church glowed with light, prismatic splendor striking through the multitude of stained-glass windows that pierced the heavy walls, transforming them into an impossibly delicate tracery of stone.

She smiled. She had discovered that the vaulting geometry of ancient Christian architecture kindled a deep response in her. It was perhaps the facet of this faith that most helped reconcile her to being ripped away from her old life. Like walking through the mind of Telos, all light and space and structured beauty.

There were others in the Cathedral, of course — it was never empty — but they all moved in their own orbits, dwarfed by the immense space, intent on their own communion with Telos and the triune holiness of an ancient faith. She was beginning to perceive a rhythm to this life, a dance-like structure, wherein the faithful moved at times in solitude, and then were drawn together in the solemn measures of the Mass and other rituals, and then apart again, but never really separate.

Eloatri desired solitude, to meditate upon the words of

Captain Nukiel, now waiting impatiently in orbit above Desrien. And on what her advisers had told her. The xenologist had been especially insistent. That ship was almost certainly their hive now. Without it, they very likely would not survive Desrien.

She slipped into the sanctuary and genuflected deeply before the altar. She stood quietly, looking up at the carven agony of the crucifix. She still found it deeply disturbing, repulsive even.

"You did not think you drank this for yourself?" The words of Tomiko in the vision came back to her, nearly a rebuke, and she forced herself to look at the man on the cross as others might see him — those others, for instance, who waited in orbit, each with their own pain to bear, past and future. Even though, as High Phanist, she was the defender of all the faiths of Desrien, this one had been chosen for her to live, now, but not for her alone.

The image's eyes were calm beneath the crown of thorns. He is all of us, as a thousand years of peace dissolve in agony. And the words of an ancient warrior of Lost Earth resounded in her inner ear: It is humanity, hanging on a cross of iron. Then, looking around for a moment longer, she settled into the lotus position and breathed out slowly.

Clearing her mind, she entered into her own communion.

Some time later, Nukiel stared at the holo of the High Phanist, almost unable to believe what he had heard. "You want me to what?"

Eloatri sighed. "Put them on their ship — all of them, including the Aerenarch and the other two Douloi, the Eya'a, and the animals — and send them to me."

Nukiel looked over at Efriq, out of view of the High Phanist. Efriq shrugged and spread his hands.

"I'm sorry, Numen," Nukiel said finally. "That would be an abrogation of my oath and my responsibilities. You are welcome to interrogate them here, but I cannot release them."

"I don't wish to interrogate them, Captain," she replied, a hint of irritation sharpening her words. That was enough to bring back the image of her head crowned in a flaring corona as Ferenzi disintegrated around him. "In fact, it is not for my benefit at all that I make this request, although I must admit to more than a little curiosity about their adventures, after what you have told me."

She paused, considering. Then her face hardened into a greater severity. "Captain, I assume you have a console there in your cabin."

Nukiel blinked, taken off guard. "Of course."

"Good. I hereby invoke the Gabrieline Protocol and command you to do as I have requested. You will find the protocol under code Aleph-Null in Fleet Standing Orders."

Nukiel snorted, convinced he was dealing with a madwoman. "There is no code Aleph-Null in the Standing Orders, and no such protocol." He heard Efriq tapping at the console as he glared at the gray-haired woman in the holo, wondering if he would be allowed to take the *Mbwa Kali* out of orbit after defying her. Efriq's story, funny in the telling, was now assuming a different, altogether unfunny dimension.

There was a sudden inhalation of disbelief from his first officer and Nukiel wheeled about to face him. Efriq looked up at him with no trace of his customary insouciance. He swiveled the data console around to face Nukiel. There, glowing under the Sun and Phoenix, was a protocol he'd never seen before.

He looked at Efriq. "It's authentic," said the first officer. "Countersign matches."

Nukiel read quickly — the Gabrieline Protocol was short and succinct — and then turned back to the High Phanist. She watched him calmly, sympathy in her expression.

"It seems I have no choice," he said.

Then Efriq spoke in the tones of a quotation, although Nukiel had never heard the words before: "This has been willed where what is willed must be."

To his astonishment, the High Phanist gave a delighted cackle. Efriq's demeanor was expressive of rueful amusement as he stepped into the view of the holo imager.

"You have a classicist on board, I see." Eloatri laughed again. "Well said, ah — " She peered more closely at Efriq. " — Commander. But some would say that applies to the Mandala, as well as Desrien. Certainly I make no claims to omnipotence."

"You might as well," Nukiel said grumpily, motioning at the console, "for all the choice that leaves us."

"No choice, but I do not expect you to leave your ass swinging past the radiants."

Nukiel choked and Efriq smiled as Eloatri laughed again. "I'm sorry, Captain," she said. "But you need to know we're not all folded hands and stained glass down here. My father was a career Navy man, chief petty officer on the *Sword of Asoka*. So I take your responsibilities seriously. You may assign two Marines to accompany them as guards, and to take whatever other precautions you deem necessary." Her face sobered. "But mark this well: no one else of your crew is to leave the ship."

Again the image of the Goddess amidst the destruction of Sync Ferenzi possessed his mind. "But I thought. . . *I* was summoned."

And then the woman's face, formerly soft and almost grandmotherly, settled into an expression of almost inhuman pity. Nukiel couldn't say why, but a thrill of terror spiked into his vitals. And as she spoke, the reality of Desrien reached out and grasped him in a grip that he knew would never be relaxed."I'm sorry, Captain, but the Goddess ha s given us no message for you. Your time is not yet come."

The image dwindled away like a flame and vanished.

Artorus Vahn stood against the wall of the Captain's dining room, thinking about the grilling he and the steward would get later from shipmates about what they'd seen and heard, even though they knew they'd get nothing from either of them. But this meeting had been so long deferred that their exigent curiosity would be excusable.

The dinner itself was done, the steward efficiently laying out the after-course and silently vanishing, but not before a glance passed between her and Nukiel when Commander Efriq raised an eyebrow at the Pnahian offering among the cheeses, safely restrained under a bell jar. Thankfully, no one decided to sample it. Vahn couldn't imagine which of the rare liqueurs and wines would go with it.

Laughter interrupted his thoughts. Krysarch Brandon — now Aerenarch — dropped his napkin back in his lap and reached to move some of the silver about on the table as he illustrated his story.

"So then the Kug jumped the Draco at this intersection, and while they enthusiastically tried to quarry each other's innards, we fell into an access hatch here — and into the waiting arms of a gang of feud-bent Yim, who were hoping we'd be Draco. . . "

The Aerenarch was describing his run through Rifthaven before he and the Rifters lifted off in the Columbiad. He made it vivid, and funny, and Nukiel and Efriq seemed to be enjoying it. The tone of hilarity also, Vahn noted, appeared to inspire a joking answer to the occasional direct question from captain or commander. There was certainly nothing overtly evasive in the Aerenarch's manner, and he readily described in detail certain things they asked for.

"My younger brother is the smartest of us," Krysarch Galen ban-Arkad had said once. He'd added thoughtfully, *"I hope he discovers it before anyone else does."*

The 'anyone else' had to refer to Semion, then Aerenarch, who had posted Vahn to Talgarth with orders to report every conversation he overheard. For security reasons, he'd been told. *"Galen ban-Arkad's mind is always on music and he wouldn't know if an assassin or a spy was among the loyal."* It had taken almost half a year before Vahn could see past the distorted lens of the training he'd received on Narbon, to appreciate Galen's freedom of thought and speech not as weakness but as something quite different. And he also had realized that the only people permitted around Galen for any length of time were Semion's spies — and that the older brother was the only inimical thing in Galen's life.

Though that turned out not to be true, Vahn corrected himself, as the men before him refilled their glasses and toasted the Panarch yet again before drinking. The news passed on by *Grozniy* ate at him sometimes, at night: could he have saved Galen if he hadn't transferred away from Talgarth?

". . . so these Rifters have no allies, as far as you are aware, Your Highness?" Commander Efriq asked after a pause. The dapper man's finicky manner hid a very acute mind.

"Their allies were killed when one of Eusabian's Rifters found their base," the Aerenarch answered. "I don't suppose you've ever heard of Hreem the Faithless?"

The captain shook his head, and Commander Efriq murmured, "Would we find the name on the bonus chips?"

"Safe bet," the Aerenarch replied.

"The vids the *Grozniy* captured at Treymontaigne," Nukiel said. "They make it look as if the Rifters armed by Dol'jhar have embarked on a sacking spree that Eusabian has done little to control."

"That's certainly the rumor on Rifthaven," the Aerenarch agreed, showing no reaction to the oblique reference to the looting of the Palace Minor by the Rifters of the *Telvarna.* "No controls at all. But that doesn't make a lot of sense."

"I expect we'll see a pattern develop as more intelligence comes in," Efriq put in. "Loose control in peripheral areas to spread terror and confusion, and more coordinated attacks on strategic points. The two sector capitals we have some data on don't seem to have suffered as much."

Nukiel set his wineglass down and steepled his fingers. "Your Highness, do you know what Captain Vi'ya planned to do once the *Telvarna* was safely away from Rifthaven?"

"That was under discussion right before Karroo sent half the ships in orbit after us," the Aerenarch said, smiling. "I know they had a second base, where perhaps they could hide out until things got resolved one way or the other—or supplies gave out."

Efriq said mildly, "Did those plans include you and the Omilovs, Your Highness?"

Vahn knew the Aerenarch perceived how carefully the question was worded. He didn't seem unduly worried as he drained his third glass of wine and reached for the decanter.

One goal of this dinner was certainly to establish whether the Aerenarch was with these Rifters by accident, or by design. Having spent as much time as he had with Brandon on the long flight from Rifthaven, he knew the captain and his XO were unlikely to discover the answer tonight.

"Perforce," Brandon said presently. He grinned over the cut crystal in his fingers. "As you doubtless know, one of the other things they discovered while on Rifthaven was that the Dol'jharian taste for thoroughness in revenge had inspired Eusabian to put a price on my head worth a few dozen planets. I get the impression that some of Vi'ya's crew wavered between the dreams of trying to collect and the reality of how long they'd live under Dol'jharian ministrations if they did try to turn me in. Right before your ruptor finished off their drive, we had just established that Vi'ya was disinclined to put us down anywhere. Thought we'd be easy targets."

Which answered the superficial question and sidestepped the real one, Vahn thought appreciatively.

He'd been born on Arthelion—both parents had been Marines—and he'd grown up absorbing the lacework of protocol that dictated life there. The problem here was a potentially messy one: there was not only the matter of civilian hierarchy, but military vs. civilian, augmented by the Aerenarch's sudden departure from military life ten years before. If he held even nominal rank, Nukiel could have ordered him to talk and be protected by regs.

"True." Nukiel's expression sobered. "And she'd be afraid that you'd lead the Dol'jharians right back to her and her crew."

"Willingly or not," Brandon said, again putting a spin on the direction of the questions. "Sebastian would not live long under one of their torture machines again, despite their best efforts."

"So the medics tell us, Your Highness," Efriq said softly. "Our CMO has offered him the reconstructive work his heart needs, but the gnostor insists on waiting until we arrive at Ares. He says his oath requires it."

A glance went between captain and commander, no more than a flicker. Vahn knew that the old gnostor was a Chival of the Phoenix Gate, but how did he think that would help the now-Aerenarch? That rank would be of little account on Ares, and less here. The interchanges between Brandon and Gn. Omilov had not offered any clues — they were as opaque as any Douloi interactions Vahn had ever witnessed.

And there was certainly no clue in Brandon's face now, still hard to read under myriad healing bruises, nor in his posture, relaxed as he watched the play of light on the liquid in his glass.

"But all that must wait until we finish our business here at Desrien."

"Ah. Desrien," the Aerenarch said, looking up. "How did this side journey come to pass?"

Vahn realized that this was the first time he had asked a question this evening. He wouldn't ask anything that might require Nukiel to define his status — as citizen or prisoner. What was he trying to protect?

"You appear to have business there," Nukiel replied. "The whole matter is still mysterious to me, but the High Phanist was quite clear in her orders—"

The Aerenarch cocked an eyebrow and Nukiel paused.

"'Tomiko was on Arthelion' was what the Numen said to me," the captain interjected. "But she now has the Digrammaton."

The Aerenarch blinked, the humor vanishing from his expression, to be quickly replaced by the same bland mask that Vahn had seen Galen assume whenever discussion of Semion arose.

"In any case," continued Nukiel, "you, the Omilovs, the Rifters, the Eya'a, and even the dogs and the cat—who, by the way, spends each night in a different cabin, so popular is he among the junior officers—are to be sent down in the Columbiad, I assume for a meeting with the High Phanist."

The skin around the Aerenarch's eyes tightened very slightly, a subtle sign that Vahn wasn't sure either the captain or the commander noted, or understood if they did. It momentarily increased Brandon's resemblance to his eldest brother.

He wasn't pleased, not pleased at all. Vahn could hardly blame him. No royal had set foot on Desrien for nearly 150 years, not since Burgess III at the end of his long reign. He had abdicated in favor of his daughter, taken the robe of an Oblate, and vanished forever among the shrines of Desrien. Jaspar Arkad had accepted the nascent Magisterium as one of the poles of power in his reconstruction of interstellar politics a millennium ago, but no Arkad was likely to be comfortable with a power that had once overthrown a reigning Panarch.

"Have you told the Rifters?" the Aerenarch asked.

"I have not," Nukiel said. "My interview with Eloatri—the new High Phanist—took place directly before we came here." He indicated the table, then turned to Efriq, who looked back with dry humor. "It appears you have been more successful at communicating with them than we have, Your Highness. Would you like to be the one to tell them, since you're visiting Ivard regularly?"

"I will," the Aerenarch said slowly. "When do we shuttle down to the planet?"

"At oh eight hundred."

And Vahn would be with them, a thought that brought no particular pleasure. What he'd heard about Desrien did not appeal to him at all.

"Thank you." The Aerenarch rose. "Perhaps I'd better do it now," he said. "So we all get what sleep we can before the ordeal." His tone made a joke of the word "ordeal," which deflected attention—at least superficially—from the fact that he, and not the captain, had brought the interview to a close.

As he jeeved out behind Brandon, Vahn reflected on the Aerenarch's masterful handling of the interview with Nukiel and Efriq. He wondered how that skill would serve Brandon on Desrien.

FIVE

"**B**eacon acquired," Lokri said.

Data leaped to Vi'ya's console in a brief twitter. Montrose took in Lokri's hot flush of irritation and Vi'ya's cold fury as she set up their course.

The rest of their flight down to Desrien was accomplished in silence. On a viewscreen assigned to the aft imager the massive battlecruiser dwindled. They fell toward the planet, the stars fading as the glowing limb of Desrien slowly filled the forward view.

The entire crew was on the bridge, even the Eya'a and the Omilovs. Jaim stood at the com console, working with Marim to repair the damage caused by Nukiel's ruptors. The engineer's bitter sadness—his mate Reth had often spoken of making a hejir—contrasted with Marim's flippant attempts to hide her fear. For Jaim, at least, there was no other place to be: the captain of the *Mbwa Kali* had ordered the fiveskip of the *Telvarna* disabled and the engine room sealed shut.

To distract himself from his own ghosts, Montrose looked around the bridge as the atmosphere of the planet began to whisper over the ship's hull. Vi'ya sat still at her console, the unusual precision of her movements revealing her fury. Nearby the Eya'a stood unmoving, facing her. They paid no attention to the viewscreen.

Marim kept her eyes away from their destination. Instead, her attention was divided between Jaim and Ivard, the latter prompting fascinated disgust.

Montrose sighed. It was unlikely that Ivard would survive to return to the *Mbwa Kali*. The cruiser's medics, despite their best efforts, had been unable to arrest the deterioration of his immune system, or the increasing dementia that the Kelly ribbon had triggered. The dogs had helped, but the visit of the Aerenarch the night before had been the occasion of Ivard's last coherent words. Now he sat on the deck, rocking slightly back and forth and buzzing to himself from time to time; his skin was almost translucent, greenish yellow and badly bruised, like that of a victim of a blood disease. His arms twitched, fingers and head writhing ceaselessly in spasmodic movements. Despite this, Trev and Gray remained lying pressed up against him on either side, their ears twitching uneasily. Gray whined softly from time to time.

At the fire-control console, sealed and dark, Brandon sat looking down at the ring on his hand, ignoring Lucifur cheek-stropping one of his boots and purring loudly. The two Marines assigned to accompany them stood against the bulkhead, alert and silent.

Sebastian Omilov sat at Ivard's station, his eyes closed, his aspect tired. Beside him his son stood, radiating distrust.

Montrose looked up at the viewscreen, feeling curiously empty. It was as though the planet now filling the viewscreen had sucked some vital essence from him. Bleakly he realized that alone of all those on the bridge, he knew that there was no limit to the changes this planet could ring on the human spirit.

For Tenaya, his wife, had been a haji. He had seen the change in her, in the few short weeks they'd had together between her return from her pilgrimage and her death. She had been different, vastly different: even more loving and vital, yet somehow distant, as if ever hearing some music that was inaudible to him. They had had too little time for him to fully come to terms with that: he would never know what life might have held for them after she was touched by the Dreamtime.

He blinked, fighting back memory. A once-familiar voice whispered in memory, *"But in the Dreamtime there is neither past nor future."*

The ship shuddered and the plasma jets whined to life as the *Telvarna* entered aerodynamic flight, arrowing across the face of Desrien toward their unknown goal.

They landed without a bump.

As the engines spun down into silence, Vi'ya cleared her board with a swipe of her hand. Then she stalked off the bridge toward the mid-ship hatch. Osri moved hastily aside as she passed him. He didn't have to look at her face to know how angry she was. Everybody was angry, except poor Ivard, who seemed beyond human emotions entirely. One thing they all shared: no one wanted to be here.

One by one the others followed the captain, the two Marines shadowing the Aerenarch.

The ramp whined down and thumped onto the ground, and a brisk breeze whirled into the open lock, bringing with it the scent of grass and damp earth, overlaid with a heat smell from the hull of the *Telvarna*, pinging softly as it cooled. At first no one moved, then Lokri snorted and pushed past Marim. He trotted down the ramp, the metal booming underfoot.

Outside, the sky was a rich blue-green between towering clouds, gray underneath and blinding white above in the light of the yellow-white sun. Before them a long meadow stretched up toward a hill crowned with a few twisted trees. A racing cloud shadow sped across the slope toward them; the air chilled Osri as the sun vanished.

The opening of the lock seemed to have focused Ivard somewhat. He got to his feet and approached the lock. The dogs began to follow, but then bolted past him down the ramp with a scrabble of claws, giving the high-pitched bark that hitherto they had only used to greet Brandon. Lucifur swarmed after, vanishing into the riot of greenery behind the dogs.

Ivard gave an incoherent shout, and Marim cursed. Everyone else was quiet and wary. The only sound was the wind, and then the soft booming of the ramp as the others slowly began to debark.

The rich smells of earth-like soil and flora crowded into the lock, shouting in Ivard's skull. The blue fire around his wrist pulsed in delight; images fountained from two faceted flames nearby, quicksilver brightness, multiple flashes that broke through the veil that hung between him and the world he had once known. The muttering pain slashing across his back hung red behind him, pushing him forward.

The two small flames on either side of him flashed by, followed by another, smaller one. He called out to them, but they vanished swiftly. He felt incomplete, isolate, but the blue fire rose up in him and his distress dwindled somewhat.

The other, taller flames around him flowed, their anxiety, borne outward by the complex stew of chemicals they generated without a trace of control, hooking him with invisible claws so that he stumbled after them.

He tasted the clangor of metal. One of the new flames spoke; this time the words broke through to Ivard: "New Glastonbury."

Ivard didn't know what that meant, but the blue fire leapt higher, a shimmer of satisfaction welling from it. Around him small flames flickered in a web of life and movement, slow and fast. Around the base of one of the tall flames — he'd exchanged life-stuff with that one — some of the tiny flames changed color, some flickered out. He danced a protest, but received no response.

Abruptly the veil cleared, revealing a tall building intricate beyond any he had ever seen. It tugged at him, rhythms in stone and glass drawing him on. He responded with a dance of celebration and recognition. One of the others had shown him, had played this — no, there was no room on the *Telvarna*. The confusion dropped the veil across his vision once more; he tasted comments from the others without comprehension, wandering in a blue-shot haze.

Marim ignored him.

"I hate this blunge-suck of a cesspit," she snarled, kicking at some kind of greenery growing alongside the pathway.

Fronds scattered across the dirt before her, leaving a sharp scent in the air that made her sneeze. Her toes were covered with sticky greenish goo.

"Sgatchi!" she squawked, grubbing her toes into the dirt to clean them. Then she noticed small wiggly things scrabbling wildly in the dirt she'd dug up, and she gave a bellow of disgust. "I *hate* dirtside!" she wailed.

Everything about planets offended her. The smells in the unfiltered air, the disgusting way things degraded, and worst of all were the bugs.

Something touched her shoulder. Ivard! He was back, his nasty freckled face blank, his arms waving around and his head bobbing as he honked at her.

Marim grimaced and sprinted away from him. Ugh! She'd bunnied with that?

She spotted Vi'ya stalking on the pathway ahead, which meant her mood was rasty. The Eya'a drifted behind her.

Lokri was at the end of the straggling line, his arms folded and face grim, but his mood was clearly even more vile than Vi'ya's, and he refused to talk.

Jaim looked around with interest. That was weird. He'd grown up on Rifthaven, and dirtballs spinning around suns were just as alien for him as for Marim. But he didn't seem to mind uncontrolled weather or the unplanned clutter of geography, or the tiny creatures doing their best to eat people; she slapped irritably at a tickle on her wrist.

As for that cursed Schoolboy! Damn him anyway, for cheating her out of that coin. He stalked, his father puffed, and Montrose wore an evil smile. As for the Arkad, who knew, or cared, what he thought? He was a prisoner, same as them. She liked him as a person, but ever since Nukiel's nicks had grabbed the *Telvarna*, Brandon was no longer Vi'ya's tame nick, he was one of *them*. You could see they all thought so. Only he was the worst kind of nick, one with a flashy title but no actual power. He couldn't get them freed, so she hoped he suffered, too. Fair's fair.

Sebastian Omilov inhaled sharply, as if in pain and wonder. "New Glastonbury," he said, staring at the vaulting lacework of gray-white stone of the cathedral emerging from behind the sheltering garden.

His face was gray. "The god who died," he whispered. "Is that why we're here? To be put to death?"

Osri swayed, dizzy: against the moving clouds the twin spires of the edifice looming above seemed to topple toward them. He put out a hand to steady his father, who grasped his arm. Then, looking down at Osri's sleeve, Omilov touched the embroidered emblem of the Phoenix there, ringed in flame. On his other side, Brandon appeared, concern in his demeanor.

Omilov's face cleared. "Ah, I lost more to Eusabian's henchman than I knew, if I've so thoroughly forgotten my mythology."

"What do you mean?"

Sebastian shook his head. "No matter." He moved off, apparently lost in private thoughts.

"Let's get this over with," Brandon suggested.

Osri fell in step beside him, the Marines trailing after them.

Marim kicked savagely at the low shrubs defining the gravel path they were following; Ivard honked and moved toward her, his arms writhing. She ignored him and he dropped back.

As they approached, the cathedral gradually swallowed the sky, shouldering it aside until it defined the world. Osri reflected on how little he knew of this faith—it had been, he remembered, a long time since a High Phanist had resided here. His only recollection was a dim wonder, in a history class long ago, that humanity should have remembered so long a brutal death by torture thousands of years past. Torture? Was that why Father reacted so?

He studied the cathedral as they walked into its shadow, puzzled at the exuberant architecture, the sense of turbulent joy embodied in the frenzied explosion of figures and carvings of trees and beasts and other, more abstract forms, trying to reconcile it all with that image of violent death.

He touched the crumpled ribbon and the coin through the fabric of his pocket, remembering the warmth they had held, and the slippery feel of blood when he had picked them up from where they'd fallen out of Ivard's grasp.

Vi'ya strode up to the massive doors, towering high above them, and grasped one handle. The muscles in her back bunched; the door swung out silently. She walked through the widening opening, followed by the Eya'a, and then the others.

As the door swung open behind the Dol'jharian captain, Artorus Vahn placed his palm against it, gauging its heft, and was astonished as it pushed his hand away even as he leaned into it. He looked thoughtfully at the Dol'jharian woman, conscious of the weight of the neurojac holstered on his belt. He sent a glance at Roget; the other Marine whistled soundlessly, rolling her eyes.

They followed the Aerenarch inside and stopped, amazed by the majesty of the cathedral's interior. All except the little blond Rifter. Marim. Raised on an unchartered habitat. Gennated for plantar free-fall adhesion.

Vahn shook his head as the information came unprompted. His brain still buzzed with the effects of the mild Augment session he'd undergone to study the interrogation chips on the Rifters and the others. Fortunately, it had been low-level enough to avoid visual migraines.

Marim trotted forward a few steps, then turned back and looked at them exasperated, hands on her hips. Clearly vast spaces meant little to her. Jaim's posture also reflected this habitat-bred   attitude—Rifthaven—but   his   shadowed expression indicated some emotional impact that Vahn couldn't clearly read.

The towering windows, explosions of color and complex form, transmuted the uneasy sky into restless beams of light sweeping through the interior. To either side tall columns marched toward the distant front of the cathedral, drawing the eye toward the elevated dais with the white-clad altar on it, and above and beyond it, the glorious mandala of colored glass that dominated the east wall.

From the distance voices chanted in a melody of eerie beauty, too muted for words to be distinguished. A sweet, resiny smell lingered in the air; close by chimes tinkled as Jaim looked around.

They approached a small figure in black, which resolved into a short, stout woman with gray hair and a grandmotherly face. She was buttoned into a long garment with a high white collar. She seemed comfortable in the majestic cathedral, assuming an aura of power quite at variance with the smiling openness of her face.

Vi'ya's stance projected obduracy. In contrast Brandon vlith-Arkad stood with elegant grace, his Douloi mask unreadable.

"I am Eloatri," the woman said, her gesture taking in them all. "Welcome to Desrien."

Her gaze passed quickly over Vahn, but he felt her full attention in that moment, without any sense of judgment or appraisal. Her gaze came to rest not on the Aerenarch, but on Ivard, whose limbs and head moved in a ceaseless rhythm with a subtle triple beat. She stretched out a hand to him in welcome, kindness transforming her worn features.

"Three il-Kavic," she began.

"Ivard," the boy managed to whisper.

"Ivard," she repeated, in a voice so soft that Vahn triggered his augmentors to hear her more clearly, "be at peace here, and find your heart's desire, in the name of the Father, and of the Son, and of the Holy Spirit." She traced a cross on the boy's forehead, lips, and over his heart.

"For much the same reason that underlies their appreciation of the waltz and the Abbasiddhu triskel, the Kelly appear to find only Christianity, with its triune image of holiness, intelligible among human religions."

Vahn's memory triggered another dollop of data; he had

no idea what a "triune image of holiness" referred to. But whatever it was, it seemed to reach the ugly, pale-skinned Rifter. Ivard's eyes focused on Eloatri. The movements of his arms and head quieted during her gesture, but when she lifted her hand the spasmodic movements resumed and the boy's bruised face settled back into vagueness. The High Phanist appeared untroubled: she caressed his cheek and then stepped aside as he loped off in his bizarre fashion toward the distant altar.

Eloatri took a step closer to Vi'ya and Eya'a. Vi'ya stared down at her, expressionless; the two Eya'a looked up, their diamond-bright eyes gathering the soft light of the cathedral into lambent prisms.

Then a shrill, ear-stabbing trill erupted from the Eya'a. They threw their twiggy hands over their eyes and cocked their heads back at a jagged angle that made Vahn uncomfortable, exposing their throats to the High Phanist. She reached forward and touched each beneath the chin with a single finger. As their heads came down, she bowed deeply to them.

"In the name of Telos, and the Fulfillment of Humankind to Come, and of the Magisterium, I welcome you, Second Mind of. . ." She trilled on a high note, "to the Thousand Suns. May you find what you seek."

The Eya'a ran their attenuated fingers over the woman's wrists and forearms as they uttered high chirping sounds.

A flicker of — disbelief? anger? surprise? — widened Vi'ya's eyes. Eloatri turned her attention to the Dol'jharian. "It is there, deny it as you will," Eloatri said.

Vi'ya looked down at her, expressionless as stone.

"As the *one-who-hears* you will not be able to avoid it."

Vi'ya walked out of the cathedral. The Eya'a took off in another direction, vanishing behind a pillar.

Eloatri turned to the Aerenarch and executed a formal deference: a bow exquisitely judged, conveying recognition of his formal status with the reservation of judgment concerning its permanence.

Brandon's lips curved into a wintry smile. He returned the deference: the unique Royalty-to-Numen mode paid only to the High Phanist, but with the conditioned-on-proof modulation. Vahn suppressed a desire to laugh. That, too, was nicely judged — there'd been much speculation on the *Mbwa Kali* on how the Digrammaton could have gotten from Arthelion to

Desrien.

Eloatri smiled and held up her right hand, displaying a white raised weal — now fully healed — burned into her palm that echoed in reverse the shape of the Digrammaton on her chest. "It had not yet cooled from red heat when I received it from Tomiko, and even now it is not entirely safe to wear."

The Aerenarch's face blanched. Montrose turned a startled look at the High Phanist.

Vahn's stomach griped with an empathetic response to the ugly weal seared into Eloatri's hand. But his mind was even more disturbed: only if she had received it at the moment of her predecessor's death on Arthelion, hundreds of light-years away, would the wound have had time to heal.

"Pay your respects and then go to the north transept," Eloatri said to Brandon. "Await me there." She turned to the remaining Rifters.

The Aerenarch pursed his lips, and after a pause, obeyed. Vahn followed.

The High Phanist said to the rest, "You have the freedom of Desrien. Make what use of it you will."

The great organ came to life, weaving complex patterns of brilliant sound around them.

SIX

ontrose followed the sound to the base of a steep stairway. Music thundered around him, spilling from mighty constructs of gleaming metal pipes and wooden-shuttered boxes in the sides of the cathedral. He climbed the staircase.

At its top a man sat on a polished bench before an immensely complex console: ranks of keyboards over an array of pedals, and row upon row of large knobs at the ends of protruding rods, some pulled out, some flush with the console. The man lifted his hands from the keyboards. He had a snub nose and pudgy cheeks; his eyes were vivid under a high forehead and fringe of sandy hair.

"I've seen pictures of this," said Montrose. "It's an organ, right? A mechanical synthesizer?"

The musician chuckled, a cheerful wheeze. "You could say that, although it is perhaps the one instrument that's never been successfully synthesized." He held up his hand. "Oh, I know. Theoretically you can duplicate any sound. But look. First, each tone comes from a different pipe."

He ran his hands across first one keyboard, then another; then, quickly pulling and pushing some of the knobs, did it again. The sound rolled across the spacious interior, coming from a multitude of sources, filling the space with a variety of chordal sounds.

"There are thousands of pipes. You can't get that sound from a single sound source. And come here." He motioned Montrose closer, grabbed his hand and pressed his index finger against one key. "Feel that. There's a direct physical link between the key and the valve that controls each pipe." The man slid off the bench and Montrose took his place.

Montrose pressed first one key, then another. The keys felt like nothing he'd ever experienced from a musical instrument: alive under his touch, and there was a slight delay he found disorienting at first.

"Your touch controls the attack. Hear it? And it takes time to start the column of air vibrating. Hear the 'chuff'?"

The man pulled on some more knobs. "These here are stops. Like the waveform tabs you're familiar with. Sets up what ranks of pipes speak from each keyboard."

Montrose pressed the keys again. He could hear how the pipes in each rank spoke differently. And it got harder to push them down as the man pulled out more stops.

"Use your bodyweight. The organ demands all of you, hands, feet, and heart."

Montrose essayed a brief segment from Markham's favorite composer. The musician looked delighted. "KetzenLach! A lot of his music might have been written for a tracker-action organ like this. Not surprising, if you consider that his teacher was organist here, 400-some years ago."

Enchanted by the almost living response of the vast instrument to his touch, Montrose began to play, launching into the Impractical Etudes: light-hearted technical exercises, joyful and rapid as flame.

The man adjusted the stops; the sound brightened, became more complex. Montrose groped for the pedals, provoking a discord at first, then, bolstered by past experience on a four-limb multisyn, brought them into the music.

Stern columns of deep-toned sound mounted up around him, woven about by shimmers of lucid clarity from the higher registers. But slowly the music changed, shifting to minor keys, and developing melodic lines that cried, and hungered, and wept. Montrose played on, frightened by the sounds that he did not choose — that chose him.

Montrose could not resist that which he had avoided most, KetzenLach's *Memoria Lucis*, once his wife's favorite piece of music. He tried to lift his hands from the keys as pain shot through him, and failed as he fell into the Dreamtime.

Death wept.

Montrose lifted his hand from the keys of the synthesizer

and looked up at the Justicials in their red robes. The Janus wiped his eyes; they glittered in his cadaverous face.

He really did look like Death himself. Montrose shivered at how appropriate it was for the hapless folk of Timberwell 40,000 kilometers below.

To either side of the sallow jurist sat his fellow Justicials, arbiters of the Quarantine now imposed on the planet. To his right, the Judge of the Descent, her white hair tightly curled, her rheumy eyes near-hidden in pouchy eyelids under heavy brows. To her he had applied for permission to descend to the surface of Timberwell, in search of Tenaya and their children, Barin and Seda.

On the left of the Janus sat a short, red-faced man, his eyes bulging in a permanent expression of choler and disdain: the Judge of the Ascent. From him alone came the right to leave Timberwell, enforced by the Quarantine monitors now established in orbit, and the guards here on the Node at the top of the S'lift, and far below, at its base.

And the Janus himself: final arbiter of a planet's fate, sitting here in judgment for a year and a day before the S'lift was finally sealed and all hope lost. The old man looked at each of his fellow Jurists in turn, then lifted up the golden two-faced mask that gave him his title, rotated it about, and settled it down upon his head. Relief shot through him, the aspect that faced him was smiling.

"Go," said the Janus, his voice hollow from within the shining metal hood. "We cannot deny you, whose music touched us so. Timberwell is open to you."

Montrose bowed. As he backed out, the Judge of the Ascent spoke, his voice a chilling hiss. "But be very sure to obey each dictate of the proctors. On this depends your egress from the planet."

Montrose bowed again, and left the judgment chamber to begin his descent to the planetary hell that had been his home.

Much later, he hurried across the terminal at the base of the S'lift. The space rang with shouts and shrieks, and the ululation of countless crying children, as a crowd of citizens pressed against the Marine cordon, frantically seeking space on the last departing modules on the S'lift. The whip-fields crackled and snarled, limning those unfortunates pushed up against them in blue light before hurling them back in convulsions.

As he reached the exit light flared, and dyplast shattered

behind him. A body hurtled through the window high above, turning slowly head over heels before it crashed in red ruin to the terminal floor beyond the cordon, a smoking hole in its chest.

"Telos-damned rebel!" he heard from above as a Marine pushed his head past the edges of the jagged hole in the dyplast. "Slipped something into the computers. . ."

From farther back he heard, faintly, ". . . or worm, can't quite tell. . ."

Montrose turned away. The guard briefly inspected his cachet and waved him through. Other guards directed him to a service tunnel: anyone emerging from the terminal proper was a target for agents of the Vox Populi, the popular terror that had overrun the planet in reaction to the Archon Srivashti's excesses.

Montrose slipped into the smoky daylight of a city on the edge of ruin, heading away from the S'lift. No one challenged him as he worked his way farther into the city, heading for the neighborhood where his cousin Almand was sheltering his wife and children.

The smoke from the dying city, eddying through the artificial canyons of its center, caught at his throat and stung his eyes. The sunlight was the color of a suppurating wound, the hazy light blurring the streets.

His route took him past the Archonic Enclave, where a huge mob shouted, the noise crescendoing to a frenzied scream of anger and satisfaction at regular intervals. Thousands of shabby people gazed up at the Archonic Palace towering far above them; an orgasmic shout bellowed up to meet the body twisting down from a window hundreds of feet above. The victim's screams were lost in the tumult, but not the crunching thud as the body, richly garbed in Douloi attire, slammed into the flagstones of the square with a spray of blood that hung for a moment in the air. Another frantic victim appeared in the window, clutching at the edges. Montrose turned away, sickened, angry that the Archon was safe far above among the Highdwellers he still ruled, albeit under Panarchic supervision.

Finally he reached Almand's house. The gates to the villa hung askew, wrenched off the hinges. He rushed through the opening and tripped over a body burned beyond recognition; the mishap saved his life as a jacbolt sizzled overhead, followed by a woman's scream.

"Montrose!" Tenaya threw himself into his arms, weeping and laughing.

Seda clung to his leg with six-year-old intensity, the other arm clutching her stuffed Wug-dog. Barin pressed up next to his sister, awkward on the edge of manhood, a happy grin twin to Seda's.

"There is little time left," Almand said, gripping a jac in one grimy hand. "They will return soon. You must be well away by then."

"Come with us, then, cousin," replied Montrose. "The Judge of the Ascent will surely. . ."

"No," replied Almand, "this is my home." He nodded towards four fresh mounds of earth in the garden nearby. "I will join them soon." He hefted the jac and grinned, a humorless rictus of a man once civilized. "But first I will burn many torches to light us to the Underworld."

Montrose grasped his shoulders, and then kissed him on the forehead in the ritual of farewell. As the last light of day faded from the sky in a bloody sunset, he and his family slipped away into the night.

The journey back was an exercise in terror. They cowered in the shadows as a mob thundered by, in pursuit of a hapless victim little less miserable than themselves. Only the darkness saved them, the stars withdrawn behind a choking pall of smoke as if loathe to witness the death of the planet below.

The terminal was worse. The lines seemed interminable; even with his priority cachet the wait stretched into hours as they inched towards the doors to the S'lift modules. Fatigued almost beyond endurance, he responded to Tenaya's questions with monosyllables until she fell silent, drawing Barin and Seda closer to her.

Finally he reached the door; beyond a module awaited, its interior lights glowing softly. Numbed by the long wait, Montrose stepped into the module, but when he turned, he discovered that Tenaya and the children hadn't followed him.

A Marine stood in their path, his hand upraised. "This one's full," he said, his voice raspy with fatigue.

"But I have priority," Montrose said, holding up his cachet.

"I don't care if you have the Green-chatzing-Plague," growled the Marine, pushing it aside. "If you hold up this one you're staying here, cachet or no." As Seda started shrieking, the Marine's face softened. "I'll make sure they're first on the next one."

"Go," said Tenaya. "We'll catch up."

"Go on," the Marine said, eyeing the crowd pressing forward. "I give you my word. They'll be on the next."

Four, five, seven people began shouting, insisting on taking Montrose's place if he got off. The Marine keyed the door, which shut on Tenaya's determined face and Seda's tears.

A harried proctor worked her way forward, pushing passengers into their seats until a light glowed on a console. "Your attention please, genz. The S'lift computer system has been compromised." The proctor held up her hands. "There is no danger to the transport system proper."

Montrose could see that she wasn't completely sure of that as she continued, "But all non-essential services, including in-termodule and intercapsule communications, will be suspend-ed for your safety. Do not attempt to access these services."

Montrose remembered the saboteur falling from the computer room. He felt the seating module loading into the S'lift capsule, the slightly queasy sensation as the entire assembly was elevated ninety degrees to fit up against the S'lift proper, the modules gimballing about to keep level. There was a muted thump as the mag-rails engaged, and then acceleration far beyond the norm, as the capsule leapt away from the planet. They were running the system at its limits to get as many people out as possible.

As they cleared the terminal the viewports snapped open, revealing the city below limned in flames. An entire section went dark. He leaned back in his seat and tried to relax, tried to visualize the module with his family in it going through the loading process and leaping up after him to safety.

He couldn't. Montrose leaned over again, hard against the viewport, craning his neck to look down. As he watched, at the limit of his vision far below, under the end of the capsule, the terminal went dark.

He lunged, bruising his nose against the triple dyplast pane, but the city had dwindled into invisibility under a pall of smoke. Tenaya was probably frantic with worry—no, he realized with a surge of honesty, since her hejir, that was not part of her anymore. But Seda, she would be frightened, and Barin, he was trying so hard to be a man. Montrose hoped that meant he'd be a help to his mother, and not a hindrance, uttering empty threats and posturing as teens sometimes did.

The loudspeaker crackled to life. "Passing Shield termination point."

The capsule had cleared the point at which the S'lift would be severed if the planetary defense shield was activated. According to Panarchic law, they were officially off-planet now. There was a hoarse cheer from the some of the other passengers. Montrose tabbed his boswell into location mode.

Had the Marine kept his promise? Yes! Tenaya and the children were in the first module. "Tenaya."

"Montrose." Tenaya's eyes widened, her voice concerned. "What are you doing? Didn't your proctor tell you not to boz?"

There was a squeal of static. Her image tore across and vanished as the loudspeaker came to life. "Vox populi, vox dei," it said in a harsh gargle. Montrose realized in horror he was hearing a computer artifact — or worm. . . can't be sure. The proctor pounded past him to her console at the front of the module.

"You have rejected us, we reject you —" The voice ceased in mid-word.

The proctor whipped around, eyes distended in horror. "You've triggered the worm!"

A brilliant red light flared from a small dome overhead, attended by a deafening siren. "Brace yourselves!" shouted the proctor. "The Shield is activating!"

There was a tremendous thump and the capsule decelerated abruptly. He was strapped in, but banged his head against the seat in front nonetheless. Others were less fortunate: the proctor flew backwards against her console; Montrose heard bones snap as she rebounded and went limp. Amid screams and moans of pain he peered out the viewport, and this time the view was clear.

Below an electronic haze glowed as the Teslas excited the complex space-time resonance of the Shield into being. At its intersection with the S'lift, the monocrystal cable simply ceased to exist as the momentum of the molecules in their bonds was transformed through ninety degrees. Radiants flared; emergency gravitors triggered to carry the severed portion of the cable up into a higher orbit, past the Node.

But Montrose had eyes only for the capsule directly behind his. As its momentum carried it past the severed end of the S'lift, the energies of the Shield seized it and dispersed it in a flaring haze of metal and organic molecules. In a brief display of light, Tenaya and her children joined the aurora glowing ever brighter above Timberwell as their atoms fled into the void.

Montrose wept.

He lifted his hands from the keyboard. The cathedral was silent. The musician was gone; he was alone.

"It didn't happen that way!" he shouted, and the groined ceiling far above returned and multiplied his words.

But grief still tightened his throat and drummed his heart, the grief so sharp the memory of the truth seemed merely a dream. He dug his knuckles into his eye sockets, fighting against desolation. The *uselessness* of the vision clawed at him, and he shook his head, every breath hissing between locked teeth as he fought for control.

"Can you tell me what happened?"

The voice was so soft he almost thought he'd dreamed that, too. But when he dropped his hands he saw Eloatri standing where the little musician had been. The slight emphasis on the verb meant, he sensed, not *are you able*, but *can you bear to?*

"It didn't happen like that at all," he said, then stopped as his voice came out shaking like Barin's had when he couldn't control his adolescent emotions.

The old woman's brows lifted in question. He didn't know if she'd seen the vision or not. Maybe it didn't matter.

He sucked in a deep breath. "I was off-planet, attending a medical conference. The officials had assured us that the troubles were temporary. Then. . . the Vox Populi triggered a small nuclear device within the Archonic Enclave. And—" He pressed his fingers hard against his eyes again, sending stars shooting across his vision. "—Tenaya and the children were visiting the museum in the Enclave. I should have been there." He groaned.

"Why?" Eloatri asked. "They would be just as dead if you had died with them." She made a slight gesture, difficult to interpret. "Or do you mean, you should have died in their place?"

"Either. No," Montrose said. "The last."

"So you would bequeath your grief to your wife." Eloatri smiled whimsically. "You would wish me to be trying to comfort her right now?"

"Your predecessor did once," Montrose said. "Talked to her, anyway."

"Ah," Eloatri said, the wrinkles in her face shifting as she smiled. "She made her hejir?"

"Two months before," Montrose said. The words came unwillingly, but talk was better than the lash of grief.

"She made her hejir alone, then?" Eloatri asked. Montrose studied her, and found no accusation there. Nothing but an interest so open it seemed childlike.

"She wanted me to come. . ." Montrose said. He shrugged. "I might have, but there were the children, and once she was back, I had my professional commitments to meet."

As he spoke, Tenaya's face replaced the old face before him. He recognized the same expression, the smiling patience. He forced words past his teeth, "She had changed. She was different."

Eloatri accepted that with an open-handed gesture.

"But don't think I was running away, or we'd quarreled — nothing like that," he added in a rush. "I had to go to that conference. I'd promised a year before. And she. . ." Tears burned. *"We will be together in spirit."* That was what she'd said. He couldn't speak that absurdity out loud, not with her dead, and gone.

But as he looked around at the clear light slanting in through the Cathedral windows, for a heartbeat he felt her presence beside him, as if she really was with him in spirit. He frowned. It was too easy. "Do you use some kind of tianqi here?" he asked. "Dispersing mind-altering drugs?"

Eloatri lifted her hands, revealing the burn on her palm. "Desrien is what it is," she said. "But we do not manipulate those who come to seek."

"I didn't come, I was forced, and I don't 'seek'," Montrose retorted.

"We all seek," Eloatri corrected, utterly without rancor. "What we find. . ." She lifted a shoulder, and then leaned out to look below. "As for Desrien, sometimes even here some achieve the tangible." She gestured and again he saw her palm. "I believe you will find your patient improves with time."

Montrose looked down at where Ivard was moving away from the altar. From a distance he did not seem different, but Montrose was surprised at the surge of hope he felt. He turned to Eloatri. "You're trying to tell me that Tenaya's faith was real?" He shook his head. "That all her talk of spirits and soul-paths and all that —" He ended, waving a hand.

Eloatri said, "Your regret. That is real."

"True." Montrose laughed, a harsh sound. "It's been riding me like a devil since —"

He looked up, self-mockery providing his access to humor at last. Humor, so steadying, so diverting. He could make a joke and end this right here, but the woman's gaze was still steady, and he knew he would probably never face such undemanding compassion again.

"In the vision," he said, "I was told to obey the proctors, and I didn't do it. I didn't believe them, I *had* to look back at the other module, and make sure my wife was on it. And it blew up."

He struck his hand lightly on the carved wood below the magnificent keyboard. "The officials assured me Timberwell was safe to leave. I never really believed them. I didn't believe Tenaya, either. Yet I blamed. . ."

"Your wife for coming here, and being away for two months? Or for her beliefs, which separated you more surely than the distance had?" she asked gently.

"I didn't blame her for that —"

"And so you blame yourself for believing the officials, and for believing her when she promised you that she and your children would be safe whatever happened." She smiled. "Where would you have been if you had not left your planet? At the museum with them?"

He started to say yes, but then he shook his head. "Probably in another part of the city."

"Ah."

"'We are all carried forward in the hands of Telos, to our ultimate fulfillment. Never doubt that, whatever happens.' That is what she said to me," Montrose said. "I wish — beyond any amount of money — that I could believe that."

Eloatri touched his shoulder lightly. "You want to be assured what is real, and what is dream," she said. "I think you know it already. As for the demon of regret. . ." She smiled. "May I offer you one of our platitudes that also happens to hold true?"

"You can try me. I can't promise to believe it, either." His fingers ran lightly over the keys of the organ, but as yet there was no sound.

"Here there is neither past nor future, only act. . ."

Which was what she had said. He sensed Tenaya's proximity again, and tentatively, even reluctantly, explored the notion that if he felt her close, it was as real as the grief and regret. That's what this woman was trying to tell him. He couldn't claim the one was real and the other not; either both were — or were not.

He looked around, breathing deeply. He could envision — so clearly! — Tenaya doing exactly the same. Holding the image, and permitting the reluctance, the distrust, to recede. And with it the anger of regret. Truth? Not truth? He didn't know, but right at this moment it didn't matter.

The demon of regret might come back to ride his shoulders, but it didn't in this moment. A new idea: when it did come, perhaps he could evoke this other reality.

For the first time in years, he felt a measure of peace.

"Play for her," Eloatri said.

He brought his hands down on the keyboard, launching again into KetzenLach's *Memoria Lucis*, but this time with understanding, and around him the cathedral of New Glastonbury filled with glorious sound.

Osri stayed close by his father, looking about him with increasing uneasiness. He watched the old woman in the cassock talk first to Ivard, and Osri's gut twitched with bleak humor when he recognized the habitual reaction of outrage at the inversion of precedence. Vi'ya, who stalked out. Then Brandon. Then the Rifters. *Freedom of Desrien*, he thought scornfully. The phrase meant no more than anything else here.

Osri was determined to follow the Rifter captain as soon as the audience was over. The Marines had left a telltale in the *Telvarna's* lock that would report their return. "We can go as soon as she's finished with us," he murmured behind his hand, conscious of how the stone overhead made sounds carry.

His father did not reply, and Osri jerked around, irrationally afraid. His father gazed in the direction of the altar, his profile tense. Ivard, face upraised, stumbled a step or two, then crumpled slowly to the ground. "Telos," Osri breathed. "What happened?"

"He was drinking, I believe," Omilov replied in a curiously absent tone. "I only saw him from the back."

"Well, I would say that drinking or eating anything here seems an invitation for drug-poisoning. How else could they inflict their ill-famed nightmares on people?"

Omilov did not answer. Osri suspected that he hadn't even

heard as he watched a pair of dark-robed figures approach Ivard. They seemed in no hurry. Before they reached Ivard, the boy stirred. The Marine who hadn't followed the Aerenarch joined them.

Sebastian let out a sigh of relief as the two figures gently brought Ivard to his feet and walked him slowly around the altar. Ivard's head lolled back, as though he could see the organ music that poured down from the intricately groined ceiling far above.

Then Omilov blinked. "What's that, son?"

"I said," Osri raised his voice slightly, "we'd be wise not to eat or drink anything here."

"We poison people, of course," an amused female voice came from behind them.

Father and son turned, Osri flushing.

"We poison them so that they freeze into statues, which we put out in the gardens. Then we send back in their places clones made from carnivorous fungoids." The small, grandmotherly woman in the many-buttoned cassock smiled, her eyes crinkling in silent laughter. "It was a great story. I saw it on a serial chip when I was a girl."

The gnostor chuckled, and Osri burned with the old rage again, just as he had as a boy when his father had found Brandon's and Galen's meaningless jokes so funny. "Why were we brought here?"

His voice sounded a little louder and ruder than he'd meant it to, but the woman merely raised her shoulders. "I don't know. It is for you to tell me."

Osri gave a sigh of annoyance.

His father spoke quickly, deflecting attention. "I'm worried about young Ivard. If we don't get him to proper medical attention on Ares soon. . ."

The woman smiled. "We are not ignorant of the healing arts, here on Desrien. I don't think that this diversion in your path will have harmed him any."

Osri's ironic reaction must have showed in his face, for the woman looked up at him in inquiry.

"We started out for Ares weeks ago," he said. "Every nightmare since has been a diversion not of our choosing. This is just another."

The woman smiled, but she looked past him at his father, who shook his head. "If something about this place does that boy any good, then I will consider this diversion well worth the time it took."

It was a diplomatic reply, in a peacemaking tone. The woman nodded to them and passed on toward the stairway to the organ loft.

The gnostor sighed again, studying the nearest of the huge wall murals. "Some of the Panarchy's finest artists are represented here. We shouldn't miss this opportunity to examine their work."

Osri assented, trying to get control of his anger. He recognized this as another manifestation of the obligation towards the Aerenarch that his father felt imposed on him by his Chival's oath: he would not leave until Brandon did. So even though Osri had little interest in artwork of any kind, much less religious, he followed along with his father and obediently looked at the paintings, mosaics, and statues along one wall.

And indeed, some of them began to absorb his attention. If nothing else, one had to admire the way the painters could use a few splotches of color to paint figures that seemed to live and breathe, and to move in three dimensions. He could appreciate with his aesthetic sense the way light and dark were used to infuse the figures with power and majesty.

His father lingered, looking intently at a painting of a dark forest, with a man in archaic costume confronted by some sort of beast. He bent down, reading the inscription on a small plaque below the canvas, but Osri couldn't catch the words.

"What's that, Father?" Osri asked.

His father shook his head again, as if something pained him, but made no reply.

Osri walked on purposefully, determined to get something out of this imposed diversion, but some of the art defeated him. He glanced back to make an observation, to discover that his father had vanished.

Osri turned in a circle in his effort to locate him. Then he peered more intently into the alcoves along the wall. No one else was visible, not even the Marine guards.

Unsettled, he began to retrace his steps until a flicker at the periphery of his vision caused him to jerk around, wariness tightening his shoulders. The twinkling of stars in a broad field make him blink with vertigo. The painting he stood before looked real, like a window on space.

But he laughed at himself, forcing the image to remain a painting, a panorama of a galaxy. With reality re-established, he bent to examine it more closely. In the foreground, tiny against the swirl of stars, the painter had placed a small asteroidal habitat, a bubbloid, like Granny Chang's. Lights glowed from viewports scattered over its craggy surface. Near it hung a decrepit ship painted in garish colors.

Rifters again, he thought in disgust. Then he bent lower. Below, a small brass plate gleamed at the bottom of the picture's frame: *The stone rejected by the builders has become the chief cornerstone.*

He snorted, only to find he couldn't pull his gaze away, and the Dreamtime took him.

Osri discovered he was standing before a vast painting, a panorama of a galaxy. Under his heels, firm stone, and around him the massive cathedral of New Glastonbury.

He blinked dry, itchy eyes, then rubbed them, trying to banish the terrible images crawling through his mind. Vertigo made him tremble as he backed away.

The painting was only a painting again, but Osri could feel it between his shoulder blades as he slowly made his way back towards where he thought he'd left his father.

Roget turned as the two medics led Ivard away, and spotted Jaim approaching.

Jaim stopped a few paces from her, respecting her space, and so she answered him mildly when he enquired after Ivard.

Then alarm burned through her: the cathedral was empty, no sign of the Rifters, or the High Phanist, or —

Roget relaxed as she caught side of the gnostor and his son in a gallery along the south wall. Then she spotted Vahn in the north transept. The conversation with the medics and Jaim must have taken longer than she thought. She checked her boswell; still green, but time had definitely slipped past. The light was fading from the windows all about, the great rose window darkening.

She walked toward the Omilovs as Osri touched his father's arm, and peered into the gnostor's haggard face. She triggered her enhancers.

"What have they done to you?" Osri asked.

The gnostor closed his eyes, then raised his hands to shade them. "It is what I have done," he murmured, his voice hoarse with barely controlled emotion. Then he dropped his hand, his face working into a semblance of a smile. "Or what I did not do." A tear jumped down the furrows of his face and splashed onto his tunic.

"I had a kind of dream," Osri said. "I knew it was a dream, but I could not break it until it was done with me."

"Tell me."

But Osri stopped as Lokri walked past, intent on the distant door through which they'd entered. Roget followed. The two Omilovs were harmless; the handsome, charming parricide was not. She'd make sure he was headed for the ship.

"I thought the main thing that marked Rifters from our culture was their insistence on living outside of our laws. . ." Roget lost the rest of Osri's reply as she followed Lokri.

Before he reached the doors, Roget's boswell burred in her inner ear. (ROGET! I'VE LOST THE AERENARCH!) Roget whirled around and ran toward the north transept.

"I thought the main thing that marked Rifters from our own culture was their insistence on living outside our laws," Osri had been saying. "Their insistence, if you will, that virtues of loyalty and service are meaningless."

Omilov rubbed his thumbs along his upper eye sockets. "You ought to know by now," he said finally, "that speaking for all of them is a dangerous thing. But one generality I will allow: I think some of them are as capable of loyalty as anyone else, should they perceive something worthy of their loyalty."

Images from the dream whispered in Osri's mind. *They need leadership.* Osri fingered the ribbon and coin in his pocket. *They have resources.* Then he started, his heart hammering, as the second Marine charged by, her weapon drawn. As she vanished into a kind of gallery on the other side of the cathedral, Lokri passed by more slowly from the other direction. The man's light gray eyes cast restlessly around, taking Osri and his father in only as details.

Omilov murmured, "Whom do you seek?"

"No one. I'm leaving."

Osri stared at Lokri. "Are we locked in here?"

Lokri murmured with an air of puzzlement, "Not that I know of. Vi'ya left, and nothing stopped her."

A tremulous echo of vertigo rippled through Osri.

His father pointed past Lokri's shoulder; when the Rifter turned to look, he gave a hiss of surprise, then walked off. Omilov gazed after. He still had not wiped away the tear tracks from his haggard face.

Then he turned to Osri. "Lend me your arm, my boy," he said tiredly. "Let us see if we can find our way out. I am afraid I am badly in need of rest."

SEVEN

Metellus Hayashi took a deep breath, savoring the air of excitement and satisfaction that pervaded the bridge of the *Falcomare*.

Only four additional ships had made it to the Arthelion mustering point, all frigates, while increased surface-to-ship activity suggested that the *Fist of Dol'jhar* was preparing to leave Arthelion.

On the viewscreen the *Lady of Taligar* hung unmoving, its angular form barely discernible against the stars — one of which, slightly brighter than the rest, was Arthelion's primary. The other ships of *Hainu* squadron, the *Barahyrn* and the three frigates now attached, were not visible.

This was the kind of action every destroyer captain dreamed of, the violent, high-speed slash-and-parry that only these vessels could deliver. Not for him the ponderous, near invulnerability of a battlecruiser, bludgeoning its opponent into scrap with the ripping terror of a ruptor beam, against which the teslas offered no protection.

The thought sobered him. That was what they would face in minutes. For the first time in twenty years, the Thousand Suns would see an engagement pitting destroyers against the kind of ship they'd been designed to kill. Only without their best weapon. They couldn't use their skipmissiles on the *Fist of Dol'jhar*, not if it hugged the planet.

"D'you think we're up against Juvaszt?" asked Orriega, his

first officer.

"Who knows?" Hayashi shrugged. "With their fondness for purges we might get lucky. I just hope whoever it is doesn't figure out what we're really up to until it's too late."

"Not likely," Orriega drawled, adding a wiredream version of a villain's gloating laugh. "He'll be too busy tracking down and vaporizing drones full of vatbeef."

Hayashi chuckled. It was an old trick, loading drones masquerading as lances with slabs of vatbeef, to simulate the right mix of organic and metallic debris when they were blown apart by the defenders. And the best kind of trick: you always had to assume they were real even if you figured it out.

"Just an old-fashioned Dol'jharian cookout," Orriega said, rubbing her hands.

But they only had enough meat for the first three waves of drones, one from each destroyer in turn. *Falcomare* and *Lady* would deliver the first blow against the *Fist*, while on the other side of the planet, the three frigates would simultaneously take on the Rifter destroyer *Satansclaw*. Best case, they'd destroy or cripple it, but Hayashi was worried: VSA observation and close-up stealth surveillance runs had revealed that the Rifter destroyer was now running a new tactical set. SigInt and Moral Sabotage agreed it was unlikely Tallis Y'Marmor was still in command. That would have made things easy.

Well, he'd settle for simply driving *Satansclaw* off station. Whatever cleared the way for the first wave of drones, launched by *Barahyrn*.

Orriega glanced at her console. "Fifteen seconds."

"Well," said Hayashi, raising his voice for the benefit of the entire bridge, "let's show them what's wrong with battleblimps. Engines to tac-level five, arm missiles, lock down for full-ruptor drill."

The hatches to the bridge engaged their locking bolts, echoing through the ship in muted clanks as the *Falcomare* segmented itself into self-sufficient domains in preparation for ruptor attack. Hayashi's stomach knotted — if anything qualified as a terror weapon, the ruptor was it — but he let nothing of his disquiet reach his voice as the countdown reached zero.

"Engage."

The fiveskip burred harshly, making his teeth ache, but Hayashi was conscious only of the breathless excitement preceding action.

"Emergence minus twelve, eleven, ten. . ." He could hear the same excitement in Orriega's voice, and sense it in his primary crew at their consoles. In moments they would emerge over Arthelion at nearly one-quarter light-speed, hurling shaped-charge missiles at their vast enemy, while in the middle system, the real battle would be fought. . .

He recalled Margot's face, their last night together; a brief stab of regret, and then the fiveskip disengaged, and there was no time for anything but the fierce concentration on the here and now that is the experience of battle.

SATANSCLAW

The attack took Anderic by surprise, but not the logos. Battle stations threw him out of muzzy semi-sleep into near-panic alertness. Words burned against the air in his darkened cabin.

MISSILE ATTACK BY TWO FRIGATES. SUSPECT THIRD. TACTICAL SKIP EXECUTED. STANDING BY.

The panic ebbed, just a bit. The logos had obeyed him. For now. It was the only thing that could save *Satansclaw*, Anderic thought as he plunged a stim into his arm and stumbled out the hatch.

Although his cabin was only steps away from the bridge, the stim had boosted him into clarity touched with a euphoria that washed away much of his concern about the logos by the time he jumped into his pod.

Under its direction, he tried to take the ship back towards Arthelion. The logos wasn't worried about the destroyer they detected just as it skipped out. It had dispatched a swarm of smaller vessels that were executing a spectacular burn towards the surface. A second frigate attack washed speculation from his mind.

"Hit him!" shouted Ninn. "Frigate One!" Brightness flickered on the flank of the Panarchist ship. A skip pulse swelled in its place.

Anderic began to understand Tallis's exultation during and after the battle at Charvann. He could see the same respect dawning on their faces, submerging the resentment.

Except for Kira Lennart.

But he had no time to think about that as the action continued, especially since Lennart passed Juvaszt's orders onto him only moments later. They were terse, but behind them, Anderic sensed the Dol'jharian captain's anger. But failing Juvaszt was better than disappointing Barrodagh, whose last demonstration of the mindripper had effectively silenced rumors that it had been destroyed in the Arkad's raid on Arthelion.

As the attacks continued, chivvying *Satansclaw* farther from the planet despite the logos's best efforts, Anderic wondered if Juvaszt had really taken the logos into account in his strategic planning. He was sure that cold mind didn't take the mindripper into account.

FIST OF DOL'JHAR

The shuttle slid through the lock field into the *Fist of Dol'jhar*, throwing off rainbow rings of light, and settled to the deck, seemingly cushioned by the spray of static discharges from its hull. Outside, another shuttle slowly approached, silhouetted against the limb of Arthelion vast beyond.

Guardsman Tanak grounded his weapon briefly, presented arms, and snapped to attention with the others of his squad as the shuttle hatch slid open, revealing the form of Anaris rahal'Jerrodi, the conditional heir. Tanak shivered and would have straightened up even more, had there been any slack in his posture. This was the one spoken of in whispers, favored of the ancestors — Arzoat, second in the squad, had seen that with her own eyes. Even the shades of the Panarchists, down below in the haunted precincts of the Mandala, obeyed him, they said.

Anaris stepped to the deck to receive Kyvernat Juvaszt's salute. Taller and stronger-seeming even than his Tarkan honor guard, he paused as his black eyes swept across all in the hangar bay. Those eyes were set in a strong face whose nose and mouth recalled his father the Avatar. Shadowing him, a short, astonishingly ugly Bori Catennach scuttled out of the shuttle, glancing nervously around.

Juvaszt took them aside, joining a small group of officers as a group in plain prison garb began to disembark. Tanak watched with avid curiosity. These were the enemy, who'd humbled the Children of Dol twenty years ago. He wondered which one was the Panarch, and then a short, slender man emerged, and all doubt fled. Not just the way the others deferred to him, not even the sudden alertness shown in the postures of the conditional heir and those around him, but the man's own carriage. Despite the way ship gravity dragged at him, there was no sign of defeat. He stepped down onto the deck, holding himself in spite of the 1.2 gravs as though he owned the ship and the loyalty of everyone within. The only sign of strain was in how carefully he moved.

As their guards led the Panarchists past, impatient with their slow pace, Anaris raised his hand. The guards halted, and the Panarch looked up with an air of inquiry into the face of the conditional heir. Tanak strained to hear, not daring to move or even change the angle of his head. Only long years of discipline prevented him from jumping when a whooping siren pulled all heads around.

"Emergence pulses, two, closing at point-two-two cee, missiles detected!" The voice boomed even louder than the siren.

Juvaszt grabbed his communicator and began shouting orders. He ran for the inner hatch to the transtube that would take him to the bridge, followed closely by Anaris and the Bori. The guards from the shuttle began herding the Panarchists, but the prisoners were slow and clumsy. So the Tarkans picked them up and ran through another hatch. Despite the indignity, Tanak saw a smile flicker on the Panarch's face, reflected in the other prisoners by exchanged glances.

The immense doors of the bay slid shut with startling speed. Outside, the curve of Arthelion blurred as the ship's defensive fields energized, seizing the hapless shuttle still outside in a merciless grip and shredding it into a haze of debris under the lash of the teslas' momentum transformation. Beyond, as Druashar, their squad leader, double-timed them to another hatch, Tanak spotted a spark of light swelling rapidly. Then the shuttle blew up with a blinding flash just before the bay lock slammed shut.

Tanak was the last Tarkan through the hatch. As Druashar tabbed the go-key, long habit turned Tanak with the others to face the door.

Afterward, his memory sorted the events into order, but at the time, it all seemed simultaneous. The doors began to slide shut as a frantic technician ran toward them, shouting, but his voice was drowned by a shattering compound roar. The massive lock door bulged, then burst into a flare of white light. The technician vanished in the burst of ardent heat that struck at them through the narrow slit as the transtube doors slammed shut. Tanak's skin prickled sharply, like a sunburn, as the concussion hammered them to the deck plates. After an agonizing delay, the module jerked into motion, accelerating them away from the wreckage of the hangar bay, now dissolved into a plasma hotter than the sun.

The roar of the sequenced missile strikes on his ship drowned the tinny shout of Juvaszt's communicator as his transtube accelerated toward the bridge three kilometers away. In his mind's eye he could see vividly the multiple strikes at the same spot, each detonation cumulatively weakening the shields until only bare metal stood in the way of a million-degree plasma moving at a quarter-cee.

Another concussion wave caught up with them. The module shuddered and squealed as it hit the sides of the transtube, throwing them to the deck, then reaccelerated. Juvaszt climbed to his feet and spat out a tooth. He shook his communicator experimentally, but the impact with his mouth had crushed it. He looked around, but the junior officers with him had comms that couldn't access his command channel—a standard precaution against mutiny.

Then Anaris's secretary stumbled toward him and pressed a communicator into his hand. Juvaszt noticed three more communicators dangling from the Catennach's belt as he snarled at the man reflexively, irritated by the useless gesture. But then he recognized the voice of his second squawking from it.

". . . Juvaszt! Are you able to respond?"

It was tuned to the command channel! He turned a speculative glance from the Bori to Anaris, surprising an expression of irony of a sort he'd never seen from the Avatar.

"Juvaszt here. Report." His tongue probed at the hole in his gum.

"Two destroyers in fractional-cee attack, sir," so-Kyvernat Chodalin responded. "No ID. Tactical skip executed, ruptors on-line, skipmissile charging. . ."

"Cancel that, you. . ." Juvaszt bit down on the next word before it emerged, chagrined at his loss of control. "Cancel that. Neither we nor the Panarchists can afford to use skipmissiles. Arthelion is unshielded. The Avatar is in the Mandala. Damage?"

"Aft second bay not reporting, minor damage to forward ruptor one."

Then the damage wasn't severe, except for the bay. "And the prisoners?"

"Safe, on their way to the brig."

Now, as the surprise of the attack dissipated, Juvaszt began to speculate. What were the Panarchists up to? Without skipmissiles they could do no more than sting the *Fist of Dol'jhar*, although, he admitted ruefully, their first sting had been a telling one.

The module began to decelerate. Juvaszt discovered Anaris regarding him coolly. The conditional heir appeared completely in control, in contrast to his secretary, whose fear-paled brow was oozing oily sweat.

The module halted; the doors jerked open. Juvaszt smelled the tang of heat as he caught a glimpse of seared metal on the outside of the module—a fraction of a second longer and they would have been vaporized. He ran down the short corridor onto the bridge, followed by Anaris and the others.

His second jumped out of the command pod and saluted as he approached. "Kyvernat Juvaszt, *Satansclaw* reports an attack by two frigates that has driven them away from their assigned position, enabling a Panarchist destroyer to discharge a wave of small vessels that they could not stop. These are now burning down into the atmosphere." He looked grim. "Their signatures match that of Panarchist Marine lances; their courses appear to intersect the Mandala."

"Weapons!" Juvaszt shouted as he threw himself into his pod. "Ready missiles for atmospheric entry, ship-to-ship. Target lances and fire upon emergence." He wiped his lips and swallowed; his mouth ached and his speech was becoming less intelligible. A glance at a secondary screen revealed that *Satansclaw* had instantly skipped away from the planet when the attack commenced. He'd deal with Anderic later.

Juvaszt looked up at the plot screen that echoed Chodalin's report graphically. A targeting diamond appeared in response to his input. "Navigation, take us in, two skips, maximum safe angle." They would have to skip out and then back in to go around the planet in the least time, and the larger the angle formed by the two legs of their route, the closer they would be to radius each time. But the Avatar was in the Mandala.

Juvaszt had a sudden, vivid image of the deadly, needle-shaped lances closing in on the palace, disgorging their cargo of battle-armored Marines. He had no illusions about their efficacy: trained in a tradition of small-squad, independent action, they would slice through the rigidly hierarchical

Tarkans like monothread through flesh.

"Nonsense," Anaris snapped as the fiveskip burped in the first skip. Juvaszt turned, startled, as his mind threw up a brief image of the spectral hands of Urtigen hovering over the conditional heir's head at the ghost-laying ceremony; but Anaris was looking at the viewscreen. Favored of the ancestors, yes, but surely not Chorei. He could not possibly hear others' thoughts.

Anaris glanced down at him, still with that expression of irony. "The Panarchists wouldn't waste their time attacking the Mandala. It makes neither tactical nor strategic sense. It must be a ruse."

The fiveskip burped again.

"They are striking at the Avatar, who has usurped their ruler and claimed his palace," said Juvaszt, turning back to the viewscreen. Now he was irritated. This was his ship. He was responsible to the Avatar, not to the heir. No, *conditional* heir.

On the viewscreen the green spears of laser-boosted missiles leapt away; coins of light blossomed above the night side of Arthelion as they found their targets.

"Sensors, scan those explosions."

"They don't think that way," said Anaris.

"Spectrum indicates organic debris consonant with human remains," reported the sensors officer after a moment.

Anaris said nothing more, and Juvaszt decided not to follow up on his advantage. The sensor report said it well enough.

"Communications, get me *Satansclaw*, *Kali* and *Mojyndaro*. Then contact the Mandala and request an audience of the Avatar." Better that he call down—even though he couldn't really spare the time—than have the Avatar call him demanding an explanation.

In the meantime, the *Fist* could handle destroyers forbidden their best weapon, and with two frigates supporting it even a Rifter destroyer, especially one equipped with a logos, should be able to fight its way back to orbit to deal with further lance attacks. He'd like more, but he needed the rest of his Rifters to locate the Panarchist forces. At least he knew they had to be clumped within a few light-seconds to start with, with their lightspeed-limited communications. That would make it easier.

He ordered the three Rifter ships to take up position antipodal to *Fist of Dol'jhar*, noting that *Satansclaw* claimed damage to one of the attackers. Perhaps Barrodagh had been right, then, about the logos. Even a stopped heart holds blood.

Juvaszt tabbed his console, summoning a medic to give him something to cut down on the flow of saliva and blood from the empty tooth socket so he could speak clearly. He motioned his tactical officer over as he resumed giving orders, with a priority on identifying his attackers so he knew whom he was fighting. He had no doubt he had very little time before the next attack.

Watching from the side, Anaris felt the old familiar rage mount up behind his eyes, but he rigidly controlled himself, letting nothing of it show. The report from the sensors had been a blow, shaking his certainty that the lances were a feint. Would the Panarchists throw away lives like that? Then he remembered the looks on the faces of the men and women around the Panarch in the hangar bay during the missile attack, and the Arkadic Marines he'd known while a hostage. That was the wrong question. Would they spend lives like that?

The fear of defeat seized him in spite of his stance on the bridge of a ship armed with the unstoppable power of the Sun-eater. The Panarchists would pay whatever price was asked of them, if they thought the prize worth it. So what was the prize? One thing he was sure of: it was not the Mandala. The fact that the other Dol'jharians around him saw the Mandala as the logical goal of the Navy's attack merely confirmed the deception.

He listened to Juvaszt snapping out orders, and though the consonants of his speech were mushy from the missing tooth, Anaris was impressed with the man's command of himself and the situation; but all the while his mind worried at the question of their enemy's real purpose. They couldn't be trying a desperate — and stupid — rescue of the Panarch?

Then so-Erechnat Terresk'jhi turned around from the communications console, a mixture of fear and awe on her face that revealed what her next words would be. "Kyvernat Juvaszt, the Avatar will speak to you," she said.

Juvaszt motioned her to open the channel, and a window swelled on the main viewscreen, revealing Eusabian's face and shoulders. The image was slightly rough; Anaris could see Terresk'jhi tapping at her console, but it didn't help. He guessed that the useless chatter and images loading down the hyperwave from their Rifter allies were stressing the discrimination and decoding circuits.

Anaris did not recognize the room Eusabian was in, but

from the furnishings guessed it was one of the Panarch's private chambers in the Palace Minor. He noted the smile of excitement, almost satisfaction, in his father's face; a glance at Morrighon made it clear that the Bori saw it as well.

"Kyvernat Juvaszt. Your report."

As Juvaszt gave Eusabian a précis of the attack and his assessment of its goals, Anaris saw in Eusabian's reactions the same culture-blind assumptions as in Juvaszt. His father had studied the Panarchists for twenty years, but he still regarded them as weak versions of Dol'jharians. There must be some way to use this blindness, but how?

Then, in full view of the bridge, the Avatar handed Anaris the lever he needed. "Bring the Panarch to the bridge and show him to the attackers. Hold the sword of their oath against their own throats."

That was a lethal mistake; Anaris kept his expression strictly controlled. Twenty years, and the Avatar still did not comprehend that the Panarchists lived and died by symbolism; it was the foundation of their culture and their lives. Did he really think they swore their oath to merely a living man?

The Avatar turned his way. "Anaris ji-rahal," he said, using again the conditional form, "I lay my paliach in your hands for now. Return my enemy to me, or kill him."

Anaris bowed deeply. "As my father commands, so it is done." He heard an intake of breath from Juvaszt as he straightened up. He had claimed the kinship without the conditional form, a response both respectful and defiant.

On the screen Eusabian regarded him with that uncharacteristic quirk of humor, then the image vanished.

"*Satansclaw*, *Kali*, and *Mojendaro* reporting in position and engaged with three enemy frigates," said Communications.

Anaris stepped toward Juvaszt. "Kyvernat, you must obey my father, but I tell you now, it will not work."

Juvaszt's dark eyes were steady and considering. "You are right," he said at length. "I must obey the Avatar." The faintest of stresses on the title was the only indication of his disbelief.

Anaris stepped back. That was enough for now.

FLAMMARION

Stygrid ban-Armenhaut sat stiffly in his command pod on the bridge of the *Flammarion*, glowering at the viewscreen.

"Ready for the skip to first coordinates, Captain," came the voice of Bar-Himelion at the navigation console. "Ten light-minutes out for long-ranging."

Armenhaut blinked. "Engage."

The fiveskip hummed then ceased. The screen cleared, and Siglnt reported acquisition of their target.

"Signature ID'd. *Ghostmaker*, frigate."

Armenhaut's tactical officer began tapping at his console, analyzing the movements of their quarry, and looking for a pattern that would enable them to emerge with enough precision to put a narrow beam through its engines, rather than relying on the broader, deadlier stroke of the *Flammarion's* ruptors. Acidly, Armenaut noted again how little Lieutenant Commander Rajaonarive hesitated over the new Tenno.

Armenhaut bit his thumb moodily. Ng's assumption of the rank of commodore, fully within the Standing Orders as it was, still rankled; being under her command was even worse because it gave form to the worry that with Aerenarch Semion dead, his career might truly have reached its zenith.

The silent activity on the bridge stretched out to minutes. Armenhaut had no doubt that the bridge of the *Grozniy* was full of chatter. What could you expect of a jumped-up Polloi? She cultivated that image of hers, of promotion through pure merit, but he'd like to see where she'd be without the Nesselryns behind her. He still remembered his encounter with the long arm of her patron family, just after their graduation from the Academy.

Politics is the continuation of war by other means. That had been a favorite epigraph of Aerenarch Semion. Merit could take you only so far, Ng would find someday. Did she think she could have refused the order to investigate reports of Adamantine activity at Xiao Hua III, had *she* been stationed at Arthelion?

Armenhaut shifted in his pod, grateful when Lieutenant Commander Rajaonarive's voice interrupted his thoughts. "We've got a pattern, sir," said the tactical officer. He snorted. "He's using the Omega tactical algorithms, with the destroyer optimization sets. Telos knows what good he thinks that'll do in a frigate."

Commander Matir leaned toward Armenhaut. "Some noderunner got lazy."

Armenhaut grunted. He really didn't care about some nameless Rifter computer tech right now.

Matir turned back to his console and tapped at it. "Attack profile is now entered, sir. Tac-level four, narrow-beam lazplaz attack, engines only, then drunkwalk skips while we wait for a response."

"Very well, Commander. Navigation, take us in to point-five light-seconds. Engage."

The fiveskip snarled. Then the screens cleared, a narrow thread of light lanced out toward their target. One second later a rosette of light bloomed where the frigate had been, churning as it faded away.

"Chatz," snapped Armenhaut, jumping to his feet. "Weapons, I wanted a Rifter frigate, not a logos-loving ball of plasma."

"I can't be held responsible for shoddy maintenance on a Rifter frigate, sir. I put the lazplaz right on target."

The answer should have been a simple *Yes sir*. It would have been, had 'Weapons' been anyone but Gertrud ban-Freyhart, cousin to one Archon, niece of another, and granddaughter of the primary Cartano line.

Armenhaut stood a moment longer, glaring at ban-Freyhart, who gazed back with the eyebrow-lift of moral superiority. He wanted so badly to throw her off the bridge that he could taste the words, but he didn't dare for the same reason she was here in the first place. The same reason she was a Lieutenant Commander, promoted (he'd found out too late) from place to place as her long line of former captains got rid of her. Her fitrep full of empty phrases that might as well have been summarized in two words: *powerful relatives*.

He turned to Commander Matir, and forced his voice to the cool Douloi cadence of control. "One of the hazards of dealing with Rifters. Since we can hit any Rifter vessel several times before they can react, we'll dial down the power."

Matir stared at the viewscreen, his face wooden, and Armenhaut hated the necessity to finesse ban-Freyhart's failure. He could just hear her talking to her relatives, "We were there to fight Rifters, weren't we? Captain Armenhaut made his opinion of Captain Ng clear, and so I thought, an officer shows initiative. . ."

"*Flammarion* is going to take this hypothetical communications device. *Flammarion* is going to show the fleet how it's to be done, as we always do. After which we will have some target practice." He paused, and when the bridge responded with *AyKay, captain!*, he said, "Communications, signal the squadron. Target volume two. Navigation, take us to the next position. Engage."

GROZNIY

"Target pattern confirmed," Rom-Sanchez sang out, proud of the steadiness of his voice. "We've got them." He turned to the captain.

The tactical plot showed a god's-eye view of the middle system, with the *Grozniy*, its attendant ships, and their target, the Rifter destroyer *Finality Jones*, in the ecliptic just sunward of the asteroid belt.

"They haven't changed their tactical algorithm since the last update to the signature banks," he continued. "They're still using the Salim set. . . at leg five now." On the viewscreen the Tenno shifted, echoing the new information with the added dimensionality of Warrigal's L-5 mods. He knew she was down in the plot room, fine-tuning the Tenno response as they fought, with the help of Commander Hurli and her team.

"Weapons, prepare for narrow-beam lazplaz attack," Ng said. "Target the engines and accelerator only. Fire on emergence. Navigation, take us in to point-five light-seconds." She paused, then said, "Engage."

The fiveskip snarled; it was set to a high tac level for precise control and high real velocity.

"Retargeting," said Lt. Herrick at the weapons console, as the fiveskip fell silent. "Firing."

Rom-Sanchez found Herrick's balding head and his grizzled profile oddly reassuring, but then his life had been full of opposites since Treymontaigne. The presence of an older office recalled to the bridge after being promoted away somehow underscored the captain's confidence in the younger officers. Among whom Rom-Sanchez counted himself.

On the viewscreen a glowing thread marking the complex beam of coherent light and near lightspeed plasma lanced out, intersecting a twinkle distinguished from the stars around it only by the targeting cross imposed upon it by the computer. It vanished, then lanced out again, then finally ceased altogether.

The Tenno flickered again, poised in ambiguity.

Rom-Sanchez watched, aware of his heartbeat thumping in his temples, yet grateful that Captain Ng had confirmed him as alpha crew for this engagement. He'd been afraid that all the time he had to spend training other officers would let Nilotis catch up with him; fellow Loonies had feared the same for their positions.

He glanced at Wychyrski and Ammant, who was now resigned to his new nickname, Vomit Comet. "*Better than Prettyboy,*" he'd said when the Loonies met up for a private celebration of their promotions. And Nilotis, who had been an enormous help, hadn't suffered by Rom-Sanchez's promotion. He was now alpha tactical on *Babur Khan.*

Rom-Sanchez thought back to his debriefing after Treymontaigne, once the most pressing of the repairs had been made. He'd planned all kinds of stirring, heroic responses, but then he'd sat across from the captain, and had her steady gaze on his face as she asked, "So how did you feel about combat?"

The stirring words had dried up, and he said, "I hated it. But I wouldn't want to be anywhere else."

Her chin had lifted in that expression he'd come to know as approval. He saw that same expression now as she surveyed the bridge crew.

DESRIEN

"You have the freedom of Desrien. Make what use of it you will."

Marim snorted a laugh as she bustled away. She felt a whole lot lighter—she'd definitely make use of the place. After all, if a person didn't look out for herself, who would?

The cathedral was a typical dirt-bound construct, with a heavy symmetry that dragged at her bones. All up and down. Marim considered the groined stonework far overhead. That was kind of hoorah, sort of like old Benewal's palace at the spin axis back home. Everybody said he'd had treasure. All nullers did. Maybe they had treasures here. Probably up high.

She looked around for a staircase. Somehow she was pretty sure they didn't have lifts here, and surely not lev-tubes. She checked a couple times to make sure the old woman hadn't followed her, like the busybiddies in Scerren, where she'd grown up. She didn't need a lecture about religious stuff from some old bore.

She found a foursquare staircase with a central well that dwindled above her into distance. Here!

Marim bounded up the first layer of steps, but that soon became plodding. Seriously out of breath, she cursed the lack of tech, and her aching thighs.

She finally reached a huge room with a confusion of bronze bells clustered overhead, ropes depending from them through the floor. There was a single large cupboard—no lock on it—that she swiftly opened. Nothing. Just rags and cans, and a neat rank of odd tools.

No treasure there. A groined arch framed a vista of soft distance which Marim merely glanced at. Looking out a different way, she saw other towers, but she'd have to go all the way back down and back up to check them out.

She was tired. She climbed out the opening and stretched out on a wide ledge that seemed to run all around the top of the tower. It was warm in the sunlight. She yawned and stretched herself full length. Just for a moment, until her legs stop hurting. She shut her eyes, and the Dreamtime took her.

She fell and fell, the useless broken wings flapping around her for kilometer after kilometer until the inner hull rushed up to smash her—

Marim's entire body wrenched, shocking her awake. She sucked in air, and discovered she lay on a ledge hundreds of feet up, but not in the safe, sane low-gee part of a habitat. She was stuck in a full planetary gee field. She could have rolled off!

She wiped her eyes, sobbing for breath as she scrambled back into the tower. This place was trying to kill her!

It was late, the horizon gobbling the sun. She wanted to find the others. She wanted to tell Ivard about the dream because he would get scared, too, and when you share fear, that somehow makes it less. She wanted to get Lokri to joke her out of the fear. She wanted to hear Vi'ya condemn dreams as foolishness, like ghosts and demons. She wanted to be with them.

Her thighs hurt even more on the way down, which seemed endless. She didn't even care about treasure anymore, just getting away. Even a Navy brig was better than this.

Ng's eyes flicked back to the viewscreen as it flickered to a close-in view of *Finality Jones*. Plasma sparkled from a rent in the destroyer's aft section. Its radiants flared, then guttered out. There was a blast of plasma from midway along the ship's missile tube. It bent, its complex struts crumpling as the stricken ship began to yaw.

"That's got it." Ng drummed her armrest. "Resume assigned drunkwalk."

The fiveskip burped again as the navigator re-engaged the evasive program known to other ships in the fleet to make it easier to find each other, which would increase their chance of avoiding surprise attack by ships responding to the distress call of their victim. If it had a hyperwave. The program was harder on the engines than the standard drunkwalks devised before the hyperwave had overturned so much Naval experience.

They waited, time crawling as each time they emerged and relocated *Finality Jones*. Finally, as the commander stirred impatiently in his pod, Ng shook her head.

"That's it, then. No hyperwave on this one." She paused, distaste souring her throat at the necessary next order. The heat of battle was the proper setting for death—not deliberate executions. "Weapons, shoot ruptor, one turret, full power."

The *Finality Jones* disintegrated into a blast of light and glowing threads of light that dissipated rapidly.

"Communications, signal the squadron. Target volume two. Dispatch this engagement record for tacponder distribution, full-sphere burst."

The communications console twittered. "Record dispatched, Captain."

"Navigation, take us to the next battle coordinates."

As the fiveskip engaged, Ng wondered what kind of luck Armenhaut and KepSingh were having. She wasn't worried about the older officer. KepSingh had jumped at the offer of Mdeino Nilotis as tactical officer for the battle, and had drilled himself and his crew mercilessly while they waited at the rendezvous. "I just wish I was young enough for Augment," he'd said.

But Armenhaut. The new Tenno had defeated him, she was sure—he'd attended only the first briefing—and his wounded pride had moved him to refuse her offer of Sublieutenant Hjivarno for tactical support onboard *Flammarion*. She could have ordered him to accept the transfer, but there'd be no cooperation and thus no tactical advantage. She refused to put one of her officers—not to mention one of her Loonies—in that situation.

"Courier from *Shahmat*. Possible contact, destroyer."

Ng redirected the squadron—or rather, issued the orders that would redirect each ship when the orders reached it via courier, beam, or transponder.

She wasn't surprised by how quickly the frigate had reported. The Navy had centuries of stored tactical sets to render operations outside light cones easier. With three squadrons, each composed of a battlecruiser, three frigates, and assorted corvettes, the odds had been they would encounter what they sought fairly soon—especially considering how thickly strewn with tacponders the Arthelion system was. Even Ng had been surprised at their density. But then, they'd had almost a thousand years to place them. The combination of thousands of tacponders and efficient use of courier ships gave them communications almost as good as if they had Eusabian's FTL comms in each ship.

But not quite.

And Eusabian had that advantage across the entire Thousand Suns. The thought reassured her of the rightness of her actions, but that didn't stop the ache of awareness of the cost they would doubtless pay. She could not prevent her mind from shooting straight to Metellus, slashing at the *Fist of Dol'jhar* above Arthelion.

"*. . . and I will pay whatever price demanded by my oath and honor. . .*" The fragment of the Naval Oath resonated in her bones, and though she meant to keep busy and rational, the viewscreen replaced itself with memory of Metellus's ardent face their last night, his warm touch, the tickle of his breath on her throat. They paid the price of honor with each separation, but she knew that the one left behind would bear the cost of loyalty.

EIGHT

Gelasaar hai-Arkad sat between two Tarkans as the transtube decelerated with distressing force. The prison tunic the Dol'jharians had issued him itched, but that was not half so distressing to his fastidious nature as the smell. His captors' ideas of hygiene fell well short of his own.

It hadn't been so long ago that his worries were planetary economies and millions of lives; now his concerns had narrowed to bad laundry practices and barely palatable food. All under the cruel drag of 1.2 gees. A soft laugh escaped him as he remembered his former longings for a simpler life. "Prayers which heaven in enormous vengeance grants."

He spoke out loud, provoking a change from alertness to wariness in one of the Tarkans. Did he understand Uni? Perhaps only the word "vengeance": that, a Dol'jharian might be expected to understand in any tongue. Probably assumed he was curse-weaving against the Avatar.

He laughed again as the module came to a stop. His own success had cursed the Avatar worse than any enemy could wish, had he but the wit to see it.

Then the doors opened, and Gelasaar comprehended how far short of understanding his victorious enemy fell as the Tarkans pushed him down a short corridor to the bridge of the *Fist of Dol'jhar*. He knew what was coming now, and he looked forward to its inevitable denouement.

The bridge of the Avatar's flagship was quieter than a

Navy battlecruiser's would have been under the circumstances, and lacking the tianqi, it reeked of anxiety-tinged sweat. Gelasaar thought he also somehow tasted the harsh tang of pain-driven Dol'jharian discipline, perhaps sensing it in the stances of the men and women moving purposefully about.

The activity on the bridge intensified. The main viewscreen split into two windows, echoed by others. In each a point of light swelled rapidly. He strained to understand the rapid-fire Dol'jharian, catching only fragments. Two destroyers in a fractional-cee attack, no skipmissiles. . . A subliminal rumble vibrated up through his feet, consoles lit up and repeater screens flared. He strained to hear . . . "and [something about] the Mandala." A shock of surprise. An attack on the Mandala? With lances? Ridiculous. It had to be a ruse.

Then he noticed Anaris standing with a short, misshapen Bori a few paces behind the captain's command pod. The young Dol'jharian was engaged in conversation with the Bori—no doubt his secretary—and hadn't yet seen him.

The attack ceased. On another screen the lance attack on the other side of the planet dwindled under an onslaught of missiles from a destroyer and some other ships. He caught a fragment of a report—organic debris confirmed—and looked away from the screen, his gut churning with grief.

Then he remembered. And studied the deck plates in front of his toes until he was certain his expression was rigidly schooled. He knew this maneuver. Jaspar had used it against the Battersea Demagogues. It was still known by an acronym—BBQ—whose meaning had long been lost. Apparently the Dol'jharians hadn't figured out yet what was happening.

Relieved, he studied Anaris, the amusement replaced by melancholy. Poor amphibious spirit. Caught halfway between two worlds that were nearly antipodes of the human experience: iron and ice against elegance and generosity, Anaris was neither Dol'jharian nor Douloi. Not for the first time the Panarch wondered if his fosterage had done Anaris a service, or scarred him beyond healing.

Gelasaar reconsidered the aborted meeting in the hangar bay before the attack, and saw again the pride and certainty of purpose in Anaris's countenance. What had he intended to say?

During a lull in the action, Anaris acknowledged him at last. As Juvaszt stood up with the easy courtesy that the military life demands for a respected enemy, Gelasaar watched

Anaris. Eusabian's son had always been hard to read, but the Panarch had long been a careful observer, and he detected signs of ambivalence, of pride and uncertainty, which would seem to confirm the polarities of the young man's spirit.

In Dol'jharian fashion, he'd carefully constructed a set piece for the meeting in the hangar bay, but now was at a loss for words in this unplanned meeting. And yet. Gelasaar suspected that the Douloi in him had seen the failure of Dol'jharian understanding that his, the Panarch's, presence on the bridge implied, and was ready to profit from it.

Anaris's smile widened, and the Panarch recognized irony, appreciating its sting: Anaris was not going to speak.

Gelasaar looked away, feeling a new wave of grief for his dead sons. He recalled his insistence that his own people treat Anaris not as a prisoner, or as a hostage, but as his own sons were treated. The gesture had been a gift, intended as a bridge. Would it aid or harm his people now?

Perhaps there was a fourth son, safe from the Avatar's paliach. Though he was aware of the emotional yearning behind that thought. That *wish*. And even were it true, Anaris would face dangers of his own.

Gelasaar considered Anaris as Eusabian's son watched the screens.

DEATHSTORM

Aziza bin'Surat shifted in her pod, monitoring the ceaseless flow of messages from the Urian relay webbed and bolted to her console on the bridge of the Rifter destroyer *Deathstorm*, now patrolling the middle system a light-hour out from Arthelion. Most of them were coded, from the Dol'jharians to other ships throughout the Thousand Suns, but many were sent en clair or in various Brotherhood or Syndicate codes, from other Rifter ships. That seemed to gall the Dol'jharians, but there was little they could do. And some of the images. . .

She forced her attention back to the small windowed image from the *Fist of Dol'jhar* that her console was echoing to one of the secondary screens on the bridge. The image was almost surreal: the Panarch of the Thousand Suns, in a tunic she wouldn't let a wattle nest in, surrounded by hulking Dol'jharians on the bridge of his enemy's flagship. It was like something out of a serial chip. She wondered how the Panarchists receiving it via ordinary EM felt.

She knew how her fellow Rifters felt. The volume of messages had increased dramatically since the Panarch's image went out over the Urian comm system. Some were comments and jokes about the Panarch, others were suggestions on how to wage the battle, aimed at the *Satansclaw* and the two frigates, or even at Juvaszt on the *Fist*. Any moment she expected that slug Barrodagh to show up on the comm and threaten them all with various horrid Dol'jharian punishments if they didn't shut up. Lotta good that'd do. But she had to admit, it was getting pretty hard to filter out all the trash on the hyperwave, and she wondered how the Ur had done it. Maybe they had eyes and ears all over their bodies, or something.

She snickered, then stifled it as the captain, slouching broodily in his command pod, shifted irritably, not taking his eyes off the viewscreen. Something about the Panarchist attack obviously bothered him, but he wasn't the sort to confide in his crew, and should anyone be stupid enough to ask, he might alleviate his boredom by carving ears or other extremities with one of his knives. Why was he worrying? The nicks'd have to stop now. They wouldn't shoot at the Panarch.

When Qvidyom caught her gaze and glared at her, she busied herself with unnecessary key taps.

"Lipri," the captain snapped.

The navigator straightened up in his pod.

"Take us to our next position." Qvidyom didn't hide his irritation at the necessity of following that stiff-nackered Juvaszt's patrol orders. They had little choice. The Dol'jharians controlled the Urian power source. Their own reactors were cold and dark — it would take hours or even ship-days to bring them back on-line, unless they wanted to risk the Plasma Wager. They'd be helpless to resist if a ship showed up to carry them off to the rebuilt mindripper. Obedience was their only choice.

On the viewscreen the long lance of the ship's missile tube swung across the starfield as the ship came about. Aziza quashed another snicker. It was typical of Qvidyom to leave the launcher visible in forward views. She doubted that the one between his legs worked.

A message from the *Satansclaw* dragged her attention back to the task at hand, but it was just a status report, noting the destruction of the last few Marine lances from the second attack. They were better off than those poor blits, anyway, and obedience had been rewarding, so far. Aziza began to drift into pleasant memories of their looting of the Achilenga Highdwellings. Highdwellings were easy: nobody carried firejacs, and anyway, the nicks had pretty much abandoned them and fled. It had been like going shopping, only with no one to take your sunbursts in trade.

Aziza jerked alert as the lights flickered. A low rumble shook the bridge.

The sensor console bleeped. "Emergence!" Odruith shrieked. "Big one!"

The captain slapped at the go-pad on his console, but nothing happened. Glare spilled from the main viewscreen as a beam of plasma so bright the electronics transformed it to a finger of blackness limned in light traced a line of destruction along the missile tube, billows of gas and gouts of flaring metal erupting from its point of contact.

"Damage control!" Qvidyom yelled.

"Engine room not reporting!" Eglerda stabbed at his console. "We've got power, but no drive."

The beam ceased. Plasma leaked from the wreckage of the missile tube.

"Skipmissile not charging," Eglerda continued.

"I can see that, you chatzing nackerbrain!" Qvidyom screamed, tobacco-stained spittle spraying from his mouth.

"Skip-pulse," reported the sensors tech. "They've skipped out." Her voice shook, a mixture of fear and confusion.

"What? Are you sure? What in the name of Prani's Nine Bronze Balls is going on?"

Aziza's brain started working again as the imminence of death receded a bit. What were the Panarchists up to? Why hadn't they used their ruptors, and more bewildering, why hadn't they followed up? Then a horrid certainty possessed her: they were going to be boarded.

"Bin'Surat, you stupid chatzrip, stop dreaming and put me through to Juvaszt on the *Fist*."

The captain's insult jerked Aziza out of a fearful vision of Arkadic Marines, invulnerable in battle armor, rampaging through the ship. The Panarchist attack was failing, with the Panarch as hostage, but it was too late for the *Deathstorm*. She patched in the channel with trembling fingers, hoping it wasn't also too late for the *Deathstorm's* crew.

FALCOMARE

To the unassisted eye the naval staging point looked empty. Only the small circles drawn by the computer around otherwise undistinguished points of light enabled Metellus Hayashi to detect the other two destroyers of his squadron preparing for the third attack on the *Fist of Dol'jhar*. The three frigates were doing a good job of distracting the Rifter destroyer and the two frigates that had joined it. But *Satansclaw* was definitely fighting better than expected, despite its forced proximity to the planet and the vulnerable Highdwellings—now the property of Eusabian of Dol'jhar, Moral Sabotage had noted.

It was *Falcomare's* turn to deliver the mock lances, while *Lady of Taligar* and *Barahyrn* slashed at the enemy battlecruiser.

"Look at this, Captain," said Mbezawi at Siglnt. "Got a great shot of the *Fistula* during the last pass." He tapped at his console as Hayashi nodded. "Couldn't have done better with a skipmissile."

A window bloomed on the viewscreen, revealing a close-up of the aft-portion of the Dol'jharian battlecruiser, shifting rapidly in perspective. There was a low whistle from someone on the bridge; Hayashi smiled broadly. They'd hit one of the ship's hangar bays; a notorious weak spot, it was now a glowing pit lined with snarls of metal, glowing puffs of gas and dust billowing from it at random intervals. The image flickered out.

"Good work, Ushkaten," said Hayashi. The weapons officer beamed. "'Zawi, pass that image along to the armory, with my compliments."

The lieutenant turned back to his console, but as he started tapping at it his motions froze. He stared at his screen for a moment, eyes wide with horror.

"Captain," he said, all the triumph gone, "you'd better take a look at this. There's a broadcast from the *Fist of Dol'jhar*. From the bridge."

"What, is he asking for terms?" said Hayashi, but the joke fell flat as a grim atmosphere gripped the bridge. "Put it on-screen."

The starfield on the viewscreen was replaced by the *Fist's* bridge. Hayashi recognized the Dol'jharian uniforms. He and his crew were possibly the first naval personnel in twenty years to see such a view. Then came the shock of recognition.

"Telos protect us," someone whispered as Gelasaar hai-

Arkad, forty-seventh of his line, holder of Hayashi's oath and that of every person on the Falcomare, gazed gravely at them from between two enormous Tarkan guards.

Despite the fact that he knew this was a one-way link, Hayashi almost saluted, so commanding was the man's presence. "Communications," he said, not taking his eyes from the screen, "signal *Barahyrn* and *Lady of Taligar*. Hold position."

There was movement in the image; as the other destroyers acknowledged, Hayashi felt certain that this was not a recorded loop, but an ongoing broadcast, a window onto the bridge of the *Fist of Dol'jhar* from minutes in the past. And then he smiled as he realized the message implicit in the Panarch's stance, a message the Dol'jharians had no chance of intercepting. It was a command no less compelling for being unspoken.

A harsh laugh escaped Hayashi, throat-scraping and bitter. "Those Telos-damned fools," he said. "They're trying to bind us with our oath of fealty. What does a Dol'jharian know of loyalty? They only understand fear." He tipped his chin at the image. "You know what *he* expects of us."

He turned away from the viewscreen, seeing understanding and grim agreement in his crew. "Communications, raise *Barahyrn* and *Lady of Taligar*. Conference."

Ensign Mellieur tapped at her console. Two windows popped up on-screen, revealing Doial and Somsri. Hayashi could see the same mix of anger, question, and resolution in their faces that he was feeling, and wondered how even a Dol'jharian could so misread an enemy.

"The captain of the *Fistula* has made a terrible mistake," he said. "I propose we explain it to him." He paused, tapping up a tactical plot and echoing it to both of them, as a snort of laughter escaped from Captain Doial.

"I propose we execute the third attack as planned, with us dumping the mock lances, but instead of meeting at the next staging point, *Falcomare* will skip behind Lunaire. The moon's mass will hide us as we relay a beam through a drone to talk to Juvaszt, and watch him as well. In the meantime, you two join our frigates and chase off those Rifters. Whichever of you can, dump a fourth wave here in relation to the *Fist*." The tactical plot responded to his touch as he sketched out the geometry of the attack.

"We'll be talking to him at that point and powering up in a Katy Wheel, so when he skips up on the first leg of his circum-planetary jump and starts to come about, we can wheel past him and get off a shot at his radiants without endangering Arthelion or the Highdwellings."

A ship always emerged from skip on the same heading on which it entered, with conservation of any rotation. By imposing a yawing spin on the *Falcomare* and skipping at just the right moment, the ship would emerge with the missile tube already swinging into alignment with the *Fist of Dol'jhar*.

He held up a hand as he saw the objection on their faces. He knew it wasn't to the danger of the maneuver — the *Falcomare* would emerge headed more or less straight for Arthelion, since that was the only way they could get off a shot aiming safely away from the planet.

"Sorry, Bea, Jarnock. Rank hath its privileges." He smiled. "This one's mine."

"Pretty iffy," Somsri growled. "That's a double Katy you're planning. *Falcomare* up to it?"

"Green thoughts, Jarnock." Hayashi laughed. "The *Fistula* didn't connect with any of us, so we're as ready as you are."

They laughed at him. He knew they didn't begrudge him the shot.

It was too bad that there was no safe way to plan a follow-up attack on the battlecruiser. This close to the planet, the risk was unacceptable. Only one ship could deliver their response, and that ship would be the *Falcomare*.

They conferred a few minutes longer, agreeing that they'd keep up the mock lance attack even after they ran out of BBQ materials, to keep the ships guarding Arthelion out of the main battle as long as possible, and signed off. Moments later, the *Falcomare* skipped out toward Arthelion to begin the third attack.

FIST OF DOL'JHAR

The radiants of their two attackers dwindled, vanishing in twin bursts of reddish light as the third attack ceased.

"Possible ruptor hit on one destroyer during the last attack. No IDs."

Anaris noted the obvious relief in Erechnat Chikhuri at the weapons console as the sensors officer reported. Dealing with a fractional-cee attack was difficult, especially from two directions at once, but so far the *Fist* had dealt nothing to its enemies to compare to the destruction wrought on the aft second hangar bay during the first attack. It didn't help that since the Highdwellings around Arthelion were now the Avatar's possessions, their use of the ruptors was severely constrained.

The Panarchists were probably aware of that, too. So far, the enemy's tactics had shown a thorough understanding of Dol'jharian thought patterns, an understanding unmatched by Juvaszt and the other officers on the *Fist of Dol'jhar*, especially since the enemy's ECM had so far prevented them from identifying their attackers other than ship class.

It galled Anaris that though he recognized a ruse, he did not yet comprehend the purpose of the attack. A battlecruiser was capable of absorbing this kind of warfare indefinitely; since the destroyers couldn't use their skipmissiles, they couldn't hope to disable the *Fist*. But there was no sign of any other activity, although he was certain there were other Panarchist ships out there. It had to relate to the Panarch, some desperate, madly heroic rescue-attempt, as happened so often in Panarchist wiredreams.

The Panarch stood at ease between his Tarkan guards, intent on the viewscreens. That was the only other person on the bridge who realized that this was all a sham, but did *he* know what the Navy's real thrust was? No, were there standing orders pertaining to his situation? Anaris deeply regretted his total lack of insight into Panarchist naval training.

The fiveskip snarled as the *Fist of Dol'jhar* made the first of the skips that would take it around Arthelion to assist the Rifters dealing with the latest wave of lances.

So-Erechnat Terresk'jhi stiffened in her pod, tapping at the communications console. "Real-time message from *Deathstorm*," she reported. "They are under attack by a battlecruiser. . . " Her brow crinkled in puzzlement. "It did not use ruptors, and skipped out after disabling the drives and the skipmissile accelerator."

And then it all crashed together in Anaris's mind. Real-time! They had real-time communications at any distance through the Urian communicator, and the Panarchists hadn't. *That* was what they're after—it had nothing to do with the Panarch; he'd let himself be distracted by the Panarch's presence.

He stepped toward the command pod. "They want an Urian communicator," he said. "This attack is merely a diversion."

Juvaszt gave him a brief glance, tapped at his console, and then looked up again consideringly. "Diversion it may be, but we cannot leave the Avatar undefended."

He turned away. "Communications, I want a real-time feed on that secondary screen—" He tapped his console and one of the smaller screens near the main viewscreen flashed. "—for all Rifter vessels in-system."

The communications officer worked at her console, and a number of windows began popping up on the indicated screen. They flickered. The images were grainy, and Terresk'jhi's movements became steadily more jerky and frantic, signaling severe stress. Occasionally another image would bleed through for a moment. The discriminators were having trouble dealing with the overload caused by the comments and images flooding in from all over the Thousand Suns as the battle at Arthelion engaged the interest of their Rifter auxiliaries.

Juvaszt began issuing orders, dispatching all the Rifters in the system to converge on the *Deathstorm's* position. His speech was clearer now; the medic had packed his wound with an absorbent, but Anaris could hear his irritation as he dealt with the increasingly unclear communications with the Rifters in the Arthelion system.

When he was finished he leaned back in his command pod. "If that's what they want, then they will commit all their forces to gaining it," said Juvaszt. "Now we can force the engagement and use the full weight of our weapons against them."

"Message incoming," said Terresk'jhi. "From the captain of the Panarchist attack squadron. He's hiding behind the moon, relaying the signal via drone. Two-point-five-second delay."

Juvaszt glanced up at Anaris again, his expression difficult to read. "Navigation, hold position. Put him on."

The viewscreen flickered to reveal a powerfully built man with a strong, hawk-nosed face, seated in his command pod. The bridge around him was out of focus. Anaris studied him while the lightspeed delay elapsed, then shifted his attention to the Panarch, whose smile was gone, replaced by the mask of command. It was happening as Anaris expected.

After five seconds the image spoke. "Captain Metellus Hayashi, of His Majesty's destroyer *Falcomare*, commanding. I assume, as is your nature, that you intend His Majesty as a hostage against the safety of your ship. I will need to confirm his well-being before speaking further."

Juvaszt smiled thinly in triumph as he motioned to the Tarkans. They prompted the Panarch forward, as Juvaszt said, "That, and cessation of your attacks against the Mandala, and of the action in the middle system. . ." He broke off as the communications officer motioned to him and pointed to a screen reporting *Satansclaw's* engagement with a Panarchist destroyer whose ID matched one of their previous assailants. The Rifter auxiliaries were being drawn out of position again as the enemy committed more forces against them.

As Juvaszt's reply reached him, the Panarchist captain's eyes shifted from the kyvernat to the Panarch. He saluted, but remained seated, within reach of his controls. "Your Majesty. I regret the circumstances. Are you well?"

Anaris watched the Panarch as he replied, "As well as can be expected." Anaris wondered if Juvaszt had an inkling of the formal emptiness of the exchange between the two, an emptiness that hid a fullness of meaning that needed no explicit statement. I congratulate you on your tactics," the Panarch went on in his measured Douloi cadences, so pleasant to the ears, and so fraught with hidden meaning. "I'm sure Kyvernat Juvaszt here will confirm their effectiveness. . . "

As the two talked on, Anaris sustained the visceral flare of conviction, but hid it. The lightspeed delay made the conversation seem even more dance-like and ritualistic: it was utterly Douloi, right down to the polite hand gestures. He could see Juvaszt's gaze begin to shift between the two Panarchists; he sensed something wrong, but didn't have a chance of figuring out what it was. Exultation accelerated Anaris's heartbeat. This Hayashi was giving him the keys to power on the *Fist of Dol'jhar*.

". . . and so I thank you, Your Majesty. That is good to know." Hayashi's gaze moved back to Juvaszt. "Well, Captain, you leave me no choice. Please stand by."

"By no means," replied Juvaszt quickly, his uncertainty evaporating. "We will not stand by while your lances attack the Mandala. We will discuss terms after we have dealt with them." He motioned decisively and the image flickered and froze.

Gelasaar's eyebrows lifted fractionally, and somehow the gesture, freighted with meaning that no one else on the bridge could grasp, left Anaris feeling even more alone than usual. For the one man who saw and understood his coming triumph was one with whom he couldn't share it.

And on board the *Falcomare,* the engines groaned on a rising note, accelerating the ship into a yawing spin that was taking it dangerously close to the stress limits imposed by its elongated form.

On the viewscreen the image froze. The Panarch looked out of the screen directly at Hayashi, his gaze as compelling as if they were still in contact.

Metellus Hayashi laughed, a savage sound; his bridge echoed his emotions.

"Skipmissile charged and ready," reported Lieutenant Ushkaten.

"Engage," Hayashi said.

There was a fractional pause—the computer would actually decide the moment of skip. Then the fiveskip burped, taking them out from behind the moon on the first leg of the skip that would hurl them in for the attack. It ceased, and the stars whirled madly across the viewscreen. The ghost of inertial pulled at Hayashi's inner ear; the gravitors were not designed to compensate for this dramatic a rotation.

The fiveskip burped again, not so harshly. They couldn't afford too high a real velocity, since they'd emerge pointed at the planet. The lower speed would leave them exposed to the enemy's ruptors all that much longer, but Hayashi was counting on the Dol'jharian inability to believe that they would fire on a ship carrying their liege.

Fools! Juvaszt—not purged, dammit—would be shot, if he was lucky, for doing so. He'd be shot, and rightly so, if he didn't.

"Emergence," sang Navigation.

Arthelion was too close behind them, fleeing across the screen as the ship yawed, and then the bright star of the *Fist of Dol'jhar* came into view. The screen flickered to maximum magnification. The vast battlecruiser began to come about for its second skip to deal with the fourth lance attack. Its radiants flared brightly, then were overlaid by the reddish pulse-wake of a skipmissile. A gout of light briefly blackened the screen.

Then, as the nose of the *Falcomare* swung past their enemy, the computer engaged the fiveskip, launching them away from the engagement.

DESRIEN

Coolness wrapped Ivard round as the light dimmed and changed, echoes pressed on him, a sweet scent clanged in his skull—where were the cymbals, then?

". . . love is stronger than death. . ."

A one had sung that.

And then there was a woman's face, gray-haired, kindly. Ivard tasted love, felt coolness, delicious, on forehead, lips, and chest. The blue fire leapt up, delighted, and withdrew a measure, and he returned to himself.

"*. . . find your heart's desire. . .*" He smiled at the woman. Then the haze returned, blue and smothering. Ivard struggled against it. The woman caressed his cheek and stepped aside, so Ivard moved on, hating the way his stupid body wouldn't *move* right. He was glad Greywing couldn't see him.

Anger doused the blue fire, leaving him aware of the vaulting space around him. But the blue fire flared up insistently, conjuring crowds of ghosts around him: he could see them—or was it smell? taste?—moving in soothing patterns, centered on the white table at the other end of the long room, where he beheld a glint of silver.

He was drawn along with the ghosts. The air around him tasted uncertain, as if the boundaries of the now had bled away, leaving him walking in past, present and future, all three suffused in the light from the colorful windows, under the vaulted ceiling so high above.

A swell of music freshened the air. Somewhere ahead a man sat at a tall console raised above the floor, his hands playing over the keys.

As Ivard neared the table, the splendor of his surroundings reminded him of the palace and all the beautiful things they'd taken. They were going to be rich, until the nicks caught up with them. He saw Greywing's face again, and the little metal disc with the bird on it, that he'd lost. Heart's desire. . .

The music broke into a discordant series of tones as Ivard, alone and lonely, limped up the steps of the dais on which the white-and-gold-clad table stood. His crewmates had vanished. Even the ghosts were gone.

Ivard looked at the table. The cloth covering it was richly

embroidered. On its surface stood two tall candleholders, intricately worked in gold and silver.

Ivard blinked as the blue fire leaped so high that it blurred his vision. Sitting in the center of the table was a battered old silver goblet, looking entirely out of place. He touched it with one trembling finger, acutely conscious of his unnaturally pale skin, and the rusty blotches and scattering of reddish hairs.

"If you are thirsty, drink."

Ivard spun around so fast he fell against the table, pain shooting through the unhealed wound across his back. A few paces away, an old man stood.

"I wasn't going to steal it!" he blurted.

The man smiled. "I know. Drink, if you desire. That, none of your treasures could buy for you."

Ivard stared at the old man. He was sure he'd never seen him before, yet he seemed familiar. But why did he think him old? There were no lines on his face. His hair was dark and glossy. Yet he was *very* old. Ivard was sure of that.

Ivard was also thirsty. He grasped the cup. It was cool in his hand. Inside, the clear water caught the light from the huge window high above, shimmering with color. The blue fire mounted, but this time it did not swallow him. A rich scent welled from the cup. He tasted life. He tasted years and multitudes as a kaleidoscope of flames infused him, voices whispering and murmuring in comforting patterns.

He drank.

It tasted like the old woman's fingers had felt on his forehead, like the approval in Greywing's eyes when he got something right without prompting, like the gentle rumble of Markham's voice, joking and teaching by turns, like the genuine interest in the blue eyes of the Aerenarch. . .

Ivard carefully set the cup down. When he looked up, he gazed straight into Greywing's eyes.

He opened his mouth, but no sound came out. She put out her arms and caught him in a fierce hug.

"Greywing, you were. . . in the palace. . ."

"Hush, Firehead." She pushed him out at arm's length, smiling; like the old man, nowhere to be seen, she looked old, but young, too, younger than he'd left her, under the palace, her body lifeless. . . He pushed the memory away. It didn't fit here.

"I lost your coin," he said.

"No, it's here." There was her old special smile. "I'm proud of you, Ivard."

He understood. In truth she stood a long way off, even as she was here, now, and when she spoke his name she meant all of him, as he had been, was, and would be, a three. To the blue-fire part of him it was perfectly clear, for its memory reached far back in time; but for the part of him that was a young and tired human boy on the cusp of manhood, it was too much, and darkness shot through the blue fire like veins of smoke, whirling him away from her smile into an echoing peace.

FIST OF DOL'JHAR

Anaris watched as Juvaszt stretched in his command pod. Anaris perceived the gesture as the assertion of control that it was and smiled in response. Juvaszt's brow furrowed.

The viewscreen cleared from skip, stars fleeing across it as the *Fist of Dol'jhar* began to come about for the second skip that would take it back over Arthelion to deal with the lances that *Satansclaw* and the other Rifter vessels had failed to stop.

"Emergence pulse!" shouted Durriken at the sensors console. "One-seventy mark 8, destroyer, course 262 mark 33, coming about for skipmissile attack. . ."

"What?" shouted Juvaszt, his eyes wide with disbelief. "Ruptors! Fire at will. . ."

A savage blow jolted the bridge. The lights flickered and a wave of gravitational distortion from unstable gravitors threw several officers off their feet or out of their pods. Gelasaar stumbled against one of his Tarkan guards.

As Anaris clutched at the back of the captain's pod for support, he exulted. Captain Hayashi's timing was impeccable!

Juvaszt's mouth snapped shut. He stared at Anaris, eyes distended as they'd been at the eglarhh hre-immash, the ghost-laying ceremony. Then he slapped at his console.

"Damage Control!"

"Skipmissile impact on radiants, severe damage to engine one, automatic shutdown sequence engaged; engine two destabilized. Skip aborted."

"Enemy vessel has skipped out, no other traces detected," reported the sensors officer.

"Communications, raise *Satansclaw* and the frigates."

The unexpected sound of a chuckle turned the heads of everyone on the bridge. The Panarch gazed at Juvaszt. Anaris very nearly burst into laughter himself. Morrighon's lips twitched as well. Juvaszt wore an expression of utter outrage, almost betrayal.

"He told you the truth," said Gelasaar, his Dol'jharian distorted by a heavy accent. "You left him no choice, nor did his oath."

The Tarkans on either side of him looked confused until Juvaszt motioned to them with a savage slash of his hand while he issued a rapid volley of orders to the Rifter defenders of Arthelion on the other side of the planet. The guards grasped the Panarch under each arm and marched him toward a hatch.

Anaris waited until they reached it before he gave in to impulse and signaled them to halt. They obeyed, dropping back when he approached, so that he and the Panarch faced one another alone. Anaris waited, studying Gelasaar's face. There was no hint of defeat, only the well-bred inquiry that indicated tight control.

Anaris pitched his voice so that only Gelasaar could hear, and said, "Brandon is alive."

The physical reaction was all he could have wished; the Panarch's head jerked up, one of his hands going to his heart before dropping to his side. His lips parted, but Anaris waved to the Tarkans, who stepped forward, one clamping a hand on the Panarch's shoulder.

But before Gelasaar was taken away, he shook off the Tarkan's hand and bowed, graceful despite his unaccustomed weight in the deliberate deference of unalloyed gratitude.

Then he was gone, leaving Anaris to face the covert curiosity of Juvaszt and his bridge officers. Anaris knew they would have misjudged the meaning of the Panarch's reactions, having only seen him from the back, they would assume that a bow of surrender, of defeat. They had not seen the Panarch's joy.

Anaris examined his own reaction to that, which had surprised him. Laughing at himself, he began considering ways to use his fellow Dol'jharians' misperception.

EIGHT

Margot Ng closed her eyes as the subtle pulse of the ruptors died away. On the viewscreen another Rifter ship dissipated in shreds and tatters of glowing debris.

"It's your empathy that makes you such a good captain," Metellus had said to her once. *"You can put yourself in their minds, see as they see. . ."*

And feel as they feel. Maybe that was the core of her success, but she sometimes wished it didn't hurt so much.

"That's another empty," grumbled Commander Krajno. "I wonder if KepSingh or Armenhaut is doing any better."

"Evidently these FTL coms are less common than those Rifters thought," said Rom-Sanchez.

"That's good news, of a sort," rejoined Krajno.

"Navigation," said Ng, "take us to position three."

As the stars slewed around on-screen, Ng wondered if their luck, or lack of it, would hold. As the battle progressed, if you could call such a spread-out, cold-blooded hunt by that name, their information on enemy positions became older and less accurate. They'd jumped right on top of their first victim; the second one had taken almost ten minutes to locate. They could expect an even longer search for the next one, and eventually their chances would be no better than a random search. And they hadn't heard from *Hainu* squadron since the third attack commenced.

"Emergence pulse, courier," said Siglnt.

"Navigation, hold position," Ng snapped.

"Message incoming," Ensign Ammant said. "*Flammarion*'s got one, a destroyer. Two frigates and a destroyer have already responded. Coordinates transferred."

Ng checked the timing on the message, automatically noting the uncertainty—still not too bad—encoded by the tactical com protocols. The courier had taken less than ten minutes to find them. She dispatched one of her own to find KepSingh, just in case the one Armenhaut reported sending didn't make it.

"Navigation, take us in, eight light-minutes out at forty-five degrees, your discretion." She tapped her console plot-pane to clarify her request.

The fiveskip burred harshly. The viewscreen cleared, and a tactical plot windowed up. She studied the information as the Tenno shifted and stabilized, hearing without attention the twittering from the communications section as tacponder information flooded in: reports from Armenhaut and others in his squadron. Rom-Sanchez's fingers flickered as he sorted the data, applying temporal filters.

She sighed. Armenhaut was fighting with his usual parade-ground style, a flourish of bravado as if he expected his enemy to quail before his righteousness. He'd not yet gotten his lances away. KepSingh's squadron should be showing up soon.

"Let's grab this one," she said finally, tapping at her plot-pane. A red circle ringed a Rifter frigate. She turned to Rom-Sanchez. "I want updates to and from the tacponders as often as you can handle it. Navigation, take us in to these coordinates, three light-minutes out for an update. Prepare for high tac-level attack. Weapons, charge skipmissile."

She paused, feeling the lift in spirits on the bridge. Not for the first time, she wondered at the human preference for danger to boredom, a failing—if that's what it was—that she fully shared. Perhaps it was as simple as that waiting for danger to strike was worse than actually dealing with it. "Engage."

SATANSCLAW

Anderic moved his hands over his console, trying to keep up with the actions of the logos as that cold intelligence fought the ship for him. It was using the hyperwave masterfully to coordinate *Kali* and *Mojendaro*. One of the Panarchist destroyers had taken damage, and they'd failed to keep him away from the third lance attack. On the viewscreen green fingers of light reached out and clawed at the last few lances, transforming them into bursts of plasma and debris that shredded away in the upper airs of Arthelion.

His hands ached, both with the tension of keeping up appearances and with the effort to keep them from trembling. His exultation had died away. Loathing filled him at his former captain's stupidity, and worse at his own cowardice. What credit was there in following the motions of a machine? He was just a chatzing puppet, and he was beginning to think that nothing the Dol'jharians could do to him would be as bad as what he'd done to himself. He was damned, in inescapable slavery to the machine that haunted the *Satansclaw*.

"ALL ATTACKING VESSELS DESTROYED," reported the logos in his inner ear. Anderic slumped back in the command pod, wringing his hands in his lap as he tried futilely tc relax them. At least they were here pot-shotting lances, instead of dueling with Panarchist battlecruisers in the middle system, or sitting dead in space like the *Deathstorm*.

He was distracted by a long, considering gaze from Lennart that he found vaguely threatening. Something had changed. He snorted. No wonder. That image of her and Luri with the chocolate had become a favorite of every Rifter ship with a hyperwave. Anderic grinned. Some inspired tech had dubbed in a new sound track with outrageous noises; just thinking about it made his sides ache all over again.

Lennart turned away as her console beeped. She listened, her head cocked. "Signal from *Fist of Dol'jhar*. New attack, coordinates transferred."

That was on the *Fist's* side. Why wasn't Juvaszt dealing with them? "Take us around," said Anderic, his heartbeat accelerating again.

The fiveskip burred, ceased. The ship came about, then skipped again. As the screen cleared, targeting crosses sprinkled the limb of Arthelion below, while above, tiny with distance, the *Fist of Dol'jhar* hung, with vapor leaking from its radiants.

Because they didn't have a logos.

Wearily, Anderic began his deadly charade anew as the logos mercilessly slaughtered the lances diving toward the surface they would never reach. He wondered how long the Panarchists could keep this up.

"DEBRIS SIGNATURE INCONSISTENT WITH HUMAN OCCUPANCY," said the logos. "INSUFFICIENT ORGANIC TRACES."

Anderic frowned. That was strange. Were they throwing empties now?

"Sensors, scan the debris for organic residue again."

After a moment the tech replied: "Different signature, Captain. Not enough organic molecules." He looked up, brows raised. "I think they're empty."

"Communications, signal the *Fist*."

The harsh features of Kyvernat Juvaszt windowed up. "Report."

"Scans indicate the lances are now unmanned," said Anderic, too weary even to attempt an ingratiating manner.

Juvaszt stared at him, then the image froze. A few seconds later it jumped to a new view of the Dol'jharian captain as transmission resumed. "Cease fire and skip to these coordinates," said Juvaszt. "You will cooperate with the destroyers *Hellmouth* and *Nirvana's Fire* and the frigate *Golden Bones* to destroy the Panarchist battlecruiser attacking the *Deathstorm*. Stand by for further orders after emergence. Juvaszt out."

The screen blanked. Anderic stared at it for a moment, empty of emotions, and then began issuing the commands that would take them into battle again, conned not by flesh and blood, but by the crystalline incarnation of warriors long dead. Did they even care, he wondered, if they died again?

FIST OF DOL'JHAR

Anaris watched Juvaszt issue orders to the Rifter destroyer and frigates that had been defending Arthelion against the lance attacks. Despite the hammer-blows the man's assurance had taken in the last few minutes, his actions were precise and accurate.

It helped that the reports from Engineering were fairly hopeful. One engine was down for at least forty-eight hours, but even so, the *Fist of Dol'jhar* was still a formidable engine of war with the Urian-enhanced skipmissiles. Now that they knew there was no threat to the Avatar, events would turn rapidly against the Panarchists in the middle system.

As for his own campaign, Anaris was fairly sure that he had the edge with Juvaszt. He hoped so. It would be a shame to have to purge him.

Well, that was still in the future. There was much to do in the meantime. He motioned to Morrighon, then held up his hand and stayed him as he heard the next orders.

"Navigation, as soon as Engineering reports ready, take us in to ten light-seconds out from *Deathstorm's* position. Weapons, charge skipmissile."

He meant to deny the hyperwave to the Panarchists by destroying the ship. Anaris stepped forward. Juvaszt turned to him, his air of deference deeply satisfying.

"Kyvernat," said Anaris, pitching his voice for Juvaszt alone, "perhaps this delay is for the best."

Juvaszt seemed puzzled "Well, the Panarchist forces will be concentrated around *Deathstorm* longer, so our auxiliaries will have more time to find and kill them."

Anaris was chagrined at having revealed his tactical ignorance — in hindsight it seemed obvious that using the Rifter destroyer as bait would make the enemy easier to find. But he didn't miss a beat. "I leave that to you. I was merely concerned that our Rifter allies not lose heart." He smiled, inviting Juvaszt to share his joke. "They are not, after all, Dol'jharians."

A short bark of laughter escaped Juvaszt. Anaris sensed his appreciation — never to be expressed in words — at the lack of gloating on his part. "No more than I am a Panarchist, it seems."

Anaris burned with triumph. That was the equivalent of surrender in a proud Dol'jharian noble like Juvaszt. He gestured dismissal. "I'd be a fool if I lived on Arthelion as long as I did and learned nothing of their ways." He paused for effect. "And even more a fool if I learned too much."

Juvaszt laughed again. "A fool, or dead," he agreed. "Among the Children of Dol it's usually the same thing, which is our strength."

He turned back to his console. Anaris could see the real-time feed changing as he queried various Rifter ships fighting around the *Deathstorm* and called more to the engagement. After more reports from Engineering and Weapons, Juvaszt issued new orders and the *Fist of Dol'jhar* finally skipped out of Arthelion orbit to join the battle.

EISENKUSS

Dyarch Ehyana Bengiat watched as the *Flammarion* fell away behind her lance and then vanished in a pulse of reddish light.

She switched the viewscreen to the forward view. Ahead a dim spark of light marked their target, the Rifter destroyer *Deathstorm*, dead in space.

There was no other sign of the struggle all around them. Space was too large, and human ships, even battlecruisers, far too small. She couldn't even see the other lances. Had she known where to look, their stealthed hulls would have defeated her eyes, just as their other countermeasures defeated the far keener senses of enemy ships. In silence, against diamond-sprinkled night, the *Eisenkuss* lunged toward its prey.

It would be several minutes before they reached the sprint point, where the engines would trigger into overload to take them through the destroyer's shields, past any weapons that might be brought to bear. And they had to know the Marines were coming for them. As Meliarch Abrams had pointed out in the briefing, the fact that Captain Armenhaut hadn't used the ruptors was a flagrant giveaway.

Well, there was no use worrying about that. She stretched against the dead weight of her battle armor, not yet energized, and then triggered the diagnostic sequence.

"Again?" came a dramatic groan over the general access channel.

"You'd look pretty funny wallowing around in half a ton of inert dyplast and battle alloy, Jheng-li," she replied. "Yeah, again."

She grinned privately. Solarch Jones Jheng-li affected an aversion to any effort that went beyond the usual Marine avoidance of scut work, but his squad was consistently near the top of the ratings in simulations and exercises. A few mocking comments followed, but quickly subsided. A Marine's battle armor was serious business: the thirty men and women on board—five squads—busied themselves confirming the status of the servo-armor that made them the deadliest fighters in human history.

A web of colored lines swept across her faceplate, followed by a flux of alphanumerics as the eyes-on display cycled. All AyKay there.

The diagnostic sequence completed as the navcomp warned of the approaching sprint point, just as she'd intended. Now the *Deathstorm* had a shape, long and angular, slightly blurred by the gas and debris leaking from its wounds.

Bengiat tapped the big go-pad with one gauntleted hand,

the only part of her yet powered up, and that at only five percent. Her faceplate sealed. She felt the clamps engage around her armor.

'Time to shut your face or suck vacuum, Mary," she said, observing the ancient tradition. "Prepare for gees."

"Will you respect me in the morning?" yelled Jheng-li, his voice near manic in one of the many traditional responses, provoking a flurry of similar cracks as her five squads pumped themselves up for attack.

Then the heart-lifting cascades of the Phoenix Fanfare's trumpet chords filled the com channel. The navcomp triggered the engines, and no one had any breath left for talking. Everything in a lance was aimed at one goal: taking it safely through the space-time distortion of a fully driven tesla field behind the fierce jet of a shaped nuclear charge. Only the bare minimum of energy was spared to cushion the Marines from gee-forces. It was a ten-gee ride all the way in.

On the screen the destroyer swelled alarmingly, filled the view, and vanished in a flare of light that blanked the viewscreen as a shattering roar rattled her bones. The lance's hull rang like a vast bell struck by an avalanche as the engines were triggered into destructive overload, carrying them through the savage deceleration of an impact that would otherwise have reduced them all to blobs of jelly in their armored boots.

After a pause of ringing silence, another roar as the front of the lance exploded outward. The interior filled with smoke, which whipped into madly rushing streamers of gray that were pulled around the edges of the opening into the destroyer, escaping toward the vacuum of space. They slowed into random eddies as white sealant pumped out.

"Was it good for you?" yelled Jheng-li, provoking a wave of laughter and bawdy comments.

Bengiat's faceplate flashed, the clamps on her limbs disengaged with a rattle, and her suit came to life. The gee-tank elevated and she stepped out.

"Let's go," she yelled, waving the five other Marines in her squad forward.

FALCOMARE

"The starboard hangar bay's pretty much done for, but we're still fit, otherwise." Bea Doial grimaced. "We got off lightly, considering."

Hayashi nodded. Captain Doial and her crew had learned something that often killed the student: that no simulator could duplicate the real impact of a ruptor. But he saw only eagerness in her face now, and in Somsri's, too, in the other window. They were at the fifth staging point, preparing for the fifth attack on Arthelion.

"Courier report incoming," said Ensign Mellieur. Her console twittered. She looked up, startled.

"From Captain Ng. The *Fist of Dol'jhar* has joined the battle around *Deathstorm*. The Marines are on board."

"Damn," said Hayashi.

"We knew they'd tip to it eventually," said Somsri.

On the screen a tactical plot windowed up with correlated transponder and courier data; he saw Doial's and Gait's expressions tighten as Mellieur echoed it to them.

"Even though it's just what Juvaszt wants, we've got to attack the *Fistula* every time it approaches *Deathstorm* until the Marines get clear with the FTL comm. Give him no rest, and free up the battleblimps to smash Rifters."

"While he and said Rifters get lots of shots at the fleet." Doial's tone was matter of fact.

"And we at them." Hayashi started sketching on his plot-pane, the screen echoing his movements with bold lines of color.

"Here's how we'll start. . ."

DEATHSTORM

Bengiat's squad spilled out the front of the lance in drill-perfect form, covering each other, but as was almost always the case, there was no one waiting for them. It was impossible to predict just where a lance would impact. Her squad deployed, positioning themselves to defend the other four squads as they emerged.

She scanned the wreckage of the hold they'd penetrated, looking past the gruesome blotches of shattered flesh decorating the twisted bulkheads. The hatch to the corridor outside hung by a single hinge; a Marine grasped it with one gauntlet and wrenched it off, sending it spinning to one side.

She felt a grinding shock as another lance struck the destroyer, then another. Her comm crackled to life.

"Bengiat, status," came the voice of Meliarch Abrams. The

rest of the lance's contingent spilled out into the hold.

"Secure the corridor," she commanded, then switched to the command channel.

"Breach secured, sir. No casualties, all full effective."

"Good. You're farthest forward and up. Proceed to the bridge and secure the FTL device. Extract the comm codes and grab the comtech if you can." A tactical map spidered up on her faceplate. "Secure these points on your way." Circles bloomed on several corridor junctions and stairs—they couldn't use the transtubes. The map shifted, with other points highlighted. "We'll secure the port and starboard hangar bays and the ships for evacuation, and shut down what's left of the power."

"AyKay, sir. Understood."

"You heard the man," she shouted. "We haven't got much time. When the Dol'jharians figure out what we're after they'll try to blow up the ship. Move it!"

They double-timed down the corridor, following the green traces in their faceplates supplied by their tactical computers. Every Navy ship had the plans for every type of vessel ever built; thanks to their tac-comps, the Marines probably knew this destroyer better than most of its crew.

From time to time red targets flashed on the bulkheads or overhead, answered by bursts of plasma from the jacs of the Marines: imagers and other sensors identified by the tac-comps.

At the critical points identified by Meliarch Abrams she deployed small groups of three to hold them—half a squad. A lance contingent, five squads of six, was an almost infinitely adaptable force. They moved as a unit, effortlessly coordinated by years of training, and yet as individuals, immediately responsive to any situation. Nothing could match them, and they knew it.

As they approached the bridge her suit discriminators picked up sounds indicative of some sort of defensive effort. She halted the two squads short of the last corner and popped a Scuttler out of her suit. The little device shot around the corner, relaying a clear picture of the six Rifters in half-armor clustered behind two plasma cannons before a flare of energy from a jac vaporized it.

"Jheng-li, deploy two for splash-n-burn, smoggers at minus three. Sniller, stun-bombs to follow up. Amasuri, you and I with the wasps." She looked around as the other Marines scrambled into position, the two Jheng-li had assigned for splash-n-burn dialing their jacs to wide aperture. The rest not called out took up positions to cover their rear. She called up the wasp setting with her eyes-on, felt the little missiles click into readiness below her wrists.

"AyKay. Five, four, three. . ."

FIST OF DOL'JHAR

Kyvernat Juvaszt could feel a titanic headache building. The grainy flickering of the real-time feeds from their Rifter allies in-system gnawed at his eyes; his irritation was compounded by the ghost images and jeering voices from other Rifters throughout the Thousand Suns that the discriminators couldn't entirely eliminate.

He glanced at Serakhnat Mekhli-chur at the tactical console. Was he keeping up with the flood of information? The tactical plot was jumpy, but appeared to be updating properly. It was hard to tell. Juvaszt tried to shed the fretful question. He had the best officers Dol'jhar had to offer. He must rely on their competence.

And they all knew the price of failure.

The presence of the conditional heir didn't help, either. Anaris had refrained from gloating, and his suggestions had been genuinely useful, but having him standing behind the command pod was almost as bad as having the Avatar there. Except that his understanding ran deeper.

Juvaszt shifted in the command pod, shocked by the dangerous direction of his thoughts.

His tactical officer leaned toward him. "I suggest these new coordinates for the *Satansclaw* and *Nirvana's Fire*," he said. Above, a screen echoed his comments graphically. Juvaszt nodded. Serakhnat Mekhli-chur turned away and began issuing the orders.

"Sensors indicate boarding in progress on *Deathstorm*," said the sensors officer.

Juvaszt glanced at Anaris, who shrugged fractionally.

"Navigation, after next tactical skip, new heading, 44 mark 272, prepare for skip, *Deathstorm* minus ten light-seconds. Weapons, status?"

"Skipmissile charged, all ruptors on-line. . ."

The ship shuddered. The fiveskip moaned in a tactical skip.

"Skipmissile, glancing impact," said Damage Control. "Minor damage in forward third."

"Destroyer signature, skipped, reading 145 mark 13."

That was the first sign of Panarchist destroyers in the battle around the *Deathstorm*. They must only have the three. And now the positions were reversed: he could move freely, unconstrained by the need to defend Arthelion, while their maneuvering was limited by their need to defend *Deathstorm*. That would make them much easier to kill than destroyers usually were.

He raised his voice. "Navigation, new course. . ."

DEATHSTORM

Jheng-li tossed the smoggers around the corner. Bengiat imagined them scuttling toward the Rifters, then bursting into thick clouds of energy-absorbing particles, cutting down the efficiency of the plasma cannons.

Jheng-li slapped one of the Marines waiting at the corner. Suza dived across the corridor, her armor deflecting the coruscant burst of one of the cannons for the brief time she was exposed. Then she swiveled, and with the other Marine Jheng-li had chosen for the splash-n-burn, triggered her jac into the corridor. She aimed at the deck, creating a wash of intense heat that rolled down toward the Rifters, under the clouds from the smoggers.

"... two..."

Sniller stepped forward and lobbed the stun-bombs around the corner. Their faceplates automatically filtered out the visual stutter-pulse, the audio in their suits stopping down at the same time to save them from the stunning ultrasonics.

"... one, go!" Bengiat launched herself into the corridor, twisting in midflight, extending her arms toward the Rifter positions hidden in the smoke and flipping her wrists palms-up. Plasma splashed off her armor in a burst of radiance and she felt the little wasp missiles discharge as her momentum carried her into the cross corridor. The coolant system of her suit whined. Twin explosions slapped at the air as Amasuri followed. Two more explosions, then silence.

She stepped cautiously back into the corridor. Nothing happened. She moved forward, her jac ready. The smoke from the smoggers cleared, revealing the cannons as twisted wreckage, surrounded by dead Rifters, mostly in pieces, armor melted around cooked flesh.

"All clear. Let's blow the hatch."

The tac-comp flashed charge-points on her faceplate, outlining the weak points in the sealed hatch onto the bridge. She motioned Jheng-li forward; he slapped two hand charges onto the spots that his tac-comp, too, was showing and stepped back.

"Clear."

There was a muffled whomp, twin spurts of light, and the charge casings fell away, revealing neat holes with blue-white edges. Bengiat stepped forward, using her eyes-on to bring up a new setting in her armor. This time, flipping her wrists ejected two stout hooks which she pushed through the holes, along with a fiber-optic probe. A quick scan of the bridge revealed nothing their armor couldn't handle.

She retracted the probe. "AyKay, Mary. It's show-time." Four Marines turned to hold the corridor, the rest poised themselves in readiness.

She pulled smoothly, reveling in the incredible amplification of her strength lent by the servos, and pulled the hatch out of the opening. Stepping back, she waited as the other Marines pounded past her, yelling fiendishly with amplified voices that boomed from the bulkheads, then threw the hatch down the corridor and followed them onto the bridge.

FLAMMARION

"Hit on *Babur Khan*," said Siglnt.

The viewscreen flickered to extreme magnification, Armenhaut saw plasma billowing from a glowing gash on the flank of KepSingh's battlecruiser before the big ship vanished in a burst of bluish light.

"Severe damage; he's skipped. Enemy destroyer bearing 82 mark 66, 6.2 light-seconds, skipped, heading 234 mark 16."

Armenhaut leaned forward, ignoring the sweat trickling down his forehead as he scanned the tactical plot on his console that Lieutenant Commander Rajaonarive was relaying to him. He ignored the main tactical screen with all the new Tenno — "loony" was a good word for it. He'd ordered his tactical officer to deliver him a digest view based on his best estimate of enemy positions, plans, and probabilities. So far it seemed to be working well. Just like the sims. He kept reminding himself of that. Just like the sims.

But the sims that he'd drilled *Flammarion* to perfection with hadn't covered an enemy with irreducibly interior lines of communication, and weapons that made one destroyer a serious enemy instead of a nuisance. At least he'd gotten his lances away in good order.

The main tactical screen flickered, and Armenhaut flinched. It was taking Rajaonarive longer and longer to deliver the digest, despite his earlier confidence. The strain was showing in the man's increasingly hesitant movements, something the rest of the bridge crew had noticed. Their movements looked increasingly brittle.

Now Hayashi's destroyers were harassing the *Fist of Dol'jhar*, keeping it away from the *Deathstorm*.

"Emergence pulse, battlecruiser—" The moan of the fiveskip modulated SigInt's voice as the *Flammarion* executed a tactical skip. "ID *Fist of Dol'jhar*, 34 mark 208, heading 65 mark 40. . . firing skipmissile. . . coming about to new heading, firing ruptors. . ."

A few seconds later a gout of light erupted on the screen. It flashed to a close-up, revealing a sphere of light expanding against the stars, with the missile tube of a destroyer spinning away from the explosion. SigInt's voice tightened.

"*Barahyrn* destroyed." Then, "Skipmissile impact on *Fist of Dol'jhar*, minor damage, engines destabilized, estimate back on-line fifteen seconds."

Another spark of light flared. "*Falcomare* hit. Severe damage, skipped. . ."

As SigInt continued, Armenhaut caught up again. The fog of battle had swept away the Panarchist defenders of the crippled ship and the Arkadic Marines on board. Armenhaut hadn't really believed that the Dol'jharians would delay destroying *Deathstorm* just to keep the battle going, and he'd seen nothing to change his mind. Now there was nothing standing between the *Fist* and the destruction of the FTL comm that so many lives had been sacrificed for already.

Nothing except the *Flammarion*.

The bridge crew saw it, too. Here and there faces turned to him. But he saw no confidence in their eyes, only sick fatalism echoing his own.

Anger burned through him--at his crew, at Ng, at Semion. And then, with icy clarity, at himself: he had failed them all.

The realization cramped his guts into an agonizing knot as the fear of death rose up in him. And evaporated.

It was almost a relief to have no choices left.

"All ships to converge on *Deathstorm* to assist Marine evacuation. Tactical, we'll try for a shot up his radiants." He snapped out the heading that would take them in against the Dol'jharian battlecruiser. "Weapons, status?"

"Skipmissile fully charged, all ruptors on-line and tracking."

Armenhaut quickly dictated a situation report. "Communications, tactical full-sphere burst."

Then, as the stars slewed to a halt on the viewscreen, "Navigation, take us in."

NINE

Aziza cowered behind her pod, shaking with terror, her jac forgotten in her hand as the hatch ripped away and the Marines thundered onto the bridge of the *Deathstorm*. Their amplified battle cries hurt her ears, jac-bolts sizzled overhead, a console exploded, someone screamed, a horrible sound that ended in a gurgle.

It was over in a moment. The surviving members of the crew, including Captain Qvidyom, who'd dropped his jac almost instantly, were quickly rounded up by the Marines, faceless in their bulky armor. Aziza could feel heat radiating from the armor of the one who pulled her from behind her pod, the only sign of the jac-bolt that had hit him.

Three of the invaders went directly to the Urian hyper-wave, glowing weirdly against the communications console. Tools extruded from their gauntlets and began to gnaw at the fittings holding down the device. Another began tracing its cable connections, while yet another went to the main computer console and began working at it. Aziza watched in fascination, her terror slowly subsiding, at the delicate whisker-like feelers that sprouted from his suit.

"Which one of you chatzers is the comtech?" came a booming voice. Aziza stared as the faceplate of the suit from which the voice issued popped open, revealing the face of a woman who wouldn't have looked out of place in one of the fancy fashion chips her mother had been so fond of.

"Well?" said the Marine, her voice more human without amplification.

"I am," Aziza squeaked. Captain Qvidyom glared at her.

The Marine swiveled and stomped toward her, her armor whining. Aziza snickered. She couldn't help it — she knew she was on the edge of a hysterical fit — but she had a crazy image of the woman in a fashion show, stumping down the runway in her armor. What kind of lingerie does the well-dressed Marine wear, or is she naked in there?

"You know how to work that thing?" the woman asked as two other Marines herded the others a short distance away and made them sit down on the deck.

Aziza nodded, swallowing. The smell of burned flesh was making her nauseous. The woman's eyes scanned her face, her expression softening slightly. "What's your name?" she asked, her voice somewhat less brusque.

"Aziza. Aziza bin'Surat."

"AyKay, Aziza. Where are the codes?" The Marine at the computer looked up. "Can you identify them?"

"Yes."

The woman pushed her toward the main computer console. Aziza was astonished at how gentle her touch was, despite the heavy armor. "Help him find them."

She turned away as another Marine entered the bridge. Qvidyom stared at Aziza, eyes full of hate. He mouthed an obscene threat at her, shocking even for him. She shuddered and concentrated on the console, stealing a glance at the Marine standing next to her. His face was craggy, his expression tense.

As she worked she heard fragments of a conversation: ". . . can't pick us up, corvettes on the way. . . out of time. . ."

"That's it," said the Marine finally, straightening up from the computer. The console twittered and went dead, and he disconnected his probe.

"Dyarch, we've got. . ." A gargling noise from the front of the bridge interrupted him. Aziza looked up to see a hideously burned figure flop out onto the deck from behind a pod, moaning. She guessed it was Nigal, though she couldn't be sure; evidently the Marines had thought he was dead. She hoped he soon would be. No one should suffer like that; unlike the captain and his particular cronies, Nigal had been pretty decent.

As the Marines guarding the prisoners turned, Captain

Qvidyom rolled onto his side, reached for his boot, and jackknifed to a sitting position, his hand cocked back. His arm jerked as the woman Marine reached for him. Aziza shrieked in pain as a knife sprouted from her shoulder.

"Chatz!" the Marine shouted, took two long steps toward Qvidyom, and lashed out with her foot. There was a wet crunching sound, followed by a squelching thud as the Rifter captain's head bounced off a bulkhead and came to rest in the middle of the deck, staring upward. The eyes blinked twice, the mouth worked briefly and was still as his headless body toppled over, spouting blood all over the luckless Rifters around him.

"Medic!" shouted the woman, and then, "That's it! We've got what we came for. Prepare to evacuate, we're going straight out."

The bridge blurred around Aziza as the medic pulled the knife out of her shoulder and packed the wound with synflesh. He slapped an ampoule into her upper arm; the pain abruptly fuzzed away. Another Marine strode toward her, shaking out a silvery bag. Aziza shrieked again and tried to scramble away as they started to stuff her into it and the bridge buzzed into darkness and whirled away.

DESRIEN

"You have the freedom of Desrien. Make what use of it you will."

Lokri looked away from the old woman and around the immense stone church with its elegant carvings, seeking the nearest exit. The damn nicks had forced him along on this farcical pilgrimage, the devil knew why. He would not stay to find out.

He had not expected a chance to escape nick 'justice,' once he'd been identified. But that chance had been presented in this senseless side trip to Desrien, and he did not intend to waste the miracle.

Lokri headed for the doors they had come in through. The nicks were so confident in the mystery of Desrien that they thought he would go back to *Telvarna*, back to Naval custody and certain death. Well, anything Desrien had to offer would be better than that. Most of the stories Archetype and Ritual spread about the planet were about as realistic as a wiredream, anyway.

Lokri saw Schoolboy and his father standing nearby, and sensed the Marine shadowing the three of them. She probably had orders to see that they all returned to the ship. Muscle memory ached with the absence of a hideout knife or the comforting weight of a holster. He'd have to use his wits. He considered some subject that would get the Omilovs talking, and maybe draw the Marine in. Lokri could slip away while Schoolboy was busy ranting about the evil Rifters.

But then the clatter of footsteps behind Lokri abruptly reversed. Lokri risked a glance. The Marine was running full out in the opposite direction, her weapon drawn.

Grateful for whatever had distracted her, Lokri began walking again. The two nicks looked his way, and Schoolboy made a typically inane comment.

Lokri passed them by, and his heart thudded in his ears as adrenaline burned through him. He'd been walking *away* from the doors! Was that incense tang he'd noted, like and unlike the scents Jaim and Reth had used, actually some sort of drug? There had to be other doors not so protected.

He scowled at the two nicks, still standing there like fools, then started trying every door he came to.

Locked. Locked. Locked.

DEATHSTORM

Aziza came back to consciousness. For a few nasty seconds she was unable to orient herself. Then memory flooded back, and the thin, slick fabric around her resolved into the interior of the rescue bag the Marines had stuffed her into. One of them had slung her over his back. Aziza squirmed around, feeling the tug of the synflesh in her wound, until she could see through the semitransparent dyplast.

Sounds came through the fabric blurrily; she heard the woman say to Aziza's fellow Rifters, "Go. Save yourselves. This ship is going to blow. You can't stop it."

They scrambled to their feet and vanished through the ruined hatch. The Marines dogged down their visors and turned to a bulkhead.

The lights vanished, then came back in the red of

emergency power. Gravity failed. Aziza heard a sizzling roar, and the creaking of metal stressed beyond its limits. As the roar grew louder, Aziza twisted, trying to see over the shoulder of her captor. The rescue bag torqued up, leaving her suspended upside down, but now she could glimpse a sliver of what was going on ahead of her.

The roar ceased. Two Marines stepped forward and placed a number of small objects against the bulkhead. They stepped back; jets of flame spurted from where the objects were leeched to the metal.

Escaping air screeched as the two Marines triggered their jacs at the weakened bulkhead. The rescue bag crinkled and expanded. Aziza's nose began to bleed as the pressure dropped. Something popped at her feet, stinging her calves: oxy-poppers. As the crystals released the precious gas, she took a deep breath and wiped her nose. Everyone knew how a rescue bag worked. No one ever wanted to use one.

The bulkhead blew out, noisy for a second followed by abrupt silence. She couldn't hear anything except the crinkling of the dyplast as the Marine towed her out of the hole. She stared in astonishment: instead of more ship, there was only a tangle of wreckage, and then space.

Her captor launched himself away from the ship, small thrusters flaring at the sides of his armor, aiming for a small ship not far off. A reddish pulse of light bloomed beyond it. Abruptly the Marine twisted, putting himself between her and it. Then the ruined bulk of the *Deathstorm* lit up with the reflected light of a distant explosion. Aziza felt her right foot tingle, the skin burning, and jerked it toward her body. She was in the middle of a battle in space, with nothing between her and the vacuum but a plastic bag.

She considered that with a kind of quiet hysteria and did the only logical thing. She fainted again.

GROZNIY

"Skipmissile impact, aft beta section, aft beta ruptor off-line and not reporting, fiveskip destabilized. . ."

The grim litany of the damage-control officer rose above the pulse of the ruptors as they fired. Ng scanned the tactical plot and snapped out the orders for a new ruptor barrage.

". . . estimate ten seconds to skip. . ."

"Skipmissile charging, forward gamma ruptors in

harmonic cycle, shutdown in fifteen seconds."

The battering the *Grozniy* was taking from the Rifter skipmissiles gritted her teeth, but the battlecruiser had a long way to go before it was no longer a danger to its enemies. The hyperwave was turning out to be unexpectedly effective in the melee. *Babur Khan* had given up trying to join the defense of *Deathstorm*, and was fighting for its life against Rifter destroyers, trying to kill as many as it could before the end that now seemed inevitable. *Grozniy* had taken some serious hits even though it had yet to encounter the *Fist of Dol'jhar*. At least she knew who she'd be fighting on that ship, although she'd rather have heard that Juvaszt had been purged.

A flare of light erupted on the screen. "Multiple ruptor hits on *Nirvana's Fire*. Target destroyed."

A quick, grim cheer rang out. That was one less Rifter destroyer to worry about. Then a shift in the Tenno brought her gaze back to the viewscreen. Another courier had reported in. The tacponder web that helped them find ships was still holding the fleet together, but uncertainty was way up. The clock was smearing as low tac maneuvers boosted ship speeds towards cee and their relative velocities diverged farther and farther.

The tactical plot resolved into clarity as she integrated what the new Tenno were indicating. Oh, Armenhaut. He'd started fighting as though the *Fist of Dol'jhar* was truly intent on taking out *Deathstorm* — charging in and taking tremendous damage in the process. And now he'd passed up his last chance to withdraw. Had he even seen it?

"Fiveskip up."

"Tactical, take us in."

When the screen cleared from skip, Ng saw that the temporal fog of battle had finally caught up with her and Armenhaut's *Flammarion*. *Grozniy* could only watch.

A wash of pity welled up in her, partly for him, mostly for his crew. Armenhaut was never stupid, just inexperienced. That, and his inner conviction that the Panarchy had to prevail because of innate superiority, was a lethal combination.

But he was not a coward.

Even though she knew it was futile — they were seeing the action many seconds in the past, at extreme skipmissile range — she snapped out a new heading, watching the screen intently. "Shoot on acquisition."

"Tacponder message, relay from *Deathstorm*," sang out Ensign Ammant at Communications, absurdly beautiful even under stress, sweat beading his brow. "The Marines have the FTL comm and are withdrawing in good order."

That was good news; but it made all the more bitter the solemn inevitability of the tragedy unfolding on the viewscreen. Slowly the *Fist of Dol'jhar* came about on its new heading. A targeting cross sprang up across its image, overlaid by the skipmissile wake.

"Target acquired, skipmissile away, skipmissile charging."

The *Flammarion* yawed desperately, trying to bring its skipmissile to bear on its opponent. The chain-of-pearls trace of a skipmissile lanced out from the *Fist*; the *Flammarion* vanished in a flare of light. When it dimmed, the ship was still there.

Moments later, the Dol'jharian battlecruiser skipped out, well ahead of *Grozniy's* skipmissile. Ng held her breath.

"I think. . ." began Commander Krajno, then a billow of bright plasma shot out of the radiants of the *Flammarion*. Small dots of light shot away from the stricken ship. Some of its personnel were escaping—Armenhaut had evidently given the order to abandon ship. Then there was nothing but an intricately-featured rosette of light fading against the stars.

Ng shook her head, then straightened up in her pod. "Navigation, new heading. . ." she began.

The Marines were still on the *Deathstorm*, their lives so far bought and paid for by *Flammarion* and many others. She would do whatever she must to complete the transaction.

BEREITTE

Lieutenant Gristrom tapped at the nav console of the corvette *Bereitte*. The little ship responded handily, crabbing closer to the stricken destroyer less than half a kilometer away. The voice of the Marine dyarch came through the comm; in different circumstances he'd have fantasized about the owner of such a voice.

"We're ready here."

"Still clear," said Ensign Appleby, crouching intently at another console, set for Siglnt functions. A flare of light washed through the con from a distant explosion.

"Big one," she said. "One of theirs, I hope."

Gristrom ignored her, concentrating on the targeting cursor for the corvette's lazplaz. If he was off by as much as a meter he'd fry the Marines and their prize. Finally satisfied, he locked in the setting. The fire-control computer would handle it from here.

"Beam incoming," he said. A brilliant lance of plasma glared out, metal puffing away in brilliant coruscations where it hit the destroyer next to the bridge. He tapped the internal comm.

"Stand by at the locks."

The lazplaz beam dimmed and ceased, its job done. He glanced at the viewscreen. Nearby, other corvettes hung in space, waiting for the Marines. Beyond, another coin of light bloomed in the darkness, now shot through with new-made nebulae marking the deaths of ships.

"Emergence pulse," shouted Appleby. "Big one, a cruiser, I think."

The viewscreen flickered to full magnification. Gristrom stared at the silvery hull looming a few hundred kilometers away, the red fist clutching thunderbolts bold on its side.

They were effectively dead. He wondered what a ruptor felt like.

TEN

"**R**uptors, fire at will," said Juvaszt. "First target ships closest to *Deathstorm*." On the screens, Panarchist corvettes and cutters began to disintegrate.

He glanced at the main tactical screen again to reassure himself. Yes, the last remaining Panarchist battlecruiser—finally identified as *Grozniy*—was still locked in battle with *Satansclaw*, *Hellmouth*, and *Nirvana's Fire*. No, that one was gone.

The ID had been a shock. He had to kill that ship. After what Margot Ng had done against the Avatar at Acheront, Eusabian would not forgive the man who let her escape death. Juvaszt must kill the rescue ships and trap the Marines on *Deathstorm*, then join the battle against *Grozniy* and. . .

The main tactical screen jerked and froze. Multiple screens smeared into unintelligibility. The hyperwave discriminators had finally overloaded.

"Communications!" Juvaszt shouted uselessly as Terresk'jhi stabbed frantically at her console.

Then he sat back as an image appeared on the main screen.

Juvaszt's jaw dropped. The entire bridge crew stared.

Anaris blinked, but the image on the main viewscreen was still there. Incredibly still there: two naked women, one small and spare, one tall and spectacular, writhed in a tangle of limbs, their tongues following streaks of some viscous dark liquid across each other's body, while a one-eyed man looked on, clutching his bulging crotch and whimpering. In Dol'jharian terms it was unspeakably depraved.

Static crackled. "Whip me, beat me, make me speak Dol'jharian," a voice said lasciviously, while others moaned and panted in the background.

"Hey, Juvaszt, send that to the Panarchists! They'll be so busy flipping their nackers you can blow 'em away easy," shouted another.

Anaris understood now: the Rifters throughout the Thousand Suns were all watching the battle in total safety, adding to the entertainment by baiting their Dol'jharian masters.

After a heartbeat of frozen astonishment Juvaszt leaped from his pod and strode over to the communications console, knocking Terresk'jhi to the deck. He stood over her, his mouth working, but he couldn't find words.

The unknown Rifter onlookers, however, could.

"Jump her, Juvaszt!"

"Ooh, Dol'jharian sex! I love it! Hurt me, you beast!"

"Juvaszt kim Karusch-na bo-synarrach, gri tusz ni-synarrh perro-ti!"

Anaris bit his lip against a fierce desire to laugh. The unknown Rifter had an excellent command of Dol'jharian, and had concocted perhaps the worst insult imaginable, equating Juvaszt's performance in the conquest-rituals of mating with solitary sex.

Juvaszt raised his fists as if to slam them down on the console.

GROZNIY

"Target identified, nine light-seconds, 62 mark 19, coming about."

"Skipmissile charged."

"Fire on acquisition," said Ng.

The *Fist of Dol'jhar* hung near the ruined Rifter destroyer, dwarfing the little corvettes swarming around it. As she watched, several of them puffed into dust and glares of light.

"A little bit of target practice, the chatzer," said Krajno, his teeth gritted.

"That's odd," Ng commented. "You'd almost think he'd lost track of us."

"Target acquired, skipmissile away." With all the dust and

debris from the battle its impact would be severely diminishes. But then, so would that of the enemy's skipmissiles.

"Navigation, new heading, 30 mark 10, skip ten light-seconds, tac-level five. Weapons, fire all bearing ruptors on emergence."

The *Grozniy* came about, the fiveskip snarled, ceased. The ruptors pulsed even as the viewscreen revealed the target's shields still flaring from the skipmissile impact. "Ruptor hits on *Fist of Dol'jhar*. Target coming about. . ." The fiveskip snarled again as the edge of a ruptor pulse shuddered through the ship.

They'd bought the rescue ships a little more time. Ng issued new orders to continue the attack.

FIST OF DOL'JHAR

A soundless blow jolted the ship. The gravitors hiccupped, and Anaris's stomach lurched as the lights flickered.

"Skipmissile impact, forward first segment, forward first ruptor turret not responding, fiveskip destabilized, estimate ten seconds to skip. . ."

"Ruptors fire on heading 135 mark 16, wide barrage, now!" Juvaszt shouted as he leapt back into his pod.

"Communications, give me clean channels to *Satansclaw* and *Hellmouth*. . ."

The shuddering squeal of a ruptor pulse shook his voice into silence. A gravitational eddy ripped open a bulkhead at the front of the bridge, spinning a crewman away in a tangle of broken limbs as a console exploded.

"Multiple ruptor hits, engine two destabilized, fiveskip still stabilizing. . ."

'Tactical skip when able," Juvaszt snapped. "Fifteen light-seconds." He motioned to the luckless communications officer's second, who took over on his console, and then to the Tarkans posted by the second aft hatch. They ran over and hauled the dazed woman away.

The fiveskip pulsed. "Tactical skip executed."

Anaris glanced at Morrighon, who made a note. If Terresk'jhi was still alive after the battle, he would intercede for her. Another ally would be useful, especially in communications.

Juvaszt glared around the frozen bridge.

"Communications reestablished with *Satansclaw* and *Hellmouth*," reported the second communications officer in the flattest possible voice.

Juvaszt began issuing orders again. Anaris watched, thoughtful, then noted his own reaction of relief as Damage Control reported that the section of the ship housing the Panarch and the other prisoners had escaped injury. Anaris would consider the implications later. He looked up at the tactical plot; the Panarchists were taking tremendous losses.

He smiled. On more than one level, the Battle of Arthelion was going very well.

BEREITTE

Dyarch Bengiat pushed her burden ahead of her into the lock of the corvette, easing it to the deck as gravity grabbed at it. She looked thoughtfully at the unconscious woman within.

Woman? She was barely more than a girl. The girl's short curly hair was matted down, her skin smudged; Bengiat could see a vein throbbing in her temple. How'd a child like that end up with a ship full of blungebags? Then she shook her head as the inner lock door cycled open. For all she knew this Aziza could have grown up with the likes of Qvidyom.

She pushed through the hatch into the corvette and triggered her comm.

"Sound off, Marys, I need a head count." Anyway, she had more important things to worry about now. She looked at Jheng-li, who cradled the alien machine in his arms. They had what they came for. All that remained was to get the hell out of the system alive.

SATANSCLAW

"But, Kyvernat," Anderic stammered. "There might be a chance they can get their repairs done. . ."

"Do not argue with me, unless you want to be left powerless to face that Panarchist battlecruiser," Juvaszt cut in. "Destroy the *Deathstorm* immediately and stand by for further orders. Juvaszt out." The image disappeared, leaving stars in its place.

Anderic looked around the bridge, sensing the pressure of the crew's attention, even though none of them looked directly at him. Didn't they realize he had no choice?

But it made no difference. It wasn't a matter of logic. Even as allies of Dol'jhar, Rifters still thought in terms of us versus them, and the Dol'jharians were more ferociously *them* than even the highest Douloi. He remembered the Panarch standing on the bridge of his enemy's flagship. He had every reason to hate the nicks, but somehow the Panarch had looked like someone you could actually talk to, who would actually listen.

Anderic snorted. He'd talked to Eusabian instead, who would never hear anything but what he wanted to from the fearful scuttlers around him.

"Navigation," he said. "You heard him. Take us in to three light-seconds. Fire Control, status?"

"Skipmissile charged," came the answer. Anderic could hear resentment in the man's tones.

"Course laid in," said sho-Imbris.

"Do it."

The fiveskip hummed. The screen cleared, and stars swung across it. The screen flickered to a close-up. The *Deathstorm* was a wreck, great holes punched in its hull where the lances had penetrated, its missile tube bent and torn, plasma leaking from a rent near the engine room. Several small ships hovered nearby. Before Anderic could issue an order to determine if they were rescue ships for their damaged Rifter ally, they began to vanish, leaving behind the spherical pulses of the fiveskip.

A targeting cursor bracketed the dying ship.

"Target acquired."

"Fire," said Anderic.

Nothing happened.

Anderic looked hopelessly around the bridge, seeing no friendliness anywhere. He realized that the only thing that would keep him alive from this point on was the logos, which he hated. With a snarl of self-hatred he brought his hand down on the firing tab. Three seconds later the *Deathstorm* blew up, fragments spinning away through a scintillant cloud of dust and glowing gas.

A short time later, Juvaszt appeared on the viewscreen, demanding a report.

"The *Deathstorm* is destroyed," Anderic reported.

Juvaszt said, "Were there any remaining Panarchist ships?"

No 'good job,' no acknowledgement of loyalty. Anderic stared at the scowling captain, realizing that he hated the Dol'jharians even more than he did the logos. He'd seen Panarchist ships leaving before he killed *Deathstorm*. What would happen if the Dol'jharians thought the hyperwave had been destroyed, but it hadn't?

He smiled, knowing Juvaszt would misinterpret it. "They were all destroyed in the explosion," he said.

Juvaszt issued new orders, then cut the com. Anderic looked around the bridge; the atmosphere had changed again. It would be too much to say that he'd regained his crew's respect, and certainly not any liking. But he saw in their grim faces that every one of them agreed with what he'd just done.

GROZNIY

Captain Ng watched again the replay from the courier. As the remains of the *Deathstorm* faded she tapped her console. The image vanished.

"That's it, then. Ammant, any news?"

"Nothing, sir."

She sighed. The battle was evaporating now. The Navy had taken too many losses to continue. *Flammarion, Barahyrn,* and *Lady of Taligar* destroyed, *Babur Khan* missing. . . Her throat tightened. *Falcomare* missing. . .

And they didn't know if they had the FTL comm or not. They could only wait, staying out of the way of the victorious enemy while the slow pulse of relativistic communications spread through the tacponder net, invisible to their opponents.

"Emergence pulse," said Siglnt. The fiveskip burped in an automatic tactical skip of 2.5 light-seconds. "Corvette, the *Bereitte.*"

"Message incoming." Ammant put it on the screen before Ng could respond.

The viewscreen cleared to an image of a very small, very cramped bridge. A Marine, a dyarch from the insignia on her rumpled jumpsuit, stood beside a small olive-skinned woman with a bloody nose. But Ng's gaze shifted past to the Marine next to them, standing with his hand possessively on the weirdest piece of — what? Her heart slammed.

The naval lieutenant in the foreground saluted. "Lieutenant Gristrom reporting, sir, attached *Flammarion.*" He smiled, weary and proud. "We got it." And he added grimly, "Paid in full."

The bridge erupted in cheers, a release of emotion greater than anything Ng had ever experienced. And rightly so. They'd paid a terrible price for that red-glowing lump of metal, but now they had the key to the greatest of the enemy's two advantages.

They now had a chance.

After a time she became aware of Ammant trying to shout above the tumult.

"Tacponder update incoming. We've found the *Babur Khan*. It's in bad shape."

The noise died away abruptly as people leaped back into their pods.

"Get on board, Lieutenant," she said. "We've got more to do."

ELEVEN

Jaim noticed the flame the moment they entered the sacred place, but he kept his distance until the elder's gaze caught his, and he recognized in her the long practice of a Discipline. Not Ulanshu, he was sure; her body denied that. But her expression—completely present, relaxed, without anticipation and yet with certainty—was one he'd faced many times across the mat. "You have the freedom of Desrien. Make what use of it you will."

She had to be a shaman.

He saw Marim skip away, no doubt on the lookout for anything not nailed down that she could conveniently fit into her pouch, and Lokri, whose anger at the Panarchists for baring his past had not diminished, searching for an exit. Montrose was drawn to the music, which after some discordant hooms and sqwonks, took on his familiar style. Memory clawed at Jaim: Reth, the shimmering tones she'd brought from the twelve-tone cymbals, interweaving bright treble flame with the deep bass of Jaim's sansa drums.

The memory drew his eyes back to the red flame. He saw Ivard lying on the floor in front of the altar, two robed forms bending over him, with the Marine looking on.

He started that way, walking in and out of slanted shafts of reddish light from the windows overhead. The ruby coloration was due to patterns in the glass, bringing once-heard words: The Rouge Gate, whose aspect is actuality.

Two figures disappeared around the altar with Ivard. By the time he reached the altar, they had vanished.

"Where did they go?" he demanded of the Marine.

Her wary gaze took him in. "You'll have to ask the High Phanist," she said finally. "I didn't see where they went."

Jaim looked around helplessly at several doors, but that would be a fruitless quest. The Marine left him without a word.

He stood there, not knowing what to do. He had no desire to speak to the High Phanist, to argue truth and non-truth with a shaman. No matter what they said, the truth was that Reth was gone. There was no joining of spirits, despite the years of ritual, despite the unswerving love they had had for one another. If anyone should have been able to bridge the Valley of Mystery, it was Reth. He had never known anyone so serene, so strong with the Flame.

He glanced again at the red glow in the lamp. Actuality: a flame existed here, but nothing There. Here, flame burned you.

Nearby Omilov and Osri pored over the artwork. He might as well use up the time by studying the glasswork, having always liked vitrine art.

Turning his back on the flame, he scrutinized the sacred art of an unfamiliar branch of the Path. The triune imagery, the depictions of a human suffering a hideous death, made him wonder at first if this might be a Dol'jharian religion, but there were no demons or other signs of violence. The triune symbols were overlaid by the more familiar balance of fours: even the building itself was laid out in a rectangular form.

He glanced up the light slanting in the west windows as the horizon rose towards the sun, again hearing words: The Phoenix Gate, whose aspect is irreversibility.

Appropriate, he thought as he strolled along the northern wall. Phoenix: the bird that was destroyed in flame and then reborn. Another splendid fantasy. But fantasy only. Irreversibility: Reth was gone, and she was not coming back. But he would send Hreem after, that he promised. The Ulanshu Path—it also promised irreversibility. The flame of anger burned steadily for vengeance. That one was no fantasy.

He glanced at the altar. The strong light from above cast the east end of the building in shadow; the flame was no more than a tiny gleam. Anger burned brighter than spirit.

Flexing his hands, he walked on.

More art. There were the Omilovs again, probably killing

time in the same way. Only now the old gnostor looked sick, and Osri bewildered instead of angry. Had the Dreamtime gripped them with unsheathed talons?

All to little purpose. Be at peace, he was inclined to tell them, but of course he did not. His opinion meant nothing; Schoolboy would react with scorn, and his father with the bland smoothness of Nick manners—Douloi. Smooth as ivory—

The Ivory Gate, whose aspect is autonomy.

Now he had it: the Mandala. The nick art treasures had been kept in the Ivory Hall's antechamber, and Ivard had looked all this up. Jaim remembered him talking about it while doped up, just before they reached Dis.

Autonomy. He liked that.

Breathing in the scent of incense, he approached the altar. The huge rose window at the east end gleamed with muted color. Its shape was the eternal circle, which corresponded with the last of the Panarchist four: The Gate of Aleph-Null, whose aspect is transcendence.

Beauty with no meaning.

He stopped before the altar. But then beauty was beauty. He could appreciate it for itself; it did not, in the final analysis, have to have meaning. "Transcendence" simply meant that one could look away from the bone and grit of everyday life for a short time, and contemplate grace and color and joy in form, but when the eye turned back, it was gone. As when the body died, the spirit was gone.

Gone.

The flame burned steadily. Gazing at it, Jaim felt the lure of the Dreamtime and willed it away. Exulting in his victory, he became aware of the sound of slippers whispering over stone. He found the High Phanist standing next to him, turning a glance of question up at him.

"Ivard," he said.

"He is well. Do you wish to see him?"

Jaim remembered the sensation of initiating a blow and meeting only wind as his opponent accepted his movement to deflect the engagement to another direction.

He spoke: "This is a nick religion—a Douloi religion."

She smiled. "When it began, it was for the lowly, the poor, and the outcasts."

Jaim shrugged. He wasn't interested in a history.

The High Phanist said, "There is an enclave for the

Serapisti at the other end of this continent."

Jaim shook his head impatiently, aware of the keening ring of the chimes in his braids.

Her eyebrows lifted. "Mourning braids?"

The question was oblique enough to make an answer possible. "The rituals bring someone closer in memory for a short time, and they are beautiful."

"You treasure beauty," she said, not quite a question.

He nodded, transferring his gaze to the steady tongue of fire. How still the air was that high! The flame rarely flickered.

"But now you have chosen the Path of the Warrior."

Surprise made him turn. "If I have?"

She smiled, her eyes crescents of mirth. "Bear with me, Ulanshu flame-seeker. I think you are the very person I was hoping might exist. . ."

He crossed his arms.

She touched his wrist with one finger. "It is not a game. But I'm going to intrude, and I sense that privacy has been your armor. With your permission, then?" She gave him a short, antiquated bow, dignified, but she smiled at him, as if sharing a confidence.

"Go on."

"You have denied the Spiritual Path, because access to someone's presence seems to have been denied you. This suggests to me that you have chosen the Warrior's Path because you've found a worthy leader. Yes?"

"Why?"

She gave a short sigh of relief, then glanced northward. Curious, he followed the direction of her gaze. In the north transept, light flooding from high western windows illuminated a familiar profile: the Arkad.

"Where he is going next," the High Phanist said, "he will be alone among many dangers. He has to steer a course through these shoals, but I would find someone to guard his back while he sleeps."

The objections came to Jaim's mind first, but he sensed that she knew them, she even saw past them. For she could have asked those Marines, whose job it surely was to guard Brandon. And yet she had come to Jaim.

He met her gaze. She gave a short nod, suggesting covenant.

Unaware of either of them, Brandon shivered in the cold

draft blowing from the vaulted ceiling far above as he approached the altar. He noted Vahn's presence nearby. Ahead of him Ivard limped up the steps before the large white-clad table and stood quietly, his limbs and body weaving their strange triple rhythm.

Brandon bowed, the appropriate gesture of respect for this face of Telos as required by his position, and then moved off towards the north transept, leaving poor Ivard to commune as he would.

Why had they been brought to Desrien? He had seen a wariness, even a flare of fear in Captain Nukiel, the night before, and he was sure it wasn't simply the spectre of the court martial undoubtedly awaiting him on Ares, which must certainly be their next destination. At least that's what he'd thought after their interception at Rifthaven. Once again events were pushing him around on a game board he could not perceive, but at least he wasn't alone in that. Nukiel had betrayed something of the same feeling.

He half sat on the edge of a stone ring around the base of a column, his eyes closed, subliminally aware of a choir, and then organ music.

But when the great organ began to peal out KetzenLach's masterpiece, the *Memoria Lucis*, there was Markham again. The two of them had played this and many other pieces by that composer while they studied, Markham certain that KetzenLach's music made their brains work faster.

Markham. . . and Vi'ya.

The dead seemed to crowd around Brandon once again, as they had on Dis, and in the Hall of Ivory. The airy interior of the cathedral resonated with echoes of the past and future melded into an eternal instant, while the flagstones underfoot felt insecure, evanescent, barely supporting him above a yawning gulf that could swallow him without a trace.

Brandon pushed away from the column and walked aimlessly, his intent to take in the art while he waited, although he knew that he could not escape either music or memory. Beams of light struck down from the vast windows, bold strokes of dusty color that were as much a part of the architecture as the stone walls themselves, or the evocative tang of incense on the air.

His sense of a gulf underfoot intensified; he walked on the balls of his feet next to the east wall, as if the floor there were more secure.

There were statues in niches along the wall. Brandon moved from one to another. A trick of the filtered light made them appear to stare out over his head, not blindly, but without interest in him below. He came to one he recognized: Jaspar hai-Arkad, in vigorous middle age, clad in courtly raiment. In one hand he held a sphere with stars carved in its surface, perhaps symbolic of the Thousand Suns he'd imposed his peace upon. The other arm cradled the Mace of Karelais. The sculptor's art had reproduced with uncanny realism the complex facets of that ancient symbol of power.

Brandon felt comfort in the presence of his ancestor until he became aware of a light shining past Jaspar's figure, revealing that the statue stood not in a niche with the others, but in the mouth of a narrow corridor. The light had the quality of sunbeams, but shone from the east, against the shafts striking through western windows high above.

He squeezed past the statue, following the widening corridor towards the light, and stepped into the Dreamtime.

. . .The hull of the courier ship pinged and crackled as it cooled, the underside sizzling and emitting jets of steam as it sank into the muck of the ruined wheat field. A last rattle of hail struck spitefully at the little ship as the storm moved on, trailing hollow thunder as the sun struck wanly through thick clouds in a sky the color of a bruise.

Brandon jumped out of the lock. His glossy boots sank deep into the half-grown wheat and mud that the storm had left behind. Nearby a road emerged from a forest, stretching toward the setting sun. There, silhouetted on a distant rise of land, rose a castle, battlements jutting like teeth against the sunset light.

Brandon squelched towards the road, and set off towards the castle. He passed an orchard, the fruit and leaves stripped from bare branches by the hail that still lay in thick drifts upon the ground, crunching mushily underfoot. From time to time he passed people working in the fields, their motions listless with abandoned hope as they hacked wearily at the sterile mud.

He called out, "Where am I?"

The people watched him with dull, incurious eyes, unresponsive to his call. He trudged on in silence.

The bright peal of trumpets greeted him as he approached the castle. Surprised—looking around for whom the welcome was really intended—he passed inside.

Lights blazed up against the encroaching night. A crowd clad in finery welcomed him and he forgot the misery outside the walls. A young, cheerful page brought a silver ewer to him, and with cool water he washed the dust of travel and the grime of long confinement from his face.

And then, as they ushered him towards the hall whence the sounds of merriment beckoned, he spied a tall figure silhouetted against the golden light spilling out between the opened doors. He couldn't see the face, but as the figure moved with familiar lanky grace down the steps towards him joy banished all questions and he rushed forward.

"Markham!" Words failed him as they embraced.

But words never failed Markham. "Brandy! You made it after all." He laughed as he slung an arm around Brandon's shoulders and pulled him close. "I wondered, watching that landing. Didn't I tell you, never argue with a thunderstorm?" He stepped back with his hands on Brandon's shoulders, his swashbuckling grin both merry and tender. "Come on," he said, sliding his hand down his arm and seizing it in a warm, strong grip, "let me show you to our host."

They moved into the hall, Markham talking with the old, familiar ease. Soon they were laughing together, trading rapid-fire jokes and insults back and forth, moving at the center of a constellation of brightly garbed young Douloi, some dressed like them, others in fashions favored a hundred years ago, five hundred years ago, older, but all these young people moved in orbit round the double star of Arkad and L'Ranja.

In the banquet hall Markham laced his fingers through Brandon's and tugged him past tables laden with food and drink from a hundred worlds, threading easily through the crowd of revelers, but as they approached the high table at the end the noise gradually fell away, and Brandon was aware of an expectant hush. Even Markham spoke rarely, finally silent as he halted before the throne-like chair at the head of the hall.

The man who sat there wore the aspect of vigorous middle-age, but his stern, high-browed face was marked with pain, lined with the memory of many sleepless nights. Withal, his eyes were steady and intelligent, his countenance solemn, yet hinting at a humor undefeated by long-borne pain. Brandon bowed; shock thrilled through his nerves as his lowered gaze descried bright blood, seeping slowly, marring the clothing of his host. What was this untended wound—and why?

Brandon controlled his reaction as he straightened up.

"Be welcome, Brandon of Arthelion," said the man, his resonant voice courteous. "I am Jaspar. If there is aught you lack, only ask."

"Thank you, my liege."

Jaspar motioned them to seats on either side, and the night progressed in delicacies, fine wine, and finer conversation—history, philosophy, music, art, all the range of human endeavor passed under review, discoursed with ease and grace by the guests of all ages who were gathered there. Occasionally he shifted carefully in his seat, his face betraying nothing of the discomfort of his wound.

"Will you have more to eat?" he said to Brandon at length. "You have come a very long way."

Brandon replied politely, his mind on the long flight—and a double awareness flickered through his mind like lightning, present and past overlaid.

He turned to Markham, trying to retain both images: though he didn't quite have them, a sense of urgency possessed him. "I tried to join you at Dis," he said. And as he spoke, memory flooded back. The urgency metamorphosed to grief. "But I was too late, and you had—"

"—died." Markham leaned across to smile at him, the torchlight twin flames in his eyes. "Why did you wait so long?"

Brandon wanted to protest that it was impossible to escape before that, but he did not utter the words: they were not completely true. It was not the possibility of escape, but the rightness of it that had kept him vacillating for three years.

And he still felt ambivalent. He had abandoned the world established by Jaspar himself. His gaze returned to his host, who smiled at his guests enjoying themselves.

Brandon turned back to Markham, who breathed and smiled again, impossibly alive. "I've got so much to ask you." The exclamation was wrung out of him.

Markham's twisted grin was a blend of affection and challenge. "You have the answers, Brandy. You have everything I had. Take them and—" He gestured, slashing one hand through the air.

"Take everything," Brandon repeated, "and run?"

Markham laughed soundlessly.

"Wherever I run," Brandon went on, "people fall down

dead."

"Not flight." Markham snapped his fingers. "*Fight*." He jabbed his forefinger in the air.

The solemn stroke of a brazen chime rang through the hall and the merriment diminished to a quiet murmur that died away, yielding to the silence of expectation. All heads turned.

A door that Brandon hadn't noticed opened and a young ensign walked into the hall, carrying before him the double-handed burden of a glittering mace. Its facets cast back the radiance within the hall in spots of light that danced across the faces of the guests therein assembled. He walked solemnly across the room; somehow no table, chair, or gathering of diners obstructed his slow straight progress.

Shock again, again controlled rigidly, as Brandon saw the fresh bright blood welling from the mace, running down the ensign's arm from wrist to elbow in a slow crimson braid that traced his path across the shining marble floor.

The chime resounded once again as the young man left the chamber with his burden, and the conversations once again resumed. Brandon glanced at his host, now bent in conversation with an old woman dressed entirely in black.

Markham gazed into the depths of his cup, silent and abstracted. Distant. After a time the sound of young voices rose above the genteel tumult in the hall, and silence fell once more. From the same door there issued forth a band of maids and youths, singing wordlessly, finely clothed, bearing a variety of vessels; but Brandon's gaze was captured by the burden of the first. She bore a sphere of silver, wrought so fine and polished such that the eye could grasp it not at all, except as a distortion of the forms around it. She placed it on the table before their host and then withdrew.

Jaspar leaned forward. "This is the Stone of Exile," he said to Brandon, "fallen from the grasp of those whose pride destroyed them, in a battle fought long before we left the womb of Earth now lost."

He placed his hand upon the sphere. "It is a thing of power, Brandon of Arthelion. It will grant you your heart's desire."

Brandon stared into the polished surface. It pulled his gaze deeper, he lost the hall and all within it, and then. . .

He opened his eyes to an empty hall in the cold light of dawn, his body cold and stiff with seated sleep.

Brandon jumped to his feet. "Markham!" he shouted,

looking wildly around.

The great room threw his voice back in a mocking echo. It was not only empty, but long abandoned, spun with the tattered webs of spiders long departed for more rewarding hunting grounds. The furnishings were crazed and crumbling with age, and dust arose in strangling puffs from underfoot as he ran out to the courtyard, now choked with brambles under a flaring sun in a sky the color of heated brass.

He ran through the gates of the castle, coughing as heat seared at his throat. The land lay dead around him, bones whitening in the fields, still clutching useless tools. All was silent save the wind and the dry scratching of the dead brambles, stirred to a mockery of life behind him.

A faint rumble fell from the sky. He looked up; a single contrail etched the sky and vanished.

"Coward!"

The cry spun him around in startlement and gladness for a human voice, but its owner had no comfort for him. She was tall, as tall as he, strong-shouldered, dark of skin and eyes, and the ends of her night-black hair brushed against her thighs.

She strode towards him, the hem of her battle-tattered garment dragging in the dust. "Coward!" she cried again.

"Why do you say that?" he demanded, falling back. "I've done nothing to warrant it."

"You've done *nothing*." Her white teeth bared. "You could have healed him."

"How?" Brandon raised his arms. "I haven't the power to heal anyone!"

She advanced on him. "Now Jaspar's peace is the peace of death."

"But I can't—"

She grasped him by the throat, raised him effortlessly off the ground, then threw him across the courtyard, to lie tangled in the thorns.

"The dishonor is yours," she cried. "For as long as death."

He struggled to get up, but the thorns tore at him and pulled him farther into their dry tangle, gray bones of a spring that would never come again. Hatred distorted the woman's face, and then she vanished.

Brandon tried to shout, but the brambles clamped themselves around his throat and choked him to a whimper.

"Markham," he said with his last breath, and then opened

his eyes to the calm consideration of the High Phanist, with Jaim at her side, as the last light died out of the great windows in the west wall of the transept and night came to New Glastonbury.

Solarch Vahn stretched his aching neck and exhaled slowly. The Aerenarch had stood a long time before the cathedral altar watching Ivard, then he'd moved to this side room, the "north transept" the Numen had called it, contemplating the statues in wall niches as if he were going to buy one.

Vahn followed, checking his surroundings. He knew all the exits, so he fell back, giving the Aerenarch more space. Bored, his mind still buzzing from the Augment session, he looked back into the nave of the cathedral. No one was visible save Roget on her circuit near the Omilovs, who both observed the parricide sauntering in the direction of the ship.

Vahn shrugged. His responsibility was the Aerenarch; Captain Nukiel had made it plain that if only one person returned from Desrien, it must be Brandon vlith-Arkad. Roget would take care of the rest.

He turned back. Terror gripped him: the west windows were dark, lights kindled far above, and the transept was suddenly empty. He ran toward it. There was no sign of the last Arkad heir. He slapped his boswell. (ROGET! I'VE LOST THE AERENARCH!)

He heard her footsteps clattering in the distance. But Brandon vlith-Arkad was there after all, his face sweat-sheened and his eyes wide and shocky. Before him stood the High Phanist and the tall Serapisti, Jaim. (CANCEL THAT. IT'S THE FADING LIGHT IN HERE.)

Roget acknowledged with justifiable irritation, but Vahn didn't take his eyes off the Aerenarch as he tightened his grip on his weapon. It wasn't the light; more now than ever he didn't trust anything about Desrien. Nothing would take him from the Aerenarch's side, from now until liftoff.

"Highness." The High Phanist's hands brushed her long robes as she bowed. "I crave a boon." It was said in a grand manner, but not at all disrespectfully.

The Aerenarch gestured for her to speak, his fingers tense.

"For my own peace of mind," the High Phanist went on. "I feel I owe it to your esteemed father."

"What can I do?" The light voice was almost lost in the

huge room.

"You can stay alive." The High Phanist made a grand gesture, presenting Jaim. "And I propose to offer you this fine young man to see that you do."

Brandon's gaze shifted from Eloatri to Jaim, his expression uncomprehending.

Annoyance flashed through Vahn. That was *his* job.

The High Phanist turned his way. "Your place is at the official functions." She turned back to Brandon. "But there is a need for someone within your own walls."

The humor was gone now, and Vahn got the impression that two conversations were going on, one with meaning opaque to him.

The Aerenarch turned. "Jaim?"

"My life," Jaim said, "for yours."

Brandon winced. He said in a hurried undertone, "But my life is —"

He did not finish. With unprecedented rudeness, the High Phanist cut in, still in that odd tone blending humor and formality: "I must be assured that every precaution will be heeded before I let you be taken to Ares."

The Aerenarch's eyes narrowed. "Ares?"

"You are free to go," the High Phanist said, smiling. "Whenever you wish. After I have my assurance."

The Aerenarch bowed, the sovereign granting the petitioner's boon. The irony in the gesture silenced Jaim and made Vahn hold his breath, but the High Phanist seemed pleased.

"Well, then," she said, "why don't you find your companions and see what they wish to do? Of course, you are all free to stay here as long as you desire."

The Aerenarch's gaze moved to Vahn's face, and the Solarch said woodenly, "I'll have Roget round them up for immediate departure."

Jaim had expected the others to have already joined Vi'ya back on *Telvarna*, but all except the Eya'a were clustered before the great doors of New Glastonbury, now open to the cool night air. Montrose had the sleeping Ivard in his arms. Sebastian Omilov leaned on his son's arm. Marim's face was flushed. Lokri was tense, in spite of his lounging pose.

As they left the cathedral, Jaim realized he had no idea how much time had passed since their arrival, whether the remainder of the day, or many days. It didn't seem to matter.

The night sky was clear, the stars more brilliant for the lack of competition from Highdwellings or any other human constructs. Time still seemed curiously suspended, as it had within the stone walls.

He looked about him, his senses heightened to an almost unbearable degree. The scents of loam, of trees and herbs, the sounds of whispering leaves and feet crunching the gravel, all were clear and distinct. Breathing deeply, he relished the dust and the chilly breeze. Each sensation moored him incrementally more strongly to this world, veiling that other world with its false shadows and seductive dreams.

The Aerenarch walked alone, contemplating the stars overhead. Jaim knew that his mind had gone ahead to what had to come next: Ares.

A step beside Jaim made him look away, glad for the distraction. The dimming light outlined Lokri's bony cheek and jawline. "Do you think they use drugs?" he drawled, pointing lazily back toward the cathedral.

Jaim heard the bravado in Lokri's voice and guessed at the fear that probably lay just underneath. "Nothing so simple," he said.

"I take it you saw — things — too. Is that what they hit every-one with who lands here? No wonder it has a rotten rep. I can't figure out how they do it," Lokri said. "I know it can't be real, though it seemed so. If I had time to look for the holojacs. . ."

"You'd never find them in that gloom," Osri's acerbic voice broke in from their other side.

"Discussing the medium," Omilov put in, "is as good a way as any of avoiding the message."

The conversational dam had broken. Brandon said nothing, but he was smiling slightly. Jaim wondered if he, too, questioned the physical reality of whatever it was he had seen within the cathedral. He seemed uninterested in the discussion of whether they'd imagined the whole as a result of some smokedrug slipped into the altar censers, or if they'd stepped through the stone walls into some other dimension.

"The truth is in the experience," was what Reth Silverknife used to say. The familiar pain gripped him.

Then the Aerenarch spotted *Telvarna*, and he flexed his hands; whatever was on his mind, he was preparing himself for a confrontation. And the only one there was Vi'ya.

Osri's voice splintered his thoughts. "If what I saw was

real, then I'll have to go back to school to relearn navigation."

Everyone laughed, even Montrose. Jaim hadn't heard the guarded tone the nick navigator had always used around *Telvarna's* crew. He wondered how long that would last.

Montrose frowned, shifting his grip on Ivard as he glanced around. "Where are the Eya'a?" he asked.

"Telltale recorded them back at the ship a good while after the captain went on board," Roget spoke up. She added in a dry voice that raised another laugh, "We had no orders concerning them."

When they reached the *Telvarna*, Jaim heard the soft thump of paws and Lucifur raced past up the ramp, pursued by Trev and Gray, their tongues lolling. Brandon spoke for the first time since they had left Eloatri. "I wonder what they encountered here," he said, as he looked down at Ivard's face, illuminated by the lights inside the ship.

Jaim fell in step beside Brandon. Though Ivard's bruises were still livid on his gaunt, feverish face, there was a changed quality to his breathing, and in the eyes that opened, clear and blue, to smile upward before closing again.

"I almost think," Montrose said, "that he will live. He spoke back there, before he dropped off again, and he actually made sense."

"What did he say?" Jaim asked.

"'Got a bad case a' vacuum-gut. What's to eat?'"

"Very cogent," Omilov said. "As well as encouraging. In fact, his suggestion has a great deal of merit."

Montrose's chuckle rumbled in his chest. "If Nukiel's minions haven't raided my stores, I shall see what I can contrive. Let me get him settled first."

"C'mon, Lokri," Marim said, tugging on Lokri's good arm.

"What?" The comtech looked down into her eyes, which lacked their usual merry brightness. "You're coming back with us?"

"Anything's better than this place," she said, folding her arms across her chest and giving a dramatic shiver. "I'll take my chance with the nicks."

"So will I, it seems," Lokri said, his voice edgy.

Marim said fervently, "This place is crazy, and maybe it'll be worse where we're going. So right now I want to hole up in our bunk, and until that chatzing cruiser grabs us let's bunny till our eyeballs steam."

Lokri choked on a laugh and they disappeared, hand in hand.

Most of the others headed slowly for the rec room, accompanied by the two Marines. The mood was akin to after-battle exhaustion, a peculiar mix of euphoria and sadness. No one had the energy to plan anything, and the Marines seemed to know it, functioning less as guards than as extra passengers.

Brandon said to Roget, "I'll be on the bridge." He started away, then paused when he saw Jaim. "A moment," the Aerenarch said.

Jaim nodded, stopping.

"Is your offer — don't think I do not value it — something Eloatri forced onto you?"

Jaim shook his head. "No."

"Then. . ." Brandon lifted his hands. "Why?"

Jaim wondered how much to say — or if he should say anything.

Then the Aerenarch said directly: "It seems that everywhere I go people die, and I can do nothing to halt it."

"That can change," Jaim said. "You can change it."

Brandon's expression was pained, somewhere between a soundless laugh and a wince. "Maybe you'll tell me how," he said.

Jaim dipped his head in a sober nod, then moved on past to go into the bridge.

Vi'ya was alone on the bridge. She sat in her pod, calm and smooth-faced as always, the strength of her body hidden by her dark jumpsuit, the midnight hair banded back in an uncompromising long tail.

Jaim silently took the communications pod. Brandon leaned against a bulkhead inside the access hatch, to all appearances unnoticed, his eyes on the captain. Waiting?

Vi'ya had just begun her status check when Jaim grunted in surprise, then tabbed a key. "Someone's outside," he said, transferring the image to the big screen.

Eloatri stood outside the lock holding a small valise, a patient-faced clerk by her side with a larger valise in one hand and clutching a glowglobe-topped staff with the other. "Captain," she said, "permission to come aboard?"

Vi'ya pulled her hands away from her console. "What is the problem?"

"It's not a problem," Eloatri replied. "It's a joining of paths:

mine and yours converge at Ares for a time. It would be simpler if I could share your vessel."

Vi'ya's hand hovered over her console as she glanced Jaim's way.

"I wouldn't want to make her angry," he said.

"No," Vi'ya agreed. She tabbed the key. "Lock opening." Then she added sardonically, "Jaim will be right there to conduct you through the ship."

Jaim slaved the com console to hers with a swipe of his hand.

"Put her with the others," Vi'ya said. "I don't want her on the bridge. Arkad, you go with them."

Brandon hesitated, then said, "Not yet."

Jaim's eyes lifted; he'd guessed right. He walked out.

Vi'ya closed the hatches, then started the flight sequence. On the screen the grassy knoll fell away, backlit by the *Telvarna*'s radiants, then forest land raced below, rapidly vanishing in the darkness.

She did not look up from her work, but she was aware of the Arkad moving from the hatch to the nav console. Even without sound and sight, she could track him by the energy of his distinctive emotional spectrum. It took effort to block him out under the best of circumstances; she felt tendrils of vertigo around the edges of her senses, a little like inadequate window-fittings against the sear of Dol'jhar's sun.

She looked past him at the screen. The stars brightened as the ship accelerated, a subsonic whispering under the hull. The Arkad sat, motionless, as she located Nukiel's battle cruiser and locked in a course.

Then he spoke. "There are fewer women than men on Dol'jhar?"

It was a strange sort of opening salvo, causing her to glance at him. The pose, the vocal intonations, were so familiar; she turned her gaze back to her console.

"Perhaps not at birth, but more of them are exposed," she said.

"Defects? Or just low birth weight?"

"Weakness." She hazarded return fire.

It forced a laugh out of Brandon, and she felt his focus sharpen, narrow-beam, laser-bright. An answering echo reached her from the Eya'a in their cabin: *one-who-gives-fire-stone, is there danger for Vi'ya?*

No danger. She shaped the words in her mind, but her inner thoughts, too fast for them to scan, amended: *no tangible danger.*

Out loud she said, "It's true enough on the mainland, though in some of the island Matriarchies, things differ." She crossed her arms. "It's a harsh planet. Early in our history, women — burdened by their own weight during pregnancy — were often crippled by joint disease at a young age."

She glanced up again. The Markham pose was still there, but this was not a lanky blond man with a twisted grin. Instead the head tipped to one side was defined in bone, the skin marred by healing bruises, the eyes wide and blue, the dark hair curling, uncut these long weeks, on his neck. She could feel him listening intently, and she looked away.

"If this is a discussion of syntonics," she said, "we've adapted."

Brandon laughed again. A subtle alteration, no more than a ripple, flickered through his emotional spectrum, but still behind it waited a vast, dark pool. She did not want to define what lay below it.

"Do you always disarm before you destroy?" he countered.

"You sought this interview."

"'Offense is the best defense,'" he said. And then, at last, a direct hit: "Why have you avoided me these past weeks?"

She realized belatedly that his initial indirection had been a gesture, not an attack. He knew how little Dol'jharians liked to give form to the intangibles by utterance. She said, "My priorities did not involve lengthy interviews with Panarchists."

"To avoid me," he went on pleasantly, "you left your crew to eat alone, train alone, and finally to lick their wounds alone." He waved a hand back toward the rec room. The movement caught the edge of her vision: the long fingers, the flash of the signet.

He knows us: she acknowledged the sense of threat she felt in his perception of Dol'jharian psychology.

"You avoided me at the risk of losing your crew," he finished. "You would have lost them, had Rifthaven gone differently. I've been trying to figure out why you were willing to let that happen." He got up and walked slowly about the bridge. "And the only answer that makes sense is that you wanted me to think that you'd betrayed Markham, and arranged his death."

He was prodding at the tangential target that she'd offered

him. A plaintive interpolation from the Eya'a distracted her: she caught reference to one-who-gives-fire-stone and one-in-mask, which was their old identification for Markham.

"Of course it could have been a purely philanthropic gesture," the agreeable voice went on. "Giving me something to do all those hours we spent in skip. And probably afforded you some entertainment, laughing from afar at my attempts to break into your system."

"It was entertaining," she agreed.

He looked up, an arrested expression in his blue eyes. The attempt to deflect failed: this one did not emulate Markham, he was Markham's model. Within the inner citadel, pain gripped her being. The time to deal with the implications would come. It was not now.

"I can't reconcile it," he said, no longer hiding behind the mask of politeness. "Mates. Not merely lovers: *mates*. Why did you not tell me?"

She could breathe again. He did not, after all, see the real issue. The shield had worked. She was safe. It was now possible to observe him, to endure the backwash of emotion — though just barely. From their hidden perspective, the Eya'a sent: *one-who-gives-fire-stone contemplates "trust" in sorrow.*

Trust: another of the intangibles. What fools her ancestors were, to teach that emotions were weakness, that everything could be conquered through force.

"Who was he to you?" the Arkad went on, coming at last to face her.

She let the silence build, though she could feel the cost. Soon — minutes — he would disappear forever into *Mbwa Kali*, which would carry him to Ares and the silk-and-glitter prison of High Douloi ceremonial. Those who were clever enough, or powerful enough, to have escaped Eusabian's clutches would be waiting on Ares to subsume him by whatever means. It was not, after all, her war.

But here, and now, she was alone with him, and she still had to decide what to say — whose integrity to protect.

A throb in her temple presaged the forfeit this interview would take from her, but that would be later. She said, "Why did you let him go?"

"Because I could not save him," Brandon answered, his eyes wide with pain.

"He warned you what Semion was."

"I didn't believe it—no," he amended quickly, "not the extent of it. How could I? All my life people shielded me from unpleasantness, from any hint that life on the Mandala was not gracious, perfect, the order that the universe strove for. The first break was when my mother died. Then there was the hostage Anaris—" He shrugged. "No matter."

The steady throb stabbed into her jaw; she was clenching her teeth.

"My point is, life was a game." His voice was quick and soft, but the tide of memory-fueled emotion beat at her. "Semion was a stern figure of authority, someone to play off, but he was also my brother. And I had no real ambition—" He faltered, and the tide stilled. He looked across the bridge at Vi'ya. "Is that it? Markham's ambition?"

He was so fast. She kept forgetting it. Once again she waited, cursing inwardly at her inability to sustain this kind of duel. But once again there was reprieve.

"I had no ambition," Brandon went on. "He must have thought I was incapable of serious commitment. For I see now that, close as we were, though we talked about everything else, we never talked about the future." He smiled, full of self-mockery. "Did he think it would bore me?"

The effort it took to withstand the battering of emotion made her mind begin to haze. But release came at last. The comm flashed. She hit it with a fist, and a moment later acknowledged the docking order from Nukiel's comtech.

Brandon turned to the screen, his entire body radiating regret.

She felt the approach of the rest of her crew and the others, and heard the rise and fall of voices.

And she could not, after all, leave him believing a lie.

"He trusted you," she said. "He always trusted you."

He looked up, the blue gaze intense. He *is* fast, she thought through the increasing red haze, but now events were faster. If at last he saw what it meant, it would be afterward, when they would no longer see one another: the repercussion, if any, would not be hers to deal with.

The docking tractor seized the ship and there was nothing more for her to do. She deactivated the console and placed her hands on it.

"Hit the comm," Montrose said, coming in first. "See if Nukiel will let me chip some of our music."

"How about the coffee?" Marim put in, appearing messy-haired and cheery as the *Telvarna* set down in the docking bay, and the engines spun down into silence.

Chatter rose on all sides. Through it Vi'ya saw Brandon watching her, but he said nothing, and when one of the Marines addressed him low-voiced, he responded with an order concerning Jaim that she could not comprehend.

She no longer had to comprehend. Control had been taken away, for the last time; they were all someone else's responsibility. She waited, sitting in the captain's pod, until the last of them had left the bridge, then she stumbled into the disposer and was rackingly sick.

TWELVE

It was almost a day later that they finished evacuating the *Babur Khan*, which had been battered into scrap by three Rifter destroyers. Captain KepSingh transferred his command to a frigate and volunteered to wait for any remnants of their forces that might still find their way out of the battle area.

"I think we can even manage a few search-and-rescues," he said. "With the tacponder net still running, we should be able to find just about anybody with a functioning comm."

Ng nodded wearily. Her duty was clear: the FTL comm had to get to Ares as soon as possible. A courier would be one way, but there were hundreds of wounded — including Mdeino Nilotis — urgently needing medical care that could now be found only on Ares. Only the *Grozniy* could get them there.

"Very well, Captain KepSingh. We'll be on our way, then. You have everything you need."

The older man nodded. His face softened. "We'll keep an especially sharp watch out for Metellus and his crew." He smiled. "That pirate's got a lot more light-years' travel in him, I'm sure."

'Thank you, Captain." She paused. There was so much to say — but not now. She took refuge in ritual. "Light-bearer be with you; *Grozniy* out."

"And with you, Captain Ng."

The connection terminated.

"Navigation," she said, when she could trust her voice.

"Take us to Ares."

As the fiveskip engaged, she turned the con over to Commander Krajno, who would release her exhausted alpha crew.

She left the bridge. The transtube took her to a hold deep within the *Grozniy*; the Marine on duty saluted and let her in.

The lights sprang on, revealing the rounded glowing form of the Urian communicator set on a table. They'd decided not to attempt any use of it — there were techs better fit for that on Ares.

Margot Ng laid her hand gingerly on the weird device, then snatched it away. It was warm, body temperature, and felt uncannily like human flesh. Like muscular human flesh, hard yet yielding.

Like Metellus.

A tear tracked down her cheek, then another. She was alone, she let them flow, remembering him, the twenty-five years they'd known and loved one another, snatched in brief, oh so brief moments. Brief, intense, loving, always knowing each might be the last.

Twenty-five years. She remembered his teasing about their bet. It had seemed a long time then. She'd been so sure she'd track down the port wriggle long before that. A sob caught in her throat. She'd give anything to have him there to claim the forfeit.

It wasn't that she thought him dead; she wouldn't think that. It was worse than that: she might never know. Space was large, and human lives were short.

. . . and I will pay whatever price demanded. . . The Urian device blurred as the tears came freely, but she didn't look away.

"You'd better be worth it," she whispered fiercely.

Mbwa Kali

As the *Mbwa Kali* sped toward Ares, Captain Nukiel entertained his two most exalted guests. He had out the best china, and everything was fresh.

The High Phanist Eloatri and the Aerenarch were the only ones who seemed at ease. Efriq sat, straight and still, and opposite him the Numen's clerk waited with folded hands for the others to finish their coffee. The young man's round face was impossible to gauge, but his eyes were never still.

Nukiel wondered if the magisters would be hashing over this conversation as closely as he and Efriq would be directly they left, and the thought made him smile.

Eloatri returned the smile. "Have I exhausted your patience with my questions?"

"That's all I know about Ares," Nukiel said, backtracking rapidly. "I was only there once, as a very green sublieutenant, and that was only in the Cap—the military sector. I never set foot in civilian country. Leontois?" He looked up at his first officer.

Efriq gave a quick shake of his head. Brandon looked from one to the other, his pleasant face completely unreadable. What did the prospect of Ares mean for him?

"It gives us enough to go on," Eloatri said, sitting back in her chair. "I thank you genz for your patience."

Nukiel hesitated, then essayed a gamble. The High Phanist had taken them by surprise when she joined the Aerenarch and the Rifters on their voyage from Desrien. Her arrival had thrown his crew into almost as much turmoil as the appearance of the Arkad heir on the Rifter ship had.

But she had been a perfect guest, self-effacing, content for the most part to remain in her own quarters after the official tour, except for attendance at various religious observances she was invited to, in which she firmly declined any official participation.

"I confess to curiosity," he said. "Is it the war that brings the Magisterium to Ares?"

Eloatri gave a small chuckle. "It's not war," she said. "It's your passengers."

Nukiel exchanged a quick glance with Efriq. On his other side, Brandon just smiled.

"All of them," she said. Adding sympathetically, "Their appearance—so sudden—must have been quite a shock for your crew."

Efriq choked on a sip of tea.

The clerk's lips thinned, obviously suppressing a smile. Eloatri did not hide her amusement. "I thought so. Well, it was no less of a shock for us." Then a pucker appeared between her eyes. "But there's one more I . . . saw," she continued, her voice musing. "Not here. I've no idea where, or even who it is."

Her face smoothed. "But no mind. For now, I find I must

try to communicate with the Eya'a better. And as for the youth bearing the Kelly Archon's genome. . . " She made a large gesture. "I am delighted, by the way, that your medical technicians report that he is on the mend."

"Well, his fever is gone," Nukiel said cautiously. "And his burn seems to be healing a little."

Eloatri nodded. "He has excellent care. I will have much to say in your praise when I do meet your Admiral Nyberg."

Relief ballooned inside Nukiel. Perhaps he would not face a court martial after all, but merely an inquiry. Regardless, he could hardly wait to hand all his passengers over to a higher authority. He knew that once he had done so, every action, every conversation would be picked over by anyone who had enough clout to get clearance. Aerenarch Brandon would be the civs' responsibility — the civs and the Navy high brass, he corrected silently. There were laws set up, just to protect citizens against military encroachment, and these laws would in turn protect the military.

"Tell me, Your Highness," Efriq said. "What did you think of Desrien?"

The Aerenarch looked up, his gaze abstract, then he smiled. "We only saw a small portion," he said. "But what we did see was unforgettable."

Eloatri chortled in delight. Even the clerk smiled.

"So I would imagine," Efriq murmured, his tone so devoid of innuendo the High Phanist laughed anew.

Brandon glanced at her appreciatively and then introduced an unexceptionable topic: the artwork in the New Glastonbury cathedral.

They were still on the subject of art when Nukiel signaled to the waiting steward to clear away the dishes. The interview was at an end; his job was officially over, all except for delivering them to Nyberg.

He resisted looking at his chrono, but he did glance at Efriq, to see understanding in his old friend's steady gaze. He was counting the hours.

The chronometer in his cell seemed broken even as it remorselessly counted off each hour that brought Lokri closer to Ares. He stood up and banged on it, then began pacing. He couldn't sleep. Whatever drugs had guarded the secrets of New Glastonbury were still buzzing in his mind and through his limbs, days after their departure from Desrien, despite what the Navy medics said. They wouldn't let him see Montrose.

His pacing brought him to the door of his cell. He raised his arms and slammed both fists against its hard-locked rigidity. Locked, locked, locked.

Locked, locked, locked. Lokri thought religious people were supposed to be more trusting. But here was a set of stairs leading down. Maybe there'd be an exit somewhere beneath the cathedral. The *cathedral?* He had to get away from this damn place!

The halls below were cool, smelling of ancient stone, lit at intervals by iron-wrought sconces. The air was cool and still, as if it had not stirred for centuries. He never passed anyone, and all the doors he tried were locked.

From time to time he heard distant noise, and saw a rhythmic flicker around a corner. The first half-dozen times he saw this evanescent light he plunged down an adjacent hallway to escape populated areas.

But the seventh time he neared the end of a long, cold hallway and saw the now-familiar purple flicker he suspected that he was wandering around in circles. So he turned toward the light and noise, figuring he could hide among the crowd, and make his way to an exit.

Rounding the last corner, he was surprised to see an open door with lumensquiggles in an unfamiliar script above it, giving off the pulsing light. The noise, the smells, reminded him of the Galadium on Rifthaven. He laughed, breaking into a run. Why had he not guessed that the high-end religious nicks would have their own gambling den?

Was there one for every superstition? All designed to take money from the gullible, just like those long-faced thieves upstairs did. And of course this place would give their off-duty clerics something to do with their time and money.

He passed through the door. A hulking masked man held out a hand.

Lokri lifted his own, palms out. "I'm broke," he said with cheerful honesty. "But I won't be long if you'll point out the Phalanx or Xi tables."

The man shrugged massive shoulders, reminding Lokri — uncomfortably — of one of Vi'ya's Dol'jharians. "We don't play in that kind of coin." The man's voice rumbled.

"I'll play in any kind of coin," Lokri said. "Let me in." And if he didn't like it, he was out the other side.

This time one shoulder lifted, and the hand waved him on. Lokri passed on inside, breathing deeply the head-twisting scents of expensive dream-smoke. The room was crowded with flash and shadow pleasure-seekers, their outlines diffused by a weirdly glowing red haze. Lokri watched the smoke swirl up from censers, under-lit by the ruby lumens overhead. The affect was like something from the lowest precinct of hell, an observation which Lokri found highly entertaining.

"Jes," came a pleasant tenor voice, one Lokri hadn't heard for a long time.

Stung at first, for he hated reminders of his real name and origins, Lokri swiftly turned to see the crimson outline of a short, thin man with long, wispy hair.

Lokri choked on a laugh. He would never have expected to find in a place like Desrien the most dangerous man in Rifthaven. "Digge Kelar," he exclaimed aloud. "I thought you were dead."

Kelar lifted his hands, his round, young-seeming face beaming with boyish delight. "Appearances belie."

"What brings you *here?*" Though Lokri was beginning to appreciate Desrien — the *real* Desrien — more each moment.

"To play," Kelar said. "For greater stakes. The greatest."

Lokri laughed. "I might have known."

"Come, Jes. Join us."

"Willingly," Lokri said, "but please. Call me Lokri."

Hearing his old name reminded him of the damned nicks and their battlecruiser, waiting to take him to his execution — if he didn't escape them. Except he met Kelar after he'd changed identities, not before. The anomaly made Lokri wary, but Kelar just laid his hand on Lokri's shoulder. "Come within. I'll have you know that we play for souls here."

"Souls," Lokri repeated, instantly diverted.

"Everything open and understood, always, in matters of play or pay." It was the same thing he'd said when he first started the Galadium out of nothing but a plasma-scarred derelict ship he'd flown in, empty except for a mysterious case in the cargo bay, and no hint where he'd been or how he'd gotten it. Within two years he had the best club in the station.

Lokri laughes. Souls. He'd walked into the Galadium

without money before, which had not stopped him from the risk of betting anyway. How much easier to stake something that didn't exist. But what did you expect on a planet like this? Still, finding Kelar talking religious came as a surprise.

"Xi games are this way," Kelar said.

Lokri followed to the most elaborate Xi setup he'd ever beheld. Twelve circles of speeding lights intersected in a tall, revolving column, with brief lineups of one color, then another, at odd intervals. Gathered around the base of the holographic display were intensely focused players, hitting their freeze-key when they thought the next color bar would line up.

Lokri watched. The circles spun faster than he was used to, and he'd never seen a tower of more than eight bars. But the odds for Xi had always been a lure — sometimes as much as fifty to one for color bars, and exponentially higher for repeated patterns.

Lokri gauged the players. In his experience, pilots and navigators were drawn to Xi; anyone who had a knack for seeing patterns in objects moving in space.

He remembered Ivard's sister Greywing being drawn to Xi, and felt mild regret at her loss, followed by a jolt of recognition. He blinked, tried to rub the reddish dreamsmoke haze from his eyes, and stared at the short, scrawny young woman in the old flightsuit. Short spacer-style haircut, ugly pale, freckled skin, guarded expression: it was Greywing. Alive.

A player fell away from his position, giving a low cry, and Kelar, who had slipped into the dealer's cage, motioned Greywing to take the man's place.

Greywing stepped forward, her thin, wary face underlit in ghostly hues by the glowing colors on the console at her fingers.

"Five tries, pilgrim, five tries," Kelar said. "Your call or mine?"

"Mine," Greywing said. It was definitely her voice. Lokri stood back, nausea crawling up his gut; he knew he'd seen Greywing fall to a Tarkan jac in the Mandala.

"Red," Greywing said.

"Try red," Kelar repeated.

The whirling lights reflected in Greywing's unblinking eyes as she watched the tower, her chin uplifted, shoulders braced. She'd always faced the universe in that stance, ready for attack, but she'd had courage. Lokri hoped she'd win now.

"Bets?" Kelar turned to the crowd. Some raised hands,

betting for or against Greywing's ability to call a solid line of red lights intersecting. Her head moved unconsciously in the rhythm, her gaze abstracted, then her hand pounced on the large key—and the tower froze, nine red lights, two yellow and one blue.

"Ooooh," a sigh went up.

"Four left," Kelar said, smiling. "Your call or mine?"

"Mine," she said firmly. "Red again."

This time she hit only seven; she caught all the rest orange. She called for red a third time, and lost to three lights.

"Two left," Kelar said. "Your call or mine?"

"Yours," Greywing said, looking uncertain.

"Green."

A green line-up was promised, and she only had to watch for it. But the lights whirled faster, and when she hit the key, she was badly off. A cry went up from the watchers.

"Last try," Kelar said. "Give you four to one. You get this, walk free. Pattern: blue-white-yellow."

The patterns were the hardest, and took the longest to pay off, but when they did, the payoff was great. Bets ran up into high numbers among the watchers, but Lokri's focus stayed on Greywing, who stared up at the tower, her lips parted and her breathing still.

She slammed her hand down—and missed the pattern by four lights. As Lokri watched, her eyes flashed wide with horror and a neat red hole appeared in the center of her chest, then she fell away into the crowd, swallowed by the shadows.

"What's—" he started to say, but the roar of the crowd swelled, and a new victim took Greywing's place: a huge, broad-faced man who Lokri recognized as his very first captain.

"Ghosts," Lokri whispered as Kelar told the man he had five tries. "The place is filled with ghosts."

Lokri watched, tightlipped and silent, as the old man lost. At the end, his face grayed and he too disappeared into the shifting shadows behind the game.

Whatever the game behind this game was, he refused to play. Lokri turned to go, but the crowd pressed against him, keeping him in place. He fought the urge to shove his way out and smash his knuckles against Kelar's smiling teeth. But when he looked at the nearest players, he recognized people he'd killed in action, others he'd crewed with or had known. All dead.

The ones who played the Xi game appeared as he had seen them last, and when they lost, their death-wound took them from sight. Four times this happened as Lokri tried gently to sidle free, a step at a time. Yet somehow the smoke and shadows led him inexorably right back. So he crossed his arms, his jaw aching around clenched teeth, determined to wait it out. Three more people from his past came and lost and disappeared, and then a tall, rawboned figure sauntered through the crowd, his grace and assurance painfully familiar.

Lokri tried to look away but couldn't. It was Markham L'Ranja, alive again—tall and ranjy, laughing blue eyes and long yellow hair. Markham smiled crookedly at Lokri, then stepped up to the Xi console.

Markham had always admitted that Lokri was his superior in this game. The urge to push through and take his place gripped Lokri, but he shook his head. Markham was already dead; whatever Lokri did would make no difference to the nightmare being spun out here.

"Blue," Markham said.

"Blue!" Kelar repeated, his teeth showing in challenge.

Markham lost, and lost again. And when his fifth time came and went, Lokri tried to look away, but he couldn't. He saw Markham's features crimson and run together and his smoking skull gleam, bony and white, while around him the crowd yelled and laughed.

And then he, too, was gone.

Lokri drew in a shaking breath, and then the last blow knocked his lungs airless. Through the crowd glided a small figure, no older than Ivard and already beautiful: Fierin ban-Kendrian, Lokri's little sister.

She looked this way and that, and her face changed when she saw him. Uncertainty gave way to delight. He stared at her, unable to move or speak. How could she be dead? Four times he'd checked on her, always from a distance. The latest one was mere weeks before Eusabian's attack: she'd been alive.

More unsettling, she looked just like she had when he last saw her, which had been years ago. He *knew* she was an adult now. She'd inherited Lokri's place. She could not be this child. But she came right up to him, and threw herself in his arms. He hesitated, then closed his hands about her thin shoulders, and hugged her warmth against him.

"Jes," she whispered, tears of joy gleaming in her eyes. "I

found you at last. How happy I am! Where have you been?"

"Hiding," he said, trying to force a distance, to regain control. "What are *you* doing here?"

"I've come to play." She lifted her hands and spun around, her glinting silvery dress the same shade as her eyes. Silver eyes, the same shade as his — the same shade as the dead eyes of their father —

"Get out of here," Lokri said.

Fierin looked hurt. "But I found you at last!"

Lokri met Kelar's gaze. He knew what this was, now. He was already dead. He'd gone through the farce at Ares and had been executed. Except how could he be alive? What he did believe was that Fierin, the only one of the family worth anything, was in danger.

With one hand he thrust his sister behind him. "You go home," he said. "I'll run their damned play for them."

"You know the risk," Kelar said.

"Yeah, you told me. Souls." Lokri didn't bother to keep the sarcasm out of his voice.

"You have to understand," Kelar said. "This is not for a night's fun, and it's not for a decade of bond-slavery like Piriag's favorite forfeit. This is *forever*."

The platitude *There is no forever* came to Lokri's lips, but in his mind was a terrifying image of falling, falling, through the void of space.

"Call it blue," he said.

Fierin's thin fingers gripped his tightly.

The circles whirled, faster than ever, but Lokri watched, feeling the patterns. . . losing them. Catching them — losing — catching — *Hit*.

He slammed his hand down, then looked up the line. Blue. . . blue. . . blue. . . blue. . . blue. . . green —

The crowd yelled.

"White," Lokri said.

Murmurs around him splintered his attention. He shut them out, concentrating, and again thought he had the pattern, and missed. Kelar laughed, his face cruel. "Give up, Kendrian? Give up?"

Lokri tried again, this time letting the house declare the pattern. When he lost for the third time, fatalism seized him. He clung tight to his sister's fingers, feeling her pulse racing under his hand.

Kelar's words echoed in his mind. Give up? That meant there was a choice, and that meant there was an exit somewhere. . . a way out. "If I lose, does she go?"

Kelar gestured back toward an open door. At either side stood two shadowy figures with ready weapons. It was either Lokri or Fierin. He studied her face, her steady, trusting gaze. He could leave her and try his own escape, or he could—

"Call it," he said.

The lights whirled, this time so bright it hurt the eyes. The roars of the gamblers rose to a scream and then died in a weird echo. Lokri felt a cold wind blow against his face, and he staggered, righting himself against a wall.

Opening his eyes, he stared straight into one of the flaring torches. He shifted his gaze to his own hand, fingers spread against a stone wall. His hand slipped, leaving a sweat-mark.

"Kelar?" He swallowed. "Fierin?"

His voice echoed. He was alone.

Rage burned through him. He began to run, faltering when he rounded a corner and nearly ran down a short figure in a long robe standing just before a stairway.

It was the High Phanist. Without slowing, he raised his fists to strike her out of his way. She remained still, even when he was three strides from her. He was angry enough to slam her against the wall, but he made the mistake of looking at her face first.

Not that she had any arcane powers. She just stood there, her eyes steady with the same sort of stillness that rested in Jaim's gaze just before a fight. But Lokri sensed no threat. She was just. . . there.

As was he.

The realization shocked him into dual awareness. He was lost under New Glastonbury. No, he was in a cell on *Grozniy*. He perceived himself standing before the door of his cell; for a moment the thin, bruised figure leaning against the door with upraised fists, his head hanging down, was the teenager who'd discovered that justice was just another word.

Lokri didn't know if anything he remembered after that moment under New Glastonbury was real. Or even since that day his teenaged self had found his family—

He faltered to a stop, and lowered his arms, but his fingers were rigid with anger. He was still on Desrien after all. "Damn you," he said hoarsely, "and *damn* this chatzing hellhole."

"It is not an easy one, I take it?" she said.

He glared down at her. "No, it *wasn't*," he said, trying to force the experience into the past, where it belonged. "How do you arrange these things?" he asked. "And where," he felt his voice rise and forced it to flatten, "do you get the ghosts?"

"You bring the ghosts with you," was the reply.

He shook his head, expelling his breath in a strangled sound midway between a laugh and a shout of anger. "Are they all dead, then?" A chill shook him. "Am I?"

She gestured invitingly, and sat on the next-to-lowest step. "Tell me what you saw."

"Ghosts. In your gambling den."

Her brows lifted.

"You're going to tell me there is no gambling den here."

"If you wish."

"What I wish is to be out of here, and free," he said. "And I want to know why my sister was forced into your farce." Her jerked his thumb back over his shoulder.

"I don't know anything about your sister," the woman said. "But I would hazard a guess that there is business left undone, perhaps something on her behalf, which you might attend to. Does that strike a chord?"

"It strikes a death knell," he said sardonically. "Any business I try to take care of will end with me in the execution dock, for a crime I did not commit."

"Ah," she said. "Then there's a question of justice."

"There is no justice," he rejoined. "There's power, which buys all the 'justice' it needs. I don't have any power."

She pursed her lips, then looked up at him. Her eyes in the flaring torchlight were tired, but very kind. "You are from Torigan, are you not?"

He said nothing, disgusted with himself for letting his speech fall back into the unmistakable Torigan cadence after so many years of successful disguise.

She shook her head slightly. "Never mind. You need tell me nothing."

"Then why are you here?"

"It seemed the right place to be just now," she replied. "My clerk reported an angry young man ranging about the corridors down here, probably lost. I wouldn't want you to miss your flight. . . should you choose to leave Desrien."

"'Choose.'" He scorned the word.

"Well, you could stay and become a pilgrim," she said, smiling teasingly.

Pilgrim. It was the word Kelar had used. The echo made the hairs on the back of Lokri's neck prickle, and he knew that he could spend his lifetime denying whatever it was that had happened in that lower-level gambling den, but it would never leave him. There was power here, something he could not even remotely understand, much less subvert.

"Maybe it'll be easier to take my chances with Panarchist notions of justice," Lokri said, leaning against the wall to disguise his trembling.

The woman put her hands on her knees and pushed herself to her feet. "I am not one given to predictions, but from what little you told me, it seems there is a family member important to you who might need your aid. And," she added, frowning a little, "it may transpire she will aid you."

He shook his head.

"Will you run forever, then?"

"The universe is big," he said.

"And often leads back to the same path, and the same nexus, to be confronted yet again."

He thought of the gambling den. "So," he said finally, "if I do go to Ares—I assume that's where we're headed when you let us go—and face their justice—do you promise me I'll get out of it alive?"

"In the end we get out of nothing alive," she said with irony to match his. "And I promise nothing. But I ask you again: will you run forever?"

He heard the other, unspoken question clearly: how many times do you want to go through this?

"This way," she said over her shoulder, and Lokri opened his eyes on the familiar blandness of his cell.

THIRTEEN

Morrighon stared into the darkness from his bed, watching the glow on the ceiling intensify.

Not again, he thought wearily. Several times since they'd returned to Arthelion after the battle, the computer phantom wearing the visage of Jaspar hai-Arkad had materialized in his room, watching silently for a time and then vanishing. He closed his eyes, waiting for it to go away.

Then he started as he heard his name.

"Morrighon." It was only a whisper, but the apparition had never spoken before. "Listen," it said, and pointed one glowing finger at the communicators on the table near his bed. There was a crackle of static, and Morrighon heard the voice of Barrodagh, issuing a series of orders. As he listened, his eyes widened.

The eglarrh demachi-Dirazh'ul! 'The Avatar has decided!'

Now Anaris would no longer be conditional heir, but heir in fact. After a short, predawn ritual of preparation, Anaris would be taken. . .

Predawn. Now, remembering his private worry, he scrambled out of bed to begin dressing with frantic haste.

He'd seen the signs soon after their return. Anaris had become more irritable, more distant—signs, Morrighon was sure, invisible to anyone else. But to the Bori they presaged the conditional heir's disappearance into his quarters for a day and a night, not to be disturbed under any circumstances, and on his eventual emergence looked haggard. This was the third episode since his assignment to Anaris.

He had no idea what it meant. He hoped devoutly that it wasn't drugs or something similar; that would mean he'd tied himself to a fool, and the only outcome of that would be a horrible death at the hands of Barrodagh. But it seemed so uncharacteristic.

He hopped around the room, frantically trying to balance as one foot became tangled in his trouser leg, peripherally aware of the ghost — *it is not a ghost* — watching him.

But it didn't matter what it was that Anaris did during those periods of withdrawal. If the Avatar found him in the state Morrighon thought he might be in. . .

Morrighon fastened his shirt tabs with shaking fingers, belted on his communicators, and hurried out. As he turned to close his door, he saw the apparition nod approvingly, and fade back through the wall.

His breath came in short rasps as he hurried down the corridors toward Anaris's quarters. He tabbed the annunciator frantically, ignoring the curiosity of the two gray-clad guards posted there. There was no answer.

Morrighon stared at the door in an agony of indecision. No, he couldn't take the chance. He didn't know what Anaris would do to him for disturbing his retreat, but he did know what the Avatar would do, if Morrighon's suspicions about Anaris were correct.

With shaking hands he entered the override code he'd pried out of Ferrasin.

Slipping through the door, he slammed it behind him, doing his best to block the gaze of the guards with his body. Inside, he stared, and his breath caught in his chest.

Anaris rahal'Jerrodi sat cross-legged in the center of the floor, his back to Morrighon, surrounded by a snowstorm of white dots. They were bits of the expanded foam used for packing, but what was impelling them in their frantic dance around Anaris? There were no air currents.

Acid crawled up Morrighon's gullet as the bits of foam slowly coalesced into a tenuous representation of the features of Eusabian of Dol'jhar. For a moment the face held; then it melted into another: the Panarch of the Thousand Suns.

Morrighon began to tremble. It was worse than he could have imagined. If the Avatar walked in at this moment and saw

Anaris practicing one of the forbidden arts of the Chorei, he would have him killed instantly.

He stepped forward and timidly touched Anaris's shoulder. There was no reaction, save that the face of the Panarch melted into another, a woman. Morrighon gathered his courage, grasped Anaris's shoulder more firmly, and shook him.

The bits of foam collapsed to the floor. Morrighon stepped back as Anaris stilled, then slowly got to his feet. He turned around. Morrighon stepped back further, terrified to the point of nausea. Anaris's nose was bleeding, his eyes bloodshot, the veins in his forehead distended and pulsing wildly.

He stared at Morrighon without recognition. Then his eyes focused and the prachan slowly distorted his features.

"My lord," Morrighon gabbled, barely able to articulate the words. "The Avatar has decided. They are on their way at this moment to begin your preparation for the eglarrh demachi-Dirazh'ul."

Anaris recoiled as though he'd taken a blow. He righted himself, his eyes wild, his breath coming in ragged gasps. Then he rushed out of the room, and Morrighon heard him vomiting. When he came back he sank exhausted into a chair, but his eyes were alert. No trace of the terrifying anger remained in his features.

"You have done well," he said softly. And with a grim smile, "There are no more secrets between us."

Then he moved swiftly, and seized Morrighon's shoulder. Morrighon barely restrained a cry of pain as the Dol'jharian's merciless grip compressed the bones and nerves.

"No one alive," said Anaris, speaking each word with precision, "knows of this." After too long he released him and turned away, crossing the room and stripping off his clothes.

As Morrighon watched Anaris reclothe himself in the unadorned black appropriate for the ceremony, he reflected on the emphasis the conditional heir had placed on the word "alive," and was amazed to find resentment in himself for that.

He suppressed the dangerous emotion. And yet, an unnecessary threat was a weak one. That was a fault that would have to be dealt with, if Anaris was to gain the throne and keep it.

Then the annunciator chimed. Anaris's face had smoothed out by then; not even Barrodagh would find fault. The waiting shuttle quickly took them out of predawn darkness into light as it accelerated toward the *Fist of Dol'jhar*, where the ceremony would be held, free of the taint of Panarchist weakness.

Anaris gazed out the viewport, enjoying the symbolism of a course that forced an early dawn as they flew east. The flight passed in silence; even had he been inclined to speech despite the throbbing headache that still gripped his temples, the presence of the Avatar forbade it. Next to him Morrighon sat quietly, making occasional notes on his compad.

An honor guard headed by Kyvernat Juvaszt and the senior officers of the battlecruiser greeted them in the hangar bay. After a short passage via transtube, the module decanted them at the entrance to the gloomy chamber where the skull of Eusabian's father Urtigen guarded the Mysteries. Morrighon and Barrodagh stepped aside as they entered; only the True Men could witness the ceremony that would empower Anaris as a fit vessel for the spirit of Dol.

Inside it was cold; their breath smoked in the still air, echoing the twin pillars of incense twisting up from the altar below the skull. Between them a skein of black silk cord rested, animated to the semblance of life by the flickering light of the tall candles smelted from the flesh of Urtigen by his son Eusabian.

They arranged themselves in silence. Eusabian approached the altar, Anaris behind and to his right. The Avatar raised his hands, the wide sleeves of his dead-black robes falling back to reveal his heavy forearms, their wrists stippled with lancet scars from innumerable ceremonial bleedings.

"Darakh ettu hurreash, Urtigen-dalla. Tsurokh ni-vesh entasz antorrh, epu catenn-hi breach i-Dol," he began. Bestow upon us your presence, great Urtigen. Turn not away your eyes, for through you are we linked to the spirit of Dol.

The syllables resonated harshly in the cold air; on the edge of his vision Anaris perceived awe in the faces of Juvaszt and the others gathered to witness his formal inheritance.

At the proper moment he stepped forward, joining his father in the bloodletting that marked all high Dol'jharian rituals. The hand-forged iron of the lancet was cold against his wrist, then hot with pain as the steaming blood splashed onto the coals of incense, adding the tang of heated copper to its pungent scent.

But as he raised his voice in the austere antiphony of the eglarrh demachi-Dirazh'ul, Anaris found his mind wandering.

Images, not of Jhar D'Ocha and the wind-savaged rock and ice of the Demmoth Ghyri, but of the marble grace of the Mandala and the gardens of the Palace Minor, possessed his mind. He tried to dismiss them, but they did not yield. Even here, before the frigid sanctity of his family's altar, they owned a power that could not be denied.

. . . hemma eg shtal . . . His mind fastened on a fragment of the litany. *Blood and iron.* The image of Gelasaar's face persisted, expressing that very different amalgam of gentleness and power that Anaris had never fully understood. The face melted into that of the Panarch's youngest son, sparking anger's heat, spiked with anticipation. He knew that Brandon would be taken to Ares; there he would assume his father's mantle. Or would he? Could he? Did the two of them face similar struggles, each in the mold imposed by their culture and upbringing?

Anaris's spirit expanded beyond the confines of the gloomy chamber. Exalted, he perceived the Thousand Suns as somehow wholly present to his senses. Something to be grasped, like a game board, and across it the familiar, hated face of his opponent.

Beside him his father had entwined his own *dirazh'u* with the one lying on the altar, weaving a complex, lengthy knot. He turned to Anaris, who faced him, the image still holding his mind.

"*Pali-mi kreuuchar bi pali-te, dira-mi bi dira-te, hach-ka mi bi hreach-te,*" the Avatar intoned. '*Be my vengeance entwined with yours, my curses with yours, my spirit with yours.*'

He touched the complex tangle of silken cords to Anaris's forehead, lips, heart, and groin in a fluid motion. Anaris took one end of the knot and pulled; the two cords separated, each now knotted in identical complexity.

"*Ejarhh!*" The sharp syllable from the lips of the Avatar shattered the silence. *It is done!*

"*Ejarhh!*" Anaris echoed.

"*Ejarhh!*" responded the watchers.

But as he and his father bowed before the altar, turned, and left the chamber, Anaris relished the game that was just beginning.

ARES

Osri Omilov held his arms a little away from his sides, hoping sweat wouldn't mark his uniform. His armpits were sticky and he felt a sudden, nearly overwhelming urge to pee.

They were here at last.

He stood in front of one of the deck-to-overhead viewports of Nukiel's gig, staring out at Ares, the command station that every naval officer hoped someday to be posted to. Remembering the day he and Brandon had set out from Charvann with Ares as destination, he shook his head slightly. It seemed not weeks, but years ago. Another lifetime.

An ensign stood next to him, a grin quirking his mouth. A flicker of amusement eased Osri's tension as he contemplated what must have been fierce competition to be assigned to the captain's gig, which was conveying both the Aerenarch and the High Phanist to Ares, along with the captain who had brought them there.

A commander had overseen the transfer. Precise military ritual made the transition from cruiser to gig smooth. Now for the last journey: the transfer from naval control to civilian.

It was time to reenter Douloi governance.

Osri sweated, trying to distract himself. But his mind kept reviewing the past weeks as he wondered where the triumph was, the elation he'd expected to feel when they finally reached safety, order, and justice.

He looked around. All were on the shuttle, even the animals, the two dogs sticking close to Ivard, and the big cat, which unlike the dogs was leashed, on Montrose's lap as he sat next to Vi'ya. The Rifters were being carefully watched, and Lokri had been fitted with a shock collar. Their presence had surprised Osri, until his father, wearing a brand-new tunic, and looking haggard but alert, had murmured as they boarded the gig: "No one knows what to do about any of them yet, until Brandon finally tells them whether he was rescued or kept prisoner."

It was both, Osri thought, touching his breast pocket where the coin and ribbon lay. How does one secure justice for that?

He kept silent, aware how his own status had been falsely raised by a few light words from Brandon. Somehow Osri had been credited with saving the Aerenarch's life after they left Charvann, though the truth was, Brandon had taken over the piloting, and had chosen their destination.

But word had gone ahead the moment the cruiser emerged outside the station, and while Osri was making ready, one of the other lieutenants had appeared at his door, saying with a mix of pride and envy, "High-end welcome at fifteen hundred on the civ side. You're included, as Rescuer of the Heir. Com says your family is in on the shuttle bay Greet List."

Family. That meant Osri's mother. She was alive, then, possibly his half-sisters as well, and they had managed to make their way to Ares. His mother would be gloating over the social coup.

Osri gazed out the viewport as the shuttle slowly emerged from the huge cruiser bay and started toward Ares. The military section was a huge saucer of metal, pocked with depressions large enough to moor a battlecruiser. There were dozens of them. Depending from the underside of the military saucer was a standard oneill habitat, giving the entire assemblage the appearance of a steel mushroom, whose stem rotated against a stationary cap. Unlike a standard oneill, the diffusers of the habitat derived their light not from the dim red sun now serving as the station's primary, but from a vast spin reactor in the saucer, making Ares entirely independent of location. The military saucer also housed the largest fiveskip ever built, the field of which encompassed the oneill as well. Ares was the largest mobile construction ever built by humankind.

Normally, Osri knew, they would have docked on the saucer, but protocol demanded the Aerenarch and High Phanist be received on the civilian habitat.

As they approached the oneill, Osri saw a swarm of ships of every description. His eye was caught by an immense glittership among them, every line evocative of wealth and power.

Someone's breath caught. "Whose yacht is *that*?"

"Archon Srivashti's," the ensign said in a colorless voice.

Everyone looked up as Lucifur gave a sudden low growl. Montrose's stiffened fingers stroked the big cat's raised hackles.

Brandon, in a plain white tunic, sat still and blank in one of the best seats before the big viewport, with Jaim standing behind his chair. Nukiel on one side and Eloatri on the other exchanged low-voiced comments.

Ivard prowled around the little cabin, his thin face excited as he watched the bewildering display of ships through the huge viewports. Then his breath caught.

Osri followed his gaze to a battlecruiser, seared and pitted, huge holes blasted in its hull, choked with twisted metal. Osri gasped; it seemed inconceivable that a ship could take such punishment and still fly.

"That's *Grozniy*," the ensign said with pride. "Just got here ahead of you. Straight from the Battle of Arthelion."

Osri caught a warning look from Nukiel. The ensign's face blanked and he said nothing more.

As they passed the long length of the terribly scarred ship, Marim bounced up next to Osri, standing close. "Sanctus Hicura," she said, and whistled. "Blits! Why didn't they skip out?"

Ivard appeared on her other side, his gaze intent on the *Grozniy*. "Only cowards skip out," he breathed, absently rubbing the head of each dog.

Marim snorted. One hip bumped against Osri; he shifted away from her uneasily. But for once she seemed to have forgotten about loot. As the shuttle's course took the cruiser out of sight, replacing it with the looming immensity of the Ares oneill, her sharp face tightened into uncharacteristic grimness. "Sgatshi! Chatzing big prison," she muttered.

Ivard looked puzzled. Marim jerked her thumb over her shoulder. "You think they're gonna have time for a bunch a' outlaw Rifters, in the middle of a war? We're gonna be spending a long, long time here."

Osri realized it was as true for him as for the Rifters, and an invisible vise squeezed his heart. When he was in the hands of the Rifters, he thought of this place as a haven, but now all he could remember was childhood, and feeling himself the outsider among his own kind.

Marim plumped down near Lokri, whom she engaged in a muttered conversation.

The shuttle curved around to the far end of the civilian habitat, approaching the center of the end cap where a vast bay loomed, a confusion of sensors and less identifiable protrusions around it. Osri moved up next to Jaim, looking out the viewport past the Aerenarch. His inner ear sensed a subtle shift as the shuttle began to match spins with the oneill.

Framed by the viewport, the Aerenarch gazed outward, and Osri's perspective shifted dizzily. Brandon vlith-Arkad, the last heir of a millennial power, awaited by all aboard the station, each with their own expectations of him—for a moment he was the fixed point in space, while the ponderous, multitrillion-ton mass of Ares slowed to match its spin to his. Then the navigator in Osri reasserted itself and the shuttle was again but a sliver of metal approaching a human-made planetoid.

The glowing discharges of the electronic lock snaked across the viewports. An unexpected chitter from the Eya'a caused a ripple of reaction, nervous twitches and little laughs. A gentle bump in the shuttle indicated they'd grounded in the bay.

Everyone stood up, including Brandon. The Navy officers moved to the hatches, standing at attention. Mutters of conversation went on around, but Brandon stood silently, an island in the middle of a restless sea.

"You four will wait," a Marine said to Montrose, Marim, Ivard, and Lokri. "Captain Vi'ya, as translator for the Eya'a, you are permitted to accompany —"

"I will remain with my crew," the woman said, her accent pronounced. "The Eya'a will know where to find me when they wish."

Brandon glanced her way, only to encounter her back, bisected by the long tail of hair.

Osri moved slowly to his father's side.

The hatch opened and the Marine honor guard presented arms. Beyond the ramp, Osri glimpsed a decidedly unmilitary scattering of people waiting, their elegant formal dress startling after weeks of either uniforms or Rifter excess. To the uninitiated eye the scattering might seem random, but Osri knew that a rigid hierarchy defined who stood where along the path; within the hierarchy the perilous minutiae of deference dictated who stood forward, and who behind.

Brandon gestured to Nukiel, and together they moved to the hatchway. Just before he passed through, Brandon turned his head slightly, and his eyes met Osri's. The perfect Douloi mask broke, revealing a wry, curiously rueful smile.

Brandon looked back and smiled reassuringly at Ivard as a hand motion summoned the dogs to his side. Then, as peal after peal of the Phoenix Fanfare shivered on the air, Brandon's Douloi mask smoothed his countenance, and in step with Nukiel the Aerenarch walked down the ramp.

"Oh," Ivard sighed, bringing Osri's attention back to the Rifters that he would leave behind momentarily.

Osri remembered another Rifter he'd left behind, the young Rifter woman at Chang's with her priceless gift of tenderness and passion. Priceless. He never even asked her name, nor she his, he'd remembered as the bubbloid dwindled behind *Telvarna* and then winked out when the fiveskip engaged. Their passion was a shared gift, free of obligation or expectation. . .

Around him the shuttle cabin dissolved. The stars slewed around in a loose spiral as Osri fell away from the mother ship. He sat up on the deck plates, his head aching. He looked out the viewport, terrified to see the big ship falling away rapidly in the vertiginous loop of a ship out of control.

He sprang to the con and fought the little courier, which bucked and strained as the speed increased. The viewscreen flickered and interference sparkled across it in nauseating swirls.

"I command you to go to Rifthaven."

Osri tried to clear visual, but only audio came through. He recognized that voice — the captain.

"But I don't want to go to Rifthaven," Osri said. "I hate that place—"

"You have to deliver the vaccine to Rifthaven," the captain cut in. "Do not evade me a second time."

Second time? Osri whimpered to himself, rubbing his aching head. He peered out at the mother-ship, now a distant star. Was that how he got this knot on his head? *I don't remember.* There was something he ought to remember, and it wasn't a ship, it was. . . a church.

"A *church?*" he squawked.

"You will take the vaccine to Rifthaven, or they will all die in the plague," the captain said.

"I don't care if Rifters die of a plague! It would be great if they die in a plague, and the nastier the better!" Osri yelled at the blind comm. "In fact, they *are* a plague!"

But the viewscreen cleared to space. The communication had ended.

"I don't understand." Osri smacked the log tab with a trembling fist.

There was the initial command. And then there was Osri refusing to go, and trying an evasion tactic. He'd been caught in the mother-ship's tractor. . .

The ship bucked, and Osri fought the controls. Tiredness

strained his neck and shoulders, and bleared his vision. There was no fiveskip; the courier flew under geeplane, whizzing through system after system—

It was a dream! Relief flowed through him. It couldn't be real. There was nothing like this in the universe. He was only dreaming.

Relief! He looked around the shadowy little courier. "I can wake up now," he said out loud. "I'm asleep, but now I'll open my eyes, and I'll find myself asleep, in my—"

Where? Confusion vanished when the courier bucked and plunged, forcing his attention back to the controls.

"Why me. . ." he muttered, slapping the scan magnification. "Why me?" Exhaustion and depression pressed on him, so when at last he saw the familiar Bloodclot and Bruise, it was akin to relief—at least he recognized where he was. The relief soon disappeared. As he slowed for the approach to Rifthaven, he found himself floating past windows and corridors.

"Who are you?" the comm demanded.

"Special courier," he said, staring into a window where an old man hunched over a console, hacking at his gangrenous arm with a knife. In the chair next to him a body, stiffening in death, sat in a grotesque parody of efficiency.

"Who are you? Why are you here?"

The next com came from an ugly, scar-faced woman who huddled in her pod, the lower half of her body a rotting mass of bleeding blisters.

"Special courier," he said again. He wanted to get away as fast as he could.

She passed him through.

Disgust churned in Osri as he moved down the long, pitilessly lit corridors with their piles of corpses. The plague worsened steadily. Everyone was losing limbs, or hacking at extremities in a desperate attempt to fight the contagion.

At last he reached a command center, a huge space filled with the dead and dying. Osri clenched his jaw to keep down the acid burning the back of his throat as he tried not to see the corpses stacked along the walls, the dying near them, their limbs worming futilely, and the extremities with black-rotted connective tissue lying strewn in his path.

He carried a heavy case in both hands. He knew it contained the vaccine; the silver case bore a carved bird on it, a symbol of freedom for —

Ivard. The coin. What was this nightmare? It couldn't be real.

Osri stopped before a great console streaked with drying blood. Transfixed across it lay a woman, her face stiff and cold in death. Great claw marks had slashed down her body, the blood dark and congealed.

Reth Silverknife, Osri remembered, sickened. Jaim's Rifter mate aboard the *Sunflame*.

He shut his eyes. This was a dream, and dreams could be ended. He simply had to end it, open his eyes, and go back to his proper post, at the Academy. But the Academy was gone.

That wasn't the dream. He shook his head violently, but when he opened his eyes, the young woman was still there before him, eyes gazing sightlessly upward.

"Why have you come?" husked a hideous old woman with one leg amputated and an eye sewn shut. "What do you hide there?" she went on, groping, groping.

"The vaccine," he said. The bird on the top of the silver case gleamed. In spite of the tug of possession he thrust the case at the woman. "It's yours. Take it." It's not mine! Why did I pick it up?

"We accept your shipment," she cried in gratitude.

Osri found himself once more in the courier, maneuvering through the red-lit streets. Everywhere, deformed Rifters lurked or sidled, staring as he floated through in his little ship.

Disgust and fury grew in him until he finally found his way out of the labyrinth of horror. Then he tabbed his comm and sent a plaintive message to the ship: "It's done, and you may's well hit me with a ruptor if I'm to be forced into any more worthless duties like that."

He ended the communication, but the comm lit anyway. "Why do you complain, Omilov? You took the duty. You took it yourself."

Osri cut the connection and lifted his hands from the controls, determined to let the ship continue on autopilot; if it made it, fine, if not, well, what was the worth of living in a universe where the decent people are being blown up by Rifters? But who would save the Rifters?

They didn't deserve to be saved. By committing the Riftskip they abrogated all their rights to the protection of the law.

But not their rights as human beings.

It was an inner voice, not an outer one. "I hate this dream!" he shouted. "I want it done!"

He opened his eyes, blinking against the light of a sun. He reached for the con to steer away, then dropped his hands to his lap. He'd force the dream to end — or he'd die. But as he neared the sun, the temperature in the cabin rose until he was faint from the heat. Still, he sat back, enduring what he hoped would be the last of a humiliating life, until the comm came on, again without his having used the controls.

"Omilov," the captain said, "where are you?"

"Near a sun," Osri answered.

"You've plotted a false course," said the captain. "Correct it. I have more for you to do."

A false course — a stupid dream. He had never plotted a false course in his life. "Why?" Osri said bitterly, to the swirling miasma of color in the viewscreen. "I'm better off dead."

"What are you angry with?" replied the Captain. "The sun about to burn you up?"

"At least it obeys natural law," Osri said. "I hate Rifters. They ruined the Panarchy."

"The Panarchy is not yours to declare ruined, or not," said the captain. "Our duty is to save the third overculture. They need leadership. They have unexpected resources."

Third overculture. That was the phrase his father had used, long ago, in a conversation about Rifters.

His father. Osri blinked, and there was his father, sitting beside the High Phanist, his eyes closed. The shuttle had landed. The hatch was open, Brandon and Nukiel just exiting.

For once Osri acted on an impulse prompted by something besides anger. As everyone moved toward the shuttle door, he threaded through them, grasped Ivard's skinny arm, and stuffed the coin and the ribbon into the breast pocket on the ill-fitting flight suit someone had donated to Ivard. Osri zipped the pocket closed, and before Ivard could say anything, he joined his father and walked down the ramp, grimly aware that he'd sweated through his shirt after all.

Osri scanned the faces waiting: curiosity, politeness, interest, wariness, but no friendly eye in sight. These were the High Douloi; their ineluctable formality seemed to close around them like an icy force field. Even the dogs orbiting Brandon seemed to move in preordained paths —

But formality did not triumph, after all.

A high, clear keening like a wind instrument beat the air above the formal music, and a Kelly trinity danced along the path, stopping before Brandon. As the Kelly performed a kind of obeisance, ribbons fluttering and headstalks whirling, Osri heard a snorting sound from inside the shuttle.

A muffled "Hey! You can't—" sounded, and then footsteps pounded down the ramp.

Ivard bounded past, nose twitching.

The Marines whirled, pointing their weapons, but Nukiel quickly raised his hand.

The Kelly passed the naval officers and swarmed around Ivard, tweeting and blatting, touching and gently slapping him all over. He responded in kind, his arms writhing. He hooted frantically, his adolescent voice cracking, joy informing every part of his body.

Then the two Eya'a moved swiftly down the ramp, their twiggy feet scratching. A whisper went through the gathered humans there; several attempted bows, and others backed away with rather more haste than grace as the little white figures moved past without noticing.

Two people, a man and a woman, stepped up to Brandon, dropping smoothly to one knee. Osri recognized the tiny, exquisitely gowned woman: Vannis Scefi-Cartano, the former Aerenarch's consort. Her smile was as brilliant as gemstones, with about as much warmth. Next to her, in formal Navy dress uniform, a man, older and suave: Admiral Nyberg.

Their obeisances were elegant and protracted; together they managed to draw the eye away from the Kelly and Ivard. Once again, Douloi formality prevailed.

But it had been shaken, Osri reflected as the silent stewards led away the four figures. A hint that things were not, after all, the same, and could never be again.

Osri smiled.

ABOUT THE AUTHORS

Sherwood Smith writes fantasy, science fiction, and historical romance for old and young readers.

Dave Trowbridge wrote high-tech marketing copy for over thirty years, which made him an expert in what he calls "pulling stuff out of the cave of the flying monkeys," so science fiction comes naturally. He abandoned corporate life for good in 2013, but not before attaining the rank of Dark Lord of Documentation. He much prefers the godlike powers of a science fiction author (hah!) to troglodyte status in dark corporate mills, and the universe is slowly coming around to his point of view.

Dave lives in the Santa Cruz Mountains with his writer wife, Deborah J. Ross, a retired seeing-eye German Shepherd Dog, and two cats. When not writing Dave may be found wrangling vegetables — both domesticated and feral — in the garden.

ABOUT BOOK VIEW CAFE

Book View Café is a professional authors' publishing co-operative offering DRM-free ebooks in multiple formats to readers around the world. With authors in a variety of genres including mystery, romance, fantasy, and science fiction, Book View Café has something for everyone.

Book View Café is good for readers because you can enjoy high-quality DRM-free ebooks from your favorite authors at a reasonable price.

Book View Café is good for writers because 90% of the proceeds goes directly to the book's author.

Book View Café's Newsletter includes new releases, specials, author news, and event announcements. Click here to sign up.

www.bookviewcafe.com